The Ihaka Trilogy

Old School Tie

Inside Dope

Guerilla Season

WHAT THE CRITICS SAID

OLD SCHOOL TIE

The most explosively funny New Zealand novel yet written.
— Tom Scott/*Sunday Star-Times*

Thomas is a true original, energetic, scintillating and quite mad. I devoured *Old School Tie* in one gulp, then suffered the indigestion of laughter for a week.
— Vincent Banville/*The Irish Times*

As significant a debut as *The Bone People* – and with jokes.
— Nigel Cox/*New Zealand Listener*

The plot is sufficiently convoluted to satisfy the most fastidious whodunit fan and the pace never flags. The most entertaining New Zealand work of fiction I've read in years.
— Karl du Fresne/*Evening Post* (Wellington)

INSIDE DOPE

If you haven't read Paul Thomas' books, commit the name to memory. He promises to do for home-grown entertainment fiction what Cloudy Bay did for New Zealand wine and *Once Were Warriors* for the film industry.
— Simon Cunliffe/*The Press* (Christchurch)

One of the funniest writers to emerge on the New Zealand literary scene in recent years.
— Kate Coughlan/*Evening Post* (Wellington)

Tightly plotted, studded with eccentric characters, roars along like an express train, refreshingly literate.
— Susan Geason/*The Sun-Herald* (Sydney)

World Class
— Stuart Coupe/*Sunday Age* (Melbourne)

GUERILLA SEASON

Thomas has carved out his own niche in New Zealand fiction. Possibly he is to 1990s urban New Zealand what Ronald Hugh Morrieson was to post-war small-town society. He's certainly in the same class.
— George Kay/*New Zealand Listener*

Paul Thomas's murders are among the best that money can buy. When you're reading [him], you've just about got everything: thrills, laughs, social comment and – irrespective of genre – a very good book.
— Bernard Carpinter/*New Zealand Books*

One of the funniest writers in this part of the world.
— Neil Jillett, *The Age* (Melbourne)

A relentlessly riveting read.
— Jenny Breukelaar/*Who* magazine

PAUL THOMAS

The Ihaka Trilogy

Hodder Moa

Disclaimer

The three books which make up *The Ihaka Trilogy* — *Old School Tie*, *Inside Dope* and *Guerilla Season* — are works of fiction. Names, characters, places and incidents are either the product of the author's imagination or are used fictitiously. Any resemblance to persons living or dead is purely coincidental.

A catalogue record for this book is available from the National Library of New Zealand

ISBN 978-1-86971-194-8

A Hodder Moa Book
Published in 2010 by Hachette New Zealand Limited
4 Whetu Place, Mairangi Bay
Auckland, New Zealand
www.hachette.co.nz

Text © Paul Th omas 1994, 1995, 1996, 2010
Themoralr ights of the author have been asserted.
Design and format © Hachette New Zealand Limited 2010

Designed and produced by Hachette New Zealand Limited
Printed and bound in Great Britain by Clays Ltd, Elcograf S.p.A.

Contents

Old School Tie   7

Inside Dope   187

Guerilla Season   391

About the Author   576

To Harry & Georgie

Old School Tie

1

It was entirely appropriate that Wallace Guttle, the private investigator, should have spent the last hour of his life looking at pictures of other people having sex.

Such pictures were both Guttle's stock-in-trade and the basis of what could be termed his sex life. As he studied these particular photographs for the first time, he congratulated himself on a job well done: the definition was superb given that they had been taken from a distance of ten metres and through a window. The object of the exercise had been accomplished: there was absolutely no doubt as to the pair's identity or the nature of their relationship.

Mingled with Guttle's self-satisfaction was disdain for the couple's carelessness in not bothering to draw the curtains; it offended his sense of professionalism when his quarry made things too easy. Not that it surprised him in the least. In the course of his long experience of such matters, Guttle had frequently observed that people engaged in illicit love affairs often took infinite pains to conceal the fact from those they lived and work with in their day-to-day existences only to behave with a remarkable lack of caution as soon as they stepped outside that environment. He supposed it was the pent-up desire. Guttle was seldom affected by desire; for him sex was a solitary activity undertaken under controlled conditions.

He fanned the dozen large colour prints out on the desk in front of him. Six months they'd been at it the wife reckoned. She was probably right; Guttle had built up a very healthy respect for his female clients' ability to sense when their partners' libidos were focused elsewhere.

Guttle was one of those lucky people who love their work. He was a private investigator who specialised in personal and confidential enquiries. The changes in the laws relating to adultery, divorce and matrimonial settlements had driven some practitioners out of the industry and persuaded others to find new niches. Guttle, however, had stayed with what he knew and loved. As long as men and women lusted, lied, coveted, cheated, betrayed, suspected and succumbed to the green-eyed monster, he would make a living. In other words, he had a job for life. Guttle was aware that some of his acquaintances in the industry, particularly those involved in what could be broadly termed industrial espionage and counter-espionage, made more money than he did. But they were forever fiddling around with complicated and expensive equipment. Furthermore, their clients were often high-handed and demanding; those who employed Guttle's singular talents were generally prepared, in their consuming suspicion and fragility, to give him a free hand.

And the work itself! Guttle liked tracking people, spying on them, watching them in their most abandoned moments, figuring out their subterfuges, anticipating their moves, employing his ingenuity to obtain photographic evidence that could not be denied.

An aspect of his work which Guttle particularly enjoyed was reporting to the clients. Even clients who were unwaveringly convinced that their partners were having affairs reacted gratifyingly when presented with the photographic evidence. It tickled Guttle to hesitantly push the manila folder containing the photos towards the client then, leaving his hand on the folder and adopting an expression of solicitous concern, to say: "Maybe you shouldn't look at these." He knew that once he'd said that, they'd no sooner follow his advice than run naked up Queen Street.

Guttle reshuffled the photos, noting what a fine physical specimen the female participant was. She was at least twenty years younger than his client, the betrayed wife. He thought, life's a bitch when your arse drops, your tits sag and your husband starts bonking his secretary. When he showed his client the photos, first she'd be angry, then she'd cry; over what? The fact that her husband was porking a twenty-three year old with a hot body and a dirty mind? Get real. Only the month before, Guttle had handed a young and attractive woman a set of prints showing her husband performing oral sex on a male street kid in the back seat of his car. Now that, said Guttle to himself, is what I call a real kick in the guts.

The private investigator interrupted his reverie to glance at his watch; it was 7 o'clock on a Friday evening. He knew he'd be the only person left in the three-storey Newmarket office block, just off Broadway. Under normal circumstances, he would have mixed himself a generous Scotch and water and reviewed the contents of the folder in his wall safe which contained the most salacious photos he'd accumulated in the course of his twenty-year career. Tonight, though, he had an appointment with a client at 7.30.

The prospect left Guttle unenthused. It was not his usual type of case; it in no way catered to his perverse inclinations and was, in his opinion, essentially a waste of time. However, the client had been insistent and, more to the point, prepared to pay the exorbitant rate Guttle had quoted with the aim of deterring him.

Guttle sighed, gathered up the photos and put them in his briefcase, turned off the lights, and locked his office. In the lift down to the basement carpark, he wondered how much longer this new client would be prepared to throw good money after bad. Not much longer, he supposed.

Guttle exited the lift and headed for his car, the only one left in the dimly lit basement, mentally rehearsing the speech he would use to put the best gloss on his modest progress. As he fumbled to insert the key in the lock of his car he was asked:

"Mr Guttle?"

Guttle, simultaneously, dropped the briefcase he was carrying in his left hand, jumped backwards a foot, and exclaimed "Suffering fuck!" in a voice several octaves above its usual timbre.

The speaker was standing in the shadows of a pillar half a dozen metres away, virtually invisible. Guttle was not a particularly brave man and had long feared that one day someone whose life had taken a turn for the worse as a result of his professional efforts would come seeking revenge. The speaker stepped out of the shadows and Guttle relaxed slightly; he'd never set eyes or trained a lens on him before.

"Jesus, I just about shat myself," he said.

The stranger chuckled, brought up his right arm, and shot Guttle three times through the head, which was twice more than was absolutely necessary.

Wallace Guttle had lived alone and, understandably, was largely shunned by his neighbours. Under normal circumstances, therefore, his body would have lain undiscovered in the basement carpark until the following Monday morning.

He was shot at 7.12 p.m. At 10.25 p.m. Margo Dugdale, who worked as a receptionist for the law firm which occupied the second floor of the building containing Guttle's office, drove her ten-year-old yellow Datsun, at a speed several kilometres per hour above what was sensible, into the carpark and over the recently deceased private investigator.

Mrs Dugdale had come from the Iguaçu bar and restaurant in Parnell where she'd just recently consumed three strawberry daiquiris in the space of forty-five minutes. That was on top of the several beers she'd had at the regular Friday night office drinks session, the two Bacardi and Cokes in the bar before dinner, and the half bottle of Hawke's Bay chardonnay with dinner which she'd eaten in the bar's restaurant with two colleagues from the secretarial pool. Back in the bar and halfway through her third daiquiri, she'd decided that the best possible way to complete these celebrations marking the arrival of the weekend was to engage in sexual intercourse, preferably several times.

By the time she drained her third daiquiri, she'd settled on a partner. The gentleman in question, a real estate salesman named Tony Rispoli, was quite amenable to her proposition which was worded in a manner precluding the remotest possibility of misunderstanding. Since he was married, chez Rispoli was out of the question as a venue for the assignation; since Ms Dugdale lived with her parents, staunch members of a particularly irrational branch of fundamentalist Christianity, her residence was equally unsuitable. They therefore settled on Ms Dugdale's office; she hoped that none of her colleagues had the same idea.

Twenty-four hours after Margo Dugdale's stomach had spasmed horribly as she stepped out of her car into Wallace Guttle's brains, some 20,000 kilometres away in Toulouse, south-west France, Reggie Sparks, remittance man and failed gigolo, sat on the windowsill of his sparsely furnished apartment and read the handwritten facsimile from his mother, Mareena. It was short and to the point:

Dear Reggie,

I was sorry to hear of your trouble with the police or whatever they were. I presume you and your friend Mr Khong were very drunk at the time. You were certainly very silly but that's no excuse for the way the police behaved. I hope Mr Khong's jaw is mending.

I am sending the money to pay your fine to your account with Banque Populaire and some extra to cover an air ticket home. Whether you decide to use it for that purpose is up to you but I'm afraid to have to tell you there will be no more money from me should you decide to remain where you are. You've had a good run. How long have you been living in France — is it four years? Living rather well I might add. You seem no more able to pay your own way for any length of time than the day you left. As far as I'm concerned, this is the last straw — 20,000 francs is over 7000 NZ dollars, which is hardly to be sniffed at.

Reggie, I'm sorry if this seems harsh but I really think it would be for the best if you came home. You can stay with me, just like old times.

Please let me know what you're going to do.

Your brother sends his regards.

Your loving mother.

Sparks re-read the fax, which had been sent to the café on the ground floor of his apartment building, with a mounting sense of resignation, grimacing at the reference to his brother. He folded it up, slipped it into the back pocket of his jeans, stood up and stared out onto Place Wilson, a circular space in the centre of Toulouse, which is known as the Pink City on account of its ubiquitous rose-coloured terracotta walls and roof tiles. It was a glorious morning and already the outdoor cafés and the expensive boutiques were well patronised. Now that the gendarmes had dispersed the winos and beggars, old men sat reading their newspapers in the little park in the middle of the Place, which was full of life and bustle and steadily circulating traffic.

Goodbye to all this, thought Sparks. There was no question that he was going to have to do as his mother suggested and fly back to Auckland, which he'd left over a decade previously to wander the world. Despite his mother's wounding assertion, he had managed to support himself for the majority of that time; it was true, admittedly, that since settling in Toulouse his income had been a little irregular and had required topping up from time to time. But even leaving aside the ugly matter of money, it had been made abundantly clear to him that he was now a marked man as far as the French forces of the law were concerned and he was well aware of what that meant. Look at poor old Khong.

The events to which his mother's fax referred, and which would precipitate Sparks' return to New Zealand, had occurred one month earlier. It had started when Sparks, out for a Sunday evening promenade, bumped into Larry Khong in Place du Capitole.

Khong, a fiftyish English-educated Lebanese, was a notorious figure among Toulouse's English-speaking community, virtually all of whom had some connection with the aircraft manufacturing consortium Airbus Industrie, which was based on the outskirts of the city. Khong himself worked for Airbus as an aircraft salesman; his patch, broadly speaking, was the Arab world. He had several major deals to his credit which his numerous detractors, who habitually referred to him as "the filthy Arab", attributed to his alleged talent for bribery and corruption and the fact that he supposedly had every high-class call-girl from Paris to Monaco at his beck and call. They insisted that Khong's deals owed more to his willingness to bribe anything that moved when in the field and his ability to arrange the satisfaction of the depraved whims of Middle Eastern government and the airline officials on their frequent visits to France, than to any aeronautical expertise or persistent salesmanship.

According to *Radio Couloir*, as the unofficial information system at Airbus headquarters was known, Khong was also in the habit of fiddling his expenses on a colossal scale, a cost ultimately borne by the taxpayers of France, Germany and the United Kingdom who funded Airbus. It was also whispered in the long corridors that he'd been caught red-handed by customs agents at Orly airport trying to smuggle diamonds into the country on his return from a trip to North Africa. In each instance, the gossip went, he had retained not only his freedom but also his job because of the intervention of some Arab princeling with a direct line to President Mitterrand. Whereas many in the English-speaking community, whether out of jealousy or fastidiousness, detested Khong heartily, Sparks found him engaging company. Sparks was also intrigued by the talk of Khong's network of call-girls.

Sparks had never intended to stay long in Toulouse. It was a difficult place in which to scratch out a living; he was a journalist by trade and, apart from a few pieces for the British rugby magazines, there was precious little scope for it. Eventually, in order to make a few francs before moving on, he'd undertaken some casual work as a translator and tour guide for the local tourism industry. It was there that he met and fell in love with Gisele Bacarat.

Gisele was a thirty-year-old administrator in the tourism authority. She had short brown hair, big brown eyes, long brown legs and a slim, firm, flexible brown body. She was by a considerable margin the most uninhibited, inventive and energetic lover Sparks had ever had. She was also married.

That didn't seem to trouble her in the least. Sparks never ceased to be amazed at the way she'd sit up in his bed after a prolonged and fiercely passionate session of love-making and prattle on cheerfully and affectionately about her husband Pierre — what they did last weekend, where they were going for their summer holidays, what he'd given her for her birthday, what they'd had for dinner at her parents-in-law's place the night before and so on. One sultry late afternoon in July, as he lay naked on his back gazing in wonder at the bite marks and streaks of sweat on his torso, half-listening to Gisele complaining about how badly Pierre, who did something in a bank, was paid, he finally raised the subject.

"How do you do it?" he asked. "How can you spend the afternoon in bed with me and then go home to Pierre as if nothing's happened?"

Gisele shrugged in that Gallic way which involved eyebrows, mouth, shoulders, arms and hands. "I don't understand. What do you mean, how can I go home to Pierre? He is my husband; it's completely normal that I go home to him, n'est-ce pas?"

"But how can you just switch from me to him? Doesn't what we've been doing affect you, you know, like the way you react to him?"

Gisele sat upright in the bed and waved a finger at Sparks. "Ah oui, now I understand. I didn't think you were so much the Anglo-Saxon, chérie. It is the English way that one has only so much love and to give it to a new man means taking away from the old. C'est vrai, non? You think that if I love you, I cannot love Pierre?"

"I was just asking," said Sparks. "Is that right? You really love me?"

Gisele's eyes flashed. "What do you think — I'd do this if I didn't?" she asked indignantly. "Of course I love you; I've loved every man I've had an affair with. But Pierre is the one I'll always love."

Sparks failed to grasp the significance of this remark and never really understood Gisele's ability to compartmentalise her life and control her emotions. Some eighteen months later he discovered what it meant in practice. Early one evening after they'd made love, she got straight out of bed and went to the bathroom. That was unusual but Sparks assumed she was going out for dinner. When she reappeared, she began getting dressed.

Sparks propped himself up on an elbow. "Going out?"

She regarded Sparks solemnly. "Reggie, this was the last time. I can't see you any more. Pierre and I want to have a child, so . . ." She shrugged as if further explanation was entirely unnecessary. As her words sank in, Sparks' heart began thundering; a terrible feeling of nausea was spreading from the pit of his stomach. He vaulted off the bend and went to embrace her. She held up her hands to stop him.

"Please, Reggie. You must understand. I must go now." She smiled a sweet, sad smile. He dropped his head, unable to look at her. She kissed him tenderly on his bowed forehead, whispered, "Au revoir chérie," and was gone.

Sparks' recovery from heartbreak was slow and difficult. For several weeks he left his apartment only to go to the market or the laundromat; after five months he remained resolutely disinterested in any sort of relationship. The celibate life, however, was starting to make him fidgety. He found his thoughts turning in the direction of depersonalised sex. While the well-used ladies who patrolled certain side streets off Allées Jean Jaurès held no appeal, the prospect of an encounter with one of Khong's exclusive stable — who were all stunning-looking and immensely skilled in his imagination, whatever they were like in fact — increasingly did.

He had attempted to broach the subject with Khong a few weeks before that fateful Sunday night, at a party in the old English enclave of Pibrac, a village just outside the city. However, Khong, a gregarious fellow at the best of times, was in social butterfly mode, flitting from one conversational cluster to another, quite unconcerned as to whether he was welcome or not. By the time Sparks was finally able to manoeuvre him far enough away from the other guests to feel comfortable discussing the topic of prostitution, Khong had consumed a stupendous quantity of Armagnac. Sparks was still wallowing in euphemisms when Khong cut him short.

"Excuse me old boy, I must have a puke."

Two minutes later a hellish row broke out when the hostess discovered Khong, on his hands and knees, throwing up into the bottom of a wardrobe where she kept her considerable shoe collection. The hostess, a demure and retiring woman, began ranting obscenely at Khong, betraying a long-suppressed working-class accent and vocabulary; he affected not to notice the string of vile names he was being called, apologised fulsomely, presented her with a signed blank cheque, and made as graceful an exit as was possible with a trail of richly coloured vomit down the front of his cream cashmere jersey. The encounter in Place du Capitole was the first time Sparks had seen him since.

Khong, dapper as ever in a dark-blue silk shirt and cream chino trousers, had greeted Sparks warmly and insisted on buying him a drink. Once seated in a bar Sparks, conscious of Khong's unpredictability, wasted no time in getting to the point.

"Larry, I hear you're on good terms with some very classy, shall we say, ladies of the night?" he blurted.

The good cheer disappeared from Khong's black eyes.

"You've obviously been talking to some of my admirers," he said.

Sparks went a shade pink. "Shit, it doesn't bother me — in fact, I'd like to meet one."

Khong took a hard pull on his Glenfiddich and water and looked appraisingly at Sparks.

"I don't mean to pry, Reggie, but are you liberally endowed with discretionary income?"

"Absolutely," said Sparks glumly. "Loaded."

"I take it, that's a 'no'?"

Sparks nodded.

Khong pushed away his empty glass and leant back in his chair. "My dear chap, these ladies of the night, as you so delicately call them, are used to getting five thousand US and a Rolex for licking some sheik's backside. Now given that you're a white man with no visible diseases and" — he sniffed noisily — "no obvious stench, they might give you a discount; a tenner maybe."

Sparks started to protest but Khong gently but firmly interrupted.

"Reggie, even if you could afford it, why waste your money? These bitches are sharks — I'd rather spend the night with Yasser Arafat."

Sparks sipped his beer morosely. "It was a bit of a fantasy I suppose . . . "

Khong, restored to his customary joviality, clapped Sparks on the shoulder.

"Fantasies should remain fantasies Reggie," he boomed. "Reality is always a disappointment. Now where shall we eat?" It was clear that the subject was closed.

They bar-hopped for a while before deciding on L'Entrecôte, on the corner of Allées President Roosevelt and Boulevard de Strasbourg where diners have only to decide how they'd like their steak cooked and which house wine they'll drink: red or rosé. Khong simplified things even further by ordering a bottle of each.

Afterwards Khong insisted that they went clubbing. He draped an arm over Sparks' shoulder: "Why a presentable chap like you should be contemplating going to a tart is beyond me. This town's awash with delicious soubrettes. We'll get you fixed up — just leave it to your Uncle Larry."

On the stroke of midnight, they were forcibly ejected from Ubu Club in Rue Saint-Rome. Khong had taken his vow seriously despite Sparks' protestations. He approached a number of young women to ask, in his flawless French, if they'd like to meet Mickey Rourke, the film star. The offer was accompanied by eye movements and twitches of the head towards Sparks, by then too drunk to be embarrassed. Khong was rebuffed with various degrees of brusqueness but remained unfazed until an outstandingly pert mademoiselle spat "Vaste faire enculer" which amounts to an instruction to go away and submit to sodomy. Khong reacted to the implication by depositing a massive gob of mucus and saliva in her lemon cordial.

After being refused admittance to a couple of other nightclubs, they ended up drinking Armagnac in Khong's apartment in an elegantly crumbling old building in Place des Jacobins. Shortly before 2 o'clock, when both were on the verge of falling asleep in their chairs, a savage catfight broke out in the courtyard below. Khong was galvanised. He sprang cursing from the sofa, rushed out of the room, and returned with a small black pistol. He flung open the double windows opening onto the courtyard and loosed off half a dozen shots. The caterwauling ended abruptly.

Khong returned to the sofa, giggling.

"Only blanks more's the pity," he said. "God, I hate cats."

There the matter may have ended had it not been for an unfortunate coincidence. Khong's apartment was on the third level; the apartment directly across the courtyard was occupied by a Palestinian surgeon, one Abu Fazali, and his family. Fazali periodically invited Khong over for a couscous but they were not intimate friends; Khong wasn't aware, for instance, that Fazali's brother, Naim, was a senior figure in the revolutionary council in the Palestine Liberation Organisation. Naim in fact happened to be visiting Abu from his base in Tunis that weekend and, Khong's gunplay notwithstanding, was at that moment sound sleep in his brother's spare bedroom.

There is a significant Arab community in Toulouse and most of the various strands of Arab radicalism are represented there. For reasons of protocol and security, given that several of the more extreme of these groups regarded the extermination of the leaders of the PLO as an absolute priority, Naim had quietly informed the French Foreign Minister of his private visit to Toulouse.

The French Government regarded his visit as a major security issue; over the years it had been embarrassed more than once by the Middle Eastern blood feuds spilling onto French soil. As a result, stationed around Place des Jacobins that night were a dozen or so highly trained killers from one of the various shadowy paramilitary outfits at the disposal of the French state.

Less than five minutes after the cat-scaring episode, the door to Khong's apartment was smashed off its hinges and in stormed six heavily armed, black-clad figures. Luckily for Khong, he had discarded the pistol; if he'd held on to it or kept it within reach, he most certainly would have been machine-gunned into bloody shreds where he sat. As it was, he was struggling to his feet when the leader of the raiding party hurdled a low coffee table and kicked him with sickening force on the point of the jaw. Khong did a back-flip over the sofa and crashed to the floor where he lay very still. Paralysed by a combination of fear, fatigue and intoxication, Sparks remained sprawled in his armchair, which saved him from similar treatment. He suffered nothing more than a swollen upper lip when the muzzle of a sub-machine gun was rammed under his nose and held there while the intruders proceeded to lay waste to Khong's apartment.

Sparks was taken to an airforce base south of Toulouse and questioned for a day and a half. It was conducted with a minimum of brutality; Khong's firearm, it transpired, was a starting pistol. On the Wednesday morning Sparks was visited in his cell by an urbane civilian who appeared to know every detail of his life since he arrived in France. His visitor told him the affair had been "an unfortunate misunderstanding". It would already have been sorted out, he said, were it not for the fact that Monsieur Khong was proving difficult.

It turned out that Khong, speaking in a bubbling hiss through his wired-up jaw, was threatening, amid repeated references to his friends in high places, to take the matter further. What eventually persuaded him to change his mind was a visit from a prosecuting magistrate who told him bluntly that unless he cooperated, he would be put on trial for firing on members of the security forces; exhibit A, he was promised, would not be his little starting pistol but a 9 mm Beretta which ballistic tests showed had been used in an attempted assassination of an Israeli diplomat in Paris some months before. If it came to that, said the magistrate, Airbus would be building flying saucers by the time Khong got out of jail.

They were tried and convicted of unspecified anti-social behaviour and fined 20,000 francs. The day the money from his mother came through, Sparks paid his fine and bought an air ticket home. He then packed his bags, vacated his apartment and caught a train to Lyon where he spent his remaining funds on a gastronomic binge in that city's famed grand restaurants. At the end of a week of relentless self-indulgence and suffering the worst hangover of his life, Reggie Sparks took the fast train to Paris where he boarded a 747 bound for Singapore.

2

The police investigation which commenced upon the discovery of Wallace Guttle's body was initially complicated by confusion over the precise cause of death. That he'd been run over was clear; how he came to be lying on the floor of the carpark and what state he was in when Margo Dugdale's Datsun trundled over him were, for the time being, matters of conjecture. Having rung the police from her office, Ms Dugdale was of little assistance to them on their arrival; befuddled by alcohol and convinced that she'd done terminal damage to her employment, her right to drive a car, and whoever it was down below with his head squashed beyond recognition, she was reduced to tearful incoherence.

Tony Rispoli was no help at all since, having assessed the situation as being fraught with the potential to ruin virtually every aspect of his life, he'd departed the scene even before Ms Dugdale had dialled the emergency number. Taking advantage of Ms Dugdale's disorientation, Rispoli slipped quietly away, thanking his lucky stars that the lady had been more interested in exchanging bodily fluids than life stories or even names for that matter.

Constables Crane and Drinkwater from the Newmarket police station responded to Ms Dugdale's call. Their first thought was that the deceased had passed out, either drunk or ill, and, in doing so, had by pure bad luck positioned his head in the spot which Ms Dugdale's front right wheel would later also occupy. A swift perusal of the photographs in Guttle's briefcase suggested other possibilities and persuaded them that the safest and most sensible course of action was to alert higher authority. That arrived on the scene shortly after midnight in the forms of Detective Inspector Finbar McGrail and Detective Sergeant Tito Ihaka.

Constable Crane had been put through to Ihaka when he'd rung Auckland's Central Police Station to report a suspicious death. He informed Ihaka that the contents of the briefcase indicated that the deceased was Wallace Guttle, a licensed private investigator; that said briefcase contained photographs of highly personal if not scandalous nature; and that a second and closer inspection of the deceased revealed what could be entry wounds. A quick search of the area had failed to turn up any firm evidence of foul play, such as ejected shell casings.

Ihaka listened with growing perplexity. He'd been on the point of going home where he'd planned to have several beers with his takeaway dinner and, in the unlikely event that he'd managed to programme his VCR correctly, watch the rugby league match. He thought about what Crane had told him for several seconds, then snapped: "Was the fucker shot or not?"

Ihaka considered Constable Crane's answer to be less than satisfactorily concise, covering, as it did, an hysterical woman, the partially crushed head and a mysterious male companion who'd vanished from the scene. He cut Crane short, hung up, alerted forensic, then walked down the corridor to McGrail's office.

Finbar McGrail, forty-four, had grown up in Belfast, Northern Ireland, and joined the Royal Ulster Constabulary straight from school. By the age of thirty he was regarded as one of the RUC's rising stars. At least that was how he was described in a front page story in *The Belfast Telegraph* relating how he'd led a team of detectives which had tracked down an Irish Republican Army hit squad. All four members of the hit squad had died the previous day in a British Army ambush involving careful planning, clinical execution and sufficient firepower to have sunk the royal yacht *Britannia*. As he read the article, McGrail reached two conclusions: firstly, that the so-called troubles in Northern Ireland would more than likely continue for the rest of his career; secondly, that being the case, the odds of his reaching retirement age were no better than even. Finbar McGrail put down the newspaper and rang directory service to obtain the telephone number of the New Zealand High Commission in London. When he got through to the immigration department, he asked whether they were interested in acquiring the services of a trained detective and devout Presbyterian whose hobbies were jogging and military history.

Tito Ihaka was well aware that McGrail was a lay preacher, that he'd run a dozen or so marathons and that he needed very little encouragement to talk at length about war in general or his favourite practitioner, Field Marshal Montgomery of El Alamein, in particular. In Ihaka's view, none of these things was as close to the Ulsterman's heart as a good murder.

He knocked on McGrail's door and went in; McGrail looked up from his paperwork, his thin, dark face expressionless. McGrail's dourness was a byword among his colleagues; a bold constable had once slipped a tape of the children's song "The Laughing Policeman" into a tape deck when McGrail was expecting to hear the confession of a housewife who'd beaten a vagrant to death with a hockey stick for trampling her daffodils. McGrail had maintained a poker face as the song, punctuated by frequent bursts of braying laughter, filled his office. Those who witnessed it swore that a flicker of a smile did cross his face when he told the constable in question that he was being transferred to Otara, or "Jungleland" as it was known to those who worked there.

This ought to cheer you up, you gloomy prick, thought Ihaka: "Sir, Newmarket just reported a guy run over in a basement carpark. Looks like it's a private investigator, fella named Wallace Guttle. The boys on the scene think he might've been dead already."

McGrail took off his glasses. "I know of Guttle," he said. "He takes dirty pictures."

"That fits," said Ihaka. "He had a briefcase full of fuck photos — not porn, more like shots of someone caught doing a bit of sly rooting by the sound of it." Most junior officers watched their language around McGrail in deference to his churchiness; Ihaka made no effort to temper either the foulness of his speech or the crudity of his observations. He lived in hope of provoking a reaction but thus far not even his most imaginative clusters of obscenity had ruffled McGrail's sang-froid.

McGrail's thin-lipped mouth twitched; there was a perceptible stirring of interest in the dark-brown eyes. He stood up, six foot tall and lean as a lifeguard, carefully rolled down his shirtsleeves and reached for his jacket.

"It looks like we'll be working this weekend, Sergeant," he said, leading the way out of his office.

Yes Deacon, thought Ihaka. Sex, murder, perversion — beats the shit out of family service any day.

Reggie Sparks' usual policy when flying was to drink steadily from take-off to touchdown. He did so not because he was a nervous flyer or found air travel too disagreeable to be undertaken sober. It was simply that he was temperamentally almost incapable of declining free drinks. This time, though, to his mild surprise, he found himself sipping his vodka and tonic disinterestedly, having to make a conscious decision to accept the offer of a glass of wine with dinner, and allowing the liqueur trolley to proceed down the aisle. Sparks was preoccupied; he knew he'd reached a watershed and the realisation had prompted some soul-searching, although reviewing his achievements required only a few of the twenty-eight hours it took Singapore Airlines to transport him from Paris to Auckland.

Sparks had been born in Auckland thirty-nine and a half years before, the son of Stanley and Mareena Sparks, née Hazard. His father owned a scrap metal business, the earnings from which he supplemented with income derived from a black market meat racket. Every Thursday night he'd drive an old Bedford van into the carpark at a South Auckland freezing works; his accomplices would then transfer fresh meat, which they'd smuggled out of the works, from the boots of their cars to the van. In the evening Sparks would tour the rugby and rugby league clubs selling the meat at a carefully calculated discount to butcher shops' prices.

The management of the freezing works knew all about the meat smuggling ring. Seeing that it comprised the site representative of the freezing workers' trade union and his entourage of enforcers, management felt that the weekly theft of a few hundred pounds' worth of meat was an acceptable price to pay for a quiet life: it ensured comparative industrial relations stability and meant the bosses could stroll around the works without worrying about the possibility of having a meat hook embedded between their shoulder blades. One Thursday night, however, Stanley drove his meat-laden van out of the freezing works carpark and into a police road block.

By that stage Stanley had profitably off-loaded his scrap metal business so the two years he spent in Mt Eden Prison were not a great hardship for his family, although Mareena had to put up with regular unannounced visits from male admirers keen to capitalise on her husband's absence. On his release, Stanley bought into a milk run. The 5 a.m. starts left him with plenty of spare time in the afternoons, which he spent fishing, doing the odd job and stalking his former accomplice in the meat racket.

He'd learned, via the highly effective intelligence network in Mt Eden Prison, that he'd been sold out by the union representative, who'd since become a Labour Party member of parliament. Although now based in Wellington, the MP returned frequently to Auckland to — in ascending order of priority — see his family, consult with his trade union masters and visit his mistress who resided in a small block of flats in Epsom.

While in prison Stanley had also learned about the mistress and where she lived. He often spent an hour or two of the afternoon parked across the road from the block of flats in the hope of encountering his betrayer. Eventually, his patience was rewarded.

When Stanley saw the MP and his girlfriend pull up in front of the block of flats, he slid out from behind the steering wheel and walked round to the rear side of the van, in the back of which his carpentry tools and gardening implements were arranged on a blanket. He selected a mini-crowbar, about a metre long. Head down and holding the crowbar down his leg, he crossed the road and approached the couple. He walked straight up to them and, without a word of warning, or introduction, took a good backswing and cracked the man on his right knee. He collapsed on the grass verge, moaning loudly. The woman squealed. Stanley told her to clear off.

Stanley was contemplating where to strike next when the MP spoke urgently through gritted teeth: "Leave it mate, leave it. I'll make it worth your while."

Stanley rapped him crisply on the left ankle. The MP switched his grip from his right knee to the new source of pain and swore feebly.

"No bullshit," he gasped. "Lay off and I'll give you some red-hot bully. Deal?"

Stanley nodded. He fully intended to carry on until he'd broken several bones but thought he might as well hear what the man had to say.

"They're going to build a harbour bridge," groaned the MP. "It'll be announced next month."

Stanley bashed him once more then walked back to his van, threw the crowbar in the back and drove off.

Despite Mareena's protestations, Stanley sold the milk run and sank the receipts, plus most of their savings, ill-gotten and otherwise, into North Shore real estate. The Harbour Bridge was opened in 1959. In mid-1962 Stanley sold one of his several Takapuna Beach waterfront properties at a handsome profit and bought himself a second-hand Jaguar. He sold two more some eighteen months later and moved the family into a two-storey house with a swimming pool in Victoria Avenue, Remuera, which he regarded as the poshest street in the poshest suburb. They moved in on the hottest day of that summer. After he'd mowed the front and back lawns, Stanley stood in the shallow end of the pool with a beer in one hand and a cigarette in the other and told his wife he'd never mow another bloody lawn as long as he lived. The following day he rang the headmaster of Prince Albert College to discuss the enrolment of his two sons.

As an ex-jailbird, it tickled Stanley's fancy to send his boys to the most exclusive school in town. Prince Albert College had been founded in Meadowbank 100 years earlier by a group of God-fearing Auckland merchants who profoundly admired Queen Victoria and her German consort. The school had promoted the values associated with their reign — religiosity of the Anglican persuasion, hard work, puritanism and conformity — ever since.

Despite the pleasure it gave Stanley, the decision to send Reggie and his older — by eighteen months — brother Gavin to Prince Albert was not a complete success. Gavin — conscientious, obedient, eager to please — was highly regarded in the college's staff common room. He passed through in the top form and was made head of his house.

If Gavin inherited his mother's social ambitions, Reggie was very much his father's son. He was a schoolmaster's nightmare — lazy, disruptive, always looking for the short cut and, most disconcertingly, apparently blessed with a cast-iron bottom which made him impervious to the threat of the cane, even when wielded by the headmaster, Dr Foster Hogbin. A towering, angular figure who only removed his mortarboard to eat, sleep and worship and who was prone to mood wings of unnerving suddenness, Dr Hogbin could go from a state of beatific serenity into a paroxysm of frothing rage in the blinking of an eye. If he considered the boys were making too much noise as they changed classrooms between periods, he was likely to gallop down the corridors with a cane in each hand and his university cloak billowing behind him, howling, "Scoundrels, scoundrels!" at the top of his lungs, and flailing indiscriminately at those too slow to take refuge.

At the end of Reggie's fifth form year, Dr Hogbin wrote on his end-of-year report: "To say that Reginald is a disappointment would be an understatement of grotesque proportions. The consensus among those unfortunate enough to teach him is that he is a shiftless lout, devoid of even the slightest redeeming feature. I urge you to consider whether he would be better suited to the state system where, for all I know, those tendencies of his which to us seem thoroughly anti-social might scarcely attract notice."

When Dr Hogbin was in an implacable frame of mind, his comments in reports could be brutally frank. But even by those standards, those were harsh words. They were written in the hope of shaming the Sparks into withdrawing

Reggie from the college since he hadn't actually done anything which in itself justified expulsion. Such subtlety was wasted on Stanley. Before long, however, the doctor's prayers were answered.

Early the following year, a few of Reggie's classmates organised a party. Reggie wasn't invited since the venue was the home of a boy who regarded him as insufficiently house trained. The snub rankled because the boy's parents were overseas and parties without parental supervision were rare events promising unimaginable decadence. In retaliation Reggie anonymously tipped off a gang, the Boot Hill Mob, which drew its membership from the Glen Innes state housing area, about the party. He'd expected that a few of the gang members would crash the party, swagger about threateningly, commandeer whatever booze they could find, and then go on to something more their speed than a bunch of private school kids playing Beatles records and postman's knock. He seriously underestimated the surge of class resentment felt by the Boot Hill Mob as they barged into what was indeed one of the grander properties in the eastern suburbs.

Things got rapidly out of hand: a motorbike was ridden through the house and out onto the grass tennis court where a series of high-speed manoeuvres involving violent braking were performed; a piano was pushed into the swimming pool; a double bed was heaved through a first floor window onto the street; girls were pawed, boys were punched; a great deal of methodical damage was done.

The anonymous tip-off came to light when the police rounded up the Boot Hill Mob later that night. Under pressure from the owners of the sacked mansion, Dr Hogbin launched a witch-hunt to find the culprit; Reggie was a prime suspect. As the enormity of the situation dawned on Reggie, so did the realisation that if he wavered for one second in his denials, he was doomed. Even when Dr Hogbin's interrogation went well outside the most broad-minded view of what constituted acceptable headmasterly behaviour, Reggie stuck to his guns. He was not believed of course and even Stanley accepted that his son's position at Prince Albert had become untenable. It was not to be the last time Reggie Sparks failed to last the course.

Sparks completed a relatively incident-free schooling in the state system and astonished all who knew him, even given the accreditation system's lack of rigour, by gaining university entrance. He then passed an undistinguished year and a half at Auckland University before being cast out of the grove of academe.

It was not so much his failure to pass any units which annoyed the authorities as his habit of producing ever more elaborate and heart-rending excuses for failing to hand in assignments. In order to mollify and disarm his various tutors Sparks invented the comprehensive maiming or deaths — lingering in some cases, traumatically unexpected in others — of grandparents, aunts, uncles, sisters and brothers. The hospitalisations, touch-and-go fights for life, or funerals inevitably took place in the remotest parts of the country necessitating his absence from Auckland for periods of a week or more.

Sensing that his English tutor was becoming suspicious, Sparks produced the excuse that brooked no scepticism. He wrote off his parents, claiming they'd been obliterated when their hired car had been crushed like a bug by a ten-ton truck somewhere on the endless highway which crosses the Nullabor Plain from Adelaide to Perth. At a film society wine and cheese that evening, the English tutor mentioned Reggie's orphanhood to a colleague in the history department. The historian was surprised to hear of Mr and Mrs Sparks' fate since Reggie had told him only the week before that they were confined to a decompression chamber in Honolulu, having suffered serious attacks of the bends in a diving accident. The English tutor then surveyed Sparks' other tutors and pieced together a chronicle of carnage involving car crashes, plane crashes, rare diseases, hunting accidents, shark attacks, botched operations and acts of God. It was clear that either Reggie was a compulsive, shameless and sick-minded liar or, that when it came to ill-starred families, the Kennedys had had a dream run compared to the Sparks.

Reggie then startled his parents by announcing that he wanted to become a journalist; he subsequently amazed them by gaining a cadetship at *The Auckland Evening Standard* and making a success of it. He endured the abject existence of a cadet reporter without complaint; he dutifully covered numbingly boring local body meetings; he did little to antagonise his superiors and even managed to ingratiate himself with the chief reporter by happily running down to the TAB to place his bets. Reggie, it seemed, had found his vocation.

By the time he reached his mid-twenties and after six years at *The Standard*, Sparks had become a valued member of staff, regarded as a young man with a real future in the game. While this lifestyle was messy, it was quite unremarkable by the standards of the newsroom. His writing, excitable at first, had adapted to the narrow discipline of the news story — the one sentence intro; what, when, where, why and how; arrange the facts in descending order of importance. Hard news was really his forte — no one chased an ambulance with greater zeal or gathered facts more single-mindedly — but his mentor, the chief reporter, decided he should gain experience in politics. Few had attained a senior editorial position at *The Standard* without a stint in the parliamentary press gallery in Wellington, an experience which supposedly imbued one with the wisdom and gravitas to pen weighty leaders on subjects ranging from the crushing of the Prague Spring uprising to the meaning of Easter. To groom Sparks for the gallery, he was promoted over the heads of more senior reporters to cover the Auckland City Council.

At this pivotal point in his career, Sparks discovered the work of the American journalist Dr Hunter S. Thompson. Thompson scorned the principles of detached observation and impartial reporting by which news journalism traditionally operated. He became part of the story; he was aggressively partisan; he frequently attacked those with whom he disagreed in savagely abusive language. He also celebrated in his writings a wild and bohemian lifestyle fuelled by relentless consumption of alcohol and drugs.

Sparks was captivated by Thompson's rebellion, his flouting of convention, his zany insights, his roaring outlaw behaviour, his twisted humour, his thundering, exhilarating, biblically uncompromising prose. However, New Zealand journalism in the late 1970s was not ready for Hunter Thompson imitators, no matter how pale.

Warning bells sounded when Sparks submitted a feature about the deputy mayor, a large man of forthrightly conservative views, whom he described as being "as piggishly greedy as King Farouk and also sharing the late Egyptian monarch's absolute indifference to the plight of the dispossessed and disadvantaged". The line was sub-edited out. Subsequent stories from the city council roundsman needed pruning to delete unsubstantiated allegations of graft and gratuitous denigration of council officers. The mounting concern about Sparks' copy coincided with a barrage of complaints from councillors and council officials about Sparks' behaviour which had changed from not unpleasant directness to crusading abrasiveness in the space of a few weeks. Within a month of embracing gonzo journalism, Sparks had been removed from the city council round.

He was transferred to a new section of the paper called *City Beat* which had been launched with the aim of attracting a youth readership. Perhaps it was felt that his newly truculent attitude would strike a chord with alienated teenagers but, after a series of corrosive record reviews peppered with comments like "If pus made a sound, this would be it", the feedback from readers indicated that they would prefer a less trenchant approach. His career as a reviewer was terminated when a record distributor filed a writ against the paper claiming damages for loss of sales after Sparks had written that "Clinical tests at Harvard University have established that listening to disco music can cause rectal cancer".

By that stage Sparks had precious little support among the paper's hierarchy. He was put on final notice and transferred to the sub-editors' desk where he was kept under constant supervision. Unable to imitate Dr Thompson in his work, Sparks sought to do so in his lifestyle. He stepped up his alcohol intake and began taking whatever drugs he could lay his hands on. However, among the attributes which Thompson possessed but Sparks did not was the doctor's self-proclaimed "mule shark" constitution. After a month-long spree of whisky, marijuana and LSD, Sparks threw the newsroom into an uproar by stabbing the shipping reporter with a copy spike, apparently in the conviction that he was a giant lizard. After being subdued, Sparks lost consciousness for thirty-six hours; when he woke up, he was unemployed.

3

Wallace Guttle was shot on Friday, 13 August. Seeing no more than a second separated Guttle's realisation that he was about to die and his demise, he didn't have the chance to reflect on the significance of the date. On the Wednesday of the fifth week after that event, Constable Jarrad Renshaw was working the midnight to 8 a.m. shift at the Harbour Bridge police station. It turned out to be an eventful night.

There was the usual paperwork, the distasteful task of cleaning up after an incontinent drunk who'd staggered in looking for somewhere warm to spend the night, and a barney in one of the Fort Street knock shops between an Estonian seaman and the manager over whether the "hostess" of the client bore ultimate responsibility for the achievement of an erection. Then just after 4 o'clock a mate who was working the same shift at the Papatoetoe station rang to tell him about something which had happened on his patch. Renshaw understood why his friend wasn't wasting any time spreading the news. The incident had the two hallmarks of your classic on-the-job story: it was bizarre, even by cops' standards, and it reinforced their basic working premise that most people out there are pretty fucked up. A man who'd been woken up by the barking of the dog next door had beheaded the canine with a chainsaw and flung the severed head through his neighbour's bedroom window. His neighbours' reaction was vociferous rather than violent; although they were mightily upset at having their three-year-old Alsatian's head and a fair amount of broken glass land on their bed in the early hours of the morning; they also had enough sense to keep their distance from someone wielding a blood-stained chainsaw.

What with one thing and another, the duty constable didn't notice the car on the monitor screen until 4.27 a.m. Even as he picked up the phone, the presence of a stationary car on the Auckland Harbour Bridge was reported by Beryl Baptist, a twenty-year-old welfare beneficiary of Whangarei.

When she'd woken at 1.35 a.m. that morning to discover that her live-in boyfriend of two weeks' standing hadn't returned from what he promised would be "a quick beer with the boys", Ms Baptist had made a snap decision. She threw some clothes into an overnight bag, strapped her year-old son Axl into the baby chair in the back seat of her heavily rusted Honda, and drove south with the intention of spending a few days in Auckland with her sister Eve.

Driving south across the Harbour Bridge at 4.18 a.m., Beryl noticed the stationary car in the far left north-bound lane at the bridge's highest point.

She found it ominous that the driver's door was open but there was no sign of the driver. When Beryl arrived at her sister's flat in Grey Lynn, and following their short but vicious exchange, she rang the emergency number and reported what she'd seen.

At 4.21 a.m. Fred "The Freckle" Freckleton left his villa in Herne Bay to drive to the studio in Takapuna from which, each weekday morning, he broadcast the mixture of semi-hysterical gibberish, juvenile smut and pop music which had made him the undisputed king of Auckland's early morning air waves. At 4.28 The Freckle stopped his Porsche behind the newish Saab 9000 parked on the crest of the bridge blocking the far left-hand lane. He peered in the windows, front and back; the car was empty. Shivering a little from the early morning chill and a vague sense of apprehension, he peeped tentatively over the railings; in the darkness he would have been lucky to spot a school of whales frolicking in the sea forty-three metres below. The Freckle was on his car phone explaining to his producer why he was going to be late when the police car arrived.

The Saab belonged to Victor Appleyard. Three hours after Eve Baptist had called her younger sister a "bludging slut" and three and a quarter hours after he'd plummeted into the still, grey waters of Waitemata Harbour at a speed approaching 100 kilometres per hour, Victor Appleyard's body bumped ashore at the Chelsea sugar refinery in Birkenhead.

In the following forty-eight hours policemen and women shuffled, for the most part apologetically, through the existence out of which Victor Appleyard had, seemingly, opted although neglecting to formally announce the fact in a farewell note.

Appleyard had been the forty-one-year-old director of sales and business development for Berkeley Enterprises, a substantial property and construction company. The small police team which arrived at Berkeley's five-storey Onehunga headquarters at 11 a.m. was led by Senior Sergeant Ted Worsp who, over the course of his three decades in the police force, had gained a reputation for sensitive handling of such situations.

Worsp's experience had taught him that when men like Appleyard went off the rails in some shape or form, their secretaries were invariably excellent sources of information and insight. The late sales director's secretary was Janet Gabites, forty-nine. On meeting her, Worsp noticed her age, homeliness and the absence of a wedding ring. When she volunteered that she'd served Appleyard for eight years, his satisfaction was complete. He dispatched his underlings to interview Appleyard's fellow executive and settled down with Miss Gabites and a cup of tea.

After half an hour of Miss Gabites, who turned out to be every bit as infatuated with her ex-boss as he'd guessed, Worsp felt he knew as much about the saintly Appleyard as he wanted to know.

"You know what it's like Sergeant," said Miss Gabites, dabbing away with what Worsp estimated was the tenth tissue she'd immersed in her moist eyes since the interview began. "I'm sure it's the same in the police; the people who care, who can't simply shrug their shoulders and switch off, just get taken advantage of. As if Victor didn't have enough on his plate, they" — her eyes swivelled like anti-aircraft guns across the office to the boardroom — "dumped Australia in his lap, so he was spending a lot of his time over there trying to sort out the mess they've got themselves into. No wonder the poor man hadn't been on top of the world lately — he was working himself into the ground."

Miss Gabites nudged her chair slightly closer to Worsp's, lowered her voice and continued: "I'm not a gossip Sergeant — I'd like to think I haven't got a malicious bone in my body — but I have to say that Victor could've done with more support at home. Maybe I'm speaking out of turn but Louise — that's Mrs Appleyard — never seemed to accept the hours Victor had to work, the travel, the stress, or the importance of being the corporate wife from time to time. Mind you, on the other hand, she certainly gave the impression that she was only too happy to have the rewards — the lovely house, the skiing holidays, the clothes. It's not for me to say so but there are people here who'd tell you that she enjoyed the benefits of being Mrs Victor Appleyard but resented the sacrifices and, as you know Sergeant, you don't have one without the other."

The picture of Victor Appleyard which emerged when the police team had their debriefing session late that afternoon was of a good bloke, solid citizen and dedicated company man. Some of his colleagues had commented that he'd seemed preoccupied and somewhat withdrawn in recent weeks but put it down to the extra pressure that went with being given the responsibility for Berkeley's troubled Australian subsidiary. There were hints of tensions on the home front. A check of his diary had revealed nothing untoward. He'd appeared to be okay the previous evening, ruefully resigned to working until past midnight. No one at Berkeley had ever entertained the idea of him committing suicide.

"That proves bugger all," pronounced Worsp. "People who go round saying they're going to top themselves either end up in loony bins or dying in bed at the age of ninety."

Louise Appleyard did not conform to Senior Sergeant Worsp's expectations or experience of widows.

Slim, elegant, darkly attractive, and seven years younger than her late husband, she sat at the jarrah table on the deck overlooking Lake Pupuke smoking a Dunhill and drinking coffee. There was a mobile phone on the table. Every few minutes it would ring and Mrs Appleyard would pick it up and listen for a while. Then she'd murmur a thank you and say she'd better go, she was being interviewed by the police and no doubt they were anxious to get back to catching criminals.

Constable Beth Greendale admired the fact that little more than twenty-four hours after learning of her husband's death, Louise Appleyard's only visible concession to the situation was dark glasses, which were really unnecessary in the weak early spring sunshine. Senior Sergeant Worsp felt otherwise. Sure it's black, he thought, but the skirt could be a bit longer, for Christ's sake. It wasn't that Worsp was averse to long legs in black stockings but he was used to grieving women responding more favourably to his snowy hair and breezy personality and what, in his frequent moments of conceit, he thought of as his reassuring, even comforting manner. When, on their way out to the deck, Worsp had laid a solicitous hand on Mrs Appleyard's elbow, she'd reacted with a slight but perceptible recoil and a tense little smile which altogether amounted to an injunction to keep his hands to himself.

Constable Greendale who, after a day's exposure, was starting to tire of Senior Sergeant Worsp, had picked up on the body language immediately. She was looking forward to the interview.

Worsp began by asking Louise Appleyard if her marriage had been a happy one. She lit another cigarette and exhaled luxuriantly causing the sergeant, a reformed smoker, a moment of acute discomfort.

"Is that a polite way of asking if I drove him to despair?" she replied with another tightly controlled smile. "I'd say we were at least as happy as most couples that I know. If you ask me, 'Was I in love with Vic?', the honest answer is 'No' but then I can't imagine anyone still being in love — in the giddy, head-over-heels sense — with their partner after ten years. That's not to say I didn't love him because I did. I take it the distinction's not lost on you Sergeant?"

She looked at Worsp curiously. He has no idea what I'm talking about, she thought.

"If you ask me did Vic and I still make love," she continued coolly, "then the answer would be 'Occasionally', certainly not as often as I would've liked. But then twelve-hour days don't do much for the libido. If you ask me whether I made up the shortfall elsewhere, then the answer's 'No' but, in the spirit of candour you've so skilfully encouraged, Sergeant, I'll admit that it crossed my mind from time to time. I doubt that makes me much different from most wives — and certainly not from most husbands."

What a bitch, thought Worsp. He cleared his throat and said, "One or two people at the office had the idea that you didn't go much for his job and the company scene generally."

Mrs Appleyard traced her right eyebrow with a bright red fingernail. Constable Greendale got the impression that she'd already decided that talking to Worsp was a pointless exercise.

"You've obviously been talking to Janet — my number one fan," she said offhandedly. "The company's okay as companies go but it forces people into a very narrow existence. Some of them probably don't have to be forced — as far as they're concerned, the world outside Berkeley and their areas of business may as well not exist — but there was a lot more to Vic than that. I thought they were using Vic, just dumping more and more on him. I suppose he could've said no but that wasn't Vic's way; he'd just take a deep breath, square his shoulders and carry on. Lately, though, I think he'd started to question whether he wanted to spend the rest of his working life in such an environment."

"So you think this questioning process led to him . . ." Worsp left the question hanging in the air.

Louise Appleyard looked at Worsp with almost clinical interest. Constable Greendale caught the look. Here it comes, she said to herself.

"Oh that?" said Louise. "For a while I thought we were going to sit here and talk about my sex life all morning." Worsp squirmed on his substantial buttocks, thinking, no wonder the poor cunt jumped.

Louse Appleyard re-crossed her legs and leaned forward. "Let me spell it out for you Sergeant, as plainly as possible," she said. "Vic did not kill himself. Let's say for the sake of argument that it all got too much for him — the pressure, the disillusionment, wondering what it's all about, the fact that I wouldn't give up smoking, that I didn't want babies, all my other failings that Janet would've filled you in on. The point is that if Vic was anything, he was considerate and he was also insured for well over half a million dollars. So if he was going to commit suicide, he wouldn't have done it like this — he would've made it look like an accident."

Worsp and Greendale made a no more than cursory inspection of Victor Appleyard's study on the basis that if he was going to leave a suicide note, he wouldn't leave it in the bottom drawer under the manuals explaining how to program the auto-dial into his telephone. Worsp lapsed into sullen silence on the drive back to town. That fact that Louise Appleyard had treated him with such transparent disdain was bad enough; what was much worse was that it had been witnessed by a twenty-two-year-old female constable.

"What about the insurance thing then?" asked Constable Greendale as she piloted the police car past Westhaven at 20 kph above the speed limit.

Worsp perked up: "Love, the hardest thing for a suicide's family to accept is that they were the last thing on his mind. You see, suicide is the ultimate act of selfishness," he said, grateful that the phrase he'd heard or read somewhere had popped back into his mind when it was needed. "If Appleyard had really cared about her, he wouldn't have jumped off the bridge would he, so why the hell should he worry about stuffing up her insurance? Believe me love, I've heard that line before today. The way I see it, the pressure and that got too much for him. Now ask yourself: is he really going to spend his last hours on earth trying to come up with some tricky way of doing it so his missus — who he probably couldn't stand anyway and who'd blame him? — gets her hands on the insurance? Do me a favour. And of course it might've been done on the spur of the moment — you know, he's been thinking about it for a while, then one night coming home across the bridge, he decides tonight's the night.

"See, the other thing you've got to remember when you're talking about making it look like an accident, as if it's the easiest thing in the world, is that it's not that easy. There aren't an unlimited number of ways you can kill yourself, you know? It's a question of what means are available. Plus, of course, for most suicides, there's only one or maybe two ways that they can actually bring themselves to do it. Just because a bloke might be quite prepared to poke a gun in his mouth and pull the trigger doesn't mean he could face slashing his wrists; a lot of people are just too bloody scared of heights to jump off a bridge. You know what I mean? It's illogical, sure, but that's the way it is. So it's not like they've got 101 ways to choose from and can pick the one most likely to fool us and the insurance company."

"I'm not sure that's quite what she meant," said Constable Greendale, but she didn't pursue the discussion. She'd heard enough of the wit and wisdom of Ted Worsp for one day.

The contents of Victor Appleyard's Saab were spread out on a desk. Worsp poked disinterestedly through the contents of the black airline pilot's briefcase; others had already done so without finding anything of interest. There was a fat hardback book about Japanese management techniques. As Worsp idly flipped through it, a folded card, slightly smaller than a normal-sized Christmas card, fell out. Worsp examined it. It was white with decal edging; on the front was a rather florid crest and the words "Prince Albert College Ball, 1970".

Something stirred deep in Worsp's memory. He opened the card. Printed on the top of the inside left-hand page were the words "Dance Card"; written on the dotted line below in a loopy, girlish hand was "Bronwen Ticehurst". Worsp, feeling slightly dizzy, put the card down and sat back in his chair.

After a few seconds he picked up the card again. Below her own name and on the facing page, the long-dead Bronwen Ticehurst had written the names of her partners for the various dances at the 1970 Prince Albert College Ball. One of them was that of the just-dead Victor Appleyard.

Worsp put the card down again and stood up. "The suicide note," he said to no one in particular. "He left one after all."

4

Despite his almost cherubic appearance, Jackson Pike competed with the Prime Minister, the Minister of Finance and one or two of the more nauseating television personalities for the unofficial title of the most hated person in New Zealand.

Pike was rarely troubled by this. Whenever he felt particularly put-upon, he consoled himself with the knowledge that, as the editor and joint proprietor of the monthly magazine *New Nation*, his unpopularity was more than matched by his influence.

As a young and dedicated journalist, Pike had often worried about the future of print journalism. One Sunday morning, in the course of a two-hour run along the waterfront, he realised that the remorseless decline of the quality, quantity and readership of the nation's newspapers presented a golden opportunity. Within six months he had secured backing for his venture; a further six months later the first issue of *New Nation* appeared. The print run of 15,000 copies sold out within seventy-two hours.

New Nation set out to be all things to all people. It combined news and lifestyle, weightiness and frivolity, hard-hitting investigative journalism and racy and irreverent celebrity profiles. Determined to avoid the fence-sitting blandness of most newspapers, Pike had launched his organ vowing that, whether the subject was restaurants, rugby or race relations, *New Nation* would leave its readers in no doubt where it stood. He further vowed that the magazine's stance would be determined by the merits of the case rather than the prevailing orthodoxy or current fashion: one month a sacred tenet of political correctness would be ridiculed, the next the outcome of yet another experiment in economic rationalism would be subjected to equally scathing scrutiny.

While this broadened the magazine's appeal, it also meant that, over time, it had offended virtually every shade of political opinion and special interest group. Very early on, Pike had decided that if he was going to give offence, he might as well be hung for a sheep as a lamb. Therefore when *New Nation* took aim at someone, it did so not with a popgun but with an artillery piece.

Even though Pike was widely loathed, his magazine's popularity meant that he could not be ignored by those who wished to influence public opinion, whatever their particular brand of snake oil. After more than a decade of being paid grudging tribute, Pike had become as selective as a diva about whom he hob-nobbed with. Cabinet ministers could bombard his secretary in vain with luncheon invitations; tycoons could spend months trying to entice him to a weekend at their rural retreats. The exception was a man who was so old, he was widely assumed to be dead; in thirteen years Pike had never missed his monthly lunch with Garth Grimes.

Pike and Grimes had instituted their monthly lunch when Grimes retired. There had been a period, after *New Nation* had really taken off and when Grimes still ventured out, during which the lunches would take place at one of the few and invariably very expensive restaurants in Auckland which found favour with both of them. But since reaching the age of ninety, Grimes' excursions had been limited to his twice-daily shuffles along Takapuna beach.

From then on Pike would arrive at the old man's seafront bungalow with a hamper of food, a month's supply of overseas magazines, and a very good bottle of wine. He would make Grimes his first gin and tonic of the day and himself a Campari and soda. They would discuss current events, both domestic and international, and Grimes would give a brisk analysis of them which Pike usually found more illuminating than anything he'd come across in the seven daily newspapers and fifteen periodicals which he made it his business to read. Grimes would then deliver a detailed critique of the last issue of *New Nation* while Pike took notes. They would then have lunch either at the table by the full-length window or on the deck overlooking the beach, depending on the weather. Over lunch Pike would pass on all the unprintable gossip which he and his team of writers had picked in the preceding four weeks.

When Pike ran out of gossip, they would reminisce about the defunct *Auckland Evening Standard* where they'd both worked in the 1970s, Pike as a feature writer and Grimes, as he had been since returning to New Zealand in 1952 after thirty-two years overseas, as the star columnist. Occasionally, when Grimes was feeling particularly frisky, his reminiscences would include the unusual, even bizarre, sexual fantasies he had entertained about some of the *Standard*'s female reporters. As he listened to Grimes' mellifluous purr, Pike would reflect that he was in the presence of almost certainly the dirtiest-minded nonagenarian in New Zealand and possibly the world.

After lunch, Pike would make coffee and take notes as Grimes proffered story ideas and any leads or tidbits he'd picked up from the surviving members of what had been a legendary network of contacts. Thus it was that on one of the few rainless days that spring, Pike and Grimes sat on the deck and discussed the strange death of Victor Appleyard which had occurred four weeks previously.

Garth Grimes regarded himself as fortunate to have been born in 1900. It meant that he was too young for the First World War and too old for the Second. He'd enjoyed what he referred to as "the last fluttering heartbeat of civilisation" — the 1920s — and the post-1945 boom during which he'd managed to position himself for a comfortable retirement. Now and again, when he was advancing this view, someone would ask: "What about the Depression?" Grimes would reply that he'd spent most of the 1930s in Shanghai smoking opium and hadn't noticed. This was something of an embellishment of the truth which was that, during his time in Shanghai, he'd never been so short of funds that he couldn't afford both "a fine meal and an evening with the innkeeper's daughter".

Grimes had left New Zealand in 1920 and spent the next three decades roaming the world as a foreign correspondent, mostly for Reuters. Being inclined to pessimism, he'd concluded in the late 1930s that only the United States was likely to be spared the chaos that he foresaw engulfing the world and accordingly had taken steps to secure himself a posting in Washington. When the threat of nuclear war between the USA and USSR emerged in the early 1950s, Grimes decided that, in the event of hostilities, his apartment building less than a mile as the crow flew from the White House would be vaporised by the first Soviet missile. It was time, he felt, to go home. In 1965 Grimes' American wife died suddenly. Virtually overnight he ceased to care a great deal either way about his and the human race's continued existence; ever since he had maintained a sunny, untroubled disposition which was the envy of all who knew him.

Grimes had always assumed that the rather self-indulgent, at times debauched, life he'd led and the fact that the only exercise he'd ever done was ascending stairs two at a time would ensure he was spared the indignities of extreme old age. It came as something of a surprise therefore when, on reaching seventy and on the brink of retirement, he underwent a thorough medical examination and was pronounced to be in rude health and good for a couple more decades.

Taking the doctor at his word, Grimes, to the consternation of those journalists at *The Standard* who had been jockeying to take over his thrice-weekly column, announced that he wouldn't be retiring after all. For another decade he continued to produce his urbane columns, melanges of opinion, gossip and arcane knowledge, and to supplement his income with what he called his "letters to friends".

To the rest of the trade, this was known as "ratting"—writing, usually on the sly, for other publications. The fundamental principle of ratting was maximum income for minimum output; the ideal rat was done during work time and involved only the most superficial changes to a story which had already been written for the newspaper which paid one's wages.

Grimes was King Rat. Each afternoon he methodically went through the tray on the news editor's desk containing copies of all stories filed that day, tut-tutting gently over grammatical imperfections, stylistic gaucheries and inept intros. Selecting any story that might be of interest to his paymasters on four continents, Grimes would re-nose and re-angle them where necessary then stroll down to the main post office to arrange for their transmission to various overseas newspapers and magazines. Their voraciousness for New Zealand news never ceased to amaze him.

Under normal circumstances, the fact that the highest-paid journalist on the paper was at least doubling his income through the labours of others could have caused resentment in the newsroom. However, Grimes, as well as being regarded with something approaching awe because of his age, reputation and exemplary professionalism, played the role of mentor to many *Standard* journalists. Any reporter, no matter how lowly, could go to him for general guidance or help on a story in the knowledge that it would be provided with the utmost affability. The young Jackson Pike, despite his burgeoning reputation as a feature writer, never filed anything until it had been given Grimes' seal of approval.

Grimes finally retired on his eightieth birthday. After long and careful calculations based on the assumption that he would live to the age of 95, he established that he'd accumulated sufficient wealth to afford his daily intake of a quarter of a bottle of gin, a bottle of decent wine, a glass of cognac and ten cigarettes for the rest of his life without having to sell his house for which in 1979 he'd been offered just over $1 million. He had absolutely no desire to live anywhere else.

In retirement he'd settled into a routine from which he seldom deviated. He rose at 8 a.m. and made himself a cup of tea and boiled an egg, read the paper and smoked two cigarettes. Regardless of the weather he would then go for a walk on the beach. Several of the organisations for which he'd ratted had neglected to take him off their mailing lists when he'd retired so each day's post brought newspapers airmailed from Hong Kong, London and New York. On his return from the beach, he would sit at the table by the big window which looked out to where sea met sky and read them with care. At midday he'd mix himself a gin and tonic; at 12.30 he'd have lunch, usually cold meat and salad, and a glass of wine from the bottle he'd finish with his evening meal.

After lunch he'd walk on the beach again, then take a nap from which he'd be roused by his middle-aged daughter who did his shopping and some cooking and often daydreamed of the house she and her husband would build on the site when Grimes died. She was sometimes troubled by her inability to suppress a twinge of resentment whenever anyone remarked on her father's durability.

Before dinner, which was always unfashionably rich when his daughter cooked, Grimes would drink two gin and tonics while reading a book or one of the magazines supplied by Pike. Sometimes he would watch the news on television, although doing so usually caused a deterioration in his mood. After a leisurely dinner he would retire to bed with a book, perhaps something by P. G. Wodehouse — he re-read all the *Blandings Castle* and *Jeeves* novels each year — and a digestive. After reading for an hour or so, he would turn off the bedside light and lay his head on the pillow. As he lay in the darkness, he'd wonder if this would be the sleep from which he'd never wake up. Just in case, he'd select one incident from his extensive and varied sexual experience and recollect it in every detail. Garth Grimes did not believe in an afterlife.

"This might make something for you," said Grimes, stirring his coffee. "Remember the Appleyard business?"

"The Berkeley guy?" said Pike. "Goodbye cruel world off the Harbour Bridge?"

Grimes, who remembered Pike when he'd been less callous about such matters, nodded. "That's the fellow. I seem to remember the coroner hedged his bets somewhat."

"Had to; Appleyard didn't leave a note. What about him?"

"Had a ring the other day from my man Worsp," said Grimes. "The sergeant at Central. The man's as vain as an archbishop; I mentioned him in a few columns twenty years ago and he's been ringing me ever since, mostly to tell me how clever he is. For once he had a rather interesting tale to tell. I don't suppose the Prince Albert College hanging means anything to you?"

Pike shook his head.

"It happened in 1970. I made a few bob out of it as it happens — *The Daily Mail* couldn't get enough of it, although they kept asking me to get some sex into it. What happened was that a girl named Bronwen Ticehurst, who'd been at the college's annual ball, was found dead in the bell tower. She'd hung herself using a school tie."

Pike nodded. "Yeah, it rings a bell."

Grimes smiled thinly at Pike's unintentional joke. He tended to think that all that held Pike back from being a great editor was that he took everything, himself included, a shade too seriously. He continued: "Well, as you can imagine there was a tremendous palaver. By all accounts she was a radiant little creature from a nice home; in those days, parents who allowed their daughters to go to private school balls rather expected them to come back alive. It was all too much for the headmaster, a very queer fish called Hogbin; he took to barking like a half-witted sheepdog in the middle of communion and had to be confined to a padded cell."

Pike pushed aside his notebook. "This is absolutely riveting Grimy but what's it got to do with Appleyard?"

Grimes regarded Pike placidly over his half-moon glasses. Perhaps, he thought, he could do with a little more patience as well. "Is my narrative too discursive? I hope not; one associates long-windedness with senility. The connection is that the police found Bronwen Ticehurst's dance card from the ball in Appleyard's briefcase; his name was on it."

Pike had a quick mind and Grimes enjoyed watching him use it. Pike put his elbows on the table, pressed his folded hands to his mouth, and then looked intently at Grimes for half a minute. "He was with the girl that night, kept the card ever since, then bales out," he said slowly. "So what's the theory — he killed her and then went through twenty-odd years of torment till he couldn't bear it any more?"

"That seems to be the sergeant's theory which in itself is cause for scepticism. The coroner made no mention of it; couldn't really I suppose — it does involve a couple of hefty assumptions and I don't suppose there's much inclination to re-visit the girl's death." Grimes took a piece of notepaper from his cardigan pocket and spread it on the table in front of him. "I persuaded the sergeant to give me all the names on the card; you might find a couple of them interesting."

Pike's eyes narrowed and he reached for his notebook.

Grimes read the names slowly: "Appleyard of course; Dermot Looms — he must've been her partner because he was down for several dances; Maurice Trousdale; Basil Batrouney; Caspar Quedley and Trevor Lydiate."

Fuck me gently with a chainsaw, thought Pike. Baz Batrouney had been a big name of the local rock music scene in the 1970s; at the height of his fame and amid suggestions that he was severely drug-addled he'd abruptly retired to Waiheke Island and become a recluse. Quedley was a high-powered public relations man, while Lydiate was a debarred lawyer who'd been imprisoned for embezzling a couple of million dollars from a client.

He reached across and picked up the list. "What about these two characters, Looms and Trousdale — they mean anything to you?"

"Looms no," said Grimes. "I suspect Trousdale's one of the carpet Trousdales."

"Perfect," said Pike. If Grimes was right, that made him a member of one of Auckland's wealthiest families. "This could be a beauty. It'll take a bit of work, though — we're bloody stretched at the moment. I might have to put a freelancer on it. Any suggestions?"

"As a matter of fact I have," said Grimes. Pike noticed a glint of amusement in Grimes' watery eyes; look out, he thought, the old trickster's up to something. "Guess who I heard on the radio the other day talking about being run out of France? Our old chum Reggie Sparks."

Pike's smile vanished. He pushed his chair back hard, stood up and began pacing around the deck. "Grimy, this is a brilliant story idea and I'm extremely grateful and all that, but Sparks? You've got to be joking. He's a fucking psycho — remember the time he stabbed Col Dumpley?"

Grimes chuckled. "How could anyone forget? A great day for journalism. Surely you're not going to hold that against him? The boy was on drugs at the time. Good Lord, I remember when I ate magic mushrooms in Mexico — the very last thing you'd want in that state is to be confronted with a sight as horrible as the Dump. I'd have gone for him with whatever I could lay my hands on too."

Pike continued to pace. "Grimy, you know I normally follow your advice without question but not this time; I'm not having that maniac running around town representing my magazine."

"Well, it was just a thought," said Grimes imperturbably. "It simply occurred to me that since Reggie would've gone to Prince Albert with these fellows" — he waved the list — "he might have a bit of a head start so to speak."

Pike stopped pacing and stared at Grimes. He came back to the table and sat down heavily.

"If you change your mind," said Grimes, selecting a cigarette, "you should be able to get in touch with him through his mother; she lives somewhere in St Heliers. I think you're being harsh on Reggie, Jackson — I always found him a pleasant young man. By no means the worst reporter either. Not a lot of flair, I grant you, but quite a toughie behind that dishevelled exterior. I knew his father Stanley you know — the original likeable rogue. He bought property over here around the same time as I did; we probably got advice from the same source."

5

Contrary to his and Detective Sergeant Ihaka's expectations, Detective Inspector Finbar McGrail was not enjoying the Wallace Guttle investigation.

The post mortem had established that the private investigator's death had been caused, not by Margo Dudgale's well-worn Goodyear, but by the three .32 calibre bullets which had penetrated his forehead in close formation. The fact that the killer, using a handgun in poor light, had been able to place three rounds into such a small target — Wallace Guttle's forehead had been more simian than professorial — strongly suggested that he, or conceivably she, was a professional.

Getting to grips with Guttle's shambolic files had been a major undertaking in itself. McGrail's preliminary review of their contents had been conducted with the grim fastidiousness of a man who doesn't own a dog removing dogshit from his front lawn. His distaste for the whole exercise was in sharp contrast to Ihaka's lip-smacking enthusiasm which extended to marking the subjects of Guttle's photos out of ten for appearance and technique. After three painstaking weeks, they'd compiled a list of people who might have held a grudge against Guttle. It was a long one. They and their team then embarked on the slow, often embarrassing and ultimately fruitless process of checking out everyone on the list. After more than a month of interviewing, there was only one name left.

McGrail paused outside the half-open door of the small meeting room at Central Police Station from which the Guttle investigation was being coordinated. He listened to the guffaws from within with disbelief tinged with irritation. Wouldn't he ever get bored with those damned photos?

He went in. Ihaka was flourishing a photograph of a man performing cunnilingus and telling a pair of constables: "I didn't recognise this bloke when I went to see him — I was expecting someone with a moustache."

The constables tittered nervously. McGrail said, "May I interrupt the gynaecology lecture?" The constables slipped out of the room, closing the door behind them. Ihaka sipped his tea.

McGrail looked at the photo. Extraordinary, he thought; Guttle must've been close enough to smell them.

"Well Sergeant, what can you report?"

"I'm seeing Mrs Broome, the one who's been overseas, at eleven this morning. She's the last."

"We haven't got a lot to show for six weeks' work, have we?"

Ihaka shrugged. "We got fuck all."

McGrail sat down opposite Ihaka. The desk between them was piled high with files, photographs and transcripts of interviews.

"We had to go through this process of course but if it was a hit — and I'm sure of that — the answer isn't in there," he said, pushing a pile of folders a centimetre or two.

Ihaka nodded. He and the inspector had had this conversation before.

"All anyone in here," said McGrail, giving the stack another nudge, "would've got from killing Guttle is satisfaction. For them the damage had been done — getting rid of him wouldn't repair their relationships. You've got to feel pretty strongly to kill someone just for revenge — it's got to be churning your guts day and night. And when you hate that much, you're more likely to do it yourself than hire someone."

Ikaha knew McGrail didn't expect an answer so he didn't give him one.

McGrail opened a manila folder and began sifting through it. "You've talked to them, sergeant, you've read the transcripts. Most of these people were well off, professional types. How many of them would know where to find an assassin?"

Assassin, said Ihaka to himself. He thinks he's back on the Bogside. "Very few, sir," he said. "I don't suppose there's a lot of call for assassins in Remuera."

From the start of the investigation, McGrail had urged Ihaka and his team to look beyond Guttle's files and photos. "Nine out of ten times," he told them, "hiring a killer is a business decision rather than an emotional act."

McGrail's theory was that Guttle hadn't been killed because of something he'd done; he'd been killed to stop him going any further with something he was working on or to stop him acting on something he'd found out. Ihaka thought the theory made sense the first time he'd heard it; he still tended to think so even after hearing it repeated twice a week for six weeks. The problem was that Guttle enjoyed his secrets too much to share them with anyone. No one knew what he'd been working on when he was killed; he hadn't kept a diary or notes of work in progress. Plus, he was a one-man band; he'd had a woman who came in for a couple of afternoons a week but only to do the administrative chores.

They'd wasted a week tracking down Tony Rispoli, Margo Dugdale's mystery companion. Rispoli had been subjected to one of McGrail's legendary interrogations — dispassionate, detailed and demoralising — at his home in front of his wife. Ihaka had gained the impression that Rispoli would have the distinction of being Guttle's last victim. Even in death it seemed, Wallace Guttle was able to put asunder those whom God had joined together.

McGrail stood up. "Okay, see this woman then give me a progress report. When I've seen that, I'll review this whole investigation. Doesn't look like either of us are going to make our names on this one Sergeant."

Ihaka met McGrail's expressionless gaze and reached for his favourite file. "A pain in the bum sir," he said, "in every respect."

If cigarettes and whisky had caught up with Stanley Sparks a month early he would have died a very rich man. Not that the September 1987 crash reduced him to penury; it simple restored the status quo by wiping out the gains he had made riding the stockmarket in the mid-1980s. As it was, Stanley had left his widow with more-than-adequate capital and a large and comfortable freehold house in one of St Heliers' nicer streets. It was there that Reggie Sparks had taken up residence on his return from France.

Reggie's major achievement since his homecoming had been to persuade his mother to subscribe to Sky Television. As time passed, he strayed less and less from the sofa in front of the television set in the downstairs den. He'd seen a lot of movies and gained what he felt was a reasonable grasp of the situation in the Balkans. Mostly, though, he watched sport. South African rugby featured prominently on the sports channel and Sparks had watched enough of it to recognise the players' names, most of which, at first hearing, sounded like someone clearing their throat prior to spitting.

Although Sparks didn't realise it, the phone call from Jackson Pike was ideally timed. His mother Mareena was a patient and tolerant woman but didn't possess inexhaustible supplies of either quality. She'd accepted that Reggie would need a period of readjustment and if that meant lying on the sofa watching television for up to fifteen hours a day, so be it. Reggie had made some contribution to the household, revealing a hitherto unsuspected interest in cookery. His specialities were the traditional French casserole dishes like boeuf bourguignon, navarin de mouton and coq au vin. But the sense of well-being induced by etuvée de veau au vin rouge and a few glasses of South Australian shiraz only lasts for so long; in Mareena's case it tended to evaporate almost completely by midday the following day, particularly if the cook was still in bed.

It was nine weeks to the day since Reggie's return. That was as much readjustment as Mareena was prepared to countenance; it was time, she felt, for Reggie to get off his backside, find a job and either move out or start paying rent. So Mareena stood in the doorway to the den, arms folded, regarding her unkempt son without affection and steeling herself for confrontation when the phone rang. She answered it; it was Mr Jackson Pike of *New Nation* magazine calling for Reggie Sparks.

The previous night, Reggie had stayed up till four in the morning watching caribou racing live from Lapland and drinking malt whisky. Three aspirins and two glasses of Berocca had had no discernible anaesthetising effect on the starbursts of pain behind his eyes. Neither Jackson Pike nor *New Nation* meant a thing to him but even with his perceptive faculties dimmed to a level of barely above sleepwalking, he'd sensed that his mother was on a mission. That could only mean one thing and it was a thing he would take every opportunity to postpone. He hauled himself off the couch and picked up the phone.

"Hello."

"Sparks? It's Jackson Pike here. We worked together on *The Standard* a long time ago."

Sparks closed his eyes and made a superhuman mental effort — Pike: short, dark, wrote features, up himself.

"Yeah. How are you?"

The half-hearted note of familiarity disappeared from Pike's voice altogether. He was all business.

"Listen, what are you up to these days? You still a hack?" He didn't wait for Sparks to respond. "I run a magazine called *New Nation* and I need someone to chase down a story. Could be a good yarn. You interested?"

Sparks listened to Pike with mounting unease. The feature story the editor outlined sounded like an extremely tricky and demanding assignment and it was a long time since Sparks had attempted serious journalism. Given the state of his morale and assuming his firestorm of a hangover ever abated, he reckoned he could just about process a press release into a ten-paragraph news story. Pike was talking about something else altogether. Christ, listen to him.

". . . okay, the basic story is these six guys who were involved with this girl who died twenty-odd years go, how it affected them and what's become of them since. But I see it as, like, an extended metaphor for the way the country's changed in that time. You know Lydiate, the lawyer who's inside, could symbolise the collapse of ethics in business, the way greed and corruption have taken over; Batrouney, the musician, he stands for the dark side of sex, drugs and rock 'n' roll, the end of seventies innocence; Quedley, the PR man, symbolises the rise of the image maker, the manipulator, that whole image industry — advertising and PR — and the way it's been able to suck money out of the taxpayer by advising government departments and all that shit. Appleyard's obviously the starting point and you're going to have to get a handle on what the hell was going on inside his head — could he have killed the girl? Was he haunted by her death all this time? I don't know about the others guys but I'll bet they're good stories too. I mean, Trousdale's apparently the heir to a massive fortune. What d'you say? If it comes off, it'll be a cover story and a bloody good way for you to get back into it and get some profile."

What's this fucking maniac talking about? Sparks wondered. He desperately wanted to hang up and lie down in a dark room. He couldn't do that, not with Mareena standing right next to him looking expectant. He muttered his acceptance and half-listened as Pike jabbered on about money, deadlines, photographs and posting him out the newspaper clippings on Appleyard.

"Okay, all set," said Pike. "Keep me posted on how you get on."

"Hang on," said Sparks. "Where do I find these guys?"

"You ever heard of a phone book?" said Pike testily after a meaningful pause. "You went to school with these wankers, Sparks; if you can't even find them by yourself, what sort of crap are you going to come up with?"

Sparks said, "Yeah, okay," and put the phone down. He smiled weakly at his mother.

"Well, Mum, back to work."

He told her all about the assignment. She was doubly pleased because it meant the moment of reckoning would be postponed, perhaps indefinitely. Who knew where this might lead? As she headed upstairs to make lunch, she called over her shoulder: "I'm sure Gavin can help you get in touch with those people; he's got a couple of friends in the Prince Albert Old Boys' Association."

Sparks slumped on the sofa. There were three thoughts running through his head and he wasn't sure which was the most depressing.

There was the fact that his mother's mind had moved much faster than his when it came to tracking down the dead girl's dancing partners; there was the prospect of having to spend time with his brother and, worse, ask him for help; and there was Pike, the hotshot magazine editor — another contemporary who'd outstripped him.

In the first few weeks after his return, Sparks had made an effort to get in touch with old friends but the reunions had proved dispiriting experiences. Even those who'd been just as directionless and irresponsible as him now seemed to have something for themselves. They had homes, families, jobs that they actually seemed interested in, reputations, even a little fame in one or two cases; they had something to show for being forty-odd. What did he have? Big fat zero. Sure, some of them had changed for the worse; some of them had become conventional and boring and smug. But they had a focus and, for better or worse, seemed happy about it.

He'd come to dread the questions that invariably followed the greeting and nostalgia: So what've you been up to, Reg? What are your plans? You going to buy a place? Better move fast, the market's heating up. Don't tell me you didn't bring a little mademoiselle back with you? When do you hit the big four-O Reg — or is that a rude question? Reggie, one word of advice — superannuation; we've got to look after ourselves now, mate, because the government sure as hell won't.

All of them growing up, settling down, making it, going places, carving out their little niches, finding a meaning in their existences to sustain them through the home stretch, the hard stretch, the real thing.

Starting to feel like the train's left the station boy and you ain't on it.

Tito Ihaka parked in front of Priscilla Broome's smart Mairangi Bay townhouse with a view. He wondered where the ex-husband was living now and decided it would be somewhere just as good if not better. Despite everything you heard about blokes being taken to the cleaners in divorce settlements, it was Ihaka's experience that the legal system was piss-poor when it came to separating rich men from their money.

You sound just like your old man he thought, smiling at the idea. Ihaka doubted that his late father, despite the firebrand rhetoric, had ever laid a finger on a genuine class enemy. By all accounts, though, he'd thrown his considerable weight about very effectively in the murky and often violent factional disputes in which he and his fellow communists often engaged. In fact, continually engaged; they just never seemed to find the time to overthrow the system.

His father had been something of a maverick: a fervent admirer of the politically unsound — in Moscow-aligned circles — Josef Broz Tito, hence Ihaka's Christian name. Had he lived to see it, the gory dismantling of Tito's legacy would have been the second great disappointment of Jimmy Ihaka's life; the first had been his only son's decision to become a policeman. Although a heretic on some issues, Ihaka senior held straight-down-the-line Marxist views on the police's role in the class struggle.

Pricilla Broome had overdone the sunbathing during the six weeks in Noosa. In Ihaka's opinion, one of the few direct benefits of being born brown was that one felt little compulsion to waste summer lying in the sun cultivating skin cancers, as Mrs Broome, whose complexion bore a resemblance to the skin of a passionfruit, obviously did.

Mrs Broome was unable to contribute much to the investigation. Her attitude to violent death was essentially that she'd like to rule it out of her life altogether but if it had to happen to someone else, who better than Wallace Guttle? It was a sentiment Ihaka found difficult to fault.

Ushering Ihaka to the door, Mrs Broome decided to give him the benefit of her thoughts on the subject of death.

"I'd never known anyone who's died mysteriously or violently and then all of a sudden, it happens to two people I know within a few weeks. When I say that, I didn't really know Guttle and quite frankly wouldn't have wanted to, but I knew poor Victor Appleyard quite well. And even more of a coincidence, not long before he died, Victor rang me to ask about Guttle and get his phone number."

Like most policemen, Ihaka was not a great believer in coincidence.

"Appleyard — he was the bloke who went off the Harbour Bridge? Bit of a high flier? Hang on, let me re-phrase that — a big-time businessman?" She nodded. "What did he want Guttle for?"

"He didn't say." Mrs Broome looked slightly embarrassed. "I'm more of a friend of Louise, Victor's wife — widow I should say. I suppose she must've told him I'd used a private detective to . . . when my marriage got into trouble. Victor must've told me three or four times that it was nothing to do with him and Louise; he said it was a business matter that he wanted Guttle for. Between you and me Sergeant, I wasn't sure I believed him. I wondered if I should tell Louise — I thought my loyalty was really to her but you've got to be careful when you get involved in other people's relationships; you can do more harm than good. Then of course when Victor . . . well, it's the last subject you're going to bring up, isn't it?"

"I guess so," said Tito Ihaka thinking, is this a clue? Did Rose Kennedy own a black dress?

6

Gavin Sparks, the accountant, checked the time on his assertive sports watch again. It was a nervous reflex — so Reggie was late, so what else was new? The second pre-dinner Scotch was also a sign of nerves; Gavin drank, as he did most things, in moderation — two snorts before dinner on a week night was loose behaviour for his standards.

It was all of thirty years since Gavin had felt entirely comfortable in his brother's company so it was par for the course that he wasn't looking forward to the evening. To make matters worse, their mother had got it into her head that this story for *New Nation* was make or break for Reggie and was expecting — no, demanding — Gavin's cooperation and encouragement.

Gavin was profoundly unenthusiastic about the whole project. The thought of his erratic and disaster-prone brother and that scandal rag *New Nation* combining forces to rattle the skeletons in Prince Albert College's cupboard was gravely disturbing. It could have professional ramifications; the old boy network was good for business. Besides, his son James was due to start there the following year.

Despite his reservations, Gavin would do what he could for his brother because Mareena had asked him to and Gavin was as good and dutiful a son as he was a father, a husband and an accountant. Gavin Sparks took his obligations seriously and took pride in performing well in his various roles. He saw himself as a contributor, a good citizen. Of course he earned a good living, but that didn't mean he thought money was the be-all and end-all; he just wanted to do the best he could for his family. If everyone had Reggie's attitude, where the hell would we be?

The prickly defensiveness of this train of thought was prompted by Gavin's certainty that, in the course of the evening, he and everything he stood for would be subjected to mockery: mockery for being an accountant, a suit, for making money, for taking life seriously — mocked for not having failed! Of all the things about his brother which irritated Gavin Sparks, the most grating by far was Reggie's assumption of superiority. What in God's name did he have to feel superior about? He took a deep breath. Tonight was another night; whatever the provocation, cordiality must be maintained. Reggie, according to their mother, was taking a tentative step in the right direction and nothing could be done to derail his comeback from semi-retirement.

The doorbell chimed. Gavin let in his brother. As they shook hands, he registered that Reggie hadn't shaved, needed a haircut, and was wearing their late father's favourite sports jacket. That jacket's at least fifteen years old, thought Gavin, and it's in a hell of a sight better condition than anything else he's got on.

"G'day Gav," said Reggie, handing over a brown paper bag containing a $12 bottle of red wine. "Nice jeans. Iron them yourself?"

Heather Sparks stood, unnoticed, in the doorway to the lounge and observed her husband and brother-in-law. Gavin stood straight-backed to the left of the fireplace; Reggie was half-sitting, half-lying in the armchair, his legs splayed out in front of him.

The odd couple, she thought; nothing in common except their name and their noses. Start at the top: Gav's hair's still black; looks a lot better since he started going to that new place too. Maybe a lighter touch with the blow dryer my darling — it's just a tad too neat. Reggie boy, do my eyes deceive me or do I see a few grey hairs? God, you'd think he didn't own a comb, the way it sticks out all over the place. I bet Gav walks into one before the night's out; he'll recommend the guy who does his hair and Reg'll have that crooked grin on his face and say something like: "Why the fuck would I want hair like yours?" So sweet to each other. Gavin, why are you wearing those designer jeans I got you? You don't like the damn things, you're always saying you're not built for jeans. He's trying to avoid — what was it Reggie used to say? — looking like he's cracking walnuts in his arse. Same reason he's put on that Country Road shirt. The sweater with the diamond pattern's not quite right, though; you can never avoid the golf club look entirely, can you my dear? Reg, Jesus, where'd you get that disgusting jacket? Otherwise the old uniform, old being the operative word: old jeans, old sneakers, old shirt. More to the point, what's underneath? Gav keeps fit but he was skinny to start with; all the jogging gives him that stringy look. Reggie's got more meat on him, but the sort of life he leads, maybe it's going soft and flabby? Oh I don't know — there's nothing hanging over his belt and that backside, let's have a good look at you. That'd really make Gav's night.

Instead she said, "Which one of you boys is going to carve?"

Although Reg Sparks liked to think he didn't envy his brother one iota, it wasn't true. He envied him Heather. Watching them during dinner, he thought, as he always did, how did a quince like him get a woman like her?

Afterwards, back in the lounge with a glass of port, Gavin gave voice to his concerns.

"Do you really think this is such a good idea? I mean, dragging up all this stuff is going to upset a few people."

"Christ, the story's going to get done whether I do it or not. You should've heard Pike on the phone — the guy was raving."

"But do you have to do it? I can tell you, it's not going to make my life any easier."

It wasn't the smartest thing Gavin could've come out with. Reggie had never seen his role in life as making his brother's life easier and wasn't about to start.

"Well, it's up to you," he said. "I mean, this wasn't my idea. Mum just thought you could give me a hand getting hold of these guys but if you're not happy about it . . ."

That had Gavin protesting that he'd never said he wouldn't help and all right, let's have a look at the list, most of them would be his year so he'd probably know himself. Reggie thinking, Jesus Gav, you're such a pushover.

Darkness rolled across Gavin's face as he read the list. His brother sat in silence thinking, what's the bet one of them's his biggest client?

When Gavin finally spoke, his voice was flat and lifeless.

"Looms, he was off a farm up north. He's probably still there; the Old Boys' Association's bound to have an address. Batrouney was the pop star, wasn't he? Wouldn't have a clue where he got to. Trousdale's family used to own Fabric Carpets; they sold it for a fortune. Maurice hasn't done a stroke of work in his life — as far as I know, he sits around his apartment in Herne Bay waiting for his mother to die. Trevor Lydiate stole a couple of million off a client and blew the lot; he's in some minimum security prison. The client was actually Barry Plugge, the strip club king, so they say Lydiate's better off inside where Plugge can't get him. And Quedley — well, just look in the phone book."

Gavin handed back the list, gulped the rest of his port, and leaned back in his chair staring at the ceiling.

"What's up with you?" said Reggie.

"Quedley hasn't changed. He's still the golden boy, too much charm for his own good. We bumped into him a couple of years go. It was one of those nights when Heather overdid it . . ."

Over the years Reggie had heard the odd story about what his mother referred to as "Heather's problem". As far as he could tell, it boiled down to the fact that when she'd had a few, she became a bit of a flirt — pinched a bum or two, turned the New Year's Eve kiss into a tongue wrestle; the same sort of stuff most men do given half a chance. If Gavin's stricken look was anything to go by, she'd given Quedley a lot more than a cheap thrill.

"We went to a party on the Shore somewhere. A client of mine was there and baled me up in a corner; I just couldn't get away from him. When I finally managed to escape, I couldn't find Heather anywhere so I went looking for her."

Reggie knew what was coming; it was just a matter of how bad. He felt slightly queasy. He was also very curious.

"I found them — Heather and Quedley — in the spare bedroom, down to their underwear. Heather had played up a few times before — you know, embarrassing stuff but nothing to get too worked up over. She never took any of it seriously, you know? This time, though, she was . . . gone — way gone."

Gavin was still staring at the ceiling, replaying the scene in his mind as he'd done a thousand times. Reggie wasn't sure what he felt for him; eventually he decided it was respect. You're a tougher man than me pal, he thought.

There was one question he had to ask: "What did Quedley do when you walked in?"

Gavin shook his head slowly. "Didn't turn a hair. He just said, 'C'est la vie', picked up his clothes, walked out and left us to it. He was just the same at school — had a nerve you wouldn't believe."

On his way out, Reggie stopped by the living room where Heather was playing scrabble with James. Saying his goodbyes, he was unusually attentive to his nephew. That's nice, thought Heather. Normally, he acts like Jamie doesn't exist.

Tito Ihaka had expected more of a reaction when he broke the news to Louise Appleyard that her late husband had hired a private investigator specialising in confidential enquiries. What he got was "Really?" accompanied by expectantly arched eyebrows. The tone and expression implied that Ihaka would have to come up with something better to justify his visit.

"You don't believe it?"

"If you say it's so Sergeant, I believe you."

"But?"

"Look, I think we're at cross-purposes. I'm prepared to believe Vic hired this character but it wasn't to check on me."

"How do you know?"

"Because there was nothing to check," she said with the diminishing patience of a teacher explaining something glaringly obvious to a backward child. "Vic knew that so why would he waste money confirming what he already knew?"

"So why did he hire the bloke?"

"Obviously to find out something that he didn't know," she said in an even sharper tone.

Ihaka had checked the Appleyard file beforehand. "Could it have had something to do with the girl's dance card that was in his briefcase?" he asked.

Louise Appleyard knew all about the dance card too. Its discovery had led to another trying session with Senior Sergeant Ted Worsp.

"Possibly," she said reflectively. "The thing had stayed with him, no doubt about that. It seemed a little morbid to me, although it was never the sort of fixation that that buffoon Worsp made it out to be — all that drivel about Vic brooding on it for twenty years. If you want my opinion, Vic hadn't had the card for long; if he had, he would've shown it to me at some stage. I suggest it would be a more productive use of your time, Sergeant, trying to find out where the card came from than worrying about whether I was a naughty girl."

If you had been a naughty girl, thought Ihaka as he drove away, I sure as hell wouldn't have minded seeing the pictures.

About the time Tito Ihaka was trying to visualise Louse Appleyard in the throes of passion, Reggie Sparks was speaking to her on the phone seeking an interview. An hour earlier, the approach would have been unceremoniously rebuffed. However, Ihaka's visit had given Louise pause for thought. This had been her first exposure to the police mentality and it had left her unimpressed: their matter-of-course assumption of sexual shenanigans on her part; their apparently unshakable determination to view Victor as a suicide; their breathtaking leap of logic to link her husband with the Ticehurst girl's death. There was something to this Guttle connection but the police would just sit on their fat collective arse . . . unless she could find some way of pressuring them to pursue it. Like a story in *New Nation*.

So at 11.05 the following morning Reg Sparks, wearing a new pair of Levis, an ironed shirt and his late father's jacket, knocked on Louise Appleyard's front door. A minute went by then the door was jerked open. There was a gust of perfume, a swirl of black hair and a female voice saying very quickly, "Come in Mr Sparks, make yourself comfortable. I'm just on the phone but I'll be with you in two ticks."

She led Sparks through to a large kitchen, which opened out onto the deck, then disappeared. Sparks looked out through the condensation on the sliding glass doors at the rain which was coming down in a silver sheet. Spring wasn't like this when we were kids, he thought. It was dry and crisp and at morning break there was a race to get the best positions to bask in the sun for a quarter of an hour. Now it's always grey and gloomy and pissing down with rain. Must be the greenhouse effect — all that spray-on shit.

There was music coming from a ghetto blaster on the kitchen bench. It sounded like Lloyd Cole. He listened to the words: "Now when you're puttin' on your face/Guess that you feel kinda low/Knowin' that you're past your best/ And you got nothin' to show." Sounds familiar, he thought. Then the chorus: "Only this time round you might have to . . . pay for it."

It was not a good moment to be reminded of his short and ignominious career as a gigolo but the memory flash was so vivid that Sparks felt his cheeks burning. It was all that fucking German's fault, what was his name? Klaus something. Standing there in that bar in Toulouse, about seven foot tall, checking his biceps and his profile in the mirror, looking like the prototype for the master race, bullshitting about the money he'd made as a gigolo on the Côte d'Azur, finally coming out with why didn't Sparks go down there and try it? Sparks, ordering two more beers, saying, "All very well for you mate, but I don't look like some genetic engineer's wet dream."

"Not at all, not at all," said Klaus vehemently. "The most important things are that you can be very charming and you can get hard at the right time, even if the ladies are a little old and not so beautiful. Okay? It is not necessary that you are handsome, just that you are not ugly. Also you must not be short, you must not be fat, you must have all the hair. So you are fine. Of course" — he looked Sparks up and down — "you must dress in the correct way."

If Sparks had dispassionately assessed himself in terms of Klaus' specifications, he would have to acknowledge that he was not renowned for his devilish charms. Furthermore, his ability to stand and deliver on demand was untested. However, it was late at night and he was drunk, a combination conducive to the formulation of hare-brained schemes. Two days later he was in the bar of the Hotel Negresco on Nice's Promenade des Anglais, dressed in a pale green linen suit he'd bought in Bangkok and casting meaningful glances at any woman of mature years who entered.

His first assignation was with a fifty-year-old spinster from Somerset. When he discovered that she was staying not at the Negresco but at a much more modest establishment several blocks back from the beach, Sparks began to wonder whether they were thinking in similar ballparks with regard to his fee. As it turned out, she had no figure in mind; indeed she was quite oblivious to the fact she was party to a commercial transaction. He discovered how it was done on his second attempt when a lady, an Austrian, demanded payment from him before she'd removed a single garment. Sparks fled with guttural oaths ringing in his ears, caught the next train back to Toulouse, and avoided the company of women for several weeks.

The traumatic recollections left him ill-prepared for his interview with Louise Appleyard. After she'd spent fifteen minutes explaining why she was sure her husband hadn't committed suicide and urging him to follow up the Guttle connection, she felt compelled to ask Sparks if he possessed the memory of a chess grandmaster since he was neither using a tape-recorder nor taking notes. Half an hour later she watched Sparks trudge through the rain towards his mother's car. If that's an ace newshound, she thought, I'm Opo the dolphin.

7

While the meeting with Reggie Sparks did little for Louise Appleyard's spirits, it had quite the opposite effect on him. He sensed that she hadn't been overly impressed with him and was determined to give her cause to revise her opinion. It had been some time since he'd had a goal in life.

Gavin had supplied phone numbers and addresses for Looms, Trousdale and Quedley. Directory service provided the phone number of the prison one hour's drive south of Auckland where Lydiate was incarcerated and Jackson Pike's secretary had rung with Batrouney's address on Waiheke Island. If Batrouney was on the phone, he had an unlisted number.

Dermot Looms was indeed still on the farm. He responded with the no-nonsense gruffness one associates with the rural sector: "If you want to come all the way up here, that's up to you. Sounds like a waste of time to me." *New Nation* seemed to carry more weight in Quedley's office; his new secretary arranged an appointment the following Monday morning on the spot. Trousdale had his answering machine on so Sparks left a message.

When Trevor Lydiate, the disgraced lawyer, got the message left by Sparks, he swore under his breath and requested to make an immediate phone call. He rang a South Auckland car dealer, one of the few people in what had been his social circle who would still take his calls, and told him to drop what he was doing and get down to the prison that afternoon.

When the car dealer got back to Auckland after visiting Lydiate, he followed to the letter the procedure the lawyer had laid down before entering prison. He stopped at the first public phone he saw and dialled the number he'd memorised. The man who answered the phone said: "Service department."

"Is Danny there?"

"Yeah, speaking."

The car dealer said, "A journalist from *New Nation* magazine, called Reggie Sparks, wants to talk to Mr Brown," then hung up.

The car dealer got back into his car, his mind abuzz. He wondered who Danny was; he wondered what Lydiate was up to; he wondered if he'd been wise to agree to help Lydiate on a no-questions-asked basis. He also wondered how long Reggie Sparks had left to live. Some two months before, the car dealer had relayed another message from Lydiate to the taciturn Danny that "a private investigator called Wallace Guttle is sniffing around Mr Brown". A week later he read in his morning paper that Guttle had been shot dead in a Newmarket carpark.

Most of all the car dealer wondered if being Lydiate's go-between made him an accessory to murder.

After the call from the car dealer, the man named Danny, who repaired electrical appliances, left his workshop and walked across the road to a phonebox. He dialled a number that he'd known by heart since long before Lydiate had become a guest of the Crown. After two rings the receiver at the other end of the line was picked up. There was no greeting or acknowledgement. Danny repeated the message that the car dealer had given him and hung up. Unlike the car dealer, he neither reflected on the consequences of his action nor was he curious as to the identity of the silent party at the other end of the line. As long as his unknown benefactors continued to pay $50 into his TAB account each week, Danny was quite happy to go on being a link in the mysterious chain.

His call had gone to a red telephone, one of three on a large and tidy mahogany desk in an office above The Blue Angel strip club in Auckland's Karangahape Road. The man behind the desk groaned when the red phone emitted its distinctive ring; lately that sound had heralded nothing but bad news. After he'd heard Danny's message, the man planted his elbows on the desk, put his head in his hands, and said in a loud and troubled voice: "Just one motherfucking thing after another."

The man was Barry Plugge. Gavin Sparks had described him as "the strip club king"; a Sunday tabloid had once dubbed him "Auckland's Sultan of Sleaze"; Plugge saw himself simply as a businessman, someone who identified a need and catered to it.

At the peak of his fortunes in the late 1970s, Plugge had earned close to $1 million a year from a dozen flourishing strip joints and massage parlours around Auckland. However, the 1980s had been a difficult decade; first came the relaxation of the censorship laws which resulted in pornographic videos becoming freely available; then came AIDS; then came some serious competition.

Plugge took a dim view of all three. He considered sex should stay in the strip clubs and massage parlours where it belonged, not on the shelves of neighbourhood video rental shops. Porn videos, he felt, simply encouraged masturbation, a practice which he disapproved of as unyieldingly as did the Vatican. Plugge, who'd been happily married for twenty-seven years, could think of nothing more demeaning for a grown man than masturbating in front of a television set. However, there was also a commercial dimension to his disapproval: masturbation was bad for business. "Wank, wank, money in the bank," he would say. "A bloke's not going to go to a massage parlour if he's just jerked off."

AIDS, he insisted, was something which happened to male homosexuals and drug addicts and his girls were neither; a few of them were undoubtedly lesbians but, to quote another of his aphorisms, "no one ever caught AIDS off a dildo".

Plugge, an ardent nationalist, was proud to be a New Zealander who employed New Zealanders and who provided entertainment for New Zealanders while performing a useful social service in the process. It infuriated him the way offshore operations had tried to muscle in on his patch in recent times — the Italians from Sydney and, even worse, the Asians who flew in "students" from Thailand and Hong Kong, girls who'd work for next to nothing and were often prepared to dispense with a condom for a few extra dollars. And when Plugge, having seen his revenues decline precipitously, swallowed his pride and his principles and brought in his own Asian girls, what did those yellow animals do? They put a fucking contract out on him!

These negative trends forced Plugge both to look around for opportunities to diversify and to consider resorting to the sort of strong-arm methods he had always shied away from. And it was the combination of the two which had reduced him to sitting at his fine desk with his head in his hands, feeling sorry for himself.

Throughout his career, Plugge had followed three basic rules: never a borrower or a lender be; never take commercial advice from a lawyer; and never make decisions when in the grip of emotion, whether the extreme of mood was up or down. Brooding on his problems, Plugge reflected bitterly that he was now paying the price for having broken two of these rules. At the time, though, it had seemed too good to be true; ever since he'd been in business, he'd been ripped off by lawyers. Then, right when his cash flow was being squeezed, he'd been presented with a scheme for getting it back with interest.

It all began with an invitation to lunch. It came from Trevor Lydiate, a partner at Trubshaw Trimble & Partners, a law firm whose exorbitant fees matched the plushness of its downtown offices and the self-esteem of its principals. Plugge had had little to do with Lydiate, indeed regarded him as just another of the supercilious Nancy boys with limp handshakes of whom there were plenty at Trubshaw Trimble. But Plugge, who wouldn't shout his best friend a meat pie if he could possibly avoid it, would put up with a lot for a free lunch anywhere, let alone at Antoine's. Obviously, Lydiate would want something but he was too well-bred to raise it until after the food and drink had been ordered. And then . . . well, thought Plugge, I've told much more intimidating characters than Mr Trevor Lydiate to get fucked before today.

They lunched well. Lydiate proved to be an excellent host, avoiding any mention of business until the dessert plates had been removed and the neighbouring tables vacated.

Then Lydiate made his pitch: "Barry, I'm leaving Trubshaw Trimble to set up my own private practice and I have a proposition for you."

The liqueur trolley arrived. Plugge chose the oldest and most expensive cognac on offer and was impressed when Lydiate nodded his approval and followed suit.

"You've got $200,000 in our trust account," continued Lydiate. "Off the top of your head, how much would you have invested in the share market, sitting in bank accounts, that sort of thing — I'm talking about money which could be redirected at short notice?"

Plugge didn't need to think about it. "Nine hundred grand give or take a few bucks."

Lydiate whistled softly. "Now I gather the business is currently making around $300,000 a year after tax. You don't have to answer this but I shouldn't imagine you declare every single dollar that comes in the door?"

Plugge swilled his brandy and felt the heat rise to his face. The lawyer interpreted his smug expression as agreement.

"For the purposes of this discussion, we'll assume that's the case. Okay, here's my proposal: you clean out your bank accounts, cash in your shares, and get your money out of Trubshaw Trimble. Then you hide it offshore — I don't know, stick it in the Cayman Islands or something; we can work that out later. To all intents and purposes, though — and there'll be all the paperwork to verify it — you will've given me that money to use through my trust accounts. All right? Then, for a couple of years, you take as much as possible out of the business and do the same — hide it offshore and pretend I've got it. When we've built up the amount to, say, two million, I own up that I've stolen it and blown the lot. You get reimbursed the full amount from the lawyer's fidelity fund and I go to jail. While I'm doing time, you put my share into an offshore account so that it's waiting for me when I come out. That's basically it."

Lydiate leant back in his chair and sipped his drink. Plugge, his large ears by now bright pink, stared at him with newfound respect.

"That easy huh?"

"Yep, that easy. Believe me, I didn't dream this up last week; I've been thinking about it for years."

"Say we get two mill — how do we divide it?"

"Well, I'm the one who's taking the fall — I get disbarred and sent to the slammer — so I reckon that entitles me to a round million."

"A mill for you, a mill for me — that seems reasonable."

"Not quite. We'll need a partner, an accountant. The books are going to have to be absolutely shipshape."

"You got someone in mind I suppose?"

Lydiate smiled cheerfully. "He gets $200,000. Of course on top of that I'll need play money."

Plugge's eyes narrowed. "What the fuck do you mean, play money?"

"I'm meant to've blown two million right? That means gambling, high living, conspicuous consumption. If it's going to stack up, I'll need to've established a pattern of behaviour — you know, overseas trips, first-class travel, five-star hotels, spending sprees, and so forth."

"How much are we talking about?"

"I'd say another $200,000 should do it."

"Jesus wept. What does that bring my cut down to?"

"Six hundred thousand — but remember that's pure cream. And you don't have to do a bloody thing for it."

The lunch had taken place almost four years previously and since then events had unfolded very much as Lydiate had outlined as they worked their way through most of a bottle of 1951 cognac. It all went without a hitch; at least, it had done until the day his red phone rang and Danny relayed the message that a private investigator was asking questions about Lydiate. Plugge was not by nature or inclination a violent man. The types of characters his industry attracted meant that now and again one had to deal with people who responded more readily to a fist in the face or a boot in the groin than to reason. When such measures had been required in the past, they'd been satisfactorily performed by the large and stupid men whom Plugge employed as bouncers. But earlier that year, when Plugge found himself under siege from the Italians on one side and the Asians on the other, both groups having abandoned any inclination to peaceful co-existence and now clearly hell-bent on driving him out of business, he'd had to rethink his attitude.

In the space of three weeks, one of Plugge's clubs was firebombed, the word went out that there was $25,000 to be earned by putting him on the slab, and the head of his "security" team was dragged into an alley where his left Achilles tendon and right thumb were severed. The other bouncers decided that Plugge's wages and the occasional free blowjob were not worth the risk of being subjected to this sort of fiendish oriental cruelty and took to their heels. In fact the knifework had been performed by a forty-nine-year-old Henderson grandfather of Croatian descent who'd just returned from doing a spot of ethnic cleansing in Bosnia. It was done on behalf of the Italians from Sydney for $2,000 and the promise of tickets to see his favourite soccer team, AC Milan, next time he was in Europe.

Desperate times require desperate measures and Herman Pickrang, whom Plugge recruited on the advice of one of his heavier underworld connections, certainly qualified under that heading. Pickrang took the fight to the enemy; on his first day on the job, he walked into an Italian restaurant, seized one of the trouble-makers from across the Tasman, pushed him head first into a pizza oven, and held him there until his eyeballs pickled and popped like frying eggs.

Then he accosted the wife of the Hong Kong gentleman who'd put the bounty on Plugge's head, surprising her while she was walking her prize Pekinese. Pickrang snatched up the dog by its hind legs and flailed it against a concrete telephone pole, reducing the beast to hairy jelly. As the horrified woman tried to flee, he seized a handful of her hair and yanked it out by the roots, leaving her with a monk-like bald patch. The contract was cancelled the next day.

Plugge was not comfortable with such methods but told himself he had to fight fire with fire. The Guttle business, however, was another story; that was overkill. It was partly his fault: that was the second time he'd broken one of his rules. He'd just heard that his two best strippers had found God and were retiring to devote themselves to His service when the call came through on the red phone. Plugge didn't lose his composure very often but when he did, a search party had to be sent out to get it back. He'd rampaged round his office, throwing things, bellowing that no snotbag snoop was going to poke his nose into his affairs and get away with it, and demanding of Pickrang, was he going to stand around scratching his arse or do something about it, the long streak of piss? Pickrang did something about it all right; the fucking madman went out and blew Guttle away. Hadn't he ever heard of breaking the guy's legs, for crying out loud?

8

Rummaging through the accumulated flotsam and jetsam in his mother's basement, Reggie Sparks found his old record collection, which included Basil Batrouney's farewell album, *Going Mad in Public*.

The cover photo showed Batrouney standing in the middle of a downtown intersection wearing only a Napoleonic hat, gumboots and a pair of underpants the waistband of which had been hitched up to well above his navel, accentuating his genital bulge. Beneath the flamboyant headgear and framed by lank black hair was a pale, oval face dominated by a pair of bulging, frog-like eyes. All in all, Batrouney looked thoroughly deranged.

Mad as a snake, thought Sparks.

The only track off the album which Sparks could remember was the notorious *Smack Gets in your Eyes*, a paean to drug use which had goaded several parliamentarians into demanding Batrouney's imprisonment. These calls were resisted, although the song was banned from the state-controlled airwaves. The album's ability to offend the establishment more than compensated for its total lack of musical or lyrical merit and ensured its commercial success.

Sparks caught the Quickcat to Waiheke Island and took a taxi from the wharf to the township of Onetangi. The address he'd been given turned out to be a nondescript weatherboard house a block back from the waterfront. Sparks mounted the steps to the verandah and knocked on the front door. It was opened by a stout man of early middle age. His receding wiry grey-black hair was pulled back into what Sparks assumed was a bun or a ponytail, and bushy white muttonchop sidewhiskers emphasised the pumpkin-like shape of his face. He peered benevolently through large round spectacles with lenses like the reinforced windows on a despot's limousine.

"Does Basil Batrouney live here?"

"That's me."

It hadn't for a moment occurred to Sparks that this portly Dickensian figure was the former wild child of New Zealand rock music. He was so thrown by the admission that all he could think of to say was, "We went to the same school."

Batrouney stared at him blankly for twenty seconds.

"School," he said eventually. It was neither a statement nor a question. It reminded Sparks of the way little children utter words because they like the sound.

Off to a promising start, thought Sparks. "Yeah, Prince Albert College."

There was another long silence. "Groovy. But as my old amigo Bobby

Zimmerman said, 'That was in another lifetime'."

Jesus, what a fruitcake, thought Sparks. "Look, I'm a journalist," he said doggedly, "and I'm doing this story for *New Nation* about a group of guys — including you — who were at Prince Albert College together . . ."

"A journalist, eh? Thought I'd finished with them."

Batrouney shrugged, turned and walked down the hallway. "If you want to rap, come in," he called over his shoulder. Sparks followed. Batrouney had a bald crown and a ponytail which hung like a dead animal between his shoulder blades.

He led Sparks into a room set up as a study. There was a large desk with a computer, a printer and a fax machine, an old kitchen table covered in files, magazines and drawings, and a draughtsman's board. Batrouney sat on the swivel chair at the desk and pointed Sparks to an old sofa against the wall.

"You still in the music game at all?" asked Sparks, trying to get the conversation going.

"Man, I don't even have a transistor." Batrouney got heavily out of the chair and went to the table. "These days, I draw comic strips; just call me Walt Disney of Waiheke." He picked up a comic from a pile on the table and tossed it to Sparks. It was called *Grub* and subtitled *The Kiwi Lavatory Humour Comic*. On the cover was a cartoon of a hugely fat man sitting on the toilet. Underneath it said: "In this issue — how to leave giant skidmarks every time. Plus! Ron's Runs, Wendy's Wide-On, Perry and his Poo-Ring and much, much more!"

Sparks glanced up at Batrouney who was swinging to and fro in the swivel chair, humming tunelessly. "It's not everybody's bag," he said. Sparks put the comic down on the arm of the sofa.

"You do it all yourself?"

"No, no, a bunch of us put it together." Batrouney giggled. "I've just invented a new character — 'Jack Stack and his Magic Crack'."

I don't believe this, thought Sparks. He tried to look interested. "Yeah? What's that about?"

"Jack's a super-hero, kind of like Batman, except what he does is suck bad guys up his arse. Like a black hole out in space." He giggled again.

"Can't see it ever being made into a movie," said Sparks, "but I've been wrong before. So how many copies do you sell?"

"You'd be surprised," said Batrouney primly. "We did our homework. Scatological humour — that's like to do with arseholes and farting and stuff — is the big growth area in comics. So," he beamed at Sparks, "can I put you down for a subscription?"

"No, thanks. I'm more your *Doonesbury*, that sort of thing."

Batrouney looked a bit miffed. "Suit yourself."

He lapsed into silence. Christ, thought Sparks, now I've upset him. However, after a minute or two, Batrouney came abruptly to life: "Now this school thing: fact is, there's nothing I can tell you. All I remember from those days is this stuff." He waved the comic. "You know, schoolboy humour. See, I divide my life into BD and AD — before drugs and after drugs. What I remember from the BD period doesn't amount to shit."

Sparks was curious. "What about the bit in between when you were actually on drugs?"

"It's a big bit. They really are missing years, man — just a blur."

"So all the fun, the groupies . . ."

Batrouney shook his head slowly. "You tell me. I might as well have been a clerk."

"That's tough," said Sparks sincerely. "But getting back to BD, to your Prince Albert days — surely you remember Bronwen Ticehurst, the girl who hanged herself? You danced with her at the ball."

Batrouney blinked rapidly behind his heavy glasses. "Man, all I remember is it was a heavy scene. What did we used to say — bad karma? Yeah, that was it — it was bad karma."

The class of '70 isn't holding up too well in the hair department, thought Sparks as he watched Dermot Looms, the farmer from up north, coming down the steps towards him. That was where any likeness to Batrouney began and ended: whereas the creator of *Grub* had the flab and pallor of a sedentary recluse, Looms was every inch the outdoorsman — tall and raw-boned, his face and exposed scalp weathered the colour of varnished wood.

"Sparks is it?"

"Yes."

"You're Gavin's brother?"

"Yes."

"You got kicked out, right?"

"Well, technically speaking I wasn't expelled . . ."

"Doesn't matter a bugger now. Let's go round the back."

Looms lived in an old colonial-style farmhouse, white-painted timber with a grey slate roof, at Tapora on the Okahukura Peninsula which juts out into the Kaipara Harbour. To the right of the house was a double garage; behind it were a rose garden and a lawn which sloped away to some farm buildings. Beyond them, the paddocks rolled down to the sea. They sat in the sun on white wrought-iron garden furniture. Sparks explained his assignment.

Looms rubbed his forehead. "Christ, what a terrible thing that was. I hardly knew Bronwen, you know. Mum was friendly with her mother and they jacked it up between them, for me to take Bronwen to the ball. I was so bloody socially backward I couldn't have had a partner otherwise but it was hard lines for Bronwen; she wasn't short of admirers. Trouble was, she wanted the one bloke who could take or leave her. I suppose that's what it boiled down to in the end, the whole sorry business."

"Who was that?"

"The Ghost — Cas Quedley. You'd remember him?"

Sparks nodded.

"We called him the Ghost after the cartoon — Caspar the friendly ghost? Good name for him too."

"What was the story between him and Bronwen then?"

"They went out a couple of times. She was pretty rapt in him; so were half the girls in town for that matter. Anyway Cas gave her the flick — I mean, she wasn't the only one that happened to; he was a terrible bugger with the birds. At the ball I had a couple of dances with Bronwen, then she says she's got to talk to Cas, she'll be back in a minute. Off she went and that was the last I saw of her. Apparently, she fronted Cas and he told her look, it's all over, don't be a pain in the arse, so she shot through. At least that's what I thought — that she'd just buggered off home. Her folks' place wasn't that far from the college. Of course, what she did was go up to the belltower and — well, you know the rest."

"What about Victor Appleyard? How did he fit in?"

"Oh Christ, poor old Vic. Well he was one of the bunch panting after Bronwen — in fact he was pretty stuck on her. He took it real hard."

"So he had the hots for her but she wasn't interested?"

Looms shook his head stiffly. "She wasn't interested in him or me or anyone but Quedley. It was Cas or no one."

"I've heard the cops think Appleyard might've jumped off the Bridge because he had a guilty conscience. Is it possible he could've killed Bronwen in a jealous rage, you know, just couldn't handle being rejected?"

Looms let out his breath explosively. "Whew, that's a bit of a shocker. Let's put it this way, Vic was just about the last bloke you could imagine doing something like that . . ."

"That's what the friends and neighbours always say, isn't it? 'He was such a nice, polite man, I'd never have picked him as an axe murderer'."

"Yeah, I guess so."

"How about Quedley? How did he take it?"

Looms sat back and folded his arms. "Well, as I said, the Ghost was a good name for Cas. You never knew what was going on there. I mean, he wasn't what you'd call sentimental. His mother died when we were at school and no one knew till weeks later. But sure, it must've upset him. I wouldn't have liked to've been in his shoes."

"Why, did people blame him?"

Looms waved a hand at an invisible fly. "Oh you know, there was whispering behind his back. I think a few doors were shut on him; he wasn't welcome in some quarters any more. But you couldn't really blame him. For a start, the birds knew where they stood with him — shit, he went through them like it was a race. And you know what it's like at that age — kids put each other through emotional hoops all the bloody time."

They walked back to Mrs Sparks' Peugeot. Looms looked in the driver's window: "You know, after you rang the other day, I got to thinking about that year. When you think about it, two suicides within a few weeks — it's a bloody wonder parents weren't pulling their kids out of the place."

"I left at the beginning of that year and I sort of lost touch," said Sparks. "Who was the other one?"

"The chaplain, Padre Swindell. He drove his Morrie 1100 straight into a wall — couldn't have been more than a few weeks before the other business. They tried to make out it was an accident but apparently there was nothing wrong with the car, the weather was okay, and the old bloke never touched the piss. It looked like he just pointed the car at the bloody wall and put his foot down."

Sparks sat in the reception area of Quedley Communications (Counsel, Strategy, Crisis Management) trying to differentiate between the various attractive young women flitting to and fro. It was no easy task; there seemed to be a distinct Quedley Communications look — long hair, short skirts, high heels. After a ten-minute wait, a statuesque brunette swayed into his line of sight, breathed, "Mr Sparks? CQ will see you now," and escorted him down a corridor to Quedley's office.

It was a huge office, big enough to house a large desk in front of which were positioned three high-backed chairs, an eight-seat meeting table, a couple of long sofas arranged around a low coffee table, a small bar and assorted foliage. There's still enough room to land a helicopter, thought Sparks.

Caspar Quedley, wearing a beautifully cut dark double-breasted suit and displaying a very deep tan and very white teeth, rose from behind the desk and advanced on Sparks, hand outstretched. The handshake he administered was impressively muscular and of precisely calculated duration: sufficiently protracted to convey enthusiastic welcome without suggesting freemasonry or arousal. The tan, the firm grip, the erect posture, the wide shoulders and the flat stomach all proclaimed that here was a man who sprang from his bed at 6 a.m. and ran ten kilometres before breakfast, a man who pumped iron, a man who played a rip-roaring game of squash, skied like a daredevil and liked the sting of salt spray in his face. What an arsewipe, thought Sparks. He sourly noted that, unlike his contemporaries, not a square centimetre of scalp peeped through the glossy black curls which tumbled onto Quedley's forehead and lent a touch of boyishness to his slightly unreal good looks.

"Thanks for seeing me Mr Quedley," said Sparks. "Or should I call you CQ?"

Quedley grinned disarmingly, "You can call me Casper or you can call me Shitface — it's entirely up to you. Take a seat."

As he poured the coffee, Quedley made small talk about *New Nation* and

Jackson Pike — "We've all got to strive to stay on side with young Master Pike."

Sparks interrupted him. "Mr Quedley, I couldn't help but notice, you seem to've surrounded yourself with bimbos. Any particular reason for that?"

Quedley put down his cup and leant forward, half-smiling. "Well Reggie, bimbo is something of a judgemental term implying that these young women perform no function save the decoration. That isn't entirely the case. To answer your question: yes, there is a reason for it. The fact is that, despite everything one hears and reads about women in the workplace, ninety per cent of the time in corporate public relations we're dealing with men. And the simple truth of the matter is that on the day-to-day stuff, most men, whether they admit it or not, would rather deal with an attractive woman than a man. The reality is that a lot of executives look upon dealing with PR issues as almost light relief, a bit of a break from the real work. So I've always had the view that it's important to ensure that there's an enjoyment factor — if you like, it's a case of giving 'em what they want, not what they necessarily need."

Sparks raised his eyebrows. "It makes it all sound pretty . . . superficial."

Quedley leaned further forward, looking thoroughly earnest. "Abso-fucking-lutely. If I can go off the record for a moment: this is a superficial industry for superficial people. If public relations ceased tomorrow, it wouldn't detract in the slightest from the sum of human happiness; in fact, you could argue that mankind would be better off. Imagine a world in which companies and governments and institutions were judged purely and simply on their merits rather than all the outrageous bullshit they spread around — on what they do rather than what they say they do. But I put it to you, it requires a certain wit and cunning to make a good living out of something so fundamentally artificial and to do so, what's more, by gouging money out of the supposedly canniest, most hard-nosed, most financially literate sector of society — big business. Which brings us back to my bimbos, God bless each and every one of 'em."

Quedley paused from his dissertation and looked at Sparks appraisingly. "So you're Gavin's brother?"

"Yes."

"I believe I've met your sister-in-law. A delightful creature — what's her name?"

"Heather."

"By God Heather, that's right," said Quedley slapping his thigh. "How could I forget? Been quite some time since I've seen either of them."

Sparks glowered at him. "You married Mr Quedley?"

"No sir. Haven't got the temperament for it."

"I suppose it's difficult for a man about town like yourself to settle down?"

If Quedley sensed the hostility radiating from Sparks, he gave no sign of it. He regarded Sparks amiably. "Man about town — I haven't heard that term for a while. If you mean that I like to do a bit of rootin' from time to time, well I'll own up to that. Don't you?"

Sparks ignored him. "I guess that was the problem with Bronwen Ticehurst — she just didn't understand your temperament?"

Quedley held Sparks' stare. "I don't know why Bronwen killed herself. That night at the ball she asked me if we could have a relationship and I said no. I heard afterwards from a couple of her friends that it hurt her — apparently, she believed she was in love with me — so maybe you could argue I drove her to it. If so, it was by being honest. Obviously, if I'd thought for one second she was going to do what she did, I would have handled it differently, although if you follow that line to its absolute logical conclusion, I couldn't ever have broken up with her — I'd have had to have married her to keep her alive. But who the hell knows? Maybe there were other things in Bronwen's life that made her unhappy, things that none of us knew about, and me giving her the elbow was simply the straw that broke the camel's back. Now, personally, you or anybody else can write whatever the fuck you want about me — I've got a fairly thick skin and I'm pretty much beyond caring what people think about me — but don't you reckon Bronwen's family could do without *New Nation* raking over it after all these years?"

"Well, I suppose that's the difference between journalism and PR; as they say, news is what someone, somewhere wants to suppress."

Quedley sniggered derisively. "Pomposity doesn't become you Reg. Besides, you know who said that? Some Fleet Street press baron, no doubt trying to justify running a 'what the butler saw'-type story. That's the sort of self-serving sound bite I'd be proud to come up with."

Sparks shrugged. "So who did you take to the ball? She must've been special — sounds like most of the other guys would've crawled over broken glass for Bronwen."

Quedley pursed his lips. "I wouldn't want this to be taken the wrong way but I don't remember. She was new, that was all."

"She was a challenge, was she? Yeah, I hear you like challenges." Quedley started to say something but Sparks pressed on. "What you were saying about *New Nation* raking over Bronwen's death, as if we're doing it just for the hell of it; that's crap. We've got something to hang it on — the Victor Appleyard connection."

Quedley sat up. "You know about that?"

"About what?"

Quedley's genial poise slipped. "Well, I'm not sure I want to . . ."

"If you mean, have we heard that Appleyard might've had some sort of fixation about Bronwen Ticehurst, the answer is 'yes'."

Quedley slumped back on the sofa. "Well, I'm sorry to hear that but at least it didn't come from me."

"Well, was it true?"

Quedley stood up and walked around in a little circle. "Look, Victor was a nice guy and I really don't want to go on the record about this but I guess you'd have to say that he seemed to have a bee in his bonnet about it. He came round and talked to me about it a couple of times."

"Where was he coming from?"

"Well, that's it. I couldn't really work it out. He just seemed to want to go over and over the same old ground. You know, no one's ever accused me of being the most sensitive soul on the block and I make no apology for not accepting responsibility for Bronwen's death, but going through it all chapter and verse wasn't exactly my idea of a good time."

"Would you say he was obsessed with it?"

Quedley grimaced. "Obsessed is an ugly word. I don't know I'd say that. But he certainly had an itch he couldn't scratch."

On his way out, Sparks asked Quedley about the chaplain.

"Old Pard Swindell? Yeah, well, there you go. Who knows what that was all about? Far be it from me to speak ill of the dead but I suspect he was well and truly screwed up. I mean, a clergyman, a bachelor, a boys' boarding school — nod, nod, wink, wink, know what I mean? He was probably a bit of a tortured soul and was punishing himself for some trivial lapse that you or I wouldn't lose a moment's sleep over."

They shook hands. Quedley's smile was full of sly humour. "Terrible things, consciences. We're much better off without them, eh Reggie?"

I can't help it, thought Sparks going down in the lift. I really ought to detest that man — but I don't.

9

When Maurice Trousdale, the heir to the carpet fortune, returned to his multi-million-dollar Herne Bay apartment after his four-day, eight-restaurant trip to Sydney, he stood in front of the big window in his upstairs living room and looked out across Westhaven Marina to Waitemata Harbour, the North Shore and the Harbour Bridge. After contemplating this scene for several minutes, he turned away, sighing. Even the view no longer worked. There'd been a time when, on his return from overseas, he'd stand at the window thinking it was good to be back, good to be home. Now even that sense of belonging failed to uplift him. He could feel a blue period coming on.

Trousdale's occasional spells of gloomy introspection resulted from his dwelling on the fact that his only role in life — that of heir — essentially involved outlasting his mother. Given that his mother was almost twice his age, it was not a lot to ask and Trousdale felt that he'd pretty much got the hang of it. He felt ready for something a little more demanding, something that would stretch him.

Trousdale spent a quarter of an hour musing on his dilemma. Having failed to come up with any stimulating projects which didn't require high intelligence or physical courage or drive and energy — none of which he possessed — he played back the messages on his answering machine. Among the invitations to weekends at Pauanui, cocktail parties and gallery openings was a message which at first gave him a nasty jolt, then triggered some furious thinking. The conclusion he eventually reached transformed his mood like a blaze of sunshine after a summer shower.

The message was from Reggie Sparks and was a request for an interview in connection with an article he was preparing for *New Nation* magazine. The message concluded with a volley of names, some familiar — Victor Appleyard, Caspar Quedley — some all but forgotten — Bronwen Ticehurst, Basil Batrouney. The common thread seemed to be Prince Albert College.

Trousdale's initial alarm was caused by the mention of *New Nation*. The magazine had a gossip column, *Aucklander's Diary*, in which Trousdale featured from time to time. There'd been a reference several years previously which he could still recite from memory. It read thus:

"A pall of gloom descends on the festive season! It is one's melancholy duty to report that yet another year has passed in which Maurice Trousdale, globetrotter, patron of the arts, bon vivant and heir to Fabrice Carpet fortune, made no discernible progress towards finding a consort.

"It defies belief that, in this savagely materialistic age, a man who stands to inherit around $200 million when Mater, the doughty Lydia, turns up her toes, can be entering his fortieth summer still a bachelor. It's hardly as if Auckland is devoid of women intent on marrying money; in the salons of Parnell and Remuera, the smart restaurants, the yacht clubs, the member's stand at Ellerslie, in fact everywhere the voluptuaries, phonies and nouveau riche white trash who make up what passes for Auckland society gather, one is in constant danger of being trampled underfoot by hordes of debs, 'models' and assorted bimbos flashing thigh and breast at anything they suspect is male, single and rich. So frenzied has the hunt become that even being of dusky hue is no longer unacceptable providing the tinted gentleman's net wealth is in the right ballpark.

"So how come, I hear you cry, Maurice is still fancy-free? Your diarist's theory is that for even the most single-minded gold-diggers, the thought of having to submit to the pudding-like albino's clammy caresses on a nightly basis is too horrific to contemplate. Plus ça change, plus c'est la même chose . . . as a lad at Prince Albert, poor Maurice was dubbed 'The Troll' because of his general unsightliness and shunned by the smart set."

Trousdale and his lawyers had debated whether or not to sue. The hawks among his legal advisers had argued that the item was so malicious, so gratuitously offensive, that no court in the land would have an ounce of sympathy for *New Nation*. The doves cautioned that defamation cases could be brutal and demeaning affairs; the defendant would be expected to leave no stone unturned in exposing every unsavoury aspect of the plaintiff's character and the resultant humiliation could far exceed that caused by the original libel. In the end Trousdale decided to turn the other cheek, swayed by the unthinkable prospect that *New Nation* might produce as witnesses the women who'd participated in his rare and uniformly gruesome sexual experiences.

Forbearance had its price. From then on, the editor of *Aucklander's Diary* felt sufficiently emboldened to preface any reference to Trousdale with the label "pudding-like albino".

What galled Trousdale most of all, though, was the realisation that the diary item was another sally in the campaign of denigration and humiliation which had been mounted against him, intermittently, for almost thirty years. He'd suspected it straight away — "Pudding Bum", "Slimefingers", "the Albino" and "the Troll" were all lampoons invented at Prince Albert College by his once and future persecutor, the diabolical Caspar Quedley. Trousdale's suspicions had been confirmed by Quedley himself when they'd met shortly after the item appeared. Not that Quedley had owned up to planting it in *Aucklander's Diary*; he hadn't needed to. The malicious gleam in his eyes, the predatory grin, the greeting — "Bugger me blue Trousers, you get paler every time I see you; you must live under a fucking bridge" — were all intended to let Trousdale know that the Ghost had struck again.

So while the very name *New Nation* had caused Trousdale to flush to the roots of his thinning hair, the remainder of Sparks' message prompted some careful thought. He'd often yearned to revenge himself on his tormentor but Quedley had seemed unassailable. If I handle this right, thought the carpet heir, I can get back at that swine through the very vehicle he used to ridicule me. Trousdale sat down at his antique writing desk, took a clean sheet of paper, unscrewed his red lacquer fountain pen and started making notes of what he would tell the man from *New Nation* about Caspar Quedley.

Sparks had two messages when he checked in at *New Nation*: the first was an invitation to join Maurice Trousdale for lunch at Le Brie restaurant the following day. The second was an instruction to call the supplied telephone number at exactly 2 o'clock that afternoon if he wanted to know the real story about Trevor Lydiate. He did so.

The call was answered on the fourth ring.

"Who's that?" said a deep male voice.

"Reggie Sparks. Who am I talking to?"

"Never mind that, pal. You want to know about Lydiate or not?"

"Sure."

"Okay, you know Potter's Park on the corner of Dominion and Balmoral? There's a kids' playground, right? Behind it, just up the rise, there's one of those round things that bands play in."

"A rotunda."

"What?"

There was a short silence.

"Sparks?"

"Yep."

"That's what it's called, the round thing — a rotunda."

"Shut your hole. You want to know about Lydiate or not?"

"Yeah, I want to hear about Lydiate."

"Okay, be at that whatever the fuck it's called in Potter's Park in one hour. How old are you?"

"Thirty-nine."

"What are you wearing?"

"Jeans, blue shirt, brown jacket. How will I recognise you?"

"I'll be the one in the hotpants."

The anonymous caller hung up.

Sparks sat in the rotunda in Potter's Park for half an hour. He would have waited a little longer, even though by then he was pretty sure that he was wasting his time, but it started to rain and the temperature dropped appreciably. He ran back to his mother's car.

Herman Pickrang, who'd been observing Sparks through a pair of binoculars from his car parked in the carpark of the Kentucky Fried Chicken outlet on the other side of Dominion Road and wondering how long it would take the dumb shit to figure out he'd been jerked, said, "About fucking time" and started his car. Pickrang had set himself two objectives for the afternoon — to find out what Sparks looked like and where he lived. Neither proved difficult. Having paraded himself for identification purposes, Sparks continued to oblige, driving straight to a house in St Heliers where he put his car in the garage and went inside. After following him there, Pickrang, who felt rather pleased with himself, decided he'd go home and play with his electric train set.

Sparks rang Jackson Pike and gave him a brief and uninformative account of his progress. Pike was unconcerned by the lack of detail: the mere fact that Sparks had found and interviewed some of the dead girl's dancing partners meant that he'd already surpassed Pike's expectations. Sparks asked Pike if he had a means of putting a name and address to a phone number he'd been given by the no-show. He hung on while Pike called a contact in Telecom who reported that it was the number of a public phone box in New North Road. Sparks had expected something of the sort. He found it interesting, in a detached sort of a way, that expecting such an answer did absolutely nothing to allay the unease it caused.

When Sparks was ushered to the table, Trousdale took a hurried slurp of his dry martini, brushed some flakes of crust from the corners of his mouth, hauled himself to his feet and extended a pudgy hand.

Like the man who doesn't know much about art but knows what he likes, Reggie Sparks had no particular notion of what the heir to a fortune should look like but his luncheon companion certainly wasn't it. Trousdale was short — no more than five feet — and plump. In the exact centre of his fat, pink face was an incongruously babyish button nose. Occasionally, women, feeling obliged to find a redeeming feature in the swollen expanse of Trousdale's face, professed to find his nose cute. Trousdale himself considered it a damn nuisance since it failed to provide satisfactory support for his spectacles. Trousdale's hair was bone-white and very fine and, beneath it, countless tiny beads of perspiration glistened on his pink scalp. Trousdale sweated a great deal. Some of his acquaintances, who considered him close to being a glutton, assumed it was excitement which made him sweat so much in restaurants.

They ordered. Sparks, recently health-conscious, chose soup and grilled snapper and a green salad; Trousdale, for whom meals were an important filler to the all-too-many hours which make up an empty life, nominated garlic snails followed by venison casserole and vegetables du jour. Suspecting that his guest might decline the offer of wine, he called for a bottle of pinot noir without consulting him.

As they waited for the food, Sparks outlined his brief from *New Nation*.

Trousdale swallowed the last mouthful of his martini. "So what did you make of the exquisite Caspar?" he asked.

"Quedley? He struck me as a pretty smooth operator."

"A smooth operator?" Trousdale arched his almost invisible eyebrows and turned down the corners of his prim mouth. "I must say that if describing Caspar as a smooth operator is any indication of the levels of insight and originality we can expect from this article, I don't think I'll bother to read it."

Only the brief flaring of his nostrils betrayed Sparks' urge to reach across the table and prong Trousdale's jaunty little nose with his fork.

"Well, to be absolutely candid, my dear old sausage," he said calmly, "I don't give a rat's arse whether you read it or not."

Trousdale dabbed his forehead with a napkin, his other hand fluttering in appeasement.

"I do beg your pardon — that sounded rather impertinent. No, what I really meant to say was that describing Caspar as a smooth operator seems rather an understatement."

Sparks' gaze remained indifferent. "Well, I get the impression that you're just itching to tell me about him so why don't you?"

Trousdale, hot and flustered, wriggled on his seat; his armpits were positively frothing. This was not how it had been meant to go at all: he'd planned to manipulate Sparks like a puppeteer, have him dancing his tune without even knowing it. Still, there was the opening. He took a deep breath.

"Well, I think one must always remember that Caspar's family was of comparatively modest means and at school he was very, very conscious of the fact. You know, see him swanning around town today as to the manner born and it's easy to forget his rather humble origins. His father was a vicar, you see, and the only reason Caspar went to Prince Albert was because of the clergy's discount on school fees — they only paid fifty per cent from memory. As I say, he was very aware, was Caspar, that he was something of a have-not compared to most of his schoolmates. I remember going to the movies with him and a few others during the school holidays, in our fifth form year I think, and someone commented on the fact that wherever we saw Caspar out of school — at a party, at the football, in town, whatever — he seemed to be wearing exactly the same clothes. I'm sure it was said in all innocence — just one of those thoughtless, flippant things teenagers say — but Caspar was quite hurt by it."

Trousdale felt a fresh outbreak of sweat on his forehead and applied the napkin. The fact of the matter was that he himself had drawn attention to the pathetic paucity of Quedley's wardrobe. It had been a put-down worthy of Quedley himself in its calculated nastiness, a moment to savour. Quedley had blushed absolutely crimson and the others, sensing the vulnerability like sharks scenting blood, had gleefully twisted the knife in the wound.

"Anyway, Caspar became terribly money-conscious. He always had some sort of money-making scheme on the go. Believe it or not — and this is strictly off-the-record by the way — in our last year he somehow got hold of an advance copy of an exam paper, university entrance history I think it was, and sold sneak previews."

"What, to a public exam? How the hell could he do that?"

"No, no, no. It was the internal school exam but he sold it to all the fellows who failed UE the year before and were trying to get accredited on internal assessment."

"Even so, how'd he get hold of it?"

"God only knows. Maybe he sneaked into the masters' common room one night and made a copy of it. As I said, he always had something on the go; he was always hatching a plot."

Trousdale attacked his food, noting with approval that Sparks was scribbling furiously in his notebook. I just hope he's up to the task, thought Trousdale. God, Quedley will hate this stuff coming out.

Sparks put his pen down and took a hurried mouthful of fish.

"What about Appleyard? Anything you can tell me about him?"

"Nothing much really — we weren't close either at school or subsequently. Although funnily enough, I did see Appleyard not that long ago — no more than a few weeks before he died, I guess — over in Sydney. I bumped into him in the lobby of the Regent Hotel and he insisted on having a drink. Now you're interested in the Ticehurst girl, aren't you? Well, I swear, that was the only subject he could talk about. He was awfully het-up about it, asking me all these questions about her and the ball. What could I say? Without wishing to appear callous, I had one rather off-hand waltz with the poor thing; it was hardly worth committing the details to memory."

"What did he say about it?"

Trousdale arranged his knife and fork on a spotless plate. He was more interested in dessert than the subject of Victor Appleyard.

"Oh, I don't know. To be frank, it was going in one ear and out the other. All I can remember was him rabbiting on that he'd come across someone in Sydney who'd shed some light on it all."

Sparks had a moment of genuine excitement. "Who? Did he say who it was?"

"Oh no. I actually asked, out of politeness rather than curiosity, but he said he'd been sworn to confidentiality or some such. I must say, I found his behaviour rather extraordinary; it did occur to me that he might've been slightly off his head and what do you know? Next thing, he's jumped off the bridge."

10

Reggie Sparks had virtually no interest in clothes. As far as he was concerned, one wore clothes to avoid pneumonia and arrest. In France he'd had two comparatively expensive items in his wardrobe: a linen suit and a Burberry raincoat. After the ignominious gigolo episode, he'd given the linen suit to the tramp who sometimes slept in the doorway of his apartment building, on the condition that, in the future, he would urinate somewhere else. He'd kept the raincoat, wisely as it turned out, since in Auckland that spring fine weather, like the ideal guests, came rarely and didn't stay for long. Sparks was wearing the raincoat when he called on the widow Appleyard for the second time. She opened her front door, looked him up and down and checked her watch.

"Is school out already?"

"What?"

"The coat, Mr Sparks. You look like every parent's nightmare."

Since their first meeting, Louise Appleyard had seldom been far from Sparks' thoughts. He'd been keenly anticipating her instant, unguarded reaction to his unannounced visit, thinking that it would be a pointer, at least, to whether her attitude towards him was essentially positive or negative. He'd envisaged a range of responses, some of them wildly optimistic, some, on the basis of being prepared for a let-down, less so; being likened to a child molester had not been among them.

He forced a stiff grin. "Thanks for reminding me; I'm almost out of boiled lollies." She acknowledged his rebound with a slight incline of the head and half-smile. He moved rapidly to the matter at hand.

"I just thought I'd drop round and let you know where I've got to. I've talked to all but one of the guys on the dance card. A couple of interesting things have come up."

He was admitted. They went into the kitchen where he sat on the bar stool at the bench while she made coffee.

Sparks began his report: "The first guy I saw, Batrouney, the ex-rock singer who lives on Waiheke, he was basically a waste of time. Guy's as crazy as a shithouse rat."

Louise raised an eyebrow.

Sparks misread her reaction. "Sorry, pardon the French. Thing is, the guy admits he gave himself one hell of a hammering with the drugs. He's only half there. You know what he does for himself these days? Draws dirty comic strips."

"What sort of dirty?"

"Stuff for grubby-minded kids."

She looked at him expectantly. "Give me an example."

"You know, it's full of . . . bodily functions," he said stirring his coffee. "The stories are 'Ron's Runs' and "Wendy's Wide On'."

Louise giggled. "'Wendy's Wide On'? You're kidding."

"Absolutely not. You wouldn't believe some of this stuff. Jesus, I thought I had a pretty basic sense of humour." He shook his head. "Anyway, as I say, old Basil's out there on his own private planet. More to the point, his memory's completely shot — he'd have trouble remembering how to get to the bathroom let alone what happened at that ball in 1970."

"Oh well, strike one. Who was next?"

"Dermot Looms. He's a farmer up near Wellsford, one of your good, keen men. He was Bronwen's partner at the ball but reckons that didn't mean much because their mothers jacked it up for him to take her. He did point out something interesting, though: a few weeks before the ball, the college chaplain also killed himself."

"What's interesting about that?"

He shrugged. "I suppose interesting's the wrong word — strange maybe. Don't you think two suicides at the same school within a few weeks is a bit of a coincidence?"

She took a thoughtful drag on her cigarette. "Hmm. What else did he say, the farmer?"

"Nothing much. He said your husband and a few others were pretty keen on Bronwen."

"Oh I knew that," she said smiling. "Under that earnest exterior, there was a genuine romantic. Vic used to say that he was hopeless when he was young, falling in love at the drop of a hat. But that one was strictly one-way traffic, wasn't it?"

"Yeah, well she had the same problem with Caspar Quedley. He was my third call."

"Oh yes, I've met him. He's rather gorgeous-looking, works in advertising or something like that? I'm thinking of the right one, aren't I?"

"I don't know," lied Sparks. "Quedley's a public relations man."

"It's not exactly a common name. What does he look like?"

Sparks shrugged, frowning. "I guess . . . smooth."

Louise Appleyard smiled enigmatically. "Okay, so what did Mr Smoothiechops have to say for himself?"

"Well, Quedley said your husband went round to see him about Bronwen Ticehurst. He said he wouldn't say he was exactly obsessed about her but he wasn't that far off. Then I talked to this strange little bloke Trousdale who said pretty much the same. Trousdale ran into Victor in Sydney just before he died and reckoned he really got into his ear about the girl and the ball and whatnot. Anyway, this is what I wanted to ask you about: Trousdale was saying your husband had met someone in Sydney who'd shed some light — those were his words — on the Ticehurst business; said he was quite worked up about it. Any idea who it was?"

She shook her head. "No. He never said anything to me."

"Did he have a diary or something, maybe an address book, that he put phone numbers in?"

"He kept a desk diary at Berkeley. I doubt if that'd tell us much — he wouldn't have taken it away with him." Her hand holding the cigarette stopped mid-arc, halfway to her mouth. "Christ, of course — the electronic organiser." She ground the just-lit cigarette in an ashtray and hurried from the kitchen, returning a minute later with the biggest briefcase Sparks had ever seen. She laid the briefcase on the kitchen table, clicked it open, rummaged inside for a moment and produced a flat black rectangular object, slightly smaller than a paperback book. To Sparks it looked like a calculator.

"The police went through his briefcase," she said. "They probably thought this was a calculator."

Sparks said nothing. She opened it out, revealing a keyboard and screen.

"Lucky I'd forgotten about this otherwise I might've wiped all Vic's stuff and used it myself, to keep track of my frenetic social life. Now let's see, when was Vic's last trip to Sydney?" She pulled a calendar off the wall and flipped through the pages, then began jabbing the small keyboard.

She peered at the instrument's small screen. "Okay, he went over on the twentieth of July and had dinner that night with TR — that'd be Toby Redsell who runs Berkeley in Australia. Wouldn't you know it, it's all bloody initials." She punched another button. "Hang on, here we go — on the twenty-fifth he had an appointment with Lloyd Chennell and on the twenty-seventh with Julian Gage. I can't remember Vic talking about either of them. They mean anything to you?"

Sparks nodded, trying hard not to look pleased with himself. "I'm pretty sure there was a teacher at Prince Albert called Chennell. Gage rings a bell too. Can I use your phone? I know someone who'll know for sure."

Herman Pickrang sat in his car parked fifty metres down the road from Louise Appleyard's house and watched the rivulets of rain run down the windscreen. He'd followed Sparks there and now he was going to have to wait for him to emerge. Although he didn't particularly enjoy sitting in a car watching rain, he would do it for as long as he had to. Among the many things Pickrang had learned during his twenty-five years in the army was the art of waiting for something to happen.

Pickrang was forty years old. On his tax return and for similar official purposes, he described himself as a security consultant. In fact he earned his living by scaring, hurting and occasionally even killing people. Pickrang sometimes wondered if he was what the newspapers called a psychopath. He'd tell himself that he couldn't be a psycho because he did what he did for money rather than pleasure. Every now and again, though, a voice from deep inside his head would point out that that really didn't prove much because he enjoyed doing it anyway. Pickrang would bring these interior debates to a close by deciding that it made very little difference to his victims whether he was a psychopath or not.

Pickrang was highly qualified for his work on several counts. In the first place, he had a frightening appearance. He was the son of Janey Wang, a Chinese-Samoan whore who'd worked the logging camps of the mid-North Island, and one of her customers. Watching Herman grow, Janey decided that his father must have been a tall Pakeha which narrowed the possibilities down but not enough to point the finger with any real conviction. Not long after she became pregnant, Janey had set up home with a Maori logger named Joe Pickrang. Janey gave her son Joe's surname and the Christian name of her first customer, the scion of a wealthy German family with large land-holdings in Samoa.

Pickrang had inherited his mother's tiny cat-like head and slightly slanted eyes. These attributes gave Janey, who was barely five foot tall, an exotic look. However, on Pickrang, who had also inherited his unknown father's long and sinewy frame and who at nineteen was six feet five inches tall, the effect was quite unearthly and had earned him the nickname "Pimplehead" when he joined the army. The unusual pattern of his hair loss over the following twenty-five years had heightened his menacingly alien appearance: he was completely bald except for a swathe of black fuzz which swung across the back of his head from ear to ear, like a hammock, and a greying V-shaped clump, all that remained of what had once been a widow's peak, which sat in splendid isolation high on his forehead. People noticing Pickrang walking towards them in the street would often wonder why he didn't wipe the bird shit off his head.

As a youth, Pickrang had been a keen and promising rugby player, his height, spring and athleticism making him an adept lineout forward. At first his brutal inclinations helped rather than hindered his career, selectors in country areas having traditionally valued "a bit of mongrel" in their forwards. One chilly afternoon in Tokoroa, however, Herman Pickrang discovered the old adage that those who live by the sword sometimes perish by it. Before the game was quarter of an hour old he'd delivered carefully targeted kicks to the heads of three members of the opposition and left livid sprig scrapes on the back and buttocks of several others. It was proving a most enjoyable afternoon until returning to earth after a mistimed lineout jump, he was struck just below his right ear by a fist the approximate size and consistency of a cannonball which had been gathering barnacles on the seabed for several centuries. His head exploded in a flash of white light and the crackle of splintering bones. By the time he came off his liquid diet ten weeks later, Pickrang had decided to quit rugby and join the army.

While Pickrang doubted, on balance, that he was a psychopath, most who crossed his path felt strongly to the contrary. In the army, an institution which has long valued psychopathic tendencies provided they are accompanied by a readiness to follow orders and a tolerance for uncomfortable uniforms and for being shouted at from close range, Pickrang found his natural home. He rose to become a sergeant-major in the SAS where his apparent relish for enduring extreme discomfort and eating disgusting things during survival exercises, coupled with his unflagging enthusiasm for making life hell for those under his command, made him a highly regarded figure.

After twenty-five years in the army, Pickrang retired reluctantly into civilian life. It was a source of aggravation to him that, having spent two and a half decades mastering numerous ways to kill people, he'd never actually had the opportunity to put his knowledge into practice. Just as disturbing was the dreary prospect of no more of the unarmed combat sessions at which he'd routinely exceeded the parameters of pain and punishment which instructors were permitted to inflict. What, he wondered, does a highly trained fighting man with powerful if controllable sadistic urges do when he can no longer serve his country? After much thought, Pickrang reached the obvious conclusion: he became a thug-for-hire.

Pickrang's second career had gone swimmingly until the mix-up over the private investigator Wallace Guttle. The whole business still gnawed at him. Not only had Plugge refused to pay for what had been an outstandingly executed job but he'd had to stand there and take some of the ripest, crudest abuse he'd received since he'd been a raw private. For a man with twenty years' experience of screaming elaborately filthy insults at others, it had been an unsettling experience. Now he was having to traipse around after this clown of a journalist hamstrung by humiliatingly restrictive rules of engagement. It was an insult to his professionalism.

If Pickrang had been less engrossed in revisiting Plugge's irrational and unjust reaction to Guttle's flawless assassination, he might have noticed Detective Sergeant Tito Ihaka driving past in an unmarked car. Ihaka, on his way to call on Louise Appleyard, recognised Pickrang's distinctive features from one swift sideways glance. Ihaka drove on past the Appleyard house and pulled to the side of the road.

Pickrang had never actually been convicted of a criminal offence, although he'd been interviewed by the police in relation to a number. Those of his victims who'd lived to tell the tale preferred not to. Ihaka wondered what a fully fledged criminal monster like Herman Pickrang was doing in this pleasant and peaceful street on the shores of Lake Pupuke and whether it had anything to do with

Louise Appleyard and her dead husband who had hired the also dead private investigator.

Reggie Sparks rang his brother Gavin.

"Got a couple of names for you; I think there's a Prince Albert connection."

"Fire away."

"Lloyd Chennell."

"Yep, he was a teacher there back in our time. He taught arts subjects, English, history, that sort of thing. He was quite good."

"Do you know where he is now?"

"He went to Australia. Last I heard, he'd done all right, got himself appointed headmaster of one of the top schools — I can't remember if it was Sydney or Melbourne. I could find out for you."

"Okay, second name — Julian Gage."

Gavin groaned. "Shit, I knew it. I won't be able to set foot in the place after this story comes out."

"Why, what'd he do?"

"Oh, even you'd remember Gage, surely? He was the character who everyone reckoned was gay. With good reason too from what I've heard of him since. I think he went to Aussie as well."

11

Ihaka waited in his car across the road from the Appleyard residence. Eventually, the front door opened and a man he didn't know came out. The man turned to Louise Appleyard, who was standing in the doorway, and went to shake hands. The gesture seemed to surprise and amuse her but she carried if off gracefully. The visitor then walked down the path, got into a Peugeot, and drove away. Ikaha watched in his rear-view mirror as Pickrang did a U-turn and drove off after him.

Louise Appleyard thought the knock on her front door meant that Reggie Sparks had found an excuse to return and found herself smiling as she went to answer it. However, it wasn't the journalist; it was the large Maori policeman whose name she couldn't remember and whom she suspected of being smarter then he pretended to be. Louise did what she always did when caught slightly off-guard, which seldom happened; she stood there saying nothing and looking good.

"Detective Sergeant Ihaka, Mrs Appleyard. How are you?"

"I'm well, thank you Sergeant. Do come in. Two visitors in one day — it's bordering on hectic."

Following her down the corridor to the kitchen, Ihaka said: "Yeah, I saw the bloke who just left. Who was he, if you don't mind me asking?"

"I'm sure you have a reason other than nosiness for wanting to know so I'll tell you: his name's Sparks, Reggie Sparks. He's a journalist."

"A journalist eh? Now why would Herman Pickrang be tailing a journalist?"

"I'm sorry?"

"While you and Sparks were in here talking about whatever it was you were talking about, a fella called Herman Pickrang was sitting in his car just down the street. When Sparks left, Pickrang followed him. Who's Pickrang? He's probably the nastiest thing on two legs in this town. In fact that's being unfair to Rottweilers. He's a hood, a heavy, someone who earns a crust by bashing people up — or worse."

Ihaka had been looking forward to testing the thickness of Louise Appleyard's coolly ironic exterior. He was glad to find that it wasn't double-glazed. Her hand jumped to her mouth: "Good God. Is Reggie in some sort of danger?"

Ihaka nodded slowly. "If Pickrang was stalking me, I wouldn't be laughing about it."

"We've got to warn him," she said, pawing through the bits and pieces on the kitchen bench. "He left me his phone number — it's here somewhere."

"If you don't mind Mrs Appleyard, I'll do that — I'd like to talk to Mr Sparks. So he's working on a story, is he?"

Louise, disorientated, rubbed her forehead. "Yes, he is, for *New Nation* magazine. I suppose in a way it's what we were talking about the last time you were here — the Ticehurst girl's dance card. He's talking to the men on the card, I think to do a story on what's happened to them since. It was Vic's death that gave them the idea."

"Yeah, well, that's the press for you. To be honest, I'm surprised you're helping them."

Louise brought her chin up. "They didn't get the names from me, Sergeant. Mr Sparks had them already. And as for helping him, why shouldn't I? At least he's going about it with an open mind; you people seem to have taken the view from the very beginning that my husband committed suicide and probably murder to boot. I can't see that I've got much more to lose."

It took Ihaka less than five seconds to work out how *New Nation* had obtained the names on the dance card. Ted Worsp, he thought; that sack of shit could talk under wet concrete.

He said, "Where do I find Sparks?"

When the *New Nation* editor Jackson Pike was told by his secretary that there was a Mr Sparks wanting to see him, he half-expected that Sparks had come to admit defeat. However, the Reggie Sparks who entered his office was not the twisted substance abuser who'd lunged at Col Dumpley with a copy spike all those years before, nor the clueless wimp to whom he'd given the assignment. While Sparks didn't look like a convert to temperance, clean living and early nights, he was by no means the burnt-out shell Pike had expected. What surprised Pike even more was that, far from weasling on the story, Sparks clearly had the bit between his teeth.

He went straight into the pitch: "Mate, I wouldn't try to tell you how to do your job but I reckon we might be coming at this thing from the wrong angle. The sort of story you were talking about, using these guys as symbols of what's happened to the place over the past twenty years — well, let's face it, you can do that state of the nation stuff any time. I mean, how interesting are these turkeys anyway? Batrouney's a rock 'n' roll casualty — what would that make him? Number 900 in an unlimited series? Quedley's a slick PR man; well, aren't they all? At the end of the day, he's a bit of a show pony. Looms is just down on the farm minding his own business and Trousdale's a pathetic little blob who's only interested in his next feed."

Pike leaned back in his excessively large chair and gave Sparks what he thought of as his "first base" look. It was intended to be both encouraging and challenging, to say: "Okay, you've got my attention, now let's see if you can convince me." Sparks, who assumed the editor was holding in a fart, was mildly flattered. Realising that the look hadn't conveyed the message, Pike spread his hands and said, "I'm listening."

"I think Appleyard found out something about the death of Bronwen Ticehurst — maybe that it didn't happen the way they said it did or that there was a lot more to it. To me, that's the story — what did Appleyard find out? Because whatever it was, it was enough to make him jump off the Bridge — or enough to make someone throw him off."

Pike lurched forward and planted his elbows on his desk. "Hang on, I must've missed something. How did we get to that?"

"You know the cops' theory is that he had something to do with the girl's death and was driven to suicide by guilt. I don't think that stands up. Mrs Appleyard's absolutely convinced he didn't kill himself. I know that in itself doesn't prove a thing, but surely to Christ she and others would've noticed something if the guy had been dragging this terrible secret around with him all these years. That's the first thing. Second, if he'd known all along what really happened to her, why does he suddenly get a bee in his bonnet and go round quizzing people about it? As far as him being murdered: well, if he didn't jump, what did happen? Either he stopped his car on the Bridge to sniff the sea air and fell — and both parts of that proposition are hard to believe — or someone shoved him. There's one other thing: Appleyard had hired a private detective."

"What for?"

"Well, we don't know, do we? Because a couple of weeks later someone blew the guy's brains out."

Pike's eyes widened.

"It was a guy called Guttle. Mrs Appleyard says he definitely wasn't hired to check up on her. Okay, again you can take that with a grain of salt. All I can say is I've talked to her and I'd be surprised if it turns out she's bullshitting."

Pike thought about it for a minute or two. No matter how much Sparks had cleaned up his act, it went against the editor's usual practice and instincts to let a freelancer, particularly such an unknown quantity, drive the story. On the other hand, sometimes the best stories, the real ball grabbers, came when a journalist got this sort of gut feeling. And Sparks did seem to have a reasonable grasp of it.

"All right Reggie, we'll do it your way for the time being. So what's the next step?"

Sparks grinned. "I'm glad you raised that."

After Ihaka had left with a promise that he, personally, would alert Sparks to the Pickrang menace, Louise Appleyard made herself her fifth cup of coffee and lit her tenth cigarette of the day and sat down to review recent events. Pickrang's sudden materialisation was genuinely alarming, but at least the police were aware of it. On the subject of the police, Ihaka was certainly a vast improvement on Worsp. There definitely was, she'd decided, a shrewd mind behind the immobile brown face. Under the circumstances, his sheer bulk was quite reassuring as well. Her thoughts didn't dwell on Ihaka and Pickrang for long; there was another, more diverting development to consider.

By and large Louise Appleyard didn't care what other people thought of her; she considered it one of her few strengths. Even so, there was one reputation she was reluctant to risk gaining — that of merry widow. Hence she'd resisted all attempts to draw her back into the social swing. These attempts had begun in earnest the previous week, exactly four weeks after her husband's funeral. Four weeks seemed to be regarded as the appropriate period of mourning and self-denial. She hadn't known whether to laugh or cry when she received that first dinner party invitation accompanied with a delicately worded rider to the effect that there'd be an unattached male of suitable age and social status among the guests for her to cast an eye over.

All the same, her own instinctive responses were now telling her it was time to get on with life. She suspected that Reggie Sparks fancied her and far from being offended or unnerved, she'd quite enjoyed the faint buzz of the electricity of attraction which flowed between them, albeit predominantly in one direction. I'm not quite sure where I stand on that one, she thought. He's not exactly every maiden's dream but, then again, he's not the tongue-tied scruff and all-round no-hoper I took him for at first.

Somewhat more tantalising than the rumpled and awkward Sparks was the prospect held out by Audrey Benn, the wife of one of Victor's colleagues at Berkeley Enterprises. While other would-be hostesses had been euphemistic, in some cases to the point of inscrutability, Audrey had been refreshingly direct when she'd called that morning.

"My dear," Audrey had said briskly, "It's time to throw off the widow's weeds. I know you've been knocking back the invites right, left and centre but be warned — there'll be high dudgeon if you don't take your place at the dinner table here next Saturday night. I've moved heaven and earth to snare Auckland's most eligible bachelor of the occasion. I'm sure you know to whom I'm referring — Caspar Quedley."

Louise had said she'd think about it. It wouldn't do to appear too eager.

Ihaka had checked Sparks' phone number against his mother's listing in the phone directory and then driven to St Heliers. There was no sign of the Peugeot or Pickrang. He rang the doorbell. After identifying himself and assuring Mareena that her son was not about to be led away in handcuffs, he was invited in for a cup of tea and a peanut brownie.

After two cups of tea and three peanut brownies and a discussion about race relations, a subject on which Mrs Sparks proved to be surprisingly well-informed and enlightened by what he assumed were the standards of St Heliers matrons, Ihaka, sitting by the window, observed Sparks pulling into the drive. He was closely followed by Herman Pickrang.

During the afternoon Pickrang's frustrations had finally boiled over. Fuck this, he thought. Any prick with a car and a pair of eyes could do this job. First chance I get, I'm going to scare the living shit out of Sparks and if Plugge doesn't like it, he can blow it out his arse.

Pickrang didn't decide to flout Plugge's express instructions solely because of his resentment at being treated as just another hired hand rather than as a highly qualified specialist. During the hours he'd spent dogging Sparks, it had occurred to Pickrang that he'd effectively rendered himself obsolete as far as Plugge was concerned. Since his retaliatory missions against Plugge's Asian and Australian rivals, peace had returned to Karangahape Road; Plugge was treating him in this demeaning fashion because he'd outlived his usefulness. If Plugge's going to give me the flick, thought Pickrang, why the hell should I worry about pissing him off?

Sparks hadn't noticed Pickrang's red Mitsubishi, which had been parked just down the road from his mother's house all morning and had followed him around town for most of the afternoon, so he was only mildly curious when it pulled up behind him. Curiosity turned to amazement when Pickrang got out of his car. Fucking hell, he thought, what sort of a mutant is that? Amazement turned to bowel-activating fear when the creature spoke.

"Hey cuntbag," it said. "I'm going to rip your fucking ears off."

Ihaka came out of the house and strolled down the drive to join them. For a couple of sickening seconds, Sparks thought he was pincered. However, when the newcomer spoke, it was apparent that he and the ear removalist were not working as a team.

"G'day Herman," said Ihaka. "Eaten any babies lately?"

Pickrang checked his inclination to fling the insolent intruder to the ground and stomp his testicles into powder. The fact that this big buck knew his name and felt bold enough to insult him could only mean one thing.

"You're a cop."

"I'm a cop and you're a headcase — that's why we're here. Whose dirty work are you doing today, Herman? Who told you to lean on Mr Sparks?"

Pickrang took a couple of paces backwards and opened his car door. He gestured rudely, got into the car, reversed out of the drive, and sped off amid the thump and whine of violent gear changes.

"He was going to rip my ears off," said Sparks. "Would he really do that?"

"Herman must like you," said Ihaka. "He usually goes straight for the nuts. So what did you do to upset him?"

Sparks noticed he was trembling slightly. He put his hands in his pockets. "I'm not sure. I guess it must be something to do with Trevor Lydiate."

"Who?"

"I'm doing this story for *New Nation* magazine . . ."

"I know about your story," said Ihaka. "I've been talking to Mrs Appleyard."

"You know about the dance card?"

Ihaka nodded.

"Lydiate's one of the names on it. He's a lawyer who's doing time for embezzlement. The other day I got this anonymous phone call from a guy saying to meet him in Potter's Park if I wanted the oil on Lydiate. Well, I went but no one turned up. The guy on the phone was your Herman whatsisname — the thing that time forgot. I recognised the voice as soon as he opened his mouth."

12

Caspar Quedley, the public relations wizard, lived in a smart new townhouse in Mission Bay. It had two bedrooms, a study, a living room with a fine view of Rangitoto Island, a heavily marbled bathroom with a large spa in which Quedley now and again stage-managed romps involving sufficient quantities of champagne, cocaine and partner swapping to constitute an orgy in these austere and unspontaneous times, a wine cellar, a dining room and state-of-the-art kitchen (neither of which was often used), and a two-car garage which housed his Lexus and four-wheel drive. He also owned a hideaway, which he liked to think of as Spartan, at one of Coromandel Peninsula's more spectacular and inaccessible beaches. Despite the various attractions of his two homes, Quedley was happiest in his office.

As he'd indicated to Reggie Sparks, Quedley was unreservedly cynical about the public relations industry. In fact, in his case public relations was just a conveniently vague term for a range of shadowy activities.

Quedley's office was the hub of a far-flung network of friends, acquaintances, contacts and informants who were constantly feeding in information, speculation, rumour and gossip. This Quedley filtered, processed and distributed in whichever direction best served the agenda he happened to be pushing at the time. His network extended across most sectors of business, through the media and to the uppermost reaches of the major political parties. Quedley's clients paid handsomely for his information, analysis, advice and, they mistakenly believed, loyalty. Most of those who dealt with him, whether as client or contact, underestimated the extensiveness of his network, his access to the highest offices and bigger boardrooms in the land and his capacity for manipulation: many would have scoffed at the notion that his influence matched their own; only the very well-connected, the real insiders, understood that Caspar Quedley was one of the two or three dozen most powerful people in the country.

Quedley also enjoyed the interaction of office life. Although he chose to live alone, he enjoyed having people around him, especially if they were young, bright, attractive and female, as most of his staff were. It was often whispered where PR people gathered that Quedley conducted staff recruitment interviews on the casting couch; he'd heard the stories and found them highly offensive. To Quedley, seduction was sport. In sport there was little or no satisfaction in gaining victory over a handicapped or disadvantaged opponent; likewise where was the challenge, where was the achievement, in getting a woman into bed through the use of pressure or inducements? It was one step up from paying for it.

He had, it was true, slept with a number of his employees, but always at their instigation and after exhorting them to look upon it as nothing more than a short-lived exercise in mutual physical gratification; it would not, he would warn, lead to a deeper relationship nor to advancement within the Quedley organisation. Sometimes these warnings went unheeded and the liaison's aftermath would be an embarrassing scene. When that happened, Quedley, who detested emotionalism, would vow never again. Those vows were seldom observed for long; Quedley was no more capable of adhering to his own rules than to anyone else's.

However, this particular Thursday morning in late October, office affairs were far from Caspar Quedley's mind. In his morning mail was a hand-addressed letter, postmarked Sydney and labelled "Private and Confidential". Quedley opened the envelope; it contained a single sheet of unfamiliar handwriting which read:

'Clifftops'
Ocean View Road
Palm Beach NSW 2108

Caspar,
I am at my beach-house for what is most certainly the last time. Although my doctor still can't bring himself to state the obvious, he no longer bothers with the customary encouraging platitudes. I can almost read my death certificate in his eyes. I can hardly do anything for myself now; even the simple act of writing is beyond me and I'm having to dictate this to my friend Dean Delamore, whose unstinting care and support has been all that has sustained me of late.

By contrast, your support has been conspicuous by its absence. I see from my diary that it is nine months to the day since I told you of my condition. When we spoke then, you promised to visit me at the first opportunity. Not only have you not come to see me but you haven't even bothered to pick up the phone and give me a single, solitary call. Surely you were well aware how much a visit from you would have meant to me and, conversely, how wounding your indifference has been. I'm deeply shocked that, after all we went through together, you could turn your back on me at this time.

No doubt a religious person — someone like poor Chaplain

Swindell for example — would say that someone in my position should feel forgiveness rather than bitterness. Personally, I've always thought deathbed conversions or transformations were cowardly. So I'm going to behave bitterly but in a way which should appeal to your finely developed sense of malice. A few weeks ago, before I became a real cot-case, I sat down and wrote a little memoir of those strange days at our dear old alma mater. It's a rather riveting read, if I say so myself. If you don't put in an appearance before I go, Dean will send it to an appropriate and interested party.

I'd better stop there and get this in the post. Time is short.

Julian.

After he'd read the letter, Quedley said "Fuckfire" in a hoarse whisper. He checked the postmark; it had been posted four days earlier. Christ, he thought, I hope the little queer hasn't croaked already. He leant back in his chair and thought furiously for a couple of minutes. Then he flipped through his address book, found a number and dialled it. The phone rang three times then there was a click and a recorded message came on:

"Hello, this is Julian Gage. I can't come to the phone right now but if you leave a message after the beep, I'll get back to you as soon as I can."

The beep sounded. Quedley put the phone down. Would it be a good idea to leave a message, he wondered? What the fuck, the sooner you make contact the better.

He rang the number again. When the beep sounded, he put every ounce of shame, regret and wheedling salesmanship he could muster into his voice and blurted, "Julian, it's Caspar. Please forgive me. I'm absolutely ashamed of myself. I've been unbelievably busy but there's no excuse for it. I'll come over as soon as I can — this weekend. In the meantime, don't . . . do anything hasty."

Quedley hung up. That's a holding action at best, he told himself. The question is, how am I really going to deal with this? Of course, Bill Tench. If it wasn't for me, Tench and that trash he employs would be breaking rocks in Mt Eden jail rather than getting fat on some of the plummest security contracts in town.

Quedley went to his address book again, dialled the number and was put through.

"Bill, it's Caspar Quedley. I need you to do me a favour old chief, bit of a delicate one. I need someone to go to Sydney straight away, like this afternoon, and perform a little task for me. It could be quite tricky — not exactly by the book, shall we say? I'll pay top dollar."

"We talking about the sort of bloke who won't take 'no' for an answer here?"

"Exactly. That's precisely the sort of operator I'm after."

"There's one bloke who comes to mind," said Tench. "Leave it with me. I'll see if he's available and ring you back. If he's on, how do you want to play it?"

"I'd much prefer to stay at arm's length. How about if I brief you and you brief him?"

Quedley ordered coffee and waited for Tench to call back. Yes, he thought, that's the way to handle it. Get someone over there pronto to intercept Julian's poison arrow.

His private phone rang.

"All set," said Tench. "This bloke's a starter."

"Billy my boy, you've surpassed yourself. Let's meet for a sandwich in Cornwall Park in an hour's time and I'll tell you all about it."

Caspar Quedley wasn't the only prominent Auckland identity to be rattled that morning.

Unease descended on Barry Plugge, the striptease impresario, as soon as Detective Sergeant Ihaka entered his office. It was the grin, Plugge decided. When a cop wore that sort of big, friendly grin, it meant he was about to shove it up you in a major way.

Plugge's secretary brought in coffee and biscuits and set the tray down on the low table separating her employee and the policeman.

"Mallow puffs," exclaimed Ihaka. "That just about amounts to bribery."

He picked up a mallow puff between thumb and forefinger, studied it fondly, and popped it in his mouth. He thought about having another then dragged his eyes away from the tray and looked at Plugge.

"Barry, they tell me you've got Herman Pickrang on your payroll these days. He's a bit heavy-duty for you, isn't he?"

"Give us a break, Sergeant," said Plugge indignantly. "You know the ructions we had around here. When it reached the stage I had a fucking contract put out on me, I decided, well, shit I'd better get myself some protection. You can't blame me for that."

"I don't think the journalist that Pickrang's been heavying is trying to put you away Barry."

Plugge frowned. "A journalist you say? Don't know anything about that; it can't have been on my account. Don't forget, Herman's a free agent, he doesn't just work for me."

Ihaka was grinning again. "Yeah Barry, but the word is he's been pretty much your man full-time since you pooed your pants over that contract. What I can't figure out, though, is why you of all people would care if a journo wanted to talk to Trevor Lydiate?"

Plugge's expression froze and he made a low grunting sound. Ihaka gulped another biscuit.

"Isn't it unbelievable these lawyers ripping off their own clients?" said Ihaka shaking his head. "So many of 'em, you can't keep track. Anyway, the point is here's your boy Pickrang following this journo all round town and threatening to do Christ knows what to him — well, shit, I don't mind admitting, it made no sense to me. I asked myself, 'Why should Plugge give a flying fuck if every man and his dog want to talk to Lydiate?' So I had a chat to a mate of mine in the Fraud Squad; he thought it was pretty strange too. He said it almost made him wonder if there wasn't more to Lydiate's little number than meets the eye. Anyway, he and his boys are going to talk to the Law Society and have a good long look at the whole thing. I just thought you'd like to know."

Ihaka wolfed a final mallow puff and stood up. Plugge sat in silence, looking as if he'd swallowed something vile and was waiting for his system to reject it.

Ihaka paused with his hand on the doorknob. "Speaking of Lydiate — you remember a private investigator called Guttle who got smoked a while back? He was working for a bloke — who's also now dead, by the way — who was poking around in something where Lydiate's name came up. I guess we're going to have to have another look at that too."

Louise Appleyard had found phone numbers for Lloyd Chennell and Julian Gage in the directory section of her late husband's electronic diary. Sparks rang them from Auckland to try to set things up in advance. Chennell was wary; to secure an interview Sparks had had to feed him a long and inventive spiel, claiming he was doing a story, using Prince Albert College as a case study, about whether private schools should be responsive to social change or maintain their traditions at all costs. The call to Gage got an answering machine. He didn't leave a message.

Sparks caught the mid-afternoon Air New Zealand flight to Sydney and took a cab from the airport to his Kings Cross hotel. There was a fax from Gavin waiting for him. It read: "LC was deputy head of history at PAC from 1968 to 1974. The head of department supervised the teaching of history at scholarship and bursary level while LC did so at UE and school certificate level. His responsibilities included setting internal exam papers."

Just after 7 o'clock Sparks went out for a stroll and something to eat. He walked through the Cross, running the gauntlet of pimps, whores and hustlers, towards Potts Point. He crossed the street to avoid a melee involving a trio of skeletal hookers, their skimpy outfits revealing decaying blue-tinged flesh, and a ragged wino whose eyes rolled comically in his plum-coloured face. Sparks didn't see Herman Pickrang in the rear seat of the taxi which halted for him at the pedestrian crossing, and Herman Pickrang was having too much fun observing the dementia of the street people to notice Sparks.

13

Adversity, it is often said, brings out the best in people. It was a moot point whether there was any "best" in Barry Plugge to be brought out but once he'd recovered from the shock of Ihaka's bombshells, the Sultan of Sleaze surprised himself with his self-possession, decisiveness and ruthless cunning.

Admittedly, the lack of histrionics once the policeman had departed was mainly due to the fact that the gravity of the situation had stunned him into a state bordering on catalepsy. After sitting virtually motionless for twenty-five minutes, Plugge cleared his mind of nightmarish visions of penury, imprisonment and being sodomised by large, brutal men with tattoos and dreadlocks, and forced himself to think.

Of the two related crises, the Guttle matter required the more urgent attention. Despite Ihaka's needling, it would take the Fraud Squad some time to get around to reviewing Lydiate's scam given the apparent epidemic of white collar crime and the fact that they already had a conviction. But murder was murder. What linked him to Guttle was Pickrang — Pickrang whose unbelievable incompetence, whose chronic inability to follow instructions, whose savage impulses had got him into this mess. Pickrang's job had been to discourage interest in Lydiate and thereby ensure that the Plugge-Lydiate connection remained hidden from view. He had achieved the exact opposite. And what, Plugge asked himself, would the useless turd do when the cops got their hands on him, which wouldn't take long? Save his own hairy arse, more than likely. There was no dodging the fact that Herman Pickrang had become a liability.

Pickrang hadn't been heard from for a couple of days which, in the light of Ihaka's visit, was in itself disturbing. First thing the next morning, Plugge dispatched his new chief bouncer to establish Pickrang's whereabouts. Just before midday the bouncer reported that Pickrang was not answering his home or mobile phone and hadn't been sighted at any of his usual haunts.

"Get out to his place and have a look," Plugge told him. "Break in if you have to."

"What if he's there?"

"If he's there, you won't have to break in will you?" said Plugge in an eerily calm voice. He put the phone down, thinking: the bastard knows he's fucked up so he's gone to ground; maybe that'll take the heat off. Even as he permitted himself that glimmer of hope, it occurred to Plugge that if Pickrang wanted to melt into a crowd, he'd have to hide in a leper colony.

Half an hour later the bouncer rang again.

"Boss, I'm out at Herman's place — I kicked the door in like you said — and I reckon he's gone to Sydney."

"Sydney?" yelped Plugge. "What the fuck would he be doing there?"

"Well, I wouldn't know. It's just that I found this thing from a travel agent on his kitchen table. It's got Herman's name on it and it's a sort of schedule, all typed up, saying when he's got to be at the airport, what flight he's on, where he's staying and all that. According to this, he went over to Sydney yesterday afternoon."

"When's he meant to be coming back?"

"Doesn't say. It says 'open return'."

"Okay. Get back here and bring that schedule thing with you."

Plugge hung up and stared at the wall. A plan was taking place in his mind. The more Plugge thought about it, the more he liked it. It was simple, easily executed and would solve the Pickrang problem at a stroke. It was one thing to identify Pickrang as a threat which had to be neutralised; it was quite another to do the neutralising. Plugge was well aware that his other employees would sooner rub themselves down with raw offal and jump into the shark tank at Kelly Tarlton's Underwater World than tangle with Pickrang; his plan overcame that problem. He went to his private bathroom and splashed some cold water on his face. As he looked at himself in the mirror above the handbasin, he said out loud, "Herman, you're about to find out the hard way that it doesn't pay to screw around with Barry Plugge."

Rocco Perfumo was just seeing out the last of the lunch customers at the inner-city pizzeria restaurant which doubled as the headquarters of his family's New Zealand business interests when a waiter told him he was wanted on the phone. He walked to the far end of the restaurant and picked up the receiver.

"Yeah?"

"Is that Rocco Perfumo?"

The caller sounded like he had a mouthful of industrial strength glue. Perfumo wondered why he was going to such lengths to disguise his voice; all New Zealanders sounded the same to him.

"Yeah. What do you want?"

"Remember Herman Pickrang?"

Remember Herman Pickrang? Was this arsehole some kind of a comedian? What does he think — that every second day some fucking gorilla who looks like Doctor No on steroids comes in here and shoves my brother head-first into the pizza oven?

Rocco's brother Martino had suffered impaired eyesight and severe facial scorching as a result of his insertion in the wood-fired oven, the virtues of which were extolled in the restaurant's advertising. He was now convalescing back in Sydney. His sight was nearly back to normal but it would require costly plastic surgery to repair his complexion. Without it, he faced the prospect of going through life looking like a sand-blasted beetroot. The brothers had demanded revenge but their uncle, the head of the family, had ruled that an escalation of the dispute might draw unwanted attention to the family's presence in New Zealand. Rocco had chafed under the veto, convinced his uncle would have put family pride ahead of profits had it been his son whose head had been baked.

"Course I remember him, the cunt," snapped Rocco. "What about him?"

"I just thought you'd like to know — he's in Sydney right now, staying at the Grosvenor serviced apartments in Potts Point."

The caller hung up. Perfumo looked at his watch. He had time to get the late afternoon flight to Sydney. He rang his mother's apartment in Sydney's inner west. His brother answered.

"Marty, it's Rocco. I'm coming over for the weekend. We got some business to take care of."

Lloyd Chennell, the headmaster of St Bartholomew's College, a private boys' school in the posh Sydney suburb of Bellevue Hill, looked at the antique clock on his antique desk. It was 4.15 on a Friday afternoon: another week over. It had been a testing week: a cache of the drug Ecstasy had been found in a stationery cupboard; persons unknown had released a cage of laboratory mice in the head of maths' new car; and a Taiwanese multi-millionaire had removed his son from the school after the lad had been left traumatised by a bullying campaign culminating in a mock lynching, dealing a severe setback to Chennell's strategy of cultivating the Asian community to make up for the fall-off in enrolments from hard-pressed country folk.

On the positive side of the ledger, the senior tennis team had won its rubber against traditional rivals Marsden Grammar. In his eight years as headmaster of St Bartholomew's, Chennell had learned that the Friends of St Bart's, the all-powerful grouping of old boys and parents which dominated the board of governors, would turn a blind eye to pure heroin being sold from the tuck shop as long as victory was achieved in the various sporting tussles with Marsden.

Chennell was spending the weekend in the Blue Mountains and was anxious to be on his way. First, though, he had to do this bloody interview. He cursed the conceit which had caused him to agree to the thing in the first place. He had done so for one reason only: being written up in New Zealand's leading magazine as the headmaster of one of the southern hemisphere's most prestigious schools would be an unwelcome reminder for his former colleagues at Prince Albert College — those patronising oafs now washing down the bitter taste of failure with cheap sherry in the staff reading room or languishing in their dim provincial colleges and second-rate prep schools — that he'd gone on to far greater things.

He vaguely remembered this journalist fellow Sparks droning on about the theme of the article, some idiotic guff about whether private schools should respond to social change. As if I bloody care, he thought. To Chennell, a private school was a meal ticket, a way to make a living without having to endure the nameless horrors of the state system. He would spend another cloistered decade at St Bart's and then take a comfortable retirement; after that, it was all the same to him whether they outlawed private schools, burnt them to the ground or turned them into loony bins. A career of dealing with children of privilege had left Lloyd Chennell with an outlook which verged on nihilism.

At 4.30 Reggie Sparks, wearing a respectable pair of corduroy trousers, a new sports jacket and his late father's lawn bowls club tie, was shown into Chennell's office. The gloom created by the dark wood panelling and the heavy drapes, illuminated only by the single lamp on the large desk in the corner, gave Sparks a nasty moment of déjà vu. However, the figure who rose to greet him bore no resemblance to the schizoid colossus Dr Foster Hogbin.

Sparks had only the haziest recollection of Chennell; he'd put it down to his indifferent memory but the fact of the matter was that Lloyd Chennell was rather forgettable. He was of medium height, slim and moved with a loose-limbed, boneless slither. He had sandy hair, spectacles, a high, brainy forehead, a loose, wet mouth and wore a tweedy brown suit and brown brogues which gave him the appearance of a boffin masquerading as a squire. Sparks was intrigued by his ears which were bright red, almost crimson, and unusually fleshy; they looked as if the slightest perforation would unleash spouts of blood one associated with decapitation. Chennell's pallor also made Sparks wonder if this build-up of blood at the extremities was depriving other organs.

For half an hour, they addressed the ostensible subject of the interview. If Chennell had been more experienced in dealing with the press, it might have occurred to him that Sparks, having opened proceedings with the broadest of catch-all questions, made no effort to shepherd the discussion in any particular direction with more follow-ups. Chennell accepted the opportunity to blow his own trumpet and was doing so tunefully, to his ears anyway, when Sparks brought the recital to an abrupt halt.

"When you think about it, some pretty strange things went on at Prince Albert back in 1970. I mean, first the chaplain steered his car into a brick wall; then the girl hanged herself at the ball; now I hear there was a black market in exam papers."

Chennell stared at Sparks, his ears glowing like horseshoes fresh from the furnace.

"You have the advantage on me there," he said finally.

"You'd remember a bloke called Caspar Quedley?" Chennell nodded. "Apparently, before the exams, he was flogging the UE history paper around the place. You were in charge of setting that paper; how do you think he got hold of it?"

Chennell rose. Something was terribly wrong here. How it had come about could be established in due course; the immediate priority was to terminate the interview.

"Mr Sparks, I have no idea what you're talking about so there's little point in pursuing this discussion. I'm going away for the weekend and I've delayed my departure on your account but I'm not prepared to do so a minute longer for this sort of scurrilous nonsense."

Sparks seemed quite unflustered by the headmaster's indignation. He flipped his notebook shut and put his pen in a jacket pocket. He looked up at Chennell who was now standing next to him.

"What about Victor Appleyard — have you come across him lately?"

Chennell decided not to wait for Sparks to get to his feet. He walked to the study door and held it open. "Appleyard? I heard he died, that's all."

Sparks stopped at the door and extended his hand to Chennell. As Chennell withdrew his hand after a fleeting touch, Sparks looked at him quizzically and said, "That's odd because I know for a fact that Appleyard had an appointment with you the last time he was over here. I suppose you're going to tell me you haven't clapped eyes on Julian Gage for twenty years either?"

The reference to Gage was a stab in the dark but the effect was spectacular: Chennell recoiled as if Sparks had requested one of his choirboys for use in a satanic rite.

"Get out of here this minute," he hissed. "And rest assured your editor will be hearing about this."

Sparks nodded. "You bet."

Herman Pickrang walked down the avenue in Potts Point checking the street numbers, enjoying the warm afternoon sun and congratulating himself on his good fortune. This Sydney job couldn't have been better timed. Even before Ihaka's appearance, Pickrang had been well aware that he was losing ground with Plugge; Plugge would've gone apeshit if he'd found out the cops had somehow got involved. All in all, it was better for everyone if he spent a bit of time out of Auckland. Maybe he should've let Plugge know about his run-in with the cop, but he could talk his way out of that if he had to — he figured the best bet was to lay low for a while, keep his head down blah, blah. Not that he particularly gave a shit about Plugge except he could do without the guy going round town badmouthing him; it wouldn't do his reputation any good. In the meantime, he was going to make sure he did the business on this job; whoever he was working for was paying bloody well and there might be more down the track — providing he didn't fuck it up.

Pickrang stopped outside a handsome three-storey terrace and checked the number against the address Tench had given him. He opened the cast-iron gate, walked up three steps to the tiny porch and rang the bell. The door was opened by a young woman whose pale face contrasted with her uniformly black colour scheme: she had black hair cut page-boy style, a black dress, black stockings, black shoes and black rings under her eyes. Pickrang leered down at her thinking, I'd give you one love if you asked me nicely.

"I'm looking for Julian Gage," he announced. "Is he in?"

The woman half-closed the door and moved nervously behind it, shaking her head. "No," she said huskily. "He's gone away — overseas."

Pickrang consulted his piece of paper.

"What about Dean Delamore?"

"He's gone too."

"Who are you?"

"Miranda. I'm house-sitting for Julian. He should be back in a week or so." She started to close the door. "Maybe you could come back then . . ."

Pickrang dropped his shoulder and rammed it hard against the door. It flew open, knocking the woman backwards. She began to protest.

"Shut your gob," snarled Pickrang. He entered the house, shutting the door behind him. "Gage's got something that belongs to a friend of mine and he wants it back. I'm going to find it so if you want to stay in one piece, just keep quiet and stay out of my way."

Pickrang searched the terrace literally from top to bottom, beginning on the third floor and working his way down. It was not a difficult task — the house was immaculately tidy and there were few obvious hiding places — but his search proved fruitless. By the time he reached the last room, the kitchen, he was in a foul mood which wasn't improved when he found there was no beer in the fridge. He summoned the woman. She came hesitantly, hands clasped in front of her.

"I'm looking for something like a letter, you know, a few pages with writing on them. It might be in an envelope or some sort of package or maybe a folder or notebook. Have you seen it?"

The woman shook her head.

Pickrang said, "Fucking shit," then brushed past her and stalked down the corridor. He stood in the doorway and said, "I'll be back," then left, slamming the door behind him.

Miranda, whose real name was Dean Delamore, stood in front of the large mirror in the hallway and remove the wig. He ruffled his hair which had been plastered to his scalp, then took a tissue from his handbag and wiped off his lipstick. He wondered what the frightening stranger would've done if he'd told the truth: that Julian Gage had been dead for two days and that the previous day he'd dropped a letter from Gage to Victor Appleyard into the airmail slot at Potts Point post office.

Dean Delamore was pretty sure lying had been the sensible course of action. He decided he wouldn't tax his already fragile state of mind by contemplating what the frightening stranger would do when he found out he'd been lied to.

14

Caspar Quedley had woken up with a hangover too often to bother berating himself for having less sense than one of Pavlov's dogs. Similarly, he had given up making pointless and self-deceiving resolutions to stay off the booze for a week, a month or a year. Even the soreness at the back of his throat and the foul taste in his mouth, the residue of one of his occasional cigarette binges, didn't cause a twinge of self-disgust. Caspar Quedley had long ago accepted himself for what he was and looked upon the various facets of his nature — the admirable and the unattractive, the healthy and the perverse — with equanimity. The simple fact was that he was going to get shit-faced from time to time; it was as inevitable as death, taxes and flatulence. Yes, he felt dreadful but experience suggested it was nothing that a ten-kilometre run, a gargantuan breakfast and a contemplative and productive twenty minutes on the toilet couldn't fix.

Quedley checked his watch — it was 9.30 — threw back the duvet, rolled out of bed, stretched, scratched and pulled on a white towelling robe. On his way downstairs he checked the answer phone in the study; the flickering light showed he had two messages. He pressed the playback and was assailed by the strident and slightly hectoring tones of Audrey Benn.

"Caspar, Audrey Benn. It's 9.30 on Friday night and this is just a little reminder that you have a dinner engagement here tomorrow evening. I'm absolutely counting on you, so don't let me down."

"Slutfire," said Quedley. "What in the world possessed me to agree to that?" Before he could grapple with that mystery, he found himself being harangued by a frantic Lloyd Chennell.

"Caspar, it's Lloyd Chennell. I've just had this journalist from *New Nation* magazine in to see me — an insolent shit called Sparks who was at Prince Albert. He made out he was doing a story on private schools but that was just a pretence to get in the door. Caspar, he brought up the exam paper; he brought up Julian. How much does he know, for God's sake? What sort of story are they going to do? Call me as soon as you can — I'll be in the Blue Mountains."

This is starting to give me a monumental slack, thought Quedley sourly as he erased the messages. *New Nation* must be taking this bloody thing seriously if they've sent Sparks over to Sydney. And how the Christ had he got onto Chennell and Gage? First things first. Quedley retrieved his address book from his briefcase, found the number for Chennell's cottage in the Blue Mountains, and dialled. Chennell answered, sounding peevish, after a dozen rings.

"Caspar here."

"Dammit Caspar, what time is it? I was sound asleep."

"Don't whine please Lloyd. The first sound I heard this morning was that of you wetting your panties, which is an extremely fucking disagreeable way to start the weekend, especially when one has a severe headache. I'm in no mood to be grizzled at."

"All right, okay. Anyway, what about this blasted journalist?"

"Exactly what did he say?"

"He said he'd heard that in 1970 you got an advance copy of the UE history exam paper and sold it to your pals; he wanted to know how you'd got hold of it. Then he threw Julian at me."

"In what context?"

"He asked if I'd seen him."

"What'd you say?"

"I refused to discuss it. I ejected him from my study."

Oh yes, thought Quedley, I can just imagine that. I bet Sparks is still shaking.

"Caspar, did you know Sparks was doing this story?"

"Yeah I did. He came to see me a couple of days ago."

Chennell, the quaver back in his voice, began demanding to know why he hadn't been alerted but Quedley cut him off.

"Stop bleating," he snapped in a voice without a trace of its customary banter. "I didn't take him seriously; obviously that was a mistake which now has to be rectified. Is Sparks still in Sydney?"

"I've no idea. He came to see me late yesterday afternoon."

"Assuming he's still there — any idea where I can get in touch with him? I mean, did he leave you a contact number or anything?"

"He did as a matter of fact. When we arranged the interview, he told me to leave a message for him at his hotel if I needed to change the time. It was the Plaza, I think. Yes, the Plaza. I believe it's in Kings Cross."

"Okay, leave it with me. I'll take care of it. If you hear from him again, find out where he is and let me know straight away."

"Thank you Caspar. I needed some reassurance. I really couldn't bear the thought of that business seeing the light of day."

Quedley put the phone down. What an old woman Chennell was. The generalised throbbing in his skull had centralised to a pinprick of intense pain high in his frontal lobe; he was in dire need of a fresh orange juice and a strong cup of coffee. As he made his way downstairs, he thought of something which perked him up enormously. He remembered why he'd accepted Audrey Benn's dinner invitation: because the extremely fuckable — and now fancy-free — Louise Appleyard would be there.

Caspar Quedley was an expert and dispassionate analyst of the various forms of communication, spoken and unspoken, used in social conduct. He employed this expertise in various ways, one of which was to assess the attitudes of attractive women towards sex in general and sex with Caspar Quedley in particular. They were categorised under various headings ranging from "mattress crusher" to "convent fodder". In almost two decades of employing his system, he had only once been dangerously underprepared for an encounter. He'd made a point of avoiding politicians' wives ever since. He'd met Louise Appleyard a few times over the years and was sure he'd detected a spark of interest in her dark eyes. She was by no means a flirt: she'd simply held his look for that extra second or two; when he'd tried to catch her eye again, she'd flick him a slightly mocking smile and look away. But back then, he told himself, her husband was always lurking around, boring someone shitless on the subject of interest rates or CBD rents or something equally fascinating. After allowing for the husband factor, Quedley had categorised Louise Appleyard as a "slow burner", one of those cool, self-contained types who like to be in control of themselves and the situation; they didn't let go often or easily but when they did, it paid to be in racing condition because one was in for a wild ride.

In the course of these musings, it occurred to Quedley that there was a second very good reason for devoting close attention to Mrs Appleyard. He hadn't really thought about it in all the excitement but the "appropriate and interested party" to whom Julian Gage was threatening to send his odious little memoir could well be the late Victor Appleyard. It makes sense, he thought: Appleyard could've seen Julian on one of his trips to Sydney and Julian's probably been too busy dying to have caught up with the fact that virtuous Victor is no longer with us.

Quedley squeezed three oranges, drank the juice, made himself a cup of coffee and returned to the study. Before I do anything else, he thought, I need to get a message to my man in Sydney on the subject of Reggie Sparks, who's becoming tiresome.

The army had eradicated any inclination in Herman Pickrang to lie abed; regardless of the day of the week or the state of his health, he liked to be up and doing by 8 o'clock. So when the go-between Bill Tench tried to get hold of him to pass on Quedley's message, Pickrang was in downtown Sydney doing some shopping. He bought himself a baseball cap to protect his scalp and a diver's knife. He then followed the advice of his next-door neighbour and visited the Queen Victoria Building, Darling Harbour and the Opera House. Just before midday he picked up a hire car and drove out to Watson's Bay where, once again on his neighbour's advice, he ate fish and chips at Doyle's restaurant. When he received the bill, he made a mental note to do something moderately painful to his neighbour when he got home. After lunch, he went for a leisurely drive through the eastern suburbs. The more mansions he passed, the more resentful Pickrang became; he was so preoccupied with envy he didn't notice the dark green Ford which had followed him since he'd picked up the hire car.

When Pickrang returned to his serviced apartment in the early afternoon, there was a message to ring Tench. He did so, reporting on his lack of progress and receiving his instructions with regard to Reggie Sparks. He had mixed feelings about this new assignment: while he was pleased that someone was prepared to pay him handsomely to have a second crack at the journalist, he was puzzled as to how it had come about. Was there any connection with Plugge and Lydiate? After a few minutes of unproductive mental effort, he reached his usual conclusion — who gives a fuck? What mattered was getting the job done.

Pickrang had planned to use the afternoon to check out Gage's place at Palm Beach but that could wait. Instead he walked over to Sparks' hotel and sat in the lobby. Watching the comings and goings, he observed that when guests left their keys at reception, they were put in cubbyholes marked with their room numbers. Eventually, he walked over to the desk and told the receptionist he wanted to leave a message for a guest, Mr Reggie Sparks. The young woman handed him a small notepad and a biro. Pickrang wrote: "Meet me in the bar at 6 p.m., Bert", folded the piece of paper, and handed it to her. He watched her put the message in the cubbyhole, noting the room number. There was a key in the cubbyhole so Sparks had gone out. Pickrang selected a chair on the far side of the hotel lobby well away from the main entrance and sat down to await the journalist's return.

This time when the doorbell rang Dean Delamore looked through the peephole. He didn't know the man standing on the doorstep; he also looked too straight — with his sports jacket and uncool hair, neither short enough nor long enough — to be a friend of Julian Gage's. On the other hand, he looked a lot less threatening than the gatecrasher of the previous day. Delamore opened the door as far as the security chain would allow.

"Yes?"

"Oh hi," said the stranger. "Does Julian Gage live here?"

"Julian's not here at the moment."

The stranger gnawed his lower lip. "My name's Reggie Sparks; I'm a journalist from New Zealand. I was really hoping to talk to Julian — are you expecting him back shortly?"

"No. He's gone away for quite a while."

"Bugger," said Sparks, grimacing. "Look, you're obviously a friend of his, you might be able to help me. Did Julian ever mention a guy called Victor Appleyard?"

"I've heard Julian talk about him. What's your connection with Appleyard?"

"Before he died . . ."

"Appleyard's dead?" exclaimed Delamore. Sparks nodded. Delamore unhooked the security chain and opened the door.

"You'd better come in."

Sparks entered.

"We'll sit outside in the courtyard," said his host. "Down the corridor and through the kitchen."

Sparks walked through the courtyard which was bathed in afternoon sun and sat down at the wooden table.

"I'm Dean Delamore by the way. Can I get you something — coffee or a juice?"

Sparks declined. Delamore was in his mid-twenties with short dyed blond hair cut Roman style, troubled brown eyes and a slim, wiry build. He wore an unbuttoned checked shirt over a snug-fitting white singlet, black stovepipe jeans, Doc Martens and gold earrings. Sparks assumed he was gay.

Sparks told Delamore about Appleyard's interest in the events of 1970 and his meetings in Sydney with Gage and Chennell: "Whatever he found out, he went back to Auckland all fired up about it. Then he died and now I'm sort of trying to piece it together. Appleyard's wife's — widow's — helping," he added, as if it gave the enterprise legitimacy.

Delamore came and sat down opposite Sparks.

"Julian's dead. He died on Wednesday."

"Jesus Christ. How'd he die?"

Delamore lowered his eyes and fiddled with one of his earrings, then looked defiantly at Sparks. "He had AIDS."

Sparks, expressionless, held Delamore's gaze for a few seconds and then looked away.

"I'm sorry."

Delamore nodded. "So am I."

He went into the kitchen and came back with an apple. As he ate it, he told Sparks about the threatening note Gage had sent to Caspar Quedley and how, two days previously and according to his instructions, he'd posted Gage's letter to Victor Appleyard.

Sparks whistled softly. "What did it say?"

"No idea. I just dropped it in the post."

"Had he ever talked to you about any of this stuff?"

Delamore shook his head.

"Well, I guess we'll know soon enough. I'll ring Louise and let her know it's coming."

"There's another thing," said Delamore. "Quedley must've got a big shock when he got Julian's letter. He left this smarmy message on the answering machine — you know, please forgive me, I'll come over and see you as soon as I can. I think he sent someone over here to find what Julian wrote. This guy barged in here yesterday, really rude, and searched the place. You should've seen him — he was unreal, like maybe two metres tall and kind of Asian-looking.

And he was bald except for this chunk of hair right here," he said, pointing to the middle of his fringe.

Holy shit, it can't be, thought Sparks. "How big was his head?" he asked.

Delamore looked puzzled. "What do you mean?"

"Did he have a really small head?" asked Sparks, making a shape with his hands.

"Right, yes he did, a tiny little head, like really out of proportion with the rest of him. Do you know him?"

It must be, thought Sparks. The sort of biological quirk which results in a Herman Pickrang happens once a generation at the most. But if Pickrang works for Quedley, where does Lydiate come into it? Maybe it was Quedley all along who was trying to scare me off and the Lydiate stuff was just a smokescreen.

"I'm pretty sure I do and if it's who I think it is, just stay well out of his way. The guy's an animal."

Delamore shrugged. "Tell me about it. I'm not going to hang around here. I've got to do a show tonight, then I'm spending a couple of days at Julian's place at Palm Beach. It's my last chance; they're putting it on the market."

On the way out Sparks asked Delamore what sort of show he was in.

"A drag show," said Delamore, brightening up. "It's a hoot. If you've got nothing on tonight, you should come and see it — Oscar's in Oxford Street. It'll broaden your horizons."

Sparks paused at the bottom of the steps down to the street. "What makes you think my horizons need broadening?"

Delamore looked down at him gravely. "You might be different but I find most people's do."

Herman Pickrang's failure to intercept Reggie Sparks that Saturday afternoon was due more to nature than dereliction of duty. After Pickrang had sat in the lobby for two hours monitoring every arrival, the several beers he'd had at lunch began to make their presence felt. Stoically, he remained at his post for a further thirty minutes until the pressure from his bladder became unbearable. The sight of Herman Pickrang mincing at high speed through the lobby with his thighs clamped together and his bottom protruding in the manner of a female baboon in mating season attracted the attention of most people in the area. No one eyed him more intently than Sparks, who was about to enter the hotel through the large glass doors. Instead he spun on his heel and walked quickly away.

So what do I do now, he wondered. I'm being pursued by a violent maniac who appears to have taken up residence in my hotel; my credit card is in a safety deposit box in the hotel and I have exactly $70 on me; I don't know a single person in this entire city. Except Dean Delamore.

Sparks walked back to Gage's terrace and rang the bell. There was no answer. His mind was racing. That club, what the hell was it called? Oscar's. Sparks looked at his watch: 5.15 p.m. He found a public phone box, inserted a handful of coins and dialled Louise Appleyard's number. It was, he reflected, the only phone number he knew off by heart. She answered on the seventh ring.

"It's Reggie Sparks I'm calling from Sydney."

"Reggie, sorry to do this but I was literally on my way out the door; I've got a taxi waiting."

"Not to worry. I just wanted to let you know you'll get something in the post in a day or two addressed to your husband. It might explain quite a lot. It's from Julian Gage, one of those guys Victor saw over here. Gage died a few days ago — it's a long story. I'll let you go — have a nice night. I'll tell you all about it when I get back."

Sparks replaced the handset wishing he'd never made the call. Now he was going to feel low all weekend; it sounded like she had a big weekend lined up. Later Sparks would wonder about that call and whether things would have turned out differently if Louise Appleyard had either let the telephone ring or been in less of a rush to get to her dinner party.

15

In the large mirror above the fireplace, Louise Appleyard watched the two men eyeing her, or to be precise, eyeing her legs which were displayed to advantage in the black lycra bodysuit she was wearing under a boldly embroidered jacket. They'd been eyeing her on and off from the moment she'd arrived; she'd wondered how long it would be before their wives noticed. She also wondered when the fat man, whose name she'd forgotten and to whom she was pretending to listen, would finish eulogising her late husband and release her hand from his moist grip. Not till we're called to the table, she guessed.

The drawing room in which Audrey Benn's guests were having pre-dinner drinks was at the front of the house, close to the front door, so the words with which Caspar Quedley greeted his hostess carried clearly: "Audrey, you appalling old gargoyle, what's for dinner?"

The eyes of all the guests, even of the pair who'd been admiring what was visible of the curve of Louise Appleyard's buttocks below the hem of her jacket, swivelled to the doorway. Quedley sauntered into the room with a simpering Audrey Benn on his arm. He wore a rumpled, navy blue suit with loose-fitting jacket and baggy trousers and a black polo-neck sweater. He surveyed the gathering, inclined his head grandly, and said, "Greeting earthlings."

Audrey steered him straight over to Louise. He shot a suspicious glance at her companion, who had at last let go of her hand, and asked: "Is this man bothering you?"

"Not at all," she said, faintly embarrassed by the lack of conviction in her voice.

Quedley looked dubious. "I'm not sure I believe you. You do realise Harvey here's a well-known snowdropper?"

"A what?"

A snowdropper. You know, a person, usually of the male persuasion, who steals ladies' undergarments off clotheslines. Lord knows what he does with them — chews the crotches out of 'em more than likely."

Louise, struggling to keep a straight face, turned to Harvey, who'd gone crimson and started to pant. "Harvey, can this be true?"

Before he could reply, Audrey cut in to ask Quedley what he'd like to drink. Harvey used the diversion to beat a retreat.

"I thought you'd never ask," replied Quedley. "I'll have bourbon, thanks Aud, providing you serve an acceptable brand. Wild Turkey or Maker's Mark would be the shot; if I must, I'll settle for Jack Daniel's. Three fingers with plenty of ice if you'd be so kind."

Audrey raised her eyebrows at Louise. "I'll see what I can do."

As Audrey Benn departed on her mission, Quedley smiled benignly down at Louise. "Alone at last. Long time, no ogle. So how the hell are you, old girl?"

She shrugged. "Oh, pretty good."

"I'm sorry as hell about Vic. He was a good lad."

"He was that."

He nodded. "Managing okay?"

"Yes, I'm fine."

"Not sitting about moping I hope. You get out much?"

"As a matter of fact, this is my social comeback."

He whistled. "Strewth, you picked a beaut. Why this show? You'd have more fun at the dentist."

"Well, if I read Audrey right, she's rather relying on you to provide the sparkle."

"She's a devious critter, isn't she? She used the fact that you were coming to get me along; wild horses couldn't get me here otherwise."

Louise, wide-eyed: "And to think little old me did the trick — flattered I'm sure."

"Now Louise," said Quedley, mock-serious, "you know bloody well I've been slobbering over you from a discreet distance for years. If it wasn't for the fact that the very thought of adultery is deeply abhorrent to me, I'd . . ."

Louise, looking over his shoulder, saw Audrey Benn coming and interrupted him. "Ah here we are — here's your drink."

Audrey belligerently thrust a heavy crystal tumbler at Quedley. "All I can say Caspar is you damn well better enjoy this. I had to send my son next door for it and he wasn't impressed."

Quedley sipped and smacked his lips. "Dashed decent of him. Sorry to be a pest Aud but, as I was saying to Louise, this is no mere whim — this is a deep and enduring yearning."

They were placed next to one another at the table. As they sat down Quedley said quietly, "By the way, have you heard about the story *New Nation* are doing?"

"Yes I have," said Louise. "In fact, I've talked to the journalist a couple of times."

"That doyen of journalism Reggie Sparks? I shudder to think what sort of dog's breakfast he'll come up with."

"Oh I don't know, I suspect Reggie's a bit more capable than he sometimes appears. He rang me tonight actually — from Sydney. He went over to see a couple of people that Vic had talked about . . . well, you know what it was about; he came to see you, didn't he? Anyway, Reggie said one of them — Julian someone . . ."

"That'd be Julian Gage," cut in Quedley. "I heard he was at death's door?"

"I'm afraid he's knocked, entered and shut the door behind him — just this week. But Reggie was saying that, before he died, Gage wrote to Vic all about that business at Prince Albert. Apparently, his letter's in the mail."

Quedley shook his head. "I could probably tell you right now what it'll say." He lowered his voice. "Listen, why don't we leave the living dead to it as soon as we decently can and have a drink somewhere? I'll tell you all about little Julian. You should know the whole background before you read it — and definitely before you even consider passing it on to *New Nation*." His concerned expression lifted, replaced by a lop-sided grin. "It won't take long. Then we can talk about you and me."

At 8 p.m. Sydney time, an hour after Audrey Benn's guests had taken their first sip of toheroa soup, Herman Pickrang left Sparks' hotel. His quarry had not appeared and the long and fruitless stake-out had left Pickrang ravenous and in a volcanically bad mood. He found a McDonald's where he ate three hamburgers, three helpings of chips and an apple pie. He then bought two six-packs of beer and returned to his serviced apartment.

At 9.30 p.m. Pickrang came out of the apartment building with a six-pack under his arm and got into his hire car. He switched on the interior light and spread out a map of greater Sydney. When he eventually located Palm Beach, he swore foully; it looked a good distance away. However, as the hours crawled past in the lobby of the Plaza Hotel, Pickrang had become increasingly convinced that Julian Gage and the item he'd been sent to secure were out at Palm Beach, at the address Tench had given him. Besides, he thought, what else is there to do: sit in that shoebox watching TV or go back up the Cross and buy himself a root. Fuck that. Pickrang had decided that the prostitutes in Kings Cross were the most repulsive representatives of the oldest profession he'd ever come across. And you've blocked some shockers in your time, he said to himself, smiling grimly at the memories.

By 10.30 p.m. Pickrang was in the northern suburb of French's Forest, pulled over on the side of the road studying the map for the third time since leaving Potts Point. Fifty metres back down the road Rocco Perfumo cursed, flicked off his headlights and swerved behind a parked car.

"I'm telling you, the cunt's lost," repeated his brother Martino.

Rocco looked across at his brother. Martino's face was starting to flake again.

"Course he's fucking lost. Question is, where the fuck's he trying to get to?"

Martino opened the glovebox and brought out a .38 calibre revolver.

"Why don't we do the fucker here and now, just pull up beside him and blow him away?" He extended his arm and sighted down the gun barrel just as a man out walking his dog strolled past their car.

"That's why, for fuck's sake," said Rocco heatedly. "Put that fucking thing away." He cuffed his brother affectionately on the shoulder. "This is great, man — the longer he fucks around out here, the better for us. We'll just wait a bit longer till no one's around, then do it. He's dead meat, mate — no worries."

It was between the rack of lamb with rosemary and the caramelised pear tart that Louise Appleyard decided in principle that she should go to bed with Caspar Quedley. It briefly occurred to her that perhaps she should send him a signal that she was thus far disposed; if he carries on knocking back that red wine at this rate, she thought, sleeping with him might turn out to be exactly that. However, as she shrank from unambiguous gestures such as casually dropping a hand on his inner thigh, she was forced to pin her faith on Quedley's constitution and to hope that he could see some benefit in stopping short of intoxication.

It had been more than a decade since Louise Appleyard had seriously contemplated having sex with anyone other than her late husband so she was understandably nervous. Apart from anything else, she was not entirely sure of Quedley's aspirations. He was not the easiest person to read: he paid attention to her in short bursts, radiating charm like heat off a bonfire; in between times he had fierce discussions on sport with the other men, once even threatening, when chided by Audrey Benn for antisocial behaviour, to lead a breakaway male group into the kitchen.

The other diners hung on his every word, solicited his opinions and sought his approval of theirs, cackled at his witticisms, and cooed like pigeons at his revelations of political and commercial intrigue. They were, by and large, a staid and conventional crew, middle-aged-going-on-old in attitude if not in fact. In their company, Quedley stood out like a black panther in a pet shop. Every now and again, he bared his teeth as if to remind them that suburban dinner parties were not his natural habitat.

Harvey's wife Eleanor, a permed and powdered supporter of worthy causes, was defending the Aotea Centre, Auckland's star-crossed performing arts centre, against well-rehearsed charges of being a white elephant when Quedley intervened.

"Personally, I don't give a toss whether it makes money or not. I mean, it's there so surely to God it's only common sense to use it? Whether or not the events they stage make a profit or not says a lot more about the management and the Auckland public than about the building. If we're going to debate the merits of the building itself, we should be concentrating on the aesthetics of it: is it pleasing to behold? Is it beautiful? Eleanor?"

"Well, yes, I happen to think it is rather . . ."

"Fine. Eleanor, I take it you subscribe to the view that architecture is an artistic medium and therefore that a building can be a work of art?"

"Of course."

"Okay. I submit that the defining quality of art is poetry. Poetry has two meanings: in the specific sense, it's a composition usually involving rhyme and metre, the stuff we were taught in school. In the wider sense, poetry is that quality in a work of art — be it a piece of music, or drama, or a novel or a building — which engages our emotions, uplifts our spirits, puts us in touch with our higher selves. It's what separates art from entertainment. Now I've got a place down at Coromandel. It's pretty rough and ready: instead of a proper toilet I've got an outhouse, a long-drop — your basic little wooden sentry box built over a bloody great hole in the ground. In summer, believe me, she gets ripe in there. You get the bluebottles — they're as big as hummingbirds but their radar's not so good so they keep flying into your mouth. Anyway, the point I wanted to make Eleanor, with all due respect, is that there's a thousand times more poetry in my nasty, smelly, flyblown little outside shithouse than in the Aotea Centre."

Throats were cleared around the table; there were a few nervous chuckles. Louise looked at Quedley expecting to see his usual ivory grin. He was looking at Eleanor with an almost quizzical expression, head slightly tilted and smiling pleasantly but without showing his teeth; the smile hadn't reached his eyes which gleamed coldly. It reminded Louise of the way her brother would look at her when they were children playing Monopoly, when he'd put a hotel on Park Lane and she'd landed on it.

By the time coffee and liqueurs arrived, most of the men were the worse for drink. Quedley, though, who'd had as much as anyone, seemed quite unaffected. Someone proposed that everyone should tell a joke and the motion was carried by acclaim. Once again Louise was reminded of her childhood; the jokes were the sort of dismal, sanitised little yarns her parents and their friends used to tell when they'd had a sherry or two and shed some of their excessive decorum. The men hooted and the ladies made indulgent, boys-will-be-boys faces at one another when Harvey told the story of an engineer who came up with a new method for getting rid of the stench from the local abattoir: he suggested running pipes from the killing chain into a gigantic tank so that the odours would dissipate in water. The mayor derided his theory saying, "Come off it mate, haven't you ever farted in the bath?"

When it was Quedley's turn, Audrey Benn instructed him, "Now Caspar, no filth thank you very much."

Quedley shrugged. "I'll have to pass then. I don't know any clean jokes."

The other men, none of whom had had the nerve to tell a proper dirty joke, set up a chorus at this, demanding that Quedley should have his turn.

Quedley held up his hands in a gesture of surrender. "If you insist, but don't say I didn't warn you. It's actually a salutary little tale this: a woman gets a part-time job as a barmaid at the local pub. So, on her first day, a Saturday, she kisses her husband on the cheek and heads off full of enthusiasm. Everything's going well until a couple of hard cases wander in. They swagger up to the bar and she goes over to serve them, putting on her brightest smile. 'And what would you like, sir?' she says to the first hard case. He looks her up and down and says, 'I'd like to smear raspberry jam all over your tits — and then lick it off'."

There were a few snorts of suppressed laughter. Audrey Benn peered closely at something in her coffee cup.

"Well, as you can imagine, the woman's a bit thrown, but the boss had warned her she'd have to put up with a certain amount of crude and uncouth behaviour. So she keeps her smile in place and turns to the second guy. 'And how about you sir: what would you like?' 'I would like'," said Quedley, speaking very deliberately, "'to fill your vagina'— he didn't use that word but in deference to Audrey's sensibilities I have — 'I would like to fill your vagina with ice cream and then eat it all out'."

Eleanor, her cheeks flushed, got to her feet. "If you'll excuse me, I'm going to powder my nose."

"If I was you, old thing, I'd have a widdle while you're there," said Quedley. "Save having to make another trip. Where was I? Yes, so this is all too much for the poor woman. She bursts into tears, dashes out of the pub, jumps in her car and hightails it. She's still distressed when she gets home where her husband's got his feet up watching television. He leaps up when he sees her: 'Darling, what's happened?' So she tells him about the two hard cases and how the first one wanted to smear raspberry jam all over her breasts et cetera. The husband is outraged. 'No one talks to my wife like that,' he declares. 'I'm going down there to have a piece of these bastards.' He puts on his jacket and as he's going out the door he says, 'By the way, what'd the other one say?' 'He said he wanted to fill my vagina with ice cream, slurp, slurp, yum, yum.' The husband stops in his tracks, turns around, takes off his jacket, goes back to his chair, sits down and turns on the TV. 'What are you doing?' asks his wife. 'I thought you were going to sort those two horrible men out.' The husband looks at her and says, 'Anyone who can eat that much ice cream is too big for me'."

Louise Appleyard had felt the tension build in the room as Quedley told his joke. She knew that, whatever the outcome, she wouldn't be able to stop herself laughing. The gross and unexpected punchline came as a release; she threw her head back and roared with laughter. Some of the men joined in while the other women exchanged dazed shakes of the head. When the laughter died down, Audrey refilled Louise's coffee cup and said: "You two obviously have something in common."

"Grubby minds," said Eleanor, pinch-faced, from the doorway.

Louise, still laughing, looked at Quedley, thinking, well, that's not a bad start.

16

The ambience of Oscar's Night Club turned out to be less confrontational than Sparks had anticipated. Earlier in the evening, over several espressos in a Darlinghurst coffee bar and when not brooding about Louise Appleyard, he'd given some idle thought to what he might encounter there. His speculations were largely populated by the stereotypes of gay subculture: musclemen with shaven heads, self-mutilators with metallic items embedded in every appendage, deviates using colour coding to advertise their readiness to indulge in various unthinkable sexual practices. However, at first sight the clientele resembled a gathering of ardent young Christians, although Sparks couldn't remember whether the Mormon missionaries who'd doorknocked around Auckland during his childhood had been permitted to cultivate hair on their upper lips. Most of the moustaches sported by Oscar's patrons were understated if not apologetic affairs even when accompanied by Van Dyke beards; there were no cow-pusher handlebars or walrusy tea-strainers. Nor were there peaked caps, chains or leather trousers customised to expose the buttocks. Oscar's, it seemed, was not the favoured haunt of the flamboyant and exhibitionists among Sydney's gay community but more of a rendezvous for those who only fully emerged from the closet at weekends and even then preferred not to make a fuss about it.

The club itself was long and narrow, on three levels. At one end was a raised stage, at the other a long bar with stools and an open kitchen. In front of the stage was a small dance floor with most of the remaining floor space given over to tables and chairs and more seating along the walls. Sparks watched the show — a series of impersonations of Hollywood's grandes dames — from the bar. He thought he spotted Delamore as Carmen Miranda but it was hard to tell under the fruit. In between the acts a disc jockey played dance music. Sparks, mooching at the bar, received only one invitation to dance. Taken by surprise, he declined the invitation more emphatically than was called for. The rejected party, a well-built young man, shrugged his impressive shoulders and muttered something to his two companions which caused them to shoot oblique accusatory glances in Sparks' direction.

Shortly before 11 p.m. the MC announced the last live act of the evening. The Rexettes performed in the style of the all-girl groups of the 1960s, their repertoire including "He's a Rebel" and "Big Girls Don't Cry", which was particularly well-received. Delamore, in a black wig and abbreviated body-hugging white dress, wiggled becomingly and emitted a piercing falsetto. After six energetic numbers, the Rexettes waved and blew kisses to the audience and tripped girlishly off the stage to the accompaniment of whoops, whistles and wild applause.

Sparks decided he needed another beer before he was ready to venture backstage. He was sipping it morosely when Dean Delamore, still in full Rexette costume, tapped him on the shoulder.

"I thought it was you — it's hard to tell with the lights," he said. "I didn't expect to see you here. So — what'd you think?"

"It's good," said Sparks nodding. "Especially the Rexettes."

"Yeah, everyone likes them. I tell you, it's hard work doing that Frankie Valli falsetto, though; I start running out of breath towards the end." He patted his cheeks. "Are my cheeks red? I feel like I've got a glow on."

Sparks shook his head. "No, they're fine. Would you like a drink?"

"Yes please, a Coke."

Sparks turned round to attract the barman's attention, asking himself, what are you doing? That's a bloke, remember? You're carrying on as if he's Sharon Stone. He ordered the drink and then turned back to Delamore.

"To be honest, I didn't really come to see the show," said Sparks. "I'm in a bit of strife. You know the gorilla who turned up at your place? I didn't tell you this but I had a run-in with him in Auckland a few days ago — he was all set to give me a hiding to make me drop my story. Anyway, right now he's camped out in the lobby of my hotel. My credit card and cash are in the safety deposit box and I don't know another soul in Sydney. I was wondering if I could crash at your place tonight?"

"Well, sure, except remember I said I'm going out to Palm Beach tonight?"

"How far's that?"

"About an hour or so."

"Well, if it's not a hassle. I can get a bus back tomorrow."

"It's no problem at all. I'll just get my stuff and we'll get going. It'll be nice to have someone to talk to on the way."

Delamore was back in a couple of minutes, wearing a faded denim jacket over the white dress.

"I can't be bothered getting changed. You right? My car's outside."

Sparks finished his beer as Delamore started for the exit. As he passed the group at the other end of the bar, Sparks noticed him exchanging words with his would-be dancing partner. Outside the club he caught up with Delamore and asked what the conversation had been about.

Delamore looked at him curiously. "Nothing."

"No come on, what'd that guy say? I'm only interested because he asked me to dance before."

Delamore put the key in the car door and looked at Sparks over the roof of the car.

"If you really want to know, what he said was, 'Do you get off going with straights?'"

They got into the car.

"What'd you say?"

Delamore started the car and steered it out into the traffic. Without looking at Sparks he said, "I said that depends on the straight."

In the end it had all been resolved with a minimum of fuss: as the dinner party began to break up, Louise Appleyard had murmured that she'd better order a taxi; Caspar Quedley had offered her a lift home; she'd replied, expressionless, "Whose?"

When they got to Quedley's place, they decided, without actually discussing the matter, to postpone both drink and the discussion about Julian Gage and his letter. Instead, after some imperfectly coordinated kissing and urgent thrustings against one another and without shedding any more clothing than was absolutely necessary, they fornicated on the long leather couch in the living room which looked out to Rangitoto Island. The spontaneity suited Louise Appleyard who'd been looking forward, albeit nervously, to the sex but slightly dreading the preliminaries. Afterwards, as they sprawled on the couch breathing heavily, she reflected that, all in all, the exercise had gone better than could have been expected apart from the slight hiccup when the image of her late husband had flashed into her mind.

Quedley, noticing her pensive expression, reached over to brush the hair off her face.

"Post coitum omne animal triste est," he said.

"What?"

"It's Latin. Roughly translated it means that all creatures feel a bit down in the dumps after a legover."

"A legover?" she said. "How romantic."

He kissed her on the nose and stood up. "My dear, there was nothing romantic about what just took place. Not to put too fine a point on it, we coupled like beasts. Now if you'd care to hop in the spa, I'll fetch the champagne."

Quedley also fetched some cocaine which he deployed in rows on a silver tray. Louise thought about declining but decided it was a little early in her new career as a born-again party girl to start applying the brakes. After trying a couple of lines she concluded that cocaine was overrated. Caspar Quedley, on the other hand, wasn't.

When the champagne and the cocaine were finished and their skins began to wrinkle, they got out of the spa and into Quedley's large bed where they made love again, this time in a more excursive manner, deriving as much enjoyment from the journey as the arrival. Insufficient clothing had been discarded during their first engagement to permit a thorough review of the other's physique; in the course of the leisurely repeat, neither suffered the disappointment which often attends the sexual experiences of the no-longer young: the discovery that artful outfitting and tailoring have concealed slackening muscles, subsiding flesh and coarsened skin.

They talked about Julian Gage on the way out to Palm Beach. According to Delamore, he'd owned a couple of wildly expensive light-fitting shops which had done very well during the mid-1980s when money was no object for those who overnight conjured fortunes from their computer screens. Then, as the end of the decade approached, he'd been diagnosed HIV positive.

"He used to say he was lucky," said Delamore. "As soon as he knew, he sold his shops for a good price. Six months later the party was well and truly over — after the economy had gone south, there weren't many people still willing or able to shell out ten grand for a lamp. He reckoned if he'd sold a year later, he would've been lucky to cover his loans. He sold the terrace in Potts Point too and rented it back so he had enough money to make the most of the time he had left. He bought his place at Palm Beach and did a lot of travelling. I was lucky too — I came on the scene just at the right time and he took me with him. It was wonderful — we always flew first class and stayed in the best hotels. You name it, we went there — Paris, Venice, New York, New Orleans, Rio. We went on the *Orient Express* and the *QE2* and cruising in the Caribbean; we even went on safari in Africa, although a person less keen on roughing it than Julian would be hard to find." Delamore stared ahead dreamily. "It was like a fairy story. I said that once and he said, 'Yes and we are the fairies'." Delamore smiled for a few more seconds, then the smile faded and he continued in a voice which resonated with loss and bewilderment: "About a year ago, the symptoms started to appear. In a few months he went from being a normal, healthy person — as far as the outside world knew — to an invalid. A few more months and he looked like something out of a concentration camp, a skeleton with skin. At the end he was just a shell. It was like he'd been eaten by termites — you thought one tap and he'd crumple into dust and blow away."

They drove across the Spit Bridge in silence and headed out through Manly to the northern beaches.

Sparks eventually spoke into the silence: "So he never said a word about what happened at school?"

"Nothing specific. But seeing Appleyard definitely unsettled him. He said afterwards that he had a big decision to make because he had something on his conscience which he wanted to resolve before he died. I asked him what the decision was and he said it wasn't just him who'd be affected."

"He didn't say who else?"

"No."

"But that letter to Quedley sort of speaks for itself, doesn't it?"

"I guess so."

"Did he ever talk about Quedley?"

"Oh God yes, all the time. Once he even called him 'the love of my life'."

Sparks stared at Delamore for a moment then he noticed how far the hem of his dress had ridden up his slim thighs and hurriedly looked away. "You telling me Quedley's gay?"

Delamore looked at him coldly. "You make it sound like being a necrophiliac or something."

Sparks waved a hand apologetically. "No, no, I don't mean that. It's just that the guy's got a reputation for being a big-time womaniser."

Delamore shrugged. "I never said he was gay; what I said was Julian adored him."

"What, you think it was all one way — what's that word . . . ?"

"Unrequited."

"Yeah, unrequited. You think it was like that?"

Delamore's mouth twisted. "It's hard to say. I suppose that was my basic impression, but Julian could be coy and drop these little hints . . . I'd say it was probably one-sided, kind of a hopeless infatuation rather than a relationship, certainly as adults. But who knows what happened at that school? It was a boarding school after all. Didn't you say you went there too?"

"I was a day boy."

After that Delamore put on a tape and they listened to Edith Piaf for the rest of the way.

As forecast, a cold front had rolled through Sydney early that evening bringing steady rain and driving the temperature down. Even allowing for the hour, Palm Beach seemed abandoned; few lights showed as they drove along the sea front. Clifftops was perched right on the edge of the hill overlooking the far end of the beach. It was down a drive at the end of a no-exit road; the nearest house was about fifty metres away.

Delamore stopped in front of the white-washed wooden house and slumped in his seat.

"I've just thought of something," he said. "We're assuming that Quedley sent that guy — what's his name, Pickrang? — over here, right?"

"It looks that way, doesn't it?"

"Julian was a bit of a show-off; he couldn't help himself. When he bought this place, he had some personalised stationery done with the address on it, you know? That letter he sent to Quedley, the one he dictated to me, was on that letterhead. What I'm saying is, Pickrang could know about this place."

"Yeah, that's a point, but I wouldn't worry about it tonight," said Sparks after a few moments. "For a start, we know where Pickrang is — he's parked in the lobby of my hotel waiting for me. And even if he got sick of that, he's hardly going to drive all the way out here at this time of night in this weather, is he?"

17

Despite having set out for Palm Beach more than two hours before Delamore and Sparks, Herman Pickrang got there five minutes after they did. Peering through the half-moons of visibility created by his windscreen wipers, Pickrang was frequently tempted to abandon his circuitous expedition to try again in daylight and, hopefully, more favourable weather the following day. Each time he'd remind himself that both the hour and the foul weather were ideal for his purpose. When he finally found his way to Palm Beach, he then faced the problem of locating 5 Ocean View Road. He briefly toyed with the idea of knocking on the door of one of the few houses from which lights glowed behind curtains before deciding that it would be unwise to ask directions to an address at which one intended to commit one and possibly several crimes. There was nothing else for it but to start at one end of the small community and work methodically across it, checking the street signs. Fortunately for Pickrang, he chose to start at the right end.

To ensure that Pickrang didn't notice he was being followed, Rocco Perfumo had taken to switching off his headlights for minutes at a time. There was hardly any other traffic on the roads so it was easy enough to follow Pickrang by his tail lights.

Pickrang found Ocean View Road at exactly 1 o'clock that Sunday morning. He drove slowly to its dead end and pulled over to the side of the road. When Perfumo saw Pickrang's lights go off, he cut the engine and drifted to a halt at the top of the street. Pickrang got out of the car. He could see lights through the trees and made his way carefully down the drive towards them. A car was parked outside the compact wooden bungalow. Staying in the shadows, Pickrang approached the house and went silently up the stairs to the verandah. The rain was easing and he could hear music over the dwindling hiss. He flattened himself against the side of the house, inched up to a window and peered in.

Pickrang was not greatly prone to self-pity. Even so, his recent string of reversals had left him in a put-upon and resentful frame of mind; he'd been feeling that it was about time he got a break. One peep through the window convinced him that, at long last, his luck had changed. In the foreground was the woman from Gage's house. She was wearing a sexy little white dress and wriggling around the room in time to the music with a glass in her hand. Over in the corner, slumped in an armchair and watching the woman with an odd sort of half-smile on his face, was the journalist Reggie Sparks. Pickrang leaned against the wall and breathed deeply. His nostrils flared. He grinned horribly, the rapacious, age-old grin of the predator in the night. He took three long strides along the verandah, threw open the door, and stepped inside.

"Howdy," he said.

Pickrang closed the door behind him and looked from Delamore to Sparks. Both of them stared at him in dumbstruck horror. He unzipped his light windcheater, reached inside and, with a slow flourish, produced the diver's knife with the thick eight-inch blade. He dropped into a half-crouch holding the knife extended in his right hand and crabbed towards Sparks, who sprang to his feet and looked wildly round for something with which to defend himself. When he'd closed to about a metre, Pickrang switched the knife to his left hand and feinted a thrust to Sparks' belly. Sparks bleated like a dying sheep and dropped his hands, his eyes bulging in agonised anticipation of the knife's cold plunge. With a snap of his hips, Pickrang came out of his crouch and slung a whiplash right hook to the side of Sparks' jaw. Sparks jitterbugged backwards, his legs splaying like a new-born foal, and spilled over the armchair he'd recently occupied onto the floor where he lay face down and utterly motionless.

Pickrang slowly straightened up and turned to Delamore who was clutching the wine glass in front of him in both hands.

"Wouldn't mind a drink myself," he said. "What've you got there?"

"White wine," said Delamore in a near-whisper.

"Cat's piss," said Pickrang. "Where's Gage?"

"He's dead. You're too late — the thing you're looking for is gone too. I posted it myself."

Pickrang's brow furrowed. "Posted it — where to?"

"Auckland. I didn't notice who it was addressed to; I just stuck it in the mail like Julian told me."

"You didn't notice who it was addressed to eh? Course you didn't." Pickrang grinned playfully. "We can talk about that later — after I've shagged the arse off you." He put the knife down on the arm of the sofa, unzipped his jacket and laid it on top.

Delamore wished to God he hadn't spent so much time cultivating a girlie voice. He tried to speak in a timbre redolent of pendulous testicles and jutting Adam's apples but all that emerged was a reedy squeak.

"Look, there's something you should know . . ."

Pickrang chuckled, shaking his head. "Let me guess, it's that time of the month? I think you've got me mixed up with someone who gives a fuck."

Delamore pulled off the black wig revealing his short, slicked-down blond hair. "I'm not a woman."

Pickrang's amiable expression disappeared. He regarded Delamore through slitted eyes. "What the fuck is this?"

"I told you, I'm not a woman. I'm in a drag show — this is one of my costumes."

"What are you talking about?" snarled Pickrang. "You got tits."

"That's part of the costume too. Look." Delamore reached behind him, undid a couple of buttons on his dress and slopped it off his shoulders. He shrugged out of the padded brassiere and dangled it in one hand; with the other he pulled down the front of his dress to expose a flat, slightly tanned chest with a few clumps of downy golden hair.

"You're a fucking transvestite," said Pickrang hoarsely.

Delamore shook his head. "No I'm not, I'm a performer, a singer. I only wear women's clothes in the show."

"Bullfuck. You had 'em on the other day."

"It was a new outfit," said Delamore wearily. "I was just trying it on."

"Don't shit me." A foxy glint came into Pickrang's eyes. "I got a blowjob from a trannie once — up in Singapore. I bet you've blown the old meat trombone plenty of times."

"I'm not touching you, you animal," said Delamore, eyes blazing.

"Oh we're choosy are we? Don't tell me you haven't gobbled matey here," he said with a jerk of his head towards the recumbent Sparks. Pickrang advanced on Delamore and was unzipping his fly when the door opened and the Perfumo Brothers walked in. Rocco shut the door and leaned against it with his arms folded; Martino pointed the revolver at Pickrang's chest.

Rocco, his lip curling with disgust, took in the scene. "Well, wouldn't you know it?" he said. "Big, bad Herman turned out to be a screaming fag."

There was a long silence. Pickrang stood with his hands on his hips looking from brother to brother. Finally, he said, "Who the fuck are you?"

"So you don't remember us, huh?" said Rocco as Sparks groaned and sat up. "Take a geek at him. That's what happens to your face when it gets shoved in a pizza oven."

Pickrang nodded his understanding. He'd taken it for granted that the pair intended to kill him; now he knew why. There was one other thing he needed to know.

"How'd you know I was here?"

Rocco smiled maliciously. "I'm glad you asked about that. You're on someone's shit list, mate. A little bird told us you were coming to Sydney, where you'd be staying, the works. We've had you in our sights since you got here, just waiting for the right moment. Now here we are — I mean, this is perfect."

Pickrang's curiosity was satisfied. He'd work out who'd tipped them off in due course. First things first. These guys are a couple of fucking clowns, he thought. One gun between the two of them; following me around waiting for the right time to do it. Jesus, talk about amateurs. You want to shoot someone, you walk up, no warning, no big speeches, no nothing; you point the fucking gun at them and pull the trigger. End of story.

Rocco Perfumo was talking to Delamore and Sparks, asking them if they were in some sort of three-way homo thing with Pickrang. Delamore was embarking on a laboured explanation when Rocco interrupted.

"Forget it, I don't want to know. It's got nothing to do with what we're here for so why don't you just fuck off back to New Zealand? Sounds like you got no reason to care what happens to this cunt and if you want to stay in one piece, you'll forget you ever saw us."

Delamore picked up his overnight bag and helped Sparks to his feet. "Of course," he said. "Thank you. Thank you very much. We're out of here right now."

Neither spoke till they were out of Palm Beach and back on the main road.

"You all right?" asked Delamore.

"Yeah," said Sparks thickly. He flexed his jaw. "Nothing broken anyway."

Delamore began shaking violently, causing the car to wobble. "Oh God," he said, "I was absolutely terrified. Pickrang thought I was a she and wanted to have his wicked way with me. They turned up just in time, those two."

Sparks stared at Delamore for a few moments then leaned back with his head on the headrest. "Jesus, no wonder you're still shaking."

"What do you think they'll do to him?"

"I don't know and I don't care — the worse the better as far as I'm concerned. I just wonder if they know what they're up against." Sparks rubbed his stomach gently. "Jesus, I really thought it was all over when Pickrang went for me with that knife. I could almost feel it going in."

"I wonder what happened to the knife," said Delamore. "He didn't have it when they came in." He smiled wanly. "Maybe he thought it spoiled the romantic atmosphere."

Pickrang was propped against the back of the sofa, quite relaxed. "So what now?" he said.

"What happens now," said Rocco, "is that we shoot you and you die. Then we'll go back into town, go to a nightclub, and have a bottle of champagne to celebrate. How does that sound?"

Pickrang looked thoughtful. "I don't know about the champagne; that shit gives me a hangover."

Rocco looked at Pickrang incredulously.

"Shall I shoot him now, Rock?" said Martino.

"Hang on, why don't we just see if there's an oven in this place?" said Rocco.

Martino nodded, giggling happily. His brother's path to the kitchen brought him within two metres of Pickrang. As Rocco walked past, Pickrang, in one swift, fluid motion, pushed off the sofa, effortlessly dragged him in with his left arm and wrapped him to his chest. He clamped Rocco to him with one arm, reached under his windcheater which was draped over the arm of the sofa and brought out the diver's knife which he held across Rocco's throat.

"Drop the gun," he said to Martino, who held the .38 at arm's length, unsure of where to point it, "or I'll cut his head off."

"Shoot him Marty," screamed Rocco. Pickrang clamped his left hand over Rocco's jaw to silence him and jabbed the index finger into his right eye for emphasis. He threaded his right arm under Rocco's armpit. With the knifepoint prickling Rocco under the chin, Pickrang hoisted him a few inches off the ground, effectively denying Martino a clear target.

"Put it on the sofa now," snapped Pickrang.

Martino lowered his arm. "I have to Rock," he wailed. "I have to."

He put the pistol on the arm of the sofa.

"Now back off. Stand over by the doorway."

Martino did so. Pickrang lowered Rocco to the floor. He retracted his right arm and positioned the knife point just below Rocco's right ear. He grinned and raised his eyebrows at Martino then, with a grunt of effort, forced the knife inwards and upwards. Two-thirds of the blade disappeared. Martino screamed and darted towards the sofa but Pickrang flung Rocco aside and swooped on the pistol. Martino turned and lunged for the door but Pickrang caught him by the back of the shirt, jerked him up short, then rammed him face first into the wall. He whirled Martino around and flung him onto his back on the sofa.

Pickrang placed his left knee on Martino's chest and loomed over him.

"If I wasn't in a hurry," he said conversationally, "I'd stick your head in the oven till it melts."

He picked up a cushion with his left hand and placed it over Martino's face. Perfumo flailed his legs unavailingly, like a beetle flipped on its back. Pickrang thumbed back the hammer and pressed the muzzle against the cushion. He fired three times, moving the muzzle slightly each time. The first shot missed altogether; the second clipped the point of Perfumo's cheekbone and ploughed a furrow up the side of his head, removing part of his left ear; the third entered his face just below the nose, precisely where previously the left and right halves of his moustache had met. After the pizza oven incident Martino had found it difficult to cultivate hair on his upper lip; eventually he'd decided that a moustache which sprouted unevenly in the style of a moulting chicken's neck was worse than no moustache at all. Thus he died clean shaven, breaking a family tradition, by no means confined to the menfolk, that went back many generations.

18

Caspar Quedley lay on his back, snoring faintly. At intervals of approximately ninety seconds his mouth fell open and a fresh globule of saliva emerged to join the thin trail of dribble running down his chin, under his ear, and into a little pond of drool which had formed on his pillow. There was a whitish wedge of coagulated spittle in the other corner of his mouth and the inner corners of his eyes, on either side of the bridge of his nose, were likewise gummed with nocturnal emissions. All in all a big night for discharges, thought Louise Appleyard.

Having completed her slightly disillusioning inspection, Louise got out of bed. She paused to look at herself in the mirror above the chest of drawers. Satisfied that she could withstand early morning scrutiny at least as well as her bedmate, she put on Quedley's towelling robe, and went downstairs. She was sitting at the kitchen table drinking her second cup of tea when Quedley appeared half an hour later. He wore jeans and an old sweatshirt; his hair was damp and his collection of encrustations had been rinsed away.

He halted in the doorway and studied Louise warily.

"Hello," she said.

Quedley's expression grew more dubious. Finally, he asked, "Do I know you?"

Louise sipped her tea. "I think I come under the heading of a barge that passed in the night," she said. "Give it a little while, it'll probably all come back to you — the tedious dinner party, too much to drink, latching onto a bit of a stray. Perhaps you should keep a visitor's book by the front door and get your pick-ups to sign in as they enter. Might help you to keep track."

Quedley nodded gravely. "Not a bad idea."

He switched on the coffee machine and took a packet of coffee out of the freezer then sat down opposite Louise.

"So how'd you be?"

Louise smiled back. She hadn't been sure what to expect from Quedley in terms of his morning-after manner, although a marriage proposal would have surprised her. Above all she'd dreaded a review of the events of the night before or even, God forbid, an appraisal of her performance.

Quedley insisted on cooking breakfast. Louise estimated it had been at least five years since she'd eaten bacon and eggs; she'd forgotten what a satisfying meal it could be.

As she cleared away the plates, she said: "I seem to remember you were going to tell me about this communication from the grave? Or was that just part of the seduction process?"

Quedley raised his eyebrows. "Excuse me? I seduced you?" He sat back on his chair and assumed the air of a raconteur. "Yes, I was going to tell you about poor Julian. You've heard the line about the practising homosexual who believed that practice makes perfect? That would be Julian's epitaph. You know they're always arguing about whether someone is born gay or goes that way because his mother made him play with dolls or because he was groped in the pup tent by a scoutmaster? If ever anyone was born bent, it was Julian Gage. By the time I got to know him — he would've been fifteen I guess — he knew he was gay; what's more, he was pretty open about it when it took a bit of nerve in those days."

"I'm trying to picture him," said Louise. "What did he look like?"

"Oh he was a handsome youth, all right — good looking, olive skin, big brown eyes — and promiscuous. It turned out to be a fatal combination — he ended up getting AIDS."

"Oh no. The poor, poor man." After a pause, she said: "Some might find the accusation of promiscuity a bit rich coming from you, in view of your reputation." Quedley started to protest but she continued: "So Caspar, is all this leading up to a confession; did you fall victim to his charms?"

"I didn't as a matter of fact but not for lack of effort on Julian's part. Despite that — or maybe because of it — we ended up being quite good friends. I saw a lot of him after we left school and even after he moved to Sydney, we kept in pretty close touch. Then, a few years ago, he was diagnosed HIV positive. I did what I could: went over and saw him, lent him — gave him — some money so he could do a bit of travelling and whatnot. But it wasn't enough. He became more and more demanding; he'd want me to drop everything at a moment's notice to spend time with him or shell out a small fortune so he could get the miracle cure at some clinic in Bermuda or Turkey or somewhere. Eventually, I drew the line, I said, 'Sorry Julian, that's it pal, no more'. Well, fuck, overnight" — Quedley snapped his fingers — "I became the Anti-Christ. He accused me of abandoning him and started making these threats — he was going to expose me, destroy my reputation, God knows what. I didn't take too much notice, I just thought the poor bastard's going a little crazy. Jesus, I could understand that; who wouldn't? And he might've had a point — maybe I should've done more for him; I'm not one of nature's good Samaritans, I'd have to admit. But you know, I don't have unlimited funds plus I had a business to run. The way my business works, if I'm not there, the revenue dries up pretty quickly. My staff can handle the day-to-day stuff but the key relationships are between me and the top people in the client companies. And what they're paying for is seven days a week, twenty-four hours a day access to me.

"So anyway, just before he died, Julian sent me this letter saying he'd make me pay for turning my back on him by exposing all the terrible things I'd done at school — cheating, blackmail, driving people around the bend, you name it." Quedley shook his head wearily. "He said he'd written it all out and was going to send it to an interested party — enter, stage right, your late husband."

"Yes, Vic saw him in Sydney."

"Oh well, there you go — perfect timing."

"Are you really worried about it? I mean, who would believe it?"

Quedley shrugged gloomily. "I guess it depends what he's said but people love scuttlebutt, don't they? The thing is reputation counts for a hell of a lot in the PR game but there are a few people out there who'd just love to see me on the back foot and would be only too happy to spread the dirt around. What really scares the shit out of me is the thought of *New Nation* getting hold of it — that bloody Jackson Pike would have a field day."

Louise walked round the table and stood behind Quedley, brushing the hair off his forehead. "Don't worry your little head about it, sugar. Whatever he's said about you, no one's going to see it. It'll go straight into the fire."

That Sunday morning Reggie Sparks and Dean Delamore caught the 10.25 a.m. Air New Zealand flight to Auckland. Delamore had announced during the drive in from Palm Beach that he'd also be going to Auckland; he said he'd been planning a trip for a while and now seemed like a good time to get out of Sydney. That suited Sparks. Delamore, he felt, could contribute a lot to his story.

They boarded the aircraft at 9.50 a.m. At 9.55 a.m. Herman Pickrang entered a department lounge elsewhere in the terminal where passengers on the 10.40 a.m. Qantas flight to Auckland were waiting to board. At 10 a.m., when the business class passengers on his flight were called, Pickrang went over to a bank of pay phones. He inserted a few coins and dialled the number for the Ristorante Vesuvio in Leichhardt which he'd got off a card in the late Martino Perfumo's wallet. Pickrang had simply been helping himself to the dead man's cash but the card, which identified Martino Perfumo as the manager of the Ristorante Vesuvio, had given him an idea.

A woman answered the phone.

"Martino Perfumo's the manager of your joint, right?"

"Yes he is. He's not here at the moment though. He should be in around eleven."

"No he fucking won't because he's dead; dead as a dodo. So's his brother."

"There must be some mistake . . ."

"How about I talk, you listen? You got a pen? You'll want to write this down. The pair of them are in the boot of a green Ford parked in the garage of number 14 Clifftops Road out at Palm Beach. Right? The garage door's down but it ain't locked. Now this bit's really fucking important. They're dead because this Kiwi guy named Barry Plugge put a contract out on them — that's

P,L,U,G,G,E. He's over in Auckland. You pass this on to the right person, he'll know who Plugge is. You got all that?"

"I think so."

"What's the guy's name?"

"Plugge. Barry Plugge."

"Good on you."

Pickrang replaced the handset and strolled back to the lounge. Most of the other passengers had boarded which suited him down to the ground because he was not fond of queuing.

Steven Perfumo, the lawyer, sneaked another furtive glance at his watch. It showed the time as just after 1 p.m. Perfumo was fretful because he had planned to have lunch with his third best friend's wife with whom he very much wanted to go to bed. Her husband was due back from Ho Chi Minh City, where he'd been setting up a pet food business, early the following morning. After that, such an illicit liaison became an undertaking requiring more boldness than Perfumo possessed.

The lunch was to be the final move in a delicate and patiently conducted campaign and Perfumo had been confident of success. It was, he felt, unbelievably if characteristically inconsiderate of his clownish cousins to get themselves murdered on this particular day; it was always on the cards that they'd end up full of holes and stuffed in the boot of a car, but why the fuck did it have to be today? Not that he dared give voice to these thoughts in the presence of his father, the head of the Perfumo family, who sat on the other side of the desk, his face twisted with grief and remorse.

"This is my fault," said his father for the fourth or fifth time. "I should've acted when Martino's face was burned. I should've allowed Rocco to take revenge."

He would've only fucked it up, thought Steven, staring at the ceiling. He decided to make one last effort to bring the discussion to some sort of conclusion. "Dad, we went through all this at the time," he said, leaning forwards, elbows on the desk. "You know why we didn't respond and you know it was the right decision. The strategy was to set Plugge and the Asians at each others' throats and to stand on the sidelines looking good by comparison while they fought it out. We talked about how it was difficult over there and that we simply couldn't afford headlines about the Italians coming in; it was a sound business decision. The real question is, how do we deal with this?"

His father ran his fingers through his silver-streaked hair then shrugged and gestured in the Latin manner to indicate that he was unconvinced by his son's argument. Not for the first time it occurred to Steven Perfumo that perhaps his father watched too many gangster movies.

"Explain it to me," said the old man. "How did this terrible thing happen?"

Steven breathed deeply. Maybe they were finally getting somewhere. "As

I was trying to say, it looks like a payback that went wrong. I've just been on the phone to Gino over in Auckland; Rocco told him he was coming here for some unfinished business. Gino made a couple of calls and it turns out that Pickrang — the guy who shoved Marty's head in the oven — was in Sydney this weekend, right? So it's pretty obvious what the unfinished business was. Secondly, Pickrang was working for Plugge — he's the established operator in the Auckland market — but Gino's heard they've had a bust-up. My guess is that Plugge wanted Pickrang taken out so he tipped off Rocco that Pickrang was coming to Sydney, hoping we'd do his dirty work for him. You know Rocco — he always took things so personally. He would've decided to do Pickrang himself and Marty would've just gone along with it." He shrugged. "They must've bitten off more than they could chew. Obviously, it was Pickrang who called the restaurant this morning; he's trying to work the same number as Plugge."

His father digested the summary solemnly. "So they're both responsible?"

"Well, yes. If Plugge hadn't tipped off Rocco in the first place, I guess none of it would have happened."

"And this man Pickrang — do we have any idea where he is now?"

"It looks like he's gone back to Auckland. We've got someone out at the airport checking it now."

The head of the family rose. He put his palms on the desk and looked at his son. "I want this taken care of by the time the boys are buried, Stefano," he said in a voice trembling with emotion. "I want you to supervise it personally."

Fucking wonderful, thought Steven. Your honour, could we adjourn for a few days? I've just got to jack up a couple of hits.

"I still recommend that we stay at arm's length," he said. "I just don't think it would be a good idea if our people are involved."

"You have someone in mind?"

"Remember that Maori gang we distribute through over there, the Blood Drinkers? Why don't we get them into it?"

"Are they capable?"

"Well they're the scariest-looking people I've ever set eyes on which isn't a bad start," said Steven with some feeling. He'd personally negotiated the distribution deal with the Blood Drinkers' collective leadership, four scarcely human men-mountains who smelt like a third-world zoo in a heatwave. He shuddered at the memory. "They're animals. They'd scalp their grandmothers for a crate of beer and a Big Mac. The thing is, it would muddy the waters – the police'll see it as a turf battle."

"I'm leaving it to you, Stefano. Do it anyway you want but see to it — make sure it happens. I won't be able to look my sister in the eye until this is settled."

Steven nodded and started to leave.

"By the way," said his father, "what will the police do about Rocco and Martino?"

Steven shrugged. "They'll be a pain in the backside for a week or two. It gives them a good excuse to hassle us but in the end it'll be the same old story — just another wog vendetta.

Caspar Quedley dropped Louise Appleyard at her house at 9.30 p.m. that Sunday night. He declined her offer of coffee and a nightcap, pleading an early start the next morning. He suspected that she had more than coffee and cognac in mind and that, after the excursions of the afternoon and early evening, he would struggle to rise to the occasion if called upon to do so yet again. The widow, he thought, has taken to it like a stallion just out of quarantine.

By 10.15 p.m. Quedley was in bed. After two late nights in a row and a physically demanding day, he was looking forward to nine hours' uninterrupted sleep. However, when the luminous dial on his bedside alarm clock was showing 4.21 a.m. Quedley sat bolt upright.

"I must be out of my fucking mind," he said out loud. "I actually believed the bitch when she said she'd throw it straight on the fire."

19

Caspar Quedley was at his desk by 7.45 the next morning, quite chipper despite his fitful night's sleep. As he set up the coffee machine he sang "Oooh-ooh Brown Sugar, how come ya dance so good? Oooh-ooh Brown Sugar, just like a black girl should", concluding his recital with a violent pelvic thrust. Quedley was cheerful because he saw the light at the end of the tunnel. He'd tossed and turned for over an hour during the night, castigating himself for his childlike faith in Louise Appleyard. Eventually, he succeeded in stirring his mind into a buzz of erratic activity which made slumber impossible. Finally, however, there came a flash of inspiration among the random and unconnected images which cannoned around inside his head like dodgem cars. He'd got out of his bed, gone into his study and written three words on a piece of adhesive notepaper which he'd stuck to his briefcase. Five minutes after getting back into bed, he was sound asleep.

The three words he'd written were "Dr Carl Plews". Dr Plews was an American, a graduate of Yale and the London School of Economics, who was often described in the media as a "world expert" in the new-fangled discipline of managing cultural change within large organisations. Quedley tended to doubt this; he reckoned that an American who really was a world expert would be back in the US of A where he could make a hell of a lot more money from transforming the completely fucking obvious into some sort of profound insight by dressing it up in a lot of new-age management-speak bullshit than he could in little old NZ. That wasn't to say that the doctor hadn't done pretty well for himself in New Zealand. He'd certainly earned some juicy consulting fees from advising government departments during their transitions into state-owned enterprises. There were three reasons for Quedley's conviction that Dr Plews would solve his problem: the first was the fact that Dr Plews' most recent client was New Zealand Post; the second related to the doctor's passion for gardening which was always mentioned in his profiles, usually just after the bit about how he was renowned for his volatile temper. That was the third.

Early one sultry evening the previous summer, Dr Plews, satisfied that his bow tie was symmetrical, had picked up the jacket of his tuxedo and called out to his wife Estelle that if they didn't get going within five minutes, they'd miss out on the start of the show. She'd hollered from her ensuite bathroom that she'd almost finished doing her make-up. Dr Plews smiled, a trifle smugly, and shrugged into his jacket. There was no need to leave for at least a quarter of an hour but his little pretence would ensure that Estelle was ready on time. Dr

Plews liked things to go according to plan — his plan.

It occurred to Dr Plews that he had time to potter in the garden. He went downstairs and out through the drawing room French doors which opened onto the upper lawn. It was a beautiful evening; the light was starting to fade and assorted floral scents floated by on the soft sea breeze. Dr Plews closed his eyes and breathed in deeply. Halfway through his exhalation, he froze: a low, snuffling sound was coming from across the lawn. Although a squat bush obscured the source of the snuffles, Dr Plews knew instantly what they signified — there was as a god-damn dog in his garden. He bounded across the lawn, swerved around the bush, and was confronted with a scene which caused the worm-like vein in his forehead to judder like a high pressure hose: the bed of delphiniums, which he'd nursed through the squalls of spring and early summer from seed to glorious blossom, was in ruins, the blooms uprooted, scattered and trampled. The devastation couldn't have been more complete had a wild pig wallowed in the flowerbed. The culprit was in fact a young bulldog, scarcely more than a puppy, which stood there panting lightly and regarding Plews placidly through oyster eyes.

"Here boy," said Plews speaking in a strangulated croak.

The bulldog obediently padded towards him. When he was within arm's length, Plews released a howl of rage, dropped to his knees, seized the dog by its collar, spun it onto its back, and began to throttle it. The dog took two long minutes to die. When it was over, Plews' lips were flecked with foam and his well-pressed trousers were smeared with dirt from the clods which the dog's excavations had left on the grass. Plews stood up; his chest heaved and he was sweating furiously. He mopped his face with a handkerchief and reviewed the situation: he knew the dog — it answered to the name of "Rumpole" and belonged to his next-door neighbour, Mr Justice Smout, a High Court judge of filthy disposition. Only a few days before, Plews and the judge had discussed Rumpole over the picturesque if somewhat ramshackle lattice fence which separated their properties, after Estelle had placed her expensively shod right foot on one of the wee fellow's steaming fresh turds. The judge had been apologetic and promised to keep Rumpole on a tighter leash but his fondness for the ugly little brute was obvious. As Plews gulped in air in the gathering twilight, it occurred to him that convincing Justice Smout that his mutt had got its just deserts would be a tough assignment.

Plews reached a decision: he didn't want a vengeful and possibly litigious judge as his next-door neighbour, nor did he relish the prospect of becoming a hate figure for pet lovers and animal rights activists. He got a spade from the garden shed, carried the dead dog to the very bottom of the garden where the compost heap was located, and buried it. Having witnessed Rumpole's fate from an upstairs window, seventeen-year-old Kirsty Bolton decided that it didn't matter how well Plews paid, there was no fucking way she was ever going to babysit for them again.

When Quedley heard the story of Rumpole's demise, he laughed so hard he fell off his chair which was not quite the reaction his informant, Kirsty Bolton's mother, had expected. He made no conscious effort to commit the incident to memory. He didn't have to: Quedley never forgot anything which cast someone else in a deplorable light.

At 8.15 a.m. Quedley rang Plews and effortlessly talked the doctor's secretary into putting him through.

"Dr Plews? Caspar Quedley here. We met in the PM's office last year."

"I remember it well Caspar. How are you doing?"

"Well, I've got a little problem, I was hoping you might be able to help me out with it."

"Shoot."

"It's to do with the postal service . . ."

"Let me tell you Caspar, I know that outfit like the back of my hand. If a postie breaks wind, I get to hear of it. Tell me what the problem is and I'll put you on to the guy or gal who can set it to rights."

"Okay. Right now there's a piece of mail in the system which was posted in Sydney last week to a Mr Victor Appleyard in Takapuna. I want to get my hands on it."

"Excuse me?"

"I don't want that letter to be delivered; I want it intercepted and passed on to me."

"This is a joke, right?" said Dr Plews in a tone which suggested he was going to get very cross if it wasn't.

"Carl, if I make a joke, you won't need to ask."

"Well, buddy, you've come to the wrong guy," said Dr Plews frostily. "I wouldn't even contemplate doing that for a friend and you sure don't qualify as one of them. Now if you don't mind, I've got things to do."

"What, like strangle a dog?"

"What did you say?"

"Strangle a dog. That's what you did to Judge Smout's little pal, wasn't it — throttled the bugger with your bare hands? All dressed up in your penguin suit too — Christ, it must have been a sight."

"I don't know what you're talking about and I'm terminating this conversation right . . ."

Quedley cut in, brisk and businesslike: "Carl, here's the deal: either you do this thing for me or I get on the phone to old Smout and tell him how you choked the living shit out of his precious puppy and planted him under your compost heap. It's your call — buddy."

Thirty seconds passed. Finally, Dr Plews said: "Who'd you say the letter was addressed to?"

One hour before Caspar Quedley and Dr Carl Plews discussed tampering with

Her Majesty's mail, a taxi pulled up outside a central city hotel. The taxi driver, a middle-aged Samoan, insisted on carrying his passenger's heavy suitcase into the hotel lobby; had he known that what appeared to be an attractive young blonde woman was in fact a man, he would've left it to the bellboy.

Dean Delamore had left the Sparks residence in St Heliers without forewarning or explanation and while Reggie Sparks and his mother were still asleep. He registered under the name Lesley Gore and took the lift to the fourteenth floor, affecting not to notice the admiring appraisal of the eighteen-year-old bellboy.

Once the bellboy had departed a dollar richer, Delamore undressed, removed the blond wig, and carefully hung his outfit, a smart lime-green suit, in the wardrobe. He then got into bed and slept for three hours to make up for the sleep he'd missed out on due to the time difference between Australia and New Zealand and by getting up so early.

At 11 a.m. Dean Delamore clicked through the hotel lobby in high-heeled shoes which nicely complemented the green suit. He left his room key at reception and got into a taxi which he directed to the office building in Parnell housing Quedley Communications. He checked the directory in the foyer then took the lift to the fourth floor.

Delamore got out of the lift and looked around hesitantly. The receptionist behind the large desk smiled at him brightly.

"Can I help you madam?"

"I think I'm on the wrong floor," said Delamore. "This isn't Deco Design?"

"Next floor up. This is Quedley Communications."

"Oh I've heard of you. You do public relations, right?"

"We sure do."

"We could be in the market for some PR. Do you have a company brochure or anything like that?"

"Yes we do. Let me get one for you."

The receptionist went away and returned a minute later with a glossy brochure which Delamore put into his large black leather handbag. He thanked the receptionist, pressed the lift button, and got into the lift. The receptionist watched the lift panel light up and shook her head. What an airhead, she thought; I just told her Deco Design was the next floor up and what does she do? Goes down.

The letter-sized envelope postmarked Sydney, dated the previous Thursday and addressed to Mr Victor Appleyard, was delivered to Quedley's office shortly before 5 o'clock that afternoon. Quedley weighed it in his hand. That's odd, he thought; there can't be more than a single page in here. He tore open the envelope; it contained a note, in the same hand-writing as his recent letter from Julian Gage, which said:

Although this letter was sent to Victor Appleyard, I suppose that it's being read by Caspar Quedley.

If not, Victor, some explanation is required: not long ago, I wrote to Caspar to tell him that I'd written what I described as a little memoir of our school days. I was feeling particularly sorry for myself at the time and warned Caspar that unless he made contact with me before it was too late, the document would be sent to an interested party — your good self. In fact it was always my intention to tell the real story of what happened at Prince Albert in 1970; I have enough on my conscience without taking the truth to my grave as well. Thinking about it afterwards, I realised it was a mistake to forewarn Caspar; he is not the sort to sit back and do nothing. He would've set out to throw a spanner in the works and, given his talent for that sort of thing, he'd probably succeed.

I've therefore arranged for the material to be hand-delivered to you. If I've over-estimated Caspar's ingenuity, there's no harm done. If I haven't — well Caspar, for once you've been out-smarted.

Of course, whichever of you is reading this, the fact that it's being read at all means I'm dead and gone. But not quite forgotten, eh Caspar?

Julian Gage.

Quedley read the letter three times then laid it aside. He sighed and rubbed his eyes; he inspected his fingernails; he picked his nose absent-mindedly; finally, he sat back in his chair and clasped his hands behind his head. After several minutes' reflection, Quedley reached the conclusion that something extremely shitty was about to happen. As usual, he was right.

Quedley was pouring his second bourbon when he got the message that there was a Mr Dean Delamore on line one. He picked up the handset, pushed the button and said: "You've got it, haven't you?"

"Got what Caspar?"

"You know fucking well what I'm talking about," snarled Quedley. "The Julian Gage story — 'I was a Teenage Cocksucker'."

"Hmm, that's got a ring to it," said Delamore. "No wonder you're in PR. So Julian was right — you did get hold of the letter? How'd you manage it?"

"What the fuck does it mater? Why don't you get to the point? This whole thing's become balls-achingly tedious."

Delamore clicked his tongue and put on a posh accent. "Oh dear, one does dread being thought a bore. Okay; the point, Caspar, is that yes, I have got it and I'm taking offers for it."

"You're offering to sell it to me? I don't think that's quite what your sugar daddy had in mind."

"Appleyard's dead. As far as I'm concerned, that frees me from my obligations. Besides, you're a fine one to talk about respecting Julian's wishes — if you'd shown one ounce of common decency, we wouldn't be having this conversation."

Quedley grunted derisively. "I could've shown more compassion than Mother Teresa at a train crash and we'd still be having this conversation. Sorry to disappoint you, but I'm not interested. You see, I don't really think that what you're selling is worth buying. Why should I care? In the first place, it'd be my word against what — the lurid ramblings of a bitter and probably deranged man on his deathbed? Secondly, what are you going to do with it if I don't play ball? Give it to the newspapers? Give me a break — no newspaper here would print a word of it."

"That's not the impression I got from Reggie Sparks," said Delamore imperturbably. "And if you're so blasé about it, why did you send that animal Pickrang over to Sydney? Anyway, who said anything about newspaper? Somehow I don't think your clients would be totally comfortable with some of the things you've got up to as a lad. I've got one of your brochures in front of me as a matter of fact; goll-y, that's an impressive client list. Now, do you want to talk or should I go find myself a photocopier?"

"Is Sparks still in on this?"

"Don't be silly."

"Oh well, no harm in talking I guess. Where are you staying?"

"Come now Caspar," said Delamore reprovingly. "That's unworthy of you — Julian made you out to be so clever. I went for a little wander today and Albert Park seemed a nice spot, especially at lunchtime with all those pretty young students around. Let's say tomorrow at 12.30."

"How will I know you?"

Delamore chuckled. "Don't you worry about that. I've got your brochure remember? God, what an ego trip — there must be at least a dozen photos of you in it. Not that you don't take a nice picture . . ."

Quedley told Delamore to get fucked and put the phone down with a clatter.

20

At 11 a.m. the following day, Tuesday, Dean Delamore walked through the lobby of his hotel and out onto the street. He was unshaven and wore jeans, sneakers and a voluminous sweatshirt over a polo shirt; he didn't wear earrings or a blond wig or make-up. No one gave him a second glance. He didn't leave his room key at the reception desk. As far as the hotel staff were concerned, the guest in room 1414 was a young blonde woman and Delamore was anxious not to disturb that impression.

He had a cappuccino in a High Street café, bought a newspaper and a tuna, tomato and alfalfa sandwich, then strolled up to Albert Park towards the university. It was a mild spring day; clusters of dirty-grey cloud were blowing in from the west every half hour with metronomic regularity and the smell of rain rose from the pavement when the sun broke through.

At 12.15 p.m. Delamore sat down on a park bench opposite the university clock-tower and began to read his newspaper. There were plenty of people around, mainly students plus a few office types who'd come up from town to escape their colleagues, eat lunch and enviously eye the students who canoodled and smoked cigarettes with an abandon suggesting they were unaware of the risks attached to both activities. At 12.25 Caspar Quedley walked up Princes Street and turned into the park. He stopped and looked around expectantly then shoved his hands in the pockets of his raincoat and pretended to take an interest in the large clock-face flowerbed. Delamore studied him from behind his sunglasses for a minute or two; having decided that the photos in the brochure didn't do Quedley justice, he turned his attention to the tuna sandwich.

At 12.45 Herman Pickrang got out of the red Mitsubishi which was illegally parked in a bikes-only zone on the other side of Princes Street and crossed the road. He walked towards Quedley, his gaze tracking slowly right to left through 180 degrees and back again. As he passed Quedley, he shook his head. Quedley shrugged. Delamore dabbed his mouth with a tissue, threw the tissue, sandwich wrapper and newspaper into a rubbish bin, got up and set off across the park. There were better ways to spend the afternoon than looking at a microfiche in the city library but, he reminded himself, he was in Auckland on business, not on holiday.

Delamore got back to his hotel a 4 p.m. He thought about ringing Quedley but decided to soak in the bath first. Let him stew a bit longer, he thought. Delamore was enjoying the game of cat and mouse, all the more so because he was sure Quedley would hate being cast in the role of rodent. That was emphatically borne out when, shortly after five, Delamore finally made the call.

"What the fuck are you playing at?" the public relations man screeched down the phone. "I stuck around in Albert Park like a shag on a rock for half an hour . . ."

Delamore cut in: "Caspar, I've got to say you've been a big disappointment. All I used to hear from Julian — until he went off you — was Caspar this, Caspar that, Caspar's so smart, what an operator you were, Mr Cool. I mean, am I missing something here? I keep expecting class and style but, to be frank, all I see is clumsiness. I was in the park today, on time, ready to do a deal. If you'd just played it straight, you'd have Julian's stuff by now."

"What d'you mean, you were there? Where were you?"

"Well, you'll just have to take my word for it. I saw you — you were in an ivory-coloured trenchcoat over a navy-blue suit. For what it's worth, I thought the coat was a shade . . . well, theatrical. I'm not sure that the Humphrey Bogart look is really you."

Quedley's tone of shrill exasperation grew more pronounced: "If you were there, why the bloody hell didn't you show yourself?"

"Why the bloody hell do you think? I guessed you'd try something and I guessed right, didn't I? As I was saying, it was very clumsy Caspar. Jesus, you can spot that pet gorilla of yours a mile away."

"Okay," said Quedley sounding flat and tired. "You win. You're way ahead of me. Name a time and place and I'll be there — just me, no tricks, no frigging around."

"Uh-uh, not so fast, sugar," said Delamore in what he thought of as his southern belle voice. "I offered you first bite at the apple but you didn't take it. Now you've got to go to the back of the queue."

Delamore hung up in the middle of Quedley's protests and collapsed laughing on the bed, drumming his heels. When he stopped laughing, he went to his suitcase and retrieved the page he'd torn out of Reggie Sparks' notebook. On it was a list of names and phone numbers, one of which he dialled. The phone was answered on the second ring.

"Dermot Looms speaking."

"Hello, my name's Dean Delamore. I was a friend of Julian Gage's — a very close friend."

"Julian Gage — there's one out of the blue. I'd pretty well forgotten that name."

"You surprise me — I mean, considering what you've got in common."

"I think you've got the wrong end of the stick, my friend. You could cover all stuff Gage and me have got in common without having to draw breath."

"Well, Dermot — may I call you Dermot? — I'd have to disagree. Julian, you'll be sad to hear, passed away last week. Not long before he died, he sat down and wrote an account of his schooldays at Prince Albert College. When I read it, it struck me what a strong link there was between the two of you, a bond almost. I suppose you could say I've inherited that fragment of autobiography but it occurred to me that it might have some emotional value for you. It also occurred to me that you might be able to put a figure on that emotional value."

There was a very long silence which didn't surprise Delamore and which he made no effort to break. Eventually, Looms said that, yes, he supposed he might be able to do that.

"Good," said Delamore. "I felt sure you'd be interested. Well, I guess the next step is for us to get together and toss a few numbers around."

Never again, thought Steven Perfumo. I don't give a fuck what happens or what the old man says, I'm never doing anything like that again — full stop.

He was sitting in the business-class cabin of an Air New Zealand Boeing 767. The aircraft was only an hour out of Auckland but Perfumo was already drunk. He took another noisy gulp of his Scotch and leaned back, closing his eyes. The scenes ran through his mind like frames from a favourite movie. He was living in a little country town or maybe somewhere up the coast — somewhere where the weather was good and everyone knew everyone else and you could go out at night and leave your place unlocked. He'd be in a little one-man legal practice, working nine to five then going home to the wife and kids, have a couple of beers, throw a few steaks on the barbecue in the backyard, maybe even wear a hat and an apron with one of those dumb sayings on it — "Don't blame the cook, he's doing his best", some shit like that. Life would be simple and safe: no "family matters" to attend to, no looking over his shoulder, no hassles from the cops. Most important of all, there would be no twenty-nine-stone Maori sociopaths with yellow-rimmed, blood-streaked piggy eyes and obscene tattoos on their stupendous arms and dreadlocks down to their arses and filthy clothes stained with what looked like every type of fluid and waste matter the human body is capable of producing.

Perfumo had known from the onset that negotiating for the terminations of Herman Pickrang and Barry Plugge with the Blood Drinkers would be a nerve-wracking and unpleasant experience. It turned out to be far worse. As Gino, the acting head of the family's New Zealand operations, had explained on the way back to the airport, the Blood Drinkers Perfumo had met on his last visit were the gang's businessmen; the guys they'd just talked to were the shock troops.

What had been truly frightening about that hour in the Otara hovel was the knowledge that he was completely at the mercy of people to whom, quite clearly, the concept of mercy was as irrelevant as last month's balance of payments figures. Sure, Perfumo knew some cruel and vicious people; he was related to a few, although their number had decreased by two this weekend.

But most of the bad things those people did, they did for a reason. They could be vicious when they had to be for business reasons. When they didn't have to be, they could and did behave more or less like human beings. But the Blood Drinkers — who could imagine what atavistic instincts they followed? Who knew what savage pagan gods they worshipped? How had he felt, an eleven-stone Italian-Australian lawyer in a Giorgio Armani suit and little tassels on his beautifully polished loafers, being glowered at by a quartet of those cavemen? He'd felt like a bobby calf in the slaughterhouse pens, sniffing death in the wind; Holy Mother of God, he'd felt like dinner!

Christ alone knew what insane impulse had prompted it but he'd actually asked them where they'd got their name from. The leader, a pot-bellied colossus with a mangled ear and Maori markings on his chin, had chuckled, a sound like an underground bomb test.

"Our ancestor Te Kooti was a great warrior. He and his men killed some Pakeha in a church one time and drank their blood, eh." He shifted on the burst and tattered couch, releasing a pocket of fetid air which made Perfumo's stomach lurch. "We don't do it, eh." He looked slyly at his companions. "Maybe if we ran out of piss." As the four Blood Drinkers bellowed with laughter and shunted one another like sumo wrestlers, Perfumo made a snap decision to increase his opening offer by $10,000. He wasn't up to haggling.

Perfumo shuddered and signalled to the stewardess for a refill. At least his father would be happy; Pickrang and Plugge were dead men, utterly doomed. They had less chance of saving their skins than a cat in a Chinese takeaway.

Caspar Quedley had two couches in his office, one of them a massive affair which he'd installed following a painful experience involving a supple and adventurous secretary, some whipped cream, a bunch of grapes and the corner of his desk. But that Tuesday evening he was simply grateful that the couch was long enough for him to stretch out full-length, collar unbuttoned and tie askew, as he sought to regain his composure and find a way out of the quicksand into which he was sinking.

How could they possibly have missed Delamore in the park? That moron Pickrang — he'd actually seen the little shit in the flesh; it defied belief that Pickrang wouldn't have recognised Delamore if he'd been there. He was there all right; he'd just been one step ahead of him. A disguise maybe?

Quedley groaned as it dawned on him how he'd been played for a fool. Pickrang had been adamant that Delamore was a transvestite; it seemed thoroughly unlikely but when his receptionist had said that, yes, someone had been in to collect a brochure that day, a blonde woman in a lime-green suit . . . well, it all appeared to fit. Pickrang hadn't spotted him in Albert Park because he hadn't been in drag.

Back to square one. How do you track down someone when you don't know where they hang their hat or what they look like? You start with what you do know which amounts to two-fifths of fuck all: he's a twenty-something gay Australian man with a flair for cross-dressing. That's it.

Quedley had an idea; it was a long shot but it was all he had. He went to his desk and rang a number he knew by heart. It was the number of his favourite restaurant in Ponsonby, whose owner was an identity on the local gay scene.

"Do me a favour Jerry — I'm trying to track down a character called Dean Delamore. He's gay, an Aussie, mid-to-late twenties, slim build, just come over from Sydney. He claims to be some kind of drag artist, although I doubt he's wandering around the place in costume. He's probably staying in a hotel or motel; at a guess one of the better ones in the city — I'd say he's got a taste for the high life. Can you check around the traps and let me know if you hear anything?"

21

It was a new-look Louise Appleyard who opened the door to Reggie Sparks. She was barefoot and wore large gold hoop earrings and a long, clinging floral dress with buttons all the way down the front; it looked like she'd started buttoning up at the waist and got sidetracked before she'd got too far in either direction. Her hair was tousled and unruly, the fringe cascaded down her face, prompting frequent horsy head movements which Sparks found distracting. The lights were back on in her eyes and shining so brightly it was hard to believe they'd ever been dimmed. His phone call from Sydney had left Sparks apprehensive, sensing that unwelcome developments were in the wind; as he followed her inside, that vague uneasy feeling returned.

They were sitting at the kitchen bench.

"New look?"

She grinned happily. "Not really. I jut felt it was time to loosen up a bit. What do you think?"

"I like it. It's sort of the gypsy look without hairy armpits."

Louise snorted with laughter. "Bloody hell Reggie, I'm not sure about that. Is that meant to be a compliment?"

The conversation moved along easily until Sparks brought up Julian Gage's posthumous dispatch. Then he discovered that Louise Appleyard had changed her mind along with her appearance.

"Hasn't arrived," she said, dropping her eyes.

"What? That's crazy. Delamore — Gage's boyfriend — posted it a week ago. You should've got it yesterday or the day before."

"Oh well, I guess it'll turn up," said Louise disinterestedly. Sparks tried to catch her eye but she examined the contents of her coffee mug. Neither spoke for a while. Finally, she said slowly: "Look Reggie, I've been having second thoughts about this."

Sparks cupped his chin in his hand and stared at her unblinkingly.

"Oh yeah? What brought them on?"

Louise shrugged diffidently. "Oh I don't know. It's just that the more I think about it, the less likely it seems that one person's version of events of what happened twenty years ago is going to prove a hell of a lot. Apart from anything else, who's to say he's telling the truth?"

"Who's to say he's not? The bloke was dying — why the hell should he lie?"

Another shrug. "Well, we don't know what his motivation was, do we?

Maybe he was playing Vic along, pretending to know something about the girl's death. Maybe he had a grudge against someone and wanted to, you know, blacken their name."

Louise glanced up, caught Sparks' frown, raised her eyebrows defiantly as if to say "Well, it's possible". She looked down again and continued: "Anyway, what I'm leading up to is that I can't guarantee that you'll get to see the letter. You're just going to have to trust my judgement, okay?"

Sparks sighed and turned his head, running his fingers through his hair. He found himself looking at the small blackboard on the wall next to the fridge. In the middle of the blackboard, surrounded by aides-mémoire — "pay phone bill", "new leotard" — boxed off, underlined and written in capital letters was the name "CASPAR" and a pair of phone numbers. One of the numbers had "home" in brackets after it.

Sparks spent thirty seconds considering the implications of this discovery and deciding they were all extremely negative. He picked up a packet of cigarettes that was lying on the bench.

"May I?"

"Help yourself."

He lit the cigarette and inhaled. It made him feel even more nauseous. What the hell, he thought. Let's get it over with. He cleared his throat and said, "Are you going out with Caspar Quedley?" He wanted it to come out casually, oh-by-the-way, but, to his ears, it sounded blunt and inquisitorial.

"What makes you think that?" she said, surprised.

Sparks took another drag on the cigarette and spoke through the smoke. "Just the thing on the blackboard there. Only thing missing is the heart with an arrow through it."

She smiled wanly. "Very droll. As a matter of fact, yes; we've been out a couple of times."

"And?"

"And what?" she said, her voice rising. "You want to put that in *New Nation* too?"

"I just meant how did it go," said Sparks stiffly. "None of my business obviously." He got up. "Thanks for the coffee — and the cigarette."

Louise Appleyard followed Sparks to the door thinking that she could have handled it worse — like she and Quedley could've been entwined on the front lawn when Sparks arrived. Sparks half-turned at the door, gave her an expressionless nod, and walked to his mother's car which was parked at the top of the drive, next to the letterbox. As he reached the car, a postwoman cycled up and slipped a bundle of letters in the box. Sparks looked around; Louise had gone back inside and closed the door. He retrieved the mail from the letterbox and shuffled through the envelopes; there was nothing from Sydney.

He walked back up the path to the house and knocked on the door. When

Louise opened it, he handed her the mail.

"Is it there?" she asked. "Don't tell me you didn't look?"

"No it's not. If it's not a gross impertinence, can I ask you a personal question?"

Louise checked to see if there was a trace of irony behind Sparks' formality but found no evidence of it.

"Feel free."

"Did you tell Quedley that Gage's letter was coming here?"

She nodded.

"Could I use your phone?"

Sparks rang Jackson Pike and asked him if he thought Quedley had the clout to intercept other people's mail. Pike said he was buggered if he knew but he'd ask someone who would and call straight back. Sparks gave him Louise's number.

"Aren't we getting a tad paranoid?" she asked when he hung up.

"We'll see."

After that, they waited for Pike to call back in strained silence.

Pike called Garth Grimes and put the question. Grimes laughed. It wasn't his usual throaty wheeze; it was a full-blown cackle and it went on for a full minute. Then he said, "Jackson, you really shouldn't do that to an old man. I'm hanging up now; I have to go and lie down."

I guess that's a yes thought Pike and rang Sparks. Sparks listened to Pike, thanked him and hung up.

"Well?" said Louise.

Sparks gave her a long look which bordered on the unfriendly. "A guy who knows a lot more about your boyfriend than we do doesn't think I'm paranoid."

When Sparks had gone, Louise Appleyard went out onto the deck overlooking Lake Pupuke to reflect on the look Reggie Sparks had given her when he'd got off the phone. It took her the time it takes to smoke a cigarette to establish that the look bothered her. Working out why took a little longer.

As Reggie Sparks sat beside the pool at the Mon Desir Hotel drinking beer and thinking bitter thoughts about Dean Delamore, Louise Appleyard and Caspar Quedley, the last was receiving good news.

"I think I might've found your lad," said his restaurateur friend. "The barman at Rococo says an Australian calling himself Dean has been in the last couple of nights. He fits the description — right age, slim build and so forth. The barman and he got to chatting and this Dean chap mentioned he was staying at the Regis. I didn't bother to ask if it was in the context of your place or mine; I didn't think it was germane."

The Regis, thought Quedley as he hung up. About time I got a break. They owe me for all the business I've put their way over the years. He rang the Regis' banqueting manager who was deeply servile and only too happy to check if there was a Dean Delamore staying in the hotel. There wasn't. Any name that was vaguely similar? Strike two. Quedley racked his brains; maybe Delamore registered as a woman? Why not? He was tricky enough and he could get away with it. Look how he fooled his receptionist.

Quedley asked the banqueting manager to run a check on the young, single women staying in the hotel. The one he was looking for would've been there for the past few days; she was slim, blonde and she'd been around in a — what was it? — yeah, a lime-green suit.

The banqueting manager called back half an hour later to say that there were only three single woman guests; the one who fitted the bill most had checked in first thing Monday morning under the name Lesley Gore.

Lesley fucking Gore? thought Quedley. Wasn't she a pop singer? Christ, years ago. Did she do "C'mon baby, do the locomotion?" No, that was Edie Gorme. "It's my party and I'll cry if I want to?" Something like that. Lesley Gore's got to be a little in-joke. Just like a faggot — too clever by half.

"All right," said Quedley. "Now we're getting somewhere. What's Ms Gore's room number?"

Delamore and Looms had arranged to meet in the Gateway to the North Tearooms in the foothills of the Brynderwyns, north of Wellsford, at 2.30 p.m. Delamore set off in a hired car just before midday. The concierge at the hotel had said it was about a ninety-minute drive but he wanted to take his time and see some countryside.

The tearooms were a white-painted weatherboard box with a red corrugated iron roof and a glass frontage enabling customers to watch the lorries they'd overtaken with great difficulty fifty kilometres back down the road trundle past. Alongside was a scruffy little repair garage with a couple of petrol pumps. The tearooms were strategically located, just about the exact driving time from Auckland that it took the average family going north on holiday to start bickering. Just when the kids in the back seat would begin agitating for a comfort stop and an ice cream and Dad would be feeling like a break and a cup of tea before tackling the climb over the Brynderwyns, they'd spot the sign saying "Tearooms 200m ahead". Summer was the busy time; apart from the holidaymakers, the truck drivers and the travelling salesmen who would linger over a second scone and instant coffee to ogle the teenage girls in their shorts and tank tops.

There were only two cars in the parking area when Delamore pulled in five minutes late — a white station wagon with a car phone aerial and a Volvo. He parked and went in. A young man with frizzy red hair, densely freckled forearms and a row of cheap ballpoints in the breast pocket of his short-sleeved white shirt was debating the merits of ordinary milk versus low-fat variety with the woman behind the counter. An older man, heavily tanned and mostly bald, was sitting by himself with his back to the wall at the table in the far corner. He observed Delamore over the rim of his cup. Farmer Giles I presume, thought Delamore.

He bought a Coke and walked over to the table in the corner.

"Mr Looms?"

"That's me. Sit yourself down."

Delamore pulled out a chair and sat down. Looms put his elbows on the table and hunched forward. His sleeves were rolled above the elbow and ropey veins ran down his forearms and wrists, branching off into tributaries which laced the backs of his thick, powerful hands. Looms' jaw jutted aggressively and his hard grey eyes stared out stonily from beneath bushy brows. This was a tough hombre, thought Delamore; not that you don't know that already.

"So Gage wrote a little story, did he?"

Delamore nodded. "I'd describe it as a hair-raising tale — well, for those of us with hair."

"You're a funny little fellow aren't you?" said Looms without a twitch of reaction showing on his granite features. "How come you've got it?"

"Julian and I were friends."

"Bum chums?"

Delamore shrugged. "I've been gay-bashed three times so being called names doesn't bother me too much. But you go right ahead if it makes you feel better."

"I started losing my hair when I was nineteen; can't recall too many people taking the piss about it."

"Well, there's a surprise," murmured Delamore. "Now that we've defined our respective areas of sensitivity, can we get on with it?" He looked around. "This is very cosy but not really my scene."

Looms raised his eyebrows as if amazed that anyone could find fault with the surroundings.

"Okay. You got it with you?"

Delamore tilted his head to one side. "Get real."

"Where is it?"

"In Auckland. In a safe place."

"It's not worth shit, you know?"

"I disagree," said Delamore confidently. "I can think of a number of people who'd be riveted by it — Mr and Mrs Ticehurst for instance. I checked them out; they're still around, still living in Auckland. He's a partner of one of those big accountancy practices — a man of substance as they say; the sort of man who could get the authorities to sit up and take notice. I think they'd find Julian's recollections convincing. Let's face it, deathbed confessions do have a certain credibility."

Looms frowned and rubbed his chin. "Maybe. So what's your angle?"

"This is my offer and it's non-negotiable: I get $100,000 Australian; you get Julian's rave from the grave and never hear from me again. You've got till the weekend to organise the money. I'll call you then and tell you where it's to be deposited. As soon as the bank account confirms the transfer, I'll hand over the document."

"A hundred grand? You're off your fucking head."

Delamore smiled. "You can get help, split the cost. You're not the only one at risk so why should you bear the whole cost?"

Looms nodded dubiously. "Even if I could raise the money, what's to stop you making photocopies and coming back for another bite?"

"Now that you mention it, nothing really. You're just going to have to trust me. The reality is, you're paying me to keep my mouth shut and go away. Which I'll do. Take it from me, I don't want to make a career out of this."

"Why not?" said Looms sourly. "You seem to have a talent for it."

Delamore stood up. "You're too kind. I'll be in touch."

Delamore hurried to the hired car and got in. As he put the key in the ignition, he felt something cold and metallic on the back of his neck. He looked around. A plump, moon-faced man with a ponytail and white sideburns and wearing serious spectacles lay across the back seat. He cradled a single-barrelled shotgun pointed at Delamore.

Basil Batrouney smiled his other-worldly smile and said: "Just drive man — I'll tell you where."

22

There was nothing sophisticated about the way Dermot Looms interrogated Dean Delamore. Directed by Basil Batrouney, Delamore had driven his hire car to Looms' farm and into a lock-up garage. When Looms arrived a few minutes later, Delamore was herded at gunpoint to the woolshed which was 100 metres or so beyond the farmhouse, down a gentle slope. The woolshed was the size of a single-storey house. There were half-a-dozen holding pens, a massive wooden bench for wool sorting and a large space where the shearing was done. Even though Looms kept a clean shed, the devoutly urban Delamore found the smell — a blend of one part blood, several parts sweat and many parts sheep droppings and urine which had been stewing gently for three generations — almost overpowering. There was a rickety old highback wooden chair against the wall. Looms moved it to the centre of the shearing area and made Delamore sit on it. He pulled Delamore's arms behind him and around the back of the chair, tied his wrists together with twine and then lashed his ankles to the chair's front legs.

Preparations complete, Looms stood in front of Delamore with his large, lumpy hands on his hips. Batrouney hovered in the background, humming to himself.

"Now then Sunshine," said Looms. "Where've you got this thing of Gage's hidden away?"

During the drive from The Gateway to the North Tearooms to Looms' farm, Delamore had reached the conclusion that his best — if not only — chance of avoiding serious injury or worse was to refuse to divulge the whereabouts of Gage's letter. That in turn, he felt reasonably sure, would require him to withstand a considerable amount of pain.

As he'd told Looms, Delamore had on three occasions been a victim of the young men who, on Friday and Saturday nights, drive in from Sydney's working-class west to its trendy inner east — Oxford Street, Paddington, Darlinghurst — with the express purpose of beating up homosexual men. Delamore had taken his beatings fatalistically, assuming that there must be a genetic link between male heterosexuality, low IQ and the urge to consume huge amounts of cheap beer and gang up on gays. The third time it had happened he'd tried to reason with them, point out that if it wasn't for all the queers, they'd have even less chance of getting girls. Perhaps it hadn't come out quite right because they all went ahead and gave him a kicking anyway.

While these experiences had left him less fearful of physical assault than the average person, he suspected that what he'd be subjected to in Looms' woolshed would be far worse: it wouldn't be drunken youths, half-mad with some sort of mass hysteria, flailing and hacking wildly and getting in one another's away; when it came to dishing out punishment, Looms, he felt pretty sure, would be both vigorous and methodical, a formidable combination. As long as that fat freak with the ponytail doesn't join in, thought Delamore. He's a psycho if I ever saw one.

So Delamore swallowed hard, licked his dry lips and said: "I'm afraid that's got to remain my little secret."

Looms tut-tutted and stepped forward to position himself within easy each. He planted his feet.

"Sure about that?"

Delamore braced himself and gave a slight nod.

Looms swayed back, gathered himself, then drove his right fist into the middle of Delamore's face. The chair was flung over. Delamore lay on his side with his undamaged cheek on the floor. The stench of sheep droppings wafting up through spaces between the floorboards was several times ranker than the general atmosphere. Batrouney was shadow-boxing, hopping from one foot to another, chirping: "Pow! Biff! Whacko! Take that Mr Bad Guy!"

Looms hauled the chair upright and let fly with a roundhouse left which caught Delamore just under the eye and knocked him sprawling again. As he propped up Delamore, he cocked an eyebrow.

"Well?"

Delamore could feel swelling coming up around his right eye. His upper lip on one side felt mashed and he could taste blood in his mouth. He shook his head.

"I can do this all afternoon if I have to," said Looms with a shrug. "You're not going to be a pretty sight."

Delamore closed his eyes for a few seconds. He opened them in time to see a big, brown, gnarled fist heading straight for the centre of his face. His nose was shattered and flattened in an explosion of blood and gristle and the chair pitched over backwards.

Delamore lay on his back with his bound legs in the air. He could hardly see and his entire face was ablaze with pain. He heard Batrouney's high-pitched scream: ". . . and the challenger hits the canvas for the third time. And here's the count: a-one, a-two, a-three, a-four . . ."

"Baz, you mad bugger, pipe down," said Looms amiably and walked over to Delamore. Then: "Hello, what've we got here?" Delamore, twisting his head to spit out blood, saw Looms stoop to pick up his hotel room key which had been jolted out of the back pocket of his jeans.

"Room 1414 at Regis Hotel," said Looms. He hauled the chair upright again and peered into Delamore's face. "I'll bet that's where it is. Save it, Sunny Jim — I can see it in your eyes. Well, the one that's still open anyway." He sighed and shook his head. "Christ, I told you — you could've saved yourself a few smacks in the scone just by giving me the bloody key in the first place."

Looms hitched himself up onto the bench. He flexed his right hand a couple of times. "I take my hat off to you, mister — I wouldn't have credited it in a blue moon. I thought one decent thump and you'd be howling the roof down." He looked at the key. "If this hadn't dropped out of your pocket I probably would've been hammering the buggery out of you till teatime. Oh well, fat lot of good it did you. What d'you reckon, Baz?"

"I do declare, hanging's too good for that varmint, marshal," said Batrouney in a hillbilly twang. "I say we do what the Injuns do — string him up by his nutbag and skin him alive with a red-hot knife."

At 9.10 that Wednesday evening Herman Pickrang, wearing his best suit and tie and carrying a briefcase, strode purposefully through the lobby of the Regis Hotel. The outfit and the briefcase, which he'd bought that afternoon, were intended to make him look like a businessman. In fact he looked exactly what he was: a thug in a five-year-old suit carrying a cheap plastic briefcase. Since the lobby was almost deserted, the thinness of his camouflage hardly mattered.

Pickrang took the lift to the fourteenth floor and found room 1414. The corridors were empty. He donned a pair of tight-fitting rubber gloves. As Quedley had promised, getting into the room wasn't difficult; the banqueting manager had been by a few minutes earlier to make sure of that.

Pickrang was not what could be termed a tidy burglar, one of those who pride themselves on leaving no trace of their visit apart from the absence of the stolen items. He violently stripped the bed, wrenched the mattress off the base, and scattered the contents of the drawers and wardrobes without finding anything.

The suitcase was locked. It had been a long time between knifings for Pickrang but impaling Rocco Perfumo had brought it all back to him just how satisfying knifework could be. On his return to Auckland, he'd procured a razor-sharp flick knife which he wore taped to his right calf as he'd seen Clint Eastwood do in a movie. He popped the blade and plunged it through the suitcase's canvas exterior. He ran the blade around the frame of the suitcase, cutting out the whole of one side. As he went to discard the material, he felt the envelope which had been sewn in between the canvas and the cloth lining.

Pickrang opened the envelope; it contained several typed pages. A quick scan satisfied him that it was what Quedley wanted. Pickrang replaced his knife, put the envelope in the briefcase, checked there was no one in the corridor, and left the scene.

He came out of the hotel, turned right and headed for his car which he'd left in a side street a couple of blocks away. As was usually the case at 9.30 on a Wednesday night, the city was near-empty and quiet.

Luther "Bad Louie" Potau awoke with a start when his mobile phone rang. He was sitting in the driver's seat of a fifteen-year-old Ford Falcon parked on the one-way inner-city side street directly opposite Pickrang's Mitsubishi. The caller was a fellow member of the Blood Drinkers who'd been stationed in the bus shelter across the road from the Regis Hotel waiting for Pickrang to come out; he was ringing to report that Pickrang was on his way.

Potau sat up and rubbed his eyes. He screwed the top back on the half-empty litre bottle of rum which was propped up between his massive fleshy thighs and slipped the bottle under the seat. For the third time that evening he broke open the sawn-off shotgun to check that it was loaded. Just as he snapped it shut, he saw, in his rear view mirror, Pickrang round the corner. Potau laid the gun on the passenger's side and wound down the window on that side. Pickrang walked a little way up the footpath on Potau's side of the road then crossed over to his car. He set down the briefcase and fumbled with his car keys. As he inserted the key, he heard a car door open behind him. He looked around. A huge Maori wearing a woolly cap and wraparound sunglasses got out of the beat-up Ford on the other side of the street and walked slowly around the front of the car. He leaned against the passenger door, folded his arms, and looked at Pickrang without speaking.

Pickrang picked him straightaway as a gang member, a species he despised despite the many things they had in common. After a few seconds' silence, he snapped: "What the fuck do you want, you big fat cunt?"

When Luther Potau reached in the open car window and brought out a sawn-off shotgun, Pickrang decided that a less confrontational approach might be in order. Because such an approach didn't come naturally, he was still trying to think of the appropriate words when Potau raised the shotgun and gave him both barrels. The blast hurled Pickrang onto the bonnet of his car. He rolled off the bonnet onto the road where he lay with his head in the gutter.

Potau, who didn't believe in looking gift horses in the mouth, walked across the road and picked up Pickrang's briefcase. He got into his car, threw the briefcase and the shotgun into the back seat, and drove off. As Potau turned out of the street, Pickrang lifted his head a few centimetres out of the gutter and coughed wetly. His chest hurt horribly. Perhaps, he thought, he should call for help. It went against his code of stoicism and self-reliance but, then again, he'd never found himself face down in a gutter with a chest full of buckshot before. When he tried to shout, he found he simply didn't have enough breath to make a sound. Before Herman Pickrang had a chance to get to grips with the implications of his extreme shortage of breath, he died.

Cec Gilpin considered that he was extremely lucky to have a friend like Barry Plugge. Even though Plugge had made it — really made it — in life, he hadn't forgotten his boyhood mates. So when, at the age of fifty, Gilpin had been made redundant by the city's parks and recreation department for which he'd worked for the whole of his adult life, Barry Plugge had put him on his payroll.

Plugge called him his "chauffeur and gofer". Gilpin didn't know and didn't care what a gofer was; he just did whatever Barry wanted. Sure, the pay was pretty ordinary — not much more than the dole if the truth be told — but the main thing was that he was occupied; he had something to do with himself, somewhere to go of a morning rather than moping around at home and having a blue with the missus. There was one other great benefit: he got to drive Plugge's cherry-red Jaguar Sovereign with the personalised number plate FLASH. Since he was a boy, Gilpin had regarded Jaguars as the ultimate in automotive excellence and style. If anyone had ever suggested that one day he'd be driving a Jag on a regular basis, he would've dismissed the notion out of hand. Yet here he was most days of the week, cruising the streets behind the wheel of this majestic machine.

Gilpin might've been less positive about both Plugge and the Jaguar if he'd been aware of the background to the Sultan of Sleaze's out-of-the-blue announcement a few months previously that Gilpin could henceforth chauffeur him around. It was to do with the threat from the Italians from Sydney. On the basis of the occasional television news reports from Sicily about prosecuting magistrates being blown to smithereens by car bombs, Plugge was of the view that the car bomb was once again the preferred assassination method of the Italian criminal fraternity. As any moviegoer knows, most car bombs were rigged to go off when the car was started. Guarding against this eventuality meant going through the tiresome procedure of getting down on your hands and knees and inspecting underneath the car every time you wanted to go anywhere. The thought of a constantly cricked neck and soiled trousers didn't appeal to Plugge; furthermore, he was so ignorant of the workings of a car and things mechanical that he could conceivably have looked straight at a bomb without recognising it as such. A much better idea was to insure the hell out of the Jag and let someone else take the risks.

Thus it was that at 9.53 that Wednesday night, Cec Gilpin drove Barry Plugge's Jaguar out of the carpark, round the block, and double-parked it out the front of the Blue Angel strip club to await his employer. Knowing the wait could last anything up to half an hour, Gilpin turned on the car radio which he had tuned to a classic hits station. The first song to come on was Gene Pitney's "The Man Who Shot Liberty Valance". Gilpin gave a grunt of delight and turned up the volume. In Cec Gilpin's pantheon of heroes, Gene Pitney ranked a close second to Barry Plugge. Sitting back in the soft leather and singing along to Gene with his eyes shut tight, Gilpin didn't see the battered Ford Falcon which came up Karangahape Road from the opposite direction, stopped a few metres away to allow a car to go by, then swerved across the middle line to pull up alongside the Jaguar.

Gilpin was doing his inadequate best to stay with Gene Pitney through the descending cadence of "He was the bravest of them all", when Luther "Bad Louie" Potau bellowed at him from less than three metres away: "Yo, white bread mother-fucker."

Gilpin swivelled his head towards the source of his unwelcome interruption. Potau poked his sawn-off shotgun through the car window, waited till Gilpin's expression changed from puzzled annoyance to eye-popping terror, and pulled the trigger. He gave him one barrel only but it was quite enough. As Bad Louie told himself as he roared down Karangahape Road towards the Symonds Street motorway ramp, he was only half the size of the other cunt, so why waste a second cartridge on him?

23

Dean Delamore's evening meal consisted of two slices of slightly stale bread, a lump of cheddar cheese, a glass of water and a handful of aspirins. He was then locked up for the night in the cellar under Looms' house. It was chilly and pitch-black and each creak and rustle caused him to wonder what other forms of life inhabited the cellar. After midnight the aspirins wore off and his wrecked nose set up a fiery throb which intensified as the night dragged on. The pain was enough to make sleep difficult; the combination of pain, the expectation of being scampered over or even gnawed by foraging rats, and dark thoughts of what the morning might bring which, try as he might, he couldn't block out of his mind, made it impossible.

At eight the next morning Looms let him out of the cellar to go to the bathroom. He examined his bruised, yellowing, misshapen face in the mirror. He decided it wasn't really the Rexette look. Suddenly, he felt the delayed effect of all the pain and shock and fear which he'd gone through and he began to shake violently. When the shaking died down, he took a last look in the mirror. Remember, he told himself, big girls don't cry.

He came out of the bathroom. Looms, who'd been waiting outside the door, gripped him by the arm and pushed him down the corridor.

"I suppose you're wondering what's happening?" he said. "Well I would in your shoes. I drove all the bloody way to Auckland and couldn't get within five blocks of the hotel. I don't know what the hell was going on but there were police everywhere, roadblocks, the works. So, I'm going to have to do it all over again tonight. I should charge you petrol money." He stopped Delamore by the kitchen door and breathed in heavily. "Smell that? Bacon, eggs, tomatoes, fried bread and farm mushrooms — Baz's speciality. What did they used to say — 'the condemned man ate a hearty breakfast'?"

Having reviewed the events of Wednesday night, Detective Sergeant Tito Ihaka felt that, on the whole, it had been one of the better nights for the forces of law and order.

True, there was a shotgun killer on the rampage who didn't appear to draw the important distinction between legitimate targets and law-abiding taxpayers. But even then, Cec Gilpin hadn't died in vain: the shocking sight of his chauffeur's face plastered across the windscreen of his Jaguar had put a hurricane-strength wind up Barry Plugge. He'd drawn the obvious conclusion — that he, rather than his employee, had been the intended victim — and immediately sought sanctuary at the Central Police Station, the only place in Auckland where he felt safe. To ensure that the police didn't throw him back on the street, Plugge had demanded a tape recorder and started owning up. When Ihaka switched off the tape recorder four hours later, he estimated that Plugge would be eligible for parole sometime around the year 2015.

Plugge began by outlining the ingenious scam he'd cooked up with the jailed lawyer Trevor Lydiate. Then he'd explained the circumstances surrounding the demise of the private investigator and candid photography specialist Wallace Guttle. No sooner had Plugge confirmed that Herman Pickrang had done for Guttle than the news came through that Pickrang himself was past tense; he'd been the first of the unknown shooter's brace of victims.

Although Ihaka felt the shooter deserved society's heartfelt thanks for getting rid of Pickrang and couldn't suppress a twinge of admiration for his industry and no-nonsense approach, the pressure was on for a swift arrest. While Ihaka took a detailed view of the previous night's events and, as always, was unable to get too worked up about what civilians did to one another — as far as he was concerned, the only sensible attitude for a policeman to adopt — the media were busy scaring the daylights out of the citizenry with its coverage of the double slaying. Ihaka didn't think the manhunt would be a long one. The way the merchant operates, he thought, he ain't exactly the Scarlet Pimpernel. The only question was how many people would be wiped out in the process of taking him out of circulation. Keep your wits about you, fat boy, Ihaka told himself; whatever happens, don't you be the first poor bastard through the door.

Detective Constable Johan Van Roon hovered nervously in front of Ihaka's desk, waiting for the sergeant to acknowledge his presence. Van Roon, who was twenty-four, was a first-generation New Zealander, the son of Dutch immigrants whose fair northern European complexion he'd inherited. Ihaka had a sharp eye for others' distinguishing features or physical peculiarities and Van Roon's milky skin had immediately caught his attention. Van Roon, he'd announced to a crowded station room on the constable's first day at Central, was the whitest white man he'd ever seen.

Eventually, Ihaka looked up.

"Well, if it ain't the Milky Bar Kid. What's your problem?"

Van Roon tried to smile but didn't quite get there. "Sarge, there's something a bit odd about this Pickrang thing; it looks like he might've pulled a burglary at the Regis Hotel just before he got hit."

"Oh yeah?" said Ihaka disinterestedly. "I'll bet it wasn't the only thing he pulled."

Van Roon soldiered on. "Pickrang copped it about 9.30. A bellboy saw him in the lobby just after nine and some time around then a guest's room got really turned over."

Ihaka sniffed noisily and looked at his watch. "Is this going to take long, constable?"

The constable, who'd heard that Ihaka's bark was worse than his bite but didn't believe it, swallowed hard. "Sure Sarge, I'm just about there. The guest whose room got done over is Ms Lesley Gore from Sydney but immigration has no record of anyone of that name entering the country. There was an Aussie passport in the suitcase which the burglar took to with a knife — Pickrang had a knife on him by the way . . ."

"Hold it, what did he take to with a knife — the fucking suitcase or the fucking passport?"

The constable nodded hurriedly. "Sorry, sorry — the suitcase. He cut one whole side panel out of it. Anyway, that's a bit beside the point . . ."

"What is the point, son?" said Ihaka with quiet emphasis.

"The passport belongs to a twenty-seven-year-old man called Dean Delamore who flew in from Sydney on Sunday; the guest registered as Lesley Gore, and there were men's and women's clothes and toiletries in the room. The women who made the beds say that they never saw any bloke's gear — it must've been kept in the suitcase — and they're certain there's only been one person in the room."

Ihaka said, "Hmmm," and stood up. "How do they know that? They sniff the sheets or something?" He walked around and sat on the edge of the desk in front of the constable. "Have we tracked down the mystery guest?"

"No. There's no sight of him — or her. The staff at the front desk say they haven't seen Ms Gore for a couple of days. She always hangs out the 'Do not disturb' sign when she's in the room. We showed Delamore's passport around and a couple of people seem to think that Delamore and Gore are the same person but they wouldn't swear to it. Yesterday morning a guy the concierge identified as Delamore from the passport photo was asking about driving up north, somewhere round Wellsford."

"You check the car hire companies?"

"Yeah we did. Delamore picked up a Honda Civic from the Hertz place in town around midday yesterday. He used a New South Wales licence and said he'd have the car back by the weekend at the latest. I sent the number up to Wellsford and asked them to keep an eye out for it. We also faxed Sydney but haven't heard back yet."

"So Herman Pickrang burgled a man who's pretending to be a woman; then a few minutes later, a party or parties unknown spread his lungs over half of downtown. You seem to be right on top of things, son — so what's your theory?"

"I haven't really got one, Sarge. I just thought it was all a bit strange. If Delamore and Gore are one and the same — and it sure looks that way — you kind of think he must be up to something to go through all that carry-on. Oh by the way, we found this in the suitcase too."

He passed Ihaka a folded sheet of notepaper. Ihaka opened it. On it was a handwritten list of names, addresses and phone numbers; some of them had a line through them, some had ticks beside them, some question marks. It was the second time Ihaka had seen these particular names; the first time was on the long-dead Bronwen Ticehurst's dance card.

Ihaka stared at the list for a full minute.

"Son, you're absolutely right. This is definitely strange. You've got something else to tell me, haven't you?"

Van Roon racked his brains. "I think that's it, Sarge," he said uncertainly.

Ihaka looked at him wide-eyed, shaking his head. "Uh-uh. If Pickrang did the break-in, what'd he nick and where is it?"

"Nothing as far as we can tell. I mean, we didn't find anything on him or in his car. Oh shit, hang on — the bellboy said Pickrang was carrying a briefcase."

"But you didn't find a briefcase, right? So it's reasonable to assume that, A, whatever he nicked from Delamore's room was in the briefcase and, B, whoever pinged him took the briefcase."

Van Roon was so angry with himself for having overlooked the briefcase that he almost forgot to pass on his final piece of information. He had to go back and interrupt Ihaka's paperwork again.

"One other thing, Sarge," he said. "When Delamore filled in his immigration form, he didn't say he was going to stay at the Regis. He put down a private address somewhere in St Heliers — I've got it written down if you want it. It's the home of a Mrs Sparks — Mareena Sparks."

Mareena Sparks and Tito Ihaka greeted one another like old friends. After they'd finished assuring each other that they were in the pink, Mareena escorted the policeman to the downstairs den where her younger son lay on the couch watching TV. When she'd gone, Ihaka asked Reggie Sparks how his story was going.

"Shithouse," he said. "Next question."

"Yeah, it's good to be alive isn't it? I've got some news that might cheer you up — it's about your old sparring partner, Herman Pickrang."

Sparks rolled into a sitting position.

"Hang on — let me guess. Pickrang's body was found somewhere in the vicinity of Palm Beach, a little place on the coast just north of Sydney. He was shot by someone using a handgun, probably in the early hours of last Sunday morning. Am I right?"

Ihaka looked at Sparks as if he'd announced his intention to roller skate to the South Pole. "You quite finished? Pickrang's dead all right. His body was found in a side street in the centre of Auckland, a city situated on an isthmus separating the Waitemata and Manukau harbours. It happened around half past nine last night. And handgun, my black arse — he bought a full load from a double-barrelled sawn-off from as close as me and you. What's all this shit about some place north of Sydney?"

Sparks leaned forward, staring at Ihaka. "What? He was killed here? Last night?" He slumped back on the sofa. "Last week I went over to Sydney, for *New Nation*. Pickrang was over there as well. I was at this place at Palm Beach when Pickrang turned up doing his 'I'm going to rip your ears off' routine. Then these two other guys showed up. Don't ask me who they were but they were dirty on Pickrang in a huge way — something to do with he'd shoved one of them in a pizza oven. Anyway, these guys had a gun, a pistol. They told us to get lost; it was pretty obvious what they had in mind."

"What was Pickrang doing over there?"

"I'm pretty sure he was sent by a guy called Caspar Quedley." Sparks told Ihaka about Julian Gage. He finished: ". . . but by the time he got there, Gage was dead and the stuff was in the mail. Gage didn't know about Appleyard — that's why he sent it to him — but it hasn't arrived; I reckon Quedley's got his hands on it."

"How could he do that?"

"He's an operator, you know, he's got fingers in all sorts of pies, knows everyone who's anyone."

Ihaka nodded slowly. "Well, if he's got the juice, I suppose he could. You know a guy called Dean Delamore?"

Sparks sat up again. "Yeah I do. He's was a friend of Gage's; he posted Gage's stuff for him. Delamore was at Palm Beach when Pickrang turned up. He came over here with me on Sunday."

"Well, that explains that. Where is he now?"

"No idea," said Sparks flatly. "He stayed here Sunday night then shot through without a word."

"Tell me something Sparks, how friendly are you and this character? The reason I ask is that I hear he likes dressing up in women's clothes. You don't have showers together and take turns picking up the soap, that sort of stuff?"

Sparks gave him a sour look. "Yeah, that's us all right."

"Hey, don't get me wrong; I've got nothing against it. Matter of fact, I wouldn't be surprised if the boy I sleep with is a bit that way."

Sparks' lips twitched. It was as close to a smile as he'd got in twenty-four hours.

"What about Delamore?"

"After Delamore left here, he checked in at the Regis — as a woman. Called himself Lesley Gore — that mean anything to you?" Sparks shook his head. "Looks like Pickrang's swansong was a B and E on Delamore's room. Typical Pickrang — tore the fucking place apart. Now what do you reckon he was after?"

"The stuff Gage wrote? Doesn't make sense. Delamore posted it in Sydney last week . . ." Sparks stopped in mid-sentence.

"You only got his word for it, right? I think your little mate's playing his own game." Ihaka passed Sparks the sheet of paper with the list of names on it. "We found this in his room."

"This is out of my fucking notebook, the little shit." Sparks put his head in his hands and thought hard. "If Delamore didn't send Gage's letter, Quedley couldn't have intercepted it. So Quedley finds out Delamore's staying at the Regis — how would he even know he's in town?"

"Delamore must've been in touch with him. Quedley must want this letter thing bad to send Pickrang over to Sydney. Why? Because it dumps shit on him?"

"I'm pretty sure it does."

"Well, I'd say Delamore's trying to blackmail him."

Sparks thought about it. "I don't know about that. I can't see Delamore as a blackmailer."

"Grow up, mate. You've known him what — a few days? The way he pissed off out of here tells you he's up to something."

"We don't know for sure that he did. I mean, he left the place in a shambles but that doesn't prove he found anything. Pickrang was seen in the hotel with a briefcase which we haven't recovered, so the way it looks, if he did find it, whoever offed him has got it now."

Sparks rubbed his face wearily. "Jesus, this started out as just a story for a magazine."

"So it's a mess, so what's new? It's always this way for cops — nothing's ever simple. It's only you fucking journalists who make out it's ever any different, writing up things like they happened all nice and neat."

"Some journalist — I haven't written a fucking word yet. So where's Delamore now?"

Ihaka shook his head. "Christ knows. He's hired a car and looked like he took off up north. He was talking about going to Wellsford or something."

Ihaka gave Sparks a quick rundown on the Plugge-Lydiate scam and its repercussions for Wallace Guttle then stood up. "Well, I'll leave you to it Sparks. You're obviously a busy man, you got TV to watch, balls to scratch. Where do I find this Quedley joker? I'll think I'll go and talk to him about his ex-employee."

24

When Herman Pickrang didn't report in that Wednesday night, Caspar Quedley took it for granted that something had gone wrong. It stands to reason, he said to himself; everything else has. Bill Tench rang him in his office the next morning to report that, as he heard it from his police contacts, Pickrang had carried out his assignment in room 1414 of the Regis Hotel; shortly thereafter though, he'd found himself on the wrong end of a sawn-off shotgun. When Quedley wondered out loud who could've pulled the trigger, Tench spluttered with amusement and replied that the police didn't know where to start looking since a gathering of the enemies of Herman Pickrang would fill Eden Park. Afterwards Quedley reflected that if Pickrang hadn't found Gage's letter in room 1414, he was back to square one; if he had, then the likelihood was that at that very moment, Gage's account of life and death at Prince Albert College would be studied, with some interest he imagined, at the Central Police Station.

Thus Quedley's spirits and shoulders sagged when he returned to his office after an early lunch to find Detective Sergeant Tito Ihaka waiting for him. He recovered himself quickly, pumped Ihaka's hand as if meeting him was the fulfilment of a long-held ambition, and ushered him into his office. Ihaka, however, proved difficult to charm.

"Didn't you used to play in the front row for University?" asked Quedley, examining him closely.

"Me? Shit no. You must be mixing me up with some other big coon."

"Yes, well, a lot of you folks are impressive physical specimens, that's for sure," said Quedley, undeterred by Ihaka's barely disguised truculence. "It's something to do with the bones, isn't it? Now Sergeant, what can I get you — coffee, tea, or something stronger?"

Ihaka shook his head. "I'm right."

"Of course you poor buggers can't drink on duty, can you? Well, if you'll excuse me, I've just had a very grim lunch with one of those born-again wowsers who live on salad and mineral water. You know what alfalfa smells like?" said Quedley getting a beer out of the small fridge under the bar. "Get a whiff of it — you'll understand why they call it spunkweed." He poured the beer and raised the tall glass to Ihaka.

"Cheers. Now how can I help you?"

"Herman Pickrang's been working for you, right?"

Quedley's brown furrowed. "Herman who?"

"Pickrang. We have reason to believe you sent him to Sydney last weekend."

Quedley chuckled. "Reason to believe — isn't that what you lot say when you haven't got a shred of evidence? I'd like to know your reason Sergeant, because I've never heard of this man."

"I suppose you don't know Dean Delamore either?"

Quedley rubbed his chin. "Delamore did you say? Now that name does ring a bell. I can check with my secretary but I seem to remember getting a call from a Delamore the other day. I couldn't get rid of him; he was babbling away about Prince Albert College — I couldn't make head nor tail of it. I think he was trying to screw a donation to the chapel restoration fund out of me. You never escape them, you know. You spend five miserable teenage years there and they pursue you relentlessly for the rest of your life."

Ihaka nodded. "Yeah I know what it's like. Tamaki College is chasing me for money to re-lay the croquet lawns. What about Julian Gage — you know him?"

"Well, I used to. He's dead. If it's not asking too much, would you mind telling me what this is all about?"

Ihaka stood up. "Seeing you never heard of Pickrang you wouldn't be interested in the fact he was shot dead last night."

Quedley drained his beer. "My, is that so?" he said blandly. "Just as well I didn't know him then — funerals make me depressed. Who did it?"

"We don't know yet but we'll find him. The thing is, the shooter took Pickrang's briefcase and we have reason to believe — there I go again — that there was something in the briefcase that a few people around town are fizzing at the bung to get their hands on. I thought you might be one of them. Wrong again, eh?"

Ihaka watched Quedley's expression turn thoughtful. He walked out of his office and got in the lift. On the way down he reflected that if the opportunity arose, he'd get enormous satisfaction from nailing Caspar Quedley to the wall — by his no doubt perfectly proportioned dick.

After leaving Quedley's office, Ihaka drove down through Parnell, up the hill past the university, and across town to Grey Lynn. He parked in Williamson Avenue and got out of his unmarked car. He was wearing jeans, running shoes and a zip-up bomber jacket. He put on a baseball cap and sunglasses and walked down a side street until he reached an old stone building. It was a church-cum-social club for one of the Polynesian communities; he had an idea it was Tongans. There didn't seem to be anyone around. Ihaka followed the path down the side of the building to the rear where there was a low embankment. There was a two-metre-high wooden fence on top of the embankment which formed the boundary of the church property. Ihaka climbed up the embankment, swore, took a deep breath and hoisted himself up the fence. He squirmed over the fence and came down in a private and well-tended backyard. Ihaka walked up the lawn towards the house, a tidy old wooden villa. He tapped on the back door.

The man who opened the door was in his early thirties. He was tall and thin and had long, unkempt blond hair, an earring, and a little triangle of white fluff under his lower lip. He wore faded jeans, cowboy boots and a tight black T-shirt bearing the legend "Kill 'em all and let God sort it out" in large white lettering. The man's name was Blair Corvine and he was an undercover policeman. By and large Ihaka was sceptical of the value of undercover police work; it took forever to get undercover men in place and then half the information they provided couldn't be used because it might blow their cover. A lot of them also turned into giant pains in the arse; he suspected it was all the dope they smoked. Corvine, on the other hand, had always been cut out for it; in fact Ihaka used to wonder how someone with such obvious criminal inclinations had ever got into the police force in the first place.

Corvine let Ihaka in. "Hey, it's big chief Ihaka," he said. "You and the bros dispossessed any hard-working honkies lately?"

"Well, my man, the fight for justice is never-ending. I tell you what, they wear you down these Pakehas, bleating about how their family's been there for 150 years and how they've levelled hills and cleared a thousand acres of bush and all this shit. You wouldn't believe the crap we have to put up with. Christ, we're not unreasonable people; we let you stay here — what more do you want?"

"I'd settle for not having that oily heap of shit with the tiki on TV every other night."

"I'm afraid you'll need to be more specific."

Corvine got two cans of beer out of the fridge and handed one to Ihaka. Ihaka, who hadn't enjoyed watching Quedley savour his beer, drank it in less than a minute.

Corvine took a careful sip of his beer. "Listen, I really enjoy it when you drop in," he said, "the way you trample on my flowers and hoover my piss and that, but is there a reason for it that's got anything to do with, like, our jobs?"

"Yeah, I was going to ask you about that. I mean, what is it with you and all these flowers? Why don't you grow some fucking vegetables?"

"That's the Ihaka philosophy is it — if you can't fuck it or eat it, it's a waste of time? I guess it's difficult for someone whose great-grandfather was a cannibal to grasp the concept of aesthetic pleasure."

"Watch yourself pal, I haven't had lunch. The reason I'm here, those Eyeties from Sydney who stirred up some shit in K Road a while ago . . ."

"The Perfumos."

"Yeah, they operate from a pizza joint, don't they?"

"Sure do — up the top of Queen Street there. They do a fucking good pizza as a matter of fact, lots of anchovies. I love anchovies. You like anchovies?"

"You're a sick man, Corvine. Didn't Herman Pickrang have a run-in with them?"

"The late, great Herman? Did he ever! They sent over these two brothers to run the show for them here; the pizzeria's the front. Apparently, Herman barged into the joint and stuck one of them head first into the pizza oven. They reckoned you could hear the cunt scream in Henderson. I forget which one it was, Marty or Rocco. It was the dumb one; man, this fucker's so thick, you'd have to tell him what to do if his wang was on fire."

"That's pretty dumb. So where are they now?"

"The one who got cooked went back to Sydney; the other one's still around last I heard. What's up?"

"I just wondered if they had anything to do with Pickrang getting blown away. I mean, these guys are meant to be the Mafia, aren't they? You'd have thought they'd have been after Herman."

"Yeah you would, wouldn't you?" said Corvine. "The word was they decided to call a truce but maybe they were just biding their time. Why the hell are you chasing whoever did that scumsucker? Guy deserves a medal."

"Wheels within wheels, matey. You talk to the Sydney cops now and again, don't you? Why don't you give them a ring, see if they've heard anything about the Perfumos lately? Thing is, I heard Pickrang was over there last weekend and had a run-in with a couple of guys who sound like them."

"What, make a fucking international call on my phone?"

"Come on Blair, I've seen your expense claims. I bet you make a profit on it."

Corvine made the call. It took ten minutes, half of which was obscene badinage, and was punctuated by frequent exclamations.

"Hey chief, your source is red-hot," said Corvine when he put the phone down. "Martino and Rocco bit the big one last Saturday night: one of them got a third nostril, the other got a knife through the neck. The deal went down in a place called . . ."

"Let me guess — Palm Beach, a little place just north of Sydney?"

"You're on the ball chief, by Christ you are. So now we know who zapped Herman and why. Shit, I just thought of something."

"Must be a leap year."

"You know who moves most of Perfumo's dope here? The Blood Drinkers. Those hits last night had Blood Drinkers written all over them — drive up with a sawn-off on your lap, boom, no fucking beg your pardon. 'What? We offed the wrong guy? Shit happens, we'll try again tomorrow.' That's them to a T. I'll bet what happened was the family put them on the case when Marty and Rocco got wasted, told 'em get Plugge while you're at it. Tell you what, I pissed myself when I heard how Barry scooted down to Central waving a white flag but fuck, if he's got those guys after him, it's the only way he's going to keep a head on his shoulders."

"The Blood Drinkers," said Ihaka. "That's just lovely."

Shortly after Ihaka got back to Central, he got a call from Reggie Sparks.

"How'd you get on with Quedley?"

"He's a cutie, isn't he? In a word, nowhere — he says he's never heard of Pickrang. He's lying of course. He didn't bat an eyelid when I told him Pickrang was dead and the turd's name hasn't even been released yet. He'd be happy that whoever did Pickrang's probably got Gage's letter; better than us having it and the chances are it'll be thrown away or lost or something. By the way, those guys who turned up at Palm Beach? It looks like they fucked up in the worst possible way." He told Sparks what had become of the brothers Perfumo. "So there you go," he finished. "I guess Pickrang found out what happens when you rumble with the big boys."

Sparks rang Louise Appleyard who said what a pleasant surprise it was to hear from him.

"Let's just say a surprise," said Sparks, spurning the olive branch. "Going by what you said yesterday — that stuff about grudges and reputations being blackened — you and Quedley obviously talked about what Gage might've said in his letter?"

Louise decided to ignore the snub. "Caspar said he and Gage used to be quite close but they'd fallen out badly. Gage was all bitter and twisted and had threatened Caspar, more or less to destroy his reputation. He said the letter would just contain a lot of lies about him — he wasn't specific if that's what you mean."

"Did you believe him?"

There was a long pause. "Yes, but I suppose I didn't really think about it too hard."

"What does that mean?"

"It means I probably had other things on my mind at the time."

Sparks cleared his throat. "Look, I want to ask Quedley a few straight questions; I'd like you to be there otherwise he'll just give me the run-around. How about it?"

"I think you might be overestimating my influence but all right. When?"

"Now, this afternoon."

They met an hour later in the reception area of Quedley Communications. Sparks, frostily polite, thanked her for obliging at such short notice. She was about to ask him how long she'd have to spend in Coventry when Quedley came out to greet them. He acted as if it was the most normal thing in the world for the two of them to turn up unannounced at his office in the middle of the afternoon. He seated them on the sofas arranged in a V formation in the corner of his office, Sparks on the two-seater, Louise on the larger. He perched on the arm of Louise's in what Sparks interpreted as a proprietorial statement. Louise, wearing snug-fitting dark green leggings and a loose white top, looked slightly anxious. Sparks, in no mood for small talk, got straight to the point.

"What happened at Prince Albert that you're so desperate to cover up?"

Quedley spread his hands and looked from Sparks to Louise with a bemused grin.

"And I thought this was a social visit. Jesus Christ, I don't mind you interrupting my work; I'm not even that bothered by the 'When did you stop beating your wife?' questions. But why drag Louise into it? What's your problem, Reggie? Are you all bent out of shape because of Louise and me so you want to make me look bad in front of her? Is that it?"

"Why stop there? Why don't you throw in my sister-in-law?"

"Your sister-in-law?" said Louise. "Where does she come into it?"

"A while ago Quedley tried to seduce her," said Sparks.

Quedley grinned ruefully. "Yes, that was rather unfortunate. When it comes to married women, I try to operate on the basis that what husbands don't know won't hurt them. How was I meant to know that Gavin was going to mount a room-to-room search?" He wagged a finger at Sparks. "But in the interests of accuracy Reggie, I must pull you up on your use of the word 'tried'. To say I tried to seduce dear old Heather implies that I failed. Now you and I both know that wasn't the case."

Sparks looked at Louise and said, "You can pick 'em." To Quedley: "She's here because I thought there was just the remotest chance that you'd be embarrassed to tell bare-faced lies in front of her."

"You're full of flattery today, aren't you? So are you here in your ace reporter role or what?"

"The chances are there won't be a story. The cops are involved now. Shit, people have been murdered. It'll probably all be sub judice for months. Anyway, if you've got nothing to hide, what are you worried about?"

"So I have you to thank for the visit from Sergeant Plod do I? I wondered about that." Quedley heaved an exaggerated sigh and looked at the ceiling. "You're persistent, Sparks; you may be obtuse — you're certainly misguided — but you are persistent. Okay, if you really must know." He slipped down onto the sofa beside Louise. "This is strictly not for publication. As I was telling Louise, Julian was a bit of a slut at school. He used to tell me who he was playing doctors and doctors with and if I thought there was some mileage in it, I'd threaten to broadcast it far and wide unless they coughed up. It was hardly extortion on a grand scale — you know, it was hand over your pocket money or, I'll have that cake your mother brought today — but it's not the sort of thing you want written up in *New Nation*."

There was a long silence. Louise looked wonderingly at Quedley who seemed to be examining his expensive-looking black brogues. Sparks' derisive snort broke the silence.

"Oh right, absolutely," he said, clicking his fingers. "You sent a fucking psycho over to Australia because you don't want people to know that twenty-odd years go, you bullied a few spoilt kids out of some chocolate cake. You really think we're a couple of morons, don't you?"

"I can't conceive of any context in which I'd lump you together with Louise," said Quedley coldly. "I've answered your god-damn questions; I can't help it if the answer doesn't suit your purposes but that's it."

"That's it huh?" said Sparks. "What about selling the exam papers?"

"Oh the history paper — I'd forgotten about that. I was quite proud of that little stunt; I broke into the masters' common room to steal it and then sold copies. Fair cop, guv." He looked at Louise. "Well my sweet, now you know all my guilty secrets," he said, play-acting. "Am I beyond the pale? Does that mean you can never see me again?"

Louise looked uncertainly at Reggie, wondering if it was all over. He was sitting with his elbow on the arm of the sofa, his chin in the heel of his hand, and his eyes on Quedley. She recognised the expression; it was the same angry and disdainful look she'd got the day before.

"You know something?" said Sparks. "There's nobody dumber than a half-smart person who thinks he's really smart."

Quedley went and sat behind his desk. "I don't think that's original, is it?" he said off-handedly. He pressed a button on his telephone and asked his secretary if there were any messages for him. Sparks stood in front of the desk and looked down at him.

"You don't know why Pickrang was killed, do you?"

Quedley looked up from his diary. "You still here? You've outstayed your welcome."

"When Pickrang was in Sydney, on your behalf, he killed a couple of people — two brothers, Martino and Rocco Perfumo. The Perfumo family is involved in organised crime. Shit, why beat around the bush? They're Mafia. Now you know what those guys are like — you kill one of ours, we'll kill two of yours. Revenge is a way of life for them. If the Perfumos find out Pickrang was working for you, you'll be next in line for a shotgun facelift. And if you were going to ask 'How would they find out?' the answer is: because I'd tell them. And I'm pretty sure they'd believe me; I'd tell a good story because, you see, I was there."

Quedley sat back with his arms folded and looked steadily at Sparks who stared back. Then he picked up the phone and dialled.

"Ken? Caspar Quedley. You get *The Sydney Morning Herald*, don't you? You got last Monday's handy? You mind having a quick look to see if there's anything about two brothers — someone and Rocco Perfumo — being murdered? Yep, I'll hang on." There was a short wait. "On the front page is it? What does it say?" Quedley listened for a couple of minutes, thanked his informant and hung up. He looked over at Sparks who was standing at the window with his back to him.

He coughed politely. "Sorry Reggie, what was the question?"

Sparks turned round. "Same as before: what would Gage have written that you didn't want people to read?"

Quedley walked over to the bar. "Anyone for a drink?" Louise and Sparks said no. He poured himself one from a heavy crystal decanter, added some ice, then went back to his desk. "The chaplain, a harmless old bachelor called Swindell, was infatuated with Julian," he said slowly, looking at no one or nothing in particular. "He was also a masochist. He asked Julian to do things to him — I don't need to spell it out, do I? I blackmailed him. After a few weeks of it, he killed himself — drove his car into a brick wall."

"What about Bronwen Ticehurst?"

Quedley swallowed a mouthful of his drink and shook his head. "Julian had nothing to do with Bronwen. He probably wouldn't even remember her. It's true, some people said it was my fault but how was I to know what a state she was in? I just told her the truth — that I didn't want to be tied to one girl. Christ, I never dreamt she'd go and kill herself."

"Have you heard from Dean Delamore?" asked Sparks.

Quedley nodded. "He offered to sell me the letter," he said dully. "Then he changed his mind, said he was going to talk to someone else."

"Who would that be?"

"I don't know. I wasn't sure if he was serious. I thought he was just going to make me squirm for a couple of days then come back to me."

Louise Appleyard went over and stood beside Quedley. "Caspar, why on earth did you do those things?"

He looked at her. "My family . . . we weren't very well off. My father was a vicar and earned next to nothing. I only went to Prince Albert because clergymen's sons got a big discount. I saw how other families lived, the families of the boys I got friendly with. It was a different world, I mean money simply wasn't an issue for them. Say if little Simon wanted to go and stay with his friend in Fiji in the holidays? 'Well of course you can dear. Si-Si needs some spending money? Will $1000 be enough? Let's make it $1500 to be on the safe side.' When I wanted a new pair of shoes because I felt such a jerk wearing my black ones out of school, it was a major expenditure decision — my parents argued about it for a week. Then my mother dies. All we'd ever really had was each other and that was taken away — we weren't even a family any more. It just seemed like we had nothing and everyone else had too much."

Quedley sat with his head bowed. He reached out and took Louise's hand; she let him do it, neither withdrawing nor responding.

Sparks said, "Boo fucking hoo," and walked out of Quedley's office.

25

Reggie Sparks sat behind the steering wheel of his mother's Peugeot, which was parked a little way up Parnell Rise from Quedley's office, pondering his next move. He'd made up his mind and was about to start the car when he heard his name being called. He looked up. Louise Appleyard was running up the footpath towards him. With her trim form, her dark hair bouncing on her shoulders and, as Sparks couldn't help noticing, her breasts bobbing perkily beneath the loose top, she looked as if she'd stepped straight from the pages of some glossy healthy living magazine. He wound down the car window.

She was panting slightly. "Are you in a mad rush?" she breathed.

He shrugged. "Not especially."

She walked around to the other side of the car and got into the passenger seat.

"That was a charming exit line," she said. "Didn't you even feel the slightest bit sorry for him?"

He looked at her incredulously. "Sorry for Quedley? You've got to be joking. As for the *Little House on the Prairie* routine, Jesus Christ." He shook his head. "How I managed to keep my lunch down, I'll never know."

"Didn't you believe him?"

"The stuff about his family? Yeah, I believed him — it's pretty much what I'd heard. But so what? Most kids feel hard done by at some stage. And what about the hypocrisy of getting his hooks into the chaplain? Presumably the poor bastard was no better off than Quedley's old man."

She raised his eyebrows non-committally. "What about the rest of it?"

"Hard to say. I still think he knows more about the girl's death than he's letting on. Once I'd hit him with the Perfumos, though, I didn't have anything else to pressure him with."

"God yes, what was all that about? Did you really see those men get murdered?"

"Well, not exactly. I wouldn't be here if I had."

"Tell the truth, Reggie: would you've really gone through with it?"

Sparks' mouth turned into a tight, coldly amused smile. Louise Appleyard was no longer in any doubt that Reggie Sparks possessed a mean streak. The only question was how big and for the second time that afternoon she found herself wondering if she'd underestimated the size of it.

"Shit yes," said Sparks. He held the smile for several seconds. "I still might."

She looked back at him, eyes narrowing. "I don't believe you."

Sparks looked away. "Relax Louise, I won't set the dogs on lover boy. You can scuttle back and tell him mission accomplished."

She laughed mirthlessly. "You know, you can be extremely bloody objectionable when you put your mind to it. As a matter of fact, I'm here because I wanted to let you know that that crack he made, implying that you were jealous — I didn't put that in his head."

Sparks gave a shrug of indifference. "You didn't need to. That's just the way his mind works."

"You're not a big fan, are you?"

"I actually quite like him in a funny sort of way," said Sparks mildly. "But the guy's an arsehole; it doesn't matter what you feel or I think, that's it." He twisted round in his seat to look at her. "You know how he gets away with it? He doesn't try to hide it; he lets people in on the secret — hey folks, look at me, I'm a walking, talking arsehole. People enjoy it because he's got a bit of style and because he says and does what they'd like to do if they had the guts. Because he's upfront, they think it's an act; they think he's putting it on and, deep down, he's not half as self-centred and contemptuous of the rest of us as he pretends. In fact, it's not a façade — he really is an arsehole."

Louise would've liked to have continued the conversation but Sparks brought it to a close by starting the car. She got out and held the door open.

"Where are you off to now?"

"I think I'll head up north," he said. "Who knows? I might find a damsel in distress."

What with having to go home and make sure it was okay with his mother to have her car for the evening and getting caught in rush-hour Harbour Bridge traffic, Sparks didn't get to Looms' farm until just before 8 p.m. He followed the drive up to the house, parked right by the front door, and got out of the car. Loud rock music was coming from inside the house. Dermot Looms — rock 'n' roll animal, thought Sparks; I wouldn't have picked it. To the right of the house was a double garage. The roller door was raised and as he'd driven up, his headlights had illuminated a car parked inside. He went over for a closer look. The car was a Honda Civic sedan. It was unlocked and when he opened the driver's side door, the interior light came on. A plastic bag with a Hertz logo hung from one of the knobs on the dashboard. The paperwork showing the car had been rented by Dean Delamore was in the glovebox.

Sparks walked up the steps to the front door and knocked. There was no response. The music was incredibly loud. The bugger must be deaf, he thought. When three sets of knocks went unanswered, he began hammering. After twelve heavy thumps which shook the solid wooden door, it was opened by Basil Batrouney who blinked owlishly behind his thick lenses.

The corridor reverberated to Mick Jagger's lubricious screech: "Oh yeah, you're a strange stray cat/Oh yeah, don't you scratch my back/Oh yeah, you're a strange stray cat/I bet your momma don't know you can sweat like that." Sparks found it vaguely disturbing that Batrouney should be listening to a song celebrating sex with minors.

"Could you please turn the music down," Sparks bellowed, making a twisting gesture with his right hand.

Batrouney nodded once and ambled off down the corridor. Sparks followed him into the living room. The music was thundering out of a new-looking stereo system set on a sideboard against the far wall. Batrouney turned the volume right down and looked questioningly at Sparks.

"Who are you?" he said finally.

"Reggie Sparks," he said, his voice sounding strident in the hush. "I'm a journalist. I came to see you a while ago on Waiheke. You showed me your comic, what's it called — *Grub?*" he added in the hope the reference might trigger a reaction in the former rock star's burnt-out brain.

There was no indication in Batrouney's large moist eyes that a mental connection was in progress but something must have clicked.

"I remember you," he said, an accusatory note entering his voice. "You didn't like Jack Stack."

"Oh well, you know, I guess it's an acquired taste," said Sparks weakly. "I'm sure if I read a few more . . ." Wait a minute, he told himself, you didn't come up here to exchange toilet talk with this anal-retentive zombie. He changed the subject. "What brings you up here? I thought you were pretty much a homebody these days."

"Visiting Dermie. My friend."

Dermie and Baz? Talk about the odd couple. "Is Mr Looms about?"

Batrouney shook his head.

Sparks moved closer. "There's someone else here though, isn't there Basil? A man called Dean Delamore?"

Batrouney's large globular head vibrated violently. "No way Jose, no way."

"I know he's here, Baz. That's his car in the garage." He took Batrouney by the right arm, above the elbow. His fingers sank into soft, doughy flesh. "Where is he?"

Batrouney's head dropped and he tried to pull away. Sparks jerked him back and said in a hard voice, "Where the bloody hell is he? I want you to show me right now."

Sparks pushed Batrouney towards the doorway. Batrouney, his head still bowed, led him into the huge kitchen and took a key from a row of hooks by the back door. He went out the back door and down a few steps to a below-ground doorway. He unlocked the door and stood aside.

Sparks peered through the door into darkness. "In here?"

Batrouney nodded.

"Give us the keys."

Batrouney handed them over. Sparks took a couple of steps down into the cellar. Just then he remembered Batrouney saying at their previous meeting that he no longer listened to rock music. It occurred to Sparks that perhaps everything else the former rock star had told him was a lie but before he could advance this proposition, he was struck a fierce blow on the back of the head. He lost his footing, careered down the remaining few steps, and sprawled on the cold concrete floor. As he lay there stunned, jarred and disoriented, he felt the keys being ripped from his grasp and heard receding footsteps and the cellar door being slammed shut and locked, plunging the cellar into utter darkness.

Outside Basil Batrouney thoughtfully hefted the heavy double-handed secateurs then dropped them back into the wheelbarrow parked by the cellar door. He said, "Good work, Batman," in a deep Hollywood voice and went back inside to listen to the other side of *Beggars Banquet*.

Sparks rolled onto his back and sat up. Blood trickled over his fingers as he gently prodded the welt which had already come up on the back of his head. As it dawned on him that he'd been outsmarted by someone whom he'd characterised, a few minutes earlier, as a zombie, Dean Delamore's hesitant voice came out of the darkness: "Is that you, Reggie?"

"No it's not," said Sparks with some bitterness. "It's Sir Lancelot."

Basil Batrouney felled Sparks with the secateurs at 8.25 that Thursday night. At 10 p.m. police teams launched simultaneous raids on several premises in South Auckland believed to be occupied by leading members of the Blood Drinkers gang. Tito Ihaka led the team whose target was a flat in Otara, the last known address of Luther "Bad Louie" Potau. However, in keeping with his promise to himself, Ihaka was not the first man through the door; that distinction fell to an extremely gung-ho twenty-six-year-old constable and member of the Armed Offenders Squad. Ihaka wondered if anyone had explained to the constable that his state-of-the-art rifle and flak jacket didn't guarantee complete protection against a sociopath with a sawn-off shotgun.

At the time of the raid Potau was sitting on a sofa watching television in the living room-cum-kitchen at the rear of the flat. He was surrounded by assorted debris including the packaging which had contained his supper — $35 worth of Kentucky Fried Chicken — and the leftover bones. A nineteen-year-old girl, whose name Potau was pretty sure was Christine but whom he called "woman" or "bitch" depending on his mood and who threw a better punch than any of his four previous de facto wives, sat on his lap. Christine had consumed four large bottles of beer and three stiff bourbon and Cokes and was quite drunk. Potau, who liked to begin the day with a couple of bottles of stout but who never drank beer after sundown on principle, was just over halfway through his nightly intake of a litre of dark rum and therefore more or less sober, albeit not by any medical or legal definition.

When Ihaka banged on the door and bellowed "Police, open up", Potau went to shove Christine off his lap. However, shifting 110 kilograms of dead weight took some doing and by the time she'd tipped onto the floor, the door had been breached and he could hear the raiders advancing down the corridor. Potau carefully set down the bottle of rum and picked up an empty beer bottle. He straightened to find a rifle being pointed at him by a tall figure in a dark boiler suit who instructed him not to fucking well move. Ihaka entered just as Potau released an unearthly roar and commenced his charge. Having to negotiate his way over and around the recumbent Christine, two beer crates and the back seat from a 1966 Zodiac, which served as seating when he and Christine entertained, prevented Potau from building up much speed and saved his life. It gave Ihaka time to step around the constable and stop Potau in his tracks by clubbing him ferociously hard across the face with a baseball bat.

The subsequent search of Potau's flat proved productive: the sawn-off shotgun used on Pickrang and Gilpin was found under the bed; Pickrang's briefcase was amid the chest-high weeds in the backyard; and Julian Gage's memoir of Prince Albert College was on the kitchen table, splattered with grease and surrounded by unwashed dishes. Christine had made a shopping list on the back of one page and begun a letter to her mother in Gisborne on the back of another.

26

When Luther Potau woke up, he was taken to the Otara police station to be questioned about the murders of Herman Pickrang and Cec Gilpin. His sullen silence was standard Blood Drinkers' practice so it was some time before his interrogators realised that his speechlessness was not a matter of choice. He was ferried, under heavy guard, to Middlemore Hospital where X-rays of his spectacularly splintered facial bone structure swiftly became collector's items. At the Otara station Tito Ihaka re-read Julian Gage's letter before sending it into Central for Inspector Finbar McGrail's attention. Then he found himself a quiet corner and made three calls.

The first was to Reggie Sparks who, he learned from Mareena, had taken off up north somewhere and wasn't expected back till later. Her tone implied that it was already late. Under normal circumstances, Ihaka might've hesitated to ask her to go in search of the list of names and addresses which Dean Delamore had ripped out of her son's notebook but these were not normal circumstances. Because Mareena derived some comfort from Ihaka's interest in her wayward son, she did so. She found the list where her son had left it, in the downstairs TV room, and told Ihaka what he wanted to know, which was where Dermot Looms lived.

Ihaka thought long and hard before he made his next call. The obvious thing to do was to ring the Wellsford cops. He imagined the conversation with whoever was on duty at Wellsford station at that hour of the night: let's see, we've got a hanged girl at a private school ball in 1970, a dead witness and a blackmailing transvestite. And that's just for starters. What the fuck would they make of that in Wellsford? Christ, if someone rang him out of the blue at 11 o'clock at night with a story like that, he'd think the guy had been into the confiscated drugs. And assuming he convinced Wellsford to take it seriously, how about if they rousted a few guys out of bed and sent them out to Looms' place and the whole thing turned out to be a load of crap, a malicious fabrication? No two ways about it, he'd be the laughing stock of the entire police force.

So instead of ringing Wellsford, Ihaka's second call was to Blair Corvine, the undercover policeman.

"Mate, I need a gun."

There was a long silence. "Chief, last time I looked, we had more guns at Central than the fucking army so would you mind explaining why you're ringing me at this hour?"

"It's pretty complicated and I'm really stuck for time — let's just say it's a grey area."

"Now chief, think about this. Think about it very carefully. This sounds like it could be one of those fork-in-the-road-type decisions."

"Who wants promotion anyway? Just more fucking work."

There was another silence. "It's your career buddy. What do you want?"

"A revolver will do."

"Oh just a revolver? I can't interest you in an Uzi machine pistol, you know 600 rounds a minute? What about a shoulder-launched missile, you let it go from the top of One Tree Hill and knock down the fucking Town Hall? Really gets the job done."

"You're tempting me, you silver-tongued devil, but I'll settle for a revolver. Can you have it for me in an hour?"

They arranged to do the handover at midnight, by the Victoria Park pavilion.

Ihaka's third call was to Louise Appleyard. It was intended as a courtesy call, to let her know that they'd found Julian Gage's letter to her late husband. It turned out to be rather more than that.

"When can I read it?" was her first question.

"I don't know. We have to treat it like evidence so we can't go handing it round to the public."

"I'm not asking out of vague curiosity Sergeant," said Louise in clipped tones, "and I'm hardly just another member of the public."

"I'm well aware of that Mrs Appleyard. That's why I called in the first place."

"Well, you've obviously read it; tell me what it says."

"Look I'm very sorry but I just don't have time. I'm a bit worried about your journalist friend Sparks."

"I saw Reggie this afternoon — he was okay. He said something about going up north."

"That's what worries me and that's where I'm off to now which is why . . ."

"What's up north Sergeant?"

Ihaka was wishing he'd never made the call. "A bloke called Dermot Looms."

"He was at the ball, wasn't he? Do you suspect him of something?"

"You could say that."

"I've got an excellent idea Sergeant. I'll go with you and you can brief me — isn't that what policemen say? — about the letter on the way."

Ihaka protested but Louise became very emphatic about how her late husband had started the whole thing and didn't that entitle her to some consideration? Ihaka thought of falling back on the excuse that it was police business but strictly speaking that wasn't the case. And while Ihaka could be an accomplished liar when the need arose, he couldn't think of a single reason — apart from the obvious one of behaving like a responsible police officer —

why he should deprive himself of the company of an attractive woman for the midnight drive.

It was 1.15 a.m. but the lights were still on in Looms' house when Ihaka pulled in behind Mrs Sparks' Peugeot which was still parked right by the front door.

"That's Reggie's car," said Louise.

Ihaka grunted and got the pistol out of the glovebox. In the deep, rural stillness, the music from the house was quite audible. It was Jimi Hendrix's "Hey Joe", not that Ihaka recognised it, Hendrix having been a little before his time. "Listen to that," he said. "Sounds like they're having a party." He put the pistol back in the glovebox. "Guess I won't be needing it."

He told Louise, "You stay here — if I'm not back in ten minutes, take off," and got out of the car. He walked up to the front door and knocked. No one came to the door. After he'd knocked again without response, Ihaka made his way around the side of the house.

The knocking startled Basil Batrouney. His friend Dermie had been due back half an hour before but, late or not, why should he knock when he had keys? Perhaps it was another of the nosey parkers with whom the Looms' spread, despite its isolation, seemed to be infested. Batrouney decided to reconnoitre rather than answer the door. The upshot was that as Ihaka rounded the rear corner of the house and entered the rose garden, he trod heavily on the toes of an odd-looking specimen carrying a single-barrelled pump-action shotgun.

The former rock star received the bigger fright but not by much. Batrouney's perception of nosey parkers was largely based on Delamore and Sparks, neither of whom could be said to be physically intimidating. The third intruder had physical presence to burn as testified by the appalling pain in his left foot. For his part, Ihaka had had quite enough of lunatics with shotguns for one night. While this weirdo looked far less savage than Potau, Ihaka's instant impression was that he'd give Bad Louie a decent run for his money in the lunacy stakes.

They recoiled from the contact and eyed one another apprehensively for a few tense seconds.

"Whoa, take it easy amigo," said Ihaka, holding up his hands in surrender. "I'm not looking for trouble. Sorry about the hour but I've got an urgent message for Dermot Looms. You him?"

Batrouney tightened his shaky grip on the shotgun and shook his head. Ihaka shifted his focus to a point over Batrouney's shoulder and flashed a bright grin. "You must be Dermot, right?"

The little charade was executed so smoothly that it would've taken in more alert individuals than Batrouney. Furthermore, being left alone to cope with the influx had made Batrouney fretful and therefore more susceptible to one of the older tricks in the book. His head whipped round as if on a spring. Ihaka shot out his right arm and wrenched the shotgun from his grasp. Batrouney looked back at Ihaka, appearing not to notice that he'd been disarmed.

"I can't see Dermie," he wailed. "Where is he?"

"My mistake," said Ihaka. "A trick of the moonlight." He leaned forward and tugged gently on Batrouney's woolly pullover. "Who are you?"

"Baz."

"Basil Batrouney?"

The former rock star nodded nervously.

"Well fuck me, the gang's all here," said Ihaka cheerfully. "Where's Sparks?"

"Who?"

Ihaka tightened his grip. "Reggie Sparks. His car's parked right outside the front door."

"I haven't seen him, I haven't seen anyone," jabbered Batrouney. "I've just been grooving to Jimi and waiting for Dermie to come home."

Ihaka shifted his grip, gathering a handful of pullover from just below the neck. He jerked violently, hauling Batrouney up onto his toes. He put his face up to Batrouney's. "Do you want a fucking good hiding?" he asked in a tone of mild curiosity.

"Don't hurt me," moaned Batrouney, tears welling up in his eyes. "I'll show you."

He limped to the back door and took the key off the hook, led Ihaka down to the cellar door, and unlocked it. Ihaka stepped in front of him and pushed the door open. "Sparks," he called out. "It's Ihaka. You down there?"

"Look out," yelled Sparks from the darkness.

Ihaka whirled. Batrouney, teeth bared, stood on tiptoe with the secateurs raised above his head. As he began the down-swing, Ihaka reversed the shotgun and jabbed the butt into his face, fracturing the former rock star's glasses as well as his nose. Batrouney shrieked piercingly and buried his face in his hands. Ihaka grabbed him by the pullover and held him at arm's length. "It's okay," he called into the cellar. "Come on out."

Sparks came out first followed by Delamore who had two perfect black eyes and whose badly bruised face glowed eerily in the half light coming from the kitchen window.

"Thanks for the warning," said Ihaka. "He get you that way, did he?"

Sparks nodded and gingerly rubbed the back of his head. "He sure did."

"Well, if it's any consolation, I just gave him a fair poke right on the snotbox." He pushed Batrouney towards the door. "Okay pal, your turn in the dungeon."

Batrouney started to whimper and flap his arms but Ihaka shoved him roughly through the cellar door and locked it behind him.

Louise Appleyard was leaning back against the railing which fenced off the paddock to the right of Looms' house looking at the stars. She was getting cold and about to go back to the car when she saw headlights turn into the drive. The car came halfway up the drive but stopped when its headlights picked up the two cars parked in front of the car. The engine and lights were switched off and Louise heard a car door open and close. She moved deeper into the shadows of the garage.

Delamore, Ihaka and Sparks had just found a bottle of Scotch in the kitchen cupboard when Looms walked in the back door. He looked around slowly, took off his jacket and hung it over the back of a chair.

"Help yourself, why don't you?"

"Don't mind if I do," said Ihaka and took a hefty gulp. "You'd be Looms."

Looms nodded impassively. "You're a ways from home, aren't you?" He walked over to the table, picked up the whisky bottle and took a swig. Ihaka casually dropped a hand on the stock of Batrouney's shotgun which lay on the table in front of him.

"Still, seeing you're here, Mr Detective Sergeant," said Looms, "I'd like to lay a complaint against Nancy Boy over here." He nodded at Delamore. "The cheeky little poof tried to blackmail me."

"Really?" said Ihaka. He studied Delamore who smiled shyly. "He looks as if he's got something to complain about himself." Ihaka turned back to Looms. "You know, there's one sure-fire way to take the wind out of his sails — just own up that you murdered Bronwen Ticehurst."

Looms frowned and was rubbing his chin as if he was seriously considering the suggestion when Lloyd Chennell slipped in the back door and pointed a .22 rifle at Ihaka.

"I don't think so," he said. "That would mean an awful lot of effort had been to no avail. Now if you'll put up your hands and step away from the table . . ."

They were in the living room, Delamore and Sparks sitting by the window on a large sofa with Ihaka in an armchair to their left. Looms and Chennell were on the other side of the room by the door, Chennell in an armchair with the rifle between his knees, its butt on the floor, and Looms on his feet, handling the shotgun like an extension of his arm.

Looms was speaking. "It's been a shit of a night, I don't mind telling you. First of all, I had to flag the Regis because there was a cop stationed outside the room, then Lloyd's flight was late . . ."

"Yoo hoo, anyone home?" Louise Appleyard's voice floated down the corridor from the back door. Sparks shot a horrified look at Ihaka who gave a short shake of his head, put his chin on his chest and massaged his forehead. Chennell, wide-eyed, turned to Looms who said, "I don't fucking believe this . . ." He held the shotgun down by this side and put his head round the door.

"Hi there," said Louise advancing down the corridor. "Pardon me for barging in but I seem to have mislaid my driver."

"He's probably in here," said Looms. "Half of Auckland is."

Louise entered the room. "Oh there you are," she said brightly, apparently oblivious to the charged atmosphere. "I got sick of waiting in the car so . . ." Her face fell as she noticed Chennell's rifle. "What's going on?"

Looms showed the shotgun. "Why don't you hop over there on that sofa?"

Louise sat next to Delamore, her hands clasped together between her knees but otherwise looking remarkably composed. Sparks did his best to give her an encouraging smile.

"Is that the lot?" said Looms wonderingly. "Or are there a few more wandering out there?"

"You must be Dermot Looms," said Louise. "Is it true what Julian Gage wrote about you?"

Ihaka started to look up, then thought better of it. Looms looked puzzled. "How come you've seen that?" he asked.

"The sergeant showed it to me on the way up here," she said. Everyone exchanged glances. Louise looked at Ihaka. "Shouldn't I've said that?" she asked anxiously. Ihaka looked up, spluttered, and looked back at his shoes.

Looms guffawed. "Well, bugger me. Here's me running all over the show looking for that bloody thing and we've got a door-to-door delivery." He stopped short. "Jesus, I completely forgot about Baz — where the hell is he?" He glared at Ihaka. "You didn't shove him in the cellar did you, you lousy bastard? The poor bugger'll be going frantic."

Looms swapped guns with Chennell. "I'm going to let Baz out and get Gage's letter," he said. "If they try anything, Lloyd, let 'em have it." He left the room.

Chennell stood up and held the shotgun across his stomach, pointing away from his captives. When Louise heard the back door open and close, she reached under her loose white top and pulled Ihaka's revolver out of the waistband of her leggings. She pointed it at Chennell and told him to put his gun down.

Chennell stood stock still. Louise sat on the edge of the sofa holding the pistol at arms' length in both hands. Her eyes stayed on Chennell's face like a spotlight but she was struggling to hold the pistol steady.

"My dear," said Chennell huskily, "are you really prepared to kill me?"

The back door opened. The pistol wavered in Louise's grip. Chennell breathed deeply and shifted his hands on the shotgun.

"You do realise Louise," said Sparks conversationally, "that these fuckers killed Victor?"

Chennell saw something red flare at the back of Louise's eyes a split-second before she shot him through the fatty deposit above his right hip, the area sometimes referred to as a "love handle". He squealed, dropped the gun and clutched his wound.

Ihaka leapt across the room and snatched up the shotgun. He peered into the corridor. Batrouney was standing in the kitchen doorway fumbling with the rifle. There was no sign of Looms. Ihaka told Batrouney to drop the rifle. Batrouney squinted down the corridor, screamed "You locked me in the dark" and raised the rifle. At that moment Looms, having failed to find Gage's letter in either car and alarmed by the gunshot, opened the front door and received a bullet, meant for Ihaka, in the Adam's apple. He made a horrendous gurgling sound, fell over backwards, and proceeded to die noisily on the front porch. Ihaka hurriedly lined up on Batrouney's legs and fired. His intention was to disable Batrouney without killing him and in that he succeeded. His aim being high, he also put paid to the prospect of there ever being any little Batrouneys, not that the former rock star had shown any inclination towards reproductive activity for the better part of two decades.

27

Ten days later Reggie Sparks received a letter from Tito Ihaka. It said:

Kia ora Reggie boy,

Just to let you know where things are at. It looks like we're going to close the book on the whole thing. Batrouney hasn't said a word since the gunfight at the OK Corral — I know he wasn't too flash to start with but he's just a veggie now.

Chennell's a different kettle of shit: if we really bust a gut, we might be able to get him on some sort of conspiracy charge but those turkeys in the crown prosecutor's office aren't being much help — "in view of the most unusual circumstances of this case, we couldn't proceed against Mr Chennell with any real degree of confidence". You wouldn't believe the mealy-mouthed crap those characters come up with. Up at the farm, he didn't actually do much apart from giving Calamity Jane a bit of target practice. There is a school of thought around here (i.e. me) which feels that the precise details of what happened up there should be allowed to fade into obscurity — if you get my drift. As you'd expect, anything to do with Bronwen Ticehurst just goes straight into the "too hard" file. We let Chennell know that, whatever happens, his school in Sydney would hear all about it — his lawyer reckons he's already resigned — but we'll tell them anyway to bugger up his job prospects. Apart from that he'll probably walk.

Part of the reasons we went easy on Chennell, as I guess you've heard from Louise, is that he explained what happened to her husband. After Gage told Appleyard the answer was on the dance card, he started working his way through the names (and hired Guttle to check out Lydiate). He went and saw Batrouney on Waiheke and apparently coaxed part of the story out of him. When Batrouney realised what he'd done, he went frothing off to Looms. Looms set up a meeting with Appleyard somewhere here in town and pulled the same trick he pulled on Delores Delamore — Baz in the back seat with a gun. About four in the morning they made Appleyard drive onto the bridge with

Looms in his car right behind, stopped at the top, and Looms just manhandled him over the edge. If they'd been really unlucky, they might've been spotted on the monitor but the cameras don't cover the whole bridge the whole time and whoever was on duty was probably doing a crossword anyway. Fair go — some of the kids joining the force these days don't even move their lips when they read. He was a hard man, Looms. Good job Batrouney was such a lousy shot.

Anyway, the insurance company has been advised so Louise gets her dough after all. While we're on that subject, a word of advice — strike while the iron's hot. It's obvious that you're keen on her but a woman like that won't be on her tod for long. I didn't realise she'd actually gone a few rounds with Quedley but I gather that's history. She told me you opened her eyes to what a complete cunt he was or words to that effect. That's not a bad start. Wasn't it Mahatma Gandhi who said that if you can open a woman's eyes, her legs will soon follow? Maybe it was Errol Flynn.

Well, on that philosophical note, I'll sign off. Seeing there shouldn't be any legal complications, you can go full steam ahead on your story. Just go easy when you reach the bit about unregistered handguns popping up out of nowhere and retards getting shotgun vasectomies etc. Attached is a copy of Gage's letter which I thought might help. I don't ask much in return — just that your story should make it clear that my role in this little saga amounted to the niftiest piece of intuitive police work since the Crewe murder case. I'll also be very dark if you don't expose Quedley as a shit-eating swine. You can quote me on that.

Hasta la vista

Chief Inspector Tito Ihaka (only a matter of time after the article comes out).

PS Burn this.

Sparks turned to Julian Gage's letter to Victor Appleyard.

Dear Victor,

First of all, let me repeat how very much I appreciated your gesture in the restaurant that night. I hope I'm wrong but I strongly suspect that very few men in your position would break off from a business dinner to speak to someone whose appearance rather encourages others to assume the worst. I also enjoyed and appreciated your subsequent visits and our chats. Many thanks too for the books. I know it's customary to tell giftgivers that they shouldn't have but I'll skip that fib and simply say I enjoyed them enormously, particularly the Jan Morris book about Venice which brought back some wonderful memories.

To say that your comments about poor Bronwen Ticehurst set me thinking would be a gross understatement; I've thought of little else. I was deeply moved that you haven't forgotten Bronwen and are still troubled by her death (and deeply shamed by the invidious contrast with my own behaviour).

Once or twice I was on the verge of telling you the whole story but I just couldn't bring myself to do so. I suppose it's just a case that I've suppressed it for so long, I now find it terribly difficult to contemplate, let alone talk about. I dare say my gesture of producing Bronwen's dance card with accompanying hints struck you as self-indulgently theatrical. I apologise. As I say, I have buried the knowledge of that episode so deep within me that it requires an immense, almost physical, effort to dredge it up again and these days my physical resources are limited. I might also say, in mitigation of my coyness, self-indulgence and theatricality, that it's not easy to break the habits of a lifetime.

Anyway so much for explanations and self-justification. Today has been rather a momentous day. I have finally come to terms with the fact of my imminent death. My doctor, bless him, still goes through convolutions to avoid stating the obvious and to find an aspect of my impressive range of ailments about which he can say something remotely encouraging. Like me, however, he is fighting a losing battle, the futility of which becomes more pronounced by the day. His whole demeanour delivers an unmistakable message which he can't bring himself to put into words. In the wider scheme of things, of course, this is making a drama out of the all-too-mundane; after all, I could hardly expect the laws of nature and medicine to be suspended on my behalf, could I? Nonetheless one lives in hope. Well, I no longer do. I shall now concentrate on dying in peace.

The significance of my embracing fatalism is that it has concentrated the mind on the task of clearing out the emotional and spiritual baggage which I either won't need or don't want where I'm going. I have therefore resolved to tell you the full story of what happened at Prince Albert College in 1970. I shall write it down and have it sent to you when I've shuffled off this mortal coil. I know that's somewhat cowardly but it's the only way I can do it. It also has for me the immense attraction that I won't have to live with the knowledge of your contempt, for assuredly that is what you'll feel towards me when you've finished this letter. Your friendship and sympathy has meant a great deal to me and I am selfish enough to want to retain them for the short while I have left.

To begin at the beginning: I'm not sure how old I was when I began to suspect that I was gay but certainly by the time I started at Prince Albert in 1968. Of course, you were a day boy and I'm not sure how much naughtiness went on amongst the day boys. In most boarding house dormitories, though, there was a constant hum of furtive activity, mostly what we called "mutuals" — tossing off the boy in the next bed after lights out providing he'd return the favour.

If I had put a figure on it, I'd estimate that at least fifty per cent of boarders indulged in boy-boy sex. It had nothing to do with homosexuality in the sense of being their sexual preference; it was simply a case of deprivation, through being in an all-male environment, on one hand, and opportunity on the other. Sheer proximity is, after all, the most potent aphrodisiac. I can't say I ever came across anyone who I refused to indulge because they had fierce moral objections; most of the non-participants either had extremely modest sexual appetites or were too timid or were so repulsive that no one with an ounce of self-respect would handle them wearing ski mitts.

As I say, there was no particular opprobrium attached to it in one's first and second year but once one reached fifth form, it was a different matter. To continue from that point was considered to denote a preference; far healthier to satisfy one's urges in privacy with *Playboy* and a wankie hankie. Those who kept at it were either too ugly or socially inept to get their fingers up during the holidays (excuse the coarseness but the disgusting schoolboy phraseology keeps popping into my head), or were blessed or cursed with excessive randiness or belonged to the tiny minority who just preferred boys and didn't give a hoot for the consequences in terms of being whispered about, sneered at or bullied. With all due modesty, I was the outstanding example of the latter. I have no doubt that I was the most sexually active Prince Albertian of my era; a respectable but nonetheless distant second would have been Caspar Quedley, which is where the tale really begins.

I became infatuated with Caspar in 1969, an easy enough date to remember. He was scarcely aware of my existence; with me being a second year and him a fourth year there were, under the rigid hierarchy of the boarding houses, limited opportunities for contact. Early the following year, however, we were both in the school play, *Julius Caesar*. Caspar was a thrilling Mark Antony while I had a non-speaking part as one of the friends, Romans, countrymen whose ears he borrowed. In the course of the rehearsals, I managed to inveigle my way into his acquaintance and, at the first opportunity, proclaimed my love and put myself at his disposal. Caspar wasn't in the least embarrassed or perturbed. He said he was flattered but didn't think it was quite his cup of Earl Grey; if he ever changed his mind or felt the inclination to experiment, he'd know where to come, as it were.

We became friends. We were both outsiders, in my case because of my hotly and widely rumoured filthy and unnatural tendencies; in Caspar's because he saw himself as underprivileged — it never ceased to amaze me how someone so well-endowed could feel so deprived — and this drew us together. Caspar didn't give a damn and had a perverse sense of humour so it amused him, being the official college stud, to ostentatiously keep company with the college queer. He also took an intense interest in what I got up to and insisted on being kept fully informed of my dalliances. I thought this was rather promising until I discovered that he was extracting money from some of my partners on threat of exposure. I was furious at first but Caspar could talk his way out of anything. He was also a very skilful flirt which kept alive the tantalising prospect of my yearnings being reciprocated, in my mind at least.

I was quite a holy boy, believe it or not. I was in the choir, by that stage a light tenor after a stint as the boy soprano — you might have heard me doing the "Once in Royal David's City" solo at the end-of-year carol service. I was also a sacristan which involved helping the chaplain, Padre Swindell, with various little chores around the chapel. The chaplain took a shine to me and was forever inviting me into his flat for a cup of tea and a chocolate biscuit. I thought nothing of this until one night he completely floored me by producing a cane and imploring me to thrash him. Not wanting to seem churlish, I obliged and the poor old thing just about put his back out trying to conceal his erection.

I'm sure you can guess the rest. I told Caspar who straightaway saw the commercial possibilities. The next time I took tea with the chaplain, I left the door off the lock and Caspar just happened to wander in while I was administering the medicine. He pretended to be shocked, horrified, revolted etc. — he really was a superb actor — then told me to clear off so he could negotiate the price of his silence. Caspar told me afterwards that the chaplain was as worried about me as about his own position: he said something to the effect that "Julian is innocent in every sense of the word; he has no idea that he was providing me with gratification". That made it even worse when he drove his car into a brick wall a few weeks later.

Although it was presented as an accident, the rumours of suicide were soon rife. I worked myself into a real state. Caspar eventually gave me a talking to: yes, Padre Swindell had killed himself, he said, but it had nothing to do with us. He claimed the chaplain had an incurable disease, hence the suicide. It was a lie, of course, as he admitted a few years later. He was worried that I'd break down and confess all and had made up the story to subdue my conscience.

After that you'd think we'd have shied away from these dangerous games but not a bit of it. The next to find his way into the honey trap was Lloyd Chennell, who taught history as you'd remember and was assistant house master in my house. However, Lloyd was far from being a passive, guilt-ridden soul that Padre Swindell had been. I began picking up unmistakable signals from him and one night in his study, in the course of reviewing my academic performance, came the inevitable hand on the knee.

Although Lloyd was certainly no matinee idol, he was really my first sexual partner who was more experienced than me — he was about twenty-six then as I remember. A number of the boys I'd been with were older than me but I was always the knowing one, the one in control. Lloyd was quite adroit; he had the touch. Some do and some don't and, in my experience, it's almost impossible to tell in advance. Nor does having the touch seem to bear much, if any, relation to a person's general sexiness either in terms of their appearance or their ardour. Some of my most handsome and ardent lovers have been the most ham-fisted.

Of course I told Caspar and shortly thereafter he struck terms with Lloyd. It all seemed to be conducted in a very civilised manner. Lloyd certainly never took umbrage with me for telling Caspar, although I suppose, in hindsight, he was rather addicted to me. Quite what Caspar got out of it I'm not sure — far more, in various ways, than he let on would be my guess. There was money of course and the famous episode with the exam paper which almost gave Lloyd a heart attack. He slipped Caspar the paper in advance solely for his own benefit, never dreaming that he'd make copies and sell them. Theirs was a curious relationship, not friendship exactly but certainly not the fear and loathing you'd expect under the circumstances. Perhaps Lloyd was bedazzled by Caspar too.

I'm sure you've found all this exceedingly distasteful and boring but I assure you it is relevant. So we come to the 1970 school ball. Needless to say I didn't go. The non-attendees had a free night but I stayed in. I forget why — it mustn't have suited my parents to have me home. Lloyd was one of the masters whose job it was to wander round at the ball and discourage tongue kissing and dry uprights (there I go again) on the dance floor. He suggested to me that if I felt left out, he could slip away from the ball at some point for a quickie. We arranged a rendezvous in the belltower, above the library, at 10.45 p.m.

I don't know if you ever saw that place but if you went up that spiral staircase from the library floor, you found yourself in this series of little rooms, a bit of a rabbit warren really, which were essentially used for storage. They contained the overflow from the library, books which had been weeded out, old furniture etc. We were in the third or fourth room along, playing with one another in the dark, when we heard approaching footsteps and the murmur of voices, one of which was unmistakably female.

We froze as they advanced through the rooms towards us. They stopped in the one next to ours. There were no doors — just a series of connecting rooms opening into one another — so we could hear every word. There were two boys and a girl and they'd come up for a smoke and a tipple. They debated whether or not to turn on the light; one of the boys; obviously the ring leader, said they wouldn't be able to see what they were doing otherwise and what did it matter anyway, there were no windows and who the hell was going to come up? So they switched on a light and began puffing and swigging and sniggering. Meanwhile Lloyd and I crouched in the dark just round the corner not even daring to put our trousers back on for fear of giving ourselves away. Lloyd, needless to say, was almost paralysed with fear.

After ten minutes or so of eavesdropping, I'd worked out that the boys were Dermot Looms, a prime example of the large farm-bred louts whom Prince Albert seemed to attract, and Basil Batrouney, a creepy youth known for his musical pretensions.

It was apparent that something was amiss with the girl, whose name was Bronwen. Before long we learned that the agent of her unhappiness was none other than Caspar Quedley. From what we could gather, Bronwen had a major crush on Caspar but he'd just made it plain that it wasn't reciprocated. I couldn't help thinking, welcome to the club, sister.

After what seemed like forever but was probably less than half an hour, the booze — they had a bottle of brandy, Portuguese I think it was — was taking its toll. Bronwen started sniffling. Looms suggested that Caspar wasn't the only fish in the sea and why didn't she forget about him and have some fun. Nothing was said for a little while — I suspect she was sitting there a bit bamboozled by the brandy while Looms nibbled on her. Then the trouble started. Looms tried to force the pace and Batrouney wanted to join in. Whether they lured her up there with the aim of getting her drunk and taking turns or whether it was spur of the moment, I just don't know. Whatever, she was having none of it. She hissed at them to fuck off and leave her alone, that she wouldn't kiss Batrouney if he was the last boy on earth and that if Looms thought she'd take her panties off for him, he was even stupider than he looked. Looms called her a cockteaser; Batrouney accused her of being a stuck-up bitch. The voices got louder as the violence of their language escalated. She said they could screw each other for all she cared but she was going; Looms roared back, like hell you are; she screamed at him to let her go. There was the sound of a struggle and a sharp slap; Looms called her a fucking slut, and then I heard this indescribable rasping choke. Without thinking about it, I ran in there pulling on my pants and screaming at them to stop it.

Then the four of us were staring at each other, thunderstruck, struggling to make sense of the evidence of our own eyes. The girl lay on the floor between us. At first, of course, none of us believed she was dead — we thought she'd fainted — and our concerns centred on having been caught in the act of considerably lesser crimes, although Lloyd was staring professional ruin in the face. For a minute no one said anything. When I broke the silence by asking if the girl was all right, Looms knelt over her and tried to bring her round. Then he stood up and said quite calmly, "I'd say she's dead." She'd slapped him and he'd seized her by the throat and throttled her. It wouldn't have taken much; he was big and strong and Bronwen was quite delicate. Looms looked at Lloyd and said, "Sir, I think it would be for the best if we all forget what's happened here."

He was astonishingly cool. Batrouney was dazed — he was quite drunk and I don't think he really comprehended the situation; I was crying; Lloyd was in a state of shock, looking from Bronwen to Looms and saying, "Of course, of course" over and over. Then he seemed to snap out of it. What was extraordinary then was how he and Looms suddenly seemed to be on the same wavelength. Crises create strange alliances, I suppose. It was only later that I came to realise that from Lloyd's point of view, Bronwen dying was a godsend. Her death necessitated the conspiracy of silence which also enveloped the lesser crimes and misdemeanours, of which his was by far the most serious.

He and Looms organised it between them. The hanging was Lloyd's idea. They used my tie; I was in the ordinary evening uniform, those pants that chaffed like mad and a blazer with a standard school tie. The other two were in full black suits and couldn't go back into the ball without a tie, nor could Lloyd, so I had to provide the noose. There was a sturdy rail which must've been used for a curtain or drape to block off the doorway and they hung her from that. Lloyd looped the tie round her neck and stood on a chair to attach it to the rail while Looms held Bronwen off the ground. Then he let her go and she dangled there like a broken doll.

Lloyd told me to get back to the house and to go straight to bed, not to talk to anyone, and to see him the next morning. When I undressed, I found her dance card in my coat pocket. I didn't even remember picking it up. The next day Lloyd gave me a lecture about how it was a terrible accident, they hadn't meant to kill her, but what was done was done and nothing that happened now would bring her back. If the truth got out, all our lives would be ruined so it was better to forget about it, to pretend it never happened. He said I had to be really tough and tell absolutely no one even though there would be times when I'd want nothing more than to confide in someone to get it off my chest. It must've had some effect I suppose; until today I never told anyone. He also found me a new tie from somewhere.

I never went with Lloyd again. We did talk about Bronwen a few times; I remember asking him why it never came out that Bronwen had been drinking. He said they would've hushed it up for her parents' sake. For weeks afterwards I expected to be called down to the housemaster's study to find a policeman waiting for me but it never happened. Eventually, it dawned on me that it suited everybody — except the Ticehurst family — to treat it as suicide. If the truth had come out, the scandal would've rocked Prince Albert to its foundations and there was far too much money and power and prestige tied up in the school itself and the old boy network — the old school tie syndrome — for that to be allowed to happen. Probably still is.

Perhaps you think that's cynical. Then consider this: if they knew that Bronwen had been drinking, it would've been a reasonable, if not irresistible, assumption that she wouldn't have done so on her own. Not many sixteen-year-old girls are solo drinkers and she'd hardly have headed off to the ball with a bottle of brandy in her handbag. That opens up all sorts of scenarios, so why didn't the police make an effort to find out who her drinking companions were?

Secondly, how was she supposed to have found her way up to the belltower? Some of the boys wouldn't have even known those rooms were up there. Thirdly, remember how we had to have a name label stitched onto every item of clothing including ties? Lloyd ripped the label off my tie; did the police think Bronwen had done it herself? And where had she got the tie from in the first place?

So there you are Victor. It hasn't salved my conscience but I feel better for knowing that I won't be taking this secret with me. Now that you know, what are you going to do with the knowledge? I'm sure you've heard the old curse — Chinese? — that may you get what you always wanted? I find it hard to imagine that your peace of mind will be enhanced should you pursue the matter — if anything the reverse. On the other hand, I can vouch for the fact that to know and keep silent eats away at the soul like acid.

God bless you
Julian Gage

When he'd finished reading the letter, Sparks rang Tito Ihaka.

"Thanks for sending me Gage's letter."

"That's okay Reggie. Use it wisely."

"Was he right?"

"What about?"

"You know what I'm talking about — that the investigation was tanked because it suited everyone to call it suicide?"

"How the fuck would I know? I was nine years old."

"Don't pretend you haven't looked at the file."

"Sparks, are you asking me as a journalist?"

"Yes."

"In that case, the answer to your question is no, Gage wasn't right. The investigation was properly conducted and thorough in every aspect."

"Okay, just between the two of us."

Ihaka said, "Between the two of us, I'm surprised you have to ask," and put the phone down.

Two days later, a Wednesday, a foretaste of summer arrived unheralded to Auckland. A warm wind blew in from the north and the temperature nudged over 20 degrees for the first time in months. Reggie Sparks was driving Louise Appleyard to the airport to catch a plane to Brisbane. She was going to spend some time with her sister; an indefinite amount of time.

As they skimmed alongside the Manukau Harbour foreshore she asked, "Did you see Gage's letter in the end?"

"Yeah, Ihaka sent me a copy."

"What did you think?"

Sparks looked at Louise who looked back at him through big dark glasses. Her window was half open and the breeze whipped around her head, fluffing up her dark mane.

"I thought it was sad. Sad for Bronwen, sad for Gage, sad for Victor."

She nodded. "I've been meaning to ask," she said. "What made you go up to Looms' farm? I mean, how did you know?"

"I didn't have to be Sherlock Holmes. Delamore knew the whole story because he'd had Gage's letter; I knew he'd gone north when Quedley said Delamore had told him he was going to talk to someone else about the letter, the obvious conclusion was that he'd gone to see Looms."

"Where's he by the way?"

Sparks smiled. "Delamore? He went back to Sydney to get his face fixed up. He said if they could make him pretty again, he'd go back in the drag show. He's decided he's not quite devious enough to operate on the edge, plus it's too hard on his looks."

"Second question. How did you know Looms had co-murdered Victor?"

"Oh that was just an educated guess. It seemed to me all along that if Victor was murdered, whoever killed Bronwen must've done it. But I was just trying to give you a bit of motivation."

"Well, you did. I needed some."

After a while he asked, "So why did you go up there?"

Louise gave him a brilliant, slightly mocking smile. "Reggie, don't tell me you haven't figured that out. You've been so clever about everything else."

He shook his head. "Sorry, you got me there."

"Because," she said, stretching out the word, "Tito thought you might be in danger."

Sparks nodded slowly. "Oh that's why? And here was I thinking you just wanted the chance to shoot someone."

He pulled up in front of the overseas terminal and carried her bags inside. She thanked him for the lift and told him not to wait around.

"Okay." He hovered awkwardly. "Well, have a nice trip."

"Thanks." She gave him a long look. It was part amusement and part fondness. He thought there might have been a part something else too but seeing she was going and hadn't booked her return, he felt it was prudent to settle for amused and fond. "Reggie, I've been thinking that in a few weeks' time, when my sister and I are no longer on speaking terms, I might come home via New Caledonia. You speak French don't you?"

"Yeah, pretty well. I used to think it was my only attribute but it's not a lot of use to me here."

"Oh, it's definitely an attribute. I was wondering, perhaps you could come up and be my interpreter, you know, and introduce me to French culture and whatnot. Don't worry about the money — I'd take care of that, now that I'm rich." She tilted her head and raised her eyebrows questioningly.

"Sounds great," said Sparks hesitantly, wondering if he dared believe his ears. "But forget that stuff about paying for me — I'd feel like a kept man."

Louise nodded gravely. "Yes you're probably right. First of all I'd want to be sure you were worth keeping."

She gave him a sly smile from beneath lowered lashes that would throw his sleep patterns into disarray for several days, put one hand on his chest, and kissed him softly on the lips. "I'll be in touch."

Sparks drove home feeling slightly light-headed. He went straight to the desk he'd installed in the downstairs TV room. On the desk was a laptop computer which his brother Gavin had lent him and pages and pages of notes. Sparks studied his notes for a while, turned on the computer and stared at the illuminated screen.

Then he started to write: It was entirely appropriate that Wallace Guttle, the private investigator, should have spent the last hour of his life looking at pictures of other people having sex . . .

Inside Dope

Prologue

On a soft, overcast night in October 1983, a thirty-eight-foot yacht skimmed down the section of Coromandel Peninsula's east coast which faces Great Mercury Island on a fifteen-knot breeze from the north-west. Shortly before 3 a.m. it hove-to off the long sweep of white-gold sand which is Otama Beach.

Running Dog was owned by a charter company operating from the Rushcutters Bay marina in inner east Sydney. Ostensibly, it had been chartered to cruise the Whitsundays; however, after clearing Sydney heads six days earlier, the crew had turned *Running Dog* right rather than left and set sail for New Zealand. The crew consisted of the Dawes brothers, Bruce and Ron, a pair of minor and slightly disreputable identities in Sydney boating circles. Their fee for lying to the charter company, sailing *Running Dog* across the Tasman and back, and maintaining an attitude of total incuriosity towards the whole exercise, was A$10,000 which more than doubled their joint earnings for the year to that point.

Having to carry out their assignment on a "no questions asked" basis didn't unduly bother the Dawes brothers: Ron's intellectual curiosity hardly extended beyond marine engines and weather patterns; Bruce, who was more worldly, didn't need to ask what it was all in aid of because he already knew. There was only one reason why anyone would pay ten grand for a clandestine boat ride to New Zealand and that was drugs. He assumed that the drugs in question were in the large white plastic chilly bin which their client, who called himself John Brown, hadn't let out of his sight since they'd motored out of the marina.

Ron Dawes dropped the mainsail and the yacht rolled lazily on the gentle swell.

Only the occasional slap of the sea against the hull and the rhythmic murmur of little waves licking at the sand 100 metres away disturbed the hush which falls on an empty stretch of coast in the dead of night. No lights shone.

"This is it, Mr Brown," said Bruce Dawes. "You want me to give the signal?"

Brown nodded. Dawes stood up in the cockpit and pointed a heavy torch at the shore. He flicked the beam on and off three times, waited a few seconds, then repeated the signal. An answering signal — two flashes, pause, one flash — came from the beach.

Brown gave Bruce Dawes a quick, nervous grin. "Sweet as a rat," he said. "I'll just grab my stuff from down below."

"Drop the pick, Ron," said his brother. "Nice and quiet."

Five minutes later Bruce Dawes called down to Brown in the cabin that the pick-up boat was approaching.

"Righto," he replied. "You and Ron better hop down here. This bloke's a bit shy."

Brown came up on deck. He wore a bulky black anorak and carried the chilly bin in one hand and a nylon sports bag in the other. He put the bag down and lent over the rail to shine the torch on the aluminium dinghy which was drawing up alongside the yacht. He didn't like what he saw.

"Who the fuck might you be?" said Brown, biting off the words angrily.

The man in the dinghy, who was burly and dark with a Zapata moustache which threatened to overgrow the lower half of his face, held up a hand to shield his eyes from the torch beam.

"No names till you're off there, eh?" he said. "You Know Who sent me."

"Where the hell did he get to?" said Brown. "He was meant to be here."

"Come on, mate. Since when did you catch him up to this sort of caper — buggering around in the tide at this hour of the night?"

Brown stared down at the man in the dinghy for a few seconds then let out an exasperated lungful of air. He dropped the sports bag into the dinghy and called down to the Dawes brothers: "Thanks for the ride, fellas. Safe trip home."

Brown, whose real name was Dale Varty, climbed over the rail and lowered himself into the dinghy. He sat in the stern facing the other man, so close that their knees touched. When they'd pulled clear of the yacht, the oarsman introduced himself.

"Grills is the name, Al Grills. I do stuff for Spurdle."

"Pleased to meet you, I'm sure," said Varty sourly. "Nice of Spurdle to warn me I'd be collected by someone I don't know from a bar of soap."

"Shit, you know what he's like about security." Grills nodded at the chilly bin between Varty's knees. "In there, is it?"

"Could be."

Grills chuckled. "You're as cagey as he is."

When they were a few metres from the shore, Grills shipped the oars. "Now you just sit tight, Varty. Wouldn't want you to get your tootsies wet."

He stepped carefully into the sea which came up to his knees and pulled the dinghy to the shore. Varty threw his sports bag onto the beach and climbed out over the prow. He helped Grills drag the dinghy a little way up the beach.

"What do we do with this?" asked Varty, indicating the dinghy.

"What do you bloody think?" demanded Grills. "We take it with us. I've got a trailer on the car. Stick your stuff in there and we'll carry it."

They carried the dinghy up the beach, through some low dunes and up a track past a few obviously unoccupied beach houses clustered in a small hollow, to the shingle road where Grills' car was parked. Varty was getting the chilly bin out of the dinghy when Grills walked around from the other side of the car and said, "Oh by the way, Spurdle jacked up a little welcome home surprise for you."

Varty turned around. Grills was grinning mirthlessly and pointing a sawn-off .22 rifle at him.

"What is this — you trying to ratfuck me?" said Varty, his voice shaking with alarm. "Spurdle and me had a deal."

Grills, still grinning, raised his eyebrows. "If I was in your shoes pal, getting ratfucked would be the least of my worries." He nodded at the chilly bin. "Open it."

Varty released the clasps and removed the lid.

"Back off," commanded Grills.

Varty stepped back a few paces. Grills came forward and peered into the chilly bin. Evidently, he liked what he saw because he straightened up, nodding with satisfaction. He was still nodding when a figure materialised out of the darkness and slammed him over the head with a shovel. It was a savage blow, so savage that it wouldn't have added to Varty's bewilderment if Grills had been driven into the ground like a tent peg. Instead, he crumpled like a crushed beer can as the sharp, bony clang of metal on skull echoed faintly in the stillness.

The newcomer was tall and wide-shouldered. He wore a long navy-blue raincoat, gloves, jeans, a turtle-neck pullover and had a stocking over his head. He put down the shovel, picked up the rifle and, with his other hand, reached into the chilly bin and brought out a sealed plastic bag tightly packed with white powder.

"How much crank we got here?" he asked.

It was a voice from the right side of the tracks; Varty was sure he'd never heard it before. "Ten kilos," he said.

The man whistled briefly, dropped the bag back in the chilly bin, snapped the lid on, and put the bin on the back seat of Grills' car.

"My car's half a mile back up the road," he said to Varty. "I'll leave this one there for you."

He climbed in behind the steering wheel.

"Jesus Christ, hang on a sec," said Varty, running around to the driver's side. "Who the hell are you?"

The man in the stocking mask wound down the window. "Under the circumstances," he said, "I'd say I'm your guardian angel — especially seeing my instructions were to let him finish you off before I grabbed the stuff."

"Instructions? Who from?"

The newcomer laughed, a rich, deep, pleasant sound. "I think that'd better remain my little secret. See you."

"What about him?" asked Varty, jerking his head towards Grills, who lay in an awkward heap.

"My sentiments exactly," said the man in the stocking mask. Then he started Grills' car and drove away.

For a few minutes Varty puzzled over the mystery man's identity and how he'd been able to crash a party that was meant to be the best-kept secret since D-Day. How many people knew he was coming into Otama tonight with a cargo of cocaine? Obviously, that cunt Spurdle, but why would he want to pull some sort of triple-cross? His off-sider Grills, lying there with a caved-in scone? Safe to assume he wasn't in on plan C. The Dawes brothers, in a manner of speaking, but they didn't find out Otama was the rendezvous point until a couple of hours ago. That's it.

Eventually, Varty decided that figuring it out would take a lot more time than he could afford just then and turned his mind to more pressing matters. It was a good thing that he knew this part of the Coromandel like the back of his hand. It was an even better thing that just before he'd got off the yacht, he'd taken the plastic bags containing the ten kilos of pure cocaine out of the chilly bin and taped them to his body. When the mystery man discovered that all he'd scored was a shitload of high-grade Australian icing sugar, when Grills came to, and when Spurdle found out he'd been shafted, things were going to get too hairy for comfort. He had to hide the dope somewhere and then disappear, just get lost.

As it happened, Varty needn't have worried about what Grills would do when he regained consciousness, because he never did.

1

It was an awful scream, even by Asian prison standards. The fact that it was so quiet in the cell at the time made it all the more unnerving.

The only sounds were the rustle of magazine pages being turned; the German humming softly to himself as he listened to his Walkman; the occasional moan from the Cambodian who had a large, ugly, and, judging by the smell, possibly gangrenous wound on his right ankle — caused by the leg irons he wore as a punishment for having seriously bucked prison discipline, although no one in the cell seemed to know exactly how — and the quiet murmur of conversation coming from the corner furthest from the open toilet where Duane Ricketts was playing Scrabble with one of the Nigerians.

As usual he was being trounced. Ricketts seldom won at Scrabble against any of the Nigerians and never against his opponent on this occasion, Augustine Adeyemi, the acknowledged leader of the seven Nigerian nationals incarcerated in the Bombat Drug Rehabilitation Centre which is located on the outskirts of Bangkok.

The name is entirely misleading since there is no rehabilitation involved in doing time in Bombat. It is simply a place where men found guilty of drug offences, usually of a minor nature, are sent to serve their sentences and, for all the authorities care, rot, as the Cambodian with the leg irons seemed to be doing.

At any given time there are approximately 2000 prisoners in Bombat, which comprises five compounds, each compound having a building containing up to twenty cells. This particular cell was on the first floor of building four and was notable for the mix of nationalities it contained. Apart from Thais, there were Cambodians, Australians, New Zealanders, a Dutchman, a German, an American and a Singaporean. And, of course, the Nigerians.

The presence of so many Nigerians in a Thai jail had come as a surprise to Ricketts. With undisguised pride Adeyemi had informed him that Nigerians were the world's best and most active drug smugglers, a status which had been officially bestowed in a recent report on international drug trafficking issued by the US State Department.

Bombat is a short-stay prison. Most of the inmates have been sentenced to terms of up to two years or are awaiting trial on charges which carry sentences of that duration when — rather than if — they are found guilty. There were exceptions: Dale Varty, like Ricketts a New Zealander, was nearing completion of a ten-year term and had been transferred to Bombat to await release.

Adeyemi owed his presence in Bombat to the fact that when he was stopped by customs agents at Bangkok International Airport carrying, as he put it, "enough number one China White to put Switzerland to sleep." He'd also had ten thousand American dollars in his money belt. At Adeyemi's suggestion, the two customs agents had split the money, taken the heroin, which no doubt found its way back to circulation within twenty-four hours, and replaced it with a small plastic bag containing two dozen marijuana seeds. As a result, Adeyemi had been sentenced to nine months in Bombat as opposed to twenty years or even life — which really amount to the same thing — in an even grimmer institution.

Ricketts called Adeyemi "Jumbo" after a cricket bat he'd once had. The bat was a Stuart Surridge Jumbo, 3 lbs 2 oz of finest English willow. When he'd got used to the extra weight, Ricketts relished the extra power the bat gave his strokes. At Keith Hay Park one summery Saturday afternoon he'd played a hook shot which struck the square leg umpire on the left knee, shattering his kneecap. The ball had then cannoned off to the long-on boundary with scarcely diminished velocity. Ricketts had grown to love that bat.

Like most of the Nigerians, Adeyemi talked a great deal about — and sometimes to — his penis. Generally, these monologues dwelt on his member's size, beauty and capacity to gratify the opposite sex. Now and again, he'd expand on this theme to muse on the white race's shortcomings in the penis department and what a pity it was that prejudice, culture and circumstance so often conspired to keep apart black men and white women who, he believed, had much to offer one another. Jumbo's penis and his deep attachment to it reminded Ricketts of his bat, hence the nickname. Adeyemi thought it had something to do with elephants.

Ricketts got on well with the Nigerians. He didn't moan incessantly like most of the other first worlders — as far as the Nigerians were concerned, spending time in prisons such as Bombat was just an occupational hazard — and he took his humiliations at Scrabble philosophically. Early on he'd got into their good books by teaching them a song he'd learned at intermediate school. To the tune of "Finiculee, Finicula" the song went:
"Last night I had the urge for masturbation
And it was strong, and it was strong;
I took my penis in my right hand —
What a prong, what a prong;
I switched it to my left hand
And pulled it long, and pulled it long.
Whack it, smack it, bash it against the wall;
Pinch it, punch it, anything at all:
Because it's long, because it's strong, because it's twice the length of me!
Forty pounds of penis hanging down between my knees."

The song delighted the Nigerians, none of whom, as Ricketts had reluctantly but unavoidably observed, could be accused of singing it under false pretences. It immediately became part of the programme for their nightly choral sessions. Sometimes they would be faithful to the traditional arrangement and perform it rousingly, in the style of a Gilbert and Sullivan chorus; other nights, perhaps when homesickness weighed upon them, it would be transformed almost beyond recognition into a quiet and rather mournful African chant.

As well as being the best hung inmate in Bombat prison, Jumbo was the leading Scrabble player. This was no surprise to Ricketts who estimated that Jumbo spent approximately one third of his waking hours playing the game, one third studying the dictionary to find new words, and the balance talking about — or to — his penis.

At 4 o'clock that afternoon the prisoners, as was customary, had been allowed to escape the heat and humidity of the compound and return to the marginally less oppressive environment of their cells. The Nigerians were very well organised, having Thai bank accounts which they could access from prison to buy in supplies. As a result, they ate well by Bombat standards. Prison fare, eaten only by those prisoners who couldn't afford to feed themselves, was two helpings of brown rice with fish heads a day. That lunchtime, for instance, Jumbo had cooked a remarkably tasty chicken and rice dish on the charcoal cooker in the compound, which Ricketts, on account of his honorary Nigerian status, had been invited to share. Thus when Jumbo suggested a game of Scrabble on their return to the cell, Ricketts was in no position to decline, even though yet another drubbing was about the last thing he felt like. They'd spread out their cardboard mattresses and made themselves as comfortable as possible on the stone floor.

After they'd traded monosyllables, Ricketts added –OZE to a D to make *doze*. With Z being a ten pointer and a triple letter score on the E, this was worth sixteen points and represented a steady, even promising, start by his standards; usually when he drew high-scoring but uncommon letters like Z and X, he could never find a way to use them.

Jumbo's response was devastating: he added an R to *doze* making *dozer* then, doubling up on the R and using a blank for the second X, laid *xeroxed* down the right-hand column. It began on a triple word score and the second X fell on a double letter score.

"That's a brand name," protested Ricketts. "You can't use that."

Jumbo shook his huge head. "Oh no man," he said serenely. "That's a fine word."

He reached for his *Concise Oxford Dictionary*, opened it, coughed politely, and began to read: "Xerox: reproduce by a certain process of xerography." He snapped the dictionary shut. "Now then." He counted his score: "Your word's worth fifteen to me, Xeroxed is twenty-two times three equals sixty-six, then add fifty for using all the letters — that's . . . 131. Extremely bloody good."

A few turns later Jumbo built *adipocere* and leant back with his head tilted to one side, admiring his handiwork. Noticing Ricketts' bleak expression, he grinned massively and said: "Hey boss, you like that one?"

"Come on, Jumbo," whined Ricketts half-heartedly. "What the fuck sort of word is that?"

"Man, you've got to learn to trust folks," said Jumbo with a satisfied smile. He reached for his dictionary again. "Where are we? Okay, adipocere: greyish fatty or soapy substance generated in dead bodies subjected to moisture."

Ricketts grimaced. "Useful word for a lifeguard."

"I've been storing that little fellow up for weeks. Thought I'd never get to . . ."

It was right then that they heard the scream. It came from the stairwell through the open door on the far side of the cell. After three weeks of sharing a ten square metre cell with thirty-eight men, some of whom, perhaps as a result of habitual drug-taking or maybe because they were born that way, undoubtedly weren't altogether sane, Ricketts had got used to hearing strange, even disturbing, noises, particularly in the night. The scream was different: raw, shrill, agonised.

Whatever anyone in the cell was doing — leaning against a wall daydreaming of home, red meat and clean sheets, lying on the concrete floor hoping to doze off and wake up a year later, flicking through a dog-eared magazine or playing Scrabble — they stopped doing it.

"Holy Christ," said Ricketts. "What was that?"

Jumbo leaned back and shrugged. "Probably just another little yellow monkey getting his lumps. It's your go."

For the Thai prisoners, being beaten by the guards for such transgressions as not bowing low enough when walking past a guard or not grovelling sufficiently when speaking to one was part of Bombat routine. The beatings usually consisted of a truncheon drum roll on the skull, followed by a stomping, with a top to toe thrashing with a long stick to finish off. If he knew what was good for him, the victim would then thank the guard profusely for his time and trouble. The Nigerians, who appeared to despise all Thais, found these performances mildly entertaining and occasionally signalled their appreciation with a polite round of applause.

Ricketts shook his head. "That wasn't a Thai getting worked over; one thing about the little buggers, they take their medicine without a peep." He stood up. "I'm going to have a look."

Jumbo tut-tutted. "Duane man, it's not your problem."

Ricketts made his way across the cell, stepping carefully over and around his cellmates who followed his progress with mute interest. He went through the doorway to the stairwell and looked up the steps which led to an identical cell on the next level. Halfway up the steps, wearing his trademark abbreviated cut-off Levis and striking a dramatic pose, was the Thai ladyboy who called himself Brandi.

The transvestite looked down at Ricketts wide-eyed, one hand pressed to his mouth, then back up to the landing above. Ricketts went up past him, taking the steps two at a time. Dale Varty, the fifty-three-year-old narcotics entrepreneur, was slumped on the landing, his face screwed up in pain. He was bleeding hard from the stomach. Standing over Varty with a knife in his hand as if trying to decide where to make the next incision was a Thai prisoner whose name Ricketts didn't know.

Brandi and the Thai with the blade were known around the compound as an item. Ricketts had heard talk that if one was that way inclined or perhaps just horny in a broad-minded sort of a way, Brandi was open to offers. The fine print was that the boyfriend wasn't too keen on Brandi taking his love to town nor was he someone who, if you'd upset him, it was smart to turn your back on. Given the talk and the scene which confronted him, Ricketts guessed that the stabbing was sex-related. The fact that Varty's shorts were around his ankles tended to support that theory.

Ricketts said, "Jesus, Dale . . ."

The Thai shouted belligerently and inched forward, jabbing the air with his blood-streaked blade. It looked to Ricketts like the blade had started life as a pretty harmless piece of cutlery and, through hard work and application, grown up to be a fair imitation of a boning knife. It also looked to Ricketts as if the Thai had decided that he might as well be hung for spiking two blue-eyed foreign devils as one.

Ricketts took a step back and held up his hands in a let's-not-do-anything-hasty gesture. When the Thai stopped advancing, Ricketts pointed down at Varty.

"He's in a bad way," he said earnestly. "He needs a doctor."

The Thai's flat eyes flickered to Varty. He spat copiously, missing Varty's left ear by no more than three centimetres, and muttered something which Ricketts interpreted as Thai for 'stiff shit'. Then he scuttled past Ricketts and headed downstairs. As he did so, Ricketts flicked out a foot to clip his heel. The Thai bounced three times on his way to the lower floor where he slid to a halt in a flurry of arms and legs at the feet of a guard who'd come to investigate. The guard proceeded to lay into him with his truncheon, presumably for failing to prostrate himself satisfactorily.

"Get a doctor," Ricketts yelled. "There's a man here's been stabbed."

The guard gave the prisoner a final fierce backhander then started up the steps. He looked inquiringly at the ladyboy who was still emoting silently halfway up the stairway. On the landing he stared impassively down at Varty who lay on his back clutching his stomach. Blood was leaking between his fingers and running onto his bare thighs. The guard sat on his haunches and with surprising gentleness moved Varty's hands and inspected the damage. Having completed his inspection, he stood up, nodded curtly at Ricketts, skipped down the stairs, and led the Thai prisoner away by the hair.

Ricketts knelt beside Varty.

"Christ mate, what happened?"

Varty closed his eyes. "What a way to go," he croaked. "Knifed in mid-blowjob by a jealous slope fag. The ladyboy's been waving her tongue at me ever since I got here. Well, shit, there was nothing like that in the other joint so I figured why not? When I thought the boyfriend was asleep, I offered her a packet of Marlboros for a BJ. We came up here and were getting along like a house on fire when the little cunt crept up and stuck me. Didn't even get my rocks off." He sighed heavily. "Fuck, it's been that long, when the mutton gun went off, it would've been like a flock of seagulls flying backwards out of my arse."

Varty released a short, bitter chuckle which ended as a groan. "Talk about a fucking loser — you know I was getting out next week?"

"You'll be right mate," said Ricketts. "They'll fix you up. You'll be on the plane home before you know it."

Varty's head lolled back. He tilted it up again with a grunt of effort and focused blearily on Ricketts. "Come on, pal. He carved me like a Sunday joint. Besides, imagine the fucking bugs'd be on that knife." As if to validate his diagnosis, Varty hiccupped gently and a little wave of blood surged over his bottom lip and down his chin.

Varty spat weakly and grasped Ricketts by the wrist. "Listen mate, if I don't make it, I want you to do me a favour. Will you do that? There'd be something in it for you."

"You name it, Dale."

"You're out of here any day now, aren't you?"

"If that dickhead from the embassy gets his act together."

"You heading back to Auckland?"

Ricketts nodded.

Varty breathed laboriously and closed his eyes. As they waited for help to arrive, he told Ricketts his story. It took five painful minutes. Twice Ricketts urged him to save his strength but he carried on. When he'd finished, he made Ricketts recite his instructions to confirm that he'd got it all. Then he passed out. A minute later the guards arrived with a stretcher and a chubby little civilian Ricketts assumed was the prison doctor.

After they'd taken Varty away, Ricketts noticed Brandi the ladyboy was still hanging around.

"What do you want?" snapped Ricketts.

"My cigarettes," said the ladyboy with a toss of his head. "He owe me. You his friend, you give me."

Ricketts brushed past him. "You should give up," he said. "It's unladylike."

Dale Varty's analysis of his predicament proved accurate in all respects and he died far from peacefully at 11.42 the following morning.

2

Jason Maltby, the administration officer at the New Zealand Embassy in Bangkok, sat in the back seat of the embassy Honda Accord and made a mental note to look up an encyclopaedia to find out who invented air-conditioning.

Whoever it was, thought Maltby, he — it would almost certainly turn out to be a he — hadn't been given his due; not by a long shot. To the diplomat's way of thinking, the inventor of air-conditioning was a towering figure in scientific history, up there with Newton, Edison and Pasteur.

Maltby had come to Bangkok having previously served his nation in London, Brussels and Canberra. After two months in the Thai capital, he'd concluded that his masters in Wellington could hardly have selected a less agreeable posting for someone of his physiology and temperament if they'd tried. Possibly Cairo; probably Equatorial Macheteland whose ruler kept a freezer stocked with especially fattened piccaninnies and where every second person from the archbishop down had AIDS. But that was about it.

Maltby's distinguishing features began and ended with his over-active sweat glands. When he'd worked in Wellington, it'd been a standing joke among his colleagues in the Foreign Affairs Department that he could break out in a sweat walking along Lambton Quay in the middle of winter into the teeth of a southerly howling straight off the polar ice cap. In steamy Bangkok he had only to stray briefly from an air-conditioned environment for dark sweat stains to appear on his trousers. After fifteen minutes in the open air, one continuous stain would run from his crotch, between his legs and up the seam, marking the conjunction of his buttocks, proclaiming to the world, Maltby felt, that here was a hopeless incontinent.

And whereas in his previous postings he'd dealt with matters of some substance, all he ever seemed to do in Bangkok was traipse after reprobates who'd got themselves into trouble over drugs. Today, for example, he was on his way out to Bombat prison, which given Bangkok's more or less permanent traffic jam meant spending at least two hours staring at the back of his chauffeur's misshapen head, to finalise Duane Ricketts' release and to try to establish what on earth had happened to Dale Varty. That morning the embassy had received a garbled message from the prison to the effect that Varty had been involved in some sort of fracas and was in rather a bad way.

Maltby hoped Varty was all right. For a career criminal, he thought, Varty wasn't a bad sort; quite an engaging character in his own way. Which was more than one could say for Ricketts: he was about as engaging as a rat in a kindergarten. It wouldn't have come as much of a surprise to hear that he'd got himself sliced up in a brawl — or sliced someone else up.

Maltby remembered his first meeting with Ricketts. The police message had informed him that New Zealand passport holder Duane Kenneth Ricketts, thirty-eight, had been arrested on a possession charge. Maltby had expected an ageing hippie type who'd come up to Thailand to get stoned for a few months, bum around, live cheap, sleep on the beach: feckless, clueless, probably crapping himself at the prospect of a couple of years in a Thai jail and pathetically grateful for a friendly face.

With the benefit of hindsight, Maltby doubted that Ricketts had a grateful bone in his body. When he'd been shown into the interview room, Ricketts had looked him over disinterestedly and without even bothering to sit up straight had said, "You're from the embassy are you? Bring any cigarettes?"

No panic, no drama, no 'I won't last a week in this place, you've got to get me out of here,' no claims of being set up, no horror stories about the police, no complaints about prison food or having to have a shit on an open toilet in front of everyone in the cell.

None of that. Instead, telling Maltby how to do his job: "Varty tells me you've just arrived. Yeah? Okay, I've talked to a few guys in here and this is how it works: the first time I go to court, it's just to confirm the charge and the plea. I plead guilty, no point doing anything else. The second time they offer me bail — it'll be about fifteen thousand NZ. I put up bail — get onto my lawyer in Auckland, he'll organise it. Soon as they let me go, I jump on the first fucking plane out of this shithole. The cops'll probably play silly buggers over my passport: they're meant to hand it over to you but they'll hang out for a bribe. Well, stuff that — fifteen grand's all they're getting out of me. You can jack me up a temporary one to get me home."

Then he'd tilted his chair back, eyebrows raised as if to say, 'Any questions?'

"Does it occur to you," Maltby had replied, automatically adopting the patronising demeanour embassy staff deploy to quell outbreaks of taxpayer assertiveness, "that you're asking the New Zealand Government to collude in bail jumping?"

Ricketts had lurched forward, the legs of his chair banging on the wooden floor, and planted his elbows on the small table. His grey eyes looked like frosted-up windows.

"Tell me something," he'd said slowly. "How do they treat you, the local cops and the characters who run this place? How'd you describe their attitude?"

Maltby, caught off guard and aware that he was losing the initiative, had shrugged defensively.

"I don't know. Pretty offhand I suppose."

"Dead right. That's because we're Kiwis and we don't count. We're pretty much slugfuckers as far as they're concerned. Now if we were Japs . . . I could've been caught red-handed selling smack from a stall in the lobby of the Oriental Hotel and they'd still've been lining up to french kiss your freckle when you came to see me. If you were from the Japanese Embassy, you'd walk in here like you owned the joint, scatter around a few million yen, and I'd walk out with you. But us Kiwis don't have that sort of grunt, do we? So we have to play by their rules. But give me credit for finding out exactly what the rules are: the fact is, it's not against Thai law to leave the country when you're out on bail; they're quite happy for me to piss off. Look at it from their point of view — they get my fifteen grand, they get rid of me, and they know I won't come back. I'd say that's pretty cost-effective law enforcement."

It still annoyed Maltby that Ricketts had been absolutely correct.

Before he issued a temporary passport, Maltby needed to know a little more about Ricketts and how he'd wound up in the Bombat Drug Rehabilitation Centre.

According to him, Ricketts made his living finding people, mostly children, who'd fled the nest and, for one reason or another, broken off communications. When the parents got anxious, which could take anything from seven hours to seven years, they'd go to the cops who'd point out that the preservation of the family unit wasn't their responsibility. Some parents would be steered to Ricketts by cops who knew him or perhaps by someone in social welfare. His clients would give him their kid's last known address and he'd go find them.

A lot of it was looking for sixteen-year-old girls who'd run away from towns like Opotiki, Thames or Dargaville to have fun in the big smoke. Most of the stories had mundane endings: he'd find the runaway working behind a check-out counter at Foodtown or Woolworths. Getting them home was another matter — usually they decided that living in Auckland, while it wasn't the buzz they'd expected, was still a step up from what they'd left behind — but that wasn't his problem. Sometimes the ending came right out of the parents' darkest nightmares, the ones they didn't even share with each other, and Ricketts would find Leah or Jasmin or Shelley — 'such a pretty girl but she could be, you know, a little wild' — standing on an inner city street corner in high heels and a short skirt, with a packet of condoms and a needle in her handbag.

Ricketts also got referrals through a couple of Auckland lawyers. Now and again these led to Sydney to find daughters who were too busy getting in touch with their creative selves to get in touch with their families; or maybe sons who were pretty sure that Mum and Dad would freak out if they knew their broth of a boy, who'd captained the first XV and been a young Rotarian, now went home at night to a partner with a nipple ring, a tattoo and sideburns like Zorro the Masked Avenger.

Ricketts had arrived in Bangkok on 17 March on the trail of Toby Ellifritt, twenty-one, who'd failed to front up at Auckland University two weeks earlier to continue studying for the distinguished medical career which everyone seemed to think lay ahead of him. Four days later Ricketts had found him sitting on the beach at Phuket smoking marijuana with a startlingly beautiful nineteen-year-old German girl called Petra. Ellifritt didn't seem surprised or impressed — let alone at all embarrassed — that his parents had sent Ricketts all the way from Auckland. He said he'd decided that medicine was for nerds and he and Petra were going to South America to look at Aztec ruins and stuff. When Ricketts asked him how he was fixed for money, Ellifritt replied that Petra's old man was the twenty-third richest person in Western Europe so who gave a fuck about money? Ricketts said give him a few minutes, he'd think of someone.

Ricketts thought about pointing out that one didn't amass the twenty-third largest fortune in Western Europe by being a benefactor to every pretty boy one's daughter scooped up for amusement value on her travels. He decided against it on the basis that, if he'd been in Ellifritt's jandals, he would've regarded any such advice as sour grapes. Instead he wished Ellifritt good luck and suggested that if he had a spare moment in between looking at piles of old stones and doing cocaine, he might like to send his parents a postcard from Peru. Ellifritt said he'd think about it.

Ricketts had returned to Bangkok on 22 March, checked into the Capital Hotel in Khao San Road, and made a collect call to Dr Phillip Ellifritt of Arney Road, Remuera. He'd told the doctor that his son was alive and well and would more than likely pitch up on his doorstep in three or four months' time, a sadder but wiser young man. And possibly a full-race cokehead, thought Rickets as he put the phone down.

That evening Ricketts had purchased two heroin cigarettes from a man he'd met in a pool hall in Khao San Road. He'd returned to his hotel, laid down on the bed, and smoked one of the cigarettes. It induced a dreamy, floating sensation, slightly nauseating but on the whole rather pleasant. He assumed he passed out because when he woke up, he was lying on a concrete floor in a cell and someone was trying to steal his watch.

According to the police report, two officers had gone to the Capital Hotel at 11.15 p.m. in response to a call from a housemaid who said she'd discovered the guest in room 202 unconscious on his bed. She'd been unable to revive him and, suspecting that drugs were involved, had called the police. The officers had found one heroin cigarette in the guest's toilet bag and remains of another in the ashtray beside the bed. They'd taken Ricketts to the Central Bangkok police station and, when he came to just after midnight, placed him under arrest.

Foreign Affairs in Wellington had nothing of interest to contribute to Maltby's file on Ricketts but the New Zealand Police liaison officer in Bangkok certainly did. His routine trawl through the Wanganui computer's database turned up the fact that Ricketts had once been a policeman. It seemed he'd embarked on an alternative career path shortly after being kicked out of the police force.

Duane Ricketts was saying goodbye to Jumbo Adeyemi.

"Anything I can do for you on the outside?" he asked the Nigerian.

"Oh no man, everything's just fine. I've only got a couple more months."

"I might drop you a line one of these days. You got a permanent address?"

Adeyemi rubbed his chin. "Well, you know I'm a bit of a nomad, I move around a lot. Best idea, send it to Poste Restante, Stockholm. I'll get it eventually."

"Stockholm? That's a long way from Mama Africa. How do you handle the cold?"

Adeyemi shrugged. "I dress like a bear. I have a beautiful fur coat, gloves with fur inside, and a fur hat like a Cossack general. It's true the weather can be very hard but I like Swedish people. Especially the women." He showed his perfect teeth. "They are very open-minded — and very white."

"I guess they don't come much whiter," agreed Ricketts. "Listen Jumbo, maybe you can do me a favour. You've got contacts here in Bangkok, business associated?"

"Oh yes."

"Let me ask you a question: What do you think happened to me? I mean, how come the cops got onto me?"

"Oh man that's plain. Whoever you bought your stuff from fingered you. That's how some of the street dealers, these insects, work: they sell to you, then tip off the police. The police catch you with some drugs so you must bribe them to stay out of jail; they confiscate what you bought and sell it back to you or return it to the dealer who sells it to the next sucker. Really, quite a neat little operation. You spoilt it by being unconscious — you couldn't bribe them so they arrested you."

Ricketts nodded. "I figured it was something like that. So that little weasel in the pool hall who sold me the cigarettes, he's cost me fifteen grand. That's the bail, that's what it's costing me to get out of here. I mean shit, apart from my house, that money was pretty much it for me."

Adeyemi raised his eyebrows in sympathy or perhaps surprise that anyone could get so worked up over such a paltry amount.

"If it was your money down the gurgler," asked Ricketts, "what would you do to the fucker who set you up?"

"I would kill him of course — slowly if circumstances permitted. You want my associates to get rid of this cockroach? It can be arranged, no problem. It will be a parting gift to my New Zealand friend."

"Christ Jumbo, I don't want him killed . . ."

"I have an excellent idea. The gangs in Lagos punish informers by cutting out their tongues. A person without a tongue serves as a warning to others."

Ricketts nodded thoughtfully. "Yeah, that seems about right: cruel but fair."

Ricketts and Maltby were in the embassy Accord on their way back into town. Maltby had arranged for Ricketts to overnight in a hotel and catch the 8 o'clock flight to Auckland the next morning.

"This business with Varty," said Maltby. "I couldn't get much sense out of the superintendent."

"What can I tell you?" said Ricketts. "He went behind the bikeshed with a ladyboy and the ladyboy's steady didn't like it."

"This ladyboy as you call him — her, it, whatever. He's a transvestite I take it?"

Ricketts nodded.

"It never occurred to me that Varty was that way inclined."

"I doubt if it occurred to Varty either," said Ricketts. "I think it was more a case that after ten years without it, he would've fucked a potplant."

Maltby took a little time trying to come to terms with that concept. Having failed to do so, he moved the conversation on to less difficult subjects.

"The superintendent was saying you spoke to Varty after he was stabbed. Did he say anything I should know about?"

Ricketts looked straight ahead and cocked a bemused eyebrow. "Well, I suppose your report should mention that Varty was attacked before he shot his bolt. It's worth having that on the record in case the ladyboy sues the government for his fee — he's still bitching that he never got his cigarettes."

"Do you have to be facetious about everything?" said Malby testily. "The man's dead, for God's sake."

"Exactly; he doesn't give a shit so why should you? All it was, if you must know, Varty asked me to do something for him back home — family business."

They sat in silence until Maltby decided to do some needling of his own.

"Now that we've got you out, perhaps you can explain something: what's a supposedly intelligent person like you doing taking heroin? I mean, you should know the harm it does better than most people."

Ricketts gave Maltby a long, slightly puzzled, slightly amused look.

"Jason, you mean to say you've never thought to yourself 'I wouldn't mind trying it just once, just to see what the attraction is?'" Ricketts turned away and looked out the window. "No, I don't suppose you have."

Maltby didn't react to Ricketts' implication. Instead, in as casual a tone as he could achieve, he asked, "Actually, there was something else I was wondering about: Why were you expelled from the police force?"

Ricketts shifted on the car seat and looked hard at Maltby who willed himself to hold his stare.

"You've been checking up on me, Jason; I suppose that shouldn't surprise me. How come you didn't get the whole story while you were at it?"

Maltby looked away. "All I saw was the bald fact. I think it said something like 'conduct unbecoming for a police officer'."

Ricketts leaned back on the seat. "I kept a photo, one of a set taken at the home of a guy I'd arrested. I showed it to a few mates and a guy who was hanging around, a friend of a friend, nicked it; he turned out to be a reporter for *Truth* and they ran the photo. The family and the lawyer kicked up a hell of stink. It made no odds that they'd pinched the photo — as far as everyone was concerned, I'd given it to them. So I was kicked out."

Sensing that he'd finally found a tender spot, Maltby tried to suppress a smirk. "That's laconic even by your standards but listen, if you'd rather not talk about it . . ."

Ricketts smiled back. "Shit, it doesn't worry me. You want to know the details, fine. Come to think of it, it's probably right up your alley. I was working at Henderson — this'd be fifteen years ago now –and we got this call from a woman out near Taupaki who said her boy and a couple of his mates had seen this bloke doing strange things with a horse — farmyard frolics if you get my drift. Me and another constable talked to these kids and there was no way they were making it up. The victim — a big black mare — was in a paddock down the road so every now and again we went out there and did a bit of surveillance. A few days later I'm sitting in among the trees keeping an eye on Black Beauty and an old bloke, about sixty, comes along. He's acting a bit shifty, looking around and that, and he's got a rope in one hand and a beer crate in the other. He tethers the horse, puts the crate down behind her, hops up on it, drops his tweeds and starts rattling away."

Maltby looked incredulous. "Good grief. What did the horse do?"

"Yeah, everyone asks that. It sort of looked at the bloke over its shoulder as if to say 'Oh Christ, not you again' and just carried on grazing; didn't seem too bothered one way or the other. Anyway, I arrested the poor old bugger. Later we went to his place and" — Ricketts mouth formed a tight and, to Maltby rather nasty grin — "here's the funny part: he had horse photos all over the walls, like pin-ups. He even had bloodstock magazines in the bog. We took a few photos for evidence. The one I kept was of the guy's bedroom — there was a bloody great colour poster of a horse on the wall opposite his bed. The horse was arse on to the camera — the view from the beer crate, so to speak."

3

Jason Maltby sat in his office in the New Zealand Embassy in Bangkok staring at the telephone on his desk. He'd turned his attention to the phone after having gazed for some fifteen minutes at the cream painted wall, which he found restful but lacking in inspiration, and then, more briefly, at the painting which hung to the left of the door.

To Maltby the painting, a still life of an unremarkable vase surrounded by cylindrical, purplish objects, symbolised everything that was unsatisfactory in his life. He knew that the cylindrical, purplish objects were tamarillos because the artist herself had told him so. The artist was the ambassador's wife which explained why the painting disfigured Maltby's office instead of being where it belonged — out of sight and out of mind in a storage cupboard, behind the reams of embassy letterhead with the out-of-date telephone number which the ambassador insisted on keeping in case of emergency. Quite what sort of emergency he had in mind was unclear to Maltby; given the paper's coarse texture and sharp edges, he hoped the ambassador hadn't picked up a whisper on the diplomatic circuit that Thailand was about to experience a severe shortage of toilet paper.

Maltby regarded the telephone with as much distaste as he had *Oriental Vase with Fresh Fruit*, which the ambassador's wife had knocked off in a two-hour creative frenzy after a sudden downpour had forced the cancellation of her weekly tennis lesson. He had no particular objection to the phone itself — it worked more often than not and his vigorous cleaning had, he was sure, removed most of the germs left on the mouthpiece by previous users. What disturbed him was the knowledge that he was going to have to pick it up and make a call in the course of which he would entreat, cajole and plead. And, when each of those approaches had failed, as he was pretty sure they would, he was going to have to grovel.

It wasn't the grovelling per se which bothered Maltby. He had, after all, been in the diplomatic service for fifteen years and had therefore grovelled for his country on occasions too numerous to recall. He'd also done a fair amount of grovelling in his own cause to ambassadors he'd served under, departmental superiors and junketing politicians. And a fat lot of good it's done me, he thought bitterly.

What really bugged Maltby was that the person to whom he was about to grovel was someone he'd known and patronised for almost twenty-five years.

When he was completely honest with himself, Maltby could identify only half a dozen people to whom he could confidently condescend and they included his parents. Any erosion of this little group's membership had unpalatable implications.

Five days previously Bernie Gemmell, a New Zealand Press Association journalist based in Hong Kong, had passed through Bangkok. Gemmell had managed to talk his bureau chief into letting him make a three-week tour of the region to research what would supposedly be a weighty series of features on the Asian economic miracle. Had the bureau chief been less preoccupied with his upcoming job interview with the *Asian Wall Street Journal*, he almost certainly would have vetoed the request on the grounds that the subject had already been done to death by commentators far better equipped for the task than Gemmell.

Gemmell and Maltby had attended Palmerston North Boys High School together in the early 1970s and subsequently kept in regular if not close touch. During Gemmell's brief stay in Bangkok, they'd gone out for a meal and a few beers. Late on in the evening, Maltby had mentioned his recent dealings with Dale Varty who was about to re-enter society after a ten-year stretch.

Without taking his eyes off the bargirl gyrating on the small stage, Gemmell had replied: "Oh yeah, and who's Dale Varty when he's not in the clink?"

"Didn't I mention that?" said Maltby, enjoying the moment. "Dale Varty is probably the last surviving link with the original Mr Asia drug syndicate."

Having got Gemmell's attention, Maltby told the story hinting, at regular intervals, that there was a direct cause-and-effect relationship between his joining the Bangkok embassy staff and Varty's imminent freedom. When Gemmell began making notes on the back of a coaster, Maltby made him promise not to file a story before 14 April, Varty's release date.

Maltby was thus confronted with an extremely tricky task: he had to explain to Gemmell that events had moved along somewhat since their night on the tiles and that the story as outlined — "Deft Diplomacy Gets ex-Mr Asia Man out of Asia" — no longer stood up; he then had to persuade Gemmell not to go with the new and rather more sensational version — "Transvestite Holds Fatal Attraction for ex-Mr Asia Man". Maltby knew very well that getting Gemmell to hold fire on such a juicy yarn would be difficult; failure, however, brought to mind various appalling scenarios which could be summed up in just two words — Equatorial Macheteland.

Before Maltby began staring vacantly at the wall, he'd been in the ambassador's office briefing him on the sordid circumstances of Dale Varty's demise. As he listened to Maltby's report, the ambassador's pink, bland features had gradually arranged themselves in an expression of pure revulsion.

"My God, that's bloody charming that is," he exclaimed when Maltby concluded. "Look here, Jason, if we do nothing else, let's make absolutely sure the press don't get wind of this. The buggers would have a field day; they'd make it into an international incident and we'd get it in the neck from both sides."

Up until that moment Maltby hadn't reassessed his beery conversation with Bernie Gemmell in the context of Varty's death. He did so then, in one panic-driven flash of comprehension which triggered a full-body sweatburst: every pore seemed to dilate to the size of a gorilla's nostrils and begin pumping out perspiration like burst water mains. He exited the ambassador's office at a military jog-trot, towelled himself dry in the men's room and returned to his office to don a change of clothes, one of two full sets he always kept in his office cupboard.

Having stiffened himself for the task, Maltby picked up the phone, dialled the number of the NZPA office in Hong Kong, and asked for Gemmell.

"I sorry sir," said the receptionist in a sing-song voice. "Mr Gemmell out of town right now on assignment. He not back till next week."

"Where can I get hold of him?"

"That not possible. You see, Mr Gemmell travelling in Laos and Vietnam. We don't have contact number for him till he reach Hanoi on Friday."

"Well, surely he rings in regularly?" demanded Maltby. "To get his messages and so on?"

The receptionist giggled infuriatingly. "You never know with Mr Gemmell. Sometime he go away and we don't hear from him for a whole week."

Maltby choked off a surge of envy. "Oh for God's sake," he snapped. "Very well, I'll leave a message: if and when he does call in, tell him not to proceed with the Varty story — that's V-A-R-T-Y — until he's talked to me. Jason Maltby, at the New Zealand Embassy in Bangkok. It's very important, absolutely imperative. And get a contact number from him."

"How you spell your name, sir?" asked the receptionist matter-of-factly, as if to say that she'd be the judge of how important it was. Maltby ground his teeth, told her and hung up.

Today was Tuesday; Gemmell had undertaken not to file until Thursday at the earliest. As long as he was arsing around in Laos and Vietnam, he wouldn't be sending anything to New Zealand.

Satisfied that he still had a couple of days up his sleeve, Maltby turned his mind to other matters. The subject had never really crossed his mind but if it had, he would've guessed that his old schoolmate lacked the technological nous to microwave a TV dinner. It certainly would've astonished him to learn that Gemmell never went on the road without his lap-top computer and modem.

It really wasn't until he felt the exhilarating surge of power lift the Qantas Boeing 747 off the Bangkok airport runway that Duane Ricketts relaxed.

He hadn't slept well the night before even though for the first time in three weeks his bed actually was a bed as opposed to a sheet of cardboard on a cold concrete floor. Maltby had warned him that the flights out of Bangkok to Australia and New Zealand were chock-a-block for the next month, so he was dead lucky to have got a seat on the Qantas flight even though it meant a one-night stopover in Sydney. But if he missed that flight, he could be sitting around for weeks wait-listed on flights, dragging himself out to the airport at 6 o'clock every morning hoping for no-shows, and all the time running up a hotel bill he couldn't afford. Each day he remained in Thailand would bring his trial date closer and there was always the possibility of being hauled in and slung back in the slammer on the stroke of a pen of a malicious or simply careless clerk somewhere in the twisted bowels of the Thai legal system.

On top of all that, Ricketts felt it'd be sensible to have several oceans between himself and Thailand when the double dealer from the pool hall informed his pals in the police force, in writing and probably in a shaky hand, that he'd been de-tongued.

So he'd tossed and turned, imagining that the alarm wouldn't go off, that the wake-up call wouldn't eventuate, that he'd sink into the mattress's soft embrace and sleep on and on, not waking till around midday, by which time the aircraft he was meant to be aboard would be approaching the west coast of Australia. In the end, he avoided missing the flight by a mere three hours and ten minutes.

As the aircraft climbed to cruising altitude, Ricketts recalled Jumbo Adeyemi's parting words. They were standing in the middle of the compound; Jumbo had briefly interrupted their conversation to swap banter with his fellow Nigerians who were playing a high-spirited game of Scrabble in the shade of the compound wall.

"They're good boys," said Jumbo turning back to Ricketts, "but I worry about them sometimes. They make plenty of money, you know, but they spend it all — on cars and women; now it's the other way round. What does that tell you?"

"Dunno," said Ricketts. "Seems a bit rigid either way."

"You may be right," said Jumbo gravely. "One shouldn't be too — what's that word, doctrinaire? — in these matters. Of course in here I'm always talking about women and this big fellow" — he patted his groin — "and so on but that's just to pass the time. Out there" — he gestured expansively — "you must put your mind on the job. I tell you man, when I became thirty, I realised it made no sense — no sense at all — to do all these dangerous things and then see the money disappear. I set myself a goal — to stop taking risks when I reached forty. I began to be more careful, more choosy about the deals, I put money away in long-term deposits where I couldn't get at it, I made some investments, I didn't change my cars and women so much. Now I can stop as I planned."

Adeyemi lowered his voice as if to reveal a confidence. "I didn't have to do this run. And for sure, I would've preferred not to get caught, but in a way, it's good for business to be here with my boys, good for team spirit. Next time, instead of thinking of me as the boss who sits in his big house counting the

money while they're in jail, they'll remember I was here. But that's it; no more."
He draped a heavy arm over Ricketts' shoulders. "Duane man, it bothers me,
the fix you're in. It's no good to be like these boys — drift along, be cool, have
a good time, don't worry about tomorrow. You've got to think ahead to when
you can't run around any more. In your situation, definitely, you have to keep an
eye out for the big score. Then when you see the chance man, you go and make
it, whatever it takes."

I'll drink to that, thought Ricketts. He hailed a passing hostess: "I'll have a
couple of beers and a double scotch when you're ready."

The hostess, an experienced-looking campaigner, eyed him warily: "This is
a long flight sir. Don't you think you should pace yourself?"

Ricketts shook his head. "Don't worry about me, I won't give you any
trouble. I have those drinks, I'll be out like a light."

When the hostess moved away, Ricketts turned to his neighbour, a middle-
aged woman who now had a slightly trapped look on her face. He smiled
pleasantly and said: "I just got out of jail."

Special agent Harold "Buddy" Funke of the United States Drug Enforcement
Administration sat naked in the wingback chair in room 517 of the Royal Thai
Hotel in downtown Bangkok thinking, 'Goddamn, I love this town.'

There were three immediate reasons for Funke's fondness for the Thai
capital. They were draped across the king-sized bed wearing only the exotic
lingerie which Funke himself had provided and in poses which, because none
of them was a day over fifteen, were more artless than lewd.

Agent Funke had joined the DEA in 1981 and spent most of the years
since outside the USA. All told he'd worked in nine of the seventy-three
foreign offices maintained by the DEA, which was created by President Nixon
and progressively expanded by his successors into a vast global apparatus with
a mission to wage war on the international drug trade. As the drug trade had
grown, so had the DEA; the question of whether it constituted a sensible
response to the problem had long since ceased to be deemed relevant. Some of
Funke's postings had been pleasant but a little on the quiet side — Bridgetown,
Nicosia; some had been hair-raising — Asunción, Port-au-Prince; some hellish
— La Paz, Peshawar. None of them, even on presidential pardon days, was a
patch on Bangkok.

The thing about Bangkok, as Funke never tired of pointing out, was that
if you had greenbacks and the right connections — and outside of the royal
family and the top military brass, not too many folks were better connected
than a DEA man with some seniority under his belt — you could do whatever
you damn well liked. Didn't matter what was your bag, your thing, your kink,
no one gave a fuck. Jesus, the things some guys did! Anywhere else, they'd lock
'em up and throw away the key.

Funke regarded himself as a normal, well-adjusted American. His particular fancy, which he indulged once a fortnight, was to rent a hotel room for the afternoon and send out for a jailbait threepack from one of the girlie bars along the Patpong Road. Funke believed that a man hadn't lived until he'd been given a body massage by three bouncy, squirming, squealing, well-oiled little yellow-brown dolls. These sessions culminated in the girls arranging themselves side by side across the foot of the bed, sometimes on their backs, sometimes on their knees. As he worked his way back and forth along the line-up, Funke was reminded of a chess master playing several opponents at once, going from board to board making his moves.

Funke stood up, pulled on his boxers, and clapped his hands: "Okay kiddos, that's it for today. Uncle Bud's got to get back to work."

As the girls scrambled off the bed and got dressed, Funke rang his office at the US Embassy to check for messages. There was just one: the deputy superintendent at Bombat prison had called. Funke rang Bombat and was put through.

"Pong, Buddy Funke. What's happening?"

"Mr Funke, something happen at the prison I thought you be interested. A prisoner called Dale Varty stabbed in a fight over a ladyboy. He dead now. Before the doctor arrive, ladyboy hear Varty talk to another prisoner about a lot of drugs hidden in New Zealand. I thought you want to know, that's all."

"That's for sure Pong. Who's the guy Varty told all this to?"

"His name is Duane Ricketts, also from New Zealand. He gone now."

"Say what?"

"Ricketts get bail. Someone from his embassy pick him up from here yesterday afternoon."

"Shit, if he made bail, he's a gone goose; we won't see him for dust. What about the ladyboy, where's he at?"

"His name is Kham Phumkumpol, call himself Brandi. He due for release next month. We very much like to get rid of him now — he cause plenty of trouble."

"Ain't it always the way? Why don't you just push the little faggot back on the street? Say it's for his own safety or some shit like that."

"I think maybe you right Mr Funke. Maybe some of Varty's friends try to get even huh?"

"They surely could. I was you, I'd just get him out of there. Say Pong, you can do me one more favour — make a copy of the files on Varty, Ricketts and the ladyboy, okay? I'll see you in Chico's bar, 10 o'clock tonight. You bring the files, I'll bring something for you, pal."

Funke hung up and sat in the armchair with his elbows on his knees, staring at the carpet. He was so preoccupied that the girls had to say goodbye three times before he responded.

4

After leaving Bangkok first thing on Wednesday morning and overnighting in Sydney, Ricketts finally arrived in Auckland at 3.20 p.m. on Thursday afternoon. When he presented his passport at the immigration counter, the official studied it for a moment then turned and nodded to a customs officer standing behind the row of booths.

The customs officer came forward and quietly asked Ricketts to accompany him. Ricketts shrugged and picked up his bags. He'd had a going over from customs at Sydney airport and was reconciled to getting the treatment again. The officer escorted Ricketts through immigration to a door marked "Airport Staff Only" and then down a corridor to a small interview room. The room contained a table, three chairs and two men in civilian clothes. Ricketts knew one of them, the Maori: he was Detective Sergeant Tito Ihaka of the Auckland CID, thirty-four or thereabouts and weighing 110 kilograms, a lot less of which was fat than people tended to assume. It was a misconception Ihaka was happy to encourage. The other man was ten years younger, thirty kilograms lighter and many shades paler.

"What's this?" said Ricketts. "The black and white minstrel show?"

Ihaka displayed a broad "we're all good sports here" smile to which Ricketts attached absolutely no significance. "Detective Constable Van Roon," said Ihaka to his companion, "meet Duane Ricketts, otherwise known as Mister Ed."

Ricketts dumped his two canvas hold-alls on the table and sat down. "Can we get this over with, Ihaka?" he asked wearily. "Do what you like, put on some rubber gloves and grope around up my backside if it gives you a thrill, but please, spare me the horse jokes."

Ihaka ignored him. "Would you believe this loser used to be a cop?" he said to Van Roon. "They kicked him out because he couldn't be trusted around horses. Guess what he does for a crust these days? Finds runaways. I mean, who the fuck's going to send a smackhead to find their little girl lost?" He shook his head. "You'd be a hopeless bastard, Ricketts. I suppose you're looking forward to getting the full body search?"

Ricketts looked stonily back at the policeman, saying nothing.

Ihaka nodded to the customs officer. "Okay mate, off you go. I doubt you'll find anything; even Mister Ed isn't that dumb."

As the officer went through his bags, Ihaka asked Ricketts what he'd been doing in Thailand and how he'd managed to get out so quickly. The responses, delivered in a disinterested monotone, were models of brevity. Then Ihaka asked about Dale Varty.

"Isn't that a matter for the Thai cops?" said Ricketts. "I gave them a statement; you want to know what I said, get them to send you a copy."

"Touchy, aren't we?" said Ihaka. "We did get a report from our liaison bloke up there; Christ, it's terrible what prison can do to a man, isn't it? How long were you inside for — three weeks? Did you go queer like Varty or just jerk off thinking about Cardigan Bay?"

Ricketts rolled his eyes and went back to staring at the floor.

The customs officer zipped up Ricketts' bags. "They're clean," he said.

Ihaka stood up. "Right then, we'll leave you lovebirds to it." He paused in the doorway and said to the customs officer: "Mate, just sing out if you get your arm stuck up his ringpiece."

As Funke expected, Kham Phumkumpol aka Brandi celebrated his first night out of Bombat by putting on his glad rags and checking in at his old haunt, a Patpong Road bar renowned for its ladyboys. After Brandi sashayed in to a heroine's welcome around 10.30, Funke left the bar and returned to his car which was parked across the street. Settling down for a long wait, Funke leaned back against the headrest and recalled the incident which had changed his whole outlook on life.

At 5 o'clock one hot Friday afternoon in the summer of 1962, Buddy Funke, just turned eighteen, closed up his father's hardware store on Main Street in the small south-west Texas town of Pecos.

While his family was spending the summer vacation at Corpus Christi on the Gulf of Mexico, Buddy was stuck in Pecos minding the store and earning some money so he could buy himself a car when he went up to college in Austin in the fall. Walking down the street thinking about the swell times he'd have himself at college with his own car, Funke didn't notice the cherry-red convertible until it was right beside him.

"Well, if it ain't Funke the punk," said Lyle Gorse, braking the convertible to a halt.

It was three years since Funke had laid eyes on Lyle Gorse and he didn't look much different: he'd filled out some but he still wore his hair rock 'n' roll style, long and greasy, kind of teased up on top of his head; he still rolled his shirt sleeves way up past the elbow to show off his muscles; he still had a cigarette slanting from the corner of his mouth; he still looked like the town bad boy.

Ever since Buddy Funke was old enough to get into trouble, his mother had been warning him that if he didn't watch out, he could end up like Lyle Gorse. Lyle's father was a no-good with a petty crime sheet as long as your arm; he'd run out on Lyle and Mrs Gorse when Lyle was twelve. Then a few years after that, a travelling salesman from Amarillo had come into the diner where Mrs

Gorse waitressed. When the salesman finished up his ham and eggs and paid the bill, she'd tossed her apron on the counter and walked out the door with him.

Even so, most people figured Lyle would've gone bad regardless. It just seemed to come naturally to him: he got into fights; he skipped class and when a teacher went round to his house, Lyle pointed a 12-gauge shotgun at him and told him to get the hell off his property; he stole cars to go thrill-riding and got sent to the correctional centre in El Paso for six months; there was talk he'd gotten away with worse because he was too smart for the sheriff and his deputies (although, as Buddy's mother was fond of saying, anyone who could put his boots on in the dark would be too smart for the sheriff's department); and he got a girl in the family way. That was always on the cards because the way it went, the more their parents talked about Lyle being no good, the more the boys wanted to be like him and the more the girls just plain wanted him.

What with one thing and another, Pecos eventually got too hot for Lyle Gorse and the day after his seventeenth birthday, he just up and left. There'd been a few sightings of him since then: someone said they'd seen him up in New Mexico, working on the highway; another story had him living in Amarillo with his mother and her second husband, earning his keep pumping gas. Not many folks in Pecos attached much credence to these reports on account of the fact that Lyle hadn't done a day's work in his life. Most people, if they had to pick where he'd got to, would've said the state penitentiary but they didn't really care where it was as long as he stayed there. He hadn't.

"Hey Lyle," said Funke. "Long time no see. Where you been?"

Gorse shrugged. "Around. Arizona mostly — Silver City, Tucson, Yuma. I like to keep moving."

Funke nodded. "So what brings you back to Pecos?"

"What do you think? This is my home town, Buddy boy. Came back to see all my old amigos."

"Well, shit Lyle, you can do that and be gone before sundown."

Gorse grinned. "You always did have a smart mouth, boy. As a matter of fact, I'm just passing through on my way down south of the border. I've been working my butt off on an oil rig for six weeks straight and I believe I owe it to myself to relax a while, have some fun. Here's an idea — why don't you come along? I'm just going for the weekend; I'll have you back Sunday night. What do you say?"

"What sort of fun you got in mind?" asked Funke warily.

Gorse took a final drag on his cigarette and flicked it away. He draped an arm over the car door and leaned towards Funke. "I want to catch a donkey show, kid. Guy on the oil well was telling me about donkey shows he'd seen in TJ; says he's heard they have them down in Juarez too."

"What's a donkey show and where's TJ?"

"TJ is Tijuana, a greaser town over on the coast, just across the border, one wide-open burg. I aimed to go see for myself when I was in Yuma but something came up. Now a donkey show is what you might call a performance put on by a señorita and her favourite burro."

Funke looked at him blankly.

"Jesus kid, do I have to spell it out? The dame gets screwed by the donkey."

Funke folded his arms. "Lyle, I'm not sure I want to watch a dame getting screwed by a donkey."

Gorse took off his dark glasses and stared at Funke. "Well there's no accounting for some folks' taste. There's plenty of other stuff to do in Juarez — Christ, you can go to the fucking market if you want, buy your kid sister one of them beanie dolls." Gorse slammed his hand against the car door. "Son of a bitch, I just thought of something — you been laid yet? Brother, there's no need to answer that — I can tell from looking at you. All right, that's settled: you come on down to Mexico with old Lyle and we'll get your cherry popped, I guarantee it."

Although Buddy Funke was one of the brighter teenage boys in Pecos, not even his mother, to whom he bore a close resemblance, would've claimed he was one of the more handsome. He was short and stocky and had a flat face splattered with freckles, eyes that appeared to focus in slightly different directions like maladjusted headlights, and ginger hair which his father insisted he wore in a military crewcut. He was also shy. Funke's homeliness and diffidence meant that although he was as anxious as any of his contemporaries to lose his virginity, the best he'd been able to do was to momentarily mislay it a couple of times. With Lyle Gorse as guide and negotiator, there had to be a good chance of finding a señorita in Juarez who'd be prepared to take it off his hands once and for all.

When the two young Texans crossed back into the United States late on the Sunday afternoon, Funke was no longer a virgin. Apart from that, all they had to show for their trip were hangovers and Montezuma's Revenge.

Gorse hadn't found a donkey show. In fact his enquiries had met with undisguised hostility from the locals who clearly took umbrage at the suggestion that the ladies of Juarez would perform bestial acts for the titillation of visiting gringos. The frustration of missing out on a donkey show combined with the disorientating effect of a steady intake of tequila and Mexican beer at one end, and an equally fluid outflow at the other, had put Gorse in a mean mood.

Instead of branching left at Sierra Blanca and heading north through Van Horne up to Pecos, Gorse continued south towards Valentine. A few miles past Sierra Blanca, he turned off down a back road.

Funke asked, "Lyle, where are we going?"

"Down this fucking road, that's where," snapped Gorse.

They drove on in silence for a few miles until they came to a little general store with a gas pump, stuck out in the middle of nowhere. Gorse swung off the road and pulled up in front of the store. He opened the glovebox and took out a revolver. He pulled his shirt out of his jeans, shoved the revolver in the belt and covered it with his shirt.

"What's the gun for, Lyle?" asked Funke nervously.

Gorse lit a cigarette and got out of the car. He planted his hands on the top of the car door and smiled crookedly down at Funke: "Well, it's like this Bud — I had my heart set on seeing a donkey show but I didn't get to see one; now I got a powerful urge for some double chocolate ripple ice cream. If they ain't got double ripple in there, I'll just have to shoot someone, nothing else for it. Stay here."

For the ninety or so seconds it took Gorse to walk over to the store, mount the steps to the porch, take a long look around, open the screen door and go inside, Funke sat in a trance-like state in the convertible imagining how various people, notably his parents, would react to the news of his arrest for being an accessory to armed hold-up. Then he leapt out of the car and ran to the store. As he pulled open the screen door, he yelled "Lyle, don't do it . . ."

It was too late. Gorse was pointing the revolver at a grizzled, middle-aged man in faded blue overalls who stood behind the wooden counter with his hands in the air. The man's name was Bobby Ray Doble and right then he was just about the worst person in south-west Texas to point a gun at.

Six weeks previously Bobby Ray's wife Martha had driven up to Abilene to see her sister. The highway patrol thought she must've fallen asleep at the wheel because just north of Sweetwater, her car had veered across the road into the path of a southbound Greyhound bus. Since Martha's funeral, Bobby Ray had spent a lot of time sitting on his front porch with a bottle of whiskey thinking about the future. Whichever way he looked at it, the future didn't seem worth waiting around for. When the whiskey ran out, he'd go back into the store and reach under the counter to where he kept his army issue Colt .45 automatic. Back in '59, a bunch of bandidos had come across the Rio Grande and held up a store down near Rocks Springs, gunned down a whole family in cold blood; ever since, Bobby Ray had kept the automatic in its holster, taped to the underside of the counter. He'd pull it out and look at it, then put the muzzle to his temple. After a few seconds, he'd put it back in the holster. "It won't be long now, Martha honey," he'd say out loud. "I'm fixing to do it real soon."

When Funke burst into the store, Gorse turned his head to tell him to get the fuck back in the car. While he was doing that, Bobby Ray Doble reached under the counter and came up with his .45. He shot Gorse just behind his left eye and from where Buddy Funke saw it, it was like a grenade had gone off inside Lyle's mouth.

Doble pointed the gun at Funke, aiming it at the tip of his nose. Funke noticed that the gun was rock steady and that there was nothing in Doble's brown eyes except mild indifference.

"Boy, you live to be a hundred," said Doble, "you ain't never going to get luckier than right now."

Then Bobby Ray Doble put the muzzle of the .45 in his mouth and pulled the trigger.

Funke felt something warm on his leg and looked down to see that he'd wet himself. Later he'd reflect that there was something to be said for having spent most of the morning on the can with the squirts after all.

He drove Gorse's convertible back to El Paso, slept in it that night, sold it on the first car lot he came across the next morning and took a bus back to Pecos. He spent some of the bus trip thinking about the cars that were now in his price range. Mostly, though, he thought about how close he'd come to getting killed. By the time the bus reached Pecos, he'd concluded that seeing as how he was so lucky to be alive, he really ought to do something more exciting with his life than teach high school in south-west Texas.

It was almost 2 a.m. when Brandi the ladyboy came out of the bar, turned left and began walking towards the Surawong Road end of Patpong Road. As he started his car, Funke found himself thinking that when some of the ladyboys got all dolled up, it was a hell of a job to pick them from the real thing.

Funke eased his car up alongside the ladyboy and wound his window down. He flashed his ID and told Brandi to get into the car, then drove three blocks towards the Chitladda Palace, turned down a little side street, pulled in to the curb and turned off the headlights.

Brandi got the wrong idea. He darted his tongue between red lips and leaned towards Funke smiling coyly.

"You want that I . . ."

"Hold your horses, missy," said Funke. "This is police business, not sweet-time. No offence intended — this town's full of imitations but you beat the shit out of any fake Rolex. Truth to tell, there've been times in this old boy's life when I'd have been happier than a nigger with new shoes to let you play with my Johnson. Could be I'd be partial to a helping now, weren't for the fact that just yesterday I was sucked and fucked every which way by three — count 'em, three — of the prettiest little gals this side of Chiang Mai and the plain fact is, I'm plumb out of poke. All I want from you is to tell me what went down at Bombat the other day when citizen Varty went to Jesus."

Brandi pouted and shifted away to lean against the car door. "I told them ten times at the prison. This Varty, he say he pay me for a suck, okay? We go up the stairs but Samran find us. He crazy jealous, push me away, then — I don't know what happen — Varty scream and fall down and I see blood . . ."

"You're one hell of a witness missy but we'll let that fine body of men, the

Bangkok police, worry about that side of it. What I want to know is what you heard Varty tell his friend Duane Ricketts."

"He talk about he used to be in drug syndicate — sound like he call it Asia but that make no sense huh? He say they move some cocaine from Australia to New Zealand by boat — talking about years ago, right? — and hide it somewhere. It still there."

"He say how much?"

"Plenty — he say worth millions of dollars."

"Okay, this is the important part. Where's the coke at?"

"I didn't hear. By this time his voice get real quiet; the guy Ricketts he like bent over so his ear right by Varty's mouth. I not hearing much what he say, okay?"

"He must've said where; there must've been a name?"

Brandi sighed. "Maybe, I don't know. If he say name of a place, I don't understand. Now I told you all I hear, huh?"

Funke shook his head. "No way that's all. Like the guy's going out slow, he's not telling Ricketts all this to give his tongue exercise; he had a reason. So what did he tell Ricketts to do?"

Brandi nodded. "Okay, I think he want Ricketts to find the coke but he also talk about his daughter. He tell Ricketts to go see her. You want to drive me home now?"

"That's it, absolutely everything? You haven't left anything out, maybe because it didn't make sense to you? I mean, he didn't talk about a map showing where the coke was stashed, anything like that? He didn't mention anyone apart from the daughter?"

Brandi shook his head. "I told you, I miss some of what he say. Only other thing I hear — he say someone killed when he bring cocaine to New Zealand. Don't ask who, okay?"

"Well, now, there's a coincidence," said Funke. He reached under his seat and brought out an automatic pistol. "Will you look at this little beauty — Beretta 9 millimetre. Took it off a mule we whacked up in the triangle last year. Feels so good, could've been custom-made for me. It's a shame I have to lose it."

Brandi pressed back against the door and looked at Funke with big, scared eyes.

"That's your cue, sugar," prompted Funke with a thin smile. "You're supposed to ask why is it, if I'm so all-fired attached to this piece, I'm going to throw it away?"

"Why you do that?" said Brandi in a barely audible whisper.

Funke reached across to open the glovebox and take out a silencer which he screwed onto the Beretta. "Well now, after I've used it to pop you, it wouldn't be too smart to hang on to it, would it?"

"Please, no," beseeched Brandi. "I do nothing . . ."

"What's your problem?" said Funke. "Don't all you zippyheads believe in reincarnation? You come back with a pussy, I'd have done you a favour, ain't that so?"

When Brandi grabbed the door handle, Funke shot him first in the chest and then in the head as he'd been taught when he'd joined the CIA out of college back in 1967: first shot to the body, the big target, to stop and disable; second shot to the head to make stone cold sure of it. Taking people out like this was called 'wet stuff' in company parlance, although some of the older guys at CIA headquarters in Langley, Virginia claimed 'wet stuff' was actually a translation from the Russian of the KGB slang for any activity which involved spilling blood.

5

At 10 a.m. local time on Thursday, 14 April, Bernie Gemmell, the foreign correspondent, entered the Boomerang Bar in downtown Vientiane. He got a cold San Miguel beer and commandeered a corner table on which he arranged the contents of his large leather satchel. He lit a cigarette, sipped his beer, and discreetly studied the dozen or so other men in the bar, only two of whom were Asian.

Although few would have suspected it, Gemmell possessed a romantic streak. In his slightly overheated imagination, a seedy, dimly lit bar in the capital of Laos was the milieu of the undercover world, the world behind the headlines, and as such the habitat of adventurers, gun runners, agents, double agents and mercenaries killing time until the next war by reminiscing, over their beers and vodka chasers, about comrades who didn't survive the last one. Therefore he examined the other patrons in the expectation that they'd be exotic, sinister and probably bound for damnation. After a few minutes' careful inspection he decided that they mostly looked like sheet-metal salesmen from Stoke-on-Trent or Milwaukee or Gdansk or Wollongong. So much for the mysterious East, he thought. Gemmell finished his beer, opened up his laptop computer, and studied the notes he'd made of his recent conversation with the diplomat, Jason Maltby.

Gemmell's enthusiasm for the Dale Varty story had waned since he'd left Bangkok. Now, as he stared at the laptop's screen, he asked himself who really gave a toss about some middle-aged sleazebag getting out of a Thai jail? Dale who? Had anyone ever heard of him? The Mr Asia syndicate was past tense, practically ancient history. And compared with the likes of the Colombian cartels, they were small-time, almost quaint: a bunch of low-rent hoods who had their fifteen minutes of media attention and then took to murdering each other. Eventually, Gemmell decided that seeing he'd come up with absolutely nothing new or insightful to say about the Asian economic miracle in two and a half weeks of gallivanting around the region at his employers' considerable expense, it would be prudent to file a Varty story, however modest.

He began to write:

From Bernie Gemmell, NZPA Correspondent
Bangkok, 14 April

New Zealander Dale Varty is nothing if not a survivor.

The fifty-three-year-old Varty, a veteran of the notorious Mr Asia drug syndicate, will be released today from the Bombat Drug Rehabilitation Centre in Bangkok after serving a ten-year sentence for drug trafficking.

Officials from the New Zealand Embassy here who have been in contact with Varty confirm that he is in reasonable physical shape and good spirits.

The fact that he has come through such an ordeal — Thailand's prison system is notoriously hard on Westerners — should not come as a surprise: Varty was, after all, a member of the Mr Asia syndicate and lived to tell the tale. Many of the Mr Asia team met violent fates, usually at the hands of fellow syndicate members, when the organisation fell into internecine conflict in the late 1970s.

Fortunately, the collapse of the Mr Asia syndicate was as swift and comprehensive as its rise was spectacular and bloody.

The August 1983 death — ironically of a heart attack suffered in an English jail — of the syndicate's boss Terry Clark, or Alexander James Sinclair as he was also known, completed the disintegration of one of Australasia's most successful, albeit short-lived, and murderous criminal enterprises.

Varty, an Aucklander, was never a senior figure in the syndicate. Originally one of the syndicate's go-betweens with distributors in Sydney and Auckland, he eventually rose to become a buyer, sourcing product from South-East Asia.

After the syndicate's collapse, Varty came to Thailand intending to tap his contacts here to put together a major deal on his own behalf. However, the plan came to grief in March 1984 when he was arrested by Thai police on the resort island of Phuket on drug trafficking and conspiracy charges.

Since his arrival in Thailand three months ago, Jason Maltby, administrative officer at the New Zealand Embassy, has energetically promoted Varty's cause and personally handled negotiations with the Thai authorities to finalise his release. Although Maltby maintains a diplomatic silence over the nature of the negotiations, it can be safely assumed they were not straightforward: Thai authorities sometimes seem to delight in spinning out the release of Western prisoners and are past masters at creating obstacles where none seemed to exist.

Maltby told this correspondent that he had been impressed by Varty's resilience and his determination to leave his criminal past behind him.

"Mr Varty's come through this remarkably well," said Maltby. "He possesses that famous Kiwi adaptability and he's remained positive by focusing on getting back to Auckland and starting a new life."

That's all it's worth, thought Gemmell as he gave it a swift read. It gives the papers a hook for a "Mr Asia Revisited" feature if they've got a hole to fill. Maltby should be happy; it makes him sound like Henry Kissinger.

He walked over to the bar.

"Can I use your phone?" he asked the barman, a forty-five-year-old West Australian called Len with a beer belly like an inflated spinnaker and a nose with a radioactive glow and strange, pitted extensions as if it was in the throes of reproducing itself, amoeba-like. "I want to make a collect call to New Zealand."

Len folded his arms across his chest. "You bet your pimply arse it'll be collect. You a Kiwi?"

Gemmell nodded.

"You hear about this Kiwi joker walking down George Street in Sydney with a sheep under each arm?" asked Len. "Cop car pulls up and this cop says, 'You a shearer?' 'Get your own,' says the Kiwi, 'I'm going to root 'em both myself.'"

"I don't get it," said Gemmell, cutting off Len's guffaws.

Jason Maltby's telephone ran hot on Friday morning. His first call was from DEA special agent Harold "Buddy" Funke.

"Jason, I understand you handled the file on one of your nationals been doing time here: a perpetrator by the name of Dale Varty, now deceased?"

"That's correct but . . ."

"Look, I'm real sorry to be hassling you with this, but you know what us Americanos are like — no such thing as something that's none of our business, right? Leastways, that's surely how my outfit operates. You might not believe this but among the fun things we get to do is file reports on any, what you might call, untoward event involving known narcotics traffickers which happens to take place on our piece of dirt. You read where I'm coming from? Now I know this ruction with your Mr Varty happened in the joint and all but I'm obliged to report on it just the same."

"Yes, I see," said Maltby. "How can I be of assistance?"

"Well, Jason, it embarrasses me all to hell to waste your time with such a chickenshit matter but our procedures require me to include Varty's last known address in his home country. Don't ask me why — just more crap they can feed into their computer I guess. Now the local uniforms have a Phuket address — must've been where he was hanging out when they arrested him — so I figure if anyone can help me close off this sucker of a report, it's the good people at the New Zealand Embassy."

"Well, I'm not sure that we can, as a matter of fact. You see, Varty was domiciled in Australia — Sydney to be exact, before he came to Thailand."

"That was downright inconsiderate of him. You have a next-of-kin for this asshole? Worst comes to the worst, I can go with a NOK address. I mean, who the hell in DC's going to know different?"

"Just a moment. Let me grab his file."

Maltby collected Varty's file and returned to the phone. "Not quite a next of kin, I'm afraid. All I have here is his ex-wife."

"Better than nothing I guess. What's her story?"

"Her name's Rayleen Crouch; the address we have is 108 Crimea Avenue, Grey Lynn, Auckland."

Funke repeated the address back to Maltby, then said: "Ex-wife, huh? He have any kids?"

"I seem to remember there was a daughter but there's nothing on her in the file. If you really feel you need her details, I suppose I could try Wellington, but the department might baulk at her name going into your computer . . ."

"Can't say I'd blame them if they did. No, that's fine; you've solved my little problem. I'm much obliged to you, sir."

"Anytime."

Funke hung up. No wonder so many folks believe Elvis is still alive, he thought; some people will believe just about any goddam thing.

Maltby's second call that morning also concerned Dale Varty. The caller was Amanda Hayhoe, a reporter from Television New Zealand.

"Mr Maltby, I work for a current affairs programme called *Sixty Minutes*. We might be interested in doing a story on Dale Varty. I was wondering if he'd left Thailand yet or, if not, where we get hold of him?"

Jesus, what? "Dale Varty," stammered Maltby. "What do you know about him?"

"Absolutely stuff-all apart from what's in this morning's *Herald* about him getting out of jail," said Hayhoe breezily. "We just thought he might have a good yarn to tell."

Maltby felt a huge bead of sweat slide down his right temple like a snail. That idiot Gemmell must've sent a story to New Zealand; how the bloody hell did he manage that? This line of thought was interrupted by a voice bellowing at him to get off the phone and out of the embassy to somewhere he couldn't be contacted. It took him two or three seconds to realise the voice was coming from inside his head.

"Look Ms Hayhoe, I'll have to call you back on this . . ."

"I'm confused — I mean, what's the problem here?" asked Hayhoe. Her tone had cooled from pleasant to neutral with a hint of "don't fuck with me, I work for television". "After all, you are quoted in the story."

"Quoted?" whimpered Maltby, standing up to unstick his trousers which felt like they were glued to his buttocks. "Saying what?"

"Oh just how Varty's come through it all intact and whatnot. You should be pleased with the story; it makes you sound . . . well, as if you're on top of things up there."

Maltby closed his eyes and squeezed his slippery forehead. This was disastrous; he had to stall her, buy himself some time to think.

"Ms Hayhoe, would you mind very much faxing me a copy of the story?" said Maltby, calling on his reserves of self-control. "I really think I should see it before I say anything. I'll call you back as soon as I've read it."

Maltby's third call came through while he was reading the faxed copy of the story which had appeared in the *New Zealand Herald*.

He snatched up the phone. "Susan, what's the matter with you?" he barked. "I told you only five minutes ago I'm not taking any calls for the time being."

"I sorry Mr Maltby but this gentleman say he have a message to call you urgently. It Mr Bernie Gemmell — he ringing from Hanoi."

6

Amanda Hayhoe, the television reporter, was not the only person in Auckland to be intrigued by the single-column NZPA story about Dale Varty which appeared on page five of *The New Zealand Herald* on Friday, 15 April.

Varty's ex-wife Rayleen Crouch came across it while having breakfast in the kitchen of her two-bedroom villa in Grey Lynn. When she spotted the headline, the spoonful of muesli and banana stopped midway through its journey from the Peter Rabbit bowl, out of which she'd eaten her morning cereal since her fifth birthday in 1961, to her mouth and remained poised in mid-air as she read the story. When she reached the paragraph quoting the man from the New Zealand Embassy in Bangkok about how her former husband intended to start a new life in Auckland, Rayleen Crouch snorted. The snort expressed both surprise and amusement and was sufficiently explosive to cause the spoon to jump in her right hand. A slice of banana fell from the spoon to the bench to her lap to the floor. Crouch's gaze flicked to the slice of banana which rolled like a hoop across the kitchen floor and under the oven. She said 'pisshole', but without putting much feeling into it, and returned her attention to the newspaper.

When she'd read and re-read the story, Crouch ate the now banana-free spoonful of muesli then, chewing doggedly, tipped what remained in the bowl into the sink waste disposal. She rinsed the bowl, put it in the dishwasher, cleaned her teeth in the bathroom, picked up her handbag, and left the house, locking the front door behind her. She was so preoccupied that she quite forgot to retrieve the piece of banana from under the oven which was quite out of character for someone who was tidy to the point of being a self-diagnosed anal retentive.

It was the first weekday morning for eleven months that Crouch had left for work without having done the *Herald* crossword which usually took her between four and five minutes. Then she'd departed from her routine in response to a frantic phone call from her office informing her that one of her clients — as they are known in the welfare industry — had just walked into the McDonald's in Karangahape Road where, upon being informed that the Egg McMuffin special offer had ended the day before, he'd unbuttoned his shirt and sliced off his left nipple with a razor blade.

Another who was riveted by the story was the lawyer Bart Clegg. Clegg read the paper sitting in his leather swivel chair in his office on the eleventh floor of the

Trubshaw Trimble building in Queen Street. Like many of Auckland's high-rises, the building was actually owned by Singaporeans; as the lead and most substantial tenant, the law firm in which Clegg was a partner had been granted naming rights.

When Clegg graduated from law school in 1976, he'd joined the Auckland Legal Cooperative, a group of young lawyers whose political stances ranged across most variations of left wingery from Maoist to sandal-wearing Utopian. Clegg himself was an anarcho-syndicalist for fifty weeks of the year; the other two, he went skiing at Mount Ruapehu. The Cooperative's self-appointed mission was to stand up for the poor and down-trodden and to defend the civil liberties of put-upon minorities; the members regarded policemen as stooges of the system at best, corrupt neo-fascist thugs at worst, and the legal establishment as a mutual support group of money-grubbing fat cats.

Like many zealots, Clegg was so attached to his opinions that he took them everywhere, rather like modern parents who take their babies to restaurants and dinner parties. One Friday night he had too much to drink in the University Club and began ranting about the bench. A stout, middle-aged man waiting at the bar briskly suggested that he was talking rot. Clegg, ignoring his friends' tugs on his sleeve, eyed the interjector up and down, thrust his reddened face forward so that their noses were almost touching, and demanded in a grating snarl, "Who asked you, you fat lard? And what the fucking hell would you know about it anyway?"

The middle-aged gentleman turned a deep crimson colour which very nearly matched the dry red wine in Clegg's glass and stalked from the room. Clegg turned to his companions with a triumphant beam, expecting plaudits for seeing off a class enemy with such pungent efficiency. Instead of praise, however, he was given the news that the man he'd just publicly and gratuitously insulted was widely tipped to be the next chief justice.

Clegg awoke the next morning with a hangover and an unsettling feeling that his rudeness to Justice Gibbon was a more serious matter than he'd been prepared to acknowledge the previous evening. By mid-afternoon unease had become gnawing anxiety. He wrote a letter of apology to Gibbon which he hand-delivered to the judge's secretary. The letter impressed Gibbon, who'd thought that in his thirty-year legal career he'd seen the parameters of self-abasement extended about as far as they could go. Clegg, though, had pushed the envelope, as test pilots say. Gibbon decided to grant Clegg's request to be permitted to elaborate on the written apology in person.

It was a deflated Bart Clegg who entered Justice Gibbon's chambers at midday the following day. He cleared his throat nervously and began the speech that he'd worked on until three o'clock that morning. Gibbons listened for forty-five seconds then interrupted.

"That'll do," he said. "You've made your point. I've been apologised to by some of the biggest crawlers in the business but you lose nothing in comparison. Sit down."

Clegg did as he was told.

Gibbon studied him in silence for a few seconds. The judge's eyes were black and a little bloodshot and to Clegg they looked as cold and indifferent as those of a cat toying with a bird with a broken wing.

"Why did you take up the law, Mr Clegg?"

Clegg swallowed. "Well, I suppose I wanted to serve the cause of justice and help those who, you know, don't get a fair shake from the system — the poor, Polynesians, gays . . ." His voice trailed off.

"Hmmm . . . and would it be true to say that you believe most people in the profession don't give a damn about justice, they just want to make a lot of money?"

"Well, I'm not so sure I'd put it as bluntly . . ."

"Come on man, yes or no?"

"Yes, I guess."

"Of course they bloody well do. Let me tell you something Mr Clegg: you're hardly the first young lawyer to think that way. Nine out of ten drop all that nonsense and come to see the law as a job pure and simple, a meal ticket, a way of making quite a good living. Now on the basis of our brief and disagreeable acquaintance, I'm quite confident you have neither the character nor the intellect to achieve anything remotely useful as an idealist. If you want to be a crusader, that's entirely up to you; but in twenty years' time, you'll be in a miserable little practice in a miserable little office handling pathetic clients; no one will take the slightest notice of you except the media who'll ring you up whenever they need an inflammatory quote. Every quote you give them will only serve to make you even more of an object of derision to the rest of the profession. My advice to you therefore is to stop posturing and try to make yourself into a half-decent lawyer. If you manage to make some money along the way, then the chances are you'll have been of assistance to at least some of your clients. Now I have some matters to attend to before luncheon."

Clegg rose. "Thank you sir. I really appreciate your advice."

Clegg had his hand on the door knob when Gibbon spoke again. "Oh, two more things: go easy on the grog; you can't handle it. Secondly, if at some stage in the future you're faced with the prospect of appearing in my court and are wondering how you'll be treated" — here Gibbon smiled for the first time but it was a private smile which contained no comfort for Clegg — "then be advised that I'm not disposed to let bygones be bygones. My philosophy is that forgiveness is for clergymen; judges are society's instruments for taking the revenge that we deny the individual. So if you're ever unwise enough to appear before me, I'll take great pleasure in humiliating you."

Clegg took Justice Gibbson's advice. He quit the Cooperative and joined a medium-sized downtown firm. He'd been a jack of all trades for a few years, then specialised in conveyancing and property law. Now, even after a divorce, he was quite comfortably off and sufficiently secure in the Trubshaw Trimble hierarchy to scarcely bother trying to conceal the fact that he was sleeping with his secretary.

He'd steered well clear of Justice Gibbon's courts too. In fact, he'd only encountered Gibbon once since that audience in chambers. It was at the Northern Club. Turning away from the urinal, he found himself looking straight into Gibbon's black eyes. The shock caused him to snag several pubic hairs in his zip. The judge was greyer, stouter, more florid and his unblinking stare was, if anything, chillier.

"Clegg, isn't it?"

"Yes, your honour."

Gibbon looked him up and down, rather as Clegg had done to him in the University Club thirteen years earlier.

"You look moderately prosperous, Mr Clegg. Who are you with?"

"Trubshaw Trimble."

Gibbon grunted enigmatically.

"And what do you do at TT?"

"Property mainly."

The judge nodded with satisfaction, as if the information legitimised a deeply held prejudice. "Haven't had you in my court, Mr Clegg. You obviously took my advice."

Clegg ventured a quick smile. "Yes, I did — to the letter."

Gibbon's eyes narrowed suspiciously. "You a member here?"

"Oh no, I'm here as a guest."

"Thank the Lord for that. Now if you don't mind clearing off, I prefer to urinate in private."

A year later ill-health forced Gibbon to retire from the bench. According to legal gossip, the judge had never been quite the same since being passed over for the position of chief justice. The fact that he drank a bottle of Famous Grouse Scotch whisky every day was also thought to have contributed to his decline. To mark Gibbon's retirement, Clegg sent him a bottle of Wilson's New Zealand whisky and a 500 gram block of lard. Anonymously, of course.

When Clegg finished the *Herald* story, he leaned back in his leather swivel chair and thought about his connection with Dale Varty, for whom he'd acted in the late 70s and early 80s. Seeing that the connection involved an unsolved murder, Clegg thought about it very carefully.

Bryce Spurdle, the semi-retired investor, read about Dale Varty in what he'd come to regard as his Auckland office: the Sierra café in Jervois Road.

Spurdle lived in a sprawling mock-Tudor monstrosity on twenty-five hectares near Albany, no more than twenty minutes' drive — outside rush hours — from downtown Auckland. Several mornings a week he'd get into one of his three cars and drive down the motorway, across the harbour bridge and up Shelly Beach Road to Jervois Road. Then if the weather permitted, he'd sit at one of Sierra's pavement tables with a cappuccino, the *Herald* and his mobile phone. He'd use the phone to ring his stockbroker, his young wife to make sure she was out of bed, and his mates to organise a round of golf or a lunch.

There'd been a time when Spurdle and Varty were best friends. They'd grown up together in Ponsonby in the late 1940s and 50s; in those days, people who lived in the eastern suburbs regarded Ponsonby as the closest thing in Auckland to a slum and wouldn't have been seen there in an advanced state of decomposition. For that reason it tickled Spurdle to sit outside at Sierra and watch the svelte women pull up in their 3-series BMWs, having come all the way from Paratai Drive for a cup of coffee.

Varty's father was a seaman and rarely at home. Spurdle's father, Bevan, went off to war in 1941 with regular features and good health; he came back with a compacted nose, breathing difficulties and a booze habit. He collected the mangled nose and the associated breathing difficulties when he walked into a bar in Port Said, Egypt during an all-in brawl. Roughly speaking, the brawl was between Australian and British infantrymen; the Antipodeans had set upon their allies because they were Poms, physically smaller and numerically fewer, a combination which tended to have the same galvanising effect on Australian servicemen out on the town as red rags on bulls. Unfortunately for the Australians, these particular Poms turned out to be Welshmen, farmers from the Brecon Beacons and the Black Mountains and coal miners from little pit villages in the Rhondda Valley. Not only did the Welshmen seem impervious to pain, they also fought like rabid weasels, displaying no respect for the etiquette of the intra-alliance Saturday night knuckle.

Bevan Spurdle entered the bar shortly after one of the Australians had retired from the fray having had a forearm chewed, a tooth knocked out and his scrotum almost wrenched off its mooring by a goblin-like creature half his size and probably twice his age. Lurking by the doorway sick with pain and burning with humiliation, the Australian lashed out at the first person to cross his path. The king-hit, a whistling uppercut, landed flush on the tip of Spurdle's nose, driving the nose bone up into his forehead and reducing the nose itself to smears of blood, gristle and mucus across his cheekbones, like warpaint on a Comanche brave.

A year later Spurdle and half a dozen others from his unit were coerced into unloading a supply ship in the port of Alexandria. The exercise, which was largely unsupervised, took several days and was almost completed when they discovered several barrels of 100 proof navy rum in the depths of the ship's hold. After three days of hard labour in the North African heat, the working party felt it had earned a dip or two. They ended up drinking solidly for the rest of the day. Bevan passed out and remained in a state of suspended animation for sixty hours. He was one of the lucky ones; two of his comrades had literally drunk themselves to death. It should've been a textbook case of aversion therapy; in fact, it had the opposite effect on Spurdle who took to the bottle with increasing single-mindedness.

With one father often absent and the other often befuddled, young Spurdle and Varty were less constrained by parental control than most of their contemporaries. They roamed the streets in search of excitement and soon discovered that larceny was as much fun as anything and more rewarding than most. They learned that because some people liked to pray by themselves instead of or in addition to attending services, churches had collection boxes into which the solitary worshippers could drop their offerings. The boxes were usually left unlocked so Varty and Spurdle would sneak in and rifle them during their lunch breaks. Varty always wanted to flog the lot but Spurdle, who even then was more astute in financial matters, would insist that they took no more than half. That way, he pointed out, the priests wouldn't realise the collection money was being pilfered; they'd just think that pickings in Ponsonby were getting even slimmer.

The young thieves also learned that people who were old enough to get the old age pension were often lax about locking back doors and bolting windows; they tended to be set in their ways so they kept their savings in the same drawer or jar or under the same sofa cushion; and they were absent-minded so if you just skimmed off a note, chances were they'd assume they'd spent it or lost it, that is if they missed it at all.

After school Varty and Spurdle would catch a bus to somewhere like Newmarket or Remuera, where the shops were better stocked and the shopkeepers didn't know them and were so used to kids who behaved themselves that you could just about nick stuff off the counter under their noses. They shoplifted comics, toys, sweets, even things they didn't need or want and ended up chucking away. They stole chocolate bars by the score; they'd get the bus back to Ponsonby with their schoolbags crammed with the big two shilling blocks, go down to their den under the Varty house, and scoff till they made themselves sick. Next day, they'd take the leftover bars to school and trade them to girls who'd pull their knickers down behind the toilets. That was worth plain chocolate, your Dairy Milk; the girls who were game for a fiddle got Chocolate Crunch, the one with hokey-pokey, or Caramello.

Varty probably would've done it just for the hell of it but Spurdle was driven by an urge to accumulate. He'd seen the boys from Kings Prep School dragging their elegant mothers into Storkline, the big toy shop in Newmarket, and just pointing at what they wanted; he'd stared in wonder through the bus window at the enormous houses along Remuera Road. By the time he was fourteen, Bryce Spurdle had made up his mind that he was going to be rich.

Spurdle got rich in three phases. In the sixties he worked in the music business, managing bands and promoting concerts. By the early seventies, drugs had become part of the music scene; once Spurdle got over his amazement at the sort of money musicians and their hangers-on were prepared to part with for a little bag of what was meant to be marijuana but could've been clippings off his front lawn for all half of them knew, he set out to meet the demand. By the time the eighties rolled around, he was one of Auckland's leading drug dealers and a millionaire.

But it wasn't all plain sailing: a guy Spurdle funded into a deal got caught with a briefcase full of acid and went to jail for the rest of the century; another time, his man got himself killed and the product in question, a swag of high-grade cocaine which was going to catapult him into the big league, vanished into thin air. Then the stockmarket went crazy. It didn't take Spurdle long to figure out that playing the market was an easier and less risky way to make money than dealing drugs. By 1987 he'd parlayed $1 million of drug money into $10 million, give or take a few thousand, virtually all of which was invested in the stockmarket.

It never occurred to Spurdle that the party wouldn't go on forever. He often used to wonder why everybody didn't jump into the market and make themselves some serious money. Not that he particularly gave a shit; if some people were too dumb to see what stuck out like a big dog's dick or didn't have the nerve to get into the action, fuck 'em — they deserved to be poor.

On his way out to the airport one day in late August 1987, Spurdle dropped in to see his broker. He'd got sick of winter so he was off to Hawaii for a couple of weeks. Wanting something to read on the plane, he spotted a paperback called *Money* on the broker's bookshelf. Seeing money was the be-all and end-all of his existence, Spurdle borrowed the book despite the broker's warning that it probably wasn't his cup of tea.

The broker was right. Spurdle had assumed that the author John Kenneth Galbraith would share his uncomplicated attitude towards money and was looking forward to picking up some shrewd tips on wealth enhancement. Instead what he got was a lot of egghead blather about economic theories and all this historical crap about things that happened in Europe and American fucking centuries ago.

Spurdle flicked disgustingly through the rest of the book; it didn't seem to get any better. He was about to give up and watch the in-flight movie *Wall Street*, even though he'd seen it three times and hated the ending, when his eye fell on the following passage:

> Speculation occurs when people buy assets, always with the
> support of some rationalising doctrine, because they expect their
> prices to rise. That expectation and the resulting action then serve

to confirm expectation. Presently the reality is not what the asset in question — the land or commodity or stock or investment company — will earn in the future. Rather, it is only that enough people are expecting the speculative object to advance in price to make it advance in price and thus attract yet more people to yet further fulfil expectations of yet further increases.

This process has a pristine simplicity; it can last only so long as prices are rising reliably. If anything serious interrupts the price advance, the expectations by which the advance is sustained are lost or anyhow endangered. All who are holding for a further rise — all but the gullible and egregiously optimistic of which there is invariably a considerable supply — then seek to get out. Whatever the pace of the preceding build-up, whether slow or rapid, the resulting fall is always abrupt. Thus the likeness to the ripsaw blade or the breaking surf. So did speculation and therewith economic expansion come to an end in all of the panic years from 1819 to 1929.

Spurdle wasn't sure if he entirely got J. K. Galbraith's drift but the passage made him feel slightly queasy nonetheless. He knew very little history but he was aware of the significance of 1929: that was the year of the Wall Street crash which led to the Great Depression. His mother had often talked about the depression; Jesus Christ, people lived on turnips for five years. What Galbraith reckoned had happened in the run-up to 1929 sounded uncomfortably like what had been going on in New Zealand for the past couple of years.

Spurdle flicked on, looking for more on the Wall Street crash. On page 220 his eye was caught by a reference to one Irving Fisher, whom Galbraith described as "the most versatile and, by a wide margin, the most interesting of American economists". Fisher's economic theories were double-Dutch to Spurdle but there was one thing about the inventor of the price index which he had no problem getting his mind around; in fact, the shocking clarity of it caused him to begin hyperventilating and prompted solicitous attention from an air hostess: Fisher lost between $8 million and $10 million on the stockmarket in the aftermath of the 1929 crash.

It was the figure of $10 million that set Spurdle off. If Fisher had dropped a couple of mill, he mightn't have taken that much notice. But $10 million? Fuck me dead, that's exactly what I'm worth, he thought. And if Fisher, who was obviously Captain Cock when it came to economics and finance and that, could fuck up big-time, where does that leave me?

Spurdle rang his broker from Honolulu and ordered him to sell his entire share portfolio. When his broker tried to talk him out of it, Spurdle asked him if he'd actually read Kenneth Galbraith's *Money*.

"Oh I started it but I didn't get far. I told you it was dry balls."

"So you didn't get to the bit about Irving Fisher?"

"Irving who?"

"Irving Fisher. He was a hotshot economist, a real fucking brainbox, who sucked at the pineapple in the Wall Street crash. If you'd heard of him, I might listen to you but seeing you haven't, just pipe down and sell my fucking shares — every last one of the bastards."

Thanks to J. K. Galbraith and Irving Fisher, Spurdle sat out the October 1987 stockmarket crash and was now even richer. However, it was the nature of the beast that no matter how rich he got, it wouldn't be rich enough.

So Bryce Spurdle sat out on the pavement at the Sierra café sipping his second cappuccino, nibbling on a blueberry muffin, and thinking about Dale Varty and money. That was Dale's big problem, he thought; he never really understood money, never grasped that money wasn't just the main game, it was the only game. Personal stuff didn't enter into it — you couldn't afford to let it get in the way. Christ, just because I pulled that number on him down at Coromandel didn't mean I'd gone off him; it was just the smart thing to do.

But Varty had turned the tables on Al Grills, something Spurdle wouldn't have picked in a hundred years. And he'd taken it personally all right; by Christ he had. Two nights after the rendezvous at Otama, Spurdle's bedside phone rang at three o'clock in the morning. He'd checked the time and picked up the phone on the sixth ring.

"Who the hell is this?"

There was a few seconds silence. Spurdle started to repeat the question when Varty interrupted him.

"It's me."

"Dale, where the hell are you, mate? I've been waiting to hear from you. Jesus, what happened the other night?"

"You can knock that shit off," said Varty in a flat, hostile voice Spurdle hadn't heard before. "Grills told me all about it. 'Spurdle's jacked up a little welcome home surprise for you' was what he told me."

"I don't get it; what are you talking about?"

"You know fucking well. You lined up that bastard to get rid of me."

"Dale, just listen to me for a minute. Grills must've decided to go solo. He would've made out I had something to do with it just to rub it in. That'd be the sort of shithouse . . ."

"You'll have to do better than that, arsehole: Grills was just the hired help; it was your idea all right. You set me up, you fucking cunt. This call is just to tell you that I know what you did and that one of these days, I'm going to get you for it. When I do, I'll cut your nuts off and feed them to you, you poxy piece of filth."

Spurdle was getting up to pay the bill when his mobile rang.

"Bryce Spurdle."

"Mr Spurdle, this is Leith Grills — Al's brother."

"How'd you get hold of this number?"

"I rang your place and the woman who answered the phone gave it to me. That okay?"

Spurdle sighed and shook his head. "Yeah. What can I do for you?"

"You seen the paper?"

"You mean about Varty coming back? What about it?"

"That fucker killed my brother, Mr Spurdle. Al was working for you at the time. I reckon we owe it to Al to pay Varty back."

Owe it to Al? What was this moron talking about? Spurdle glanced around. The only other people at the pavement tables were two overdressed women trying to talk over each other; they wouldn't have taken any notice if he'd recited all twenty verses of "The Captain of the Lugger" at the top of his voice. Spurdle hardly knew Leith Grills; he vaguely remembered him as a bigger, uglier and denser version of his dead older brother — and, by all accounts, even more of a headcase. I could do with someone like that right now, he thought.

"Well, Leith, I reckon Al understood that risks were part of the job," said Spurdle in a low voice. "Went with the territory, you know what I mean? Anyway, let's not worry about that. Fuck Varty — the bastard promised he'd come back and get me too. Listen, why don't you come out to my place tomorrow, say around lunchtime? We can have a bite to eat and a few beers and talk about this."

After he'd got off the phone, Spurdle went back to thinking about Dale Varty and the deal that went sour. Varty had obviously gotten away with the ten kilos of cocaine; there was no way he'd taken it with him when he skedaddled out of the country and he obviously hadn't been back to collect it since then. Spurdle knew the local drug scene well enough to be sure the cocaine had never found its way onto the market; Christ, you couldn't have missed it, not that much top-shelf snort, even if it'd been drip fed. Where all that led was that the coke was still wherever Varty had hidden it.

It wasn't the first time that Spurdle had thought about the cocaine, but without any sort of line on its whereabouts, it had never been worth pursuing. Now the only person who knew where the treasure was buried was coming back.

Because Spurdle was a cautious man, he didn't use his mobile phone to make the call. Instead he drove around till he found a public phone box. He rang the chemistry department at the university and asked to speak to someone who was an expert on narcotics. He was put through to a Dr Wong.

"Dr Wong, my name's Bevan Jones. I'm a journalist at the *Sunday News* and I'm working on a story about drugs. I was wondering if you could tell me how long drugs last for? I mean do they have like, a use-by date?"

"Which drugs are we talking about?"

"Let's say cocaine."

"In solution cocaine has a ten year half life, that's to say after ten years, it retains fifty per cent of its potency. In powder form it could last considerably longer. Of course, that's the laboratory answer if you like; in practice, all sorts of factors could cause it to degenerate much more quickly."

Spurdle didn't like the sound of that. "Like what?"

"Well, is it pure? Is it bulk raw material? Is it moisture-free? Is it away from the light? What temperature is it being stored at? You see, the higher the temperature, the quicker it degrades."

Spurdle thought swiftly: if there's one thing Varty knows about, it's dope; he would've done it dead right.

"Let's say it's pure and it's been stored properly."

"In that case, the best answer I can give you is that I don't really know how long it would last because very little research has been done in that area. Certainly, ten years, but who knows beyond that? If it's completely air-tight and kept at a low temperature, it could quite conceivably remain potent for twenty years. Again in theory the potency would reduce at a rate of ten per cent over five years but if it was pure to start with, it would still be extremely potent."

In the phone box Spurdle grinned broadly. "Thanks, doc. You've been a big help."

"Tell me something," said Dr Wong. "Did a big drug story break today? The reason I ask is you're the second journalist who's rung this morning asking that question."

7

After the customs officer had finished going where no man had gone before, Duane Ricketts got dressed, picked up his bags and walked somewhat gingerly out of the terminal. To save money, he got a mini-bus rather than a taxi. Because he was the last passenger on board and because the mini-buses operate on a first-on, first-off basis, the trip lasted a little over an hour and a quarter which is how long it takes to get from the airport to Mt Roskill if you go via One Tree Hill, Ellerslie, Mt Eden and Balmoral. Ricketts whiled away the time thinking about what he'd do with the $10 he'd saved.

Ricketts' house was a moderately ugly white-painted wooden bungalow with a garage, a shed, front and back lawns bordered with sparsely planted flowerbeds, a washing line and a vegetable garden in which he'd once tried to grow potatoes, capsicums and lettuces but now just weeded a few times a year for the exercise. He was pleased and mildly surprised to find that his seven-year-old Toyota Corolla was still in the garage and the house hadn't been broken into. The letterbox contained a few bills, leaflets advertising everything from bulk meat to three different types of manure, and an invitation to be present at the Second Coming which apparently would take place a few doors down the street ten days hence. Ricketts, who didn't believe in anything much, let alone God, found the notion that the Lord Jesus would choose Mt Roskill as the venue for his comeback a little far-fetched.

Mt Roskill has a well-deserved reputation for religious zaniness. Ricketts sometimes amused himself at the supermarket by advising shoppers not to go overboard on toilet paper because he had it on good authority that the end of the world was nigh. Now and again a shopper would nod solemnly, say something like "Gosh, so it is; it'd slipped my mind," and put a few rolls back on the shelf. When people told Ricketts that Mt Roskill had no redeeming features, he'd reply that that was what made it affordable. He'd also point out that it was one of the few, if not only, parts of Auckland where you could get a three-bedroom house for under 150 grand within five minutes' drive of two reasonable golf courses.

After he'd had a shower, Ricketts weighed himself on the bathroom scales. He was 74 kg, almost a stone underweight in the old measurement. He looked in the mirror; the face that looked back at him was only half-familiar. His eyes had sunk deep into their sockets; there were lines which hadn't been there a month ago etched into his cheeks and his dark hair seemed faded and lifeless, like a cheap wig. Maybe you should go along to the Second Coming, he thought; you'd blend right in with the mad and the marginal. Instead he decided to go and see his sister down on the farm.

Ricketts' sister Shirley and her husband Lloyd had a dairy farm on the Hauraki Plains, not far from Paeroa. Ricketts got there just after ten the next morning, having rung ahead. Shirley took one look at him and said: "Jesus Duane, what've you been up to this time?"

He started to tell her about his adventures in Thailand, but she interrupted saying they had all day to gasbag, right now the main thing was to get some food into him, he looked like he hadn't had a decent feed since Christmas dinner. Then she cooked him bacon, sausages, eggs, fried tomatoes and mushrooms which, apart from the mushrooms, was exactly what Ricketts had expected. Lunch, three hours later, was cold leg of lamb and salad followed by bread and cheese. That evening they had roast beef, potatoes, kumara, carrots and beans with homemade apple pie and ice cream for dessert. By the time the kids went to bed, Ricketts was two shots into his bottle of duty-free Remy Martin and starting to feel like a new man.

Ricketts had intended to stay the weekend at Shirley and Lloyd's. He'd thought the rehabilitation process would take at least that long and had contemplated putting in a few hours' work around the farm to reactivate muscles and get that country air through the lungs. In the end, though, he decided to head back to town on Saturday. He had two reasons for cutting short his stay: the first was that when, following Varty's instructions, he'd rung the lawyer Bart Clegg, Clegg had said they'd have to meet on Sunday; he had a case in Wellington starting Monday morning that would probably go all week. The second was Ricketts' feeling that he was beginning to outstay his welcome.

He'd started to get that feeling just after he'd confessed, halfway through his third cognac, that "to be absolutely honest, it was heroin I got done for, not marijuana". At breakfast the next morning Shirley carried on as if she thought the moment she turned her back, he'd be sprinkling some mind-rotting addictive substance on the kids' cornflakes. And from Lloyd's reaction when Ricketts offered to give him a hand, there was obviously no way he was going to allow a dope-sucking degenerate in the same paddock as his Friesians.

On Saturday morning, just before noon, Ricketts stopped to buy fruit and vegetables at a roadside stall at the foot of the Bombay Hills. The place was busy so, while he waited to pay, he flicked through a copy of that morning's *Herald* which was lying on the counter; it was the first time he'd looked at a newspaper since he'd got back. He wasn't really concentrating so it was a fluke he even noticed the story which was little more than a filler tucked away at the foot of an inside page. The two-deck headline said "Mr Asia man's mystery death" and the story went:

Mystery surrounds the death in Bangkok of former Mr Asia drug syndicate member Dale Varty.

Yesterday the New Zealand Press Association reported that the fifty-three-year-old New Zealander was about to be released from a Thai jail after serving a ten-year sentence for drug trafficking.

However, Thai authorities subsequently informed the New Zealand Embassy in Bangkok that Varty had died of unspecified causes shortly before he was due to be released. The authorities said Varty had been taken ill suddenly in Bangkok's Bombat Drug Rehabilitation Centre and died a short time later in the prison clinic.

The embassy is now seeking information on the exact circumstances and cause of death.

What the hell's all that about? wondered Ricketts. By the time he'd paid for his fruit and vegetables, he'd concluded — correctly — that it was about people covering their arses.

Rayleen Crouch slept in on Saturdays so she didn't get around to reading the paper until mid-morning. After she'd made a cup of tea and heated up a croissant, she took her breakfast and the paper back to the bedroom and opened the curtains to let in the autumn sun. She was sitting on the bed in her dressing gown propped up on two pillows when she learned that her former husband's old life was the only one he was going to have.

The news caused mixed emotions. The previous afternoon she'd spent a frustrating hour and a half trying to get hold of her daughter Electra, who didn't look at a newspaper from one year to the next, to let her know that her father was coming back to Auckland. Electra, who was eighteen, had moved out of her mother's house a couple of months earlier after a row. Crouch couldn't remember whether the row had been over Electra's new nose-ring, new boyfriend or new rock band; seeing she'd disapproved of all of them, it was just a question of which one she'd criticised first. In fact it was the band they'd argued about: Electra was the founder member and lead singer of 'The Homo Dwarves' and Crouch, who held a range of progressive views, felt strongly that to call the band a politically incorrect name was bad enough but two was verging on shameful.

Ever since Electra was fourteen she'd been threatening to leave home — she'd actually done it a few times, although only for a day or two — so Crouch hadn't taken much notice when she'd packed her bag and stormed out. This time, she seemed to be serious. Her mother assumed it meant she'd found herself a sugar daddy or else 'The Homo Dwarves' were hot.

Electra rang in now and again to confirm she was still in one piece. Each time Crouch assured her she was welcome to come home whenever she wanted to; each time Electra replied that she'd bear it in mind but she felt it was doing her some good standing on her own two feet for a while. And each time, on hearing those words, Crouch, who was enjoying having some space, uttered a silent prayer of thanks.

Because Electra was rather vague about exactly where and with whom she was living, her mother had been unable to track her down the day before. Under the circumstances, thought Crouch, it was just as well.

Leith Grills hadn't read the paper before leaving home. That didn't really matter because when the front door of the Spurdle residence opened and he saw Jody Spurdle standing there pointing her extraordinary breasts at him, his mind went completely blank as it tended to do at moments of sensory overload.

Bryce Spurdle was sitting at the bar in his den cum snooker room having his first beer of the day and reading the racing pages when his wife ushered in their guest. Spurdle looked up. The first thing he noticed was that Jody had on a new gym outfit; in keeping with tradition, it exposed even more of her body than its predecessor. The second thing he noticed was that Leith Grills wasn't looking at him; instead he was staring at Jody's breasts, which were partly encased in a white sports bra, with the glassy, disbelieving expression of a man who's just run over his foot with the lawnmower.

Grills certainly wasn't the first man to ogle Spurdle's wife in his presence; none of the others, though, had been anywhere near as brazen about it. Spurdle noted Grills' slack jaw, his fixed, dull gaze and the thick, black, continuous strip of eyebrow which seemed to wriggle across his low forehead and the bridge of his blunt nose like a tropical caterpillar; having done so, he decided that expecting social graces from Grills was as unrealistic as expecting a sheep to play the guitar solo from "Layla".

"I'm off to the gym, hon," said Jody. "See you later." She looked briefly and dubiously at Grills and told him, with patent insincerity, "Nice to've met you."

Grills lifted his empty dark eyes from her chest to her face and attempted a polite half-smile. Jody, who was used to men looking at her with longing and worse, left the room thinking that Grills' lewd, vacant grimace was one of the most horrible sights she'd ever seen.

"Fucking hell Mr Spurdle," said Grills after Jody had closed the door behind her. "If you don't mind me saying so, your wife — she's a knockout."

"You noticed, did you?" said Spurdle dryly.

"Shit, you couldn't help it. Tell you what, you're a lucky bloke . . ."

"Yeah, so I've been told. I tried to get hold of you this morning, to tell you not to bother coming over. Varty's dead."

He handed the paper to Grills who read the story, mouthing the words.

"It doesn't make sense, Mr Spurdle. Yesterday the paper said he was coming back here."

"Well, what it said was he was going to come back when he got out of jail. He must've picked up some fucking disease at the last minute and croaked on it. You'd think he'd have been immune after that long, wouldn't you? Anyway, that's him fucked. Bit of a bummer really. You know that dope he ripped off Al? I'm bloody sure it's still sitting there, wherever he hid it. I was hoping we could persuade him to let us in on the secret."

Grills thought about it for a while. "He must've told some bastard."

Spurdle shook his head. "Doubt it. He didn't trust a soul, Dale."

"Didn't he have a wife? A fair-looking piece if I remember right — not in your missus' class but not too foul all the same. You reckon he might've told her?"

"Rayleen? No — she'd be the last person he'd tell. The reason they split in the first place was him pushing drugs, then they had a real shitfight over the kid. By the time it all went down, they were history."

Jody Spurdle had been deliberately vague when she'd told her husband that she was going to the gym since she was actually a member of three gyms — one in Mairangi Bay, one in Shore City, Takapuna and one over in the city. She found that having a choice of gyms as well as outfits provided that element of variety which helped her keep to her exercise routine.

Another benefit of belonging to three gyms was that it made it harder for Bryce to keep tabs on her which was useful when, as was the case that Saturday afternoon, she used going to the gym as a cover for seeing her lover. He was a fitness instructor and part-time model named Troy Goatley who rented a waterfront house in Belmont for $300 a week. Jody contributed $100 of that out of her allowance so that Troy didn't need to have a flatmate; having someone else around the place would've inhibited their relationship and the gymnastic and vocal sex of which it almost exclusively consisted.

After Goatley and Mrs Spurdle had had sex, which involved a lot of changing positions, sometimes for technical reasons and sometimes so that they could get a better view of themselves in the full-length wardrobe mirrors, Troy went to the kitchen to make a restorative drink. When he returned to the bedroom Jody was lying on her back, an arm behind her head, staring at the ceiling.

"You're looking serious, babe. Got something on your mind?"

"You know that cop who comes into the gym, the one who told you Bryce used to be involved in drugs?"

"Wayne? What about him?"

"Could you ask him if he's ever heard of a guy called Leith Grills?"

"Leith Grills? Yeah, sure. Who's he?"

"This really creepy guy who came out to see Bryce today; he looks like a real hood."

"You think Bryce might be going back into the drug business?"

Jody rolled onto her side. "Even if he was ever in it — and we've only got that Wayne's word for it — why would he want to do that now? No, it's just this guy Grills; he gave me the screaming shits — he looked at me as if he was, like, trying to memorise every detail about me. Coming over here I suddenly thought, Christ, maybe Bryce's hired him to check up on me. I don't know, maybe I'm getting paranoid; it's just there's been a couple of things lately made me wonder if he suspects something. The other night, right, I walked into the bedroom and found him going through the washing basket. My gym gear was in there but I hadn't been to the gym; I was here all afternoon."

She looked at Goatley expectantly; he looked back blankly. "I don't get it, babe; so what?"

"When I've done a workout, my gear's real sweaty, okay?" said Jody impatiently. "Sometimes it's, like, sopping wet. So if he touched it when he was rummaging in the washing basket, don't you think he might've wondered how come it was dry?"

Goatley shrugged his meaty shoulders. "So if it wasn't sweaty, why'd you put it in the basket in the first place?"

"Oh gee thanks, professor," said Jody sarcastically. "I just thought it was safer seeing he'd seen me walk out of the house in it. He doesn't make a habit of going through the washing basket, believe it or not."

"You don't have to bite my head off," said Goatley with a wounded air. "I just wondered, that's all. You ask him what he was looking for?"

"Course I did. He said he thought he'd left some money in a shirt pocket. He didn't find any."

"Well, did he say anything about your gym gear?"

Jody rolled onto her back, swung her long, golden-brown legs to the floor and stood up. "If he had've, I probably wouldn't be here, would I? I told you, I could be getting paranoid but this guy today freaked me out. Just do me a favour, okay, and ask that cop about him?"

"I said I'd do it, didn't I?" said Goatley a little sullenly as it dawned on him that the matinée wasn't going to have an encore. "In fact I'll do it this arvo. Got nothing better to do."

Everton Sloan III, the youngest and brightest of the CIA officers attached to the US Embassy in Bangkok, was sitting at his desk trying to catch up on his paperwork when the embassy chief of staff burst into his office.

"You seen that fucking Funke?" he demanded.

Sloan, who knew that his Ivy League appearance and mannerisms annoyed the chief of staff more than most people, slowly removed his horn-rimmed glasses.

"Buddy?" He shook his head. "Haven't set eyes on him for a couple of days. I seem to recall him muttering something about going up country. Why? Is there a problem?"

The chief of staff slumped into the chair in front of Sloan's desk. "You'd think I'd know better than to come in here on a Saturday, wouldn't you? The goddam phone rings, you answer it, and you're stuck with someone else's fucking problem."

"Anything I can do?"

The chief of staff gave Sloan a sharp look. If anyone else in the embassy asked a question like that, he'd automatically assume they were being sarcastic; either that or they'd have some outrageous favour in return up their sleeves. Sloan was his usual boyish and apparently guileless self. The chief of staff had learned long ago not to judge a book by its cover; besides, he kept hearing how Sloan was as smart as a whip and already earmarked for stardom by the big dicks at Langley.

"You mean it?" he asked suspiciously.

Sloan held out his hands, palms upwards. "I'm just doing paperwork — nothing that won't keep."

"Well, I'd sure appreciate it, Ev. I promised Milly I'd be home by one. We're having a cookout and guess who's on chef duty."

Sloan smiled pleasantly. "Well, seeing as how I'm not invited, who better than me to pick up the ball?"

The chief of staff grinned weakly. "Hey Ev, it's one of those family things — kids everywhere. You'd be bored shitless. But listen, if you get through by three or so, come on over by all means."

Sloan's smile broadened. "We'll see. Now what've we got here?"

"Okay. The other night a transvestite was found shot dead down by the Chitladda Palace. So fucking what, right? Well, it turns out he should've been in the slam instead of peddling his ass on Patpong; he'd been in Bombat, wasn't due out for another month. The call I took, it's the superintendent at Bombat and he's pissed off; his deputy's telling him it was Funke's idea to turn this character loose early. Now the transvestite's family's making waves and everyone's running around looking for someone else to blame. Shit, you know how it goes."

Sloan nodded. "You got any details?"

The chief of staff handed him a piece of paper containing a list of names and phone numbers. "Phumkumpol, that's the dead fag. The name below that is the cop handling the case and the bottom one is the deputy superintendent."

"Leave it with me," said Sloan. "I'll check it out."

The chief of staff stood up beaming. "I owe you one, pal."

Sloan put his glasses back on. "Rest assured, I'll think of something."

8

Although Everton Sloan III was philosophically and temperamentally inclined towards pessimism, he didn't expect the brouhaha over the murdered transvestite to amount to much: a twenty-four-hour wonder, he reckoned; if that.

The way Sloan figured it, if Funke really had leaned on the deputy superintendent of Bombat to spring the transvestite, he was probably just doing an informer a favour. Either that or he'd had a use for him, maybe as a stooge, witting or unwitting, in some kind of entrapment operation. It hadn't gone entirely to plan — such ploys seldom did — and Phumkumpol had been dispatched to the great sex change clinic in the sky. That was an extremely bad break for him but the Thais would be pissing against the Hoover dam if they tried to make an issue of it. Funke was, after all, a badge-carrying agent of the US of A engaged in the war against the forces of darkness. It was a war which was short on rules but long on collateral damage. That was a fact of life and the superintendent of Bombat could either like it or he could eat it raw.

It took four phone calls to persuade Everton Sloan III that the situation was somewhat more complicated than he'd imagined.

The first call was to a contact in the Bangkok police to get the basic facts about the victim and the circumstances of his demise. The contact rang back half an hour later with the information that Kham Phumkumpol aka Brandi had been in Bombat on a two-bit marijuana charge, probably as a result of getting caught up in some kind of police shake-down. He had no known links to the drug gangs, big or small. The murder had taken place in the early hours of Thursday morning, shortly after Brandi left the ladyboy hangout on Patpong Road. That indicated it might have been transactional in origin; on the other hand, he'd been blown away in a no-nonsense, even professional, fashion which tended to undermine the theory that Brandi was shot because he'd overcharged or underperformed.

Next Sloan rang the deputy superintendent at Bombat.

"I understand," said Sloan, "that it was special agent Funke's idea to release Mr Phumkumpol early?"

"Right. Mr Funke, he tell me to let Brandi go because he cause so much trouble," answered the deputy superintendent in the agitated tone of a prison administrator who's seen the future and it largely involved washing out latrines. "Also he could be in danger here — maybe some guys want to get him for what happened."

After a pause to admire the deputy superintendent's ability to utter that last sentence without a trace of irony in his voice, Sloan asked: "What did happen?"

The deputy superintendent told Sloan about Brandi's role in Dale Varty's stabbing, concluding, "Ladyboys, they make trouble all the time but this one, he the worst, for sure."

"As a matter of interest, how did agent Funke get to hear about this incident?"

"Mr Funke, he DEA, okay? So when Brandi tell me how he hear the New Zealand guys talking about their drugs, I say to myself 'you got to call Mr Funke'."

Whoa, thought Sloan. New Zealanders? Drugs? Run that by me again.

The deputy superintendent told Sloan that Varty, the one who was stabbed by Brandi's boyfriend, had told Duane Ricketts, the one who'd got bail and been driven away from the prison by someone from his embassy, about a stash of drugs hidden in New Zealand. While Sloan was trying to make sense of it all, the deputy superintendent asked the question he'd been wanting to ask since the start of the conversation: "Why you not talk to Mr Funke? He explain everything."

"Agent Funke's not around right now. He's out of town somewhere."

"Maybe he gone to New Zealand huh? Find the drugs. That his job, right?" The superintendent's voice dropped to a near whisper. "For sure he very interested in this. I know because he ask me for copies of files — for Brandi, Varty and Ricketts. I not meant to do that but, hey, we on the same side, right? We have to help each other."

Sloan hung up and stared thoughtfully at the ceiling for a minute or two. Then he rang the New Zealand Embassy and asked to speak to the official who'd collected Ricketts from Bombat. The call was put through to Jason Maltby who was tidying his desk prior to taking a fortnight's leave in New Zealand — at the ambassador's suggestion.

Sloan introduced himself and asked Maltby if he could confirm that Ricketts had returned to New Zealand.

"I believe he has. Put it this way, he was booked on a flight to Auckland last Tuesday and we haven't seen or heard from him since. You'd be aware of course that it's not against Thai law for someone to leave the country when they're on bail?"

"Is that right? Frankly, over here we don't lie awake nights worrying about what is or isn't against Thai law . . ."

"Don't tell me you've got to do a report as well? Good grief, you people must be in constant danger of being buried alive under an avalanche of paper."

"Excuse me?"

"Just the other day I had a colleague of yours — one of the anti-drug police whatever they're called — on to me, wanting details of Varty's next of kin; said he needed it for a report he was doing. The mind boggles; rather you than us is all I can say."

"Would that've been agent Funke?"

"Funke, that's the man. Seemed a nice chap. What part of the States does he come from with that accent? Somewhere in the deep south, I imagine."

"Agent Funke's from Texas — a good old boy from the Lone Star state."

Texas, thought Sloan: where everything's bigger and better than anywhere else. Including the bullshitters.

Sloan's fourth and final call was to Funke's condominium. The Filipino maid said Funke had gone away the previous evening. He hadn't said where to or for how long.

Sloan walked down the corridor to Funke's office which he carefully searched. As he'd expected, he didn't find anything which shed light on what Funke was up to. There were a few colour photographs in the top drawer of the desk; they'd been taken at a country club outside Bangkok, the expat American community's favoured R and R locale. One of them showed a grinning Funke making a pistol sign at the camera with his thumb and forefinger.

Sloan's mouth twisted into a sour, ironic smile as he looked at the photo. The blithe confidence with which he'd sallied forth an hour earlier had now dissipated completely. Perversely, he found it almost reassuring that his optimism had proved ill-founded. Like most pessimists, Sloan believed it was safer to expect the worst; that way, life held fewer disappointments.

At 10 o'clock that night Sloan went into the ladyboy bar on Patpong Road. He bought a Heineken and showed the barman the photograph of Buddy Funke in his gunfighter pose. The barman shrugged unhelpfully. Sloan showed the photograph to the other staff and a few of the regulars. One of the regulars, a petite transvestite, was sure Funke had been in the bar only a few nights before, maybe Wednesday or Thursday. The reason the transvestite remembered was that when he'd asked the man in the photo to buy him a drink, he'd told him to go rub his phoney gash up against someone else.

At 9.25 the next morning Jody Spurdle was driving back from the baker in Forrest Hill in her Volkswagen Golf convertible with a Sunday paper, a crusty white loaf for her husband and a mixed grain loaf for herself when the car phone rang. It was her lover Troy Goatley.

"Hey babe, you were right on the money about that Grills character — he's a bad dude."

"Why, what's he done?"

"Well, he hasn't killed anyone — not that the cops know of anyway . . ."

"Troy, Jesus, don't joke about it, all right? Just tell me."

"He's just a lowlife, that's all. He's been inside a couple of times, once for receiving stolen goods, once for burglary, and he got off some other stuff. How about this, though: his brother, who was also a crim, was murdered about ten years ago — beaten to death somewhere down Coromandel. They never caught the killer. Is that spooky or what?"

Over breakfast in the sun room, Jody Spurdle studied her husband for signs that she was under suspicion. There were none. As usual he didn't close his mouth as he chewed so watching him eat was like watching a paisley shirt in a tumble dryer; as usual he made wet, lapping noises of the sort she associated with cats or old ladies with wobbly teeth; as usual he dredged his teacup dry with three or four abrupt slurps, rarely lifted his eyes from the sports section, and made a beeline for the toilet as soon as he'd finished. It was all reassuringly normal.

He was still in the toilet when the phone rang. Jody answered it.

"That you Mrs Spurdle? Leith Grills here. How're you going today, kicking on?"

Over the sudden pounding of her heart, Jody heard the toilet flush down the corridor.

"I'm okay. You want to speak to Bryce?"

"Yeah, he called here this morning, left a message for me to ring him."

"I'll just get him . . ."

"Oh before you go Mrs Spurdle, let me ask you something: how regular do you go to the gym? Reason I ask, just recently my missus has porked up in a big way and I was thinking she could take a leaf out of your book. Not that she'd look like you if she worked out till Kingdom come but it might stop her turning into a complete blog, eh?"

Jody could hardly believe her ears; her cheeks lit up like a neon sign. She stammered, "Four, five times a week I guess," and dropped the phone with a clunk.

She ducked into the bathroom to splash water on her face then walked down to the den to tell her husband, who was setting up balls on the snooker table, that Leith Grills was on the phone. She went back to hang up the phone in the hall. Before she did so, she listened for a few seconds.

". . . you know what I said yesterday about the wife?" she heard Bryce say. "Well, I've had another think about it and I want you to get onto her straightaway. You reckon you can handle that?"

"Just leave it to me," replied Grills, his voice brimming with anticipation.

Jody replaced the handset shakily, terror leaping from the pit of her stomach like vomit.

Varty had told Ricketts to use the lawyer Bart Clegg as a go-between for getting in touch with his daughter. He'd explained that if his ex-wife Rayleen got wind of what was happening, she wouldn't let him get within a bull's roar of Electra. So at 1.35 that afternoon, Ricketts pulled up outside Clegg's house in Ladies Mile, Remuera. He was five minutes late. It was a still, overcast afternoon and the lack of activity in the street suggested the residents were concentrating on Sunday lunch.

Clegg lived in a gracious old white-painted wooden villa, screened off from the street by a towering oak tree in the middle of the front lawn. Ricketts walked up the path and mounted the steps to the verandah. He pressed the doorbell and waited. A minute passed; no one came to the door. He jabbed the button several times in quick succession but that too failed to draw a response. Ricketts peered in the window into a dining room which contained an expensive-looking table with seating for eight and a matching sideboard on which were arrayed several crystal decanters and a set of goblets. To the left of the house was a single garage with a tilt door which was lowered but not locked. Ricketts lifted it up. The garage housed a dark-blue Alfa Romeo 164 but, like the dining room, was devoid of anything resembling a lawyer.

Thinking that Clegg might be round the back of his section pruning his roses or playing in his treehut and hadn't heard the doorbell, Ricketts followed the path down the right of the house. Clegg's back yard was even more private with a two-metre fence and some fine old trees to block prying eyes, not that there was anyone in it to observe.

Steps led up to a wooden deck and the back door. Ricketts stopped at the foot of the steps and listened; he could hear a hissing, bubbling noise. He went up the steps. The noise was coming from a spa pool; no one was in the spa but it was on full-bore, bubbling away furiously and foaming over the rim onto the deck. On the deck beside the spa pool was a three-quarters empty champagne bottle and a long-stemmed glass.

Ricketts looked in the window; there was nobody in the kitchen. He knocked loudly on the back door and called Clegg's name; still no answer. After a minute or so, he walked over and looked down at the spa. There were a few filmy white patches, like big soapflakes, among the bubbles. Ricketts knelt and scooped one off the froth. He found the switch for the spa and turned it off. It took a couple of minutes for the bubbling to die down and reveal more flakes floating on the surface.

The spa pool was oval, about two metres long and a metre and a half across with an underwater seat protruding from the sides. As the turbulence subsided, Ricketts could make out something large and white jammed under the seat. He craned forward for a further look.

It took him a few seconds to work out that what he was looking at was a body. It took him a few more seconds to realise that, that being the case, the filmy white substance he'd skimmed off the surface of the pool was more than likely skin.

Ricketts didn't waste much time wondering what to do next; he knew he had no choice but to report his grisly find and hope for the best. He could wipe down the doorbell and clear off but the cops would almost certainly get on to him before long. His call to Clegg to set up the meeting might've been logged by the lawyer's secretary; more to the point, Clegg probably put the meeting in his diary. His car had been parked out the front for a quarter of an hour so if he did a runner now and one of the neighbours had happened to notice the car, he'd be in deep shit.

Ricketts went in the back door to the kitchen. He used the phone on the bench to ring Auckland Central police station and ask for Detective Sergeant Ihaka. It was Ihaka's day off.

"Track him down," Ricketts told the officer who'd taken the call. "Tell him it's Duane Ricketts and it's important. Get a phone number off him. I'll call him in ten minutes."

When Ricketts rang back, the officer gave him a number adding, "Ihaka said he's really looking forward to hearing from you."

Ricketts dialled the number and a little girl answered. He asked for Tito Ihaka and heard her holler, "Uncle Tito, you're wanted on the phone."

"Ricketts?"

"Uncle Tito — how cute."

"Let me guess, Ricketts: you want me to sponsor you onto a methadone programme?"

"No, that's under control — I held up a chemist this morning."

"Then what can I do for you?"

"What you can do for me is eat shit and die. What you can for the people of Auckland, who you're paid to protect and serve, is get your fat arse over to Ladies Mile; there's a death by extremely fucking unnatural causes awaiting your attention."

"Who?"

"Don't know for sure but if I had to make a wild guess, I'd go for Bart Clegg."

"Who's he?"

"A lawyer."

"A lawyer? Dearie me, we can't afford to lose one of them. What happened to him?"

"Under the rather unusual circumstances, I'll have to pass on that."

"I take it we have a corpse?"

"We sure do."

"Where?"

"In the spa pool. Been in there for quite a while I'd say — with the juice on. When you pull him out, I reckon he'll be like a great big lump of industrial-strength soap."

"I can't wait. All right, what's the address?"

Ricketts told him.

"Oh Ricketts, one more thing."

"Yeah."

"Did you do it?"

"As a matter of fact, no."

There was a long silence.

"Don't you believe me?"

Ihaka guffawed explosively. "What sort of poophead question is that? I can think of a couple of people who I'd put down as incapable of committing a murder but you sure as fuck aren't one of them. And if you did clip someone, this is just the sort of sick but tricky way you'd do it. Plus, of course, you'd have the nerve and the nous to do exactly what you're doing now."

"You know something Ihaka?"

"What?"

"That's the nicest thing you've ever said to me."

9

As instructed, Duane Ricketts reported to the Auckland Central police station at 9 a.m. on Monday. He was taken up to the eighth floor and shown into a small conference room. A few minutes later Detective Sergeant Tito Ihaka booted the door open and came in. He was dressed in jeans and a T-shirt and carried two plastic cups containing coffee, one of which he plonked down on the table in front of Ricketts.

"It's sewage but it's all there is," said Ihaka. "McGrail's on his way."

Ricketts nodded. He hadn't met Detective Inspector McGrail and wasn't particularly anxious to do so. He'd once heard a cop describe McGrail as having all the warmth and personality of a dead eel. He took a tentative sip of the coffee; it was quite horrible.

He pushed the plastic cup away. "Christ almighty, how can you drink that shit?"

"It's not easy," said Ihaka, as if he was giving the question serious consideration. "We look at it as a challenge. By the way, the weirdos downstairs tell us the thing we pulled out of the spa definitely used to be Bart Clegg."

"What sort of state was he in?"

"What you were saying about a lump of soap wasn't far wrong. We'll learn fuck-all from the autopsy, you can put the ring around that."

"Do you know what that soapy stuff on a floater's called?"

Ihaka looked at his watch. "A corpse joke at ten past nine on Monday morning — that could be a record."

"It's not a joke — it's called adipocere."

"Adi-fucking-what?"

"Adipocere. Look it up in the dictionary — it might come in handy next time you play Scrabble."

The door opened and Detective Inspector Finbar McGrail, ex of the Royal Ulster Constabulary, entered the room. He wore shiny black shoes, sharply creased grey trousers, a glossy, perfectly ironed white shirt with sleeves carefully rolled above the wrist, and a navy-blue tie with the words '1987 Boston Marathon' in yellow lettering. His face had a pink, freshly shaved tinge and his short dark hair had been combed into place while still damp. Ricketts suspected McGrail trimmed his ear and nose hairs every morning; in fact, he would've put money on it.

McGrail had several manila folders under his left arm and a bone china teacup and saucer in his right hand. He sat down opposite Ricketts, took a sip of tea and leafed through the contents of one of the folders. Ricketts glanced at Ihaka who winked at him and leaned back, tilting his chair precariously. Finally, McGrail looked up. He examined Ricketts, wrinkling his nose suspiciously like a health inspector sifting through the innards of a suspect meat pie.

"I see you used to be a police officer, Mr Ricketts," he said in his Ulster brogue. At the far end of the table Ihaka, trying not to laugh, made an unpleasant, phlegmy noise.

"Yeah. Few years ago now."

"Hmmm, you've picked up some bad habits since you left the force."

Ricketts started to ask what the bloody hell his habits had to do with anything when McGrail, raising his voice, interrupted: "Your movements, please, since you arrived back in the country."

"I got back Thursday afternoon and was met at the airport by my faithful manservant Ihaka." McGrail's thin lips formed a wintry smile. "Then on Friday morning I went down to my sister's place on the Hauraki Plains — that's sister, brother-in-law and a couple of kids in case you were wondering. I came back on Saturday afternoon and I've been at home since — apart from going to Clegg's."

"We'll check with your sister's family and you better cross your fingers that Clegg died while you were out of town; as you can imagine, establishing time of death isn't a straightforward matter. So what were you doing at his house?"

"I told one of your blokes all this yesterday."

"Now you're about to tell me."

Ricketts breathed through his nose long-sufferingly. "When I was up in Thailand, I came across Dale Varty . . ."

"That was in jail, of course?"

"No, in a Buddhist monastery. He asked me to give Clegg a bell when I got home, pass on his regards. I rang Clegg last week to do that and he said come over for a beer on Sunday afternoon. That's what I was doing there."

"Varty was about to get out of jail himself — why did he need you to get in touch with Clegg?"

"This was after he'd been stabbed. He didn't think he was going to make it."

McGrail stood up and walked around the table to lean against the wall behind Ricketts who kept looking straight ahead.

"Let's picture the scene," said McGrail in a "once upon a time" voice. "Varty's been stabbed and thinks he's going to die; with what may be his last breath, he asks you to get in touch with Clegg. Obviously, he and Clegg were bosom buddies?"

"How the fuck would I know? That's what the guy asked me to do and I did it."

"Sergeant, you spoke to Clegg's ex-wife last night," said McGrail. "Assuming

I've managed to decipher your report, she had an idea Varty was a client of Clegg's at one point but didn't think they had a personal relationship to speak of, correct?"

"Got it in one sir," said Ihaka brightly.

McGrail put one hand on the back of Ricketts' chair, the other on the desk and brought his face close to Ricketts'. "Surely you don't expect us to believe that this man's on his last legs and all he can think of is sending a good wish to his ex-lawyer?"

Ricketts turned his head to look at McGrail and said carefully: "I don't expect you to believe anything."

McGrail returned to the other side of the table, sat down and resumed looking through his folders. Without looking up, he asked, "What else did Varty say to you?"

"Nothing. The doctor arrived and they carted him away. That was the last I saw of him."

McGrail produced another of his quick, cold smiles. For a moment Ricketts thought he saw a glimmer of something approaching amusement in the policeman's eyes.

"I think that'll do for the time being, Mr Ricketts," said McGrail. As Ricketts stood up, he added: "Incidentally, why did you insist on dealing with Sergeant Ihaka yesterday?"

Ricketts glanced at Ihaka, then looked back at McGrail. "Whenever I find a naked corpse in a spa pool, I think of Ihaka. They just seem to go together."

He paused at the door. "If you haven't already done it," he said, "maybe you should check whether the champagne glass that was by the pool is part of a set. If it is, I wouldn't be surprised if the set's one short."

Ihaka went "Eh?"

Ricketts shrugged. "Call me a party animal but if I had a spa and a bottle of champagne, I'd probably get someone around to share them — in fact, I thought that was the whole idea. Maybe Clegg had someone round, someone who'd prefer to remain anonymous and so they removed all traces of their visit. But shit, why am I telling you this? You're the experts, right?"

Ricketts smiled to himself as if he found this notion amusing then exited, closing the door behind him. McGrail looked at Ihaka and raised his eyebrows. Unlike Ricketts, Ihaka was in absolutely no doubt that what he could see in the inspector's normally bleak brown eyes was amusement.

"Fuck it," said Ihaka. "I should've thought of that."

McGrail nodded. "Interesting man, your Mr Ricketts," he said. "I wonder what Varty really said to him."

Everton Sloan III's father was a colossally expensive Washington DC lawyer who was sometimes described in the press as a powerbroker or even an eminence grise.

These are terms Washington political journalists apply to obviously high-powered but low-profile individuals who from time to time have lunch in expensive restaurants with congressmen, members of cabinet or presidential advisers. It was true, nevertheless, that Everton Sloan II was widely acknowledged to be a smart cookie; whenever a new administration was taking shape, his name would be bandied about as a contender for a cabinet post or high-level staff job in the White House. It didn't really matter whether the administration was Democrat or Republican since Sloan wasn't a member of either party; insofar as he held political views, they were of the "strong defence, safe streets, sound money" variety espoused by most of those who counted on both sides of politics.

However, Sloan had never responded to the various feelers put out to him by recruiters for incoming administrations. Whenever he was accused of playing hard to get or of lacking a sense of civic responsibility, he'd reply that, as a young man, he'd made a vow never to work for anyone who wasn't as smart as he was. Because this remark was always accompanied by a gentle, self-deprecating chuckle, only those who knew Sloan well were aware that he wasn't joking.

Those who knew him well were also aware that there was another reason for his reluctance to work in the White House or for any of its occupants: Everton Sloan II was a snob. The Sloan family had been pillars of the old money, anglophile, East Coast establishment for six generations; in their scheme of things good manners, a familiarity with the higher expressions of English culture, the ability to look well on a horse, and a sound wine cellar were more admirable attributes than the dubious knack of achieving popularity among the little people. Respect was another matter, but then few presidential candidates ever seriously contemplated trying to earn the electorate's respect.

The last president of whom Sloan had wholeheartedly approved was Dwight Eisenhower. Like many New England Episcopalians, he'd been immune to the charisma of the Irish-Catholic Kennedys; his attitude to that ill-starred clan was summed up in the phrase "I told you so", which he never tired of using.

Of the others, he regarded Lyndon Johnson as a vulgar, arm-twisting fixer; Richard Nixon as capable but mean-spirited and irredeemably common; Gerald Ford as a small-town Rotarian who somehow blundered into the presidency when people's attention was elsewhere; Jimmy Carter as a cracker who talked about God as if he played rackets with Him and introduced the offensive practice of holding hands with one's wife in public; and Ronald Reagan, while a pleasant enough fellow, as an actor, a huckster, and, worst of all, a Californian. Sloan and George Bush came from similar backgrounds but Bush failed to measure up on grounds of syntax: as Sloan told his friends, "I'm too old to learn whatever language George speaks." The idea of working for Bill Clinton was an anathema on more grounds than he cared to enumerate for fear of appearing unpatriotic. Since the 1992 election, Sloan had taken to spending more and more time on his farm in upstate New York, brooding on the future of the republic.

Whatever else he was, Everton Sloan II was exceptionally well-connected. Thus when his only son rang from Bangkok on Sunday evening Thailand time seeking advice, he told him to go and see Theodore Natusch in Singapore.

First thing Monday morning Everton Sloan III caught the shuttle down to Singapore; shortly after 9 o'clock he was ushered into Theodore Natusch's office on the thirty-eighth floor of the Westin Plaza building. Natusch came out from behind his desk to shake hands, noting with approval that Sloan still dressed like an East Coast Wasp: dark-grey suit with button-down collar, expensive but understated silk tie and sturdy black brogues. It was completely unsuitable attire for South-East Asia but experience had taught Natusch to distrust men who too readily shed their skin on entering a new environment; in his view it smacked of rootlessness and a lack of fixed allegiances. Natusch himself was dressed for Singapore's enervating climate in a light cotton short-sleeved shirt without a tie, linen trousers and black leather moccasins.

Theodore Natusch was a paunchy six footer with a round face which crinkled when he smiled, which was a lot of the time, warm hazel eyes and rust-coloured hair worn in a crewcut, as it had been for nearly all of his fifty-eight years. In 1966 he'd arrived in Saigon to cover the Vietnam War for United Press International. After Nixon's re-election in 1972, when it became crystal clear that America was going to cut and run, he'd resigned from UPI and set himself up as a freelance journalist, based in Tokyo. He spoke Mandarin, Japanese and Vietnamese, he was industrious, and he possessed excellent analytical skills, a limpid prose style and laughter lines and friendly eyes which encouraged complete strangers to confide in him. It was little wonder therefore that within five years he'd gained a reputation as something of a sage on Asian affairs. What the editors of the many newspapers and magazines in which his articles appeared didn't know was that, as well as being a fine journalist who knew his way around Asia, Theodore Natusch was a CIA agent.

He came close to exposure in 1983 when a disgruntled CIA officer leaked the information to a reporter with one of the American television networks. When the news that Natusch's cover was about to be blown reached the CIA's Deputy Director, Plans (Clandestine Services), he rang a supportive senator who rang Everton Sloan II; Sloan in turn rang the network's major stockholder. They had a forty-five-minute conversation which on Sloan's side comprised equal parts charm, menace and legal razzle-dazzle, and on the network bigshot's side opened with bluster and closed with timid gratitude. The story was killed.

In 1986 Natusch quit journalism and moved to Singapore. He opened a public relations consultancy which he proceeded to build into a successful business, largely by exploiting his network of high-level contacts throughout the region backed up with a little judicious blackmail. When he turned sixty he planned to start looking around for a buyer for the consultancy — he had a figure somewhere between $US5 and $US7.5 million in mind — and, once it was successfully off-loaded, to work out the inevitable management contract via modem from a beach-house in Bali or possibly Sri Lanka if the political situation there stabilised.

"So how's your father, the great attorney?" asked Natusch as they waited for coffee.

"He seems fine. I'm not sure he finds Washington entirely to his taste these days."

"I'm surprised anyone does."

"How long since you saw him?"

"Sad to say I've never actually met him, although we've spoken by phone. He did me a great service once: saved my reputation and quite possibly my skin. Going by what you said when you rang last night, I'm about to have the opportunity to repay a little of that debt."

"I was hoping to pick your brains and perhaps get some advice."

"Go ahead."

"What do you know about Buddy Funke?"

Natusch closed his eyes for a few seconds. "Texan, joined the company out of college, by reputation a moderately good operative, perhaps a touch erratic. Went over to the DEA — would've been late seventies, early eighties. Lost track of him since then."

"He's in Bangkok."

Natusch shifted in his seat. "Ah, well, a man with his background in the DEA, you'd expect him to be either out here or in Colombia."

"Why did he switch?"

As the conversation had become more business-like, the warmth in Natusch's eyes had gradually been replaced by a cool wariness. "What makes you think it wasn't just a straightforward career decision?" he asked.

"Common sense. Going from the company to the DEA isn't a brilliant career move now, let alone back then."

Natusch nodded. "How are you on recent British history?"

"Okay."

"A rather morbid taste in one so young. In that case you'll have some idea of the state of play in Britain in the mid-seventies? The miners had seen off Heath's government; the Labour Party was back in office but the trade union bosses were calling the shots and they seemed hell-bent on wrecking the country. The majority of them, in their misguided way, were simply making the most of finally having the upper hand in the class war but we knew some were sleepers and others were taking Moscow's gold. Whatever their motivation, they were getting the job done; the place was going to hell in a handcart. As things went from bad to worse, a few right-wing patriotic organisations sprang up, GB '75 and the rest of them. It was our old friend, the man on horseback syndrome: retired generals announcing their readiness to save the country from the politicians, make the trains run on time and send Sambo back to Jamaica while they were at it.

"Funke was in the London station which was taking a pretty alarmist view of things. The way they were calling it, Britain was heading down the road to voluntary Finlandisation; it was going to be Yanks Go Home and wave goodbye to all those wonderful listening posts and airbases. Buddy was monitoring the right-wing groups. Well, he was as gung-ho as all hell and he kind of got involved with one of them, a genuine paramilitary outfit headed by an ex-SAS crazy. The long and the short of it was he offered to help them get their hands on some serious weaponry. The company was doing shady arms deals all over the place so diverting a shipment wouldn't have been all that difficult.

"I'm sure you can guess the rest. This splendid band of patriots had been thoroughly infiltrated by MI5 and Funke's kind offer got back to Whitehall in the time it takes to make a phone call. The Brits went ballistic. The ambassador was summoned and chewed out; he got on the horn to his golfing buddy in the White House and within twenty-four hours Funke was out on his ass, cast into the outer darkness."

Natusch stood up and stretched. He walked around his desk and perched on the edge of it, looking down at Sloan. "At least, that's what we told the Brits. What really happened was that Funke flew a desk at Langley for a year or so, then got reassigned — to Southern Africa, working with the Unita rebels, Jonas Savimbi's motley bunch, in Angola. He wangled some shoulder-launched SAMs for them, the idea being that if they knocked down a couple of planeloads of Cuban troops, Fidel and co might be less enthusiastic about being Moscow's Gurkhas. In the middle of all this, a Brazilian aircraft manufacturer doing a sales pitch to the Angolans sent an airplane to Luanda on a demonstration visit. The Brazilians invited a couple of ministers and assorted VIPs and their wives on board and took them up for an airborne cocktail party and a little sight-seeing.

"For propaganda reasons, the Angolan government decided it'd be a good idea if the plane landed in Huambo: Unita was claiming they had the town blockaded and nothing could get in or out. As propaganda stunts go, it left a lot to be desired: when the airplane was on final approach into Huambo, Unita blew it out of the sky using a SAM supplied by our mutual acquaintance.

"Whether it was a mistake or whether Unita knew there were ministers on the flight was never really established but all hell broke loose in Washington. No one was shedding tears over the Angolans — they were commies after all — but the Brazilians were another matter altogether. They were critical to holding the line down south — El Salvador, Nicaragua, Guatemala — you name it, we needed Brazil on side down there. Our proxies shooting down one of their civil airplanes with a Brazilian delegation, including members of a couple of the big families, on board wasn't the way to win friends and influence people. It was deemed to be a major league screw-up and someone had to take the fall. Come in agent Funke, your time is up."

Natusch refilled Sloan's coffee cup and went back behind his desk. "Well, that's the history lesson," he said. "How about you tell me what Buddy's done now?"

Sloan told Natusch briefly and dispassionately about the murder of Brandi the transvestite and what he'd learned through his detective work at the weekend. When he'd finished, the two men looked at one another without speaking for a few seconds. Then Natusch said, "Let's have it, son; what's your theory?"

"I think Funke killed the transvestite and he's gone down to New Zealand for the drugs. I don't think he's got it in mind to throw them in an incinerator when he finds them."

"How was the transvestite killed?"

"By the book — two shots at close range, chest and head."

Natusch raised his eyebrows noncommittally. "Why should Funke do it?"

Sloan shrugged. "To shut down the connection, make it harder for anyone to pick up the trail. Who knows? Maybe he gets a jolt out of it."

"Do you know for sure that he's left Thailand?"

"No. Yesterday I got a computer print-out from Thai immigration of people who'd left the country in the last forty-eight hours. He wasn't on it but I didn't expect him to be; he would've used a false passport or slipped out on a fishing boat and been dropped off somewhere down the Malay coast. Then he'd make his way to KL or here and catch a plane."

"I was under the distinct impression this neck of the woods was awash with drugs. Why on earth would he go all the way to New Zealand?"

"Less risk: no one knows him, there's no DEA presence, no one looking over his shoulder. Hell, it's about as far off the radar screen as you can get."

"So how's he going to play it?"

Sloan shrugged again. "Most likely just go in, do his thing and get out. Anything goes wrong, he'll wave his ID and say he was just doing his job." Sloan slipped into a fair imitation of a Texan accent: "'See here hoss, I'm a maverick — always have been; the Good Lord willing, always will be. I follow my nose like an old hound dog; I don't give a hoot in hell about jurisdiction and all that bureaucratic crap.' Only an idiot would believe it of course but we've got enough of them."

Natusch ducked his head to acknowledge the performance. "You seem to have it all figured out," he said.

"You think I've read it wrong?"

"No, I dare say you're right," said Natusch smoothly. "Funke certainly fits the profile of a potential rogue: he's single, amoral, unorthodox, closing in on retirement; given what must've been his aspirations twenty years ago, his career's gone down the toilet. He's operated in places where the corruption's right there, under your nose — that puts ideas in a man's head. As a wise acquaintance of mine once said, he's lived too long in a world with no respect for the laws of God or man. Unfortunately, I find it all too easy to believe he's decided it's time to feather his own nest. I mean, he's hardly the first, is he?"

"Look Mr Natusch, if I thought there was nothing more to this than Buddy Funke topping up his superannuation, I could probably be persuaded to look the other way. But this is a dangerous man and he's out of control; he's likely to kill anyone who gets in his way. Okay, that might be a drug dealer or a scumbag of one sort or another; on the other hand, it might be a policeman or a civilian who happens to be in the wrong place at the wrong time — or a harmless lost soul like Brandi. He's got to be stopped."

Surprised and a little nettled by Sloan's sudden and uncharacteristic vehemence, Natusch responded more tartly than he'd intended: "What are you telling me for? Blow the whistle on him."

Sloan resumed his air of thoughtful detachment. "If I did that, following correct procedure, what would happen? Assuming it was taken seriously, by the time it was all checked out, it'd probably be too late. More than likely, though, it'd be deep-sixed. I can hear them over at the DEA now: 'Can you believe this little Yalie fuck, trying to sell Buddy down the river?'"

Natusch sighed. "Okay Everton. Tell me what you want me to do."

Sloan leaned forward. "How high can you reach at Langley?"

Modesty and pride struggled briefly for squatter's rights to Natusch's face; pride won. He smiled smugly: "I'm godfather to a certain deputy director's daughter."

"That's high. Can you tell him what Funke's done and what he's going to do?"

Natusch nodded slowly. "If that's what you want, I'll do it. Then what?"

Sloan took off his glasses and held them up to the light, then polished them with the back of his tie. He put them back on and looked at the older man with a level gaze.

"Then they'll send a cleaner after him."

"You know about the cleaners?" asked Natusch, quite unable to keep the incredulity out of his voice.

"Before I went to Bangkok, I did a couple of research projects. They came down from the top and involved pretty major security clearance."

Natusch studied Sloan with a mixture of surprise, respect and faint embarrassment. You're going to go a long way son, he thought. I wonder how many more terminations you'll initiate before you're through.

10

Special agent Harold "Buddy" Funke left Bangkok on the evening of Friday, 15 April on a Thai Airways flight to Hong Kong where he treated himself to an overnight stay at the Peninsula Hotel. As Everton Sloan III had suspected, Funke travelled on a false passport, according to which he was Donald Edwin Surface, a native of Oklahoma. Funke had obtained the false passport in Macau six months previously, on the principle that one never knew when it might come in handy.

The false passport was the work of a seventy-eight-year-old Portuguese who'd spent much of his adult life labouring under the misapprehension that he was blessed with artistic talent. The considerable bitterness he felt over the art world's total lack of interest in his extensive output was only partially alleviated by the handsome income he earned from forging US passports, mainly for Hong Kong Chinese who wished to reside in the land of the free and the home of the brave.

However, as well as being very bitter, the old forger was also extremely greedy. So on the last Friday of every third month, he'd catch the 8 a.m. jetfoil ferry from Macau to Hong Kong. At some point during the fifty-five minute voyage, another passenger — it was always someone different — would sit down beside him and surreptitiously slip a fat wad of US$100 notes into his navy blue British Airways flight bag. The money came from the US Immigration Service, although establishing that would have required a lengthy investigation by people experienced in the workings of the international banking system. In return for his quarterly US$15,000 retainer, the forger would pass the courier an envelope containing the details of the false passports he'd produced during the previous three months.

Although Funke wasn't aware of it, the passport in the name of Donald Edwin Surface had the distinction of being the Portuguese forger's final creation. A few days after the DEA man had picked it up, two hard-muscled young Chinese men burst into the forger's apartment, tied him up, and proceeded to torture him by the crude but effective method of pulling out his teeth with a pair of pliers. After he'd confessed that he routinely betrayed his customers to the American authorities, his assailants yanked out his remaining teeth just for the hell of it, then doused him with several litres of petrol and set fire to him. Mercifully, the old man died of shock within seventy-five seconds of being set ablaze which gave him just enough time to work out that at least one of his recent customers had been a member of the Triads.

Funke left Hong Kong the next afternoon on a Cathay Pacific flight bound for Los Angeles. When the 747 reached cruising altitude, Funke requested a scotch and 7-Up and was about to settle back and listen to some country music when the passenger in the next seat sought to strike up a conversation.

"Listening to that accent, I'd say I'm sitting alongside a fellow American," said his neighbour, extending a pudgy hand. "Gene Pokorny's the name, coming to you from Bakersfield, California."

Funke sighed and turned his head to look at Pokorny. He registered blow-dried hair, puffy features, a fixed, beaming smile, a loud tie and a louder tie-pin. Just my luck, he thought: sat next to a fat fucking salesman all the way across the Pacific. He placed a lifeless hand in Pokorny's.

"Howdy," he said without a trace of warmth. "Donald Surface."

"Where are you from, Don?"

Funke went back to fiddling with his Walkman. "Oklahoma."

"Uh-huh. I'm a computer man myself. What business would you be in?"

Funke slowly looked up at Pokorny. "Well, since you ask, friend, white slavery's my line of work. I just got through delivering a matching pair of fourteen-year-old chickees to a middleman in Hong Kong who'll sell 'em to one of the people's tycoons in Shanghai. I'm talking serious dinero."

Pokorny's professional smile faded. He studied Funke very carefully, as if attempting to count the blackheads on his nose. Funke put down the Walkman and twisted further round in his seat.

"I'll let you into a secret, Gene," he said, dropping his voice. "These days, the biggest status symbol in the third world isn't a chopper or a goddam big pleasure boat or a private jet; no siree, it's having your very own all-American fuckdoll. No shit, I can't keep up with the demand. Problem is, these niggers — I use the term in the widest sense — all want the same thing: blue eyes, blonde hair, no zits and a hymen. Believe me, Gene, that package doesn't grow on trees. You think the coloureds like to fuck? Well, let me tell you, they ain't got that all to themselves. I had to snatch these little cuties right off the sidewalk as they walked home from bible class."

Pokorny continued to stare at Funke. Eventually, he said, "Fella, that's a very dangerous sense of humour you got there. I was you, I'd be real careful who I laid that stuff on."

Funke chuckled and snapped the George Jones tape into his Walkman. "Had you going for a minute there, didn't I?"

"I guess you're not into conversation right now, huh?"

Funke turned his strange, unaligned gaze on Pokorny again. "No offence, Gene, but I've just got this feeling in my bones that we look at life from different perspectives."

With the lawyer Bart Clegg no longer available to act as a go-between, all Duane Ricketts had to go on in tracking down Dale Varty's daughter was her

Christian name — Electra — and the fact that she was in a punk rock band. He assumed that Varty's ex-wife would've reverted to her maiden name and the daughter would've followed suit. Unfortunately, Varty hadn't got round to sharing that information with him.

After his session with McGrail and Ihaka at the Central Police station, Ricketts walked across town and up the hill through Albert Park to the university. The first person he asked was able to tell him where to find Radio BFM, the student radio station.

Radio BFM operated from a scruffy collection of rooms on the second floor of the student union building which was behind the cafeteria. When Ricketts explained his mission to the receptionist, a plump twenty-year-old with a shaved head, she told him, "Gabby's your best bet." She walked over to a door off the reception area, knocked quietly and opened it.

From within came a husky female voice speaking in a conversational tone: " . . . and that was Tracy Chapman and 'Talking 'bout a Revolution'. Nice song but did you listen to the lyrics? 'Poor people gonna rise and get their share/ Poor people gonna rise up and take what's theirs.' Course they are Tray, you daft bitch. Just like I'm going to be the next dean of the law school. Coming up next, a track for all you psychos out there — music to cut up the family photo album by. It's from The Doors. Remember their lead singer, Jim Morrison? He thought he was a poet and, to prove it, he pulled his knob out and waved it at the crowd. Then he went off to Paris, took loads of drugs and croaked in the bath. Way to go, Jimbo. As the saying goes, he lived fast, died young and left . . . well, as a matter of fact, it wasn't such a good-looking corpse; he was a bit of a fat bastard by the end. And speaking of the end, that's the name of the song; it's an everyday tale of mass murder and incest, about a bloke who wants to kill his brother, sister, father and mother; in Mommy's case, he wants to play hide the salami before he knocks her off. Weird scenes inside the goldmine indeed."

The music began. A tall fine-featured young woman wearing a woollen skullcap, jeans and a T-shirt with the message *Smells Like Teen Vomit* emerged from the studio. She flicked Ricketts a disinterested glance and walked past him over to the coffee machine behind the receptionist's desk.

"This is Gabby," said the receptionist, tripping along in her wake. "One of our deejays. She might be able to help you."

Gabby was making herself a cup of coffee. "I'm trying to get in touch with a girl called Electra," said Ricketts to her back. "She's in some kind of punk band."

"A punk band?" said Gabby. "How quaint." She flopped onto a battered couch against the wall. "Who are you and what do you want her for?"

"My name's Duane Ricketts. I've got a message for her from someone I met overseas."

"The meaning of life perhaps? A recipe for the perfect date scone?" Gabby took off her woollen cap and scratched her short dirty-blonde hair. She made a noise like a siren and chanted "Dandruff alert" several times, then tugged her cap back on. "She a dyke, this chick?"

"Wouldn't have a clue. Why?"

"She a midget?"

Ricketts shook his head in bemusement. "Look, for all I know, she could have two heads and a hump — I've never set eyes on her."

Gabby raised her eyebrows. "Now that'd be a good look. The reason I ask is I seem to remember the chick who fronts 'The Homo Dwarves' calls herself Electra."

"'The Homo Dwarves'? That's the name of the band? How would I get hold of her?"

"You could try Jerry Naismith — he promotes a lot of the gigs round town."

"You got a number for him?"

She pointed with her chin. "If you can read, it's right there on that socking great poster behind you."

Ricketts borrowed the receptionist's ballpoint and wrote the number on the back of his hand.

"Thanks for your help. You ever do requests?"

"Sometimes. You want one?"

"How about Tom Petty — 'Even the losers get lucky sometimes'?"

With the sixteen-hour time difference, Buddy Funke arrived in Los Angeles an hour and a half before he'd left Hong Kong. He bought a ticket on that night's United Airlines flight to Auckland, then checked into an airport hotel and slept solidly for seven hours.

The United flight arrived in Auckland on schedule at 6.25 on Monday morning. Funke entered New Zealand on his other false passport, the one in the name of his boyhood partner-in-crime Lyle Gorse, which he'd had for almost twenty years. He bought a taxi into the city and, on the advice of a stewardess, checked into the Regis Hotel. After a nap and a long, hot shower, Funke was sitting on the bed towelling his hair when it dawned on him that, for the first time in his adult life, he was unarmed and without immediate access to a firearm.

Weaponry hadn't been an issue for Funke in the past. Whichever godforsaken and hostile corner of the globe he'd found himself, he'd been there in an official capacity; obtaining a weapon, therefore, was simply a matter of rendezvousing with the local friendlies or slipping into the embassy.

Funke had a vague idea that New Zealand was like a little outpost of England stuck down at the ass-end of the world. That being the case, they probably shared England's communistic attitude to gun control; in other words, it wouldn't be the sort of place where you could walk into your friendly neighbourhood gunshop a sitting duck and walk out with enough firepower to turn the Dallas Cowboys defensive line into two tons of steak tartare.

A stroll around town later that morning confirmed his fears.

There wasn't a gunshop in sight and when Funke raised the subject with a passerby who had the gimlet eye and vaguely paranoid demeanour of a shooting man, he'd been informed that the first step to obtaining a firearm was to discuss the matter with the police.

Shortly at 10 o'clock that evening, Funke walked out of the Regis and asked the concierge to whistle him up a cab. When a taxi pulled up, Funke checked out the driver. Satisfied by what he saw, he climbed into the back seat. The driver, sixty-one-year-old Stan Mattamore, looked at Funke in his rear-view mirror and asked him where he wanted to go.

"How long you been driving a cab?" asked Funke.

"Thirty-odd years, on and off."

"I guess you must know where the action is in this town, right?"

Mattamore swivelled round. "You want a root, is that it?"

"You mean, do I want to get laid?"

Mattamore nodded.

"A root, huh? That's a new one on me. Okay amigo, how about you take me to the best root in Auckland."

Mattamore shrugged. "I'll take you to a knockshop but whether it's any good or not . . . from what I hear, you've been to one, you've been to them all." After a pause he added, "I'm a married man myself," as if that explained his unfamiliarity with the vice scene.

Mattamore drove Funke to The Pink Wink, a massage parlour in Fort Street. As Funke paid the fare, he asked, "You folks haven't legalised prostitution, have you? You know, like the Dutch?"

Mattamore stared at him blankly for a few seconds. "Mate, if you're worrying about getting arrested, believe me, the cops have got better things to do."

"As long as it's not legal," said Funke. "I find that takes the fun out of it."

He was offered his pick of two young women who stank of cigarettes and paraded for his inspection with the enthusiasm of virginal peasant girls summoned to an audience with the Marquis de Sade. Funke, who surmised from their vacant expressions and waxy skins that they were junkies, decided he'd seen more desirable armadillos. He chose the marginally more alert of the two who led him upstairs. In the bedroom Funke told the prostitute to sit on the foot of the bed and keep her clothes on. He sat up on the bed with his back against the wall.

"Okay sugar, you can relax," he said. "I don't want to screw. Just let me look at you a while."

The prostitute, who often felt slightly sick when she looked at herself in the mirror, thought this was just about the oddest thing a punter had ever said to her.

"You want me to play with myself?" she offered helpfully. "Or I could talk dirty — I'm pretty good at that."

"I'll bet you could come out with stuff that'd make a tugboat captain puke but I'll pass on that, thanks all the same. Tell me this, though: that gal downstairs who's kind of organising things — she the manager?"

"Nadia? No, she just like runs the shop."

"So who's the boss?"

"Guy called Ronnie."

"He around tonight?"

"Think so. Why?"

"Tell me about Ronnie."

"What's there to tell? He's a pimp."

"Is he a rough guy?"

The prostitute thought about it for a few seconds. "He only hits us if we miss a shift."

"What a prince. Is he your source?"

Her eyes widened. "Hey, what the fuck is this . . ." She stood up and made for the door. "I'm getting out of here . . ."

Funke rolled off the bed and intercepted her. "Don't go making a fuss now sugar or you'll piss me off," he said calmly. "I want to talk to the man, that's all, but first I want to know if he's worth talking to. Just tell me yes or no: does he deal?"

The prostitute knew that it was extremely unwise to discuss Ronnie's unlawful business activities with a complete stranger. On the other hand, she was a hell of a lot less scared of Ronnie than she was of this Yank even though, to look at him, you'd think he was harmless enough: just another drab little middle-aged bloke losing his hair. Christ, though, the way he moved — when she went for the door, he'd come off the bed like a scalded cat. But what really freaked her was the way he looked at her. Not even the pimps who rented her out like a hire car — 'we don't mind if you thrash the shit out of her, just bring her back in one piece' — or the worst sort of customers, the misfits who'd never had a woman reach for them without being paid or frightened, looked at her that way — like she was nothing more than a speck of dirt he'd just noticed under his fingernail. She dropped her eyes and nodded.

"Good," said Funke. "Ronnie sounds like my kind of guy. Let's go see him."

Ronnie Traipse, the manager of The Pink Wink, was in his dirty, pokey office reading a bodybuilding magazine when the prostitute put her head round the door and said a customer wanted to talk to him.

Traipse sat upright and threw the magazine aside. "Jesus, Leanne," he said threateningly, "you didn't fucking fall asleep again, did you?"

Funke slid past Leanne into Traipse's office. "No sir, she was just dandy. What I want to talk about is a business matter."

Traipse, who had a big chest, a bigger gut, stupid eyes and a jaw that harked back to the Palaeolithic era, stood up and flexed his shoulders in what was meant to be intimidating fashion. "Oh yeah?"

Funke nodded to Leanne. "You run along now, my dear." He closed the door behind her and took a good, long look at Traipse. If this boy's not dirty, he thought, granddaddy never stepped in buffalo shit.

"I'm in the market for a pistola," said Funke. "A handgun. I thought maybe you could advise me on how I'd go about getting one."

Traipse squinted at him moronically. "A gun? What makes you think I could help you get a gun?"

"I just thought you might have the connections," said Funke with an ingratiating smile. "A man in your position."

Traipse sat down. "What you want a gun for?"

"Well, you see, I come from Texas where we believe very strongly in a man's inalienable right to bear arms. Fact is, I've carried a gun since I was this high and I feel downright uncomfortable without one. So how about it son — reckon you can rustle me up a piece?"

Traipse scratched his chin. "Could be. How much you prepared to pay?"

Funke shrugged. "I'll pay the going rate, whatever it is. Mind, I want a man's weapon, not some itty-bitty purse gun — nothing smaller than a .32. And I want it ASAP, like tomorrow."

"Sounds to me like you'd be up for a couple of grand."

"Holy shit, two thousand dollars? Son, in Vladivostok I could buy me a truckload of plutonium for that sort of money."

Traipse, who had no idea what Funke was talking about, heaved his shoulders. "You want a pistol in twenty-four hours, that's what it'll cost. It's up to you."

What the hell, thought Funke, I'm not exactly flush with options. "Okay son, this is the deal: you get me a .38 revolver, clean and in prime condition, plus say a couple of dozen rounds, by this time tomorrow night, I'll pay you 2500 of your dollars. Are we talking turkey?"

Traipse nodded slowly. "Sounds good. I'll ring around, see what's available. What's your name?"

"Well, now, I don't see as there's any need to bring names into it."

Traipse's eyes took on a stubborn glaze. "Have to mate. First question these guys are going to ask is 'Who's it for?' They might want to check you out."

Funke thought about it for a few seconds. "If that's the way it works, I guess I don't have a choice. I'm called Donald Surface."

11

On the days when he didn't have a luncheon meeting, Richard Thames, the Deputy Director Intelligence of the CIA, ate his midday meal alone at the conference table in his large office at the agency's headquarters in Langley, Virginia. These solitary lunches generally consisted of sourdough bread, peppery Italian salami, black olives, a tomato, some cheddar cheese and an apple. He washed his food down with half a litre of the dark Prussian beer for which he'd developed a taste during his seven years in West Berlin.

Thames drank the beer from an old pewter mug which his twenty-two-year-old daughter, who'd always had an acute sense of how to gain entry to her father's good books, had given him for his most recent birthday. Thames' twenty-eight years as a spy — half of it spent in the field, half in Washington — had planed away the outer layers of his personality. At the age of fifty and having attained a level of seniority which allowed him some leeway, Thames had decided to add a dash or two of colour to what had become a study in grey; he began accumulating old and anachronistic objects and incorporating them in his daily routine in the belief that they would make him appear quirky or even mildly eccentric: he told the time by a sixty-year-old Rolex watch, scrawled comments on documents with a fountain pen of similar vintage, played golf in plus fours, and went for walks with a knobbly wooden walking stick even though both legs were in reasonable working order. Six months after his birthday, by which time the pewter mug had become part of the Thames persona, his daughter confessed that she'd stolen it from a village pub with a thatched roof somewhere in south-west England, not far from the town with the wonderful Georgian architecture. Thames assumed she meant Bath.

As he drank his beer, Thames thought about his daughter and her troublesome habit of simply commandeering things which took her fancy, the latest of which was her former best friend's fiancé. That train of thought led to her godfather, Theodore Natusch, who'd rung from Singapore the night before to raise the alarm about Buddy Funke. Natusch had repeated word for word what he'd been told by Everton Sloan III and when Thames had asked him what he made of it all, he'd replied that Sloan's reputation as a bright young man appeared to be merited.

When he'd finished his lunch, Thames picked up one of the three phones on his desk and asked Leon Rehbein to step into his office. Rehbein worked in the Office of Central Reference in Thames' department. In addition to being a computer wizard, Rehbein was an irredeemable social misfit with a major personal hygiene problem. Thames frequently used him to carry out sensitive and confidential little research projects. He chose him on the basis that Rehbein's interaction with his colleagues was pretty well confined to saying "hello" in the morning and "goodnight" in the evening, while they in turn seldom, if ever, leaned over his shoulder and asked him what he was working on.

Rehbein knocked and entered. Thames greeted him and pointed him to the chair in front of his desk. The computer wizard was tall and thin and very pale, and had frizzy blond hair which he wore in an Art Garfunkel afro. The consensus among his colleagues was that Rehbein looked a lot like Kermit from *The Muppet Show* but that was as far as the comparison could be taken since, personality-wise, the frog left him for dead.

Even though Rehbein was thirty-two, much of his face and neck was covered with angry red acne which he fingered incessantly when nervous, as he invariably was in Thames' presence. Once Thames had been explaining an assignment to him when he'd prodded a ripe, white-crested crop of boils on the point of his chin a little harder than, presumably, he'd intended. There was an audible popping noise and a trail of pus had splattered across the sheet of crisp, white blotting paper on Thames' desk. Because the memory of that incident still caused him to tremble with nausea and because Rehbein's body odour attacked the senses like nerve gas, Thames had taken the precaution of shifting the visitor's chair a further two metres away from his desk.

"Leon, I've got another little assignment for you," said Thames, forcing himself to smile. "Needless to say, it's a sensitive matter."

Rehbein nodded eagerly and clawed at his cheek, which caused Thames to flinch and push his chair back a few centimetres.

"I want to locate a man named Harold Funke, usually known as Buddy. He used to be one of us, went over to the DEA about 1980. His details will be on file. He disappeared from Bangkok. He would've used a false passport so what you'll need to do is get on to the embassy in Wellington and have them send you a list of passport holders who've entered New Zealand since last Friday. Break out the males in the right general age bracket and run them through the computer. I need to know for sure that he's down there and what name he's using.

An hour and a half after Thames had briefed his computer wizard, at 7.30 on Tuesday morning New Zealand time, Buddy Funke checked out of the Regis Hotel. He took a short taxi ride across town to the Hyatt Kingsgate hotel on the corner of Princes Street and Waterloo Quadrant. He paid the driver, got out of the taxi, and entered the hotel by the main entrance. Inside, he sat in an armchair in a corner of the lobby pretending to read the paper for almost half an hour, until he was absolutely satisfied that no one was taking any notice of him. Then he stood up, picked up his bags, and walked through the lobby and out of the hotel by a side exit which took him onto Princes Street. He walked down Princes Street, turned left into Eden Crescent and walked down the hill till he came to the Crescent Lodge boarding house.

The manageress of Crescent Lodge greeted Funke as if she'd known him all her life, which she obviously hadn't otherwise she wouldn't have called him "Mr Williams". That was the name Funke had used when he'd walked in off the street the previous afternoon and booked a room.

After five years in the police force, Detective Constable Johan Van Roon had more or less come to terms with the unpleasant aspects of the job. He'd lost count of the number of dead bodies he'd seen, something that not that long ago he wouldn't have thought possible; whenever he thought about them, which he tried to avoid doing, they tended to merge into one asexual, featureless lump of flesh.

The family in Howick were the exceptions. The husband was slumped over the kitchen table; the wife was on the floor in the corridor looking like she'd got tangled up with a propeller; and their twin daughters were tucked up in bed with their throats cut. They were eight years old with blonde hair and blue eyes, just like Van Roon's niece. In fact, put the three of them together, you might've picked them as triplets.

They worked it out that the wife had been in the lounge watching TV when her husband had come up behind her and stabbed her with a short-bladed kitchen knife. After seventeen goes at it, he must've decided the knife wasn't really designed for stabbing people to death and gone back to the kitchen to find something better suited to the task. While he was doing that, the wife had started crawling down the corridor towards the bedroom where the twin daughters were asleep. She'd got halfway along the corridor when the husband had come back with a carving knife.

Afterwards, the husband had sat down and written a note of explanation. It was all his wife's fault, he said. She'd announced that at the end of the school term, she was off and taking their daughters with her, even though she knew full well that he couldn't face life on his own. Seeing that she didn't deserve to live, and he no longer wanted to, and it would've been unfair on the twins to leave them all alone in the world, the only solution was for them all to die. Then he'd taken just enough sleeping pills to qualify as an attempted suicide. Van Roon's guess was that the husband would be released from the mental hospital around the time his niece brought home her first boyfriend.

Afterwards, Van Roon had had to take some time off work. Detective Sergeant Tito Ihaka had turned up at his flat one afternoon, claiming he'd been in the neighbourhood and decided to drop in for a beer. Seeing Van Roon didn't drink, he'd brought his own. For a while they avoided the subject. Eventually, Van Roon had said he thought he was going to be okay, he just never wanted to see anything like it again. Ihaka had looked at him with a sad little smile on his bulldog face and gently pointed out that it didn't really matter a fuck what he saw or didn't see from then on because he was going to keep seeing the little girls and their mother till the day they put him in a box. When, after a minute or so, Van Roon nodded to indicate that he understood what Ihaka was telling him, the sergeant had punched him sickeningly hard on the upper arm and told him it was time to get back to work.

Until that afternoon, Van Roon had basically been shit-scared of Ihaka. While most of the guys rated the big Maori as a hell of a cop, Van Roon had also heard him described as a thug, a slob, a degenerate, a vindictive bastard and his own worst enemy; the word around Auckland Central was that Ihaka had gone as far up the ladder as he was ever going to go because senior officers considered him "unsound". On the basis of this personal experience, Van Roon had been inclined to believe that all of these opinions, even the contradictory ones, had some validity. Even though Van Roon now felt something approaching fondness towards Ihaka, he still dreaded having to pick him up from his place.

For a start, you never quite knew what to expect. Once Van Roon had turned up at the Sandringham bungalow to find Ihaka's car in the vegetable garden. Apparently, Ihaka had come up his drive at high speed, failed to negotiate the left-hand turn into the carport, and just ploughed straight ahead, across the lawn and into the garden. Another five metres and he would have parked in his next door neighbour's back bedroom. Ihaka had blamed it on antibiotics he'd been taking for a sore throat, claiming they'd affected his night vision.

Another time Van Roon had discovered a blow-up sex doll in a deck chair on the front porch. The doll had a large cucumber jammed into its mouth slot and a sign around its neck which said "I claim this house in the name of Satan". Ihaka's explanation was that he was being harassed by God's door-to-door salespersons.

Secondly, Ihaka lived alone and was as undomesticated as he was lazy, so his place was always a mess. Whenever Van Roon called there, Ihaka would try to browbeat him into doing a week's worth of dishes or a few loads of washing or — horror of horrors — changing his bed. Thirdly, if Ihaka had a hangover, you could bet he'd be in a foul and abusive mood, not that he was Mr Sweetness and Light at the best of times.

It was just after 10.30 a.m. when Van Roon pulled into Ihaka's drive. He got out of his car and went up the steps to the front door. He rang the bell; it got no response. Van Roon sighed. Ihaka was still asleep: that meant he'd been on the piss the night before so it was odds-on he'd be grumpy all day. Van Roon knew that Ihaka never bothered to lock the door when he was at home so he opened it and went in. He found Ihaka stretched out unconscious on his bed, fully clothed. On his chest were the remnants of fish and chips in newspaper wrapping and a fat ginger cat which was nibbling on a piece of fish in batter.

Van Roon shook Ihaka's right foot. After a few seconds Ihaka opened his eyes. He looked at the cat, then at Van Roon, then back at the cat. He said, "Help yourself, you ginger cunt," then punched the cat in the face. The left jab knocked the cat, yowling, to the floor. It bounced to its feet and scrambled past Van Roon's ankles out of the bedroom.

Ihaka screwed the newspaper containing what was left of the fish and chips up into a ball, dropped it on the floor, and heaved himself into a sitting position.

"Shagnasty," he said, rubbing his eyes. "How'd you be?"

Van Roon, who'd been called far worse names than "shagnasty" by Ihaka and considered it a hopeful sign, said, "I'm okay. How's your head?"

"My head?" said Ihaka, feigning puzzlement. "What about my head? You trying to suggest I got pissed last night, you cheeky little ape?"

Van Roon shook his head. "Why would I think that?"

"Why indeed?" said Ihaka. He gulped in air and unleashed a thunderous, reverberating burp which filled the room with the odour of beer and takeaways. "Give us twenty minutes for a shit, shower, shampoo, shave and shoeshine, and I'll be right with you."

An hour later Ihaka and Van Roon and Jody Spurdle were having tea and biscuits in the sunlit living room of a house in one of the short no-exit streets which run off Hurstmere Road down to Takapuna beach. The house belonged to friends of Jody's. Van Roon was in a jacket and tie, Ihaka in his usual outfit of jeans, sneakers and bomber jacket. Jody wore a low-cut lambswool sweater, a short black skirt and black stockings with high heel shoes. She sat on a sofa and crossed her legs at intervals of approximately two minutes. At first Ihaka was flattered by this; after a while he realised she was completely unaware that she was doing it.

Jody looked anxiously from one policeman to the other. Ihaka was expressionless; Van Roon smiled encouragingly. She addressed herself to the detective constable: "As I said on the phone, I know I sound like a drama queen but I think my husband has hired someone to kill me."

"Because he found out about lover boy?" asked Ihaka with a directness which made Van Roon uncomfortable. For a moment he thought Jody was going to burst into tears. She bit her lip and looked away while Ihaka glanced at Van Roon and made a grotesque face simulating sexual ecstasy. To Van Roon's relief, Jody swiftly composed herself and counter-attacked.

"That makes it okay, does it?" she demanded. "Like, if a woman's unfaithful, she deserves everything she gets?"

"Shit no," said Ihaka, quite unabashed. "Especially not if they're married to an old weasel like Spurdle."

Jody started to say something but Ihaka interrupted: "Listen, why don't you just tell us exactly what makes you think your husband wants you out of the way — right from the word go?"

Surprising herself as much as Ihaka with her matter-of-factness, Jody told them about her affair with Troy Goatley, finding her husband going through the washing basket, the sudden appearance of Leith Grills, and the scrap of overheard phone conversation.

"What did your husband say?" asked Ihaka. "The exact words."

"He said, 'You know what I said yesterday about the wife? I've had another think about it, I want you to get onto her straight away. Can you handle that?'"

"Does he normally call you 'the wife' when he's talking about you? As opposed to 'my wife' or 'Jody' or 'the war office' or 'that bitch'?"

"I don't know, probably not. I guess he'd usually say 'Jody'."

"Mrs Spurdle, I don't want you to run away with the idea that we're not taking this seriously but it's not a hell of a lot to go on."

"What about that creep Grills? I thought he was a well-known criminal?"

"Sure he is but that doesn't prove anything — your husband's been hanging out with ratbags for years. Look, we'll check out Grills, see if we can find out what's going on. In the meantime, I suggest you and the boyfriend give it a rest and let us know if anything else happens."

On the way back into town, Van Roon asked Ihaka what he thought.

"What I think is that Spurdle would've had her sussed ages ago. She's obviously a bit of a sausage jockey — with a body like that, it'd be a crime against nature if she wasn't — but she's not tricky enough to pull the wool over his eyes. Spurdle's so crooked, he couldn't lie straight in bed. That sort of bloke suspects everyone; if the Mother Superior told him she was just off for a quick crap, he'd follow her to the bog to make sure."

"So you reckon there's nothing to it?"

"I didn't say that. Spurdle wouldn't have that shithead Grills around for his conversation. He's up to something — the question is, what?"

12

The village of Manacle is situated on the east coast of the Coromandel Peninsula. It was founded in the early 1880s by six married couples who felt that the gold towns of the Thames-Coromandel area were unsuitably volatile environments for growing children. The would-be settlers by-passed a few likely sites on their trek up the peninsula before they reached a little bay just north of Whangapoua Harbour. It was a pretty spot, autumn was approaching and reserves of stamina and stoicism were running low, so they decided that they'd found what they were looking for. Since they couldn't agree on what to call their settlement, they drew straws; naming rights fell to a Cornishman whose father had gone to Davy Jones' Locker, along with a smuggled consignment of French brandy, just off a part of the Cornish coast known as Manacle Point.

Nothing of any great interest happened in Manacle during the next fifty years. Then one fine afternoon in March 1938, an Englishman by the name of Errol Swarbrick, who was eighteen months into a world tour which didn't have a schedule or an itinerary but was simply proceeding as the spirit took him, rode over the ridge on a dapple-grey mare. Swarbrick got off his horse, stretched his legs and admired the view: green hills rolled gently down to a gold sand beach which stretched almost half a mile from the point, where he could make out children paddling in the rockpools, to a native bush-covered bluff. After contemplating the scene for a few minutes, he decided that he'd chanced upon the most beautiful, most peaceful place on earth. That would have been a minority view even among Manacle's 175 residents, but being in the minority didn't worry Errol Swarbrick in the least because he was quite odd and very, very rich.

Swarbrick's father, the late Sir Ned, had laboured all his life to build Swarbrick Breweries into the dominant brewing company in the north of England. Having achieved that goal, he'd then dropped dead from a massive brain haemorrhage at the Headingly cricket ground in Leeds. England were playing Australia and Sir Ned keeled over shortly after stumps had been drawn on a day in which the visitors had accumulated 455 runs for the loss of one wicket with Don Bradman contributing 271.

Four years earlier, in 1930, Sir Ned had spent a day at Headingly watching England play the Australians and suffered apoplexy brought on by the build-up of seething, impotent rage as the men from down under made 458 runs for the loss of three wickets. Bradman's share on that occasion was 309. On the advice of his physicians, Sir Ned had, in the intervening years, abstained from all activities which excited his passions, particularly watching cricket matches involving Yorkshire or England.

Encouraged by the situation after the first day's play of the 1934 test match — Australia were struggling at 39 for the loss of three wickets in reply to England's first innings of 200 — and in the conviction that lightning on such a scale couldn't possibly strike twice, his physicians had lifted the ban to allow him to attend day two.

While Sir Ned was fond of his only son, he was, in his hard-headed Yorkshire way, well aware that the lad was as daft as a brush and quite incapable of running a whelk stall, let alone a multi-million pound business. Under the terms of his father's will, Errol became a twenty per cent shareholder in Swarbrick Breweries provided he did not take a seat on the board. In addition to dividend pay-outs, he received an annual income of £20,000; all he was required to do to earn that staggering sum was refrain from setting foot on any company property. The arrangement suited Errol down to the ground since he heartily loathed the north of England and everything connected with it, particularly Swarbrick's Bitter, the company's flagship brand.

Swarbrick camped in Manacle for a few days which did nothing to diminish his enthusiasm for the place. He then travelled to Auckland and paid a visit to the offices of the law firm Prawle Prawle & Mulvany where he outlined his plans to a startled Sefton Prawle KC, the senior partner. Swarbrick instructed Prawle to arrange the purchase of a large block of waterfront land in Manacle and to commission New Zealand's leading architect to design and oversee the construction of a residence along the lines of an English country house, complete with appropriate landscaping, on the property. He would contact his bank in London forthwith to arrange the transfer of £100,000 for the purpose.

A fortnight later Swarbrick boarded a ship bound for California where he intended to rent a house on Malibu Beach, bathe in the Pacific Ocean, assess investment opportunities in the motion picture industry, and have sex with as many female movie stars as possible; his plan of attack was to begin with Mary Astor and work his way through the alphabet till he got to Mae West. Swarbrick believed that every woman had her price and nothing he'd heard about the prevailing moral code in Tinseltown suggested that screen goddesses were any different. Sefton Prawle went down to the wharf to see him off and inform him that negotiations over the purchase of the section were proceeding satisfactorily. He never saw or heard from Errol Swarbrick again.

Construction of the Swarbrick house was completed in December 1939, three months after the outbreak of the Second World War, at a total cost of £113,000. Prawle didn't hear a peep of complaint from Swarbrick's bankers or the London solicitors administering his affairs over the fact that the project had gone over budget.

Prawle journeyed to Manacle to inspect the house and surroundings.

They were magnificent. The house was an imposing two-storey, thirty-room Edwardian-style mansion with a panelled entrance hall, a large and ornate dining-room, a library and a billiards room. The broad verandah, bay windows and upper floor balconies looked out to Great Mercury Island. Built of kauri and painted white, it had heavy eaves, blocks of timber at the corners to represent stone quoining, and a grey slate roof. Its four landscaped acres contained a tennis court, a croquet lawn, a gazebo, a variety of flower gardens and shaded walks.

Back in Auckland, Prawle wired Swarbrick's solicitors in London to inform them that their client's new residence had been completed, that it was entirely splendid and now only required his presence. In the meantime, he enquired, should he undertake the recruitment of domestic staff? The solicitors wired back to say that Swarbrick had taken himself off to an artists' colony in Mexico for an indefinite stay. They would send funds to cover the upkeep and maintenance of the house and grounds and would appreciate Prawle providing them with a quarterly accounting of disbursements.

Three years passed. Prawle heard nothing from Swarbrick or his solicitors. When the funds in the property maintenance account had all but dwindled away, Prawle wired London again. He received a prompt but barely civil response, the gist of which was that it appeared to have escaped his attention that there was a war on. A few days later he received a follow-up cable advising that money was on its way to restore the property maintenance account to its original balance.

Early in 1945 Swarbrick's solicitors in London received a wire from their client. The cable, sent from San Diego, California, was the first communication they'd had from him for twenty months. It instructed them to transfer a quarter of a million pounds to his account at the San Diego city branch of the Wells Fargo bank forthwith. They wired back to Swarbrick, care of the San Diego post office, pointing out that their explicit instructions forbade them from releasing more than £1000 in a calendar month without written authorisation from Swarbrick himself. Written authorisation duly arrived. Worried by the shakiness of Swarbrick's signature and aghast at the thought of losing the income which flowed from their administration of such a vast amount of money, the solicitors dispatched one of the partners to New York to hire the Pinkertons' National Detective Agency to track down their client.

Three weeks later a Pinkertons' operative found Errol Swarbrick in the basement of a house in the Californian coastal town of Carmel. He was existing on a diet of pet food and water provided by his captors, a failed painter and his failed poet girlfriend who'd met Swarbrick a year earlier on the beach at Mazatlan and who were the authors of the recent instructions to his solicitors. Swarbrick weighed seven stone and had a bushy beard and hair down the small of his back; he was wearing a cowboy hat and boots, leather chaps and a fringed buckskin jacket and told the man from Pinkertons' that he was the legendary gunfighter, Wild Bill Hickok. The Pinkertons' man, who was a wild west buff, didn't bother to tell Swarbrick that Wild Bill Hickok had been shot dead in the Number Ten saloon in Deadwood, South Dakota in 1876. Even though the private detective knew a lot more about the wild west than about mental health, he was pretty sure he could recognise stark, raving insanity when he saw it.

Shortly thereafter the London solicitors instructed Prawle to sell the Manacle mansion to the highest bidder. Prawle did the deal over lunch at his club the day after receiving the instructions, although he didn't advise London until a couple of months later. The buyer was a prominent Auckland businessman, a client and close friend of Prawle's, who'd often waxed lyrical about the mansion which he admired whenever he sailed past Manacle during his summer holiday cruise. They agreed on a price of £9500, only £9000 of which were sent to London. The shortfall was Prawle's cut for not telling anyone else that the property was for sale.

The mansion, which had come to be known as "Swarbrick's Folly", remained in the businessman's family until 1986 when a newly and enormously rich corporate criminal made his grandson an offer he couldn't refuse. In 1989 the owner went bankrupt and ownership passed to his principal creditor, the Bank of New Zealand. In view of the disparity between the failed entrepreneur's assets and his liabilities, it could be argued that the bank paid close to $40 million for the privilege of owning Swarbrick's Folly.

Swarbrick's Folly was then the focus of six months' frantic activity on the part of a number of real estate agents galvanised by the depressed state of the property market and its effect on their lifestyles. Eventually, the mansion was purchased, for the proverbial song, by an Indonesian company which planned to convert it into an exclusive hotel.

Fleur Wolfgramm, the manager of Manacle Grange, as the Indonesian hotel company had named Swarbrick's Folly, stared resentfully at the fax she'd just received from Jakarta. It was from her boss, a twenty-nine-year-old South African who was the company's sales and marketing director, and it read:

> Next week I have to give the board a property by property breakdown on how the group is performing. Having just reviewed the figures for the last six months, I'd have absolutely no concerns about my presentation if it wasn't for Manacle Grand which, unbelievably, is doing worse than ever. This isn't the outcome we envisaged when we hired you; in fact, I distinctly remember you expressing complete confidence that MG would be operating profitably within six months. Not only hasn't that happened, the occupancy rate has continued to head south.

Fleur, I'd like to know what you propose to do about it. I accept the fact that my arse will be kicked around the boardroom over MG's pathetic performance; my objective is to make sure that's as far as it goes. I'm counting on you to reply, by week's end, with a summary of your planned marketing and promotional initiatives to enable me to demonstrate to the board that we're doing more than just shuffling the deckchairs at MG.

Wolfgramm had been around for long enough to know that the fax meant she'd soon be out of a job. The sales and marketing director's fallback position, if the board started heavying him, would be to suggest getting rid of her. Even if it didn't come to that, she was on borrowed time. Regardless of what the fax said, she knew for a fact that at least two other properties in the chain were losing money so in order to keep his CV clean, the sales and marketing director would soon jump before he was pushed. The first thing his replacement would do would be to sack the managers of the non-performing properties: it was much easier than actually analysing the situation and doing something constructive and it would make him or her look tough and decisive, a hands-on, kick-butt trouble-shooter. After the new boss had axed a few people, he or she could focus on the things that mattered — like spending their entertainment allowance and flying around the world first class to attend travel exhibitions.

Wolfgramm re-read the fax. What a little turd, she thought. She was amazed that he remembered any of her waffle at the job interview; he'd spent the whole time staring at her tits.

A lot of men stared at Fleur Wolfgramm's tits, partly because they were jolly nice tits by any standards and partly because she tended to dress in a manner which made it difficult to ignore them. She was a statuesque forty-year-old brunette with expressive green eyes and a wide, full-lipped mouth which admiring men and envious women alike took as evidence of an ardent, even lascivious temperament. She'd worked in the hospitality industry in New Zealand, Australia and the South Pacific since she was twenty-one, acquiring a modest reputation for professionalism and a stupendous one for her prowess between the sheets. As is often the case with reputations for being good in bed, it was bogus to the extent that most of those whose testimonies had contributed to it weren't in a position to know one way or another. As it happened, Wolfgramm was quite proficient in a range of sexual activities; she was also extremely selective about whom she was prepared to be proficient with.

She'd taken the position at Manacle Grange for two reasons: she'd thought it would be a cushy number and hence an opportunity for recuperation and stocktaking after a frenetic few years involving frequent changes of jobs and addresses, marriage, divorce and a wealthy fiancé's death of a heart attack a fortnight before their wedding and eighteen hours prior to an appointment with his solicitor to discuss changes to his will. Wolfgramm had witnessed her fiancé's death after a fashion: she was sitting on his face at the time.

Secondly, she'd calculated that many of the male guests at Manacle Grange would fit the age/income profile of her ideal second husband. While she was correct in this assumption, there was a major flaw in her logic: unattached plutocrats rarely visited Manacle Grange; generally, the wealthy middle-aged or elderly gentlemen who came to stay there had either wives or companions. Those companions, often sharp-witted adventuresses of similar outlook to Wolfgramm herself, could sense the presence of a rival predator the instant they set foot in the hotel.

The Grange had thus failed to live up to its promise. She wouldn't be sorry to leave but would prefer to have something lined up before she did so. That meant buying herself some time; in other words girl, extract digit and at least make out you're doing something to bring in a few punters.

Wolfgramm had an idea. She rang the Tourism Board's Auckland office and asked for the public relations department. She was put through.

"Hi, this is Fleur Wolfgramm at Manacle Grange, down at Coromandel. I'm looking to get some international exposure for the Grange. Would you happen to know if there are any overseas travel writers in the country at the moment?"

Duane Ricketts met Jerry Naismith, the rock promoter, at the Atomic Café in Ponsonby Road, at three o'clock on Tuesday afternoon. Naismith was fortyish trying to look twenty-five with the mandatory ponytail and mobile phone. They ordered coffees. Ricketts asked if Electra was meeting them there. Naismith said yes, she was, but his evasive expression said otherwise. Ricketts was a little surprised; he'd assumed that to be a rock promoter, you'd have to be a reasonably good liar.

"Does Electra use her old man's surname or her mother's?" asked Ricketts.

"It's Crouch; I wouldn't know whose it is."

Ricketts nodded. "And this band of hers — 'The Homo Dwarves': Is that a full-time thing or does she do something else?"

Naismith glanced at his watch. "There's not a lot of full-time musos in this town. She goes to varsity."

"Oh yeah? What does she study?"

"English. She's right into literature — poetry and that. She reckons it helps her song writing."

Naismith had been watching the door over Ricketts' shoulder. He raised his eyebrows to greet someone, then stood up.

"Well, I'll leave you guys to it."

A tall young man, early twenties, wearing jeans, motorcycle boots, a leather waistcoat to show off his tan and biceps, and a few bits of junk around his neck slid into the seat Naismith had vacated. He had earrings in both ears and his long brown hair was gelled and swept back off his forehead.

Ricketts stirred his coffee and looked up at Naismith. "Who's your boyfriend?"

The newcomer reached across the table and grabbed Rickett's right hand, bending the thumb back.

"What the fuck did you say . . ."

Ricketts was stirring his coffee with his left hand. He took the teaspoon out of the coffee and pressed it down on the back of the newcomer's hand; he swore and jerked his hand back, letting go of Ricketts' thumb.

"Hey, hey, take it easy guys," said Naismith in a high, nervous voice. "This is Jake, Electra's partner. You want to meet Electra, you've got to square it with him first, okay? Right, I'm out of here. Catch you, Jake."

Ricketts put the teaspoon in the saucer and sipped his coffee. It was very hot. He smiled at Jake who was rubbing the back of his right hand and giving him the dead eyes look.

"So Jake," he said. "You're Electra's social secretary?"

"Fuck you, man. Try something like that again and you'll be fucking sorry."

"Okay, I get the message: the reason you walk like that is you've got great big balls. Good for you. Now can we get on with it? All I want to do is talk to Electra — for five minutes."

"Electra doesn't know you and she's pretty sure she doesn't want to know you. That's why you're talking to me. You got a message for her, you give it to me and I might pass it on or I might not." It was Jake's turn to smile. "Depends what sort of mood I'm in. Right now it's seriously shitty."

Ricketts shrugged. "I met Electra's father up in . . ."

"Her old man? He's dead."

"Yeah well, before he was dead, he was alive. That's the way it works, see? I met the guy in Thailand; when he found out I was coming back, he asked me to get a message to his daughter. That's all it is — he asked me to do him a favour and I'm trying to do it. Personally, I don't give a shit if I never set eyes on Electra."

Jake leaned forward and put his elbows on the table. "Is that right? Well, take it from me pal, she feels the same way about you. So what's the message?"

Ricketts shook his head wearily and got to his feet. "It's personal. Look, how about you explain the situation to Electra? If she's interested in hearing what her old man wanted to tell her, she can leave a message with Naismith. If she's not, then to hell with it; I've kept my side of the deal."

Ricketts headed for the door. Jake followed, talking to his back. "You know what I think? I think you're full of shit. I think this stuff about a message from her old man is all shit."

Ricketts stopped and turned to face him. "So why am I wasting my time trying to get in touch with her?"

Jake's lip curled like a breaking wave. "You've probably got the hots for her. I bet you saw her at a gig and she gave you a rat-on. You wouldn't be the first jerk-off to come crawling around."

Ricketts winked at him. "You're getting warm."

After their meeting with Jody Spurdle, Detective Sergeant Tito Ihaka and Detective Constable Johan Van Roon went over to Remuera where they interviewed some more of the late Bart Clegg's neighbours. They got back to Auckland Central just before 6 p.m. Ihaka had a message to ring Kit Fawcett. It was code; what it meant was: ring Blair Corvine and do it now.

Corvine was an undercover policeman. Paranoia is an unavoidable by-product of undercover work and Corvine's head reached the stage where he distrusted everyone, police included; hence the code. Ihaka sometimes got tired of Corvine's elaborate security procedures. When that happened, he'd remind himself that if certain people around town did happen to find out that Corvine was a cop, it was odds-on that within twenty-four hours his body would be discovered floating in the Manukau oxidation ponds; where they'd find his head would be anyone's guess.

The way the code worked was that if Corvine had to leave a message, he'd use the name of an obscure All Black. The degree of urgency depended on what position the All Black had played, working from front row to fullback. So, for instance, if Corvine called himself Perry Harris, who was a prop, it meant don't bust a gut; a second five, say Phil Gard, meant get your skates on and a fullback like Fawcett was red alert.

Ihaka found an unoccupied office and rang Corvine.

"Yeah?"

"Kit Fawcett?"

"That's me."

"Kit, something I always wanted to ask you: you know how when you went on that tour to South Africa, you said you'd score more off the field than on? Well did you?"

"You'd fucking hope so, wouldn't you?"

"What's up?"

"You know Ronnie Traipse, runs that scrub and tug joint The Pink Wink, down in Fort Street?"

"Vaguely. What about him?"

"He put the word out today for a shooter. Apparently, he's got a guy prepared to shell out two and a half grand for a .38 revolver."

Ihaka whistled. "Someone's keen."

"You'll love this; the buyer's a Yank tourist called Donald Surface."

"A tourist? Jesus, you wouldn't want to fuck up his bookings, would you?"

The squad car Ihaka sent to The Pink Wink got there twenty minutes too late. By mid-afternoon Traipse had found someone who would supply the goods; by 4.30 the goods had been delivered. Funke called just after five to check what was happening and was told the item was ready for collection. By the time the police, flak jackets and all, got there, the gun had gone and so had the mysterious Mr Surface.

13

Duane Ricketts had never met a writer, at least not that he knew of, so after he got out of the shower on Wednesday morning, he stood around in his old dressing gown getting cold and trying to decide what to wear. Eventually, he settled on a woolly jumper, old corduroy pants and brown suede shoes with rubber soles, the sort his father used to call "brothel creepers"; not that Tom Ricketts would've known where to find a brothel, let alone what to wear to one. He had some fruit and cereal then got a couple of second-hand paperbacks from the bookcase and wrapped them in brown paper. On the way down Dominion Road towards the city, he stopped at the Mt Eden post office to buy stamps. He parked in the Victoria Street carpark and walked up through Albert Park to the university. It was 9.45 a.m.

He asked a group of students where English lectures were held. They said they thought some of them anyway were in the big lecture theatres on the basement floor of the library building and pointed the way. A crowd of students was milling around in the basement floor corridor, obviously waiting for a 10 o'clock lecture. Ricketts went up to a young woman wearing jeans and a man-size blue shirt who was leaning against the wall by herself, reading a book.

"Excuse me, is there an English lecture in here at 10 o'clock?"

"Sure is — Shakespearean tragedy."

"Who's the lecturer?"

"Davenport."

"Is Davenport he or she?"

The student seemed amused. "There are people round here — Dr Daniel Davenport for instance — who think he's the sexiest male since Lord Byron."

Ricketts raised his eyebrows. "What do you think?"

"Well, Byron died in 1824. Call me sceptical but I find it hard to believe that Davenport's the best your gender could do in 170 years."

Ricketts agreed that, when you looked at it like that, it did seem unlikely. He asked her where the English Department's administrative offices were and was told the fifth floor.

Ricketts waited till five past ten, then took a lift to the fifth floor. He went through a set of glass doors with a sign saying "English Department Administration". A middle-aged woman was sitting behind a reception desk working at a computer terminal. She looked up at Ricketts and offered to help him.

"Is Dr Davenport about?" he asked.

"I think Dr Davenport's lecturing at the moment. I'll just check." She punched a key.

Ricketts clicked his fingers. "Course he is — Wednesday mornings, he's got Shakespearean tragedy."

The receptionist was peering at the screen. "That's right, stage two." She looked up at Ricketts. "If you'd like to come back in an hour or so . . ."

Ricketts grimaced and glanced at his watch. "Look, I'm in a bit of a rush — perhaps you can help me. I'm Phillip Quayle, the writer . . ." He paused; the receptionist met his expectant look with a blank stare. Ricketts cleared his throat and continued: "Anyway, I'm a friend of Dan Davenport's. A while ago he introduced me to a student here, Electra Crouch. I promised I'd send her a couple of my books" — he put the parcel on the reception desk — "but wouldn't you know it, I've gone and lost her address. You couldn't give it to me, could you, so I can get this lot off to her? They've been sitting around for two weeks, all wrapped up ready to go. I've even got the stamps, look?"

"Well . . ." The receptionist hesitated. "Under the circumstances I suppose it would be all right." She hit the keyboard a few times. "What was that surname again?"

"Crouch. Electra Crouch."

"Here we are." She passed Ricketts a pen. "Flat 3, 13 Datchet Terrace, Westmere."

Ricketts wrote the address on the parcel and thanked the receptionist. As he headed for the glass doors, she reminded him that there was a post office on campus.

At 6.10 on Tuesday evening Washington time, Leon Rehbein rang his boss Richard Thames to say that he'd made some progress on the Funke assignment. Although Rehbein spoke in his usual nasal drone, Thames knew that the computer wizard had struck paydirt; he wouldn't have rung him otherwise. He told Rehbein to come straight up.

Although the prospect of having Rehbein in his office for the second time in as many days caused a fluttering sensation deep in Thames' abdomen, he consoled himself with the thought that no matter how proud of himself Rehbein might be, he'd deliver his report without embellishment or theatrics. Some of Thames' staff could make tailing a seven foot tall African diplomat in full tribal regalia through Central Park in broad daylight sound like mission impossible.

Rehbein knocked, entered, sat down, briefly consulted his notes and embarked on his report: "Sir, from Friday April 15 to Monday April 18 inclusive, 137 male US passport holders aged between forty and fifty-five entered New Zealand. I ran all of them through the computer and cross-referenced them against Harold Funke. I eliminated a number because of the discrepancy in height and weight; eventually, I narrowed it down to eighteen possibilities on the basis of rough physical resemblance and southern background. One in particular stood out because the gentleman in question and Funke have the same place of birth: Pecos,

Texas. This party is named Lyle Gorse; he was born two years before Funke. From 1973, when Mr Gorse's passport was issued, till now, it hadn't been used to enter or exit the US. I tapped into the Texas state police computer in Austin and found that a Lyle Gorse, born Pecos 1942, was shot dead in the course of a suspected hold-up in south-west Texas in 1962. I also got into the computer holding Texas' education records and it seems that this Lyle Gorse and Funke were at the same high school in Pecos at the same time. I think it's safe to assume the Gorse passport is false; my guess is it's one of ours. I assumed you wouldn't want me to pursue that line."

"Correct. What you've got there seems pretty conclusive anyway, Leon. Excellent work."

"Thank you sir. There is one other thing. The embassy in Wellington has received an urgent query from the New Zealand police concerning a man described as an American and using the name Donald Surface. It seems Surface obtained a handgun by way of an illegal transaction. As you may be aware sir, New Zealand has very strict regulations concerning firearms. This took place in Auckland — which is the gateway for most international flights — yesterday, Tuesday their time. The embassy has checked and no US passport holder by that name has entered New Zealand in the past two months. On a hunch I contacted Bangkok." Reinbein's mud-coloured eyes warmed and he permitted himself a brief smile; it was as animated as Thames had ever seen him get. "A Donald Surface left Bangkok for Hong Kong on a US passport last Friday night. The next day Surface flew to LA which is where Lyle Gorse flew out to Auckland from."

"How many false passports does the son of a bitch have?" asked Thames.

It was a rhetorical question but Rehbein answered it anyway: "Probably one more."

Rayleen Crouch wasn't a big drinker. She'd sometimes have a glass or two of white wine when she ate out or a light beer, which she'd sit on for an hour, when she went for a drink after work. If Crouch's friends and workmates, who regarded her as a borderline teetotaller, had seen the litre bottle of Chivas Regal in the cupboard above the sink they'd have assumed it was for visitors who wanted or needed a stiff drink; maybe, given that Rayleen kept pretty quiet about her love life, she had a man friend with expensive tastes. They would've been taken aback to learn that not only did she drink the Chivas herself but she got through it at the rate of one of those litre bottles every few weeks.

Crouch went to the cupboard above the sink on the nights when the job really got to her. She'd be sitting in the lounge with the TV on but not seeing anything, not hearing anything, just wondering why she was wasting her life running after fuck-ups, losers, loonies and misfits, putting up with unbelievable crap to try to help people who half the time resented you or abused you or tried to stab you in the back — sometimes literally.

On those nights, Crouch would get out the bottle, drop a few ice cubes in a glass, pour in some scotch and throw it back. She actually quite liked the taste but that was a bonus; what she was after was that jolt when it hit the stomach and the way the tingles went all the way out to her fingertips. Pour another dollop and do it again. Starting to feel pleasantly light-headed now; no need to gulp, just settle back on the couch and nibble at it. It was as if she'd pulled the plug on the connection between her mind and her emotions, what she'd been thinking about and how it made her feel. Instead of feeling bitter and guilty for feeling bitter at the same time, she just felt like "fuck 'em all".

Rayleen Crouch was a thirty-eight-year-old social worker. Over the years her beat had covered psychiatric hospitals, crisis centres, refuges for battered wives and halfway houses for ex-criminals. These days she mainly worked out of youth hostels, dealing with state wards, abused children, runaways, kids who'd gotten into trouble with the law. She had a sociology degree, a hefty mortgage, a dead ex-husband, a semi-estranged daughter, a sixth of a bottle of premium scotch whisky, and a portfolio of clients who covered the spectrum from social cripples to sociopaths and included some of the most dedicated, hard-core substance abusers this side of the point of no return. And when she woke up tomorrow morning, nothing much would've changed: she'd feel like shit and the scotch would be all gone, but her clients would be getting ready for another day with their demons.

The ones with genuine psychiatric disorders weren't so bad. Even like now, when she was in one of her fuck 'em all moods, she couldn't blame them. The poor sods couldn't help it. When they were up, when the moon was in a certain phase or whatever the hell it was, they were fine and, what's more, they understood what you were trying to do for them and were grateful. But then just when things were going well and they seemed to be making progress, they'd hear a voice from somewhere — maybe from the old gumdigger in the painting at the top of the stairs — and it'd set them off again. When that happened, you had to be on your toes because you never knew what was going on behind those shining eyes.

The ones who really got her down were the kids who hated the world and everything in it, most of all themselves. Even after fifteen years as a social worker, Crouch could still be chilled by the sheer force of their self-destructive impulses. There was one kid who slashed himself with a razor blade when he couldn't score any drugs. They'd take him to hospital to get him patched up and when the nurse's back was turned, he'd steal used alcohol swabs. He'd smuggle the swabs back into the hostel, squeeze the fluid out of them, and inject himself with it.

Her black mood had been triggered by a confrontation with this particular kid that afternoon. He'd asked her to lend him some money. The line he spun was that it was to buy a few car magazines; he was getting really interested in cars and thinking maybe he'd like to be a mechanic.

She's stared at him and asked, "Steven, do you really expect me to believe that? This is me you're talking to, not some church group do-gooder."

Steven, who wouldn't be a bad-looking boy if he stopped doing drugs, ate properly and got a decent haircut, looked at her as if he was going to burst out crying. Instead he said, "Dried-up old cunt," and spat on her blouse.

Crouch had fought down the urge to slap the little shit till his ears bled. Instead she'd wiped away the spit with a handkerchief and said, as calmly as she could, "I'd rather be a dried-up cunt than a pathetic little junkie."

Then Steven really had burst into tears.

Crouch had been so angry that she'd completely forgotten about the note one of the girls at the hostel had given her, telling her not to read it till she got home. This girl, Merelle, was a tragic case. She'd been sexually abused by her mother's de facto, although the way Merelle preferred to tell it, she'd seduced him. They got her out of there but the damage was done. She went through a phase of offering herself to any adult male who as much as looked sideways at her; lately she'd got herself together a bit but that side of her, a mix of exhibitionism and self-humiliation, was never far away. Crouch doubted that she'd ever forget the time she and Merelle were at a crowded outdoor café in Parnell; Crouch went inside to get something else to eat and when she came back, Merelle had her dress up around her waist, one leg up on the table, and one hand inside her panties, diddling away.

Crouch was stretched out on the sofa near the bottom of her third scotch when she remembered Merelle's note. It was kind of sweet the way Merelle had come up to her, all shy, and slipped the note into her bag. Crouch stood up and swayed. She walked a little unsteadily through to the kitchen where she'd left her handbag on the bench, found Merelle's note and unfolded it.

In her surprisingly neat handwriting, Merelle had written: 'Get a life lezzo-slut.'

Crouch stared at Merelle's note for ten seconds. Then the grim line of her mouth slowly curled into a sour smile. She chuckled. The chuckle became a laugh. She put her head back and hooted with laughter for a full minute. Then she abruptly stopped laughing, said "little slag" out loud, screwed up the note and dropped it in the rubbish bin. She was pouring herself a final scotch when the doorbell rang. She looked at her watch; it was 9.20. That'll be Electra, she thought; about bloody time she put in an appearance.

She negotiated the corridor with just the single ricochet off the wall. If she'd been sober, she wouldn't have just taken it for granted that it was her daughter at the door and she certainly wouldn't have opened the door without taking the elementary precaution of asking whoever was on the other side of it to identify themselves. But she wasn't sober and she didn't ask; she just opened the door. It was only then that her mental machinery ground into action: this is not my daughter; this is a large beetle-browed man with a very dark 5 o'clock shadow and thick, blunt-fingered hands. All the better to strangle you with. Oh Jesus, no.

Crouch went to slam the door but the man was too quick for her; he flung out his right arm and blocked the door with the heel of his hand then jammed a foot in the doorway.

"Hey," he said. "That's not very nice."

Crouch shoved as hard as she could but the man stepped right up to the door and leaned his shoulder against it. She couldn't budge it.

"Please," she gasped. "Go away."

"Keep your hair on, Rayleen," said the man in a non-threatening, almost reasonable tone. "I just want a quiet word."

He pushed the door open and came inside. Crouch backed away down the corridor.

"Who are you?"

"You mean you don't remember me? Leith Grills? Fair play, though, it was a while ago now, not long after you got hitched to Varty. You know that shitrag killed my brother?"

She retreated into the lounge. Grills sauntered in after her and looked around like a house hunter at an open home.

"You've got the place looking nice," he said, nodding his approval.

"When?"

Grills looked puzzled. "When what?"

"When did he kill your brother?"

"1983 it was. Varty brought some dope over from Aussie on a boat, I mean millions of bucks worth. It was a fifty-fifty deal, him and this other guy. Al, my brother, was working for the other guy. Al went down to Coromandel to meet Varty and got his head bashed in for his trouble. Varty wanted the lot, see? As a matter of fact, that's what brings me here."

Crouch had never sobered up faster. "What's it got to do with me?"

Grills grinned. His eyes gleamed with greed and dumb cunning. "Varty had to shoot through in a big hurry, right? So he never had a chance to shift the stuff. Well, me and his partner, the bloke he ripped off, want to get our hands on it; trouble is, we don't know where the prick hid it. But we reckon he must've told someone." Grills' grin disappeared and he moved closer to her. "Maybe his pretty little wife."

Crouch, who'd relaxed a fraction and was half-sitting on the arm of the sofa, sprang upright and retreated behind it.

"That's ridiculous," she exclaimed. "Varty and I had split up way before that. I didn't see him or speak to him from one year to the next."

There was a sharp rap on the window of the French doors which opened out to the back yard. A short, stocky middle-aged man stood in the half-light. He smiled and made a little waving gesture.

"Who the fuck's that?" snarled Grills.

"I don't know," said Crouch, starting towards the French doors.

Grills pushed in front of her. "Get out of it. I'll take care of him."

The key was in the door. Grills turned it, pushed the doors open, and told the stranger, "You can shove right off, whoever you are."

"Well now," said the stranger in a lazy American drawl, "I was sitting in my car across the street there when you sort of barged in without a real big come on in and set yourself down, far as I could tell. I've been standing out here observing the two of you and I assessed from the lady's demeanour that you ain't exactly a long lost friend. So maybe you should take your own advice and shove the hell off yourself."

Grills, flabbergasted, stared down at the American for a few seconds. He began to make a low growling sound then suddenly yanked back his right arm and let fly. The American ducked under the haymaker and counter-punched, snapping off a short right which thudded into Grills' throat as he lunged forward. Grills made a noise like a sink waste disposal unit trying to cope with a bucketful of gravel and clutched his neck. The American slipped his right leg behind Grills' and judo-threw him. Grills went down, hitting the back of his head hard on the floor. He felt something cold and metallic rasp between his teeth and opened his eyes to discover that he had two inches of gun barrel in his mouth.

"Okay compadre," said the American who was squatting on his haunches beside him. "What happens now is either you haul your sorry ass out of here or I pull the trigger and blow whatever's inside your skull all over the little lady's nice, clean floor. Would you care to indicate a preference?" There was a click, a very loud one it seemed to Grills, as the American cocked the revolver.

Grills' eyes bulged in supplication and he gagged on the gun barrel. The American looked up at Crouch and smiled.

"I'm picking he'll go for the tactical retreat. What do you think, ma'am?"

Crouch, utterly bewildered and half-expecting that at any moment she'd awake from this whisky-induced nightmare with a thundering hangover, responded with a dazed nod.

The American stood up and gave Grills a casual kick in the ribs. "Scram, asshole. Be advised that if we meet again, you won't be getting a vote on the outcome."

He followed Grills down the corridor, the pistol dangling in his right hand, and watched him get into his car and drive off. Then he slipped the gun into the waistband of his trousers and returned to the lounge. He reached inside his jacket and produced a badge for Crouch's inspection.

"Allow me to introduce myself, ma'am: special agent Buddy Funke of the United States Drug Enforcement Administration at your service. Begging your pardon for crashing the barndance but it seemed like a good idea at the time."

14

Tito Ihaka didn't have a telephone beside his bed on principle. He believed that having a phone in your bedroom was an invitation to people to ring you at all hours of the day or night, including those normally set aside for sleeping. The phone beside the bed implied, he felt, not just that you didn't mind being rung at ungodly hours, you expected, if not actually welcomed, it. Ihaka didn't welcome it at all. Among his friends, ringing Ihaka at the wrong time and for anything less than a matter of life and death — say, for instance, that a giant meteorite was about to land in his street — was known as 'Dial-A-Diatribe'.

Thus when the phone rang at 6.27 that Thursday morning, Ihaka didn't curse or groan because he assumed it would be important. There was a second possibility — that it was a wrong number — and Ihaka spent the short time it took him to get out of bed and walk through to the living room considering what he'd say to the caller if that was the case. When he picked up the phone, he'd progressed no further than a couple of old stand-bys — leprosy, consumption of animal droppings — so he was almost relieved when it turned out to be Detective Inspector Finbar McGrail.

"Sorry about the hour," said McGrail. "If it's any consolation, I got a wake-up call too — half an hour ago."

Pull the other one, it's got warts on it, thought Ihaka who knew that McGrail got up at 5.30 every morning and went for a run.

"Not to worry, sir," said Ihaka. "I'll catch up on my sleep at work. What's up?"

"You're on a plane to Wellington leaving in just over an hour. You'd better get weaving."

"What about the Clegg briefing? Isn't that this morning?"

"Forget it. You won't miss much."

"Autopsy a fizzer, eh?"

"Well, it simply confirmed that there's no physical evidence to show that someone drowned him, then jammed him under the seat. The pathologist believes the body had been in the spa for thirty to forty hours — since Friday night in other words . . ."

"That's Ricketts off the hook."

"Indeed. You saw the body — if there ever were marks indicating the use of force, they're not discernible now. The coroner will bring in an open verdict; he couldn't do otherwise."

"Pretty fucking weird way to commit suicide, but."

"Agreed. And quite how the body could get under there if it'd been some sort of accident escapes me, but there we are."

"What about that missing champagne glass? The cleaning woman says there was a full set when she did the place last Wednesday and the rubbish had already been collected."

"Interesting but hardly conclusive. The point is that whatever logic and instinct tell us, at the moment we've got no actual physical evidence of foul play, no reports of disturbances, no one seen coming or going from the scene and no apparent motive; therefore we can't as yet make a watertight case for murder — if you'll pardon the expression. And with all due respect, Sergeant, I don't think anything you might contribute at the briefing will substantially alter that state of affairs."

"I hear you," said Ihaka thinking, Christ, he's in fine fettle this morning. "So what's the go in Wellington?"

"You've got a 10.30 meeting at the Beehive, in the Police Minister's office . . ."

"That tosser . . ."

"Sergeant, can I suggest that for once in your life you just play a straight bat — if for no other reason than self-interest. The American ambassador will be at the meeting as will a few high-ranking officials from various government departments; I think you'd be wise to proceed on the assumption that these people are unlikely to share your rather unusual sense of humour."

Ihaka smiled to himself and asked what it was all in aid of.

"It's to do with your man Donald Surface. It seems he's some sort of American agent who's gone off the rails. I dare say the minister and the US Embassy want the thing handled as discreetly as possible."

"Has Surface got diplomatic immunity?"

"I shouldn't think so. I doubt the Americans would be being this polite if he had."

"Sir, this is bloody silly. You should be at the meeting, not me — you're far more cut out for this sort of shit."

"How kind of you to say so, Sergeant," said McGrail, "but it's not up to me; as soon as the district commander knew you were in the loop, he was adamant that you should represent us."

"For Christ's sake, why? Hang on, let me guess: has it got anything to do with the fact that I'm Maori?"

"Oh, I don't think I'd care to speculate on the district commander's thought processes."

Ihaka's brow furrowed as he picked up the undertone of amusement in his boss's voice. Where's McGrail coming from he wondered; he's probably hoping I make a goose of myself and the DC ends up getting kicked in the nuts.

"Well, did you warn him about my lack of — what do they call them? — people skills?"

McGrail chuckled dryly. "My word, yes, but he's confident that cometh the hour, cometh the man. Your ticket's at the Ansett desk. Enjoy your trip, sergeant."

He hung up. Ihaka put the phone down thinking: this is a hell of a time for McGrail to develop a sense of humour.

At 7.45 that morning, Duane Ricketts parked his seven-year-old Toyota across the road from 13 Datchet Terrace, Westmere. It was a three-storey brick and plaster block which someone with a real estate agent's jaunty attitude towards the unvarnished truth might have described as art deco. The pale pink paintwork was flaking but probably not fast enough to suit the neighbours. Datchet Terrace sloped down towards the harbour; Ricketts guessed that if flat three was on the top floor, Electra and Jake would be able to admire the view down Waitemata Harbour to Hobsonville and Greenhithe, in the unlikely event they ever got bored with admiring themselves.

Shortly before 8.30 a young woman came out of the building and began walking up the hill to the main road. She was quite tall and slim with short, spiky reddish-brown hair and walked with an eye-catching, loose-limbed sway, swinging her free arm like a sergeant-major on parade. She wore black boots, black leggings, a black denim jacket slung over her left shoulder. Her nose-ring glinted in the early morning sunshine which was bright without being warm. Experience had taught Ricketts to be cautious in making assumptions about people's appearances; on the other hand, he told himself, it hasn't taught me how to do the perfect boiled egg. He got out of his car, locked the door and followed the young woman who was on the opposite footpath.

On the corner where Datchet Terrace met the main road was a little grassed area, about ten square metres, containing a large rubbish bin, a bench and many dog turds of varying chalkiness. When the girl reached it, Ricketts crossed the road. She heard his footsteps and glanced over her shoulder. He said, "Electra Crouch?"

She looked at him warily. Up close he could see that she had several studs in both ears, huge black eyes like wet stones, a slight pout and flawless pale skin. She was very good looking. I bet a lot of guys tell her she's beautiful, thought Ricketts, and some of them would believe it. He wondered if she believed it herself.

"Who are you?"

"Duane Ricketts. I saw your father in Thailand."

"Not you again? Jake says you're a jerk-off."

"I'm sorry to hear that. I thought he was a wonderful human being."

"Is that your idea of a joke?" she sneered. Ricketts couldn't quite understand how she managed to sneer and look attractive at the same time.

"He's your boyfriend — you tell me."

She looked at her watch, a garish, plastic thing the size of a small landmine. "I've got a bus to catch."

"Don't worry about that: I can give you a lift — my car's back there."

"Oh wow," she said, batting her eyelashes. "It's been ages since a strange man tried to get me into his car." She switched from facetiousness to suspicion. "How'd you find out where I lived?"

"It wasn't very difficult; I make a living out of finding people. Look, I don't know what all the drama's for — I only want to pass on a message from your old man. It'll take five minutes, tops."

Electra kept the suspicious look in place for a while longer. Then she shrugged and went and sat down on the bench. When Ricketts joined her, she said, "I haven't seen him since I was seven and he wasn't exactly the model father."

"Yeah well, I guess old Dale did make a couple of bad moves along the way. It seemed to me that he felt he'd let you down and wanted to make it up to you."

She was completely unmoved. "Spare me the soppy stuff. You got something to say, say it."

Ricketts had known all along that this would be the tricky bit. He'd considered various approaches but none of them, he decided, was going to make it: this girl was too bright to con and too cynical to get sentimental. When all else fails, he thought, try telling the truth.

"I talked to Dale just before they carted him off to hospital. He told me about a shipment of drugs — cocaine — he brought over from Australia in 1983. He walked straight into trouble: he was double-crossed by his partner, a big-time drug dealer called Bryce Spurdle, someone ended up getting killed, and he had to hide the dope and get out of the country. He said he hid it in a special place, somewhere down at Coromandel he took you when you were a little kid." Electra's eyes widened. "What he wanted was for us to find it so you could, you know, benefit from it."

She frowned. "Have I got this straight: he wanted me to tell you where this special place is so we could find the coke, sell it, and I get the money — Daddy's parting gift? Sort of like, and to my darling daughter Electra, I leave an absolute shitload of cocaine?"

"Yeah, that's about it."

"And what's in it for you? Or would you be doing it out of the goodness of your heart, wonderful human being that you are?"

Ricketts detected a hum of suppressed anger beneath sarcasm. He shifted on the bench, re-crossing his legs.

"Well, I think the way Dale saw it, there'd be something in it for me if I, you know, did the work and took the risks."

Electra took a packet of cigarettes out of her bag and lit one. She leaned back on the bench and stared straight ahead without speaking, sucking in her cheeks with violent drags which burnt the cigarette down a centimetre at a time. Maybe she's taking a while to get used to the idea, thought Ricketts hopefully; after all, it's not every day a complete stranger offers to make you a millionaire.

She stood up. "Look, I'm really flattered that Dad thought I've got what it takes to carry on the family tradition but I'll have to pass."

She started to walk away, then stopped. She walked back to Ricketts, now on his feet, and fixed him with a look of sheer loathing. There were tears in the black eyes and her voice was an acid hiss: "Drugs ripped my family apart and me and my mother are still a bit screwed up because of it. My father's dead because of drugs. The very last thing he did was to send you sliming around trying to suck me into a drug deal. What sort of fucking father does that? And what sort of dreg does that make you?"

Ricketts met her accusing stare for a few more seconds then looked away.

"I'm sorry," he said. "It was a bad idea, okay? Don't be too hard on your dad. He was dying, don't forget; he just wanted to do something for you. The thing to remember is that when the time came to think about the people who really mattered to him, he thought of you."

Large, pear-shaped teardrops swelled from Electra's eyes and slid slowly down her cheeks to the corners of her mouth. Soon there were steady trickles. A drop splashed onto her denim jacket. She reached up with her right hand and, with two abrupt movements, wiped the tears off her face with the back of her hand.

Quietly but without the slightest quaver in her voice, she said, "Fuck the fuck off."

The Minister for Police was shorter and seedier than he appeared on television, which didn't surprise Ihaka; in his experience, most politicians were. He shook hands, coating Ihaka's palm with an oily film, then introduced him to the other participants in the meeting: the US ambassador, a tall, bulky, almost completely bald, almost elderly black man; his chargé d'affaires who, apart from being male, was none of those things; a matching set of bureaucrats, one from the foreign affairs department, the other from the minister's staff; and a woman from the Attorney-General's office who wore tartan and looked disgruntled, as if being there had made her miss her bagpipes lesson. Ihaka was seated next to her at the meeting table.

"I guess the transsexual dwarf couldn't find a park for the wheelchair, eh?" He said to her in a low voice. She pulled a hideous face, which Ihaka interpreted as a glare of disapproval, and transferred her attention to one of the bureaucrats.

The minister sat at the head of the table. He cleared his throat to bring the meeting to order and set off in a squeaky, cartoon-character voice: "Mr Ambassador, Ms McHarg, gentlemen — thank you for attending at such short notice. I called this meeting because we seem to be confronted with an unusual, if not unique, situation. Mr Ambassador, perhaps I could ask you to start the ball rolling."

The ambassador bowed his gleaming cranium and opened a manila folder.

"Thank you, minister," he said in a double-bass rumble. "After the Auckland police notified us about this guy Donald Surface procuring a firearm, we put it back to Washington. They tell us his real name is Harold Funke; he's a senior officer in the Drug Enforcement Administration, currently on a posting to Bangkok. Seems he's operating under two aliases, the other being Lyle Gorse. He entered New Zealand on a passport in that name."

The ambassador's mouth twitched with distaste or perhaps discomfort and he adjusted his tie. We're about to get to the guts of it, thought Ihaka.

The ambassador continued: "Our people in Bangkok and Washington have been on Funke's case since the beginning of the week; their conclusion is that he's come here after a drugs cache. Under the circumstances and given that he has absolutely no jurisdiction here and has made no effort to inform us or the authorities of his presence, we must assume his intentions are criminal."

The ambassador paused and looked at the minister who smiled, nodded and turned to Ihaka: "Detective Sergeant, I gather you found no trace of Surface last night?"

Ihaka shook his head. "He moved out of the Regis Hotel on Tuesday morning and got a taxi over to the Inter-Con but he didn't check in there as Surface or anything else — we went through the guests and none of them matched up. We tried all the main pubs and the car hire companies and came up empty. We should get that other name circulated right away."

"It's under control," said the minister's assistant. "It was passed to Inspector McGrail earlier this morning."

"Sergeant, any questions or comments on what we've heard from the ambassador?" asked the minister.

Ihaka didn't try very hard to keep a straight face. "Well, I think we're on safe ground assuming this bloke's a baddy. Sir, you said your guys had been onto him since Monday — before he went looking for a gun. Why was that?"

"Someone in our Bangkok embassy seems to have had an attack of initiative," said the ambassador, sliding several typed sheets of A4 paper across the table. "This should explain a few things."

It was a copy of a report prepared by Everton Sloan III, summarising his investigation. Although not noted for his animation, Ihaka did a double-take worthy of a churchgoer coming across an advert for a dominatrix in the parish magazine when he spotted the names Dale Varty and Duane Ricketts. What really worried him, though, wasn't anything he read; it was the bits he couldn't read.

He looked up at the ambassador. "In among all the stuff that's been blacked out, would there be anything we — as in the police — ought to know before we go any further?"

The ambassador sighed and flexed his jaw. "Funke used to be in the CIA," he said.

"Oh right. What as?"

"He was an operative." The ambassador gestured vaguely. "An agent in the field."

Ihaka looked around with a cheerful but slightly puzzled smile. "Is that what simple folk like us would call a highly trained killer?"

The minister intervened: "Sergeant, the ambassador is well aware of the seriousness of the situation. Indeed, he brought it to our attention."

Ihaka's smile withered to a thin, cynical line. "Well, that's fine. Maybe he'd like to make the arrest as well?"

The minister's face fell. The man from foreign affairs embarked on a prolonged and, by the sound of it, productive, throat clearance. The ambassador's offsider looked at Ihaka with respectful curiosity, as if he'd declared that he was about to undertake some insanely risky activity, such as nude fencing.

The ambassador himself seemed unperturbed. He stroked his chin contemplatively and, when the man from foreign affairs had ceased gargling phlegm, said: "If you're waiting for me to volunteer, Sergeant, you might want to make yourself real comfortable — maybe order in as well. Fact is, I wouldn't go up against a guy like this with anything less than an Abrams tank. I take it your attitude, in a nutshell, is that seeing as how he's our loose cannon, we ought to put him back in the rack?"

Ihaka raised his eyebrows in agreement: "Well, put it this way, sir: I didn't join the police force to see if I could out-draw the Man from U.N.C.L.E."

"No, I don't suppose you did," said the ambassador with a slow smile. "You just had a thing about handcuffs, right?" He put his elbows on the table, clasped his hands together, and looked around to take in everyone present. "Contrary to the impression you might get from the movies, the vast majority of the men and women in the US security agencies are highly principled and dedicated servants of their country. But we have to face facts: there is the occasional rotten apple in the barrel; every now and again, one of these people goes rogue on us. Like a lot of things we could do without, it really started during the Vietnam War: what happened up there, particularly in Laos, has been well enough documented not to need my two cents' worth. There've also been some well-publicised instances of renegade officers running guns and other hardware to terrorist organisations and nations like Libya. Security considerations prevent me from telling you any more but the bottom line is this: we have a system for responding to these situations; we have people trained to deal with the likes of Mr Funke. One of them's heading this way as we speak."

The minister stood up. "Thank you Mr Ambassador," he said with a cheesy smile. "On behalf of my government, let me reiterate how much we appreciate the speed and scale of the United States' assistance in this matter." He rearranged his face and looked unaffectionately at Ihaka. "Okay Sergeant, that's the assignment: you and your team find this character; the specialist sent by Washington will do the rest. If it should come to that, of course; hopefully, it can be resolved in a peaceful manner. Geoffrey here will fill you in on the rest of it. You're to act as the liaison officer. I trust I can count on you and your colleagues for the fullest co-operation."

Ihaka's participation in the meeting was clearly finished. He stood up and nodded at the ambassador who nodded back.

Outside in the corridor the minister's offsider told Ihaka that the specialist was flying into Auckland from Los Angeles first thing the next morning; Ihaka was to meet the flight.

"Shit hot," said Ihaka. "Do I get to wear a shiny suit and hold up a sign? Tell me, has this new role of ours — sniffing out targets for visiting hitmen — been cleared with McGrail?"

"Look Sergeant," said the bureaucrat crossly, "the commissioner of police was in the minister's office at midnight last night dealing with this matter. The decisions were made at that level and now you have a small role to play in carrying them out. If I was in your shoes, I'd focus on making it happen." He walked a few paces down the corridor then stopped and looked back at Ihaka. "Besides," he said, a transparently malicious smirk spreading across his face, "it's not a hitman, it's a hitwoman."

15

Electra Crouch and her boyfriend Jake Latimer met for lunch at a new café in Kitchener Street, across the road from the art gallery. The café's décor was dominated by mirrored glass and stainless steel, giving it the clinical, high-tech sheen — and the atmosphere — of a state-of-the-art abattoir. Jake's gaze was drawn to the reflective surface like a rat to a rubbish dump and he was still shooting 'do you come here often?' looks at himself when the waitress arrived. It was only then, when he glanced across the table to check if Electra was ready to order, that he noticed she was sniffling tearfully into a handkerchief.

In the almost three months they'd been together, Jake had seen Electra cry twice. The first time was when an album deal fell through; the second was when she heard her father was dead. The album deal was a bummer but he'd been surprised at how hard she'd taken the news about her old man — going by her rare comments on the subject, she seemed to have as much filial affection as he did and the way Jake felt towards his parents, if he won five million bucks in Lotto, he'd buy them a garden gnome. Second hand.

Jake got rid of the waitress with a jerk of his head and asked Electra what was the matter. She stopped crying, mopped her eyes, blew her nose, drank most of a glass of mineral water and told him about her encounter that morning with Duane Ricketts. Jake blew his top, pounding the table so hard that the cutlery bounced and vowing to find that fucking Ricketts and kick his fucking head in. Despite her flushed cheeks and red-rimmed eyes, Electra was somehow able to look coolly unimpressed by this display of vicarious outrage.

"Quite finished?"

"Screw you," he snapped. "Why shouldn't I want to get the fucker back?"

"Get him back — what for? He didn't do anything to me."

Jake, bemused, shook his head. "What was all the blubbing in aid of then?"

Electra propped up her chin in the heel of her hand and looked away. "Partly because I'm slutted that my father, on top of everything else, would try to get me involved with drugs. And partly, I don't know, the thought of him dying the way he did with nothing to show for it except a few bags of coke." She stared at him defiantly. "Pathetic I know but it just seemed to call for a few tears. Forget about Ricketts: I told him what I thought of him; that's all he's worth."

Electra went to the toilet. When she got back to the table, she was still trying to marshal the welter of thoughts and memories and feelings that Ricketts had set loose, otherwise she might've picked up the overly casual note in Jake's voice.

"So, this special place of yours; where is it, just as a matter of interest?"

"Dale's dream home," she said with a hollow laugh. "The summer I turned six, Dad came over from Sydney and we went camping down at Coromandel — our last family holiday as it turned out. I guess it was make or break for him and Rayleen and it broke. She was a beach babe in those days — just wanted to lie around in the sun and go for swims and that — but Dad had ants in his pants, you know, he couldn't hack doing nothing; plus with his complexion, a day in the sun and he looked like a saveloy. Anyway, one afternoon he took me for a drive. We ended up in this place called Manacle, just north of Whangapoua. It's a neat little spot with a great beach and right there on the beach was this house you wouldn't believe, I mean a real mansion. It was weird in a way, seeing it there: you know how in the movies, some guy in the desert sees a mirage, a castle or something, out in the middle of nowhere? It was sort of like that."

Electra's eyes took on a faraway look. "So we're standing there doing the tourist thing, right, gawking at it, when this old guy, like doddery old, came down the drive and said hi. He was wearing shorts and a daggy old towelling hat — Dad said afterwards he thought he was the gardener but the guy actually owned the place. Dad and him got talking about the house; it all went over my head but I read up about it later. It's famous; it was built, in the 30s I think, by this crazy English millionaire who just disappeared, never to be seen again; they used to call it Swarbrick's Folly after him.

"He asked us if we wanted to look around. Dad said sure so we got the big guided tour. It was awesome, these amazing rugs and antiques everywhere, all done out in this dark wood: the sort of place you see in glossy magazines — lifestyles of the rich and famous sort of thing. Dad couldn't get over the master bedroom: it was as big as a tennis court with this humungous four-poster bed. The old guy even made Dad lie on the bed to try it out. As we were going, the owner bent down and looked at me and said, 'I think this little girl could do with a cold drink, let's see what we can find.' We went into the kitchen and he got me a lemonade and a chocolate from a box of chocolates, Continental I think they were. It was almost full, the box, but he told me to take it; he said, 'Don't eat them all at once, darling, save some for a rainy day.'

"On the way back to the camping ground, Dad said — I'll never forget this — 'One of these days I'm going to buy that house and you know what, sweetheart? You'll spend your wedding night in that big bed.'"

Electra looked at Jake. The faraway look was gone; the black eyes were as flat and hard as tarmac.

He said, "So what's the moral of the story? Don't make promises you can't keep?"

She nodded. "Especially to six year olds. They actually believe them."

"Well, maybe if his drug deal had worked out . . . who knows? So according to Ricketts, what happened was, this guy Spurdle pulled a swifty but your old man got away with the coke? And then, it sounds like, went to this fucking mansion? Is the place still there?"

Electra shrugged. "Far as I know. I read something about it being turned into a hotel."

"So he must've broken in and hid the coke somewhere inside?"

Electra nodded disinterestedly. "I guess — probably right in that big old bedroom he took such a fancy to." She picked up the menu and began to study it. "One thing's for sure, when it came to special places, I wasn't spoilt for choice: that was it — the one and only."

The back porch of Duane Ricketts' Mt Roskill bungalow caught the afternoon sun which made it a good spot to rest and regroup after a setback. For instance, if a scheme which he'd been counting on to deliver him once and for all from financial insecurity had just been blown away like dandelion seeds, he'd go and sit out there in an old armchair with a book and a beer and eventually doze off.

Ricketts had made an early start that day so he got only halfway through Jack Nicklaus's chapter on wedge shots and not much further through a Steinlager before he nodded off. He dreamt.

He was at a ball, a full black tie affair. Across the dance floor Electra Crouch was talking to a man with his back turned so Ricketts couldn't see his face. Electra's hair was different, darker and more natural, framing her oval face, and she'd discarded the nose-ring and ear studs. She wore a low-cut, flared turquoise evening gown which reached to the floor. Her companion looked around to take in the scene; it was her father, Dale Varty. His hair was plastered down and parted in the centre and he wore a crimson cummerbund.

As if she felt Ricketts' eyes on her, Electra turned her head and looked at him. The look went on and on until its meaning became unmistakable. He walked across the room to ask her to dance. Before he could get the words out, she smiled enchantingly and glided into his arms. They danced without speaking, gazing into one another's eyes. Electra moved closer to him until they were joined from thigh to chest; her body was sinuous yet firm. She tilted her head back and slightly parted her lips and her eyes grew cloudy with desire. As he leaned down to kiss her, someone tapped him on the shoulder.

He glanced over his shoulder. Jumbo Adeyemi stood there, at once exotic and urbane in white top hat and tails, twirling the cane with which he'd administered the tap; in his other hand he had a small box which was gift-wrapped in gold foil.

"A little something to brighten up your dreary existence, man," said Jumbo, handing him the box. Ricketts opened it. The box contained a curled and blackened slab of tongue which leaked blood from its serrated edge into the bed of cotton wool on which it rested. Jumbo winked at him, then bestowed a dazzling grin on Electra.

"Don't go wasting your time with this white boy, Miss Electra," he told her. "Why, his weeny little nudger would fit through that ring you've got on your pinkie finger with room to spare."

Electra removed the ring and held it up in front of her face. "Crikey," she said. "He must be hung like a hedgehog."

"Indubitably," said Jumbo. "I, in sharp contradistinction, am blessed with a dangle like a bull elephant's trunk which is why folks call me Jumbo." He bent to kiss her hand. "My vocabulary is even bigger; would you care for a game of Scrabble?"

Electra dimpled coquettishly and took his arm. "That sounds too stimulating for words," she giggled.

As Jumbo and Electra strolled off arm in arm, Ricketts became aware that silence had descended on the ballroom; the music had stopped in mid-waltz and the revellers had broken off their conversations to stare at him. Then, as if responding to the baton of an invisible choirmaster, they bellowed in unison and at mid-jarring volume, "Ricketts, you cocksucker."

Ricketts awoke with a whimper of relief which slid up the scale into an anxious bleat when he saw Tito Ihaka's contorted face hovering ten centimetres from the end of his nose; for a couple of unnerving seconds he thought the policeman was going to chew on his face, like a pit bull terrier. Instead Ihaka slowly straightened up, although he continued looking at Ricketts as if trying to decide where a bite would do the most damage.

"The neighbours are God botherers," said Ricketts, a little shakily. "They're not too keen on that sort of talk."

"Fuck the neighbours," said Ihaka crisply.

Ricketts noticed that Ihaka was, by his normal standards, formally attired. "Nice tie," he said. "Hundred per cent polyester?"

Although Ricketts wouldn't have thought it possible, Ihaka's expression became several degrees more malevolent; abruptly he turned on his heel and stomped into the house. He came back with the neck of a beer bottle protruding from his meaty fist, leant against the side of the house and glared down at Ricketts who was still in the armchair.

"Where's the dope, Ricketts?"

Ricketts had gathered that this wasn't a social call but the question still took him by surprise. Even as he mouthed the automatic response "What dope?", he could feel his face giving him away.

Ihaka poured beer down his throat for a while. "The dope Varty told you about in Bangkok. You got it here?"

Ricketts shook his head. "Look, I don't know what you're talking about."

Ihaka nodded as if the discussion was proceeding in line with his expectations. "Tell you what: I'll get myself another beer and I'll take my time over it. While I'm doing that, you go and get the coke and put it in my car, out the front. Then I'll piss off and we'll forget the subject ever came up. Just bear in mind pal, this is it; this is the one and only favour you're ever getting from me. You pull another stunt like this, I'll put you away so fast you won't even blink."

Ihaka went inside. Ricketts stayed where he was. When Ihaka returned, so did his scowl.

"All right cunty, you've had your chance . . ."

"I haven't got it."

Ihaka's eyes narrowed. "Okay; where is it?"

"I don't know."

When Ihaka started to call him filthy names, Ricketts interrupted again: "Varty didn't tell me; he just said go and see Clegg."

"Clegg? What the fuck was he meant to do?"

Ihaka studied Ricketts thoughtfully for a few seconds. "This is going to put a rocket under the Clegg investigation — you realise that, don't you?" Ricketts shrugged. "What I'm saying," continued Ihaka, "is if you're bullshitting, I'll come back and trample your balls into fish-paste."

Ricketts shrugged again.

"I'll be on my way then." Ihaka looked back from the foot of the porch steps. "You've got nerve Ricketts, I'll give you that. If I thought a trained fucking killer might turn up on my doorstep any moment, I wouldn't be sitting out on the porch having a wet dream."

Ricketts yelled after him wanting to know what the hell he was talking about but Ihaka walked to his car without a backward glance and drove away.

Back at Auckland Central, Ihaka went straight in to see Detective Inspector Finbar McGrail.

"Ah there you are, Sergeant," said McGrail looking up from some papers. "I hear you excelled yourself this morning."

"Oh yeah?" said Ihaka guardedly, thinking, here we go.

"The minister's secretary said the American ambassador found you — and I quote — 'a breath of fresh air'."

Ihaka managed to look both surprised and slightly relieved. "Yeah well, he seemed like a decent bloke — easy enough to do in that company, I suppose. You heard what's happening?"

"I did indeed. Extraordinary business, but ours not to reason why."

"What's new, eh?" Ihaka's wary look faded. He tried, briefly and unsuccessfully, to squeeze self-satisfaction out of his expression. "Still, the day hasn't been a complete dud — I reckon I know why Clegg was killed."

McGrail's mouth quivered. "Let me hazard a wild guess: does it have anything to do with the shipment of drugs Dale Varty brought across from Australia in 1983?"

Ihaka shoved his hands into his pockets. "I thought you said the briefing would be a non-event?" he said resentfully.

"Oh it was, completely," said McGrail blandly. "Sergeant, why don't you close the door and take a seat?"

When Ihaka had sat down, McGrail opened a desk drawer and produced a cassette.

"This morning I had a ring from one of the partners at Trubshaw Trimble — Clegg's law firm. He asked if he could pop in for a chat — about this." McGrail indicated the cassette; he put it in the tape machine on his desk and pressed a button.

A voice Ihaka didn't know said: "Monday October 17th, 1983, recording meeting with client Al Grills to discuss receiving stolen goods charge."

McGrail stopped the tape.

"That's Clegg. The fellow who came to see me is the executor of his estate. In the course of going through Clegg's files — no doubt also with his Trubshaw Trimble hat on looking out for any nasties which might pop out of the woodwork — he found a key to a bank safety deposit box. That's where the cassette was." Knowing instinctively what was running through Ihaka's mind, the inspector added: "No Sergeant, he didn't tell me what else was in the safety deposit box and, under the circumstances, I thought it would be churlish to ask."

Ihaka feigned a polite smile. "Fair enough."

McGrail fast-forwarded the cassette to the point he wanted. "Now then," he said. Intrigued despite himself, Ihaka sat up in his chair and craned forward.

A telephone rang. Clegg said, "Clegg . . . yep . . . right now? I'm actually with a client . . . how long will it . . . a few minutes? . . . Okay, be with you in two ticks." He hung up. "Al, sorry about this, I've just got to duck upstairs and see the senior partner. Won't be long. Can I get Cath to bring you another coffee?"

Another voice, obviously Grills': "No, she's right."

"Okay, be back in a sec."

A door opened and closed. A telephone receiver was picked up and a number dialled. Then Grills: "Yeah, it's me . . . You've heard from Varty? Shit hot, when's that story . . . right . . . right . . . hang on, let me get a pen . . . okay, what was it again? . . . Otama beach, Thursday night? Okay . . . you bet . . . oh he'll be shitty all right . . . yeah, what you said before, you don't do this sort of crap any more . . . yeah, well, let's face it, he's not going to turn round and fuck off back to Oz . . . yeah . . . yeah, picked it up this morning, a sawn off .22" — Grills laughed — "he can't complain — hanging out with Terry Clark and co, he's fucking lucky he's lasted this long . . . and I'll bring the stuff straight over to your place? . . . Yep . . . ten kilos, right? Sweet as . . . okay, I better get off the phone, Clegg'll be back any mo . . . yeah, see you."

McGrail punched a button and the machine stopped. "What do you make of that, Sergeant?"

"Varty set the deal up with whoever Grills is talking to but his partner decided to shaft him; the call was putting the finishing touches on the shaft. Except Grills fucked up big-time, right?"

McGrail opened the file on his desk. "Grills' body was discovered by the side of the road that runs along Otama Beach on Friday, 21 October. He died from massive head injuries as a result of a single blow with a shovel. The murder weapon belonged to the owner of one of the beach houses down there, near where they found the body. No one was staying there at the time; the shovel had been left under the back steps where anyone could've picked it up."

Ihaka snapped his fingers loudly, lurching forward. "Clegg must've warned Varty. When he heard the tape, he got in touch with Varty and told him what was going on." He leaned back and closed his eyes. "Grills is getting set to slot Varty; before he has a chance, Varty sneaks up on him and beats him like a drum; probably didn't mean to kill him. When he realised the guy was dead, he thought Christ, I've got to get out of here, dumped the dope somewhere, and buggered off."

McGrail nodded. "Makes sense."

"You bet. I've just talked to that lying turd Ricketts; you know, the real reason he was out at Clegg's place that day? Because Varty told him Clegg knew where the coke was. Varty must've cut him in on the deal as a payback. Then when Varty shot through, they probably agreed to leave the stuff where it was till he got back. You could just about say this gives Leith Grills — Al's brother — a motive for killing Clegg; speaking of Leith, you know he's working for Bryce Spurdle these days?"

"The drug dealer — supposedly retired?" McGrail shuffled through his papers. "He's down here as a known associate of both Al Grills and Varty. Maybe it's Spurdle Grills is talking to on the tape."

"Could be," said Ihaka. "Put it this way, it's a lot more likely that Spurdle's got Leith on the payroll to help him get his hands on that dope than to get rid of his missus."

"Say again?"

"I told you about Spurdle's wife, didn't I, how she's got it into her head that he's hired Leith Grills to knock her off?"

McGrail, whose most fervent detractors acknowledged he had a mind like Colditz — once something had entered, it rarely escaped — shook his head very slowly from left to right and back again. "Negative, Sergeant. Why should Spurdle do that?"

"Oh, she thinks he's found out she's been getting a knobbing from her gym instructor."

"Well, if he has found out, she might have a point. Men have been known to kill their wives for less."

"Men have been known to kill their wives for patting the family dog too often but we're talking about Spurdle here. Maybe if she was renting studs on his Amex card, but that's about it. And let me tell you, there's no way this chick's paying for it; shit, she'd find herself a root in the Vatican."

McGrail rubbed his chin reflectively. "I see. Tell me Sergeant, exactly what did you and the American ambassador talk about?"

16

It was a tense time in the Spurdle household. For reasons which escaped Bryce Spurdle, his wife Jody had been in a diabolical mood the past few days. She'd bristled and snapped every time he opened his mouth and when he'd asked her if it was that time of the month, a reasonable question under the circumstances, she'd thrown a wobbly and refused to make dinner. Discreet monitoring of the packet of tampons in her ensuite bathroom had ruled that out, so Christ knew what was eating her, the crabby little mole.

That was Monday night. Spurdle had dined on hamburger patties which, by the end of the meal, he'd come to suspect could have done with a little more defrosting in the microwave. Later, he lay in bed flinching at each gurgle from under the sheets in case it heralded the agonizing abdominal ructions which often accompany food poisoning. Fortunately, it was nothing more than a particularly heavy build-up of the nocturnal wind which, in happier times, had provided him with much innocent amusement.

On Tuesday night, emboldened by an excellent bottle of American red wine and a large Cointreau and ice, Bryce had suggested to Jody that she might care to don a few choice items from her lingerie drawer and drape herself over the king-size bed to await his pulsating presence. She'd been unimpressed by this love-talk; she'd called him "a pisshead", threatened to throw up if he got within an arm's length of her, and snidely added that he'd pulsate about as much as the shrivelled-up parsnip which had been languishing at the back of the fridge since Waitangi Day. Then she'd plucked her dressing gown from the wardrobe and flounced off to the spare room.

Wired on alcohol and unsated lust, Spurdle had, for the second night running, found sleep elusive. He'd flopped this way and that in the big bed, like a fish in the bottom of a boat, and tormented himself with bitter thoughts. Fuck, it wasn't as if his demands were excessive — he only put the hard word on her once every couple of weeks, if that. She'd been happy enough to lie back and think of her credit cards in the early days, when he'd spent more time in the saddle than Lester Piggott; she hadn't even baulked the odd time he nudged her awake for a dawnbreaker — or "the waterjump" as he'd once heard it described, in reference to the physical and mental challenge of performing with a bulging bladder. That was then, before the deal was signed and sealed, he thought; now that the bitch has got everything she wants, including a bloody long leash, one lousy squirt a fortnight's too much to ask.

Then on Wednesday night, the shit-train rolled through town again. He'd got himself fizzed up at the prospect of finally getting his hands on Varty's boatload of cocaine, but that'd turned out to be another pie in the sky. He'd sent Grills off to heavy Varty's ex-wife, a simple enough mission for someone as vicious and ugly as him, you'd think. Not on your fucking nelly; Grills had drifted back, red-faced and shaken, mumbling about how he'd been jumped by a short-arse Yank who'd stuck a pistol in his face. Then the deadshit dug his heels in and refused point-blank to have another go unless he got some firepower of his own. He was all set to head out to Pukekohe to collect a shotgun from a bloke he knew but Spurdle had given that the thumbs down, double quick: retrieving a swag of drugs which everyone had long since forgotten about was a very worthwhile exercise as long as it could be done nice and quietly, without attracting any attention, let alone that of the boys in blue. Leith Grills fired-up and brandishing a shotgun was not Spurdle's idea of stealth.

On Thursday morning Spurdle went into town and had breakfast at the Sierra café. He took his golf clubs and on the way back stopped in at the driving range in Northcote where he flailed wildly at golf balls until his frustrations subsided.

He got home just before one o'clock and was pleasantly surprised to find there was a lull in the hostilities. Jody was in a civil mood and in the kitchen, preparing lunch. After grilled snapper salad, a couple of glasses of chardonnay, and some bile-free conversation, Spurdle felt less at odds with the world. The phone call, which Spurdle answered, didn't hurt either.

"Is that Bryce Spurdle?"

The caller was male, the voice unfamiliar. He sounded young, whoever he was.

"Who's this?"

"You're the only B. Spurdle in the phone book but the question is, are you the B. Spurdle who went into a let's say business venture with Dale Varty a few years ago which didn't pan out?"

Who is this arsehole? thought Spurdle.

"Because if you are, I've got good news for you. I've located the product. The stuff that was brought in from overseas and went missing? I know where it is."

Spurdle remained silent, wondering if it was some sort of set-up or perhaps someone pulling his tit.

"Are you out there?" asked the caller. "Is there life on planet Spurdle?"

"I'm listening," said Spurdle.

"Okay. I assume that means you're the guy. As I was saying, I know where the product is and I thought you'd be pretty keen to find out."

"Maybe."

"Yeah, right . . . and maybe dogs like sniffing other dogs' backsides. How about we make a date to talk about it?"

Spurdle looked at his watch. "You know the Sierra café on Ponsonby Road?"

"Sure do."

"I'll see you there in an hour."

"An hour's good. That'll give you plenty of time to top up the bank account."

Spurdle took the Porsche this time but on the motorway he got stuck behind a cop cruising at right on the speed limit. He was almost ten minutes late when he pulled into a parking spot outside the Sierra. There was a long-haired guy, early to mid twenties, in dark glasses and black leather jacket sitting by himself at one of the outside tables. When Spurdle walked up to the entrance to the café, the guy took off his glasses and said, "Yo Bryce, you're late, dude."

Spurdle stared down at him. "Don't 'yo' me, don't call me Bryce, and don't call me dude." He sat down. "Who are you, pal?"

Jake Latimer smiled confidently and shook his head. "I think I'd prefer to remain anonymous . . ."

"Is that a fact?" said Spurdle, raising his eyebrows. He leaned forward and lowered his voice. "Let me explain how we're going to do this: first, you've got to convince me that I should take a blind bit of notice of you or anything you say. If you can do that, we'll go on to the next step. If we get to the stage of negotiating, then you're going to have to tell me who you are and where I can find you, otherwise forget it. See, the thing is sonny, you're selling information and information's only worth anything if it's kosher. Now you, being so fucking sharp, are going to want money up front, right? Because otherwise you've got no leverage. You see the problem? I don't find out if what I've paid for is worth shit until after I've handed over the dough. So you're going to ID yourself; that way, if I pay for information which turns out to be bodgie, I can send someone round to your place to get my money back — and while they're at it, to stick a crowbar so far up your arse, you'll think you're getting dicked from both ends. Which probably wouldn't be a new experience for you."

Latimer laughed, a little nervously. "Hey, that's cool. I can dig it."

"Well hoo-fucking-ray. Let's hear it, flash."

Latimer gave Spurdle a brief account of the events of October 1983, managing to avoid any allocation of blame for the collapse of the enterprise, and of Varty's death in Bombat prison.

"So what?" demanded Spurdle. "All that proves is you can read."

"What else can I tell you, apart from where the stuff is?" asked Latimer plaintively.

"For a start, why don't you explain how you found out?"

Latimer took a deep breath: "A guy I know was in prison with Varty, up in Thailand. Varty told him about, you know, the deal and how he hid the dope. He didn't tell him where but he dropped a few hints. I put that together with stuff I got from someone here, someone who was really close to Varty."

"It sounds a bit fucking vague to me."

"Shit, I can tell you which room in which building in which town: how much more do you want?"

"Have you actually seen the stuff?"

"Come on — would I be sitting here if I had? I only found out where it is myself a couple of hours ago."

"Who else knows?"

"Only one other person; take it from me, they don't want anything to do with it."

"How far out of Auckland?"

Latimer shrugged. "Bit of a drive."

"Coromandel?"

"Hey," said Latimer holding up his hands. He smiled tentatively at Spurdle. "Nice try."

The older man didn't smile back. Either this guy's not a bad actor, thought Spurdle, or he really believes he knows where the coke is.

"Okay, let's say I believe you. How much?"

Latimer grinned twitchily and cleared his throat. "Fifty grand."

This time Spurdle did smile; it was an indulgent, almost fond, smile. "You want to try again?"

"Jesus, there's a shitload of it . . ."

"Well, off you go and get it then. It's all yours. Of course, that means you have to take a few risks: you've got to find buyers, deal with all sorts of nasty bastards, shitting yourself the whole time they're going to stiff you or turn out to be undercover cops. And soon as word gets out that you're sitting on a big supply, there'll be a few hard shots around town making plans to take it off you."

"Okay, okay. Tell you what, why don't you make me an offer?"

Spurdle stroked his nose and pretended to be doing some complicated mental arithmetic. "Five."

"Oh man, get real; that's a fucking insult."

Seven minutes later they agreed on a price of $12,500 cash. Latimer waited at the Sierra while Spurdle went down to a bank in Ponsonby village and withdrew the money. On the way, Spurdle rang Leith Grills on his mobile phone and told him to put some gas in his car because he was going to be doing some distance.

Rayleen Crouch had her professional expression in place, nodded frequently and said 'yes', 'is that right?' and 'uh-huh' at regular intervals. Despite the appearance of solicitous interest, though, she was only half-listening. That was quite an achievement since most people would have been either fascinated or horrified — or perhaps even physically sick.

Rayleen was in a counselling session with Jon, one of her clients. Jon was a twenty-two-year-old heroin user with a fashionably wasted look and an Adam's apple which jutted as if he'd swallowed a large padlock; that was entirely possible since he was in the habit of swallowing metal objects. It wasn't altogether clear to

Rayleen why Jon swallowed knives, forks, spoons and other, even less digestible, metallic items. A psychiatrist had told her that Jon had a death wish which was possibly the least illuminating statement she'd ever heard. After she'd informed the psychiatrist that the same could be said about many, if not most, of the people one came across in welfare work, she pointed out it wasn't even all that logical an explanation seeing Jon had swallowed the contents of the average household's cutlery drawer several times over without succeeding in killing himself. Rayleen tended to believe that, as was the case with most of the bizarre things her clients did, it was about half and half exhibitionism and a cry for help.

At this session, however, Jon was showing off by relating anecdotes about life on the street with a drug habit to support. The key to it appeared to be a willingness to engage in sadomasochistic homosexual acts for an appropriate fee; under normal circumstances, Rayleen would have taken a professional interest since it was one of the few branches of deviant behaviour with which she was unfamiliar. On this particular afternoon though, not even Jon's lurid accounts of amyl nitrate, sodomy and the lash could hold her attention. Rayleen couldn't get her mind off what had happened at her house the night before: the intrusion of the very scary Leith Grills and his subsequent rout at the hands of the little American anti-drug policeman, who'd managed to be courtly and ever so slightly sinister all at the same time.

Like Grills, Funke had wanted to talk about her late ex-husband and his drugs but the combination of shock and Chivas Regal had left Rayleen incapable of holding up her end of a chat about the weather. Fearing that Grills might return, she'd asked Funke to drive her to a friend's place in Epsom where she'd spent the night.

Jon eventually managed to gain Rayleen's attention but by then it was too late. He'd just started telling her about well-known Aucklanders for whom the excretory functions formed an important part of sexual and para-sexual activity when she remembered she'd arranged to meet Funke at her place at five o'clock. She made her excuses and left.

Funke was already there, sitting behind the wheel of the dark-grey Fiat Tipo in which he'd ferried Rayleen to her friend's house the previous night. They went inside and she made coffee while he explained his assignment: the location and destruction of the shipment of cocaine which Dale Varty had talked about, in the process using up breath he could ill afford to waste.

"That's what that goon last night was after," said Rayleen. "He's in it with Dale's partner back then."

"Would you happen to know who that was?"

Rayleen shook her head. "I could make an educated guess, no more. Dale was thick as thieves with a shady character called Bryce Spurdle."

Funke nodded. "Well, ma'am, it doesn't surprise me one little bit that the underworld is showing an interest," said Funke. "There's a considerable quantity of cocaine involved here so as you'll appreciate, it's real important that we get to it ahead of the likes of your gentleman caller."

"I'm sorry Mr Funke . . ."

"Please, ma'am, call me Buddy."

"Buddy, I'm sorry but I just don't have a clue where Dale would've hidden it. You see, Dale and I had split for good by then. I wasn't in touch with him at all."

Funke sighed. "Ma'am, I'm sure sorry to bring this up: when Mr Varty was telling this Ricketts fellow about the cocaine, he mentioned a daughter — she'd be your daughter too I presume?"

"Electra?" yelped Rayleen. "How the hell did she come into it?"

"According to the person who overheard the conversation, Mr Varty told Ricketts to go see her; our informant got the impression your daughter could point him in the direction of the drugs."

Rayleen waggled her head emphatically. "That's ludicrous. I mean, for God's sake, Electra's only eighteen now. She couldn't have been much more than six when she last set eyes on Dale."

Funke shrugged. "Well, yeah, it does seem kind of strange but that's what our informant heard Mr Varty say. Now the thing that worries me is this Ricketts, who doesn't sound like a model citizen, is bound to try to get in touch with your little girl."

Rayleen considered this statement for a micro-second then bounded to the phone and rang her daughter.

"Electra? It's Rayleen."

"Hi there."

"Darling, are you all right?"

"Yeah, I'm okay. Why?"

"Have you seen or heard anything from a man called Ricketts?"

"Are you psychic or something? The guy bailed me up on my way to varsity this morning . . ."

"Honey, you stay exactly where you are; don't move, right? Promise me?"

"I'm not going anywhere but would you mind telling me what this is about . . .?"

"I'll be there in five minutes."

Funke drove Rayleen over to Datchet Terrace where Electra made them a pot of herbal tea and told them about Duane Ricketts, what he'd wanted, and how she'd sent him off with a flea in his ear. Then she told them all about the beautiful house in Manacle where the old man had given her an almost-full box of chocolates. All she left out was the promise her father had made on the way back to the camp-site.

When she'd finished, Funke looked from Electra to Rayleen and said, "That's a fine young woman, right there. If more young people had her attitude to drugs, I'd be out of a job. Say, would you happen to know where can I pick me up a road map?"

17

Digby Purchase, the travel writer, had dined well: game soup to start, then seafood risotto and a half-bottle of Marlborough sauvignon blanc; that was followed by grilled tenderloin of beef, asparagus and gratin potatoes with a half-bottle of merlot from Martinborough. After a contemplative pause, he'd pressed on: a slice of orange syrup cake with mango sorbet and a glass of dessert wine, then cheese and port. And fingers crossed, the best was yet to come! As the grandfather clock in Manacle Grange's old billiards room chimed midnight, Purchase looked over the rim of his brandy balloon into Fleur Wolfgramm's tantalising green eyes and felt his thought processes disintegrate into a kaleidoscope of depraved images. In the course of his extensive travels and twenty-year association with the tourism industry, Purchase had bedded a number of hotel managers — none of them, as it happened, of the female persuasion. It was an anomaly he fervently hoped to put right before taking his leave of Manacle Grange.

Digby Purchase was forty-six years old, pink, slender and bisexual. He had thick, very blond, almost flaxen hair which he wore longish, the Hitler-style fringe descending diagonally across his forehead to his left eyebrow. From time to time it would interfere with his vision, prompting an imperious toss of the head. With his expensive and somewhat fogeyish clothes, plummy drawl and air of languid boredom, Purchase did a passable imitation of a well-bred Englishman. The further afield he ventured, the more successful the impersonation tended to be; in London, where they occasionally come across the real thing, he was usually picked as an imposter in next to no time.

Over dinner Purchase had reflected on the events which brought him to Manacle Grange. There was no doubt about it, he decided; his guardian angel, who'd been conspicuous by his or her absence of late, was back in business. If that reception in Auckland hadn't been so naff, he wouldn't have drunk himself paralytic; if he hadn't done that, he wouldn't have slept through his alarm and missed the flight to Christchurch. And if he'd made it to Christchurch, he'd be facing the prospect, on the morrow, of a hike up a glacier or white-water rafting or whatever other hellish, not to mention life-endangering, activities the New Zealand tourism flacks could devise; here, on the other hand, he faced the immediate prospect of a prolonged and sweaty grapple with the delicious Ms Wolfgramm. He made a mental note to ring and thank the public relations woman in the tourism board's Auckland office who'd suggested the alternative of a visit to Manacle Grange.

Indeed, Manacle Grange was most agreeable. And the wonderful thing about it was that, with an ounce of luck, he wouldn't have to write a single, sodding word about the place. The tiresome part of being a travel writer was that after the trip, when the fun and games were over, one had to write about it. But if the highlight of the trip was a stay in an exclusive hotel which had since gone out of business, you were off the hook. He'd lay odds the Grange would've closed its doors before his article was due — it was obviously a complete frost. When he'd arrived the day before, there were only two couples in residence: the Lees from Taiwan, who'd smiled a great deal, hadn't said a word, not even to each other, and, at breakfast, had done stomach-turning things with their eggs; and the Australians, Barry and Marcie Pyves from the Gold Coast, who'd been rather more loquacious, cheerfully admitting to his bankruptcy and her plastic surgery within fifteen minutes of being introduced. But the Lees and the Pyves had checked out that morning, leaving Purchase as the sole guest. And now the kitchen was closed, the staff had gone home, and Digby Purchase had Manacle Grange and its manager all to himself.

Purchase was the tourism writer for *Travel Weekly*, a London-based newspaper for the British travel industry. He'd been the editor for several years but he had been demoted after spectacularly disgracing himself three times in quick succession. The first blot on his copybook came to light when he submitted an expenses claim relating to a trip to New York. Normally, these were authorised without quibble, *Travel Weekly*'s publisher being too much of a gent to actually check how much of the company's money Purchase had spent, let alone assess the validity of the various items of expenditure. On this occasion, however, the publisher's eye was caught by the column entry showing that, during a three-day stay in the Big Apple, Purchase had run up a £365 laundry bill. Even allowing for the stratospheric charges of big-city five-star hotels, this seemed excessive.

Curious and uncomfortably aware that, as the authoriser, he was a major link in the chain of responsibility for fiddled expenses, the publisher called the accounts department and obtained Purchaser's expense claims for his recent trips; all featured huge amounts for laundry. When an explanation was sought, Purchase confessed that, to avoid doing or paying for his laundry, he took a suitcase of accumulated dirty washing whenever he went on a trip and had it done in hotels at the paper's expense. While the publisher took a dim view of this, he would've been positively outraged if Purchase had told him the truth: that the clothes in the extra suitcase belonged to some of Purchase's bachelor acquaintances who paid him the going High Street rate to have their suits dry-cleaned and shirts laundered to five-star hotel standards.

Purchase was given a stiff warning. Nevertheless, two months later the publisher received an irate phone call from the marketing director of an upmarket holiday company who was aggressively insistent on knowing why the *Travel Weekly* representative on a just-concluded, no expense-spared press trip to the Caribbean had been a semi-literate motor mechanic, when both the invitation and accepted practice specified a journalist. The mechanic concerned had posed as a freelancer commissioned by *Travel Weekly*, but his habit of throwing away press kits in the presence of the PR functionaries who'd prepared them, rather than in the privacy of his hotel room, aroused suspicion. The publisher's investigation established that Purchase had sent the mechanic on the junket as a contra payment for keeping his temperamental Triumph Stag roadworthy.

The incident in the sex club was the final straw. While attending a big annual travel exhibition in Berlin, Purchase had hosted the boss of one of Britain's largest tour operators, a major advertiser in *Travel Weekly*, to a night on the town. After dinner and visits to a few of the little bars along the Kurfurstendamm, Purchase took his guest to Mitzi's, a sex club in which he'd spent some horizon-expanding times during previous exhibitions. The tour operator had never seen a live sex show so they sat at the very front to enable him to savour the raw lubricity of the performances. Halfway through a protracted and disappointingly orthodox copulation routine, the late nights, long hours and booze caught up with the tour operator who fell asleep in his chair. While his guest took time out, Purchase slipped away to a back room to renew acquaintance with a sparky little Uruguayan.

The humdrum fornicators were followed by the star of the show: Madame Herta, the Prussian Mistress of Pain. Herta wore stiletto heels and a skin-tight black leather bodysuit complete with zippered balaclava and stalked onto the little stage cracking a whip and promising that all the naughty boys in the audience were about to get the spanking they so richly deserved. She was laying into her first victim in fine style when his ecstatic squeals were drowned out by an explosive series of snores from the tour operator, slumped in his seat at the foot of the stage.

Herta, who was actually Spanish rather than Prussian and possessed a haughty Castilian temperament, reacted angrily to what she interpreted as a provocative critique of her work. She strode to the front of the stage, wound up and lashed the slumbering tour operator across the chest. The blow was sufficiently violent to do three things: it woke the tour operator up, it caused his left nipple to bleed profusely, and it shattered the expensive pair of designer spectacles in his shirt pocket. A scene ensued which ended with the tour operator being hustled out of the club by two bouncers, beefy neo-Nazis, who dragged him into an alley and gave him a methodical kicking as a small token of their admiration for Madame Herta and their resentment over Britain's role in the destruction of the Third Reich.

However, as the chimes of midnight died away, the humiliating demotion which followed the debacle at Mitzi's couldn't have been further from Purchase's mind. While, sexually speaking, a man of catholic tastes, Purchase did have a slight weakness for the youths of North Africa; at that moment, however, the juiciest catamite in the casbah could've materialised in the old billiards room without attracting a second glance. There was something about Fleur Wolfgramm, about the faintly wicked gleam in her green eyes and the sensual mouth, which proclaimed that here was a woman who'd been around and enjoyed every stop on the circuit. If this one isn't a sack-artiste extraordinaire, thought Purchase, I'm Yoko Ono.

Noticing she'd finished her Sambuca, Purchase threw back the rest of his cognac and reached for her glass.

"Allow me."

She looked at her watch. "Just a smidgin."

Purchase hustled across to the small bar in the corner. The Sambuca bottle was empty.

"Out of this stuff, I'm afraid," he said, holding up the bottle. "What about a cognac?"

"Oh God, no thanks," said Wolfgramm. "It's far too late to be mixing drinks. I think I might call it a night."

Purchase was seized with something close to panic. "There must be more of it somewhere?" he gabbled.

"Probably in the library bar," she said disinterestedly, "but I can't be fagged getting it."

"Don't worry, I'll get it," said Purchase hastily. "You stay right where you are. It's the second on the right down the corridor, yes?"

Wolfgramm shrugged. "Yep, that's it."

Galvanised by the two imperatives of delaying Fleur Wolfgramm's retirement and getting more alcohol into her, Purchase broke into a run down the corridor. He yanked open the library door and was groping for the light switch when he heard a footfall in the corridor behind him. Thinking she'd come to cancel the Sambuca, he turned to plead. Largely because Purchase's mouth was open when the shotgun butt slammed into the side of his face, he sustained a multiple fracture of the jaw as well as being knocked senseless for several hours.

When Wolfgramm heard the bumps in the corridor, her first thought was that a guest had woken up with the dry horrors and gone on the prowl for a fizzy drink. Then she remembered that the only guest they had was the English ponce whom, if she wasn't very much mistaken, she'd shortly have to tell to fuck off, thereby blowing her strategy of getting the Grange some positive overseas press coverage. She went out into the corridor and found herself looking down the barrel of a pump-action shotgun and into Leith Grills' eyes. As scary sights went, there wasn't much to choose between them.

Grills waggled the shotgun which, in defiance of Spurdle's veto, he'd picked up from his mate in Pukekohe on the way down.

"Keep your trap shut," he said in a low voice.

Wolfgramm opened her mouth but swiftly closed it again, deciding she didn't have anything to say which was important enough to justify ignoring a direct instruction from a shotgun-wielding throwback. With rising dread she saw the throwback's gaze was fixed on her bosom. For once, though, Leith Grills had things other than breasts on his mind.

"You the manager of this joint?" he demanded.

Wolfgramm nodded, feeling a surge of relief as she realised that he'd been staring at her lapel badge.

"Show us the master bedroom."

Without thinking, she stammered, "I'm afraid it's occupied at the moment."

"Too fucking bad for them," growled Grills. "Who's in there?"

She gestured hesitantly at the prostrate travel writer. "Well, as a matter of fact, it's Mr Purchase's room."

Grills glanced back at Purchase. "Hoy, blondie," he said, "I'm just going to have a geek in your room, all right?" Then to Wolfgramm: "He says 'Be my guest.'"

Wolfgramm led Grills up the stairs to the master bedroom. He put down the sports bag which he'd had slung over his left shoulder and made a careful examination. It was a large, square, high-ceilinged room dominated by the massive four-poster bed. The head of the bed was against the left-hand wall, as you entered. On each side of the bed were small tables with lamps and beyond it, in the corner, an old leather armchair. There were French doors in the wall opposite which opened out onto a balcony and the bathroom was through a doorway in the far corner. A walk-in-wardrobe faced the bed and alongside it was a chest of drawers with a mirror. Against the near wall was an antique writing desk with a high-backed chair and a wooden bench holding a battered leather suitcase.

Grills made Wolfgramm sit on the high-backed chair. He rummaged in the suitcase and pulled out three of Purchase's silk shirts which he tore apart, using the strips to tie her to the chair with her hands bound together behind the back of it. He balled up a shirt sleeve and shoved it in her mouth as a gag; she retched when the sour, mingled tang of deodorant and body odour hit the back of her throat. Then he searched the bedroom. It took him fifteen minutes to find what he was looking for.

About the time Grills, on his hands and knees in the walk-in wardrobe, spotted the scratches on the skirting board and the indentations around the carpet tacks indicating that the carpet had been lifted and replaced, Buddy Funke gently pushed open the front door of Manacle Grange and slipped into the impressive entrance hall. He cocked his head and listened for half a minute. The ground floor lights were on but the great house was quiet. Moving soundlessly in his rubber-soled walking shoes, Funke went through the hall towards the stairs with the gleaming dark-wood banisters and ornate fretwork. As he reached the stairs, he glanced down the corridor running through to the rear of the house and saw splayed feet protruding from a doorway. He investigated. The feet were attached to an unconscious man who'd either wandered into the path of a longhorn stampede or been taken out by someone who employed direct and brutal methods. Believing the latter scenario to be the more likely, Funke drew the .38 revolver from his belt.

Halfway up the stairs Funke heard the murmur of a male voice. On the landing he looked left and right; the first door on the right was open and the lights in the room were on. An exclamation of triumph — "you fucking beauty" — floated through the doorway. Funke flattened himself against the wall and inched down the corridor.

Holding the revolver out in front of him in both hands, Funke slid round the doorway moving fast and low. His eyes and the .38 moved as one, sweeping the room in an arc from left to right. A large backside poked rudely out of the wardrobe at the far end of the room; its owner, presumably the speaker, remained absorbed in whatever he was doing in there. A woman was tied to a chair and gagged. Funke held a finger to his lips as she rolled her eyes and jerked her head towards the bottom.

Funke glided across the room. The wardrobe was big enough to stable a giraffe but all it contained was a blue blazer on a hanger, a spare pillow and blanket on a shelf above the railing, and the man he'd tangled with at Mrs Crouch's place the night before.

Grills had pulled up the carpet in the corner, peeled it back and lifted a few short lengths of floorboard. There were some tools and half a dozen plastic bags of white powder on the floor beside him. In front of him, propped up in the corner, was a shotgun. As Grills lifted out two more bags, Funke placed the revolver's muzzle against the nape of the kneeling man's neck. Grills froze.

"Make a move for that shotgun hoss, you're gone," said Funke. He stepped back two paces: "Now you just back on out of there on your hands and knees."

Grills did as he was told. When he was all the way out of the wardrobe, Funke told him to get up and put his hands behind his head.

"We can't go on meeting like this," said Funke, smiling pleasantly; Grills sent back a murderous glare. "What was that you were rooting around after in the closet there, boy? Found yourself a big mess of nose candy?"

"Go fuck yourself," said Grills through clenched teeth.

"Later maybe," said Funke affably. "If I don't get a better offer. Going by the shape of that pilgrim downstairs and the way you've trussed up the little lady, you're some piece of work. Seems to me I better get the cuffs on you, pronto. We're going down the stairs and out to my car, okay? Keep in mind, you as much as shuffle and I'll give you the gun."

Grills led the way down the stairs. In the hall, Funke plucked a plump cushion off an armchair and held it behind his back.

Funke's Fiat was parked a little way down the drive behind a white Holden Berlina. As they passed the Holden, Funke asked, "Say, this your heap?"

Grills said it was.

"I got a better idea. Open the trunk."

Grills gawked at him, nonplussed. "What?"

"Open the goddam trunk," snapped Funke, pointing the pistol at the rear of the car.

Grills fished in his pocket for the car keys and opened the boot.

"Get in," ordered Funke.

Grills hesitated. Funke extended his right arm and pointed the .38 at Grills' head. "Oh, I get it — you'd prefer to die. Well, that's okay."

Grills clambered awkwardly into the boot and stretched out on his side. Funke looked down at him, smiling thinly.

"Well, ain't you a good boy? Now get on your back and put your hands behind you, underneath your body."

When Grills had got himself into a satisfactory defenceless position, Funke planted the cushion on his chest, rammed the gun barrel into it and shot him twice through the heart. The manoeuvre was executed with the deft economy of a poultry farmer wringing a chicken's neck. Funke closed the boot, stuck the pistol in his belt, slipped the car keys into his pocket and walked back up the drive, softly whistling "Rose of Alabama". He stopped whistling when a tall figure in a long raincoat and with a stocking mask over his face stepped out of the shadow of the house and pointed a sawn-off rifle at him.

"Very neat," said the masked man. "I take it you've done this sort of thing before?"

Funke adopted a quizzical expression. "If it's a room you'd be wanting," he said earnestly, "I don't think you'll need the rifle. Near as I can tell, the place is about empty."

"Thanks all the same but I'd say I'm here for the same reason as you."

"Who're you?"

"As they say in the movies, I'll ask the questions," said the newcomer who sounded as if he was enjoying himself. "Now slowly take out the gun, drop it on the ground and get your hands up. Otherwise, as you were just saying to the poor bastard in the boot, a bullet between the eyes can be easily arranged."

Funke discarded the revolver. The man in the stocking mask motioned him back and without taking his eyes or the rifle off Funke, stooped and picked up the .38 which he slipped into his coat pocket.

"Okay pardner," he said. "I presume you've found the crank; let's go and get it."

Hands in the air, Funke led the way into the Grange and up to the master bedroom. Fleur Wolfgramm stopped struggling to get free and looked in bewilderment at the man in the stocking mask, wondering why all of a sudden Manacle Grange had become a Mecca for men with guns.

The new arrival looked at her. "Well, I was expecting to interrupt something but this is downright kinky."

"It's over there," said Funke. "In the closet."

The other man seemed to smile under his stocking mask. "Then why don't you hop in there and get it?"

Funke went into the wardrobe and collected the bags of cocaine which Grills had extracted from their hiding-place. He brought them out and dumped them on the foot of the bed.

"There's more," he said.

"I should hope so," said the tall man. As Funke went back to the wardrobe, the newcomer strolled over to Wolfgramm. Holding the sawn-off rifle in his right hand braced against his hip, he used his left hand to remove the gag then perched on the end of the bed.

"I can see you're tied up right now," he said, "but when do you . . ."

Funke backed out of the wardrobe and spun around, bringing up Grills' shotgun. The buttocks of the man in the stocking mask were scarcely off the bed when Funke fired from the hip. The blast took the masked man in the chest and flung him back onto the big bed where he sprawled. With his lacerated torso and outspread arms and legs, he looked like a dissected frog.

Funke walked over to the bed and retrieved his revolver from the pocket of the raincoat. He looked down at the dead man and said, "Sleep tight, little buddy."

He went out into the corridor and listened for a minute then opened the French doors and did the same on the balcony. During the twenty minutes or so she'd been tied to the high-backed chair, Wolfgramm had formed the view that firstly she was in pretty dodgy company and, secondly, her chances of getting through the night in one piece were somewhere between poor and ratshit. After witnessing the man in the stocking mask go out backwards, she decided that she'd overestimated both the company and her chances.

Funke came back into the bedroom closing the French doors behind him. "You the manager, right?" he asked.

She nodded.

"Tell me sugar, how many more folks am I going to have to shoot?"

She shook her head. "None."

"Well, that's a relief."

Funke pulled up the dead man's mask. He was about forty with a long nose and good teeth. Although the face was screwed up in a death snarl, Funke was sure he hadn't seen him before. He wiped off the shotgun and placed it and the sawn-off .22 beside the dead man then pulled the bedspread over the body from both sides of the bed, wrapping it.

He got the rest of the cocaine out of the wardrobe, replaced the floorboards and rolled the carpet back. He put the twenty packets of cocaine into Grills' sports bag and slung it over his shoulder. Then he untied Wolfgramm.

She stood up, rubbing her wrists. "This is a drugs thing, right?" she said.

Funke looked amused. "Yeah, kind of. In case you're wondering, I'm the good guy."

She said, "Oh?"

Funke chuckled. "More to the point, I'm the one still standing. Now help me tote this boy downstairs."

With Funke at one end and Wolfgramm at the other, they carried the dead man outside and deposited him in the boot of the Berlina. Leith Grills had often dreamed of coming face-to-face with the man who'd killed his brother but the fact that they were both dead rather robbed the encounter of drama.

Funke forced the boot shut on the two corpses and flipped out his ID.

"I'm a sort of cop working for the US Government. I realise this-all ain't exactly by the textbook but shit, you know, that's the way things work out sometimes; nothing for it but to go with the flow. Right now I need you to help me out."

"How?"

"Drive this car back to Auckland — can you do that?"

"With those guys in the boot?"

"Honey, those guys are deader than Davy Crockett. They ain't going to give you any problems."

She shrugged. "Okay."

"All right. You get yourself in the car."

Wolfgramm got into the driver's seat. Funke went over to his car then came back to the Berlina.

"Here're the keys. Give me your hand."

She offered her right hand. Funke produced a pair of handcuffs; he snapped one bracelet over her wrist and attached the other to the steering wheel.

"Go nice and steady now. I'll be right on your ass. If you do anything fancy, make a run for it, step on the gas or take a wrong turn, I'm going to start shooting. You understand me? We'll drive to Auckland and head to the airport, to the carpark at the international terminal."

At 4.05 a.m. Fleur Wolfgramm steered Grills' Holden Berlina into the carpark at the international terminal at Auckland airport. She drove to the middle of the near-empty parking area and stopped. Funke pulled up beside her and got out of his car. He took the keys out of the ignition, uncuffed her, used a handkerchief to wipe the steering wheel, the driver's door handle and around the boot lever and then locked the car. He told her to get into the Fiat and got in on the driver's side.

"You're going to have to stick with me for a day or two, sugar."

"Do I have a choice?"

"Sure you do. You can stick with me or join those fellas in the boot. Be a squeeze but I reckon there's room for one more."

"You talked me into it."

Funke started the car. As they drove away from the airport towards Mangere, he asked, "You ever hear mention of a party called Bryce Spurdle?"

"I have as a matter of fact. He's rich."

"I'm mighty pleased to hear that. You wouldn't happen to have any idea where he hangs his hat?"

"You want to get in touch with Spurdle?"

Funke nodded.

"That's shouldn't be too hard. He's married to a girl I used to work with."

Funke twisted around and grinned at her. "There you go. I'm already glad I didn't pop you."

18

Whenever anyone asked her where she was from, C. C. Hellicar's eyes would light up and she'd reply, "As a matter of fact, I was born in Between."

It was quite true: C. C. — the initials stood for Candice Clara, but she'd been C. C. as long as she could remember — was born in the one-store town of Between in Walton County, Georgia. She was a home birth, arriving two weeks early and at such short notice that her mother had no chance of getting to the hospital; she'd just leaned out the window and hollered for her neighbour. When C. C. was seven, her mother died and she and her father moved a few miles up the interstate to the county seat of Monroe, an hour's drive north-east of Atlanta, where her aunts lived.

Being born in Between was the first of several unusual things about C. C. Hellicar. Another was that she'd lost her virginity and killed someone on the very same night. One assumed that doesn't happen very often; just how rarely is a matter for speculation, given the lack of statistical data: C. C. herself, for instance, had never revealed just how much she'd managed to pack into that eventful night. The fact that she shot a man dead at approximately midnight on a sultry August night in 1983 was a matter of public record, but being a well brought up young lady of good southern stock, she was extremely discreet about such matters as ceasing to be a virgin. The only other person who knew the full story was her third cousin Wesley Teuton, her partner in the necessarily brisk and furtive act of intercourse which took place in the back seat of his father's Thunderbird in the parking lot of the Dairy Queen hamburger joint and ice cream parlour. Earlier that evening they'd been to the movie *Alien* and thinking about it later, C. C. wondered if it was the sight of Sigourney Weaver in her panties which had inspired Wesley to do what she'd been waiting for him to do for the several weeks since her sixteenth birthday.

When Wesley heard next morning what his date had done for an encore, it merely served to reinforce his conviction that he'd be the worst sort of fool to flaunt his carnal knowledge of C. C. Hellicar. He'd initially come to this conclusion as he was driving C. C. home, although, at that stage, his concern was focused more on her father. Willard Hellicar was celebrated throughout Walter Country as a hard-ass, a dead shot with anything from a sleeve piece to a semi-automatic carbine, and a fiercely proud and protective parent to his only child. The closer he got to the Hellicar place, the more nervous Wesley became at the thought of having to look his date's father in the eye. Willard Hellicar had icy blue eyes — which, disconcertingly, his daughter had inherited — and

Wesley feared that when those cold orbs began boring into him, he'd go to jelly and let on what had transpired in the carpark.

So when C. C. asked him did he want to come in for a cold drink and piece of pie, Wesley declined, saying he'd be in big trouble if he didn't get his daddy's car back by midnight. In fact, time was slipping away so if it was okay with her, rather than walk her to the door, he'd get right on his way. C. C., who'd baked the pie that afternoon especially, shrugged, gave him a chilly look, got out of the car and walked up the path towards the house.

The Hellicar place was set back from the road behind a couple of old willows. When C. C. was about ten metres from the front porch, the door opened and a man came out. When he stepped into the pool of light from the lamp above the front door, C. C. observed that he was large and black. While her father was not particularly racially prejudiced — at least not by the standards of many Georgians of his generation — neither did he make a habit of inviting blacks into his home to sip his Wild Turkey. The fact that the black man had a tyre iron in one hand and a canvas sack in the other added to her suspicion that it hadn't been a social call.

C. C. and the robber, as she'd characterised him, looked at one another for a few seconds without speaking. Then she yelled "Daddy" at the top of her lungs.

"Your daddy ain't going to help you," said the robber, grinning broadly.

He started down the porch steps, lazily swinging the tyre iron. C. C. opened her purse and took out the nickel-plated .22 automatic her father had given her on her thirteenth birthday and which she practised with once a fortnight at the firing range.

The robber's grin got even wider "Well lookee here," he said. "Missy's got herself a popgun. You ever used . . ."

C. C. aimed at his gleaming white teeth and, as she did nineteen times out of twenty at the firing range, hit the target. The bullet took a deviation off the intruder's upper jaw and proceeded upwards to the brain. He was dead before he hit the ground. C. C. averted her eyes as she ran past him. She raced up the steps and into the house where she found her father lying face down at the foot of the stairs. He was in his dressing gown; his hair was matted with blood which leaked from a weal on the back of his head but he was still breathing. She was about to call for an ambulance when he groaned and rolled over onto his back.

Willard Hellicar sat at the kitchen table holding a tea towel full of ice cubes to his wound and taking hefty gulps from a tall glass containing four fingers of bourbon and the leftover ice. He was telling his daughter how he'd been upstairs waiting for her to get home and how he'd come over a little peckish and remembered the blueberry pie she'd made when she interrupted to say there was a man in the front yard with a hole in his head.

Willard put down his glass. "Darling, did I hear you right?"

"I shot him, Daddy — the robber. He came out the front door just as I was walking up the path. He was coming at me with the tyre iron so I shot him."

"Jesus Christ almighty. Is the son of a bitch dead?"

"I didn't look real close but I'd say so."

They went outside. C. C. stayed on the porch while Willard went over to where the man lay. He put his hands on his knees and peered at him. "That's a dead nigger," he said finally. "No two ways about it."

"Please Daddy," said C. C. reproachfully, "don't call him that."

Willard Hellicar studied his daughter with frank amusement. "C. C., you just blew this no-good's head off and now you're chastising me for calling him a nigger?"

"There's no call to use that word," she said stubbornly. "Besides, race didn't enter into it — I would've shot him whatever colour he was."

Willard smiled wryly. "That's my girl. Now tell me, where were you when you pulled down on him?"

C. C. came down from the porch and showed him. "I was right here. I called out for you and he said you weren't going to help me. Then he started down the steps sort of swinging the tyre iron. He was in the course of asking me if I'd ever used the gun. I guess he found out, huh?"

"You're damn right, he did. You hit him dead centre from seven paces away in the dark." Willard shook his head. "Honey, I knew you was good with a gun but that's something else."

C. C. frowned. "Well, I just didn't see any way round it, Daddy. He indicated that he'd done you harm so I figured he wasn't going to want a witness."

Willard started shaking his head again. "Dammed if you ain't got ice water in your veins, C. C. Maybe you should forget about going to college; go off to Africa, be a big game hunter instead. Now how about you run inside and fetch an old towel or something to put over this boy's face because we're going have to drag him into the house. I remember the sheriff telling me one time, anyone comes into your home without an invite, you can shoot the son of a bitch and no jury in Walton County's going to worry about the details — it's just straight ahead self-defence, no matter what. Course the fact that he's an Afro-American and we ain't won't hurt none neither."

There were other unusual things about C. C. Hellicar: for instance, that she'd spent eighteen months at the US Army special forces training camp at Fort Bragg in North Carolina; that she worked for a company based in Scottsdale, Arizona which provided security advice, training and protection to government agencies, corporations and private citizens in many parts of the world; that the company she worked for was secretly owned and funded by the CIA — a "proprietary" in CIA jargon; and that she was what Everton Sloan III had referred to as a "cleaner".

Just before 7.15 a.m. the small crowd pressed forward as the first passengers came out through the arrivals gate, pushing their trolleys and looking around expectantly for familiar faces. Tito Ihaka made his way to the front of the crowd and checked a luggage tag to make sure they were off the United flight from Los Angeles. He heaved a sigh of resignation and held up the sign saying MS HELLICAR in block letters which he'd had behind his back.

A few minutes later the crowd had thinned out and Ihaka was leaning against a wall holding the sign to his chest, staring at the ceiling and whistling tunelessly to himself when a female voice said, "Maybe you should go easy on the steroids, Ms Hellicar."

The speaker had short dark-blonde hair, high cheekbones and the palest blue eyes Ihaka had ever seen. She was standing a few metres away in a pose of studied nonchalance, one long leg crossed in front of the other and hands thrust into the pockets of her loose-fitting pleated trousers. The trousers were the lower half of a light-grey Donegal tweed suit under which she wore an embroidered waistcoat and a white shirt. With her cool gaze, athletic, square-shouldered build and lean, sculpted face, she looked conditioned and purposeful. The accent, though, was pure southern belle.

She extended a hand. "I'm C. C. Hellicar."

They shook hands. She had a firmer grip than plenty of men Ihaka had shaken hands with; the Minister of Police for one.

"Detective Sergeant Tito Ihaka."

She raised an eyebrow. "Tito? As in the late, great communist?"

"That's the one. My old man was a bit of a red."

"You say 'was' — did he lose the faith?"

"No, 'was' as in he's not around any more. He was a believer until his dying day."

"I'm sorry. My momma was a McGovern Democrat; in Walton County, that's just one step up from being a communist. She passed away too."

Ihaka nodded. "Yeah, well that's where worrying about the future of mankind gets you." He pointed at the metal suitcase on the floor beside her. "Is that the lot?"

"Uh-huh, but you don't have to carry it for me."

He shrugged. "We're old-fashioned down here." He picked it up; it weighed a ton but she hadn't bothered with a trolley. What the hell am I doing, he wondered, volunteering to carry Wonder Woman's bag?

"You got a matching pair of elephant guns in here?"

She smiled. "I over-packed. I wasn't sure what to expect in the way of weather. Actually, I do have some equipment in the diplomatic bag."

"Right, that's being taken care of. It'll be delivered to the police station in town."

Ihaka led her out to the unmarked car which was parked in front of the terminal's main entrance, in a restricted zone. He put the suitcase in the boot and they got into the car. As they drove away from the airport down George Bolt Drive she asked, "Are you a Maori?"

"Sure am."

"I'm afraid all I know about Maoris is what was in the *Welcome to New Zealand* movie they showed on the airplane."

"I bet it was full of women swinging little balls and blokes in grass skirts poking their tongues out?"

"There was some of that."

"Well, we're reasonably civilised. Personally, I haven't eaten anyone since my twenty-first birthday party."

Feeling that the conversation had taken an unpredictable and possibly difficult turn, Hellicar smiled politely and looked out the window.

"Sorry, it's not the scenic route," said Ihaka.

She shrugged. "It never is. They don't put airports in the nice part of town."

"I guess you see a few airports in your line of work?"

"A few of them."

"You're from the south, right?"

"Yes sir. As a matter of fact, I was born in Between."

Ihaka glanced at her, puzzled.

"The town of Between. It's in Walton County in the state of Georgia."

"A place called Between? You're kidding?"

"Absolutely not. We got another town's called Social Circle."

"No shit? Georgia — that's redneck country, isn't it?"

She looked amused. "The south's come a ways since the civil war, Sergeant. You gave up eating folks when you turned twenty-one; me, I freed my last slave."

Ihaka chuckled. "Those were the days, eh? So this is how you spend your life — flying round the world weeding out the bad apples as the ambassador called them?"

Ihaka had his eyes on the road so he missed Hellicar's thoughtful glance.

"What I do is classified information — I'm not at liberty to discuss my work and all that jazz. Besides, we should be talking about Harold Funke. You got a fix on him?"

"Not yet but we've got some leads," he said with more confidence than he felt. "He sounds like a dangerous bastard."

She went back to looking out the window. "That he is. You wondering if I'm up to it, huh?"

"No, just curious — we don't get much of this James Bond stuff. I mean, we've got a unit called the Armed Offenders Squad — a bit like your SWAT teams, cops who get special weapons training and dress up in black uniforms and all that shit; makes them think they're fucking Rambo. No offence but on the face of it, you sort of wonder what you can do that a bunch of them couldn't?"

"No offence taken," she said mildly. "There's guys in SWAT teams can put a round up a bug's ass halfway across town as long they've got all day to get themselves set; the same guys couldn't hit the Dixie Flyer from five yards away if they have to do it bang" — she snapped her fingers — "like that. Especially not when they know that if they don't hit the target first time, they're going to die. How many of these guys who think they're Rambo would you say have been in that situation?"

"Bugger all. But you have?"

"Uh-huh," she said. "And as you can see, I'm still here."

Neither of them spoke for a few minutes. When they stopped at the lights at Hillsborough, Ihaka turned to her and said, "So what does the C. C. stand for?"

"Candice Clara."

"Anyone ever call you Candy?"

"Not at home. Maybe every once in a while at school — some of the boys."

"Let me guess: they used to say, 'Hey Candy, you look good enough to eat,' right?"

Hellicar batted her eyelids at him. "That's truly amazing," she said in an awe-struck tone. "How in the world did you know that?"

Ihaka pretended he hadn't picked up the sarcasm. "It's a gift. My grandmother was a full-blooded Maori; she could tell things about people just by looking at them. I sort of inherited it."

"That's fascinating." She looked away. "What else can you tell about me?"

He studied her profile for a few seconds then nodded sagely. "The boys who said you looked good enough to eat? I bet none of them ever did."

Hellicar turned her head slowly and fixed her wintry blue eyes on Ihaka. The effect was slightly unnerving and left him with the strong feeling that, despite his determination not to, he'd seriously underestimated her.

"I hate to be the one to tell you this, Sergeant," she said in her honeyed drawl, "but you ain't in your grandmama's league."

By 11 a.m. that Friday the temperature in Wellington had crawled up to 8 degrees Celsius where it rested on its laurels. Depending on whether you were a local or a visitor, there was a stiff breeze or a gale whipping off Cook Strait. Lumps of black cloud bumped along the ridges above the city and drenching rain slanted in on the wind. In the office buildings and in the toytown houses clinging to the hillsides and dotted through the gorges, people shivered and moved their chairs closer to the nearest source of heat.

Perhaps the only person in the capital who wasn't complaining about the weather was the diplomat Jason Maltby. Oblivious to the elements, he plodded up the 112 steps from the street to his brother's Kelburn house, reflecting that if he had to suffer stress, far better to do so in Wellington than Bangkok; if he'd had a morning like this in Bangkok, he'd need to be wrung out like a sodden sponge. Inside, Maltby changed his shirt then sat at the kitchen table with a cup of instant coffee and considered his next move. Eventually, he reached a decision. He rang directory service and obtained the phone number for D. Ricketts, of Mt Roskill, Auckland.

It was a blustery, overcast day in Auckland with a good drying wind blowing from the west. Duane Ricketts was hanging out his washing when he heard the phone. He went inside and answered it.

"It's Jason Maltby here, from the embassy in Bangkok. Remember me?"

"Jason, I hope you're not ringing to tell me they've set a date for my trial? That'd be a waste of taxpayers' money."

"No, nothing to do with that. I'm in Wellington actually, back on a couple of weeks' leave. The reason I'm ringing is that I was called into a meeting at the department this morning, about this DEA man from Bangkok, Harold Funke. Does the name mean anything to you?"

"Not a thing. What's the DEA?"

"The American Drug Enforcement Administration. It's a gigantic anti-drug police stroke intelligence organisation; they've got offices all round the world."

"You don't mean to tell me they haven't got more to worry about than me and my two lousy heroin cigarettes?"

Despite his anxiety, Maltby couldn't help smiling; the same old Ricketts. "I think it'd be safe to say that the DEA has got one or two more pressing matters on its books. No, it appears this Funke character's swapped sides and come to New Zealand chasing after a consignment of cocaine that was once the property of our late mutual acquaintance, Dale Varty."

"Eh?"

"Hello Duane? Are you still there?"

"Yeah, I'm still here. I'm just having a bit of trouble working out what it's got to do with me."

"Not a lot really. The truth is, I'm ringing to ask a favour . . ."

Maltby paused to give Ricketts an opportunity to make encouraging noises. No noises, encouraging or otherwise, were forthcoming.

Eventually, Maltby ended the silence: "Yes, well, I suppose you've got no particular reason to do me a favour," he said awkwardly.

"Rule number one: Jason — don't promise to do someone a favour until you know what it is."

"That's sensible I suppose. Well, during your police force days or since, have you come across a detective sergeant called Ihaka?"

What the fuck is this? wondered Ricketts. *This is your Life?* "Yeah, I know the fat prick. What about him?"

"Ihaka's in charge of finding Funke, who by all accounts is a nasty piece of work. Up in Bangkok, they think he murdered the ladyboy, Brandi — the one Varty . . . got involved with."

Yesterday Ihaka was crapping on about a trained killer, thought Ricketts; this must be the guy. But what's the connection to me?

"Funke rang me in Bangkok, just after you'd left," continued Maltby. "He fed me a cock and bull story which, I'm afraid to say, I swallowed. He claimed he had to do a report on Varty and needed various details including next-of-kin; I gave him the name and address of Varty's ex-wife. The favour is this: could you alert Ihaka that Funke's got this woman's name and address? I wouldn't want to have it on my conscience if anything happened to her. If you're wondering why I don't do it myself, the truth is I'm in a certain amount of hot water as it is; if word got around that I'd dished out this information over the phone to the representative of a foreign agency, and a corrupt one at that . . . well, put it this way, I'd be for the high jump."

"Shit, that's no big deal," said Ricketts, thinking Christ, old Maltby's sounding as flat as I feel. "What's her name?"

"Rayleen Crouch. She lives in Grey Lynn."

"No sweat. I'll pass it on."

"Thank you Duane, I appreciate it. It's quite embarrassing really. I should've smelt a rat: I mean, Funke even wanted to know about Varty's daughter, God only knows why. Luckily, I had enough sense not to . . ."

"Jason, hang on a moment, would you? Just let me think." The ladyboy. Is that it? He was on the stairs; maybe he overheard what Varty told me. "You said they think this guy Funke killed the ladyboy?"

"That's right. And it's not the Thai police saying it either; that came from the US embassy."

Ricketts thought holy shit, said goodbye and hung up.

19

The telephone conversation went pretty much as Duane Ricketts had anticipated.

"Rickets," hissed Tito Ihaka, as if administering a terrible curse. "What the fuck do you want?"

"It wasn't very nice of you not to tell me about Funke."

"What's your problem, Ricketts?" demanded Ihaka caustically. "Have you lost it completely or what? I thought I made myself clear: I wouldn't piss on your face if your eyebrows were on fire."

"You're taking this rather personally, aren't you?"

"This is different: when you decided to go after the dope, you crossed the line. You're one of them now."

"Who's them?"

"Them's everyone who's not us."

"You're full of shit, Ihaka. Since when haven't I been on the outer?"

"Some people thought you were hard done by; some people still had a bit of time for you. Not any more they don't."

"Some people being you?"

"Especially me."

Pompous turd, thought Ricketts. "In that case you obviously won't be interested in any assistance from me?"

"Hang on," said Ihaka. "Who told you about Funke?"

"That's the pleasantries over with, is it? Tell me something first: have you got a handle on this prick yet?"

"Funke? We're following some leads."

"In other words, you haven't got a fucking clue."

Ihaka grunted affirmatively. "Let me put it this way: Mr Funke's movements since Tuesday night — when he purchased a .38 Smith & Wesson revolver and enough ammo to wipe out the Eden Park cheerleaders — and his current whereabouts remain shrouded in mystery. As of now, our strategy is to hope that he walks into Auckland Central and gives himself up."

"Well, they say the simple plans are often the best. To answer your question, the person who told me about Funke was the same person who told me he's got hold of the name and address of Varty's ex-wife."

"How?"

"Pass."

"What does she know?"

"Nothing, according to Varty. Funke mightn't believe that of course; he might cut chunks out of her until he's convinced otherwise. Just a thought. Her name's Rayleen Crouch, she lives in Grey Lynn. To save you looking in the phone book, there's an R. Crouch at 108 Crimea Avenue."

"Okay, we'll drop in on her. You still haven't said who told you — and don't fuck around, eh? This is serious shit and we need all the help we can get."

"Ihaka?"

"Yeah?"

"Are you familiar with the saying 'Get a big dog up you'?"

That Friday afternoon some light was shed on Harold "Buddy" Funke's mysterious comings and goings.

Ihaka and Detective Constable Johan Van Roon went to 108 Crimea Avenue where the doorbell wasn't answered. The next-door neighbours supplied the information that Rayleen Crouch was some kind of social worker; with assistance from the social welfare department, they tracked her down to a youth hostel in Mt Albert. Crouch filled them in on how Funke had popped up out of the blue with his badge and gun, shooed Leith Grills off the premises and discovered, courtesy of their daughter, where her ex-husband had hidden his cocaine.

When Van Roon went off to ask the Whitianga police to send a reconnaissance team to Manacle Grange, Ihaka commented to Crouch that the news of Funke's villainy didn't seem to surprise her a great deal.

Ihaka's exploratory prod likewise failed to draw much of a reaction. "Sergeant, I've been a social worker for fifteen years," she said in a somewhat world-weary tone. "Very little surprises me any more. Besides, it's every man for himself these days, isn't it?"

At 3.40 p.m. the Whitianga police unit reported from Manacle Grange that they'd discovered direct physical evidence of one crime and prima facie evidence of several others: the previous evening, the hotel's sole guest, an English journalist, had suffered a broken jaw when ambushed by an unknown party; there were pellets in the bedposts and wall and traces of blood on the sheets in the master bedroom, indicating that someone had been in the line of fire when a shotgun was discharged; the hotel's manager had disappeared without taking her clothes, toiletries or car with her; and three of the journalist's silk shirts had been torn to shreds. While the shirt-ripping didn't have quite the sinister implications of the other discoveries, the journalist was making as much fuss about it as a man whose jaw was broken in three places could possibly make.

Ihaka estimated that, left to themselves, the boys from Whitianga would be pushed to make sense of it all before the turn of the century so he sent Van Roon down to give them a hand. In just over two hours' time C. C. Hellicar, who'd planned to spend the morning catching up on her sleep and the afternoon working out, was coming in for a full briefing. For various reasons, some of them personal, Ihaka was very keen to have something of substance to report. The way things were going though, it looked like he'd once again be subjected to unsettling scrutiny from those frosty, eerily pale blue eyes.

When he'd finished exchanging endearments with Ihaka, Ricketts drove over to Westmere to see Electra Crouch. She wasn't home. He moved his car a bit further down Datchet Terrace and parked on the other side of the road, facing back up the street. From there, he had a good view of the building and would see her and anyone else coming whereas they weren't likely to notice him. Then he settled down to wait.

Datchet Terrace wasn't a hive of activity that afternoon. In two hours, Ricketts observed twenty-two cars, thirteen pedestrians and four children on bicycles. None of them warranted close attention except perhaps for the boy who spat copiously on his rear window and scuttled away cackling gleefully. At 2.15 p.m. a black Porsche cruised down the street, coming to a halt outside Electra's apartment building. A stocky man, well into middle-age, got out. He wore a striped, long-sleeved body shirt, jeans with a big-buckled belt, desert boots and aviator sunglasses. His hair was thick and bushy and unnaturally black: it covered his ears like eaves, curled onto his collar and smothered his forehead. The overall effect was of a man who, for some reason, had been pleased with his appearance twenty years ago and had retained the look ever since. He went into Electra's apartment building only to emerge a couple of minutes later. He got back into his car and just sat there. Ricketts found this behaviour both interesting and slightly worrying.

For the first time, Ricketts felt he could've done with a mobile phone. While it seemed unlikely that Funke would choose something as ostentatious as a Porsche for transportation, it would've been comforting to have had the option of calling in the seventh cavalry. As things stood, if he went to find a phone box, Electra might come home and Funke, if it was him, would have a free hand to do whatever he had in mind. At 2.47 p.m. Electra Crouch resolved the dilemma by walking down Datchet Terrace and entering number 13A. The man in the Porsche had a good, long look at her as she walked past, then put his head back on the headrest. Ricketts didn't read too much into the look, figuring Electra probably attracted plenty like it.

Ricketts wrote the Porsche's registration number on the back of a credit card docket. He got out of his car, crossed the road, went into number 13A, climbed the stairs to the second floor and knocked on the door to apartment three.

"Who is it?" called Electra.

"Duane Ricketts. I need to talk to you — it's important."

"No way is it important enough. Piss off."

"Electra listen, there's an American called Harold Funke who might try to contact you . . ."

"First with the news again, Ricketts."

"Eh?"

"You're only a day late, that's all. Funke was here yesterday."

"Jesus, what did he want?"

"The same as you. One slight difference, though — he's a cop. Go away Ricketts — and this time, stay gone."

"Just a sec. Did he get in touch with you through your mother?"

"What difference does it make?"

"Electra, Funke's a bad guy. He's a killer."

"Oh fuck off Ricketts, you wanker. I saw his badge."

"Yeah, I know what he is but he's bent — he's after that cocaine. Don't take my word for it: ring Detective Sergeant Ihaka at Auckland Central. Better still, ring your mother; the cops would've talked to her by now."

There was a long silence before she said, "Well, whatever he is, he got what he wanted."

"You told him where it is?" When she didn't reply, Ricketts continued: "Well, shit, how were you meant to know? There's something else: a bloke's been sitting outside in a Porsche for half an hour, waiting for someone. Do you want to have a look, see if you know him? It might be Funke."

A minute later the door opened. Her outfit — blue jeans, a man-size white shirt worn outside the jeans, boots with high heels — was less of a uniform than what she'd had on the day before. The expression had softened a little too but was still a long way from tender.

"How's business, Ricketts?" she said with heavy irony. "Got a few kids hooked today, did we?"

Ricketts let it go. "Is that Funke out there?"

She motioned Ricketts inside with a jerk of her head and shut the door. "Can't tell from up here. He wasn't in a Porsche yesterday, though."

"Maybe he's sold the dope and traded up."

Electra wasn't sure if the remark was offensive or merely inane. Before she could make up her mind, there was a thunderous knocking at the door.

Electra jumped. Ricketts motioned her away from the door. A short, narrow hallway ran from the flat's entrance through to the living room; the kitchen was off the hallway on the left. He stepped into the kitchen and grabbed a chopping knife off the bench.

The knocking started again. When Ricketts nodded, Electra asked, "Who's that?"

"Is Jake Latimer in there?" The man didn't sound young but he was definitely angry.

"Jake's not home."

"When the hell will he be?"

"I don't know."

"Give him a message — he'll know who it's from. It's real simple: tell the little fucker he's in deep shit. Tell him I didn't get what I paid for and I want my money back. If I don't get it, he'll be in a wheelchair before the weekend's out."

"I don't know what you're talking about. Jake didn't say anything about this . . ."

"No kidding? Well, let me fill you in. I paid the cunt for information — where I could find something that belongs to me. The bloke I sent to pick it up hasn't come back so either Latimer duded me or he doubled up — got greedy and did the same deal with someone else. If he did that, he'll end up in a fucking coffin, never mind a wheelchair. Tell him he's got twenty-four hours."

Message delivered, he stomped off. Ricketts put down the knife; from the kitchen window he watched the middle-aged man come out of the building, get into the Porsche and drive off. He went through to the living room where Electra was sitting at a small table with her head in her hands, staring at the tabletop. He perched on the end of a sofa, feeling the sensible course of action was to keep quiet until invited to say something. Electra sat motionless for a couple of minutes then suddenly sprang to her feet and stormed out. Ricketts heard her going from room to room. After a minute or two, she reappeared and sat down at the table, pale and stiff with tension. In a voice creaking with rage, she said: "Fucking lowlife fucking pimp."

It didn't necessarily call for a response but Ricketts decided to chance it. "He's done a runner," he said, not bothering to make it sound like a question.

Without looking up, she bobbed her head in a short, angry nod.

"You told him where the dope was; he sold the information to the loudmouth in the Porsche who would've made it part of the deal that no one else knew. When Jake found out Funke was in on the secret, he realised he was in big trouble so he took the money and ran."

Another abrupt nod.

"Well, you've got to ask yourself one question."

She turned her head slowly.

"Do I let him get away with it?"

The fury in her eyes dimmed to resignation. Her shoulders drooped and she resumed staring at the tabletop. Eventually, she said in a brittle voice: "Looks to me like he already has."

"Only if you let him," said Ricketts.

"There's stuff-all I can do about it now," she said sulkily.

"You could tell the cops: whatever's going on, it's got to be illegal and Latimer's dealt himself in. Or you could sic his Porsche-driving mate onto him — that's what I'd do."

Electra switched on the scorn: "A, I don't know who the guy in the Porsche is; B, I don't know where Jake is. Apart from that, it's a really great idea."

Ricketts produced the credit card docket. "A's not a problem. I got the number of the Porsche — I can find out who owns it in five minutes. And I bet you could work out where Jake's gone if you put your mind to it."

Electra's eyes narrowed and she sat up straight.

"Put yourself in his shoes: he's hit the jackpot but now he needs a place to hide. Where would he go? What would he do with the dough? I mean, you lived with the guy; you must have some idea?"

Electra thought about it, nibbling her bottom lip as she did so. It seemed to work: "He bought a Lotto ticket every single week; man, it was like a ritual. I must've heard him say a hundred times that if he hit, you know, if he won big, he'd buy himself a Harley-Davidson. And if he got a Harley, he couldn't help himself, he'd have to show it off to his best friend, Lenny. He lives up near Whangarei."

Ricketts asked to use the phone. He rang a guy he knew at Telecom and asked him to check if there'd been any STD calls made on Electra's phone in the previous couple of days. There'd been one — at 8.55 that morning, to Whangarei.

Ricketts passed the number to Electra. "Recognise it?"

She got a filofax out of her back-pack and checked it. It was Lenny's number.

Warily, almost formally, they exchanged nods of acknowledgement.

He said: "Okay, now let's find out who he's got on his tail."

Ricketts rang another contact, this time in the Ministry of Transport. It was obvious from his reaction that the answer struck a chord.

"Well?" she said when he put the phone down.

Ricketts gave her a careful look. "The Porsche belongs to Bryce Spurdle."

Electra, expressionless, kept her black eyes on Ricketts for half a minute then asked if he wanted a cup of tea. On her way through to the kitchen, she said over her shoulder: "They're not meant to do that, are they? You know, just hand out information to anyone who rings up?"

"I'm not just anyone — they know me."

"How come?"

"Remember I said yesterday that I find people for a living? It's a hell of a lot easier if you can access that sort of information. That's a matter of getting to know the right people — and maybe making it worth their while."

Electra brought two mugs of tea into the living room and handed one to him. "Is that how the cops do it?"

Ricketts smiled. "The cops do all sorts of things; anyway, they've got most of that stuff at their fingertips."

"Do you reckon they'd know the number of Funke's car?"

Ricketts sipped his tea and remembered what Ihaka had said. "I doubt it. Why?"

"I wrote it down." She half-smiled self-consciously. "Electra Crouch, girl detective."

"Why'd you do that?"

"When I was living at home, every time a guy came round to pick me up, when he wasn't looking, Rayleen — that's my mother — would take down the number of his car in case, I don't know, we ran away together or something — you know, the boy turns out to be Jack the Ripper Junior. Yesterday I was at the kitchen window when she got into Funke's car and I thought, hey, look at her, getting into a strange man's car, blah blah." She shrugged. "And I wrote it down."

The first thing the cops would've done, thought Ricketts, was check the car rental companies. If Funke had hired a car, he would've used false ID but they would've been looking out for that. He asked her for the number and rang his man at the Ministry of Transport again; the car was a Fiat Tipo registered to a Mrs Ada Merchant of Crescent Lodge in Eden Crescent. That's weird, he thought; surely to Christ Funke wouldn't be tooling around in a stolen car, running the risk of being spotted by every cop on the road. Unless he just used it once and dumped it.

"So?" said Electra.

He told her. "It's a bit strange. I might just check this Crescent Lodge place out."

"You find people, right? How'd you get into that?"

"I used to be a cop. When they kicked me out, it seemed about the only thing I was qualified for."

She looked at him disbelievingly. "You got kicked out of the cops?"

Ricketts nodded.

"What for?"

"How do you feel about horses?"

She frowned. "Horses? What about them? They don't do much for me."

Ricketts smiled a little grimly. "If everyone had that attitude, I'd probably still be a cop."

20

Jody Spurdle, wearing skin-tight calf-length leggings and a barely adequate halter-top, was doing stretches on an exercise mat in the TV room to a Cindy Crawford work-out video when her husband got home. She heard him coming from the letterbox 400 metres away because he gunned the Porsche up the drive at the sort of speed white people in expensive cars pass through parts of South Auckland where that particular combination is as unfamiliar as it is provocative. Oh gross, thought Jody, as the Porsche slid to a halt in a spray of gravel outside the front door; he's got the runs again.

About once a fortnight Bryce Spurdle got together with a few cronies for a long lunch. More often than not, these bouts of gluttony and heavy drinking played havoc with his metabolism; if he didn't keep his eye on the clock — for instance, if he dallied over a final cleansing ale — he ran the risk of experiencing, at some point during the drive home, a swift and terrible build-up of what he called "nozzle pressure". Faced with the messy, ignominious and downright dangerous prospect of soiling himself at the wheel of a vehicle doing 100-plus kph along the motorway, he'd put in a supreme physical and mental effort involving clenched buttocks and what sports psychologists call "visualisation" — overcoming the pain and stress of competition by imagining the moment of eventual triumph; in Spurdle's case, that was the blissful relief he'd obtain a millisecond after his bottom made a hard landing on a lavatory seat.

Jody had become well-acquainted with the syndrome; he'd roar up the drive, pull up out the front with a squeal of rubber, and hit the ground running. So when, that afternoon, he slammed the front door behind him with an impact which rattled every window in the house, it occurred to her that perhaps he wasn't answering a bellow of nature after all; usually he didn't waste time slamming doors or saying hello or doing anything at all which might slow his progress to the toilet reserved for his exclusive use which adjoined his den cum snooker room.

She stopped the video and went to investigate. She found her husband in the den. He was behind the bar sloshing dark rum into a glass and scowling like a spoilt brat on Christmas morning. He dumped some ice and a dollop of Coke into the glass and gulped massively.

"Something wrong?" she asked.

Spurdle wrenched off his sunglasses, dropped them on the bar and glared at her: "Yes, as a matter of fact there is," he said in a clipped, snide way. "But what the fuck would you care?"

"What's that meant to mean?"

He responded with a surly shake of his head and came round to the other side of the bar where he sat on a high stool with his back to her. "Forget it," he grumbled. "You'd better get back to your work-out before your arse goes soft."

She walked over to him. "For crying out loud, Bryce . . ."

"Look, it's business, all right? You wouldn't want to know. You never have before so why change the habits of a lifetime?" He looked away and swallowed more rum and Coke.

"Well, I'm interested now — better late than never, isn't it?"

"What's the matter, sweetie?" he sneered. "You worried the money tree's got dry rot?"

Jody drew in her breath angrily: "Jesus, Bryce, you can be such an arsehole when you put your mind to it."

Spurdle tossed back the rest of his drink and got up to make another one. He glanced across the bar at Jody. She was doing the petulant act: lips pursed, head on one side and hand on her hip. Look at her, he thought bitterly, standing there like a gym slut. Hey guys, check this out — flat stomach, tits like lawn bowls and a bum like a boy scout. Which reminds me; last time — when was it, Tuesday night? — I had the gall to suggest a root, I got dumped on from a great height, yeah, including that fucking crap about having as much jab as a shrivelled up parsnip.

Throughout their brief courtship and seven-and-a-half-year marriage, Spurdle had fretted at the thought of Jody learning of his murky past and had gone to some lengths to conceal it from her. But the recollection of her calculated slur on his virility, on top of the succession of maddening frustrations, caused something to snap. He was seized by an overpowering urge to jolt his glamorous young wife from the polka-dot bandana restraining her dyed-blond hair all the way down to her pink toenails.

He put down the rum bottle, placed his palms flat on the bar, bunched his shoulders and, adopting what he imagined was a silky and slightly menacing tone, asked: "You really want to know what I'm pissed off about, do you?"

"I asked, didn't I?"

He hoisted his eyebrows another centimetre. "Are you quite sure about that?"

"What's all the drama in aid of, Bryce?" she said, starting to feel faintly uneasy. "If you're going to tell me, tell me; if you're not . . ."

"Okay," he said, in an "I'm a reasonable man" voice. "I'll tell you."

And he did.

Despite Spurdle's sudden, reckless desire to lob a dirty great rock into the calm pond of his wife's pampered and complacent existence, there were, inevitably, limits to his candour. He told her that he'd funded Varty into the drug deal when in fact he hadn't put up a cent: the ten kilos of cocaine were technically the property of the moribund Mr Asia syndicate; Varty simply commandeered it and also paid for the charter of the yacht. Spurdle claimed Varty had double-crossed him — when it had been the other way around — and that Varty had murdered Al Grills, a misrepresentation which owed as much to ignorance as invention. The narrative concluded with Jake Latimer pocketing the $12,500 and Leith Grills' as yet unexplained failure to return from his mission.

Jody listened to her husband with mixed feelings which, contrary to his expectations, did not include shocked disapproval of his would-be drug trafficking, past and present. Her chief reaction was mortification: not only had she been hideously wrong to believe that Bryce wanted her out of the way, she'd also brought in the police. And now of all times, with this stuff going on! The minute she got the chance, she'd ring Sergeant Ihaka and tell him it was all a dreadful mistake.

Having dropped his bombshell, Spurdle awaited the fallout. He'd anticipated confusion, tears, anxiety rising to panic and other manifestations of scandalised dismay. What actually happened was that Jody leaned down and kissed him softly on the cheek.

"Poor thing, no wonder you're upset," she said tenderly. "God, I don't blame you one little bit. I'm just going to jump in the shower; why don't you relax, put your feet up, have another drink, and think about what you'd like for dinner."

Spurdle was deflated. He was still puzzling over it twenty minutes later when something happened to temporarily deprive him of the capacity for rational thought. Cooing noises floated down the stairs from the bedroom. Jody was calling him in a teasing and suggestive little girl voice; it was a voice he hadn't heard for several years — indeed, a voice he'd given up hope of ever hearing again — and to which he responded as instantly, eagerly and pathetically as a goofy dog to its master's summons. His heart thumped wildly; his hands shook; blood surged to his groin emphasising that his jeans were a shade too tight for comfort. He put down his drink and half-fell, half-dismounted from the bar stool.

"Yes dear," he croaked tentatively, praying that his ears hadn't deceived him or worse, that the minx hadn't decided that mere denial was no longer sufficient and the time had come for a more exquisite form of torment.

"Come and have a look at this," she said playfully. "I need a second opinion."

Spurdle shambled up the stairs. Jody sat on the end of the bed; she was wearing a diaphanous black teddy which reached to the top of her thighs, a garter belt with sheer black seamed stockings, and bright red, spike-heeled shoes which matched her lipstick. She leaned back, shoulders squared and legs slightly parted and extended, as if offering every silk-wrapped, semi-visible square inch of herself for his drooling inspection. Spurdle goggled; he felt weak at the knees and was vaguely aware that, below his belt, something was twitching and leaking like a beheaded snake.

"Well?" she said huskily. "What do you think?"

Half an hour later Bryce Spurdle lay on his back in the king-sized bed. His eyes were closed, his mouth was open and he was making little snuffling sounds punctuated, every now and again, by a barnyard grunt. Next to him, Jody sat up in the bed with her back against the headboard, one hand behind her head, one slim, brown arm draped over her now uncovered breasts. Good thinking, kiddo, she told herself: whisking Bryce off to bed had killed two birds with one stone — got him out of that filthy mood and taken the edge off her guilty conscience. A few more of those performances — she'd been a raunchy little trollop if she did say so herself — and they'd be square . . .

Jody swore under her breath as she remembered that she'd volunteered to cook Bryce the dinner of his choice. The state he was in, he'd agree to anything so she could suggest going out instead; on the other hand, maybe she should rack up the brownie points while the going was good. She was weighing it up when the bedside phone rang. She answered it as Bryce snorted and rolled onto his side.

"Jody?"

"That's me."

"Long time, no yakitty yak chickie — it's Fleur, Fleur Wolfgramm."

"Fleur! Where are you?"

"I'm in town for a couple of days; any chance of catching up?"

"You bet. When do you want to do it?"

"How would tonight suit?"

"Tonight?" Jody glanced down at her husband who'd pulled a blanket over his head. "Tonight could be difficult. Bryce and I had something planned, sort of."

"Actually, I'm meeting someone tonight . . ."

"You old tart," said Jody with a giggle. "Tell me more."

Wolfgramm coughed. "No, it's not like that. He's a client; but I was telling him a bit about Bryce and he's really keen to meet him — he thinks they've got lots in common and could do some business together. Trouble is, he's American and he's about to head off overseas."

"Hey, well why don't you and your friend come out to our place for dinner tonight? We were tossing up on eating out or staying at home; if I'm going to cook, it makes no odds if it's two or four."

"That'd be great; are you sure it's okay though? We won't be interrupting anything, will we?"

Jody said no but if she'd rung a few minutes earlier . . . Fleur said she hadn't realised the late afternoon bounce was back in fashion and they both sniggered. Then Jody gave directions and said to come any time from 7.30 on and Fleur said the Spurdles obviously couldn't wait that long and they sniggered some more and exchanged "see you soons" and hung up. It wasn't until Jody was under the shower that it struck her that the last she'd heard of Fleur, she'd been running an upmarket boutique hotel somewhere on the Coromandel. Surely, it couldn't be the same place that Bryce was talking about . . .

Duane Ricketts left Electra Crouch's flat in Westmere at four o'clock that Friday afternoon. He drove along Jervois Road, down College Hill and past Victoria Park into the city. He parked in the Shortland Street carpark, walked up the hill and turned left into Eden Crescent. Crescent Lodge was a boarding house all right. Out of curiosity he went back down the street checking cars and number plates and soon came across the Fiat Tipo that Electra Crouch had seen Funke in. Ricketts was considering the implications of it all when he felt a seismic tremor at the very back of his mind. He walked up past the Hyatt Kingsgate hotel and sat on a bench in Albert Park; after twenty minutes' concentrated thought, he had a plan.

He retrieved his car from the carpark and drove back to 13A Datchet Terrace where he outlined the plan to Electra. She listened impassively and, when he'd finished, asked a couple of reassuringly intelligent questions.

"It's a punt," he said, "pure and simple. It might be a complete waste of time but I reckon it's worth a try. What do you reckon?"

She nodded. "Definitely."

"What about your bit?"

"Yeah, I'm in."

"You realise you'll have to lose the nose-ring and look . . . normal?"

She smiled lopsidedly. "The nose-ring's no big deal; it can always go back. Looking normal's a lot to ask of a girl, though: the clothes are the worry — I mean, what do women detectives wear?"

At precisely 6 o'clock that evening a meeting commenced in a small conference room on the eighth floor of the Auckland Central police station. The participants were Detective Sergeant Tito Ihaka and Detective Inspector Finbar McGrail of the Auckland district police and C. C. Hellicar whose title, affiliation and, reflected Ihaka, no doubt shoe size and favourite flavour of ice cream were classified information. She was all in black: black Levis, a loose black zip-up jacket over a black skivvy, and black ankle-high gym shoes. Ihaka wondered if they were her work clothes.

Ihaka was reviewing the events at Manacle Grange when there was a knock at the door. A constable entered with a metal briefcase for Ms Hellicar which he placed on the table.

"As I was saying," continued Ihaka, "the coke must've been stashed under the floorboards in the wardrobe. It's gone and so's the manager; the obvious conclusion is that Funke took them both."

"Why take the manager?" asked McGrail.

"We think she might've gone feet first. At this stage, we're working on the theory that he used the shotgun on her but didn't want to leave the body. The Pommie journo was lucky; he didn't get a look at Funke."

"I'm a little confused, Sergeant," said Hellicar. "I understood Funke had a Smith & Wesson .38?"

"He did but that doesn't mean to say he couldn't have got himself a shotgun as well; they're not that hard to get hold of."

"Why would he want one?" she asked mildly. "It's unwieldy, difficult to conceal, and he's got himself a perfectly good pistol; beats me why he'd bother with a shotgun. Besides, if it was just a matter of getting shed of her, Funke wouldn't use a shotgun, especially at that time of night; he'd know that many ways of doing her with his two hands, he'd be plum spoilt for choice."

One of Ihaka's attributes, which certainly wasn't shared by all ranking officers at Auckland Centre, was that he recognised good sense when he heard it, even when it was being employed to undermine his position; allied to that, he never wasted time or breath defending a position he knew to be indefensible. Even so, he felt a rush of irrational but intense irritation when he saw, out of the corner of his eye, McGrail nodding agreement.

"I must say, that seems like sound thinking to me," said McGrail, bestowing a warm smile on Hellicar. Hello, thought Ihaka; McGrail's got a stiffy.

Ihaka nodded at Hellicar. "Yeah, you're probably right; Funke wouldn't use a gun unless he had to. Maybe someone else brought the shotgun to the party."

"My word," said McGrail turning to Hellicar. "The sergeant's a moving target tonight."

Hellicar grinned as if she was enjoying the by-play. Ihaka maintained a polite smile which didn't entirely disguise a desire to rip out McGrail's tongue and strangle him with it.

"Such as who?" asked Hellicar.

Ihaka told her about Leith Grills' barging in on Rayleen Crouch, his association with Bryce Spurdle and Spurdle's suspected involvement in the drug shipment. He added: "We tried to bring Grills in this afternoon but couldn't get our hands on the bugger; his wife said he's out of town and she doesn't know when he gets back."

"How would Spurdle and Grills have found out about Manacle Grange?" asked McGrail.

"I guess the same way as Funke," said Ihaka. "Through the daughter. Seems like she's the only one who knew the dope was down there. We'd better talk to her."

"What about your sparring partner, Ricketts?" said McGrail. "What's he up to? He's known about the drugs all along and I can't see him standing on the sidelines."

"Who is he?" asked Hellicar.

Ihaka gave her a brief and unflattering summary of Ricketts and where he fitted in. "I wouldn't bet on it," he said, "but I think I might've warned him off. Ricketts came back from Thailand looking to make a score, no two ways about that, but only if he could've breezed it: walked in, got the stuff, walked out and off-loaded it — no law, no complications, no heavy stuff. My gut feeling is that Ricketts would play the odds. Once it got too high risk, he'd flag it."

Ihaka ran them through what was being done: a nationwide alert for Funke; a watch on all ports; another, more painstaking, check of hotels, motels and boarding houses; a blitz on informants; and surveillance of known and suspected major drug dealers, including Spurdle, whom Funke might contact.

"It's a waiting game now," he concluded. "Funke won't want to take the stuff out of the country and in through customs somewhere. He'll try to sell it here and that means putting the word out, moving around, seeing people. We'll get a tip-off or a sighting — just a matter of time."

"What about this guy Ricketts?" asked Hellicar. "You got someone on him?"

Ihaka shook his head. "Waste of manpower. If we put him under surveillance, Ricketts would spot it; if we put a tail on him, he'd lose it. He's good at that shit — better than most of our guys anyway."

McGrail gave Hellicar another winning smile. "On that score at least, the sergeant and I are as one."

The meeting wound up shortly afterwards. McGrail lavished some more of his limited supply of charm on Hellicar, then left the room.

"He surely is a nice guy," she said.

Ihaka lurched over to the large plastic rubbish bin in the corner, bent over so his head was almost in it, and did a disconcertingly convincing imitation of someone being violently and noisily ill.

He turned around wiping his mouth with the back of his hand. "They don't come any nicer than McGrail," he agreed. He nodded at the briefcase. "Is that your gear?"

Hellicar stopped staring at Ihaka and shook herself to make sure she hadn't imagined the vomiting routine. It's not me, she told herself; I didn't take a sleeping pill on the plane; I'm not hallucinating; he really did do that.

"Yes, that's it," she said distractedly.

"Can I've a geek?"

"A what?"

"A look. Can I've a look at your equipment?"

"I'll show you, Sergeant, if that's what you really want," she said watching him suspiciously. "Just don't offer to show me your nightstick."

Ihaka looked affronted. "The thought never entered my head."

"I dare say there isn't room — not with the other stuff you've got in there."

While Ihaka pondered that remark, she spun the combination locks and snapped the briefcase open. It contained a sleek, compact black automatic pistol with a moulded finger-grip butt, a spare magazine, a box of ammunition and a plastic stock.

Ihaka wolf-whistled. "That's a mean-looking unit. What is it?"

She picked up the pistol and ejected the empty magazine from the butt. "A Heckler and Koch VP 70; 9 millimetre, takes an eighteen-round load."

She opened the box of ammunition and began feeding bullets into the magazine.

"What's this?" asked Ihaka tapping the stock.

"A stock; you can fix it to the pistol and brace it against your shoulder — like a rifle butt — and set it to fire in three-shot bursts. For those times when you just can't afford to miss."

"I thought they were all like that?"

She nodded. "To tell the truth, I've only ever used the stock at the firing range."

"State of the art bang-bang," he said in a hucksterish American accent.

She shrugged. "It's a good weapon for sure but it just suits me — nice weight, good feel. I got the grip — see how it's moulded? — custom-made to fit my hand." She slipped the last bullet into the magazine, slid the magazine into the butt and aimed across the room. "It gets the job done."

21

At 7.05 that Friday evening Duane Ricketts drove his baked bean-orange Toyota Corolla down Eden Crescent. He was dressed in a blue shirt with a button-down collar, a cheerfully patterned tie, a dark-green check woollen jacket and off-white chino pants. They were his good news clothes; he wore them when he took a runaway back to Mum and Dad or, failing that, gave them a phone number and a Polaroid of the stray displaying clear eyes, clean fingernails and a haircut that wouldn't frighten the neighbours. His bad news outfit was white shirt, plain tie and dark suit. He wore it when he had to explain to parents that they still had a child but he or she bore no resemblance to the one they missed; or to break the news that a long-lost brother, the clever one everybody said was going to be famous some day, spent most of his life on a bench in Myers Park with a cask of Lincoln Road Müller-Thurgau and hadn't changed his underpants since the fall of the Berlin Wall.

A transformed Electra Crouch was in the passenger seat. She'd borrowed a thigh-length tweed herringbone coat, belted at the waist, from the woman in the ground-floor apartment and wore it over black leather trousers and a black turtleneck sweater. The nose-ring, the earstuds, the chestnut dye and the gel had all been discarded; the hair — now glossy-black — fell naturally, curling onto her forehead and below her ears. Electra looked older than eighteen anyway, but Ricketts had suggested a bit of make-up might add a useful year or two; not one for half-measures, she'd put on lipstick, eye shadow, face make-up, and judging by the alluring scent, some rather expensive perfume.

Ricketts had déjà vu when the new-look Electra Crouch came out of her bedroom and struck a catwalk pose: the clothes were different but otherwise she looked uncannily like she'd done in his dream. He had mixed feelings on the more pertinent issue of whether it amounted to a convincing impersonation: she'll pass for early twenties all right, he thought, but apart from that she looks about as much like a working policewoman as Madonna does. He hoped that whoever ran Crescent Lodge based their expectations of policewomen on American TV shows.

The Fiat Tipo was still there. Ricketts drove past the boarding house, U-turned and double-parked facing back down the street. After a few minutes' wait, he got a parking spot where he wanted: across the road from Crescent Lodge and a little way up the street so anyone going from the boarding house to the Fiat would walk away from them, not towards them. It was almost dark but there was a street light right outside Crescent Lodge, illuminating the entrance.

"Okay," said Ricketts. "Let's run through it again."

"What for?" she said. "We've done it to death."

"Humour me."

Electra put her chin on her chest. "Okay," she sighed. "I don't touch anything; I don't use names; I leave the talking to you; I look reassuring and professional; I refrain from smoking. As soon as we get into the room, I ask to use a phone; I ring the flat and pretend to have a conversation with Ihaka then I keep them occupied till you're finished. If I see Funke coming, I take off."

"And if they ask you what's going on?"

"I tell them to mind their own fucking beeswax." She glanced sidelong at Ricketts who seemed to have left his sense of humour back at the flat with the nose-ring. "Sorry, got that wrong; I say I've been assigned to tag along with you but don't really know what it's all about. If they don't get the message, then I tell them to mind their own fucking beeswax."

It was Ricketts' turn to sigh. "This is not a game."

"I know, I know, I know. Don't worry about it, I'll be fine. I do this before a concert — kid around, get loose. You should try it. Speaking of music, you got any?"

"There're a few tapes in the glovebox."

She opened the glovebox, brought out half a dozen tapes and shuffled through them. "Oh I get it," she said. "You can have whatever you want as long as it's Van Morrison?"

"What's wrong with Van Morrison?" said Ricketts testily.

"To me he's like, you know, Mozart, Beethoven — guys like that."

"In other words, he's a kraut who's been dead for a couple of hundred years?"

"I didn't mean . . ."

"What you're trying to say is boring old farts listen to Van Morrison — correct?"

She said, "If the hairpiece fits," and started laughing. "What I was actually trying to say is people who listen to him obviously aren't into what's happening right now."

"Like 'The Homo Dwarves'? Choice name — where'd you get it from ?"

She shrugged. "Just made it up. We wanted a name that'd get up people's noses."

"I hate to disappoint you but it doesn't get up mine — then again, I'm not a homo or a dwarf."

"Nor's my mother; nor are most of the people who've whinged about it."

At that moment a couple came out of Crescent Lodge. The man was middle-aged and short with a broad, tanned face and not much hair. He was wearing a dark reefer jacket and light trousers and carried a shopping bag. The woman was younger, stylishly dressed and quite striking, with a mane of dark hair. They walked across the road towards the Fiat.

"That's him," said Electra quietly.

"What about the woman — you know her?"

She shook her head. "No. She looks a bit glam for him, though."

"Yeah, doesn't she?"

The couple got into the Fiat. The woman was a new factor but Ricketts couldn't see that it changed anything. A soon as the Fiat turned out of Eden Crescent, he got out of the car and got a boxy black briefcase out of the boot.

"Let's go," he said.

They crossed the road and went into Crescent Lodge. It was a narrow, three-storey wooden building which had seen better days; even in its prime, Sunday drivers wouldn't have made detours to admire it. The foyer was deserted except for three china ducks flying in close formation across chintzy blue floral wallpaper. Below the ducks was a sofa which looked old enough to have farthings in its crevices.

The little office beyond the reception counter was unoccupied so Ricketts hallo-ed loudly. A door opened down the corridor which ran off the foyer. A woman poked her head out, saw them and bustled down the corridor. She looked in her sixties: well-lined, iron-grey hair and eyes which twinkled behind the reading glasses.

She beamed at Electra. "Well, look at you," she said. "Aren't you the pretty one?" She glanced uncertainly at Ricketts who realised that she was having the same thoughts about the two of them as they'd had about Funke and his female companion a few minutes earlier. "Now then, would you be wanting a room? We do have a vacancy."

"Actually madam, we're from the police," said Ricketts, flashing his fake identification. It was an extremely convincing forgery as were the documents in his wallet identifying him as a health inspector, a Telecom engineer and an officer of the Social Welfare department. The forgeries had been done for him by a Dutch screen printer who lived in Huapai and who'd been the first person Ricketts rang after he was kicked out of the police force. The purpose of the call was to warn the Dutchman that the police knew about the twenty or thirty marijuana plants he had in his garden and would be coming round to arrest him shortly.

"I'm Detective Sergeant Wright," he said, "and this is Detective Constable Edgar. Are you Mrs Ada Merchant?"

Her eyes grew big: "Goodness me. Yes I am but what . . .?"

He produced a small notepad from his jacket pocket. "Mrs Merchant, are you the owner of a Fiat Tipo?" — he flipped the notepad open and read the car registration number.

"Yes," she nodded vigorously. "Yes, that's my car. I've had it for three years now. Everyone told me to get a Japanese car. Don't get a Fiat, they said; they're unreliable and they rust. But do you know, I've never had a problem with it —

not even the slightest speck of rust. You didn't catch me on one of those hidden cameras, did you, going through a red light? I'd be surprised if that's the case, Sergeant; I'm normally very careful . . ."

"Mrs Merchant, have you lent your car to anyone recently?"

Comprehension eventually arrived on Mrs Merchant's face, bringing up the rear in an almost comically predictable procession of expressions. "Yes, yes of course I have. I lent it to Hank — that's Mr Williams, my American guest. Did he go through a red light? I'd be a little cross if he did because he promised . . ."

"Mr Williams is a guest here?"

"That's right. You see, he was involved in some sort of dreadful traffic accident back home — Oklahoma, I think he said he's from. Not his fault he assured me, but there's going to be a court case and, in the meantime, his licence has been suspended which means the poor man couldn't hire a car; that would've completely mucked up his holiday so he suggested that I hired one — whatever sort I wanted, he'd pay for it — and he'd use my Fiat." She lowered her voice. "Guess what I did — I hired a BMW." She emitted a little squeak of delight. "You should see people's faces when they see me in it." Her face dropped. "Golly, I didn't break the law, did I?"

"Don't worry, Mrs Merchant, this has got nothing to do with you and not much to do with your car. We're only interested in it because that's how we traced your guest, Mr Williams. To cut a long story short, we don't think he's who he says he is. We believe his real name is Funke and that he's wanted by the authorities in Thailand. Is he here now?"

"No, you've just missed him — he's gone out to dinner with his lady friend."

"Mrs Merchant, we need to establish as quickly as possible whether this is the man we're looking for; for that reason, I'd like to have a look in his room. You've obviously got a spare key?"

She looked dubious. "Well, yes, but don't you need a search warrant for that sort of thing?"

"Not if you let us in," he said. "After all, it's your room; you can go in there whenever you like." Ricketts lowered his voice confidentially. "Between you and me, Mrs Merchant, this is a pretty serious matter with all sorts of international ramifications. All we're after is confirmation of identity; I'll be in and out in two ticks."

She nodded agreement, fetched the key from the office, led them upstairs and let them into room seven. It contained a neatly made three-quarter size bed, a hand-basin, a small writing desk, a bedside table with a reading light, a chest of drawers and a wardrobe. Perfume hung in the air.

Mrs Merchant wrinkled her nose like a guinea pig. "Mr Williams' friend certainly splashes on the perfume." She looked at Electra. "Yours is much nicer, my dear — much more subtle."

Electra rewarded her with a gorgeous smile. "Why thank you, Mrs Merchant.

To tell the truth, I'm a bit of a beginner when it comes to the smellies. Look, is there a phone I could possibly use? I should check in with headquarters."

Mrs Merchant, who appeared to entertain fewer reservations about Electra than about Ricketts, said of course there was. As soon as they'd gone downstairs, Ricketts closed the door and took a pair of skin-tight plastic gloves from his briefcase. He put them on and tried the wardrobe; it was locked. He took a small jimmy from his briefcase and forced the wardrobe door. Inside were a couple of shirts on hangars, a shopping bag containing a blouse, brassiere and panties, and a large Samsonite suitcase with a combination lock. He pulled the suitcase out of the wardrobe and checked it was locked, then used the jimmy to lever it open. It contained some carefully folded clothes, US passports in the names of Harold Funke, Donald Surface and Lyle Gorse, an airline ticket with an open return to Los Angeles, and nineteen plastic bags of white powder which was one less than Dale Varty had said there'd be. Ricketts removed the bags and replaced them with nineteen of the twenty bags of icing sugar he'd brought with him in the briefcase; he'd picked up the icing sugar at a supermarket earlier that evening and repackaged it in self-sealing clear plastic bags.

Ricketts closed the suitcase, returned it to the wardrobe and put the nineteen bags of what he was reasonably confident was cocaine into his briefcase. He left the room, locking the door behind him, took off the gloves and put them in his jacket pocket and went down to the foyer where Electra and Mrs Merchant were agreeing to disagree about Mr and Mrs Rachel Hunter: Electra didn't have a lot of time for either of them while Mrs Merchant seemed to think that Rod Stewart was a bit of a lad and that there were worse things in life than being rich, famous and regarded as a bimbo — running a slightly down-at-heel boarding house, for instance.

"What do you think, sergeant?" asked Electra with a malicious glint in her eye. "I bet you're a big Rach fan?"

Ricketts gave her a prim little smile and said, "I think she's a wonderful ambassador for New Zealand." He turned to Mrs Merchant. "Your guest's definitely the man we're looking for. You were saying he's got someone with him?"

"Yes, a friend of his; they met overseas apparently. She's from out of town — that's why she used his room to get changed."

That's one theory, thought Ricketts.

Ten minutes later he rang Auckland Central police station from a phone box on Dominion Road. Without identifying himself, he informed the constable to whom he was put through that Harold Funke was staying in room seven of the Crescent Lodge boarding house, driving a Fiat Tipo, the registration number of which he provided, and in the company of a rather attractive brunette. He thought about adding that the brunette could be an accomplice or a girlfriend or both or possibly even some sort of hostage, but decided against. It was complicated enough already.

At 7.45 p.m. the two-person police surveillance team stationed in a small stand of pine trees in the paddock across the road from the entrance to the Spurdle property reported in to operation control at Auckland Central. They'd got the registration number of a car which had just gone up the Spurdles' drive but weren't entirely in agreement over the make and model: Constable Beth Greendale, whose brother was a mechanic and who knew a bit about cars, had seen enough through her night-sight binoculars to be reasonably confident it was a Fiat Tipo; Constable Jarrad Renshaw, who didn't have a brother, didn't know much about cars, and whose idea of a good time wasn't blundering around in the dark putting his foot in cowpats, described it as "just another fucking Japanese hatchback". They also reported that there were two passengers, a male and a female; beyond that, their descriptions fitted every pale-skinned man and woman on the planet who didn't have two heads.

Five minutes after Ihaka received that information, along with details of the car's registered owner, he was handed a note of the anonymous tip-off about Funke. After a brief discussion with McGrail, Ihaka dispatched a police team, including several members of the Armed Offenders Squad, to Crescent Lodge. Then he walked along to the conference room where C. C. Hellicar was writing postcards and listening to John Hiatt singing about lipstick sunsets on her Walkman.

Ihaka stood in the doorway looking unusually serious. Hellicar put down the ballpoint and took off her earphones.

"Feel like going for a drive?" he asked.

"Anywhere in particular?"

Ihaka nodded. "Spurdle's place. He's got company."

Hellicar's eyes narrowed and she reached for the metal briefcase. "Is it him?"

"Could be." He paused. "I've got a feeling it will be."

She stood up with a faint smile. "Oh right, your gift. So I guess you already know how all this is going to work out?"

"Yeah — Funke's about to become defunct." He stood aside to let her through the door then caught up with her. "Listen, will you be heading off straightaway or can you stick around for the weekend? Reason I ask is my family's got a beach-house up north. I could take you up there, show you a bit of the country."

Hellicar's cool look wasn't entirely devoid of either amusement or curiosity. "You mean just you and me?"

Ihaka shrugged. "Up to you. If it'd make you feel more comfortable, bring your two mates — Heckler and Koch."

22

Buddy Funke halted the Fiat Tipo outside the Spurdle mansion and switched off the motor. He gave Fleur Wolfgramm a long, calculating look and said, "You've played it real smart so far, sugar; don't go blowing it now."

Part of Fleur Wolfgramm — the logical, cynical and therefore pessimistic part — was faintly surprised to be still alive. The other part — the upbeat, extrovert, slightly new age part which was responsible for most of the really stupid things she'd done in her life — had drawn comfort from the fact that Funke had been a gentleman when he'd had ample opportunity to be a beast. From the outset, her strategy had been to do whatever it took to stay alive till they got to the Spurdles and then hope that something turned up. The first bit had been a piece of cake — whatever it took had proved to be very little — but the menace now unmistakable behind Funke's amiable demeanour suggested that the next bit might be a lot trickier.

"What do you mean?" she said anxiously. "Why should I do that?"

"No reason that occurs to me," he said with the wry delivery of a cracker-barrel philosopher, "but folks have a habit of giving in to temptation just because it's there; sometimes they ain't even that shook on what it is they're giving in to. Me and Mr Bryce Spurdle are going to talk business tonight and I don't expect he'll want to do that in front of the womenfolk. Remember now, just because I'm not there keeping an eye on you is no reason to cut the fool. We've got along just fine, you and me, but if anything untoward happens, you'll answer for it."

Wolfgramm nodded. "Message received," she muttered. "I'll say this for you, you know how to put a girl in a party mood."

Bryce Spurdle had been stunned and immensely gratified by his wife's second coming as Susie Homemaker in crotchless panties. As the afterglow faded, however, gratitude inevitably gave way to suspicion. Whatever else he was, Spurdle was a realist and, after a few seconds' wishful thinking, he dismissed the possibility that it'd been a genuine and spontaneous expression of her true feelings. Before it began to gnaw at him, he had one of those rare moments of clarity when one grasps that the easy and obvious course of action is also the most sensible. What the fuck am I worrying about? he asked himself. Who gives a fat rat's arse what she's up to? Get your snout in the trough mate. Make the most of it while it lasts.

Bucked both by his rigorous reasoning and the conclusion to which it led, Spurdle refrained from throwing a tantrum upon being informed that a pair of strangers were coming for dinner. While Jody prepared his favourite meal — Mediterranean roast lamb and sticky toffee pudding — he browsed contentedly in the mini-wine cellar beneath the stairs, savouring the aroma of roasting garlic and balsamic vinegar which wafted down the hall from the kitchen. He liked to take his time choosing wine, especially on an occasion like this when he had to balance his ebullient mood and desire to do justice to Jody's culinary exertions against his profound aversion to wasting expensive wine on other people.

The Spurdles and their guests were having pre-dinner drinks in the lounge. Bryce was doing the honours: champagne for the ladies, scotch for Funke, more dark rum for himself. Jody and Fleur were already gabbling like auctioneers while Funke stood on his own, quite relaxed, with one hand in his pocket and the other holding a shopping bag. Spurdle eyed him surreptitiously as he poured the champagne; he wondered briefly what was in the bag before turning his mind to the much more interesting question of whether their guests were sleeping together. Not surprisingly, given that his assumptions about other people's sex lives owed far more to his dirty mind than to empirical evidence or even probability, he concluded that they were.

The drinks were distributed and toasts exchanged. The women took perfunctory sips and carried on with their exclusive conversation. Spurdle was swirling his drink around trying to think of something to say when Funke saved him the trouble.

"You got the message that I have a business proposition for you?" he murmured.

Spurdle, who associated that approach with losers, con-men and white-collar thieves, looked as unenthusiastic as the circumstances permitted and said, "Yeah, Jody mentioned it."

"How about we get to it right away?" said Funke. "Would there happen to be a little corner we can go so's we don't bore the ladies?"

Spurdle glanced at Fleur and Jody, thinking that for all the ladies cared, he and the Yank could get naked and shave each other's body hair. "Okay," he said. "Let's do that. Girls, we're just slipping down to the den. The champagne's in the ice bucket — help yourselves."

They went into the den. Spurdle was hitching himself up onto a stool when Funke plonked the shopping bag down on the bar in front of him.

"A little something from me to you."

Spurdle looked bemused and slightly apprehensive. Funke grinned and pointed at the bag. "Well?" he asked. "You going to have a look?"

Spurdle pulled the bag towards him. He peered into it suspiciously then glanced sharply up at Funke who winked back. Spurdle reached into the shopping bag and brought out a plastic bag of white powder. He looked at it for a few seconds then placed it on the bar and pushed it away.

"What's that then?" he said with a jerk of his chin.

Funke turned the bag over to show that it had been opened and then patched with sticking plaster. "That, my friend, is cocaine deluxe and I ought to know — I'm a goddam expert."

"Just what the hell makes you think I'd want it?" asked Spurdle, working up a little truculence.

"Well now," said Funke with a thin smile, "I hear tell you're a man who'd know what to do with it; a man who understands that this stuff's just about the most efficient way of generating cash money ever invented." He pushed the bag back towards Spurdle. "That's a present; call it an expression of goodwill. There's nineteen more where that came from: all up, ten kilos of top of the range nose candy."

Spurdle stared at him. "Who are you, pal?"

"Don't take this the wrong way but I work for the DEA. You know what that is?" Spurdle, eyes wide, nodded. "The Brits have got a saying about someone being a poacher turned gamekeeper. That's sort of what I am, except contrariwise."

Spurdle's eyes narrowed. "This could be a set-up."

Funke shrugged. "That goes both ways," he said mildly. "For all I know about you, you could be taking it in the tail from the chief of police. Let me tell you how it came my way; that might explain a few things. I found it in a little place called Manacle . . ."

Spurdle flashed a dark, angry red and wriggled off the bar stool. "You got it from Manacle Grange?" he demanded, his voice rising. "That makes it my fucking cocaine. I paid for it twice over and got ripped off both times. How the fuck did you get hold of it?"

"Well, let me tell you, it wasn't easy," said Funke, who seemed to be finding the conversation increasingly enjoyable. "But what counts is, I've got it; and as we both know, in this business possession is ten tenths of the law — everything else is for shit."

"Wait a fucking minute," said Spurdle. "Now I've got you taped; you're the one who pulled a gun on Leith Grills the other night, over at Rayleen Varty's place."

"Yup, that was me all right," agreed Funke. "That old boy work for you, did he?"

Spurdle caught something in Funke's tone. "Yeah, now and again. In fact I've been expecting to hear from him all day. I don't suppose you came across him down at Manacle Grange?"

"I did, as a matter of fact," said Funke. "The way he was waving that shotgun, it would've been hard to miss him."

Spurdle did a double-take. "A shotgun? Jesus Christ, what happened?"

"It's a sad story. Suffice to say, I'm here and he ain't; I got the cocaine and all your Mr Grills has got is a couple of holes that the Lord didn't give him."

Spurdle gawked at Funke, transfixed: "You shot him?" he asked hoarsely.

"Yes sir, I did," said Funke briskly. "The boy left me no choice. Like I say, he was waving that shotgun like he was John Dillinger himself. That's by the by: time's a-wasting; are you and me going to do some business or should I take my custom elsewhere?"

Spurdle shook his head in bewilderment and went behind the bar to make fresh drinks. He pushed Funke's scotch across the bar to him, took a distracted swig of his rum and Coke, then stood with his hands flat on the bar and head bowed. Two minutes passed. Then he looked up at Funke, heaved a sigh of resignation, and said, "How much?"

"All right," said Funke. "In my experience, which as I say is considerable, merchandise of this quality wholesales around 200 grand a kilo and retails at about 500 grand. I'm talking American; in your money, that's around 320 wholesale, 800 on the street. Working off those numbers, you — being the wholesaler — would aim to make around three million of your dollars on ten kilos. That sound about right to you?"

"It sounds fucking high to me."

"Sure it does because right now you're a buyer. I'm about to make you the offer of a lifetime, amigo: the stuff's yours for 750 grand."

"NZ or US?" asked Spurdle quickly.

"NZ. That means if you're even semi-reasonable, you'll make at least three times your money. If you're good, you'll quadruple it without working up a sweat."

Spurdle knew he was being offered a good deal and forced himself to keep a poker face. "Even if it's as good as you say, that's still pretty steep . . ."

"Uh-uh," said Funke waving his index finger. "That ain't a negotiating position, that's the price. It's cheap and you know it."

"Well, maybe . . ."

"No goddam maybe about it," said Funke emphatically. "Christ almighty, when I think of the shit I had to go through to get it . . . by the way, there is one condition."

"Oh? What's that?"

"We do the deal tomorrow morning at sun up."

"The fuck we will," yelped Spurdle. "Where the hell am I going to get the money? It's Friday night in case you hadn't noticed . . ."

Funke's eyes went dull and his mouth set like a closed vice. "How about you quit flapping that tongue, brother?" he said softly, hunching across the bar. "I'm not offering you the best deal you ever had on account of I particularly like you — because I'm bound to say, I've known you for half an hour and you ain't grown on me even a little bit. The fact is, I figure I've pushed my luck about as far as it's going to go; I want to be on the first plane out of here tomorrow morning so I'm giving you a discount for short notice. Now you're asking me where you're going to get the money from on a Friday night, like I'm some kind of jerk who couldn't find his dick in a double bed. If I seriously thought you had to get the money from a bank, I wouldn't be here because that would give me two good reasons not to deal with you; in the first place, it would mean you're dumb because the bank's going to report a withdrawal that size; second, it would mean you ain't a player. Anyone who buys and sells dope has access to a mess of cash whenever: either he's got a stash or he knows people whose business is selling money. Now make up your goddam mind — are you in or out?"

Spurdle didn't reply right away but that didn't worry Funke because he knew from the look in his eyes what the answer would be. While he waited for Spurdle to get around to it, Funke sipped his scotch and idly wondered how much the son of a bitch had in his secret safe.

Tito Ihaka pulled over to the side of the road about half a kilometre from the entrance to Spurdle's drive, flicked off the headlights and turned to C. C. Hellicar.

"I've got an idea," he said.

She kept looking straight ahead. "Sergeant, this is not a good time to be having ideas," she said. "Let's not complicate things. Why don't you just get me thereabouts and then stay out of the way?"

"No, this is a shit-hot idea. See, I've got a valid police reason for dropping in on the Spurdles. When I show up, Funke'll be so busy worrying about me, you can sneak in and zap the bugger."

Hellicar appeared to be considering it. "It makes sense I guess; there's just one slight flaw."

"What's that?"

Hellicar twisted around in her seat and gave him a very direct look: "Funke might just shoot you on sight."

Ihaka's forehead furrowed. "Thank Christ there's not a major flaw." He shook his head. "I doubt it; he's got no reason to think we're onto him and I've got a reason for being there. Sure, he's going to watch me like a hawk but that's what we want him to do."

"Tito," said Hellicar gently, "I appreciate it and all but I really don't think this is a good move. You being a cop isn't worth a Yankee dime to Funke. He's going to be eat up with suspicion the moment you set foot in there; half a second after he decides something's going down, you'll have a .38 in your face."

"It's just a matter of timing," said Ihaka blithely. "Shit, I'm not planning to spend the night with the prick; I'll wait till you're up there before I go so we're talking — what? A couple of minutes. It's a tried and true tactic — create a diversion and whack the fuckers when they're looking the other way."

Hellicar sighed and looked up at the car roof. "I don't understand; you're not a macho dimwit or some idiotic kid who thinks it's like the movies and the good guys always walk away. It's not even your responsibility."

In a whiny country-and-western voice Ihaka sang 'Tito, don't be a hero.' Hellicar threw up her hands and said, "Goddamit."

"You're dead right about me not being macho or naïve," he said, "but you've got the other bit wrong. Okay, Funke's one of yours but this here's" — he gestured at the surrounding darkness — "my neck of the woods. More to the point, if Funke gets past you, then me and the other blokes will have to have a go and that could get ugly — don't forget there are three other people in the house. In my professional opinion, it's the best chance of getting the job done without things getting out of hand." He paused and leant back in his seat. "Besides, I hate having nowhere to go on a Friday night."

Hellicar nodded solemnly. "Well shit," she said, "why didn't you just say so in the first place."

Ihaka started the car. "The surveillance guys say it's about 400 metres from the road up to the house. I'll drop you just before the gate and give you a quarter of an hour or so to get up there. What time do you make it?"

"Twenty after nine."

"Okay, I'll knock on the door at a quarter to ten. The back-up's in the paddock across the road; they'll block off the entrance. How long should they wait?"

"Me and Funke haven't got a whole heap to talk about; whichever way it goes, it'll be over and done with pretty damn quick."

At 9.44 p.m. Ihaka drove up to the Spurdle residence, parked behind the Fiat Tipo and rang the doorbell. A minute later, a flushed Bryce Spurdle opened the door. Ihaka introduced himself and asked to speak to Mrs Spurdle.

Spurdle liked to see himself as a man in control of his destiny but recent events had left him feeling like a body surfer caught by one of those sudden monster waves which dribble in innocuously, pause about twenty or thirty metres out from the shore, rear up and then hurl themselves at the beach like dam-bursts. He felt like he'd been picked up and catapulted by an irresistible force — churned, flipped, dragged, bounced and finally dumped on the beach, breathless, disoriented and tingling with exhilaration. The only thing missing was sand in his crack. On top of all that, he'd drunk six double rum and Cokes, a couple of beers and two-thirds of a bottle of wine in the space of a few hours. The net result was that he'd achieved a state of fuzzy detachment and while it seemed strange that a cop should turn up out of the blue wanting to talk to his wife, he couldn't actually find it within himself to give a flying fuck.

So he shrugged and said, "You'd better come in then. Bit bloody inconvenient, though; we've got people for dinner."

"It won't take a moment."

Spurdle led Ihaka down to the dining room where the others were sitting at the long, polished wood table politely waiting for him to come back before they started their desserts. Spurdle paused in the doorway, waited till he had everyone's attention, then said loudly, "Babe, there's a cop to see you," adding, as if oblivious that Ihaka was right behind him: "big bastard he is too."

Having made his dramatic announcement, Spurdle sat down at the head of the table with his back to Ihaka and began a minute inspection of his dessert. Ihaka came into the dining room which was between the lounge and the kitchen; the lounge was on his right through open double doors and the doorway to the kitchen was on his left. An anguished Jody Spurdle sat bolt upright gaping at him from the far end of the table; a woman he didn't know was on the lounge side of the table looking queasy and shaking her head at the middle-aged man opposite her. He was clearly unhappy but there was something not quite right with his eyes so it was difficult to tell whether the focus of his displeasure was the woman, Ihaka or Spurdle, who was attempting to completely submerge his sticky toffee pudding in whipped cream.

"Evening," said Ihaka, ducking his head. "Sorry to barge in but I wondered if I could have a quick word with you, Mrs Spurdle."

"What about?" she stammered.

"Well . . ." said Ihaka, hesitating. "It's to do with what we discussed the other day."

Jody had gone quite pale. "I don't know what you're talking about," she said shakily. "Please go away."

Funke got up from his chair, walked around the table to stand in front of Ihaka, and drawled: "Just what in the hell is going on here?"

Ihaka studied him with that look of barely concealed contempt which police officers automatically bestow on uppity members of the public. "I was talking to Mrs Spurdle. I'm following up a matter she brought to our attention . . ."

"She says that ain't so."

Ihaka shrugged indifferently. "That's understandable. It's a little embarrassing."

Funke persisted: "It must be pretty damn serious for you to come all the way out here at this hour."

Ihaka ignored him. "Mrs Spurdle, we talked to Leith Grills tonight . . ."

"You use a fucking Ouija board?" snapped Funke. He reached under his reefer jacket for the revolver which he had stuck in his belt at the small of his back, pulled it out and held it under Ihaka's chin.

"Do you know who I am, boy?" he said.

"Clint Eastwood's midget brother?"

Something's all-to-hell wrong here, thought Funke; this asshole should be filling his pants instead of standing there cool as you please, giving me a fuck you look.

Out of the corner of his eye, Funke saw a black shape in the kitchen doorway a few metres to his right.

"Put the gun down," said C. C. Hellicar firmly.

Funke kept the .38 a few centimetres from Ihaka's chin and turned his head slightly. A young woman was wrapped around the jamb of the door showing as little of herself as possible. She had an automatic on him, holding it very steady in both hands. Funke remembered that hot afternoon in 1962, the store on the back road down around Sierra Blanca and the white trash storekeeper who'd blown away Lyle Gorse. She's pointing her piece just like that storekeeper, he thought — still as death itself. Something tells me this little gal ain't going to chew on it.

"Where'd you spring from, honey?" asked Funke in his most laconic tone.

"Langley sent me."

"Langley huh? Well, I guess they didn't send you all the way down here to give me counselling." Funke's eyes swung back to Ihaka. "Looks like we got ourselves a Mexican stand . . ."

Hellicar shot Funke in the exact centre of his right cheek. The bullet exited through his left cheek along with a fine hail of splintered teeth and gum, went through the open double doors and shattered the most valuable piece in Spurdle's Toby jug collection before burying itself in the antique sideboard at the far end of the lounge. Funke spun around and fell face-first, losing hold of the .38. He lay on his front, groping blindly and feebly for the pistol. Holding the automatic pointed to the ceiling, Hellicar walked purposefully across to Funke and stood astride him. She extended her arms, took careful aim, and shot him twice in the back of the head.

In the echoing silence, Jody began to cry hysterically; Fleur Wolfgramm gripped the table with both hands and stared sightlessly at her untouched sticky toffee pudding while Bryce Spurdle goggled at Funke's body in drunken disbelief and reached for his wineglass with a trembling hand. Satisfied that none of them posed a threat, Hellicar turned to Ihaka who hadn't moved anything except his eyeballs since Funke had pulled the gun.

"You okay?"

Ihaka nodded and took a very deep breath.

"You know, he hadn't cocked the .38; that made the shot a little safer."

Ihaka forced a smile. "I feel a lot better for knowing that."

After thirty or so seconds, the frozen concentration began to recede from Hellicar's pale blue eyes and her mouth formed a lopsided, mirthless smile.

She hefted the automatic: "You still want to take us to your beach-house?"

23

The United States Government terminated its occasionally awkward twenty-seven-year association with Harold "Buddy" Funke at precisely 9.53 p.m.

By 10 p.m. the back-up team had completely secured and sealed off the Spurdle property. At 10.17 p.m. four unmarked vehicles passed through the police roadblock and swept up the drive; a few minutes later, two of them swept back down the drive and headed into town. The first, a black Toyota Landcruiser four wheel drive fitted out as an ambulance, was driven by an armed constable; his passenger was a police pathologist and his cargo was a body bag containing former special agent Funke. While to the untrained eye the second car looked like an ordinary old Commodore, it was in fact a modified version from the Holden Special Vehicle facility in Notting Hill, Victoria: it had a 5.7 litre V8 engine, a top speed of 243 kilometres an hour, could reach 100 kph from a standing start in 6.6 seconds and was by some distance the most sought-after car in the Auckland Central fleet. On this occasion it was being used to ferry an uncharacteristically subdued Detective Sergeant Tito Ihaka to his home in Sandringham and a characteristically enigmatic C. C. Hellicar to her city hotel.

The police contingent which remained was led by Detective Inspector Finbar McGrail whose first priority was to convince the Spurdles and Fleur Wolfgramm that it was really none of their business if Americans wanted to shoot one another in their dining room. It was a slow process: the trio were suffering varying degrees of shock and needed medical treatment and gentle handling. What with one thing and another, it wasn't until close to midnight that Wolfgramm mentioned the car out at the airport with two dead men in the boot. By the time the squad car from the Otahuhu police station got there, it was too late.

At five minutes to midnight, Derril Shine, twenty-three, had driven his lime-green Datsun Starlet very slowly and with the headlights switched off into the international terminal carpark. In the passenger seat was Apollo Laulau, a twenty-one-year-old Fijian-Samoan whose main interest in life was collecting baseball caps. Both men were unemployed; while they were vaguely familiar with the concept of earning an honest living, neither of them had ever actually given it a try.

The pair had been drinking in the public bar of a Mangere Bridge tavern. During a game of pool, an acquaintance had told Shine, who constantly advertised his availability for any criminal enterprise which didn't require seed money and didn't involve heavy-duty violence, that there was good money to be made supplying stolen cars to a second-hand car yard cum chop shop in Te Atatu. Shine had thought about this for a minute or two then left the bar and driven his Starlet to the airport. After checking the arrivals board to see when the last flight of the night got in, he'd gone back to the tavern to discuss commission, preferred models and delivery procedure with his acquaintance and to enlist Laulau as his driver.

There were fewer than three dozen cars in the carpark. After eliminating those with alarms or steering wheel locks and models which weren't in demand, Shine chose the Holden Berlina parked on its own in the centre of the carpark. He got a jack out of his boot, smashed the Berlina's passenger door window, raised the bonnet and hot wired the engine. With Laulau following in the Starlet, Shine drove the Berlina to the house in Glen Innes where he'd lived by himself since his co-tenants had taken up residence in Mt Eden prison. Shine wasn't sure how long he'd be able to stay in the $200 a week accommodation; it was really a question of when the penny dropped and the landlord realised he had neither the inclination nor the means to pay the rent.

Shine parked the Berlina out the back of the house and he and Laulau went inside for one last drink. What started as a celebratory Drambuie and beer chaser soon developed into a drinking race, the outcome of which was settled by Laulau's abrupt loss of consciousness. Shine went into the bathroom, induced a prodigious vomit by putting two heavily nicotined fingers down his throat, and then collapsed on his bed.

He woke up at 10.25 the next morning. He didn't feel refreshed or alert or particularly well, so apart from the vile taste in this mouth, it was much like any other morning. It had been a good idea to make himself sick; next time he'd have to remember to clean his teeth afterwards. Laulau was still slumped on the couch so Shine made himself a cup of tea and went outside to inspect his new car.

As he sat behind the steering wheel sipping his tea, it occurred to him that there might be something in the boot worth stealing; he pulled the boot release lever and got out of the car. That was when he noticed the smell. Fuck me, that's off, he said to himself; the coconut's probably shat himself. When Shine lifted the boot lid, the smell, a greasy, noxious, choking blend of rotten fat and open drains, intensified dramatically. The stench and even more shocking sight caused him to gag shudderingly before he could slam the boot shut and reel away.

Trembling with nausea and anxiety, Shine sat on the back steps and reviewed his options. He could simply deliver the car and its contents as arranged, thus shifting the problem of the bodies in the boot onto someone else's plate; if he did that, the someone else would probably hunt him down and beat him paraplegic with a baseball bat. Or he could transfer the bodies from the boot to another location, then deliver the car; it took him less than five seconds to decide that, on the whole, he'd rather be beaten with a baseball bat. Or he could just pull the pin and dump the frigging thing.

It wasn't a difficult decision. When he'd reached it, Shine went inside and shook Laulau awake. The Fijian-Samoan, whose complexion had taken on an unhealthy and rather unPolynesian grey sheen, groaned and sat up, rubbing his bleary eyes.

"Let's go, bro," yelled Shine. "Arse into gear time. I'm going to have a quick shower; do something useful for once in your life and check out the boot on those wheels."

Shine waited till his accomplice had shuffled outside before taking up a position at the kitchen window. It wasn't so much the amount Laulau threw up or the distance it travelled which impressed Shine; it was the fact that the yellow-green gushes continued even after he'd fallen into a dead faint.

They abandoned the Berlina an hour later behind the Remuera golf course in Abbott's Way, then Shine dropped Laulau off at his aunt's house in Mt Wellington. Laulau told his aunt he had food poisoning and went straight to bed.

The Ihaka family retreat was a rough and ready weatherboard pole-house at Tauranga Bay, on the south head of Whangaroa Harbour, about two hours' drive from Cape Reinga. It had three bedrooms and a small kitchen with a worn formica bench and a museum-piece fridge which heaved and rattled like a Sopwith Camel when Ihaka switched on the power. There was a large all-purpose room with a bare wooden floor and an assortment of battered and ill-matched furniture, cast-offs from several clan members' homes; sliding glass doors opened onto an enormous deck which extended to within a girlish stone's throw of high-water mark.

It was a fine, warm, still day. Hellicar stood on the deck and surveyed the half-mile or so of empty, yellow beach. The curtains were drawn in the other beachhouses and the only sound was the soothing rinse of the incoming tide.

"Is it always like this?" she called to Ihaka who was putting food into the fridge. "Not another soul in sight?"

He came out onto the deck and sucked down a lungful of sea air. "Yeah pretty much, except for a couple of weeks at Christmas. Put it this way, I've never seen a Jap with a camera here."

"You have a problem with the Japanese?"

Ihaka shook his head. "I just don't want busloads of the little buggers clogging up my beach. Same goes for German backpackers, Aussies in campervans, or, for that matter, dickheads from Auckland with their caravans and spastic kids."

"Isn't that a tad selfish?" She waved an arm. "I mean, there's not exactly a shortage of space."

He squinted into the sun. "Depends on your point of view," he said. "Some of us need more than others."

Ihaka manhandled a 12-foot aluminium runabout with a two-stroke Seagull engine out of the kitset lock-up shed behind the beachhouse and they carried it down to the sea. They spent the afternoon puttering along the coast and in and out of little bays where Ihaka dived and foraged for shellfish. Hellicar sat in the bow sunning her long legs and wondering how much of Ihaka's catch was edible by normal people's standards.

The sun was losing its warmth and Ihaka was thinking of calling it a day when Hellicar suddenly took off her shorts and T-shirt and slipped over the side in her bra and panties. She swam back and forth parallel to the shore, 100 metres at a time, for twenty minutes and then effortlessly hauled herself back into the boat.

She had a body off a billboard and Ihaka took his time over passing her a towel. She snatched it from him, mimicking his bug-eyed stare.

"You look pretty fit," he said hurriedly. "I suppose you have to be?"

She smiled briefly and sardonically and wrapped the towel around herself. Then she leaned back and studied Ihaka who was sprawled in the stern, fishing rod in one hand and a can of beer in the other, wearing only football shorts.

She said: "What about you — do you work out?"

Ihaka drained the can, crumpled it, resisted — only just — the urge to belch and said, "Shit no."

"You should."

Ihaka got two cans out of the chilly bin and tossed one to her. "What for? I was born fat; my father was fat; my uncles are fat; my grandfather was fat. It's a tribal tradition. You honkies don't understand such things."

Hellicar nodded solemnly, as if acknowledging a wisdom deeper than hers. "I didn't say you were fat. Right now you're just a big guy but if you're not careful, it'll sort of creep up on you. If that chest ever slips," — she clicked her tongue — "you'll be bumping into folks before you're close enough to recognise them. What'd your daddy die of?"

"Heart attack."

"How old was he?"

"Fifty-one."

"Doesn't that tell you something?"

"Yeah, it tells me that only fuckwits believe hard work never killed anyone. You want my opinion, a gym is a place where you pay for the privilege of breathing other people's body odour."

Hellicar raised her eyebrows. "How about jogging?"

"Last time I went for a run, a dog bit me."

She blinked and fought back a giggle. "Really? Where?"

"I was coming down Sandringham Road . . ."

"I meant what part of your anatomy?"

"The backside if you must know." Unconvinced by her straight face, he added: "It wasn't funny — it hurt like buggery. Plus, I couldn't crap normally for about three weeks."

Hellicar's better judgement told her to change the subject but she couldn't help herself: "Why was that?"

"The fucking mongrel took a dirty big piece out of my right cheek; I couldn't sit down so I had to get up on the dunny seat and perch there."

In her mind's eye, Hellicar saw Ihaka squatting on a toilet seat like a sumo wrestler. She bit her lower lip quite hard and said, "Forget I ever raised the subject. You're happy with the way you look, that's fine; what the hell's it got to do with me, right?"

Ihaka waited a minute then said, "I don't suppose the sort of blokes you go for belong to weightwatchers?"

She frowned. "We seem to be at cross-purposes: I was talking about looking after your health."

He nodded. "The conversation's moved on. I'm just asking: What's your type?"

"I don't have a particular type," she said firmly. "You know, it's not like having a preference for a certain brand of toothpaste."

Ihaka was expressionless but his brown eyes gleamed. "Okay, well put it this way: What does the man in your life right now look like?"

"The invisible man," she said with a finality which indicated the subject was closed. "Now turn around."

"Why?"

"Because I'm about to take off my wet things and put on my dry things."

"We're a bit tight on room down this end. How about if I just close my eyes?"

"How about I put this bucket over your head?"

They went in, showered and changed. Ihaka prepared the shellfish, steaming the mussels and pounding the black, rubbery paua tender before frying it with bacon. To Hellicar's surprise, she almost enjoyed it. He barbecued a couple of steaks which they ate out on the deck with a salad and a bottle of red wine.

A little later Hellicar brought out the ghetto blaster she'd found in one of the bedrooms and put on a tape.

She stood with her hands on her hips. "You want to dance?"

Ihaka stood up. "I'm not exactly poetry in motion."

Hellicar shrugged. "So we won't win the steak knives."

The song was a slow country lament. At first Ihaka kept a respectful distance but little by little the gap closed till they were close enough for him to feel her breath warm and ticklish on his neck. She put her head on his chest and began, very softly, to hum the song. At the exact moment that Ihaka realised he'd been unconsciously holding in his stomach, his mobile phone rang.

They stopped dancing and looked at one another.

She said, "Wrong number maybe?"

Ihaka tried to smile but didn't even get close. He went inside, snatched up the phone and snarled incoherently. Almost curtly and certainly without a hint of apology in his Ulster brogue, Finbar McGrail said: "Whatever you're doing Sergeant, stop doing it and get in here."

Ihaka held the phone away from his ear and looked out to the deck where Hellicar stood with her arms folded and head slightly cocked, watching him. He drew a finger across his throat, then said to McGrail: "What's happened?"

"We've just found Leith Grills in the boot of his car, shot twice in the chest at point-blank range. There was another body with him — European male as yet unidentified: about six foot two, forty-odd, a shotgun job; Funke's work, both of them. That's the first thing. The second thing is the cocaine we recovered from the boarding house turned out to be icing sugar. Just before we got there, a man and a woman posing as detectives showed up looking for Funke and talked their way into his room."

Ihaka said flatly: "Ricketts."

"It looks like him from the description; it definitely feels like him."

Ihaka chuckled bitterly. "You've got to give the bastard marks for persistence. You hit his place yet?"

"We're just about to."

"You won't find an aspirin. You won't find him either."

"I share your conviction Sergeant; that's why you're needed."

"Okay. I'll be a few hours, though — I'm up north."

Ihaka ended the call and said quietly, "Cunthooks." He walked out on to the deck and said to Hellicar: "We'll have to finish the dance some other time."

She turned away to look out to sea and murmured, "No time like the future."

Ihaka was right in thinking that Duane Ricketts would have more sense than to hang around waiting for the police to show up. What Ricketts did do, just to keep abreast of developments, was ring his next-door neighbour, the sixty-nine-year-old pensioner Clarrie Scudamore.

It was the first time they'd spoken for almost a year, since the night Ricketts had knocked on his neighbour's front door and asked if he could have a lemon from the abundant crop on the tree in Scudamore's back yard.

Scudamore had eyed him suspiciously: "What for?"

"I'm making someone a gin and tonic and I'm clean out of them."

If Ricketts had been aware that Scudamore, a Seventh Day Adventist, was almost fanatically anti-drink, he would've said something else. Then again, if he'd known that Scudamore was almost certainly the meanest person in Mt Roskill, a suburb where charity begins and ends at home, he wouldn't have bothered to ask; he would've simply vaulted the fence and taken a lemon off the tree.

Without really bothering to conceal the satisfaction it gave him, Scudamore had said, "Grow your own," and shut the door.

When Ricketts rang at about 10 o'clock that Saturday night, Scudamore, his voice hovering uncertainly between curiosity and indignation, demanded to know what on earth was going on over there. At the other end of the line, Ricketts smiled to himself.

"What do you mean?"

"You know perfectly well what I mean; there are police everywhere — they've even got dogs. I think you owe me the courtesy of an explanation."

Ricketts didn't feel he owed Scudamore the courtesy of an explanation or even courtesy for that matter so he hung up in his ear and dialled Bryce Spurdle's number.

Spurdle had his feet up watching television. He stared balefully at the phone on the coffee table when it began to ring; eventually, he decided that seeing everything that could go wrong had already done so, there was no reason not to answer it. He picked it up and said a guarded hello.

"Is that Bryce Spurdle?"

"Yeah."

"This is Duane Ricketts. The name mean anything?"

"Nup."

"I was the last person Dale Varty spoke to."

"I'm happy for you."

"That makes two of us: he told me where he hid that cocaine. I made the mistake of telling Jake Latimer. Does that name ring a bell?"

Spurdle sat up straight. "Loud and fucking clear. That shitbag . . ."

"Yeah, we'll get to him in a minute. The reason for the call is I was wondering if you're still interested in the dope? Because if you are, I can deliver."

"You're full of shit, pal," said Spurdle crisply.

"How's that?"

"You haven't bloody got it; the cops have."

"All the cops've got is a lifetime's supply of icing sugar. You know where the coke was, right? An American guy called Funke got hold of it and brought it back here. He was staying at a boarding house in town; when he went out, I got into his room and did a swap."

"When was this?" asked Spurdle, a note of cautious interest entering his voice.

"Last night."

"What time last night?"

"Early on, about eight."

"How much coke was there?"

"Nine and a half kilos in nineteen bags. Funke must've had one with him."

There was a long silence.

"Well?" said Ricketts eventually.

Spurdle grunted noncommittally.

"As a matter of interest, why'd you think the cops had it?" asked Ricketts.

"Because Funke was round here last night giving me the same sales pitch. The cops showed up and blew him away, right in front of us. Fucking choice, eh? My wife's a nervous wreck."

It was all the same to Ricketts whether Funke was in a hole or behind bars as long as he was out of circulation. "So what about it — are you interested?"

"Depends on the price, doesn't it?" said Spurdle. "It's going down by the hour; the heats on big-time."

Ricketts suggested a round million; Spurdle said piss off, there was no way in the fucking world he'd go over a hundred grand. Ricketts said okay, see you later and Spurdle back-tracked, saying hang on a minute, have you got a fucking plane to catch too? Eventually, they reached agreement in principle on $450,000, Spurdle saying he wanted to sleep on it, think about whether he really wanted to go through with the deal. You mean to check me out, thought Ricketts. After they'd arranged to talk again in the morning, Ricketts tossed in the sweetener: he told Spurdle where he could find Latimer.

Ricketts hung up and walked through to the living room of the house in Huapai owned by the Dutch screen printer who was sitting cross-legged on the floor rolling a joint.

Ricketts watched him for a few seconds: "Do you ever worry about what that stuff's doing to you?" he asked.

The Dutchman stroked his long beard and thought about it. "Not for long," he said eventually. "I can never remember what I'm meant to be worrying about."

24

Jake Latimer's friend Lenny had led a fairly pointless existence at the taxpayer's expense on two hectares just outside Whangarei since the day he'd stooped to pick up a ballpoint pen, with which he'd been making inane, semi-literate additions to a management memo on the staff noticeboard, and put his back out. The resultant discomfort — a conveniently imprecise measure of suffering — was his entry visa to the never-never land of accident compensation where time crawled by like a Moscow bread queue and with each month that passed, it got harder to find reasons for getting out of bed in the morning.

Not long after 9 o'clock on Sunday morning, Latimer rode his second-hand Harley Davidson 1200 Sportster down the drive from Lenny's weatherboard bungalow to the main road. He paused when he reached the road, put on his helmet, gave the machine a couple of wasteful but mildly arousing revs, then swung it to the left and roared off down Highway 14 towards Maungatapere. He didn't notice the white Toyota van parked on the verge a little way back up the road. Even if Latimer had've noticed the van, he wouldn't have given it a second glance; as far as he was concerned, the whole point of having a Harley was that people — especially the sort of dildos who drove Toyota vans — looked at you, not the other way round.

The man sitting behind the wheel of the Toyota van was called Rowan Mayweed and no one had ever accused him of being a dildo, at least not to his face which was red and lumpy with mean eyes and a nose you could clear scrub with. For a second or two he thought about going after Latimer before deciding that by the time he got rolling, the prick would be halfway to Dargaville. He'll be back, Mayweed told himself; he lit his tenth cigarette of the morning and settled down to wait.

Mayweed was forty-seven years old and weighed 125 kilograms. He owned a takeaway bar in Whangarei which did a reasonable burger and excellent fish and chips; the fish was always snapper or tarakihi and the chips were made on the premises from garden-fresh potatoes by a refugee from East Timor who found that peeling potatoes and cutting them into chips took just enough concentration to keep her mind off things she preferred not to think about. For all Mayweed cared, the takeaway bar could've served deep-fried penguin. He left his staff to run it as they saw fit; the only reason he'd bought the business in the first place was to enable him to launder money generated by his marijuana plantation in the Tangihua forest.

Mayweed was spending Sunday morning sitting in his van on the side of the

Dargaville road because his old acquaintance Bryce Spurdle was paying him to. They went back to the early seventies when Mayweed had been a bouncer at an Auckland night spot where Spurdle staged rock concerts. The law of supply and demand had brought them together: whenever possible, Spurdle avoided doing his own dirty work; Mayweed, on the other hand, was only too happy to do his own and, for the right price, anyone else's.

Mayweed heard Latimer returning from his fifty-minute spin before he saw him. He started the van and drove off the verge onto the road as the Harley Davidson zoomed over the hump 100 metres away and decelerated for the turn into Lenny's drive. Mayweed indicated that he was turning into the driveway as well; observing New Zealand's quirky rule of the road which gives right of way to the person making a right turn, he slowed to a halt to let Latimer go first.

As Latimer turned into the drive, Mayweed mashed his foot down on the accelerator. The van catapulted forward and rammed into the back of the motorbike. Latimer went over the handlebars like a human cannonball, did a ragged somersault, landed on the point of his right shoulder and slid up the gravel drive on his front. The Harley skidded away on its side in a shower of sparks, flipped and slammed into a tree, rupturing the fuel tank. There was a dull, thumping explosion and a column of bright orange flame leapt several metres into the air before dying down to little pockets of fire which licked at the charred and twisted metal.

Mayweed got out of the van and strolled up the drive towards Latimer who was staggering to his feet. His right arm hung uselessly and crimson grazes glistened through his torn leathers. Mayweed waited till Latimer had removed his helmet then said, "Bryce Spurdle says gidday," and punched him very hard in the mouth. Latimer fell over and Mayweed, who'd come prepared in heavy work boots, kicked whichever part of his anatomy Latimer was unable to shield with his functioning arm. After a dozen or so deliberate and percussive boots, Mayweed decided that if he kept it up for much longer, he'd either kill Latimer — and he certainly wasn't being paid enough to do that — or have a heart attack. He stopped kicking and bent over with his hands on his knees, gulping in air.

When Mayweed had got his breath back, he squatted on his haunches and said, "All right twat-features, where's the money?"

Latimer's lips fluttered but all that emerged were a few little blood bubbles.

"The money you rooked Spurdle out of," prompted Mayweed. "Have you got it on you or is it up there in the house?"

Latimer groaned pitiably; unfortunately, the only person who could hear him was Mayweed and he hadn't felt a flicker of pity towards anyone but himself since his voice broke.

Latimer's groans became an inaudible whisper. Mayweed hunched down and cocked an ear. "Say again?"

"I spent it," croaked Latimer. "On the bike."

Mayweed looked over his shoulder at the smouldering wreck and said, "Oh fuck."

Duane Ricketts got up late and went for a run. As often happens, the combination of fresh air and exercise cleared the head and sharpened the thought processes; by the time he got back to the German screen printer's house, having covered seven mostly flat kilometres in thirty-seven minutes, he'd worked out what he had to do.

He showered, dressed and poached some eggs for himself and his host. At midday, as arranged, he rang a service station in Albany. Spurdle answered the phone.

"So how'd I scrub up?" asked Ricketts.

"Eh?"

"That's what you've been doing, isn't it — checking up on me?"

"I made a couple of calls," admitted Spurdle. "I hear your name's getting some airplay down at Central; sounds like you're pulling a bit of heat."

"Yeah, I heard the same thing," said Ricketts nonchalantly. "All the more reason to move quick. I take it we have a deal?"

"Looks like it. What've you got in mind?"

"The sooner the better as far as I'm concerned — like tonight."

"That's as good a time as any, I suppose. Where?"

Here we go, thought Ricketts. "What about Cornwall Park?"

"No way," said Spurdle. "It's too big and too dark — a recipe for a fuck-up. Besides, you wouldn't want to be wandering around in there in the middle of the night, would you? It'd be wall-to-wall perverts — sheep shaggers, you name it; the place'd be crawling with them."

"You got a better idea?"

"What about a movie theatre?"

"Oh you want an audience, do you?" said Ricketts sarcastically. "I thought the idea with drug deals was to keep them private. Shit, if you do it at the movies, someone gets a look at you when you buy your ticket, people notice you when you get up and walk out in the middle of the film. It's asking for trouble."

They traded ideas for a few minutes; Spurdle's didn't get any better and Ricketts' were designed to be rejected. When he sensed that Spurdle had run out of suggestions and patience, he said: "Well, what about Westhaven Marina? Sunday night. If we leave it late enough, the place'll be deserted but it's not like you're in the middle of nowhere. You got easy access; we can be in and out in a couple of minutes."

Spurdle went for it.

"What time do you want to do it?" asked Ricketts. "Midnight, 1 o'clock, later than that?"

"One o'clock'll do. How will I know you?"

"If the theory's right, we'll be the only people there, won't we? On that subject, let's be sure we understand each other: this do is by invitation only and the only people with invites are you and me, right?"

"Suits me."

"I'll be driving an orange Toyota Corolla."

"I'll bring the Merc — it's a 360, dark green."

"Yeah, why not? Tell the world crime does pay."

Next Ricketts rang an old friend from his cricketing days who'd since made himself rich by writing stunningly simple-minded advertising jingles which burrowed into the subconscious like borer. Among the rewards he had to show for this curious knack was a two million-dollar, three-storey apartment in Shelly Beach Road, Herne Bay, overlooking Westhaven Marina.

When the jingle wizard answered the phone, Ricketts offered him and his wife an all-expenses paid night at the Hotel du Vin.

"I don't think so, Ricketts. You wouldn't make an offer like that unless there was a truly evil catch."

"There's no catch," said Ricketts earnestly. "Only thing is, it's got to be tonight."

"That's it? Somehow I don't believe you, Ricketts; I can recognise a bribe when it's dangled in front of me. Just tell me what it is you're up to so I can marvel at your bare-faced cheek for a moment or two before I tell you to stick the Hotel du Vin up your pipe."

"Trust me; I used to be a policeman. You might as well leave us a key, though, just in case."

In the following ten minutes Ricketts used every trick in the book, except telling the truth, to talk the advertising man round. In the end and despite his misgivings, the advertising man gave in, deciding — without being entirely sure why — that he wanted to stay on side with Ricketts.

When he got off the phone, Ricketts went through to his kitchen where the Dutch screen printer was washing the breakfast dishes.

"Go easy on the weed today, eh?"

The screen printer looked blankly at Ricketts through his granny glasses and waited for an explanation.

"I might get you to give me a hand tonight — nothing too demanding but I wouldn't want you to fall asleep on me."

The Dutchman shrugged and looked at his watch. "Sure. But that still leaves the afternoon."

Ricketts showed his teeth in a grin which the screen printer knew from experience and distrusted deeply: "Did I forget to mention that we're having a visitor? There's a policeman I want you to invite out here for afternoon tea."

At that moment the policeman in question, Detective Sergeant Tito Ihaka, was, for the second time in three days, hanging around in the international terminal at Auckland Airport waiting for C. C. Hellicar.

When she'd completed check-in for her flight to Los Angeles, Hellicar walked over to him. She produced a sheet of notepaper from her handbag and gave it to him.

"That's my daddy's address and phone number in Monroe, Georgia," she said. "You ever fixing to come to the States, doesn't matter what part, you get in touch with him, okay? He'll pass the message on. I figure the likelihood of me being sent down here again is next to zero but" — she hunched her shoulders — "I'm due a right smart amount of vacation and they've got to let me take some sooner or later." She tilted her head and looked at him, her pale eyes shining. "How about it, Tito — you being able to see the future and all: Do we ever get to finish that dance?"

Ihaka closed his eyes trance-like for a few seconds then nodded: "Yep — what's more, we walk away with the steak knives."

The smiles they exchanged were affectionate, knowing, wistful and perhaps also a little relieved.

"Okay," she said briskly. "We've both got to go. Give me some southern sugar and be on your way."

They kissed, an awkward, in between sort of kiss, half on the cheek, half on the lips. It was the kiss of a man and a woman who'd felt something happen between them, a moment electric with possibilities, but who recognised that the moment had passed and it was pointless to pretend otherwise.

She squeezed his hand. "Go carefully now, you hear?"

"You too, Candice Clara."

Ihaka turned and walked out of the terminal, as certain as he was of anything the he'd never set eyes on C. C. Hellicar again.

25

Bearing bad tidings is a thankless task, no matter how you go about it.

Members of the 'cruel-to-be-kind' brigade believe in getting straight to the point and can be recommending a crematorium before the next of kin is sitting comfortably. Others prefer to break it gently and sidle up to the unwelcome news via the weather, the soaps and André Agassi's new haircut.

Rowan Mayweed tried a middle way when he rang Bryce Spurdle on Sunday afternoon — the old "I've got good news and bad news" approach. It didn't get him very far.

"Fucking what?" barked Spurdle. "Rowan, I don't want to hear this shit. I feel like Rose Kennedy I've had that much fucking bad news lately; I'm up to here with it. All I wanted to hear from you is that you've done the business; instead, I get this fuckhead good news, bad news routine." He paused and released a deep, angry sigh. "All right, let's have it," he continued in a long-suffering voice, dragging out the words. "Give us the bad news first."

Mayweed, who was calling from his split-level brick house at Whangarei Heads, squirmed in his ezy-chair thinking, fucking Bryce, he's going to make a meal of this.

"I'll tell it to you as it happened," said Mayweed, calculating that if he arranged the facts in chronological order, there was a slim chance that Spurdle would understand and be appeased. "Latimer went out for a burn on his motorbike this morning. When he got back, I followed him into the driveway and shunted him right up the arse. He went for a row of shitcans; the bike hit a tree and boom, up in flames."

Spurdle chuckled, a low, grimly satisfied noise from deep in his throat. Mayweed was encouraged.

"He wasn't looking too flash by this stage, your little mate; he's got a busted arm for sure and I reckon they'll be digging gravel out of him for a week. Before he'd worked out which way was up, I decked him, then slippered the crap out of him. Tell you what mate, you got your money's worth; I'd lay odds the bastard's in plaster from his gob to his knob."

"Well, Rowan, that all sounds tickety-boo," said Spurdle with transparently false good humour. "Pity you have to spoil it. So what's the bad news?"

"The bad news is he's already spent your money."

"Spent it?" screeched Spurdle. "How the cunting hell does a turd like that blow twelve and a half grand in a couple of days?"

"He bought the bike," said Mayweed wearily.

"He bought the bike," repeated Spurdle in a voice filled with wonder. "Would that happen to be the same bike you shunted into a tree and blew to shit?"

"Yeah, the same fucking bike. I dragged the prick up to the house and made him show me the paperwork. He got it last Friday from a place in New North Road, specialises in second-hand Harleys. Cost him thirteen grand."

After that, things went rapidly downhill. Spurdle said you'd have to be thick as pigshit. Christ, a little arsewipe like Latimer with a Harley-Davidson, it was fucking obvious what he'd done with the money; Mayweed retorted that it was bloody easy to be wise after the event and if that was the thanks he got for putting himself out to do a bloke a favour, next time he wouldn't bother; Spurdle came back with favour my fuzzy arse, it was business and Mayweed hadn't kept his side of the bargain so if he thought he was going to get paid, he better think again and what's more . . . it was around about there that Mayweed told him to go fuck himself and hung up.

After he'd put down the receiver, Spurdle looked at himself in the mirror behind the bar and said, "Tithead."

The bike going up in smoke wasn't such a big deal. He knew a guy in the insurance game who'd dummy up a false claim for a few hundred bucks; all he needed to do was get a tow truck operator from Whangarei to pick up what was left of the bloody thing and talk the bloke in the bike shop into giving him a copy of the receipt. There wasn't any point in getting shitty with Mayweed but you just can't help yourself sometimes, can you? No point in ringing him back either: when Rowan gets that beak of his out of joint, it stays that way for a fortnight.

And a fortnight was no good to Spurdle; he needed Mayweed that night.

Half an hour later Spurdle was still sitting at the bar in his den cursing his quick temper and racking his brains trying to think of someone who could step into Mayweed's shoes when his wife walked into the room.

It wasn't the first time Spurdle had seen Jody look ropey — exhausted or ill or hung over or even, on a couple of memorable occasions, all three — but he'd never seen her in this state. Her face was drawn and blotchy and her unwashed hair hung in oily tangles; her shoulders sagged, her hands plucked at the belt of her white towelling robe and her red-rimmed eyes were darting around like a frightened bird's.

"Hi," she said in a dull voice. "I heard you on the phone a while ago, shouting. Anything wrong?"

"Shit, I didn't wake you up, did I?"

She shook her head and flopped down on a sofa. "I've been awake for ages." She yawned nervously and took a deep breath, steeling herself: "I owe you an explanation. You must be wondering what the hell that was all about the other night with the cop."

Spurdle shrugged. "Oh well . . ."

"I made a really, really terrible mistake," said Jody, her voice quavering on the edge of tears.

He joined her on the sofa. "Hon, this'll keep. Why not leave it till you're feeling better, eh?"

Her lower lip wobbled and her breathing became jerky. "I want to get it off my chest." She looked away, sniffing. "What he was talking about, Ihaka, was me going to the police because I thought you're hired Leith Grills to kill me."

Jesus, thought Spurdle, it's all got too much for the poor little bitch. The men in white coats will be here any minute; I mean, look at her, opening and closing her trap like a goldfish and eyeballing me as if I've sprouted tusks.

"Did you hear what I said, Bryce?"

He patted her hand. "Well, I heard you say something sweetie . . ."

"I picked up the phone one day when you were talking to Grills. The guy totally freaked me out anyway and when you said you'd changed your mind and wanted him to get onto the wife . . . I just got it into my head that's what you meant."

"I'm missing something here," he said warily. "No matter how much Grills gave you the creeps or what you heard me say to him, I don't see how you got from there to the idea I was . . . up to something like that. Didn't you ever just sit down and ask yourself why? Why would I want to do it?"

She sobbed and buried her face in her hands. "I thought you must've found out I was having an affair."

He frowned at his wife's bobbing head: "An affair? Who with?"

"A guy called Troy Goatley," she said in a strangled voice.

Spurdle went over to the bar, opened a beer and poured a little cognac into a liqueur glass. "Who's he?"

"I met him at the gym in Takapuna — he runs the weights room."

"How long have you and him been . . ."

"Since late last year. It's finished, I broke it off."

Spurdle drank his beer and idly wondered how Jody would react if he told her that the private detective who'd been keeping an eye on her on and off since before they were even married had reported the affair several months ago; or that in the safe under the floorboards in the wine cellar there was a large manila envelope containing audiotaped and photographic evidence of her infidelity; or that some nights when she went to bed early, he'd get the envelope out and . . . Yes well, he said to himself, I think it's safe to assume she'd react negatively; extremely fucking negatively; so fucking negatively that he might go into the kitchen tomorrow morning and find the cat having his dick for breakfast.

He went back to the sofa, gave her the drink, and draped a protective arm around her shoulders. "Look baby, we've been through a fair bit in the last few days. As far as I'm concerned, whatever's happened has happened — it's over and done with. I think we ought to just get on with life, you know, start again with a clean slate. What do you say?"

She put her face against his chest and snuffled wetly on his shirt; he rested his chin on the top of her head and patted her back, making soothing noises. They stayed like that until Jody had cried herself out which took a few minutes. Well before the tears dried up, her husband's eyes opened wide and then narrowed to a thoughtful squint. He was having an idea.

At nine o'clock that night Jody, more like her old self, and Bryce were curled up on the sofa in the TV room watching a movie; on the low table in front of them were the remnants of a home-delivered pizza and an almost empty bottle of wine. When the ads came on, Spurdle disengaged his arm, looked at his watch and said by the way, he had to pop out for a while later on.

Jody's head swivelled: "What for?"

He winked at her: "To see a man about a dog."

"No, come on Bryce," she began before noticing his foxy, guarded expression. "It's those drugs again, right?"

He nodded.

"Why don't you just flag it, babe? I mean, God, are they really worth all the agro?"

Spurdle leaned towards her, his face set and serious. "I've been waiting more than ten years to get my hands on this stuff. Remember I told you how Varty brought it over from Australia then did the dirty on me? Ever since then, it's been there at the back of my mind, nagging away at me, but there wasn't a bloody thing I could do about it; only Varty knew where it was and he was in the clink in Thailand." His voice got harsh. "Well now it's out there, up for grabs. Each time I get close, there's some sort of last minute fuck-up; each time that happens; it makes me more determined that if any bastard's going to end up with it, it's going to be me."

"Okay, okay," she said, taken aback by his intensity. "I didn't realise it meant that much to you. Who's this guy you're meeting?"

"Ricketts is his name; he was in that Thai jail with Varty."

"Can you trust him?"

He sniggered. "Babe, this is dope — you can't trust anyone."

"Will it be dangerous?"

Spurdle shrugged. "No reason it should be. I ran a check on this guy and he doesn't sound like he's a hard man — he's small-time, a bit of an amateur. But you never know: as I said, it's the dope business . . . and yeah, I would feel better if I had someone with me, preferably someone built like a brick shithouse. Unfortunately, poor old Leith can't make it."

Jody swallowed hard. "There must be someone else."

"I had a guy in Whangarei in mind — that's who I was talking to this afternoon." He smiled wanly. "The negotiations broke down."

"Bryce, I'm sorry but I've got to say, I think it's just crazy for you to go by yourself . . ."

"Well, that's fine honey but this isn't a lot of people's idea of fun. Besides, you're talking about a guy who looks the part and can handle himself." Then, tentatively: "I can only think of one possibility and that's pretty bloody remote."

"Who's that?"

"Goatley."

Jody stared at him, open-mouthed.

"You were saying he runs the weights room; I imagine he'd be a pretty well-built sort of a bloke?"

She nodded slowly. "Well, he's big and, you know, seriously into that scene."

"What do you reckon — think you could talk him into it?"

Jody Spurdle held her husband's gaze for the first time that day: "I think so."

At 12.50 a.m., Monday, Spurdle drove his dark-green Mercedes 360 down Curran Street, under the harbour bridge and into the Westhaven boat marina. He cruised very slowly past the yacht club buildings down to the parking area on the end of the seawall. To his left, Waitemata Harbour shifted and rustled like a great, dark duvet over a restless sleeper; to his right, row upon row of yachts and launches sat in their moorings like ducks, their lines flapping and creaking in the breeze. There were no cars and no lights showing in any of the buildings. The carpark was slick from recent rain and the low, starless sky threatened more before the night was much older. Spurdle turned and circled back to the foot of the harbour bridge; satisfied by what he'd seen and hadn't seen on the slow tour, he drove back to the far end of the seawall and turned off the engine.

A couple of minutes passed. Troy Goatley, who lay cramped and foetal on the back seat, deferentially broke the silence: "Jody — Mrs Spurdle — wasn't too specific about exactly what it is you want me to do."

"Just look mean," said Spurdle staring straight ahead. "And if I tell you to do something, don't ask questions, just do it, all right?" Headlights came around the harbour's edge and up past the yacht clubs. "Here he is. Stay put until I give you the word."

Spurdle got out of the car, leaving the door open. He zipped his brown leather jacket up to the throat and hunched his shoulders against the chill. The Toyota stopped a few metres away; the lights and engine were switched off. Ricketts, wearing a windcheater and jeans, got out of the car.

He said, "Yo ho ho and a bag of cocaine."

Spurdle, who didn't seem to think it was the time or place for levity, was curt: "Let's see it."

Ricketts reached into his car and brought out a sports bag. He put it on the ground, unzipped it, and held up a plastic bag of white powder for Spurdle's inspection.

"Show me yours," said Ricketts.

Spurdle smiled unpleasantly and called over his shoulder: "Troy, bring out that suitcase, would you?"

The back door of the Mercedes opened and Goatley extricated himself. He was a head taller than Ricketts; pectorals like hubcaps swelled out of the low-cut singlet he wore under an unbuttoned denim jacket and his jeans were stretched taut over slab-like thighs. Moving with a tight-buttocked body-builder's strut, he went and stood, glowering, beside Spurdle.

"This is Troy," said Spurdle. "He can benchpress 170 kilos."

Ricketts raised his eyebrows. "Who counts for him? This is out of order, Spurdle. It was meant to be just you and me, remember?"

Spurdle's unpleasant smile grew wider. "I'm scared of the dark. Troy, search him and the car."

Goatley walked across and glared down at Ricketts who shrugged and held out his arms. Goatley patted him down and then searched the car, boot and interior. He backed out of the car dangling nothing but a pair of binoculars.

"Nothing much in here except these, Mr Spurdle."

"Okay. Bring me the bag."

Goatley dumped the binoculars on the driver's seat and took the sports bag to Spurdle; Spurdle produced a Swiss army knife from the pocket of his leather jacket, slit open one of the plastic bags and dabbed some white powder on his tongue.

He winked at Goatley: "The real thing as they say."

He zipped up the bag and put it in his car. "You know Ricketts," he said putting on a reflective air, "it seems to me there's something not quite right about all this. I mean, a man would have to be a major dipstick to pay 450 grand for something that belongs to him, don't you reckon?"

Ricketts shook his head disinterestedly. "Forget it Spurdle. I don't give a shit about the history of it. I'm selling, you're buying, we agreed a price. End of story."

Spurdle's smirk faded: "Yeah, end of story's right." He knelt, flipped open the suitcase and began taking out brick-sized wads of bank notes which he tossed one by one to Ricketts. "How many's that — six? That's over twenty grand; take it and be fucking grateful. Now piss off before I change my mind and get Troy to chuck you in the tide without a cent."

Ricketts dropped the money on the driver's seat of his car and picked up the binoculars. He said 'catch' and lobbed them to Spurdle.

"See that place up there with all its lights on?" He pointed across the rows of boats to the cliff overlooking the approach to the harbour bridge and the marine. "Take a close look."

Instantly suspicious, Spurdle's eyes flicked from Ricketts to the lit-up building and back to Ricketts. Then he used the binoculars. The building was a three-storey apartment which blazed with light against the dark background. A wild, piratical figure stood on the balcony in front of the huge top floor window. He had a bushy, nipple-length beard and wore John Lennon spectacles, a camouflage jacket and a red bandana on his head. He looked to Spurdle like one of those psycho gun-nuts, the sort who subscribe to *Soldier of Fortune* magazine and either join the French Foreign Legion or go down to the local shopping centre and shoot anyone with ginger hair and freckles. The fact that he was examining Spurdle through telescopic sights attached to a rifle contributed powerfully to this impression.

Spurdle lowered the binoculars, noticing that Ricketts had switched on his headlights, illuminating him and Goatley in the beam.

"There's a guy up there with a gun," he said as if uncertain whether to believe the evidence of his own eyes.

Ricketts nodded. "Yep, a friend of mine. He's a professional hunter," he added helpfully. "He's got a night-vision scope and in case you're wondering about the range of that rifle, he was telling me before he could pick off a windsurfer coming round North Head from up there. He could drop you and that overgrown mongol like sacks of shit." He paused to let the threat sink in. "You're going to cough up Spurdle, to the dollar. You can hand it over or I guess I'll just have to step over your corpse and help myself. Up to you."

Goatley took the binoculars from Spurdle and had a look for himself. He said, "Mr Spurdle, maybe you should . . ."

"Shut up and get in the car," snapped Spurdle.

Goatley put the binoculars on the ground and got into the car. Ricketts told Spurdle to slide the suitcase over to him. He quickly checked the contents then gave Spurdle a pleasant nod: "Let's do this again some time."

Spurdle got into the Mercedes and started the engine. As he pulled away, he lowered the window. "You think you're fucking smart, don't you?" he said, his mouth twisting with pique. "Just remember this, little man — it's not over till I say so."

He nudged the accelerator and the Mercedes surged forward, hissing across the wet tarmac. Ricketts watched him go and said softly, "Dale Varty sends his best."

Coming out of Westhaven up the hill into Shelly Beach Road, Spurdle found his way blocked by three police cars parked across the road in a U formation. Before he could reverse, a fourth unmarked car pulled away from the kerb and stopped right behind him. Detective Sergeant Tito Ihaka got out of it as policemen converged on the Mercedes from both sides of the road.

Ihaka looked in the driver's window and said cheerfully, "What are you doing out and about at this time of night, Mr Spurdle? You should be home, tucked up in bed with that spunky little wife of yours."

When the police found the cocaine and Ihaka told Spurdle and Goatley they'd have to come down to Central and play twenty questions, Spurdle exploded saying it was a set-up, the dope wasn't his, it belonged to this cunt Ricketts who'd still be down in the marina, he was the one they wanted. Ihaka smiled enigmatically, shepherded him into the back seat of a police car, and climbed in beside him.

As the car moved away, Ihaka turned to Spurdle and flashed a grin of pure, cold malice. "I'll let you into a little secret, snotball," he said. "Ricketts is one of us."

26

Fingerprints taken from the unknown dead man, shoe-horned along with the also dead Leith Grills into the boot of the latter's car, matched those of Clive Anthony Nigel Balfour who in August 1976 had been convicted of robbery with violence. The then twenty year old's crime spree had begun on a Sunday evening at the White Lady pie cart in Newmarket, taken in a couple of service stations, a takeaway bar and a dairy, and culminated the following Thursday afternoon in the Royal Oak branch of the Auckland Savings Bank.

Balfour's modus operandi involved a stocking mask, a line of banter which, while glib, was nonetheless appreciated by his victims who took it as a sign that he didn't really want to shoot them and wouldn't do so unless he absolutely had to, and an imitation Colt .45 Peacemaker which his grandfather had given him for his eleventh birthday. Clive Balfour senior, a prosperous car dealer, had bought it at the Neiman Marcus department store in Dallas and it was about as realistic as toy guns get: 700 grams of die-cast steel-zinc alloy. However, it wasn't realistic enough to fool a firearms buff like Roy Codd who happened to be in the bank when Balfour entered wearing his stocking mask, brandishing his toy gun and telling the bank staff that if they didn't hand over a great deal of money, he'd have to come back next week.

Codd detached himself from the queue and confronted Balfour: "That's not a real gun," he said in a very loud voice.

Balfour looked puzzled and twisted the toy gun in his hand, examining it from several angles. "Are you sure?" he said dubiously.

"I've been a gun collector for twenty years," sneered Codd. "I know a fake when I see it."

Balfour shrugged. "Okay, let's see."

He placed the muzzle against the prominent cleft in Codd's chin and thumbed back the hammer; as sure of himself as he was, Codd couldn't help flinching and clamping his eyes shut. Balfour flipped the gun in the air, caught it by the barrel and chopped the butt down on Codd's receding hairline. The firearms buff folded up like a deckchair, rivulets of blood streaming from his split scalp to form intricate patterns on his face. Balfour looked around and tersely enquired if anyone else wanted to make fun of his gun.

That morning Balfour had held up a dairy in Remuera. Although he'd worn the stocking mask, the owner of the dairy had recognised him which wasn't really surprising seeing the Balfour family home was just around the corner and young Clive had been coming into the shop at least once a week for a decade, buying soft drinks and frozen buzz bars in summer and hot pies in winter and shoplifting girlie magazines all year round. The dairy owner had long since tumbled to the shoplifting but turned a blind eye. He did so partly because the Balfours were rich, important and good customers and partly because the Balfour kid was different: weird, disturbed, call it what you like, the guy was a loose unit. In fact, if the stories were anything to go by, the wrong side of Clive Balfour was one of the more dangerous parts of town. Better a few copies of *Men Only* and *Playboy* taking a walk, felt the dairy owner, than a Molotov cocktail through the shop window or getting home to find Maxi the Scottish Terrier nailed to the front door.

The disturbing stories which circulated about Clive Balfour dated back to his expulsion a few years earlier from Prince Albert College, the posh private school for boys in Meadowbank. He'd set fire to a prefabricated office used by a biology teacher with a reputation for being swift to send for the cane and extremely methodical when it arrived. The teacher wasn't in his office at the time but a dozen or so cartons containing the fruits of two years' research towards a doctorate were. Balfour's arson earned him a suspension; the headmaster choosing to believe his excuse that it was a practical joke which had got out of hand even though the facts cried out for a less charitable interpretation. Cynics suggested that Grandfather Balfour's generous donation to the college building fund was coincidental only in the sense of timing.

The incident which caused his expulsion took place a few months later during the college's annual cadet training week when the boys dressed up in heavy black boots and khaki serge uniforms, which chafed like sandpaper, and spent the hottest three or four hours of the day drilling on the parade ground. During a lull in the square-bashing, Corporal Balfour and his platoon were sent to the firing range to waste ammunition and be bawled at by a firearms instructor from the Papakura Military Camp.

Eventually, Balfour grew tired of the abuse; he pointed his loaded .22 rifle at the instructor and told him that if he didn't shut up, he'd shoot him; when the instructor shut up, Balfour told him that if he didn't apologise to the whole platoon, he'd shoot him; when the instructor apologised, Balfour told him that if he didn't strip naked and crawl up the drive, through the school gates and all the way back to Papakura, he'd shoot him. The instructor stripped off and started crawling; it was never fully established whether Balfour had taken into account the fact that, en route to the school gates, the instructor would crawl past two matrons' flats, the chapel, the staff common room and the playing fields where 600 boys were being trained for the last war.

Armed robbery was rather more serious than shoplifting so the dairy-owner rang the police who were waiting for Balfour when he returned to his parents' house after the bank job. He was tried and convicted. Before sentencing, the magistrate called for a psychiatric evaluation which duly pronounced Clive

Balfour schizophrenic. He was thereupon bunged into Kingseat Hospital and largely forgotten about.

On Sunday afternoon Balfour's parents were tracked down to their retirement home at Algies Bay; that evening they drove to Auckland to identify the corpse. Not that there was much doubt about it, especially after Balfour's Honda Civic had been found parked behind the church hall, two blocks from Manacle Grange.

Detective Finbar McGrail was keen to trace Balfour's route from Kingseat Hospital to the boot of Grills' Holden Berlina. Balfour's parents told him that Clive had responded to treatment and, after leaving hospital in mid-1979, had worked for a couple of years on a South Island high country farm. He'd suffered some sort of relapse and had to come back to Auckland; and the end of 1983 he'd gone overseas, working firstly on a cattle station in Australia's Northern Territory and then on ranches in Zimbabwe and Kenya. He'd returned to Auckland in 1992 and bought a cottage in Parnell and a farmlet in Clevedon with money left to him by his grandfather; since then he'd divided his time, as the glossy magazines say, between the two properties.

His parents admitted that, living up at Algies Bay as they did, they hadn't seen a lot of him and knew next to nothing about the company he kept, not that he'd ever kept much; Balfour, it seemed, had always been a loner and living on large, isolated farming properties had made him even more solitary. As far as they were aware, he hadn't been in trouble with the law since 1976, he wasn't a drug-user, and had no connection with Manacle Grange.

McGrail didn't for a moment doubt that, by their lights, Mr and Mrs Balfour had been caring parents to their only child; he also suspected that, deep down, they'd always feared he'd come to a sad or bad end. If that was so, he reflected lugubriously, Clive Balfour had died up to his parents' expectations.

Fleur Wolfgramm had testified that Balfour had been after Varty's cocaine; the question was: How had he known where to look? McGrail hoped to find the answer in Balfour's Parnell cottage.

The police search team arrived at the two-bedroom cottage in Bath Street at 2.15 on Monday afternoon. It was sparsely furnished, almost monkish, and spotlessly clean.

"It's odd this," mused McGrail to Senior Sergeant Ted Worsp, a veteran cop who'd been added to the investigation because he'd arrested Balfour in 1976 and was therefore assumed to possess some insight into the dead man; thus far he'd kept it to himself. "This could be a motel; it doesn't tell you a thing about the man. People who live on their own usually go the other way — they go overboard putting their personal stamp on the place."

A few minutes later Worsp was in the guest bedroom which contained a bed and a mattress, an empty wardrobe, an empty chest of drawers and the cheap rug on which he was standing.

"Fucking waste of time, this," he grumbled to Constable Johan Van Roon. "Doesn't look like he even lived here. What about the place out at Clevedon?"

Van Roon shook his head. "It's just a hut apparently. They found sweet FA there."

The floorboards creaked beneath Worsp as he turned to leave the room. Given his considerable weight, this in itself wasn't unusual but the creak was loud enough to make him lurch backwards. As he did so, he felt the floor sag alarmingly.

"Bloody hell, this floor's a bit dodgy," said Worsp. "Watch this."

Worsp bent at the knees and heaved his bulk a couple of centimetres off the ground. When he came down, there was a sharp, splintering crack and the floor gave way; Worsp continued to travel south, plunging straight through the floorboards and disappearing from view. It transpired that he'd conducted his little demonstration on the trapdoor to a cellar which Balfour obviously found more congenial for everyday living than the cottage's above-ground rooms. The cellar had a metal-framed camp-bed and sleeping bag, an old armchair, a small table and a chair, a mini-fridge filled with bottles of Fanta and tubes of luncheon sausage, piles of newspapers and periodicals ranging from the learned to the juvenile, and a bookcase. Among the authors represented on its shelves were L. Ron Hubbard, Erich von Daniken, Janet Frame, William Burroughs, James Ellroy, Roald Dahl, Aleister Crowley, Laurens van der Post and Barry Crump.

On the table was a scrapbook containing newspaper articles about the deaths of Al Grills and Bart Clegg and twelve hardback A4 notebooks filled with spidery, illegible scrawl. Sitting on top of the bookcase was a champagne flute which, to the teetotal McGrails' inexpert eye, looked very much like the one Clegg had been drinking from just before someone jammed him under the seat in his spa pool and left him to simmer.

Two days later, Wednesday, 27 April, Rayleen Crouch returned to her Grey Lynn villa after a hard day's social work to find McGrail and Detective Sergeant Tito Ihaka waiting for her. McGrail introduced himself and said that if she had a few minutes, there were a couple of loose ends he'd like to tie up; she said that was the best thing to do with loose ends and invited them in for a cup of tea.

While she made the tea, Ihaka leaned against the wall looking mildly curious; McGrail sat at the table in the kitchen cum dining room and did the talking.

"Ms Crouch, do you know a man named Clive Balfour?"

She screwed up her face. "Rings a bell . . ."

"Balfour suffered from a psychiatric disorder; he was in Kingseat during the late seventies and had ongoing counselling after his release. I saw your name on a document and got the impression that he'd been — I'm not sure what the term is in your field — a patient? Of yours."

"A client — we call them clients. Yes, I remember him now. God, it seems like a lifetime ago; that's social work for you — time flies when you're having fun. He was diagnosed schizophrenic, wasn't he? I seem to recall he wasn't too bad as those cases go; I mean, he had his moments, sure, but he was quite rational and socially capable most of the time. What about him?"

"He's dead I'm afraid. The American, Funke, shot him."

"What?" gasped Crouch. "What's going on? Last I heard, someone had shot Funke."

McGrail's brows beetled: "Heard from whom, as a matter of interest?"

"My daughter," she said defensively.

"Of course — and she would've heard it from Ricketts; their alliance had slipped my mind."

"Where on earth did Balfour run into Funke?" asked Crouch.

"Their paths crossed last Thursday night at Manacle Grange which is really why we're here. You see, Ms Crouch, so far we've found just the one link connecting Balfour to your ex-husband's treasure trove, which of course was the reason for him being at Manacle." McGrail's lips formed a tentative, slightly apologetic smile. "That connection is your good self."

"I'm sorry," she said with a frown. "I'm not sure what you're getting at."

"Well, it's quite simple: only a handful of people, of whom you were one, knew prior to last Thursday night where the cocaine was; as far as we know, you're the only member of that select group, if not the only person involved in this whole business, who knew Balfour." McGrail smiled thinly again but this time without a hint of an apology. "So we were wondering if you sent him to Manacle Grange."

She paused in the act of pouring boiling water into a teapot, glanced at McGrail, and then refocused on pouring. "That's pretty off-the-wall, inspector," she said casually. "I've had nothing to do with Balfour for at least ten years; more to the point, why would I do that? How do you have your tea by the way?"

"Black for me, thank you; milk and one sugar for the sergeant . . ."

Ihaka spoke for the first time: "That's two sugars."

Ihaka's sudden outburst seemed to startle Crouch and she dropped a teaspoon with a clatter. She put the three mugs, teapot, milk, sugar and teaspoons on a tray and carried it over to the table. When she'd served the tea, she took her mug and retreated to a bar-stool at the kitchen bench.

"Well, we have a genuine mystery on our hands," said McGrail philosophically. "Who or what led Balfour to Manacle Grange? We may never know." He sipped his tea. "There's an intriguing sidelight to all of this which may interest you: Balfour had a .22 rifle which we've traced back to a man named Al Grills. Does he ring a bell?"

Crouch was watching McGrail closely, even intently. She nodded.

"So here's another riddle: How did Balfour come by a rifle last seen in the possession of a man whom your ex-husband was assumed to've killed in a squabble over the cocaine? If you think about it," — McGrail raised his eyebrows as if bemused at the direction this line of thought was taking him — "there was a connection between you, Balfour and the drugs back in 1983 just as there is now."

Crouch, who appeared to be thinking about it quite seriously, said nothing.

"October 1983 to be exact," said McGrail. "You were seeing Balfour in a counselling capacity at that time, I believe?"

"What other capacity is there, inspector?" she said with a strange, almost coy smile. "I'd have to check but it sounds right; it was round about then."

McGrail studied her thoughtfully for a few seconds. "Did you know Bart Clegg, Ms Crouch?"

The sudden change of tack took her by surprise. "Well, yes," she stammered. "Vaguely. Only through Dale — he was Dale's lawyer. I didn't know him well."

"Back in October 1983, did Clegg warn you that your ex-husband was sailing into an ambush?"

Crouch looked confused. "I'm sorry, I . . . no he didn't."

"We have evidence that Clegg knew Bryce Spurdle and his man Grills planned to double-cross Varty once the cocaine was landed," said McGrail deliberately. "Did Clegg pass that information on to you?"

Crouch sat utterly still, staring at McGrail. "I told you," she said in a low voice. "No, he didn't."

McGrail continued as if he hadn't heard her. "I think what happened was this: Clegg told you that Varty was in for it as soon as the drugs were ashore. By then Varty was halfway across the Tasman where you couldn't get in touch with him. So you talked Balfour into going down to Otama; I imagine he thought it'd be a great adventure — he seemed to have a taste for that sort of thing. Unfortunately, he hit Grills a little harder than was necessary and Grills died. Isn't that what happened, Ms Crouch?"

"I'm a bit hazy on the law," she said carefully, "but it sounds like you're asking me to admit to being an accessory to manslaughter."

"Maybe I am," said McGrail as if the thought hadn't occurred to him. "But even if we pursued it, you'd have to entrust your defence to a spectacularly incompetent lawyer to run any risk of being convicted."

"I don't think that's quite as hard as you make it sound, inspector; anyway, it's certainly not a risk I'm inclined to take."

McGrail smiled benignly. "Fair enough. Well, let me ask you this, Mrs Crouch: How did you feel when you discovered what Balfour had brought back from Otama was icing sugar, not cocaine?"

Crouch's face went stiff. She took her mug over to the sink and rinsed it out. Without looking at McGrail she said, "If you're going to ask questions like that, I think I should have a lawyer present — even a spectacularly incompetent one."

McGrail finished his tea and stood up. "Next time perhaps; the sergeant and I have to run along. Have you met Ricketts by the way? You should — he tells an interesting story; I suppose re-tells would be more accurate seeing it's what your ex-husband told him very shortly before he died. Varty told Ricketts that the fellow — let's call him Balfour — who popped up out of nowhere and donged Grills made no bones about the fact that he'd come to get the cocaine." McGrail paused. "Or that his instructions were to allow Varty to be murdered."

The hostile glow in Crouch's eyes eventually faded, giving way to a heavy-lidded indifference which McGrail admired but didn't believe. She got a bottle of Chivas Regal out of her cupboard above the sink and poured some into a tumbler. "Balfour — if it was him — was mad," she said coldly. "He could — and did — say all sorts of things; most of it was meaningless, deluded crap."

"You're probably right." McGrail's tone was as innocently conversational as if they were exchanging gardening stories. "Still, it's hard to feel sorry for him after what he did to poor old Clegg. You know, after he'd drowned Clegg in his bubble bath, Balfour took a champagne glass away, obviously because it had fingerprints on it. For some bizarre reason — well, as you were just saying, the man wasn't all there — he kept the glass; we found it in the cellar under his house. So now we're running round taking people's fingerprints; I suppose we should take yours."

Despite the scotch, Crouch had gone quite pale. "Why?"

"Oh I don't think for one moment that Balfour took it upon himself to kill Clegg. Why would he? I mean, if robbery was the motive, I think even a lunatic, having gone to the trouble of murdering the householder, would steal more than a glass. No, my guess is that Clegg liked sharing the tub and a bottle of champagne with his lady friends but this particular lady friend got Balfour to crash the party and perform that rather horrible deed."

"This is fucking insane," she hissed. "Why the hell would I want to kill Clegg?"

"A very good question and one that had me stumped for a while, I don't mind telling you," said McGrail imperturbably. "Then yesterday, when I was going through the file, I had the two newspaper clippings side by side and it suddenly hit me: Clegg was murdered on the night of Friday the fifteenth, by which time your ex-husband was dead. Except that as far as everybody knew, he was very much alive and on his way back here because that's what the story in Friday morning's paper said. The follow-up story saying as you were, Varty's actually dead, was in Saturday's paper."

McGrail thrust his hands into his pockets and began to pace up and down. "Now I can only speculate on what went through your mind when you read that Varty was coming back: perhaps you had some sort of reconciliation in mind, the two of you and your daughter living happily ever after; perhaps not. Whatever, it all revolved around the cocaine. But first things first: you had to deal with Clegg double quick because when he and Varty got together to compare notes, Clegg was bound to mention how he'd found out about the ambush and warned you. And at that moment, Varty would've realised that instead of using the information to save his life, you'd used it to try to get the cocaine for yourself and to hell with him. Bang would go any chance of a reconciliation — although I suspect that would've been purely tactical; bang would go any chance of getting your hands on the drugs or sharing in the proceeds. So Clive Balfour, the faithful foot soldier, received another call to arms."

McGrail stopped pacing; his eyes gleamed with sardonic humour. "It must've well and truly put you off your cornflakes, reading next morning that Varty was dead after all."

There were beads of sweat on Rayleen Crouch's forehead and upper lip, although her face was white and pinched. She about-turned, stalked down the corridor and held the front door open. As the two policemen walked to the door, Ihaka said, "What about those notebooks from Balfour's cellar, sir? You had a look at them yet?"

"Just a glance," said McGrail. "They look like diaries to me. They'll take some deciphering, mind you — his writing's pretty well unreadable. We'll get there, though; that's what we have handwriting experts for." He paused at the door and stared impassively down at Crouch. "Till next time then," he said quietly. "Somebody will be in touch about the fingerprints."

Ihaka drove. As they cut across Ponsonby Road, he said: "I'm glad to see someone's been using their head while I've been out there risking life and limb."

McGrail nodded and tried to think of the last time he'd heard Ihaka pay anyone a compliment. He couldn't.

"We'll be pushing it uphill to nail the bitch, won't we?"

McGrail stared out the car window. "We haven't got a prayer," he said, "which is a sobering thought because that's an evil little woman back there. I was in with the crown prosecutor this morning; his advice, in a nutshell, was that we needed Balfour alive and sane to have a case. Whatever's in those notebooks, the fact of the matter, as Ms Crouch so bluntly observed, is that he was mad; madmen who kill have a long history of saying the devil made me do it. Hopefully, we've put the wind up her a bit; she might do something silly, although I can't say I'm overly optimistic. Will you arrange surveillance?"

"Sure. What about if her prints are on that glass?"

"If we had a compos mentis and cooperative Balfour, it would make first-rate circumstantial evidence. But the truth is there aren't any prints. It was a bluff: I wanted to be sure that I'd got it right about Clegg; I had to — for a few seconds there, it was written all over her face." McGrail sighed ruefully. "Brother Balfour was tidy to a fault: all the lab technician found on the glass was a very faint residue of dishwashing liquid; his exact words were:" — the Ulsterman put on a passable Kiwi bloke accent — "Tell you what sir, I wish my missus got our glasses to sparkle like that."

Neither spoke again until they were in the lift at Auckland Central police station.

"One thing I can't work out," said Ihaka.

"What's that?"

"Why didn't Balfour let Grills bump Varty like she told him to?"

"Yes, I wondered about that," said McGrail. "I concluded that when it came to the crunch, Balfour couldn't simply stand back and let it happen. He wasn't a killer, not a cold-blooded one anyway. Now you're going to say, 'What about Clegg?' I think Clegg was killed in hot blood. I'm sure Crouch and Balfour had a relationship — that's how she manipulated him; I think she knew he'd go berserk when he saw her in the bubble bath with Clegg. He wasn't wearing a swimsuit at the time and I suspect neither was she."

Ihaka nodded slowly. "That woman's wasted in social work," he said.

Epilogue

A week and a half later Rayleen Crouch skipped the country. Accompanied by her daughter Electra and travelling on a one-way ticket, she flew out on an Air New Zealand 747 bound for London. She gave her employer, the Department of Social Welfare, a couple of days' notice and most of her friends and acquaintances none at all. She'd simply held a garage sale and given away what she couldn't sell, listed her house with a real estate agent, packed a couple of suitcases and gone. It was all done discreetly rather than surreptitiously and the police had soon realised what she was up to. They maintained surveillance right to the aircraft door but didn't try to stop her.

On Monday, 4 July depositions hearings in the case of the Crown versus Bryce Spurdle began in the Auckland District Court; Spurdle had earlier entered a plea of not guilty to the charge of possession of cocaine for the purposes of supply and been remanded in custody without bail. The prosecution's star witness was Duane Ricketts who was described as an undercover policeman. Giving evidence from behind an opaque screen, Ricketts told the court of an elaborate undercover operation designed to intercept a major consignment of cocaine before it reached the market. It had involved him going to Thailand and getting thrown into the Bombat Drug Rehabilitation Centre on a minor drugs charge. Once in jail he'd set about gaining the confidence of Dale Varty, a former member of the Mr Asia syndicate whose prison term was almost up; the police were certain that Varty would come straight back to New Zealand and put the ten kilos of cocaine he'd brought over from Australia in 1983 into circulation. When Varty was killed shortly before his release, Ricketts had returned to New Zealand to locate the cocaine, using the information he'd managed to glean from him. A sting operation was then mounted against Spurdle, Varty's original accomplice, which culminated in his arrest after he'd bought the drugs for $100,000.

When Ricketts mentioned this figure, the defendant Spurdle exclaimed loudly and incoherently and clutched at his chest, prompting the magistrate to call a fifteen-minute halt to proceedings to enable him to regain his composure. A reporter trying to eavesdrop on the intense discussion between the defendant and his barrister outside the courtroom thought she heard the lawyer ask, "What about the IRD?" For a moment she wondered what the Inland Revenue Department had to do with the price of fish; then she observed the instant tranquillising effect the question had on Spurdle and decided she must've misheard.

The media were getting quite excited over the prospect of Spurdle's trial mainly because his legal team kept dropping off-the-record hints that they'd produce evidence which would be deeply embarrassing, not only for the police but also the government. The announcement at the commencement of the second day of depositions that Spurdle had changed his plea to guilty thus came as both a shock and a let-down. Ten days later Spurdle appeared in the High Court for sentencing and was given an eight-year term. The judge told the court that the period of imprisonment was half that which he'd normally impose for such a serious crime but he was mindful of Spurdle's cooperation with the authorities, cooperation which would significantly assist them in their efforts to combat the pernicious blight of narcotics. He did not specify what form the cooperation had taken.

That evening Jody Spurdle appeared on *Holmes*. She vowed to stand by her husband and to be there for him when he got out of jail; with parole, that was likely to be four or five years hence. She denied suggestions of a cover-up or that her husband had been pressured into changing his plea by people in high places. Most people who watched the interview found her deeply unconvincing, especially on the point of where she planned to be when the prison gates swung open and her sixty-something husband walked free.

At 5.35 on the mild late-winter afternoon of Friday, 7 September, Duane Ricketts parked his Toyota Corolla outside his recently acquired Grey Lynn villa. Detective Sergeant Tito Ihaka, who was sitting on the steps leading up to the verandah and front door said: "About bloody time," and got to his feet. They went inside; Ricketts gave Ihaka a beer and a quick tour of his new house.

"Very nice," said Ihaka, when they were sitting down in the living room. "How much?"

"Three hundred and ten."

Ihaka whistled. "Not that fucking nice but what the hell? It's not as if it's your money." He raised his bottle. "To Bryce Spurdle, without whose generosity you'd still be in that dump in Mt Roskill."

Ricketts toasted: "Bryce, a true philanthropist."

"What've you been up to?" asked Ihaka.

"Same old stuff. I've just been into Trubshaw Trimble to see one of the partners, the guy McGrail recommended me to. He reckons they'd have a couple of jobs a month for me. He's even talking about a retainer."

"McGrail might regret that: he asked me the other day if I thought you'd be interested in coming back."

"That yarn of mine put ideas in his head?"

"Must've. I told him you weren't suitable because you made it up as you went along; you can imagine what he said to that. Oh, I almost forgot." Ihaka pulled a postcard out of the back pocket of his jeans. "Your mail. It's from your little partner-in-crime."

Ricketts rolled his eyes. "Why don't you just give me the highlights? Save me the trouble of reading it."

Ihaka flicked the card over to him. "I had to occupy myself somehow. Highlights? I'd probably go for Mother Crouch getting her hooks into some rich old fart." He shook his head. "What an operator. Did I ever tell you McGrail reckoned she was blocking Balfour?"

"The nutter? You believe that?"

"McGrail's the biggest fucking prude I know but he can sniff a filthy secret at a hundred paces; if he says they were grunting, that's good enough for me."

"Did she get a mention in his notebooks?"

"Christ knows. It was hard-core gibberish: the handwriting bloke said it was like a cross between *The Perfumed Garden* and *Cattle Breeders' Monthly*. He gave up on them in the end."

While Ihaka went to the kitchen to get more beer, Ricketts read the postcard which had been redirected from his previous address. It said:

> Ricketts,
>
> Is this a shock to the system or what? You wondered why the swift exit, right? When I told Mum about the share of the you-know-what (you never know who reads your postcards) she said we're outa here, let's see the world. A case of all cashed up and no reason to stay I guess. Anyway, it's worked out really well — had some fab times travelling and London is excellent. I'm in a seriously cool band — when I told them about 'The Homo Dwarves', they adopted the name. Rayleen's a new woman partly because she's got a new man. He's a tad (!) older and loaded — I'm starting to see the attraction. The bottom line (as he always says) is I don't see us coming back for a while. Hope everything is OK and you had big fun spending your share.
>
> Exx
>
> PS I'm even getting into Van M! What do you say we meet on the river of time one day?

Ihaka returned with the beers. "What's this river of time crap?"

"It's from a Van Morrison song."

"What's it mean?"

"It doesn't mean anything."

"Bullfuck. She sent you a postcard — that means something for a start."

"It means she's in London and I'm in Auckland. We're what's known as inseparable."

After a pause Ihaka said: "Maybe we should've told her about her old lady."

"What's this 'we' brown boy? You want to play God, go ahead but leave me out of it. On the subject of absent friends, what about pistol-packing Annie, whatever her name is?"

"C. C. Hellicar?" Ihaka thought about it for a while. "Put it this way, I won't forget her in a hurry."

Ricketts sat up straight. "Really? Exactly what did you crazy kids get up to?"

"We went up to the beach-house and went fishing. Then we danced on the deck."

"Get down, you dancing fool!" whooped Ricketts. Then, in a hushed, dramatic voice: "I suppose one thing led to another, to sweet nothings whispered in the moonlight before . . ."

"Ricketts, shut your hole," said Ihaka almost distractedly. "One thing led to fuck all. We'd just started dancing when McGrail rang to say they'd found the stiffs, the coke had been swiped by a couple of phoney cops and would I kindly get my black arse back to Auckland." He looked bleakly at Ricketts. "I don't think I ever got around to thanking you for that."

There was a very long silence. A subdued Ricketts said, "So I stuffed up what was going to be a night to remember?"

Ihaka shrugged. "Who knows? Doesn't matter anyway. I danced with C. C. Hellicar; I saw the look on her face when the phone rang; I'll settle for that."

There was another long silence. "You really mean that?" asked Ricketts, surprised but respectful.

Ihaka threw him a pitying look. "Course I fucking don't," he said. "What do you take me for?" His expression changed to his trademark sly, cocksure, ruthless grin. "Anyway, enough of that shit: what's for tea?"

Just before the grin faded, Ricketts thought he saw a shadow descend on the brazen glitter in Ihaka's eyes. Maybe he did mean it after all, thought Ricketts; then again, maybe he's just hungry.

Guerilla Season

1

Cowards, wrote Shakespeare, die many times before their deaths. So do hypochondriacs.

The radio talkback star Fred 'the Freckle' Freckleton had both strings to his bow: in his imagination, he'd suffered most of the fates known to medical science and the insurance industry. Even at his most creatively morbid, however, it hadn't occurred to him to worry about urban terrorism.

At half past midnight on Tuesday, 22 August, Freckleton dropped his empty beer can into a wastepaper basket, said goodnight to his producer, and took the lift to the basement carpark. He felt drained but it was the weary satisfaction of a job well done.

It'd been a top show: he'd sparked, the all-important maniac factor was right up there, and the new gimmick had been a big hit. This was a sound effect of a flushing toilet which he used to terminate callers who didn't enter into the spirit of things: the temperate, the tolerant, and — worst of all — the well informed. Late in the show, he'd preceded the flush by telling one particularly dogged dissenter to "Get back where you belong — with all the other turds." It was a good line; he'd use it again.

The previous year, 40 years old and a self-diagnosed burn-out after 15 years on the breakfast shift, the Freckle had taken a sabbatical to fulfil his long-held ambition of driving coast to coast across the USA in a Detroit convertible the size of Sylvester Stallone's swimming pool. Along the way, he got acquainted with the ebullient and ultraconservative talk radio sensation, Rush Limbaugh. Limbaugh, so he read in a magazine, earned around US$25 million a year for saying pretty much the sort of stuff Freckleton himself came out with after a few beers. As he pondered the Limbaugh phenomenon, it slowly dawned on Freckleton that he'd stumbled on the solution to his mid-life crisis.

Back in Auckland, Freckleton talked his network's owners into taking over a struggling easy-listening station. It was renamed Radio Mainstream — The Station for Real Kiwis, and given a news/talkback format, alleviated only by the odd classic hit. Each weeknight from eight till midnight, Mainstream's star turn, Fred Freckleton: The Bloke Who Speaks Your Language, vented his reactionary spleen on feminists, gays, Maori radicals, left-wing politicians, environmentalists, trade-union leaders, welfare beneficiaries — in short, anyone whose agenda, activities, or mere existence were likely to annoy the suburban heartland, the majority which, thanks to talkback radio, can no longer be described as silent.

393

In empathising with this audience, Freckleton skated over his quarter-of-a-million dollar salary, his lavishly renovated villa with harbour views, his Porsche, his atheism, his childless marriages — both messy failures — and his heavy use of the amphetamine Benzedrine. Instead, he dwelt on his Little House on the Dairy Flat upbringing, the subtext to his tirades against welfare recipients.

A sample: "You know what really gets my goat? It's when the bleeding heart mob, the moaners and the bleaters — you know who I'm talking about — tell the government it's got to raise taxes, in other words, grab even more of our hard-earned dough, so they can devote more resources — don't you love that line? — to the less fortunate. Now what that means, in plain English, is taking money off people who work and giving it to people who don't — 99 per cent of the time because they simply can't be stuffed. Let's be clear what these turkeys are on about: they want to take more of your money — the money from that extra bit of overtime, the money you'd put aside for the kids' Christmas presents or the summer holiday or to chip away at the mortgage — and give it to the bludgers and the scroungers and the no-hopers and the parasites. And what do you reckon they'll do with it? Well, for a start, they'll piss a fair chunk of it up against the wall; some on cigarettes. What's left will go on junk food because even though they don't do a stroke of work from one month to the next, they're still too bloody lazy to make a proper meal.

"Well, I'd just like to ask one question: what's stopping these bludgers from getting off their arses — fat arses too, most of 'em: it's all that booze and junk food — and doing something for themselves? My old man was a fitter and turner in a dairy factory. He didn't go to the pub after work and drink himself pie-eyed; he came home, dog-tired and covered in muck, and went straight out to feed the chooks and work in his vegetable garden. Mum, God bless her, baked every day — cakes, biscuits, even her own bread. Every biscuit, every cake, every egg, every vegetable eaten at the Freckletons' was home-grown. But try telling the scroungers to grow a few spuds or bake a cake and you'll get called every name in the book. Why? Because of this crazy mentality that it's not up to them to help themselves, it's not their responsibility. You know how it goes: society has to look after them and when things go wrong, society is to blame. Well, society is you and me. Speaking for yourself, I've got a lot better things to do with my money. If it was up to me, they wouldn't get a brass razoo. Safety net, my eye — it's more like a bloody hammock. Let's hear what you think — we're taking your calls now."

Freckleton drove his Porsche 928 out of the carpark, through the empty streets of Takapuna, and over the harbour bridge to Herne Bay. In sight of home, he activated the remote control to raise the garage door. Nothing happened. He pulled up in front of the garage, held the remote out the window, and tried again. It still didn't work. He swore, reversed and parked on the street.

He got out of the car. Two men in dark boiler suits and ski masks got out of a station wagon parked over the road. They crossed the road towards him, unhurried but purposeful.

Freckleton was dizzy with fear. He gabbled: "Who are you, what do you want?"

"You can call me Betty," said the smaller of the pair suavely. "And you can call him Al. We'd like you to come with us."

"What for?" squeaked Freckleton.

"All will be revealed in good time."

Al advanced, eyes animal-bright in the slits of his ski mask. He sank fingers like shark hooks into the loose flesh of Freckleton's upper arm. He thrust Freckleton into the back seat of the station wagon and got in beside him. Betty slid behind the wheel and drove towards the city.

Freckleton tremulously broke the silence: "Am I being kidnapped?"

The only response was the driver's amused snort. When Freckleton repeated the question, Al carefully gripped his right ear and wrenched violently. Freckleton heard a squishing sound, as if sinew and gristle were being pulped, and suffered a jolt of hideous pain which receded to a slow, hurtful throb. After that, he didn't speak or even assess the damage for fear of provoking further torture.

Betty parked in a side street by St Matthew's-in-the-City. They escorted Freckleton, now thoroughly cowed, up the hill to Hobson Street. It was a clear, cold night, about five degrees. The inner city was silent and deserted, as if a neutron bomb had blotted out all life, leaving brick, mortar and reflective glass intact. They came to a fenced-off building site. The wire mesh fence was cut. Al wriggled through the gap then peeled back a section of fence for the others to follow. Cranes perched like prehistoric birds of prey on the unfinished high-rise which towered above them. Freckleton gazed up at it, shuddering.

"Now climb," Betty hold him. "I hope you're fitter than you look."

They went up 15 flights of concrete stairs. By the time they reached the top, Freckleton's face had popped sweat and he was gobbling air like a footballer in injury time.

"Showtime," said Betty, breathing easily. "We've brought you here tonight, Mr Freckle, to give you a taste of your own medicine. Right now, this building's more or less the same height as that one right alongside. We've bridged the gap with a sturdy if somewhat narrow plank: all you have to do is walk across it." His face split in what seemed to Freckleton a transparently sadistic grin. "Seeing you're so anti safety nets, we haven't provided one."

Freckleton legs almost buckled. He croaked: "What is this — some sort of fucking sick joke?"

"Oh, it's no joke. Under this flippant exterior, I'm serious to a fault."

"There's no fucking way you're getting me on that plank," blurted Freckleton. "I'm shit-scared of heights."

Betty nodded. "Well, it wouldn't be a cakewalk for a steeplejack — it's pitch black and there's a tricky breeze. Before you make up your mind, though, you really ought to consider the alternative: if you won't do it, we'll simply shoot you. Look at it this way: if you plummet fifteen floors to a horrible death, you'll be remembered as a martyr for free speech; but if you make it, you'll really have something to talk about on the show."

Freckleton implored him: "Why are you doing this? What have I ever done to you?"

Betty shrugged. "You're a hate-mongering demagogue, you're shallow as a birdbath, you're in love with the sound of your own voice, you play too much Billy Joel — take your pick. Well: what's it going to be?"

Al produced a semi-automatic pistol. He took a silencer from his breast pocket and screwed it on.

"It's up to you, Mr Freckle," said Betty. "Your fate is entirely in your hands — just as you're always saying it should be."

The talkback man stood rooted to the spot. A minute passed. Betty told Al: "I'll do the honours."

Al passed him the pistol. Freckleton forced himself to move, shuffling woozily to the edge of the building. The building seemed several postcodes away.

Betty said: "Off you go then. Take my advice: don't look down and don't try anything fancy, like a pirouette — we're hard to impress."

Freckleton extended his arms in a crucifixion pose and stepped onto the plank. He wobbled sickeningly but managed to keep his balance. He took another step. With his arms still extended, he lowered himself very slowly onto one knee, then gripped the plank with both hands. When he had both knees on the plank, he began to inch forward.

"I said walk, not crawl." Betty's tone was mildly disapproving. He sauntered to the edge of the building, put his right heel against the plank, and shoved.

Freckleton hit the ground at 113 kilometres per hour, which is just over half the maximum speed a falling body can reach — what physicists somewhat ghoulishly call terminal velocity. It was quite fast enough for Betty's purposes.

Construction workers discovered the body at 7.05 a.m.

The fact that Freckleton was a celebrity of sorts whose pugnacious glower adorned several billboards around town didn't facilitate the identification process. The examining pathologist described the corpse as compelling evidence that human beings aren't designed to jump off anything higher than a beanbag. When it came to nominating the actual cause of death, the pathologist found himself quite spoilt for choice: eventually, he narrowed it down to the lacerated liver — the organ had split open like a well-read book — and the ruptured aorta. Then again, the almost instantaneous loss of 40 per cent of his blood hadn't done the poor bugger much good either.

Although the contents of the deceased's wallet were blood-soaked, his platinum American Express card scrubbed up well enough to permit a tentative

ID. This was confirmed by dental records and Freckleton's GP who, over the years, had become more intimately acquainted with his patient's physique and physiology than he would have liked.

Thanks to its good police contacts, Radio Mainstream was first with the news of its star announcer's mysterious death. The station's head of news assured staff that the Freckle would've wanted it that way.

At 10.20 the next morning, the 28-year-old television current affairs reporter Amanda Hayhoe left the St Mary's Bay villa which she shared with her landlady.

Hayhoe liked the area: as people always said, it had character. She'd decided that having character meant it had more cafés, restaurants and weirdos per head than most parts of town. She liked the house, the rent was reasonable, and her landlady/flatmate was okay to live with most of the time. The plusses, therefore, outweighed the minuses, of which there were two.

The first drawback was that she got little, if any, sleep when her flatmate's boyfriend was in town. He was a 44-year-old married man from Henley-on-Thames who flew 747s for British Airways. The second was the amount of emotional support she had to provide when the pilot flew away. Whenever that happened, the flatmate would get it into her head that he'd be rostered on to another route somewhere like Johannesburg or Budapest, and she'd never see him again. For a couple of nights she'd go on sobbing jags which took several hours of Hayhoe's undivided attention and general jollying along to bring under control.

Hayhoe had come to find these performances irksome especially when her reward for providing a shoulder to cry on was mascara smudges and lipstick smears on her Rosaria Hall shirt. She felt that seeing the pilot had been loving and leaving for a couple of years now, her landlady, who was, after all, thirty-five, and a practising psychoanalyst, really should have come to terms with it.

What's more, when the psychoanalyst was bingeing on self-pity, it never seemed to cross her mind that in the ten months they'd flatted together, the most exciting thing that had happened in Hayhoe's bedroom was her alarm-clock radio suddenly and inexplicably picking up a rugby league commentary from Papua New Guinea.

Hayhoe was late for an appointment. That wasn't the end of the world but she had a hangover which felt like it very well could be.

As she walked to her car parked down the street, she tried to remember when she'd last had an alcohol-free day. The recollection prompted a curious half-smile and a rueful shake of the head: she'd stayed off it for a week late the previous summer after waking up one Sunday morning in an Epsom motel next to the wife of one of Auckland's wealthiest men. Hayhoe was wondering which question to ask first when Mrs Moneybags saved her the trouble by declaring that Amanda hadn't thrown up or snored or hogged the blankets or made a drama of declining the invitation to a spot of amateur lesbianism.

Whether it was the hangover or the motel flashback, Hayhoe had driven her four-year-old Honda Civic up the hill to Jervois Road and through Ponsonby village before she noticed the white envelope tucked under the windscreen wiper. She pulled over and got out of the car. The envelope was sealed but not addressed. It contained a single sheet of paper with a message hand-written in block capitals.

COMMUNIQUE NUMBER ONE

THE AOTEAROA PEOPLE'S ARMY HAS DEALT DECISIVELY WITH THE REACTIONARY BROAD-CASTER FRECKLETON.

FRECKLETON HAD METHODICALLY VILIFIED PROGRESSIVE FORCES AND SOUGHT TO INCITE HATRED TOWARDS THOSE WHO REJECT AND RESIST LAISSEZ-FAIRE MULTINATIONAL CAPITALISM. HE HAD ACTIVELY PROMOTED A FASCIST LINE AGAINST THE POOR, THE DISENFRANCHISED, MINORITY GROUPS, AND THOSE IN THE VANGUARD OF THE STRUGGLE FOR MAORI LIBERATION AND SOVEREIGNTY.

FRECKLETON DID NOT ACT IN ISOLATION; THE VOLUME OF EXTREME RIGHT-WING PROPAGANDA IN BOTH THE MASS MEDIA AND SOCIO-POLITICAL ARENA HAS INCREASED SIGNIFICANTLY IN RECENT MONTHS, SIGNALLING THE MOBILISATION OF REACTIONARY ELEMENTS. THE AOTEAROA PEOPLE'S ARMY WAS NOT PREPARED TO ALLOW THIS PROCESS TO GO UNCHECKED.

THE CRYPTO-FASCISTS IN THE GOVERNMENT-BIG BUSINESS AXIS AND THEIR MOUTHPIECES IN THE MEDIA SHOULD HEED THIS WARNING. IF THEY CHOOSE TO IGNORE IT, THEY SHOULD NOT BE SURPRISED WHEN THE AOTEAROA PEOPLE'S ARMY ADMINISTERS FURTHER DIRECT REVOLUTIONARY JUSTICE.

Amanda Hayhoe had to read it three times before the full implications sank in. When they did, she said, "Fuck a priest," which wasn't an expression she used lightly or often, and resumed her journey. Her hangover seemed to have disappeared.

2

At 3 o'clock that afternoon, a meeting began in a glass-walled, venetian-blinded, ground-floor office in Television New Zealand's state-of-the-art studios on the corner of Victoria and Nelson Streets. The only item on the agenda was the apparent outbreak of urban terrorism, a blight to which New Zealand was thought to be immune because of its isolation and the phlegmatic, some would say passionless, disposition of its inhabitants.

Taking part were the network's head of news and current affairs, the producer of the 6 o'clock national news, the wholesome mixed double who presented the news and who were called, behind their backs, various mildly satiric names such as Ken and Barbie and the Blands, a producer from *The Holmes Show*, the reporter Ainsley Tarr, a network lawyer and Amanda Hayhoe.

Earlier, the lawyer and Hayhoe had gone to Auckland Central Police Station, where he'd handed over the original of the Aotearoa People's Army communiqué and she'd been fingerprinted.

The news producer opened the meeting: "Okay, we've just heard from the cops that they're holding a press conference at five to release the text of the communiqué. They'll say they've never heard of this outfit, they're not ruling out a hoax, and all the usual shit — enquiries are proceeding, blah, blah. What that means is we don't have an exclusive but we do have an edge, due to the fact that the terrorists chose to announce themselves via our very own Amanda Hayhoe."

Mr Bland glanced uncertainly at Hayhoe. "Are you — is she doing the story?"

The head of news and current affairs said, "No, it's business as usual: Ainsley's covering the story; you'll do a live cross to Amanda in the newsroom and run through it with her."

Hayhoe and Tarr exchanged fleeting, insincere smiles. Ainsley had been to make-up before the meeting: she didn't miss a trick.

Amanda couldn't have cared less about not doing the story for news: two minutes air-time maybe, three max, most of it cops and politicians grinding out waffle and no comments. Forget it, she had a bigger fish to fry: an in-depth story for her current affairs programme, *60 Minutes*.

"How are we going so far?" asked the head of news and current affairs.

"The Wellington bureau's jacking up comment from the PM and the Leader of the Opposition," said the producer.

"They're bound to be pretty guarded so we're trawling the backbenches for someone who'll say it's the end of civilisation as we know it . . ."

The women from *Holmes* said, "How about Chas Gundry, media slut extraordinaire?"

"Yeah," enthused the producer, "he's absolutely fucking rabid. Point a camera at him and he foams at the mouth."

"And who'll speak for our brown brethren?" asked the head of news and current affairs.

Ainsley Tarr breathed, "I'm on to it, Phil." According to the network's market research, her husky delivery activated erectile tissue from North Cape to the Bluff. "Whetu Porima's agreed to front."

"What's he going to say?"

Tarr flipped open her notebook. "Whatever they are, the Aotearoa People's Army aren't tangata whenua: Maori don't need anyone else to fight their battles for them; none of the leading radicals have ever advocated violence against individuals. Off the record, it couldn't have happened to a nicer guy."

"Yeah, fine Ainsley, but don't give Porima a soft ride, eh? Put it on him that the inflammatory shit he and his mates are always coming out with might've given these guys the idea."

Tarr numbed him: "Phil, have you ever known me to give a soft ride?" Complete with slow-motion, heavy-lidded smile.

Holy creeping shit, thought Hayhoe, that was an official announcement. She scanned the table: the head of news and current affairs dropped his eyes to his blank notepad; Tarr met her glance with an unfathomable smile and a fractional lift of her right eyebrow; the others wore studiously blank expressions.

After that, Hayhoe didn't take much interest in the discussion. Instead, she thought about Ainsley Tarr: twenty-two, just out of the Canterbury University journalism school, and zeroing in on media stardom with the pre-programmed implacability of a cruise missile.

It helped that she was sexy: soap-star looks and that super-vamp voice. A cameraman had told Hayhoe that talking camera angles with Ainsley was better than phone sex.

The camera loved her, no doubt about that. And Ainsley loved it right back with a lack of inhibition which sometimes made Hayhoe envious but usually made her change channels. It was like watching a dirty movie: it wasn't so much what they were doing that bothered you, it was the fact they seemed so proud of themselves.

A secretary knocked and poked her head in: "Amanda, there's a Detective Sergeant Ihaka to see you . . ."

"Ihaka." The producer pulled a face. "He'll make your day."

"Is there anything I should know?"

"He's got a chip on his shoulder the size of a satellite dish." He paused for effect. "And he particularly hates the media."

Hayhoe's first impression was that the producer's thumbnail sketch might have erred on the side of generosity.

Ihaka was a Maori in his mid-thirties, about 180 centimetres tall, wide as a bathtub. He had a Popeye jaw, a greedy mouth and a flat, sprawling nose. After that, things improved marginally: his eyes were large and brown with long, dark lashes and would have been attractive if they'd contained a glimmer of warmth. He looked tough, cynical, not very nice.

He certainly wasn't one of your devious, roundabout interrogators. As soon as she'd sat down, he demanded: "How come they made you the messenger girl?"

She shrugged. "No idea."

"You're a journo, aren't you? Surely to Christ you've thought about it."

That was true enough. "Well, I guess, basically, they wanted a journalist to make sure it got publicised . . ."

Ihaka rolled his eyes, murmured, "No shit?"

". . . and when you're on TV, people you don't know from Adam know you — or at least your face."

"And the rest — these jerk-offs know where you live and what car you drive."

Hayhoe flapped her hands, a bit rattled. "I don't know, maybe they followed me home from work or saw me out somewhere and followed me."

"See, you have thought about it. I need a list of places you've been in the last couple of months, especially anywhere you go regularly. Anything unusual happened lately? Anyone hassled you, stared at you, watched you get into your car, hung around outside your place?"

"Not that I've noticed — you get used to the odd person gawking at you. After a while it doesn't really register."

Ihaka grumbled. It wasn't what he wanted to hear. "Freckleton sucked it on Monday night: why'd they wait a day to stick the note on your car?"

Hayhoe had to think about it. "Maybe they tried on Monday night — my car and I were otherwise engaged."

"Doing what?"

"I had dinner at a friend's place. I drank too much wine so I stayed over, responsible citizen that I am."

"What's his name?"

"Whose?"

Ihaka raised his eyebrows: "Your friend."

"Deirdre — funny name for a bloke, don't you think?"

Only two hats had been tossed into the ring when nominations for the position of coach of the Auckland rugby team closed that afternoon.

One belonged to a hulking, pock-marked, bull-necked forty-eight-year-old builder named Barney Tingle. Tingle had a brick-red complexion and eyes like trampled grapes, perhaps because he had Scotch whisky for morning tea and at increasingly regular intervals thereafter. Curiously, almost three decades of excess had done little to undermine his impressive physique.

Since giving up the game at thirty-seven, Tingle had coached several club teams with mixed results. His bulk, gruffness and the chilling reputation for brutality he'd acquired during his playing days meant that, as a rule, his teams were far more frightened of him than the opposition and competed accordingly. Tingle was, however, handicapped by the growing consensus that it was high time the tyrant coach was consigned to the dustbin of history.

Clyde Early, the other candidate, was rather more palatable. He was a trim, telegenic thirty-nine year old whose promising playing career had been aborted by injury. He immediately took up coaching with spectacular success. At twenty-seven, he'd gone to France and taken an obscure fourth-division club into the first division and the sports pages. That brought him to the attention of a rugby-mad northern Italian multi-millionaire whose sponsorship of his local club was the only thing it had going for it. The tycoon hired Early to make his feeble team a force to be reckoned with. It took him five handsomely rewarded years.

After ten years in Europe and having turned down an opportunity to coach the Italian national side, Early came home. He settled in Auckland, invested his considerable savings in property, blue-chip stocks and a highly profitable hardware retailing franchise, and embarked on the third and final phase of his carefully planned coaching career.

The first step — winning the Auckland club championship — had been safely negotiated. Step two was to be appointed Auckland coach. That, in turn, would be the springboard to the goal he'd set his sights on seventeen years ago as he sat in a hospital bed absent-mindedly caressing the livid scars on his right knee: to coach the All Blacks.

Publicly, Early downplayed his ambitions. In private, he was quite specific about both his destination and timetable. No one who'd heard him on the subject doubted that he'd arrive on schedule.

When he'd finished with Amanda Hayhoe, Ihaka went across town to the university. He had an appointment with Dr Ralph Skeet, a history lecturer who'd read a lot of books about terrorism, was toying with the idea of writing one himself, and was therefore what the media called 'a recognised expert' on the subject.

Dr Skeet was aged between thirty and fifty and had gone to a lot of trouble to look the part of the mad professor: he had frizzy, grey-black hair, a moustache like a burst cushion, and pinkish, demented eyes behind red-framed spectacles. He wore cowboy boots, black jeans, a blue denim shirt and a tie which looked as if it had been used to clean up after a seasick Italian.

He had a poster of a B-1 bomber on the wall behind his desk. The caption read, 'US Bomber Command — Nuke 'Em till they Glow.'

They shook hands. Ihaka said, "Nice poster; I bet it gets a few people going."

"You're not wrong there, bud," replied Skeet. He had a surprisingly deep voice and a strong American accent. "Matter of fact, it offends the shit out of some folks. I figure, fuck 'em if they can't take a joke."

"Fair enough." Ihaka handed him a copy of the Aotearoa People's Army communiqué. "See what you make of it."

Skeet seemed to like it. He read it giggling and looked up at Ihaka with a wide grin: "Don't you love it?"

Ihaka stared.

"Oh, man it's a classic — the jargon, the rhetoric, the euphemisms: I mean, how about 'dealt decisively with' when what you really mean is we threw the sucker off a fifteen-storey building? It's beautiful."

Ihaka dripped sarcasm: "Did I miss something?"

"Chill, baby," said Skeet blithely.

Ihaka could remember a woman calling him baby, but seeing it was tacked on to a threat to behead him with a bread knife, he'd assumed she was being ironic. He'd never had a man call him baby, ironically or otherwise; it took him a few seconds to get over the shock.

"I'm looking at it from an academic perspective," Skeet continued, apparently unaware of the stir he'd caused. "Personally, I think anyone who believes politics is worth shedding blood over should be lobotomised. But, hey, are you guys totally convinced that whatsisname, Freckleton, was shoved as opposed to maybe he took a jump and this is some sick fuck's idea of a joke?"

"That's always a possibility but we're working on the basis he was shoved. It looks like someone fucked around with his garage-door remote so he couldn't drive straight in. Why? Doesn't it ring true?"

"Most urban terrorists, in the Western world anyway, have been young, university-educated zealots from middle-class backgrounds. They talk about the class struggle like we talk about movies; they see themselves as intellectuals but all they are is exhibit A for the proposition that a little knowledge is a dangerous thing." Skeet tossed the communiqué onto his desk. "I've seen carbon copies of this from a dozen different outfits in Europe and the States: I sure as hell never thought I'd see the Kiwi version."

"Could they be students?"

Skeet scratched his head. "That's the profile but, shit, that kind of new-left campus radicalism's as passé as the Monkees. The kids today are into working their tickets, period; all they ever jump up and down about is money — grants and fees. Put your average Rotarian in Levi's and Doc Martens and he'd fit right in."

"Names are a big deal for these guys — it's like their corporate logo, their brand. They're into names that make catchy acronyms: IRA, ETA, PLO." He shrugged: "APA — voilà. 'People' is meant to give them legitimacy — this is who we're fighting for — and the military touch is standard too. Deep down, most of them are Che Guevara wannabes — what they really want is to look cool on a poster in a brainy chick's bedroom."

"Obvious question: does Aotearoa make you think Maori?"

"I guess so but, Jesus, half my honky colleagues use it as a matter of course."

"Do you take the threat of more where that came from seriously?"

Skeet took off his glasses and squinted at Ihaka. "If this is for real, then I'd say the chances are pretty good. You're the cop, you tell me, but isn't the way it works that the first one's the hard one, after that it just gets easier? I guess it's the same whether you're strangling a little old lady for her pension or striking a blow for the oppressed masses."

3

The September issue of *New Nation* magazine, which came out that Friday, had a cover story testing the claim of some publicity-seeking think-tank that New Zealand was poised to become the Switzerland of the South Pacific.

The businesspeople and economists surveyed fell into three broad camps: those who agreed, those who felt it could happen providing the democratic process was suspended for two or three decades, and those who assumed it was some kind of practical joke. There was also a story which failed to deliver on its promise to explain what the America's Cup would mean for Auckland, a fairly fawning profile of Clyde Early, the would-be coach, headlined "Early To Rise?" and the regular features and columns.

The issue departed from the usual formula in one respect. As a rule, the editor Jackson Pike used his editorials to flag the strongest or most controversial stories or to stroke the ego of whichever staff writer was agitating for a pay rise that month. This time, however, Pike had unburdened himself of some novel, if not eccentric, thoughts on the subject of capital punishment.

It was headed, 'A Modest Proposal'.

> RECENTLY, I SAW a murder victim's father interviewed on television. Asked what he thought of the twenty-year prison sentence given his daughter's killer, he replied: "We should bring back the death penalty. Scum like that don't deserve to live."
>
> I wondered how many New Zealanders would agree with him.
>
> A lot, I suspect. Anyone who's discussed crime and punishment in a public bar, a trendy restaurant, or a boardroom has heard numerous variations on the theme of "string the bastards up".
>
> But no matter how strong the sentiment in favour, there's next to no chance of capital punishment being reintroduced. Servants, compulsory military service and the 6 o'clock swill are all more likely to make a comeback. The fix is in, the establishment has decided capital punishment is not for us, and that's the end of it.
>
> But despite being unfashionable, capital punishment is, if you'll pardon the expression, an idea which refuses to die.
>
> Perhaps it's time to explore the middle ground between death row on the one hand and a system many see as soft on perpetrators of horrific crimes on the other.
>
> In the same interview, the victim's father claimed he'd be

prepared to look the murderer straight in the eye and "press the button". Well, why not? If the system isn't prepared to do the job, why not throw it open to the victim's nearest and dearest?

This is my modest proposal; if the accused is found guilty of murder and the judge considers that the crime warrants the maximum penalty, the victim's immediate family or next-of-kin should decide what form the punishment takes: life imprisonment or death. But if they chose the death penalty, they'd have to do the business themselves — pull the lever, administer the lethal injection, form a firing squad.

This would have several benefits: victims' families would no longer feel let down by a system too detached to feel and express their pain; the element of participation would restore public interest in the legal process; and the punishment would once more be seen to fit the crime without the disquieting overtones of state executions.

And we'd also find out if we really are a nation of hangmen.

It was a curious piece which caused some headshaking among the magazine's staff. Eventually, a sub-editor asked Pike exactly what he was trying to say.

Pike was short with boyish features, a combination which often led people to underestimate his age and toughness. He examined the sub-editor through narrow eyes: "Doesn't the headline give you a clue?"

The sub opened the magazine: "A Modest Proposal?" He shook his head. "Sorry, don't get it."

"Have you heard of Jonathan Swift?"

The sub shook his head again.

"He wrote *Gulliver's Travels*; surely you've heard of that?"

"Oh yeah." The sub forced a weak grin. "Have to admit, I've never actually got round to reading it."

"Course not," snapped Pike. "There isn't a serial killer in it. Swift wrote an essay called 'A Modest Proposal', about poverty in Ireland. He suggested the solution was for the Irish to breed like mad, fatten up their babies, and sell them to the English as delicacies."

"Jesus."

Pike could see the sub-editor had no idea what he was talking about. "I'm glad we've had this little chat," he said with a thin smile and walked away.

The sub reported the conversation to a colleague.

"It doesn't surprise me," said the colleague. "Pike's been very strange lately. If he was still married, I'd say he was having an affair."

It took Leo Strange most of the day to track his man down. He finally found him just before six, in the upstairs bar of the Globe.

Brandon Mules was sitting by himself at a corner table, reading the racing section; there was one decent mouthful or three sips left in his beer glass. Strange suspected he was making it last.

When Mules heard the chair being pulled out, he lowered his newspaper and ran a hostile eye over the inoffensive-looking middle-aged man who'd sat down opposite him. Satisfied he didn't owe the man money and therefore had no reason to be civil, he raised the newspaper and said firmly, "Feel free to fuck off."

A minute passed. Having heard nothing to indicate that his invitation had been acted upon, Mules lowered the paper again. He was almost two metres tall and weighed close to 120 kilograms and was used to people fucking off with alacrity when he suggested it, so there was a trace of curiosity in his glare.

"Didn't I just tell you to fuck off?"

"Well, more or less," said Strange with the conciliatory half-smile of a man who didn't want to get into a debate over semantics. "You look like you could do with a refill; allow me."

Mules stared at him for a few seconds, then shrugged and went back to his paper. "Double Jack, ice, and a splash of Coke," he said from behind the racing section. "Tell that poof barman just a splash or else he'll drown the bastard."

Strange fetched Mules' bourbon and a single malt whisky for himself. He sat down and raised his glass: "Your very good health."

Mules said, "Cin fucking cin," swallowed half his drink and went back to the racing pages.

Strange took a careful sip of his single malt. "My sources tell me you're not as dim as you sometimes appear, Mr Mules. I hope they haven't let me down."

Mules signed. He folded the racing section and dropped it on the floor.

Whoever he was, this bloke wasn't one of those all-time losers who hang around pubs hoping someone will take pity on them: he was in his fifties, balding, with placid, shrewd grey eyes. Now that Mules had a good look, he saw prosperity in the pink, smooth features, the comfortable plumpness and the expensive, understated clothes: single-breasted dark pinstripe suit, white shirt and discreet gold cuff-links, navy-blue polka-dot tie, and an oyster-white raincoat which had fallen open to reveal a Burberry label.

"Okay," said Mules. "I'll play the game: who the fuck are you and what the fuck do you want?"

"Leo Strange is my name. I have a proposition for you, one I think you'll find attractive. It involves significant financial reward — and the opportunity to get even with Clyde Early."

Brandon Mules was an ex-ruby player. In 1982, when he was twenty-three, he was being tipped for big things by a few pundits; unfortunately, the new Auckland coach wasn't one of them. At the start of the season, he'd taken

Mules aside and given him a concise, scathing and perceptive evaluation of his ability and prospects. With that door slammed in his face Mules had followed the so-called lira trail to Italy, where New Zealand players were in hot demand and the game's amateurism regulations were paid the sort of nonchalant lip-service the French pay their marriage vows.

In September 1988, Mules was about to start his second season with a struggling small-town club located two hours' drive north of Venice. It usually took a club a couple of seasons to realise that he wasn't half as formidable as he looked. Then the new coach arrived. Within an hour of parking his brand-new BMW 325i outside the club's headquarters, Clyde Early had summoned Mules to his office and sacked him.

Mules asked about his contract. Early said he didn't give a rat's arse about contracts.

Mules spluttered: "You haven't seen me play yet so how the hell can you sack me?"

"I saw you at home," said Early dismissively. "Once a sheila, always a sheila."

Mules had tried going over Early's head to the club's director, a nephew of the tycoon who bankrolled the whole show. The director was an obliging young man; Mules expected he'd be easily bullied. But before Mules could build up a head of steam, the director made Latin gestures of the fatalistic variety and asked what could he do? His uncle had given Early a free hand. Mules demanded that his contract be paid out. The director opened a folder on his desk. It contained bills and expenses which Mules, without authorisation, had charged to the club: massive phone bills, petrol accounts, even bar and restaurant tabs.

The director went through the bills, digressing to compare notes on various restaurants, before suggesting that, under the circumstances, perhaps they should just call it quits.

When Mules began to make vague threats, the director's habitual smile slowly shrank until it had disappeared altogether, like a ripple fading from the surface of a pond.

"You have a saying in English, no? When in Rome, you do like the Romans. This is Italy, my friend, but you are not Italian. You should think about that before you make trouble."

Mules did think about it. He concluded that it could mean various things, ranging from being hassled by the tax people to starting his car one nippy morning and having his ballbag blown over the Dolomites. He decided not to rock the boat.

Mules had always claimed he'd up and left Italy simply because he'd had enough of the place so he asked: "Get even with Clyde Early? What the fuck for?"

The question seemed to surprise Strange. "For dumping you from that club in Italy, of course."

"What gave you that idea? I'd just had a gutsful of the dagos."

Strange placed both hands on the table: "Mr Mules, we're wasting time. I do my homework: Early sacked you, he threw you out like last week's milk. Why pretend otherwise?"

Mules shrugged and finished his drink. "It was ages ago. Who gives a shit?"

"If you don't, I shouldn't have thought anyone would," said Strange, whose unflappable, omniscient manner was getting on Mules' nerves. "If you do, I'm offering you a chance to get your own back — and, as I say, earn good money while you're at it."

"What sort of money are we talking about?"

"I'll pay you ten thousand dollars, half in advance, for an assignment which shouldn't take more than a couple of weeks and which you can do in your spare time. If it transpires that more time is needed, we'll come to an arrangement based on the initial fee."

Mules grossed $3500 a month working night shifts as a security guard. He nodded warily: "What do I have to do? Kill his wife and kids and the cocker spaniel?"

A pained expression appeared on Strange's face. "Good Lord, no, nothing of the sort." He leaned forward, lowering his voice. "I understand Mr Early's playing up — not seeing enough of his wife but seeing far too much of someone else's. I want you to find out if that's so and, if it is, to get proof of it."

"How the hell would I do that?"

"I'll give you the woman's name. You're to observe her, record her meetings with Early, and, if possible, photograph them together."

"Why don't I just spy on Early?"

"He knows you; she doesn't: this way there's less risk of being spotted. Are you interested?"

"You got the money on you?"

"The advance? Yes, it's in here." Strange patted a tan leather satchel beside his chair.

When Mules nodded agreement, Strange took a small leather-bound notebook and a fountain pen from inside his suit. He wrote in the notebook, tore off the page, and handed it to Mules. He'd written, "MRS MAURICE TROUSDALE".

Mules shot him a sharp look. "Trousdale's loaded, isn't he?"

"I'm led to believe he's worth in the order of two hundred and fifty million dollars."

Mules slipped the piece of paper into his jacket pocket. "There're a couple of things I'd like to know."

Strange nodded. "I assumed there would be."

"If I get what you want, what are you going to do with it?"

Strange tapped a thumbnail against his teeth as he pretended to weigh up whether or not to answer the question. "I suppose you're entitled to know. I'd simply point out to Mr Early that with something like that bubbling away in the background, it wouldn't be a good time for him to be in the spotlight — as he undoubtedly would be if he became the Auckland coach, for instance."

Mule's mouth fell open. "You mean you want to stop Early getting the coach's job? What the fucking hell for?"

Strange pursed his lips in an expression of polite regret. "I'm afraid I'm not at liberty to reveal that. Suffice to say, Mr Early would like to become the Auckland coach; I'd prefer that he didn't."

Mules sat back scratching his jaw, which was blue-black, and looked as hard as a horseshoe; like a lot about him, it was a case of appearances being deceptive. He stared at Strange, who held his gaze until he became distracted by the thick black fuzz on the back of Mules' hand.

Eventually, Mules said: "Well, you've certainly come to the right bloke — I mean, you'd have to hunt high and low to find anyone who'd get more fun out of fucking things up for Early than me. But say what you like about the prick, he can coach: the other bloke belongs in a zoo. So I'm confused about a couple of things. The first is why someone would go to all this trouble to help a suckback like Barney Tingle. The second is you, Mr Leo Strange — if that's who you really are. I bet you couldn't tell the difference between a rugby ball and King Kong's left testicle. So how about you tell me what's really going on here."

Strange finished his drink. "You can look me up in the Wellington phone book, under Strange and Associates. You know what and you know how much; that's all you need to know and it's certainly all I intend to tell you. So for the last time: do you want the job or not?"

"Shit yeah, I'll do it."

Strange said, "Good," with a short, satisfied nod. He picked up his satchel. "Shall we find ourselves somewhere a little more private?"

As Strange led the way downstairs, Mules asked, "What do Strange and Associates do?"

Strange smiled primly over his shoulder: "I suppose you could call me a facilitator; that's as good a description as any."

4

The phone call that changed Meredith Fife-Crossley's life came at 7.19 a.m. on Christmas Eve 1993, a Friday.

Fife-Crossley, who was known as Rusty because of her eye-catching red-brown hair, had been dreaming of the time she and her sister Milly had netted a small trout from a stream on Fife Station, the 50,000-acre family property in the Mackenzie Country. They'd run all the way back to the house with it, uphill across three paddocks.

The housekeeper had cleaned the trout, fried it and served it with new potatoes no bigger than golf balls, and runner beans. Their parents had gone to Geraldine for the day and, at the last moment, Milly had a flutter of remorse over the trout and opted for reheated shepherd's pie, so Meredith had it all to herself. Whenever she remembered that meal, she wondered why the trout she'd had since didn't taste half as good. She also wondered what happened to Milly's conscience.

That was 1976, the year before Meredith went to boarding school and got her nickname. She was twelve years old and happier than she'd ever been since.

Fife-Crossley resented being jerked from that enormous sunlit kitchen, with its stone floor and mingled smells of roast meat and baked bread, back to her south-facing shoebox of a flat off Parnell Rise. She snatched up the bedside phone and complained about it.

The caller was Caspar Quedley, a public relations hot-shot who'd once made a women's magazine's list of New Zealand's ten most eligible bachelors. Quedley liked to claim that he was only heterosexual on the list, which wasn't quite true.

He and Fife-Crossley had been lovers for a time, a surprisingly long time given that both of them suffered from low boredom thresholds in their relationships. When the affair ended without emotional damage on either side, they'd pledged to remain friends. They'd managed to do so, despite their practice of spending the night together every now and again for old times' sake.

He asked, "Are you alone?"

A good question. "Hang on."

She propped herself up on one elbow and took stock: the other half of the double bed was empty and bore no sign of recent occupation.

"It would appear so."

"So where did you strike out last night?"

"The French Café. I went with a crowd. Actually, I did toy with the idea of dragging one home . . ."

"Don't tell me he baulked?"

"Well, things were going fine until he put tomato sauce on his confit duck leg. As you know, Caspar, I'm nothing if not broad-minded. I mean, I've done it with a Pakistani — granted he went to Eton and Oxford and was an international cricketer. I've done it with a negro, a West Indian to be precise, who also played cricket . . ."

"I didn't know you had a thing about cricket players?"

"I'd admit to a slight weakness for cricketers, although, paradoxically, only foreign ones."

"And particularly those of the dusky, loose-limbed, hung-like-a-wildebeest persuasion?"

"That does seem to help. Now, Caspar, much as I enjoy talking about big, black dicks before breakfast, I'd appreciate you getting to the point. I was sound asleep when the phone went, dreaming of better days."

"Lydia Trousdale croaked last night; I heard it on the radio."

"How terribly sad. But seeing I'd never met the woman, I fail to see why you had to wake me up to tell me . . .?"

"With Lydia out of the way, her son and sole heir Maurice, aka the Troll, is now up for grabs."

"What are you talking about?"

"Come on, Rusty, get with it. The main reason Maurice has never married is that every girl he took home for the once-over got the thumbs-down from the old hag. Trousers, to his credit, always managed to foil her match-making with passive resistance. The point is, he's now free to marry whoever he likes — and if dribble is a reliable indicator, he likes you."

"Caspar, that's a vile suggestion, even by your standards — Maurice Trousdale wouldn't win a beauty contest in a leper colony."

"He wouldn't get past the first round, but that's hardly the issue: how many lepers of your acquaintance are worth two hundred million bucks?"

Fife-Crossley rolled onto her back and stared thoughtfully at the ceiling. She'd never had much time for the school of thought which maintains that looks aren't everything but, hey, it was a woman's prerogative to change her mind.

Rusty's great-great-grandfather Jock Fife established one of the first of the great South Canterbury Hill stations in the upland valleys of the Two Thumbs Range, east of Lake Tekapo. His son transformed the stone cottage Jock built on the property into an impressive fifteen-room homestead. The house and station remained intact and in the Fife-Crossley family until late 1984 when Milly, who was three-and-a-half years older than her sister, came back from Europe with her fiancé.

Her husband, as he quickly became, was an English stockbroker. His family claimed lineage from George Villiers, a courtier noted for his dancing to whom

King James I, the Scottish homosexual, gave a dukedom for services to pillow-biting. Because Mrs Fife-Crossley was a snob and was bored with her high-country existence, she championed the son-in-law's suggestion that the family should sell up, invest the money on the buoyant stock exchange, and move to Christchurch to lead more interesting lives.

She got her way. Things went pretty much as the son-in-law had predicted until June 1987: Mr and Mrs Fife-Crossley and their younger daughter returned from a week's skiing at Mount Hutt to discover that Milly and her husband had liquidated the family's $2.5 million share portfolio, transferred the money to a bank account in the Cayman Islands, and caught a plane to Los Angeles. Where they and the money went after that was anyone's guess.

There'd been only one confirmed sighting of them since: on television, in a close-up of the crowd at the 1989 Wimbledon ladies' final. After they'd watched the replay several times, the Fife-Crossleys agreed that a least some of the family fortune had gone on plastic surgery — rhinoplasty for her, a chin-tuck for him. Opinions differed on whether it was money well spent.

In 1992, a friend of Rusty's returned from the USA adamant that she'd seen the brother-in-law coming out of a Pizza Hut in Fort Lauderdale, Florida. The friend said he'd had a red bandana on his head and a diamond stud in his left ear and was chatting up a pair of schoolies in cut-off jeans and bikini tops. When she'd approached him, he'd hustled the girls into a Honda Prelude and driven off.

Rusty doubted it. The Lolita syndrome had the ring of truth and, at a pinch, she could believe the red bandana and the diamond stud. But the Japanese car was stretching things and, as for the idea of her brother-in-law going to Pizza Hut, that was too much to swallow.

The Fife-Crossleys were forced to sell their five-bedroom home in leafy Fendalton with its grass tennis court and swimming pool and move into a two-bedroom townhouse in scruffy Sydenham. Rusty was twenty-four and had never had a proper job. When she asked her mother what she should do, her mother looked at her a little sadly and said, "My dear, why don't you do what girls like you have always done? Marry money."

It took a while but she managed it. Eight months after Lydia Trousdale choked to death on a Spanish black olive, her son Maurice married Meredith "Rusty" Fife-Crossley on the manicured lawn of Greywater, the Trousdale family home perched on the cliff above Mission Bay.

After the ceremony, a couple of male guests took their flutes of Krug '83 down to the edge of the cliff to smoke a cigarette and enjoy the magnificent view of Rangitoto Island and the Hauraki Gulf before the light faded.

"You know," said one, "I really don't know whether to envy Maurice or feel sorry for him. He's got the best address in Auckland, he's worth a fortune, he's never had to do a stroke of work in his life, and he never will. On the other side of the coin, he's the ugliest white man in the eastern suburbs, he got the personality of an ottoman, and now he's married to Rusty."

"Yeah, I know what you mean," said the other. "Someone was just saying that Rusty wanted to invite every bloke she's ever shagged but they couldn't find a marquee big enough."

At 10.45 on Sunday morning, 27 August, the electronically controlled gates of Greywater swung open and a British racing green Mercedes E220 cabriolet swept out. It was a perfect late-winter's day: still, bright and warm enough to encourage people with cabriolets to put the tops down.

All Leo Strange had been able to tell Brandon Mules about Mrs Trousdale was that the lady was a youngish, attractive redhead with something of a reputation. He hadn't elaborated on that point, the implication being that women earn reputations for one thing and one thing only. Mules was parked 30 metres up the street from Greywater; when he saw that the driver of the Mercedes was a woman with auburn hair, he started his Ford Laser and followed her down to Mission Bay and into the waterfront carpark.

The woman, whom Mules assumed, correctly, was Mrs Trousdale, crossed Tamaki Drive and sat down at a café's pavement table. Mules watched her from the carpark for a couple of minutes, then followed suit. He sat behind her, at a table just inside the open double-doors, so he could study her at leisure while she'd have to twist around and look over her right shoulder to see him.

Lustrous chestnut hair fell on her shoulders; the fringe swooped over one eye and curled around her jawline. She had a sharp little nose faintly dusted with freckles, and a wide, well-defined slightly pouting mouth accentuated by crimson lipstick. She was slim, neither short nor tall, and wore black leggings and a thick, loose-fitting, cream turtleneck sweater which reached the tops of her thighs. When she arched her back and stretched, Mules saw the tight swell of her breasts under the sweater.

As if she'd sensed that she was being watched, she took off her sunglasses, draped an arm over the back of her chair, and looked around. Her gaze swept the café, not pausing for an instant on Mules or the other customers. The way her green eyes slid indifferently over him convinced Mules, not that he needed much convincing, that he was dealing with a 24-carat, nose-in-the-air, rich bitch.

He'd seen plenty like her during his stint in Italy, in the smart shops and cafés, promenading along the canals of Venice or in the squares of Treviso. He'd based many a lurid fantasy on the premise that, behind their disdainful exteriors, those elegant creatures were on the prowl for uncouth beefcake such as himself to satisfy their yen for rough trade. The fact that, in six years, not one of them as much as asked him for a light didn't deter Mules from similar thoughts vis-à-vis Mrs Trousdale.

She was checking her Patek Philippe watch yet again when her mobile phone rang. After a brief conversation which didn't seem to please her, she ordered a café latte. She took a cloth-bound book the size of a fat paperback from her handbag and began to write in it.

Once it had dawned on Mules that Mrs Trousdale was updating her diary, it didn't take him long to grasp the implications and work out his next move. Leo Strange's sources had been as reliable as ever: Mules wasn't as dim as he sometimes appeared.

Since the break-up of his second marriage, the editor Jackson Pike had lived alone in a rented townhouse in Grange Road, Mount Eden.

At getting on for 11 o'clock that Sunday night, Pike was about to switch off his word processor and treat himself to a nightcap and half an hour of *Madame Butterfly* courtesy of Von Karajan, Pavarotti, and the Vienna Philharmonic, when he heard a noise downstairs. Fearing that he might have inadvertently programmed the dishwasher to irrigate inner West Auckland, he hurried to investigate.

At the foot of the stairs, he was confronted by a figure in a ski mask and dark boiler suit who pointed a pistol at his Adam's apple and said "Trick or treat?" Pike was trying to think of a reply when a third party rabbit-punched him behind the right ear and he fell over unconscious.

For a few awful moments after he came to, Pike thought he'd gone blind. He felt fabric against his face and realised that he had a hood over his head. He also had a gag in his mouth and his hands were tied behind his back. All he could do was roll back and forward and, even then, only a little way because he was in some kind of container.

After what seemed like an hour but was actually a quarter of that, Pike heard car doors quietly open and close and an engine start.

He was moving. He was in the boot of a car.

The car stopped. They hadn't gone far, five kilometres, if that. The boot was opened; he was hauled out and set on his feet. Strong hands gripped him. A voice said, "Walk."

They went from road to shingle path to soft, uneven ground, kicking up dead leaves and crunching twigs. Pike's mind raced on the spot, spitting out panic, like a news wire ten minutes after someone took a shot at the president.

"Stop." The hood came off.

Trees. Not dense bush, more like woods. Silence, no lights. Where the hell are we? The Waitakeres? Too far. Two of them in ski masks and boiler suits. Holy Jesus God, is that a silencer?

The one with the pistol said, "Shall we ungag him?"

"Why not? Al, see to it he doesn't make a fuss."

Al came back behind him. He slipped his left arm under Pike's and wrapped his hand around the back of the neck. He clamped his right hand over Pike's jaw, the thumb and finger digging into his cheeks. Al's hand seemed inhumanly powerful, as if he could squeeze Pike's head until his eyes popped like champagne corks.

The gunman said, "Let me introduce ourselves: we represent the Aotearoa People's Army — you may have heard of us. We've had our eye on you for some time, Mr Pike, and I'm afraid that editorial was the last straw."

"Christ, that wasn't meant to be taken literally," gasped Pike, working his jaw laboriously in Al's iron grip.

"A Modest Proposal: yes, I wondered if you were modelling yourself on Dean Swift. A little presumptuous of you, if I may so."

Al felt Pike's chest heave as he filled his lungs.

Pike heard a sound like a thousand bullwhips cracking in unison and the bank of screens in his head went to black forever.

5

Amanda Hayhoe left for work on a Monday morning feeling rested, clear-headed and a little smug. She'd had a very quiet weekend.

When she spotted the envelope under her windscreen wiper, she thought about it for a few seconds, then went back to the house and got the rubber gloves from under the kitchen sink: Sadie the Cleaning Lady meets Nancy Drew, girl detective.

She took the envelope inside. It was plain white and unaddressed, like the one from the Aotearoa People's Army. She dithered over whether to open it or ring the police; eventually, she reminded herself that she was a journalist, not a cop. Besides, for all she knew, it might be a marriage proposal from her near-neighbour, the Sultan of Brunei.

She carefully slit the envelope open with a short-bladed knife and removed the note with her landlady's eyebrow tweezers. As she read it, her eyes widened and her left hand went slowly to her open mouth.

She rang Auckland Central and was put through to Detective Sergeant Ihaka.

"You thought of something?" his voice didn't throb with expectation.

"No, it's not that. I got another letter this morning."

"From them?"

"Yes, from them."

"You opened it." It wasn't a question; a disapproving silence followed.

She gabbled into the vacuum: "I was going to ring you first, then I thought, what if it's got nothing to do with the APA, I'd just've wasted your time. I was pretty careful — I used washing-up gloves and eyebrow tweezers so there shouldn't . . ."

"Ms Hayhoe."

"Yes?"

"Who's this week's human sacrifice?"

"Jackson Pike."

"Who's he?"

"The editor of *New Nation* magazine. He's probably the best-known print journalist in the country."

"Well, if he wasn't before, he sure as shit will be now," said Ihaka with breezy callousness. "What do they say?"

"I'll read it. It's headed 'Communiqué Number Two'. 'Last week, the Aotearoa People's Army carried out revolutionary punitive action against the reactionary broadcaster, Freckleton. We issued an unequivocal warning to the media mouthpieces that we would undertake similar action against those who persist with extreme right-wing propaganda intended to mobilise reactionary elements.

"'In his magazine, J. Pike has been openly hostile towards progressive causes. In particular, he has promoted an imperialist and racist line on the struggle for Maori liberation, sovereignty and the return of lands, forests and fisheries to their rightful owners and guardians.

"'In his most recent editorial, Pike signalled his intent to campaign for the reintroduction of the death penalty. While he purported to be concerned with violent crime, it is axiomatic that judicial execution is a weapon used by authoritarian regimes to eliminate so-called enemies of the state — i.e., radical oppositionist forces. Transparently, Pike aimed to fuel this campaign — and camouflage its true purpose — by whipping up hysteria over supposed lenient sentencing.

"'Accordingly, the Aotearoa People's Army, acting on behalf of the masses, has administered revolutionary justice. No one should doubt our seriousness or our resolve to undertake similar action. Those who continue to ignore our warnings will have only themselves to blame for the consequences.' That's it."

"Same as last time — stuck under your windscreen wiper?"

"Yep. Same sort of stationery, same printing in capital letters."

"They don't say what they've actually done with him?"

"No. So nothing's . . . happened?"

"There no fresh meat in the morgue if that's what you're trying to say. Are you at home?"

"Yes."

"Sit tight. I'll send someone to pick up the mail."

About the time that Hayhoe was alerting the producer of the 6 o'clock news, Brandon Mules was getting Strange and Associates' phone number from directory service.

He rang it and got a recorded message: "You have reached the Wellington office of Strange and Associates. All our staff are occupied at present so please leave a message after the beep. If you wish to send a fax, press start after the beep."

Mules waited a few minutes and tried again with the same result. He rang every three or four minutes for half an hour but Leo Strange's brutally overworked staff didn't have time to answer the phone.

Mules left home. He stopped in at a post office to check Strange and Associates' address in a Wellington telephone directory. It didn't come as a big surprise that it was a post office box number, or that there wasn't a private listing for L. Strange.

He got back in his car and drove east to resume surveillance of Mrs Trousdale.

Mules guessed he was in for a day in the life of a lady of leisure: coffee and lunch with the big hair, year-round tan set, then hit the boutiques to try on more outfits than they've got in drag queen heaven. And if Strange's dirt was on the money, somewhere along the line she might take time out for a bounce on the mattress trampoline with Clyde Early.

It wasn't quite like that.

It was mid-morning and raining hard when Mrs Trousdale steered the green Mercedes out of Greywater. She passed Mule's Laser without a sideways glance and followed the previous day's route down to Tamaki Drive. She went into a delicatessen then drove up St Heliers Road, through Tamaki and Panmure, and across the Panmure Bridge to Pakuranga Heights. She parked outside a centre for intellectually handicapped children and went in.

The rained eased and finally stopped, patches of blue sky appeared: a pale sun came out but Mrs Trousdale didn't. Mules read the paper, listened to the radio, smoked a couple of cigarettes.

At 1 o'clock, Mrs Trousdale and another woman come out hand in hand with two small children who were well wrapped up against the weather. They got into the Mercedes and went back across the Panmure Bridge, through Ellerslie to Cornwall Park, where they went for a walk, made friends with a few sheep and had lunch on a park bench.

Fifty metres away, Mules cursed himself for not bringing something to eat. He tried to take his mind off food by working out the quartet's relationship: the kids belonged to the other woman but Christ knew where Coppertop fitted in — unless ferrying them around was her good deed for the month.

After an hour in the park, she returned them to the centre, then headed back over the bridge. This time, she turned left into Mount Wellington Highway and got on the motorway. She came off at the Market Road exit and went down Remuera Road towards Newmarket. Okay, time to thrash the plastic. But at the top of the hill where Remuera Road descends to hit Broadway, she swung off the road and pulled up outside a church hall.

Mules snarled, "What the fuck's she up to now?" and looked around for a park.

It took him twenty minutes to get one in sight of the Mercedes. He'd just switched off when Mrs Trousdale and an almost elderly woman came out of the church hall carrying covered trays. The Mercedes being a two-door, there was a bit of a performance over getting the trays onto the back seat. Then Mrs Trousdale jumped in and took off.

She went through Newmarket and up Khyber Pass to Newton, where she stopped outside a shabby old wooden bungalow. It might've fitted the first-home buyer's formula of the worst house in the neighbourhood's best street, but whoever dreamt that up probably didn't have Newton in mind.

Mules watched her take in a tray; I don't believe this — first the mongols, now fucking meals on wheels. I thought she was meant to be the town bike, not Florence fucking Nightingale.

She made drops at equally insalubrious residences in Eden Terrace and Grafton before crossing back to the right side of the tracks for another call in a quiet street overlooking Orakei Basin.

As she got out of the car, the rain fell like a silver curtain. She slung her handbag over her shoulder and reached into the car for an umbrella. She unfurled it but when she went to get a tray from the back seat, it all got too awkward. She put down the umbrella, tossed her handbag into the car, pulled out the tray, grabbed the brolly, kicked the door shut, and ran for it. Mules was idling back at the corner; when she disappeared up a long drive, he knew he'd never have a better chance.

The other visits had taken five to ten minutes. Shit, it'd be the highlight of a bedridden old fart's week; no way they'd let her dump the grub and fuck off without a bit of a yarn, even if she had left her car unlocked.

He cruised up alongside the Mercedes and double parked. It took him 75 seconds to get out of his car and into hers, grab the diary from her handbag and a leftover sandwich from the brown paper bag on the passenger seat, get back in his car and zoom.

Without checking the filling, he took a bite of the sandwich. He gagged: smoked salmon with alfalfa and cream cheese. No fucking wonder it was left over; even mongols wouldn't eat that shit.

He tossed it going down Greenlane Road and dropped in for a party pack at the KFC on the corner of Dominion and Balmoral.

Dudley Garlick, the Anglican Dean of Auckland, was forty-five when he first felt the dull ache of what turned out to be loneliness. Because it had never occurred to him to consider any domestic arrangement other than self-contained bachelorhood, it took him a while to diagnose his condition. At first, he'd wondered if it foreshadowed a loss of faith.

Identifying the problem was one thing; solving it was another matter altogether. There were, for instance, several maiden ladies among his flock who appeared to nurse fond and, he suspected, maternal feelings towards him. For his part, he was surprisingly unintimidated at the thought of embarking on a relationship with a member of the fair sex after a twenty-year hiatus.

But after some careful thought, he decided that it wouldn't work. It wasn't that he recoiled from the intimacy of marriage: after all, if it actually got to the point of conjugals, it would more than likely transpire that in the kingdom of the blind, the one-eyed man — i.e. himself — was king. No, the sticking point was that, while he accepted that marriage required some suppression of the idiosyncratic self in the interests of co-existence, he knew that he'd suited himself in too many respects for too long not be begrudge infringements on his autonomy.

After a good deal of meditation and having urged the Lord to throw in His two cents' worth, the Reverend Dudley Garlick decided to get a dog, a golden Labrador, to be precise.

Martin — named after the director Martin Scorsese, who'd made a film about the crucifixion which had impressed Garlick — was a sweet-natured animal with a quite phenomenal appetite. The dog-owners among his parishioners warned him that unless he rationed Martin's tucker with an iron hand and exercised him regularly, the pooch would bloat before his very eyes. Garlick, himself capable of shifting industrial quantities of food and drink and no fan of activities requiring physical effort, took little notice. A fat, jolly man, that was his attitude; he and Martin would exemplify the serenity conferred by a well-nourished, reflective existence.

So it came as a rude shock to the cleric when, a mere forty in doggy years and resembling a baby hippo in a fur coat, Martin simply lay down and died. After hoovering two kilos of gravy beef with his usual blinding speed and bestowing a final, loving look on his master, he flopped down in a patch of sunlight, never to stir again.

Garlick got another golden Lab when he moved into the deanery. This time he vowed to do it by the book: there would be no repeat of the indulgent regime which brought about poor Martin's premature demise.

Thus, every evening, whatever the weather, Emma — after Emma Peel, the character in *The Avengers* played by Diana Rigg and the object of roughly 90 per cent of the carnal thoughts (the other ten per cent being evenly shared among Mary Tyler Moore, anonymous lingerie models and stiletto heels) — and the dean could be found taking their constitutional in Auckland Domain.

It was cold with a moist, blustery wind and the light was fading fast when they set off at 5.15 that Monday evening. They entered the domain off St Stephens Avenue and marched up the rise to the War Memorial Museum. Coming down the slope towards Stanley Street, Emma, who had been obese and complacent, began straining at the leash, tugging Garlick towards the woods on the lower, northern side of the domain, below the road.

This was normal behaviour. On summer evenings, Garlick often took Emma into the woods, sometimes even let her off the leash so she could plunge madly into the undergrowth. Not tonight, my girl; this isn't a night for the woods. The rain was driving flat on the wind, spitting icily in under Garlick's umbrella; darkness was closing in. He had an overpowering urge to get back to the deanery, build a blazing fire and get outside several brandy and sodas.

But Emma was pulling like a mad thing. Faced with the alternative of having his right shoulder wrenched from its socket, Garlick gave in. They crossed the road and followed a track in among the trees. The dean hauled grimly on the leash to prevent Emma forcing him to break into a gallop and muttered profanely as he skidded on wet leaves and planted his brogues in sucking mud.

Suddenly, Emma surged forward, ripping the leash from his grasp, and bounded off the track into the light undergrowth. Garlick swore horribly and blundered in pursuit. It was mercifully short-lived: less than thirty metres off the track, Emma had found whatever it was that had provoked her mutiny and was giving it her full attention.

When Garlick reached the scene, she'd embarked on an exploratory chew of what proved to be the Timberland boat shoe on the dead Jackson Pike's left foot.

6

Same old scene, thought Tito Ihaka.

Blue lights flashing for no particular reason; traffic jam — cop cars, unmarked grunt machines, a dog-handler's van, the morgue-mobile; people standing around doing bugger all except pull a bit of overtime; radio-babble soundtrack.

They say the violent crime rate goes up with the mercury; there's even stats to prove it. A hot afternoon, a guy has five or six beers too many, gets one of those mean, thumping headaches, works himself up till any fucking thing's going to set him off — man, he's looking for it. So some guy he's never seen before walks into the bar and winks at his chick, maybe just gives her a little sideways smile. Whack! Stick a broken-off pool cue in his neck.

The night before, Sir Lancelot probably slapped her till her fillings rattled for changing channels on him.

They can say what they bloody well like, but it doesn't get any worse than this: going on a wet night, about seven degrees before the wind chill kicks in, to look into a dead man's face. Right on dinnertime, too.

Ihaka got out of the car, pulling on a hooded tracksuit top. A uniformed constable pointed the way with his torch beam.

He took the magazine with him, the one with the article under Jackson Pike's picture by-line which the Aotearoa People's Army had objected to. Not that he'd need it: he knew in his bones that the dead white male in the trees was Pike, just as he'd known the APA wasn't kidding the moment he'd set foot in Pike's place.

Nothing you could put your finger on: no kicked-in doors, no blood on the rug, no flesh in the waste disposal. Just something in the air he'd felt a hundred times, each time a little stronger than before: bad vibes, bad karma, bad medicine. Whatever you called it, it meant the same: someone's time had come early: someone's life just stalled on the tracks and the shit-train ran right over them.

Ihaka went along the path, towards the lights in the trees. He met Detective Constable Johan Van Roon coming the other way.

"Over there, Sarge." Van Roon pointed right, into the undergrowth.

"What's the story?"

"The doc thinks it's a broken neck but wants to get him on the slab for a good look. The bloke who found him was walking his dog, so what with its scent and the rain, our dogs are running round in circles, disappearing up each other's arse."

"Who found him?"

"A bloke called Dudley Garlick. I think we can rule him out — he's a priest." Van Roon jerked his head. "A big cheese at the cathedral over in St Stephen's Ave. A couple of the crew are up there now."

"Okay, let's have a gander."

A couple of cops and a police pathologist were in a huddle no more than three metres from the dead man's feet. Dirty-joke guffaws floated: it didn't take long before you could look at a corpse and only see paperwork.

Flashback: his first, a hippie type in a dump over in New Lynn. The guy had gobbled bad acid and decided cutting his own head off with a bread knife would be a trip. He'd got a fair way, too, a lot further than you'd think. There was enough blood to float a rubber duck and the dead kid lying there like a botched beheading. A cop and a police photographer sat on the sofa, smoking cigarettes and arguing about the Moscow Olympics.

The cop, a sergeant, beckoned Ihaka: "Hey, it's the big Maori boy. What do you reckon, fella? Keep politics out of sport, right?"

He noticed Ihaka changing colour and looking everywhere but at the mess on the floor: "Yeah, didn't this deadshit do a number on himself? Jeeze, we all cut ourselves shaving now and again but that's fucking ridiculous."

Laugh? He nearly puked.

Ihaka said loudly: "I hear there's been a murder round here — anyone seen the victim?"

The huddle broke up. Ihaka ignored the muttered greetings and squatted beside the dead man. It was Pike all right, his head lolling like a broken flower.

Ihaka headed back to his car thinking, fuck me, now they're killing each other over magazine articles.

He segued to his twenty-two-year-old niece: it wasn't that long ago, she was as normal as a kid with a Meccano set on her teeth could be. She used to follow him around like a puppy: Uncle Tito was Superman with a suntan. Even after she turned pretty and got an attitude, she wasn't a bad kid under the poses. Now she wore a hard face and raved about burning forests and blowing up dams and necklacing Uncle Toms.

The other night, he'd asked her if being a cop made him an Uncle Tom. Her voice said not necessarily, but her expression said, what do you think?

His sister shook her head, bewildered. Their mother said softly, "Something bad's coming, Tito, I can feel it, like a storm out at sea."

It's your lumbago, Ma.

A man answered the first time Brandon Mules rang Greywater. He asked for Bob and was told, a little huffily, that there was no Bob there and to kindly check the number.

He rang back a few minutes later. This time she answered — just "hello" but it was enough. He'd heard her in the café and it wasn't a voice you forgot in a hurry: cool, confident, posh — yeah, and sexy.

"Mrs Trousdale, yes or no: are you alone?"

"I'm sorry, I . . . "

Stupid bitch. "Is there anyone else there with you?"

"Well, yes . . . "

"Okay, this is a wrong number — I asked for Bob. I'll ring again in exactly five minutes — ten to eight, right? Get yourself next to a phone, somewhere private."

Mules rang at ten to eight on the dot.

She picked up after one ring: "Who is this?"

"Never mind that. Are you alone?"

"Yes, I'm upstairs but what . . . "

"Mrs Trousdale, are you missing something?"

"No. Should I be?"

"You checked your handbag since you did your bread for the poor act this afternoon?"

"Would you mind telling me what this is about?"

"I wouldn't mind at all; in fact, I'd be bloody delighted. I've got your diary."

"My diary?"

The penny hadn't dropped. Get ready, baby, you're about to spoil your frillies.

"Yeah, your diary. You know, that book you write it all down in, every little thing that happens? What Maurice got you for your birthday; how you just about broke your neck skiing; how one of your boyfriends porked you on an office desk while the blokes he was meant to be having a meeting with twiddled their thumbs next door. Ring a bell?"

Silence.

"You there, Mrs Trousdale?"

"Are you saying you've got my diary? My private diary?"

"Well, shit, if this isn't private, I'd love to read one that was."

"How did you get it?"

The indignation in her voice made Mules smile; he'd half-expected hysterics.

"What does it matter? The point is, I've got it. If you don't believe me, I'll read you some. Hang on, let me find a juicy bit. Here we go: Queen's Birthday — remember it? Maurice was in Sydney; Clyde bullshitted his missus that he had a business appointment and scooted back to town, leaving her and the kids at Taupo. Jesus, don't tell me you've forgotten already? This should jog your memory. Quote: 'Sometimes I amaze myself. For three weeks, I've hardly thought of anything else then, finally, we're in bed, Clyde's pounding away like a man possessed, and what am I thinking? M.'s coming home tomorrow and I mustn't forget to change the sheets! Zut alors! C. went at it hammer and tongs — he's no maestro but a frisky lad and fit as a fiddle. To put it crudely, he fucked the daylights out of me.' Unquote. Good old Clyde, eh? Wouldn't have thought he had it in him. Okay, what else have we got here? Oh yeah . . . " — Mules sniggered nastily — ". . . the weekend of the twenty-fifth and twenty-sixth of February. Bugger me, you do get up to some far-out . . . "

"That's enough," she said in a low, hard voice. "I'm convinced."

"Glad to hear it."

"When can I expect it to be returned?"

Mules chuckled. "Nice try, Mrs Trousdale. Full credit for positive thinking. I can see why you'd want it back, though — shit this thing's worth its weight in gold."

"Oh, I'm beginning to get the picture," she said flatly. "You want money — is that it?"

"Give the lady a stuffed toy."

"How much?"

"Now that's the sort of attitude I like — no pissing around, just get straight to the point. Well, the way I look at it, your husband's worth two hundred and fifty million bucks, so what's a lousy half a million more or less? That's just loose change."

"You're a fool, whoever you are," she said contemptuously. "Who do you think my husband is — Scrooge McDuck? Do you think he rolls around in a pile of gold coins every morning? For a start, there's hardly any cash: it's all tied up in trusts and investments. Secondly, it's looked after by an army of accountants and lawyers who might just notice if I sold off half-a-million dollars' worth of Fletchers shares. And I somehow doubt they'd believe me if I said I'd spent it on having my colours done."

Mules growled, "Who the fuck are you calling a fool? It's your fucking diary, lady, your fucking problem. I couldn't give a shit if you have to sell your nice green convertible or the family heirlooms — or your arse come to that. And while you're making up your mind, think about this: if you don't cough up, it won't be just you in the gun, it'll be your playmates as well. I bet you didn't tell them you were keeping a record."

"I'll need time."

"You've got to the end of the week. You'll be hearing from me." He hung up.

Rusty Trousdale sat on the edge of the bed with her head in her hands. Hearing her husband coming up the stairs, she scuttled into her ensuite and closed the door behind her.

He called, "Who was on the phone?"

"Vicky. I took her and the kids to Cornwall Park today. She just rang to say thanks."

"Are you almost ready? I'm a touch peckish."

There's a surprise. "Just putting on my face — I'll be down in five."

She sat in front of the mirror dabbing on make-up, her mind whirring. She had to consult someone who wouldn't be judgemental and who could give her sound advice. Luckily, she knew such a person: not only was Caspar Quedley unshockable, he also happened to be something of an authority on blackmail.

Detective Inspector Finbar McGrail looked up from the September issue of *New Nation* when Ihaka walked into his office. Although he'd been at work for thirteen hours, McGrail was his usual clean-cut, buttoned-down self: the subdued maroon tie was still tightly Windsor-knotted and his two shaves-a-day complexion shone pinkly.

"Nice night for a murder, sergeant," he said in an Ulster brogue which the fifteen years and 20,000 kilometres separating him from Belfast hadn't modified. Ihaka had grown used to it, if not fond of it. "You'd think the bugger didn't have a tongue," was his widely quoted description of McGrail's accent.

"Yep, it's nights like this make it all worthwhile." Ihaka nodded at the magazine: "You reading Pike's article? Bloody good idea, I thought."

McGrail massaged the dark rings under his eyes. "The proposition has a certain appeal, although I'm not sure Mr Pike was being altogether serious."

"It's a piss-take, right?"

"Not a particularly subtle one, either, but it still seems to've gone over our terrorists' heads." McGrail tapped a copy of the APA communiqué. "I don't suppose that should surprise us: fanatics aren't renowned for their sense of humour."

Look who's talking: Mr Fun himself.

"What can you report, Sergeant?"

"Not a lot, sir. Nothing so far from Pike's place: forensics are still over there but it doesn't look promising. We know he was home last night — someone from his work rang him there around nine. The joint looks normal — no signs of forced entry or struggle. It's like he just up and left without turning off the computer, the lights or the central heating. I'd say the front door was unlocked and they just walked in. The bed's made up, so it probably happened between nine and, say, midnight. Zilch from the neighbours: nice, quiet street, mainly families — Sunday night, they stay in and have an early one. We're still doorknocking but, meanwhile, back at the Domain, the rain's made a nice fucking mess of things. What about the communiqué?"

McGrail's thin-lipped mouth turned down at the corners: "Same story as last time — it's a cheap brand of stationery, there's a ton of it in circulation. Same writing: our resident expert seems to think this black-letter style isn't the writer's usual hand." He shook his head dolefully. "Experts — what would we do without them? No fingerprints, not even the TV woman's. Speaking of whom, is surveillance under way?"

Ihaka looked at his watch. "Started an hour ago."

McGrail put his hands behind his head and leaned back in the swivel chair, looking at the ceiling. It meant he was collecting his thoughts before delivering unwelcome news.

"I had a call from the commissioner a short while ago."

McGrail had a particularly arid tone he adopted when referring to his organisational superiors and intellectual inferiors. "He'd had a call from the minister and was merely passing on the message. The gist of it was that we can't go on losing media identities like this. Apparently, Pike wasn't just another scribbler . . ."

"I'd say he was the best-known print journo in the country," said Ihaka, as if he'd researched the matter thoroughly.

McGrail's eyebrows twitched with surprise. "You're in good company, Sergeant: the ministry — via the commissioner — said more or less the same. Anyway, the upshot is, Wellington's decided we need some help. They're sending us an expert."

Ihaka groaned. "Oh shit, no. Who?"

"An SIS man who specialises in counter-terrorism. I didn't bother to ask in which terrorist hotbeds he earned this reputation — the commissioner doesn't care for what he calls negative nit-picking."

"A counter-terrorism specialist, eh? You must've come across a few of them in Ireland?"

"You mean Ulster," said McGrail firmly.

Ihaka was briefly tempted to be flippant but thought better of it. "Sorry, Ulster."

"Yes, I did."

"What were they like?"

"They were . . ." McGrail hesitated, choosing his words.

"Cunts?" offered Ihaka helpfully.

McGrail nodded slowly. "Yes, I suppose that's as good a term as any. And rather stupid ones at that."

7

Maurice Trousdale's favourite things in life were French cuisine, Italian cuisine, South Australian red wine, his wife's smooth, responsive body, and his pearl-grey Bentley Mulsanne Turbo. In that order.

Most mornings, he took the Bentley for a spin. It was as good a way as any of filling in time between breakfast and lunch, after which his blood-alcohol count was usually too high for carefree motoring. And while experience had taught him that it was both pointless and dangerous to make assumptions about when he was likely to be granted access to his wife's body, she was seldom at her most playful — or most obliging — early in the day.

As soon as the Bentley glided out of Greywater that Tuesday morning, Rusty Trousdale set about contacting Caspar Quedley. That wasn't entirely straightforward since, to all intents and purposes, he'd disappeared off the face of the earth.

The decline and fall of Caspar Quedley was triggered by a story in the January 1994 issue of *New Nation* magazine. It revealed that as a pupil at Auckland's exclusive Prince Albert College, Quedley had blackmailed the school chaplain over his masochistic infatuation with a choirboy. A few weeks later, the chaplain drove his car into a brick wall. It also emerged that Quedley had unleashed a notorious standover man in an attempt to stop the reporter airing his dirty laundry.

Quedley had prospered and made himself influential in a shadowy, behind-the-scenes way by running what amounted to a political and corporate intelligence service in tandem with his public relations consultancy. He had the ears and, frequently, the undivided attention of some of the most powerful people in the land through his judicious dissemination of the rumour, gossip and information he accumulated from his network of contacts spanning the business, political and media worlds.

By close of business on the magazine's publication day, Quedley had taken calls from representatives of the prime minister, the leader of the Opposition, and the heads of several major companies. The message from all of them was short and sour: henceforth, Quedley was as non grata as a person could be.

By mid-January, as the nation drifted back to work after the Christmas break, the vultures were circling. With the media's habitual relish for kicking a man when he's down, a TV current-affairs programme did a bludgeoning follow-up of the *New Nation* story. Cornered by a reporter and cameraman, a haunted-looking Quedley had expressed the hope that his clients would bear with him in this difficult time. They didn't.

By February, Quedley Communications (Counsel, Strategy, Crisis Management) had closed its doors. Quedley sold his Lexus and put his Mission Bay townhouse and Coromandel hideaway on the market. Then he simply disappeared.

In May, Rusty Fife-Crossley received a postcard. Quedley wrote: "Greetings from beyond the pale. How goes the Troll hunt? Answer on a postcard to Private Bag, Rotorua. C.Q."

She wrote back to inform him of her betrothal and beg him to attend the wedding.

Six weeks later he replied thus:

Dear Rusty,

Congratulations. I hope it makes you very happy, although I wouldn't put the house on it — not that I have one to put. If that strikes you as a bit rich after my Cupid act, what the hell? This is no time for you to start giving a toss what others think.

I won't be at the wedding. Much as I appreciate the invite, Trousers would find me as welcome as an outbreak of genital warts. Besides, I'm planning to lay low for a while; as Captain Oates said, I may be some time. If you want or need to get in touch, write care of my lawyer, Paddy Tickford at Trubshaw Trimble.

Yours in disgrace,
Caspar

When Rusty returned from Mauritius, she wrote Quedley a chatty letter describing, in perhaps unnecessary detail, the wedding, the honeymoon, and her new life as Mrs Maurice Trousdale.

The reply, postmarked Tauranga, was snappy: "It sounds divine but you left out the most interesting bit — how often does the little toad expect you to spread 'em?"

Somewhat miffed and mindful of her husband's fear and loathing of Quedley, she'd allowed the correspondence to lapse.

Rusty rang Trubshaw Trimble. She introduced herself to Tickford and explained that she needed to see Quedley.

The lawyer put her on hold. Two minutes later: "Well, you are on the list, Mrs Trousdale — one of the select few — but could you tell me why you want to see Caspar? His instructions were quite clear — emergencies only."

"I can't give you the details but trust me: it's an emergency."

"For who?"

"For me."

"Surely you've got others you could call upon?"

She took a deep breath. "Mr Tickford, Caspar is the only person I know who just might be able to solve my problem. He's also the only person I'd even discuss it with."

"Well, I wish you luck, Mrs Trousdale. But I think I should warn you: speaking as one who's had a bit to do with him since his fall from grace, I wouldn't want to be relying on him."

"Why not?"

"Because I don't think my trials and tribulations concern him in the slightest — and right now I'm probably the best friend he's got."

Maybe so, but I bet he's never worn a pair of your undies to a meeting with Rupert Murdoch.

"I'll risk it," she said. "I've got nothing to lose."

Tickford gave her the address. Quedley was in Cambridge; she could be there in a couple of hours. She didn't ring ahead in case he told her not to bother coming.

At twenty minutes past midday, Rusty pulled up behind a filthy Land Rover parked outside a white weatherboard cottage in a short street four blocks back from the main road through Cambridge. She imagined that in spring, with the sun shining, the flowers coming into bloom and leaves on the trees, it could be a picture of small town, slightly olde worlde charm. But at the gag-end of a wet winter with a cold wind shaking skeletal branches it felt more like the last, drab, sad stop on a terminal decline. She shivered and shrugged into her black leather coat, pulling the belt tight.

She walked up the crazy pavement path to the front door and pressed the bell. A gaunt, shaggy refugee wearing a navy-blue fisherman's pullover and corduroy pants opened the door. They examined one another for a few seconds.

Finally, she said, "I'm in deep shit, Caspar."

Quedley looked into the middle distance. "You're just in time for luncheon. It's spécialité de la maison — baked beans on toast."

Amanda Hayhoe sat at a table in the Atomic Café in Ponsonby Road spooning down café latte and reviewing the recent phone conversation with her producer.

The way he'd gone on about Pike's murder making it a whole new ball game and what a nightmare unsolved crime gigs were, she'd got it into her head that he was going to can the story — or give it to someone else. "The punters like happy endings, Amanda, they like things cut and dried. You could spend a month on this story and not know any more about the APA than we do now. Alternatively, the cops could have someone behind bars and we'd get sub judiced."

Minor tantrum time: "Phil, don't even think about taking me off it. I just can't believe you're getting cold feet over the biggest story . . ."

"Who said anything about taking you off it? I happen to have budgets and schedules to worry about and I just want to make sure we end up with something to show for this, all right? I want you to put together some stuff on Pike so if we come up light on the APA, we can re-angle it to Jackson Pike, Media Martyr."

So now Hayhoe was waiting for Justin Hinshelwood, a *New Nation* staff writer she vaguely knew and was relying on to shed some light on the late, self-effacing Mr Pike.

Hinshelwood showed up. He was around thirty, tall and gangly with designer spectacles and dressed for the wilds of Ponsonby in a green anorak, plaid shirt over a grey T-shirt, jeans and sturdy boots. After allowing a decent period for lamentations, Hayhoe asked him to fill her in on Pike.

"Pike was a driven, workaholic." Hinshelwood talked like he wrote. "He didn't do small talk or socialise with the troops. He didn't confide — like, we only twigged that his marriage had folded because he started putting in even longer hours."

Hayhoe sighed. "What were his interests outside work?"

"You tell me. Far as we could see there was no outside work. I know he was into classical music because I bumped into him in Marbeck's one night. Come to think of it, his performance pretty well summed him up. I asked what he'd bought and, the way he carried on, you'd think I'd asked to see his will. The bottom line on Pike is this: knew how to get a magazine out but not someone you'd choose to be marooned on a desert island with."

"He sounds a bit paranoid?"

Hinshelwood took the cue: "Get this: he wouldn't use the hard drive on his office word processor. He worked on floppies and took them home because someone once tapped into his machine and went through his files."

"What did they find?"

"Big brother was watching us — that's what they found. He kept tabs on everyone: how much time we took over a story, how much rewriting it needed, how many letters of praise or complaints it got."

"So he was hands-on?"

"Yeah, but less so lately. He came back from holiday with a bit between his teeth about something and spent a lot of time on it. Typical Pike, he didn't tell anyone what it was." Hinshelwood snapped his fingers. "I'll tell you who you should talk to, if he's still alive — Garth Grimes. You know who I mean?"

Hayhoe lied: "The name rings a bell."

"He was sort of like Pike's mentor — they worked together on the old *Standard*. Pike went to see him every month, come hell or high water. Some people reckoned Pike hadn't had an original idea in his life; he got them all from Grimes. Our in-house joke was that the day Grimes died — he's about a hundred and ten — was the day to send out your CV because the mag would go straight down the tubes."

"Did you believe that?"

Hinshelwood finally showed some emotion: shame flitted across his face. "I guess all of us did at some stage — shit, you know what journos are like."

Rusty Trousdale sipped her mug of supermarket-brand tea and assessed what ruin and neglect had done to the handsomest man she knew.

Quedley had aged ten years, gone from looking five years younger than he really was — early forties — to five years older. The hair had a lot to do with it: it had lost is dark gloss and the loose curls, now flecked with grey, fanned out in a disorderly tangle, like wide brambles. The beard, almost white at the chin and temples and bushy as a tramp's, wasn't a good look while the loss of half a dozen kilos which weren't doing any harm gave him the bony, wasted appearance of the seriously decadent or seriously diseased. Eventually, she realised who he reminded her of: one of those ageing rock stars lined and leathery beneath their grizzled, lifeless mops, who criss-crossed the globe on never-ending farewell tours.

After she'd reached this bleak conclusion, she asked, "Why, Caspar?"

"Why what?"

Her gesture took in Cambridge, the beard, and the baked beans: "Why any of it?"

Quedley shrugged indifferently: "What did you expect me to do — run for Parliament?"

"Well, no, but I didn't expect you to stop shaving and become a recluse."

"Nor did I."

"What's that meant to mean?"

"I didn't plan it. The idea was to drop out of sight for a while, do penance, let the fuss die down, then slip back into town and start again. But" — he paused and looked at the ceiling — "I've found that self-denial can be addictive."

He smiled sardonically. "Think of it as anorexia of the soul."

She absorbed the explanation with a few confused blinks. "Are you working?"

He shook his head. "I'm officially unemployed. Every now and again I have to apply for a job — assistant store manager maybe, or some sort of clerk. I even get a haircut so I can't be accused of making myself unemployable. But they keep turning me down; apparently I'm over-qualified."

"You're on the dole?"

"Why shouldn't I be? I've paid enough sodding tax over the years."

"I didn't mean it that way, you goose. How on earth do you manage?"

"It's not that hard," he said mildly, "once you've renounced your vices."

"So if you've given up everything that's bad for you, what on earth do you do with yourself?"

"The trick is to have lots of sleep — leaves less time to fill. Then there're the chores: the cleaning, the washing, the supermarket. I read, I jog by the river, I potter around in the garden, I watch a fuck of a lot of TV. And I wait."

"What for?"

Quedley smiled distantly, "For Godot, for motivation, for something to turn up. And here you are."

"It doesn't sound like a lot of fun, Caspar." She couldn't keep the pity out of her voice.

He looked at her with a steady, incurious gaze. "It keeps me out of trouble — I'm not the one who needs help."

"Touché."

"What's up, Rusty?"

She heaved a long, expressive sigh. "I'm being blackmailed."

"Sex, of course."

"Of course. Someone got hold of my diary."

He closed his eyes, pinched the bridge of his nose with his left thumb and index finger, and said slowly: "You daft little bitch."

She nodded glumly. "I know. I should've given it up when I got married."

"How far back does the fucker go?"

"Oh, he's only got this year's, thank God."

"Been a big year, has it?"

"I haven't been that bad," she said defensively.

"Pig's arse. How many?"

She lowered her eyes, "Three — but nothing happened with one."

Quedley's eyes opened wide.

"We shared a bed but when it came to lights, camera, action the lady got stage-fright."

"Well, shit, that doesn't count."

"I'm not so sure about that." She blushed slightly. "The Dear Diary version wasn't entirely accurate."

He shook his head in disbelief.

Rusty hung her head. "I didn't say we did it; I just sort of left it up in the air."

"It's all spilt milk anyway. What does he want?"

"A mere half a million — by the end of the week."

Quedley whistled.

"Exactly. He seems to be under the impression I can dash off a cheque and no one will notice."

"Any idea who it is?"

She shook her head.

"Who knows you keep a diary?"

"No one."

"If the worst comes to the worst, what'll the Troll do?"

"If you mean my beloved husband, I'm pretty sure he'd send me packing."

"Come on, Rusty, he knew the score. You can't tell me he didn't expect you to play up now and again?"

She grimaced. "The trouble is, he did. Before the wedding, we had a full and frank discussion, all very grown up. Maurice said he was prepared to turn a blind eye to the occasional fling as long as I was discreet, but if I made him a laughing-stock, it'd be lawyers at ten paces."

"Hmmm. I suppose he locked you into a bomb-proof pre-nuptial agreement?"

She nodded. "You could hardly blame him for that. On the subject of laughing-stocks, I should mention that for the last few weeks Maurice has been telling the world that we're trying for a bambino."

"Jesus," said Quedley reverently. "You don't do things by halves, do you?"

"Caspar, what the hell am I going to do?"

"Stall for time, that's what," he said decisively. "You told the guy there was a problem getting the money?"

"Yes. He said he couldn't give a shit; it was my problem."

"Course he did, but the point is he's more interested in getting his hands on some loot than in wrecking your life. As long as he thinks you're going to come up with the goods — and not necessarily the full whack either — he'll hold fire. So you've got to string it out. You tell him you can get the money but it's going to take time — weeks if not months. He'll make all sorts of threats but, at the end of the day, he'll go along with it. That'll give us time to work out what to do next."

"I'll have to tell the others, won't I?"

"Some would argue that you owe it to them to warn them what's going on. More to the point, you need to find out if the leak came from them."

She moaned, "Oh God, Caspar, I don't think I can face them."

Quedley stared at her, genuinely surprised: "I assumed you wanted me to do it. Isn't that why you came down here?"

8

The last Justin Hinshelwood had heard, Garth Grimes was still in the land of the living — occupying a choice patch of it, in fact, right on Takapuna beach.

Amanda Hayhoe checked the phone book: there was a listing for G. Grimes in Minnehaha Avenue, Takapuna. She rang the number and asked the woman who answered if she could speak to Mr Grimes.

"I'm afraid not. He's had a terrible shock and he's rather under the weather. Perhaps you could try again next week . . ." She broke off. Hayhoe heard her say, "I don't know who it is, Dad . . ."

Grimes' daughter came back on the line. "Who's calling please and what's it regarding?"

"It's Amanda Hayhoe from TVNZ. I was hoping Mr Grimes could help me with a story I'm doing."

There was another pause. The daughter sounded piqued when she spoke again: "Could you try again tomorrow morning, about eleven?"

"I'll do that," said Hayhoe hurriedly. She thanked the woman and hung up.

Next morning, Grimes himself answered. His voice was rich and mellow, not the reedy old codger's crackle she'd expected.

"It's Amanda Hayhoe, Mr Grimes. I rang yesterday."

"Yes, I vaguely remember yesterday. And what do you do at TVNZ, my dear?"

"I'm a reporter on *60 Minutes*. It's sort of magazine-style current affairs."

"I must admit I haven't seen it. I watch very little television these days — too many buffoons for my liking. They're even doing the weather."

"We call them personalities."

"Do you indeed? Are you a personality, Amanda? Have you had your picture in a women's magazine cradling your mulatto love-child called, let's see, Tiffany — or perhaps Amber?"

Hayhoe let go a low, bubbling laugh. "If I had a love-child, which I don't, I certainly wouldn't call her Tiffany or Amber. They're the sort of names strippers call themselves."

"I'll have to take your word for that; it's some time since I was on first name terms with a stripper. Now, then, to what do I owe the pleasure?"

"I was wondering if I could come and talk to you . . ."

"Oh?" The velvety voice took on a thin, high note of surprise. "Oh really? Well, in that case you'd better tell me about yourself. So far we've established what you won't be calling your love-child, which is interesting insofar as it goes. I seem to remember an English lady cricketer with a double-barrelled name,

Hayhoe-something-or other. You don't play cricket, do you?"

"No."

"Glad to hear it. Dodgy lot, women cricketers."

Hayhoe felt she was starting to get the hang of it. "Mr Grimes, don't tell me you think all sportswomen are hairy-legged dykes?"

"Good heavens, no. As a matter of fact, the last time I achieved anything remotely resembling an erection was watching women's tennis on the television. An Argentinean lass caused the most excitement."

Bloody hell. Hayhoe stammered, "Gabriela Sabatini?" only just managing to get the ball back over the net.

"I believe it was. What a splendid creature: reminded me of a señorita I shacked up with down in Vera Cruz just after the war — that's the Second World War in case you're wondering. From memory, her features were somewhat coarser than Miss Sabatini's; on the other hand, given the way she plays tennis, I suspect my little Mex was the more adventurous spirit. There we are. Let's press on: how old are you?"

"Twenty-eight."

"Yes, I'd have put you around there on the basis of that knowing undertone in your laugh. Are you pretty?"

"Isn't that in the eye of the beholder?"

"Come now, Amanda, I want a dispassionate assessment. I'm a very old man and I long ago reached the stage of pleasing myself in all things. There was a time when I'd no more talk about erections over the phone to a young lady I hadn't met than wear yellow braces. Now you're obviously very nice and lots of fun but if you're not pretty, I'm afraid we'll have to confine our relationship to the telephone. No offence intended; it's just that . . . Well, I think that when one reaches my age, one's entitled to a certain amount of arbitrariness."

"Well, I'm certainly no stunner but I might just scrape in as pretty if the bar wasn't set too high. What else would you like to know?"

Grimes was suddenly all business. "What do you want to see me about?"

"It's, uh . . . Jackson Pike."

Silence. When Grimes eventually spoke, there wasn't a trace of banter in his voice. "First of all, you should know that I was immensely fond of Jackson. I'm prepared to talk to you because his contribution to journalism should be acknowledged, and better I do that than some back-biting mediocrity who wished him ill every step of the way. But I will not be party to a hatchet job — is that clear?"

Hayhoe was a little taken aback. "That's not what we've got in mind at all. In fact, the piece will probably focus more on this Aotearoa People's Army . . ." Her voice trailed off as it occurred to her that she might be digging herself into a different hole.

"Well, let's see how it goes, shall we?" Grimes' voice warmed up again:

"I have a feeling we're going to get along very well."

They arranged a time. Afterwards, Hayhoe reflected that it was a bit like her first real kiss: it took her by surprise but, once she'd got over that, she found herself quite looking forward to the next step.

Tito Ihaka would've disliked the counter-terrorism expert Wayne Cramp at first sight but he didn't see any point in waiting.

His version of the golden rule was that people were shitheads until proven otherwise — that went double for people who were going to tell him how to do his job — so it wasn't as if he needed a reason to dislike the bloke.

Cramp gave him one anyway; in fact, he gave him several.

They met early on Wednesday afternoon in Detective Inspector Finbar McGrail's office. Cramp was late-thirties, half a head taller than Ihaka and almost as heavily built. He had a round, fleshy face with a beard light enough to qualify as designer stubble. He was losing hair and tried to disguise it with the chrome dome's tablecloth: growing his hair long on one side and draping it over the scalp. Ihaka suspected he used hairspray to keep it in place.

The hair was one reason. Ihaka enjoyed mocking the bald as much as anyone but, when all was said and done, it was just another physical defect like buck teeth or knobbly knees. Your genes dealt you a hand: some guys came up trumps in the hair department and some didn't. No big deal; no one's perfect, right? But to pretend you weren't bald via a wig or a ridiculous hairstyle said something about the sort of person you were — something along the lines of "Call me Fuckweed".

The clothes were another, specifically the chunky gold cufflinks and the waistcoat with a silver back, like the underbelly of a dead fish. Ihaka reckoned anyone under fifty who wore cufflinks and a waistcoat when they didn't have to was a wanker, simple as that. It wasn't as bad as having a personalised number plate or wearing sunglasses inside or wearing a baseball cap backwards after your balls have dropped or putting some insane shit on your answerphone — but it was pretty fucking close.

They shook hands. Cramp closed his grip a fraction early, catching Ihaka's fingers rather than the palm of his hand. He might've looked like a head waiter but he had a powerful grip. Ihaka couldn't return the pressure and had to stand there looking unconcerned while Cramp mashed his fingers.

That was the third.

McGrail said: "Mr Cramp has a theory about the APA."

Ihaka slumped into a chair. "If it involves aliens, I've heard it."

Cramp plinked a meaty buttock on the corner of McGrail's desk and set off in a deep, confident voice: "I think the key is to focus on the political — as opposed to the criminal — nature of these killings. We should be asking: who has the motivation for terrorism? Who has the underground organisation and the hard core of fanatics you need to conduct a terrorist campaign? Who's indicated that they're prepared to resort to terrorism? You and I both know there's only one group out there who gets a tick on all three: the extreme Maori nationalists. Their objective — New Zealand under Maori rule — demands a strategy of what ideologues call the armed struggle simply because it's not going to happen any other way."

McGrail looked at Ihaka: "Sergeant?"

"Well, yeah, I guess they'd have to be on the list, but why would they target the media? Christ, they live publicity; they depend on it. And how fucking underground can you be when you're on TV every week?" He pointed his chin at Cramp. "I bet you blokes know where most of them are twenty-four hours a day."

Cramp leaned forward, upping the intensity: "What we're seeing here, Sergeant, is a textbook case of a transition from a political campaign to stir things up and put pressure on the government, to a terrorist campaign to sap the community's will. There transitions occur when extremists conclude that the political campaign either won't deliver the goods or will take too long about it. At that point, the hard men take over. They're not interested in winning hearts and minds. Their strategy is to intimidate society into submission. For a while now, we've been predicting the emergence of a hard-line pro-violence faction among the Maori radicals, something like the Provisional IRA: I believe that's what we're seeing now. As for targeting the media, well, frankly, we don't think the media is the target. Our theory is that Freckleton and Pike were just practice runs. The real target is always the power structure: politicians, civil servants, businessmen, judges — and the security forces."

Ihaka ended the silence that followed: "Well, you know what they say: opinions are like arseholes — everybody's got one."

Cramp stared at Ihaka, working his jaw. He turned to McGrail: "Looks like I got here just in time, inspector. I'll skip the rest of amateur hour if you don't mind. I haven't had lunch yet."

Amateur hour? That made four.

Cramp headed for the door. Ihaka said over his shoulder "Wayne, if you hit the canteen in that gear, the boys'll think you're going to do magic tricks."

Cramp exited, shutting the door with a bang which drew an irritated, slow-motion blink from McGrail. He tidied some papers which had been disturbed by Cramp's rump. Without looking at Ihaka, he said, "Pretty predictable so far, eh Sergeant?"

Clyde Early worked out of an office at the back of his Mr Fixit Hardware franchise in the Birkenhead shopping centre. He was set to call it a day when he remembered there was someone waiting to see him. The guy wouldn't tell his secretary what it was about, just that it had nothing to do with hardware or rugby.

That was three-quarters of an hour ago. Early got up from behind his desk and opened his office door. A man he didn't know sat in the small waiting area. The visitor glanced up from his paperback: he didn't seem impatient or expectant, just neutral.

Early said: "You wanted to see me?"

The man nodded. "If it's convenient. I won't keep you long."

"Sure." Early stepped back from the doorway. "Come on in. Sorry to keep you waiting — it's been one of those days."

"No problem." The man closed a slim, dog-eared Penguin with an old-fashioned cover. "I had my book."

Early saw it was by Jean-Paul Sartre, whoever he was.

He asked, "Good read?" just for something to say.

The man frowned at the book, as if he was marshalling the strands of a powerful critique: "No, it's a load of crap really." He extended his right hand. "Caspar Quedley."

That morning Quedley had spent an hour and $55 getting pruned by one of Parnell's trendier hairdressers. He was wearing a navy-blue cashmere overcoat over a dark, roomy double-breasted suit, white Oxford-weave shirt, and blue silk tie. Early, who'd become moderately fashion conscious during his time in Europe, guessed the suit was Ermenegildo Zegna.

With his slightly emaciated appearance and sober, expensive clothes, Quedley cut an elegant and, Early couldn't help thinking, faintly sinister figure. Early ushered him into his office, sat behind his desk, and waited for the pitch, which he expected to be smooth.

Quedley took his time. He sat down, had a cursory glance around the office, and a long, careful look at Early. He concluded that Early was probably smart but not necessarily bright in the high-IQ sense, tougher and more worldly than his regular-guy looks would suggest, and as hungry as a barracuda.

Whatever his other attributes, Early wasn't overly patient. He made a show of looking at his watch. "I don't mean to be rude, but it's been a long day and I was looking forward to some time with the kids."

Quedley smiled politely. "Of course, I was forgetting you're a family man. I'll get straight to the point: I'm here as a go-between, on behalf of our mutual acquaintance, Mrs Rusty Trousdale."

Early's eyes narrowed and he shifted on his seat. "I know Mrs Trousdale," he said guardedly, "but what does she need you for? She could've just picked up the phone."

Quedley had wondered how he'd feel once things got under way. He was a little surprised to find that he was enjoying himself. He brushed a speck of fluff off the arm of his overcoat and tried to look sombre: "It's a bit embarrassing I'm afraid. Rusty just didn't feel up to it."

He paused. Early leaned across his desk, eyes wide open. "Up to what?"

Quedley shook his head ruefully. "You'll have to bear with me, I'm out of practice. Up to telling you that she's being blackmailed over your relationship."

Early was starting to look quite unfriendly. He leaned back in his chair and snapped: "What fucking relationship?"

"Yep, that's the one." Quedley permitted himself a lopsided half-smile. "You see, the bugger of it is, it doesn't matter a hell of a lot whether you two had a relationship or not. What matters is that Rusty said so in her diary — at some length. I'm talking dates, places, who did what to whom, how often, and from which direction. The backmailer's got the diary."

Early paled but maintained his cold stare. He said, "And you're here to do what exactly?" coming down hard on the last two words.

"A couple of things: firstly to warn you what's happening; secondly, to ask if it's possible that you let on about Rusty to anyone. Maybe without even being aware of it at the time?"

"What do you think?"

Quedley shrugged. "Well, you'll appreciate I had to ask. Maybe the blackmailer got lucky but it doesn't look that way to me. He could've walked off with the contents of her handbag — a few hundred bucks, a chequebook and a full set of credit cards. Instead, he just took the diary, which kind of suggests that he had a pretty good idea what was in it. Now you might be an exception, Mr Early, but in my experience, a secret is something you tell one other person."

Early shook his head emphatically. "Absolutely no way. So what now?"

Quedley shrugged again. "I'll see what the others have to say."

"Which others?"

"Rusty's other partners in sin."

"Jesus Christ, how many of them are there?"

"Two." Quedley paused before adding blandly: "I'm sure you were her favourite, though."

9

At 8 o'clock the next morning, Thursday, Rusty Trousdale left her husband to his breakfast — grapefruit juice, fresh mango, scrambled eggs with smoked salmon, chocolate brioche, two double espressos — and went upstairs. She locked herself in her bathroom, ran the bath, and used her mobile phone to ring the motel where Caspar Quedley was staying. She was anxious to know how he'd fared with Clyde Early.

So-so, was the answer: "He didn't shoot the messenger but the thought might've crossed his mind. He says he hasn't told anyone."

"Damn. Not to mention fuck. One down, two to go."

"Not necessarily."

"Excuse moi? Don't you believe him?"

"I don't know him. Would he own up if he'd blabbed?"

"You tell me."

"Under the circumstances, I'd bloody well hope so."

"Ask him yourself: you'll be hearing from him before long."

An hour and twenty minutes later, in fact.

Rusty went into damage control: "God, Clyde, I'm absolutely mortified about this. I know I should've come myself but . . ."

"Forget it," said Early impatiently. "Where'd you find that guy anyway?"

"Caspar? He's an old buddy. He used to be quite a mover and shaker around town — knew everybody who's anybody — until he came a cropper. He's had some first-hand experience of blackmail."

"Oh yeah? From which side of the fence?"

Rusty tittered. Aren't we perceptive today?

"So how the hell are you going to handle it?"

"Basically, stall for as long as possible. He wants a ridiculous amount of money. I tried to tell him I can't just dip into the Trousdale fortune, not that it cut any ice. I'll just keep putting him off and hope that he gets fed up and goes away — and in the meantime, try to find out who he is."

Early was disbelieving: "That's the plan?"

"Clyde, if you have a better one, feel free to let me in on it."

"Well, Christ, what if it doesn't work? What if he won't go away?"

"Then I suppose the choices are: call his bluff; offer him whatever I can scrape together; confess all to Maurice and throw myself on his mercy; or go to the police. Or some combination of the above."

"Shit."

"Tell me about it."

"You've got no idea who it is?"

"Not the foggiest," she said flatly. "Actually, something did occur to me as I tossed and turned last night: it almost sounded as if he knew you."

"Why, what'd he say?"

"Well, he read a bit out of the diary — you and I sharing a tender moment. Naturally, you get a glowing mention and he said something like he didn't think you had it in you."

"That doesn't mean a thing — he's probably seen me on TV or something."

"Maybe. It was the way he said it, though."

"If you think about it, it's a damn sight more likely he knows you — I mean, how else would he've known about the frigging diary?" Early's voice subsided to an accusatory monotone: "Quedley said there were others."

"Did he now?" she said coolly. "That was thoughtful of him. Let me put your ego at rest: they both pre-date you and with one of them, nothing even happened."

Early sniffed as if he found that hard to believe. He said, "Keep me posted, eh?" and hung up.

Miss you too, darling.

She'd just put the phone down when it rang again. The blackmailer said: "You got the money yet?"

"It's not the end of the week."

"What's a day or two between friends? Well, have you?"

"No, and I won't be getting it in a hurry either. Remember I warned you it wouldn't be easy? Well, it's proving even harder than I thought. I'll need a lot more time."

"Don't give me this shit — I told you: how you get it's your problem . . ."

"Look, I'm just explaining the situation: it's going to take weeks to get that sort of . . ."

Mules grated: "You've got a week, you hear me? That's it: no excuses, no extensions. Either I get the dough next Thursday or the party's over lady."

It was true, to the extent such claims ever are, that Caspar Quedley knew everybody who was anybody. Obviously, he knew some a lot better than others.

Serge Le Droff, who qualified as a somebody because he displayed most of the symptoms of serious wealth, was one of the others. Quedley had met him once, at a cocktail party a few years ago. All he remembered was that Le Droff wasn't fazed by all the attention paid to his companion, a languid New Caledonian beauty who didn't look away when Quedley made eye contact.

When Le Droff's name appeared in the press, which wasn't often, it was usually with a tag to the effect of "publicity-shy millionaire". He ran a package-holiday company from the ground floor of a downtown high-rise and lived in the penthouse apartment, twenty floors up.

Quedley parked in the Customs Street carpark and walked around the block to Quay Street. He went into the Eurotours sales office, where one of the counter staff directed him to the corporate office on the nineteenth floor.

The lift opened onto a reception area dominated by a monolithic marble-topped desk. To the left of it was a badge-operated security door, to the right, a couple of plush sofas and a low coffee table overlooked by a huge picture from the chimp-with-spraycan school of painting.

The receptionist's smile dimmed when Quedley said he'd like to see Le Droff. She asked, "Do you have an appointment?" knowing the answer. He said he was representing Mrs Maurice Trousdale on a personal matter.

The receptionist told him to take a seat. She picked up the phone and murmured into it. Ten minutes went by. The phone rang; she listened for a few seconds then escorted Quedley through the security door into an unoccupied meeting room with a view of the harbour and North Shore. He was staring out the window without seeing very much when someone joined him.

It wasn't Le Droff or the blow-dried personal assistant Quedley had half-expected. It was an erect, vigorous-looking, broad-shouldered man of fifty-odd. He had thick, wavy, silver hair swept back from a low forehead, a ruddy complexion, flat, peaked ears, cobalt-blue eyes, eyebrows which curled upwards like budding horns, and a toilet brush moustache several shades darker than his hair. His wide mouth was curved in a permanent half-smile and the whole face seemed to come to a point in a sharp, upturned nose above protruding front teeth.

There was so much happening on the man's face that it took Quedley a few moments to see the big picture: *fuckfire, it's Rin Tin Tin in a three-piece suit.*

"Now then, old chap, what can we do you for?" He might've looked like a German shepherd but the accent was upper-crust English.

"You're not Serge Le Droff." Quedley tried not to make it sound too much like criticism.

"Well done. Close observation leading to a sound conclusion." Rin Tin Tin pulled a chair out from the small table and sat down, crossing his legs. His shoes were black leather, size 13 or 14, polished to a sheen, and ideal for kicking to death anything smaller than a Shetland pony. "Take a pew."

Quedley did as he was told. The man took a card from his breast pocket and dropped it on the table. It identified him as Colonel Wyatt Bloodsaw, head of security for the Le Droff Group of Companies.

"Colonel — what of?"

Bloodsaw barked, "Thirteenth Parachute Regiment, British Army," as if he was giving his name, rank and serial number. "Packed in soldiering years ago, but it seems to carry some weight in my lark."

Quedley raised his eyebrows. "This might be a silly question but why does

Le Droff need a head of security? I thought he was a travel agent."

"He'd be frightfully chuffed to hear himself described that way," replied Bloodsaw cheerfully. "In point of fact, LDG's is a varied and far-flung empire; take it from me, old son, I earn my modest keep." He strummed his bristly moustache. "One of my tasks is running the rule over bods we don't know who come calling for reasons we don't understand."

"We being . . . ?"

Bloodsaw bared his teeth in a ferocious grimace which Quedley took, from the look in his eyes, to be a grin. "We being we."

Quedley nodded. "Can I take it I won't be granted an audience with the bwana?"

"Affirmative."

"It's personal. Extremely personal, in fact."

Bloodsaw's blue eyes twinkled merrily.

Quedley shrugged: "Okay, I'm here on behalf of Mrs Maurice Trousdale. A few days ago, her diary was stolen. It contained references of a, let's say, intimate nature to Le Droff. Whoever's got the diary is trying to blackmail her and she's concerned that Le Droff might get dragged into it. She wanted to warn him; she'd also like to know if he's discussed their relationship with a third party."

Bloodsaw dropped his chin and studied Quedley from beneath his devilish eyebrows: "Delicate situation, what?"

"Very."

"So you've popped in to alert the boss that his name could be . . . bandied around?"

Quedley nodded.

"Well, that's damned decent of you, old boy, but I doubt the boss'll lose much sleep over it. You see, he's what used to be called a bachelor gay: footloose and fancy-free, no strings attached. Chaps like that are bound to roger other chaps' wives every now and again — law of averages, what? Get my drift?"

Quedley smiled. "He must be popular at the tennis club."

Bloodsaw snorted explosively. "Not one for clubs, the boss; not one for giving much of a fig what people think either."

"Lucky him. What about whether he told anyone?"

"Stand easy. We'll sort that out, toot sweet."

Bloodsaw grabbed the phone on the desk and jabbed buttons: "Bloodsaw . . . I'm downstairs with brother Quedley . . . Apparently, the lady kept a diary which has fallen into hostile hands . . . hmm, dispatched him to sound the alarm." He released an abrupt, jarring laugh. "I told him that, almost those precise words . . . He wants to know if you told anyone . . . what? what? . . . Oh, I say."

Bloodsaw laughed again and slam-dunked the handset.

"The boss says one thing a gentleman never, ever does is kiss and tell."

"Is that right? Some would say another thing a gentleman should never do is someone else's wife."

Bloodsaw let fly with another machine-gun laugh.

"Shrewd thrust, old boy, shrewd thrust. However, in these matters one must draw a distinction between your bachelor gay, who occasionally happens to find himself at close quarters with a married lady, and your cad, who goes out of his way to seduce same."

He sprang to his feet, signalling that the discussion was over.

"Did he have anything else to say?" asked Quedley.

"He was vaguely curious to know how many other chaps you're calling on."

"Someone else asked me that," said Quedley pleasantly. "But he wouldn't pretend to be a gentleman."

Chas Gundry MP was proud of the fact that he'd topped the parliamentary press gallery's Arsehole Index three years in a row.

But then perversity was Gundry's trademark. Nothing illustrated that better than his oft-quoted pronouncement that his American pit bull terrier, Sam, had been the major influence on his personal and political creed. Sam has lived to a good age despite the efforts of Gundry's neighbours, local body officials and the postal service to have him destroyed in the interests of public safety. When Sam finally passed away, he was replaced in Gundry's affections by the pick of the last litter he'd sired: a chip off the old block which the MP, to the amusement of no one but himself, named Son of Sam.

Gundry was an ex-used car salesman and repo man who'd been swept into parliament in the National Party's 1990 landslide. But with the first mixed member proportional representation election approaching and facing formidable obstacles in the form of disadvantageous boundary changes and party chiefs who couldn't wait to see the back of him, Gundry had decided to set up his own party.

The Queen and Country Party had two basic aims. The first was to ensure that the British monarch remained New Zealand's head of state. While Gundry sincerely believed that an English grandmother with an unfortunate taste in hats was all that stood between New Zealand and anarchy, the stance was also based on the hard-headed political calculation that a combination of diehard monarchists, recent British immigrants and morons who ticked the wrong box would lift Queen and Country above the five per cent of the vote threshold which guaranteed parliamentary representation. That would enable the party to achieve its other — undeclared — aim: to prolong Gundry's political career until he was eligible for an MP's pension.

The trouble was, other MPs were adopting similar strategies and the populist right was becoming a crowded corner of the political landscape. Gundry believed it was time for him to take ownership, as the fancypants consultants like to say, of another emotive, gut-level issue.

He found it that Thursday at the Wellington Club. Over lunch, an SIS officer gave him a deep background briefing on the Aotearoa People's Army. By the time the port and cheese arrive, it had all fallen into place. Later that afternoon on the floor of the house, Gundry indulged in some forthright speculation about the APA's membership and motives.

His speech would've rung a few bells with detective Inspector Finbar McGrail and Detective Sergeant Tito Ihaka, since it stuck closely to the line pushed by Wayne Cramp. This wasn't a coincidence: Gundry's briefing had come from Cramp's immediate superior, who'd decided it was time to take the initiative in the shadow war against the enemy within.

Early that evening, Gundry flew to Auckland to deliver a speech to an anti-republican meeting and spend the weekend in his electorate. At the airport he bumped into another MP who suggested, without seeming too concerned about it, that Gundry's speech might have whistled him straight to the top of the APA's hit-list.

"Do I look worried?" Gundry jerked a thumb at a tall, athletic-looking young man who stood nearby, scrutinising passers-by through narrowed eyes. "See that bloke? One of the top men from the Protective Services Unit. And he's just the backup: if those cunts come after me, I'll send him round with a hose and bucket to clean up after Son of Sam's finished with them."

10

At 4.57 that afternoon, twenty-seven minutes late, Amanda Hayhoe knocked on the door of Garth Grimes' slightly shabby weatherboard bungalow perched on a little crag above Takapuna beach.

The woman who opened the door was well into middle age. Going by her serviceable hairstyle, sensible clothes and general air of flustered irritation, she believed in acting her age.

She gave Hayhoe a dubious once-over: "You're the reporter, are you?"

"Yes."

"I was beginning to think you weren't coming."

"Sorry I'm late — there was an accident on the bridge."

It obviously wasn't the first time the woman had heard the harbour bridge blamed. "People never seem to allow enough time for the bridge," she sniffed. "Not that it matters: I decided not to wake Dad until you'd arrived."

She led Hayhoe into a living room lit by pale late-afternoon sun streaming in through sliding glass doors.

"Before I get Dad up, can I ask you please not to get him excited?" Grimes' daughter wrung her hands anxiously, a gesture at odds with her head-librarian demeanour. "He's almost ninety-five, you know. He mightn't show it — he's very good at that — but I can assure you, Jackson's death knocked him for six."

Hayhoe was out on the wooden deck admiring the view and wondering if there was some kind of inverse relationship between the father's defiance of the ageing process and the daughter's surrender to it when the glass doors slid open. Garth Grimes shuffled out to the deck, supporting himself on a walking stick and his daughter's shoulder.

Grimes mightn't have acted his age but he certainly looked it. He was stooped and shrunken; a few strands of fine white hair swayed above a nut-brown scalp and his spectacularly mottled face hung in folds like a bloodhound's. Behind half-moon spectacles, dark eyes glistened in yellowing eyeballs, like black olives floating in melted butter. They were the eyes of a man who'd seen everything there is to see and been shocked by too little of it.

He had on pleated grey flannel trousers with cuffs, brown leather brogues and a green-check woollen jacket over a washed-out heavy cotton shirt which was done up to the throat. The buttons for the button-down collar were missing and the collar tips curled like dead leaves. Hayhoe suspected that every visible item of Grimes' attire was as old as she was and would support the argument that, in the long run, it pays to buy quality.

Grimes let go of his daughter's shoulder to extend a desiccated, almost transparent hand. "Amanda, my dear," he purred, "welcome. What a pleasure, all the more so for being unexpected."

Grimes insisted they sat outside. He reclined on a padded deck chair; Hayhoe sat at the outdoor table. He introduced his daughter, then politely but firmly dismissed her. She hovered, reluctant to depart.

"Now off you go, Veronica," he said. "That husband of yours will be home shortly and you know how he performs when he feels you're dancing attendance on me at his expense. I'm sure Amanda can look after me."

The daughter left. Grimes confided: "Don't be alarmed, my dear — you won't have to undress me or lower me onto the potty. I can fend for myself passably well but I don't like to rub it in. Veronica and her booby of a husband have coveted this site for years and I suspect they regard it as monstrously inconsiderate of me to continue to dodge the Grim Reaper. I keep telling them I'm ready when he is but they don't believe me." He paused to examine Hayhoe. "You're a most attractive young woman — why on earth were you coy about it?"

She shrugged, forcing a weak smile.

Grimes tapped the deck with his stick. "I wouldn't care to be classified as one of those insufferable old bores who forever offer unwanted advice, but let me just say this: journalism is no trade for the modest: if you undersell yourself, you'll be overtaken by those whose sole ability is self-promotion. What line is your young man in? Something more lucrative than journalism, I trust?"

Hayhoe changed position on the wooden bench. "I'm unattached at the moment. Have been for a couple of years, actually."

Grimes' sparse eye brows jumped: "A couple of years? Great Scott, you must've been gallivanting like Lillie Langtry to need a break of that duration."

"Nothing of the sort," she said indignantly. "I just had a . . . messy experience."

"No self-respecting journalist should be deflected by enigmatic responses. Please explain."

Hayhoe sighed. "If I do, can we talk about Jackson Pike?"

Grimes lit a cigarette. "Perhaps," he said airily. "Before you embark on your lurid narrative, why don't you mix us a gin and tonic?"

Hayhoe made the drinks and took them outside.

She made a half-hearted plea: "Look, there's nothing special about it — in fact, just the opposite. I bet you've heard it a hundred times before."

Grimes, whose collapsed face now shone with curiosity or perhaps even excitement, was implacable: "I've heard everything a hundred times before."

She took a deep breath. "I was a late starter in journalism: I used to work for an investment bank in Wellington. To cut a long story short, I ended up getting involved with one of the directors."

"Ended up getting involved?" Grimes feigned uncertainty. "I'm not sure exactly what that means. Can you be more precise?"

Hayhoe made a face at him. "You can needle me as much as you like, Mr Grimes, but I'm not going into the sordid details. I wasn't some naive little convent girl in a tartan skirt with buckles on her shoes, if that's what you think I was implying."

"No, I can't quite see you in that light." Grimes looked pleased with himself. Dirty old goat.

"He was twelve years older than me and married with a couple of kids. He told me he'd leave his wife and I sort of believed him. At the time, I think he sort of believed it himself."

She asked herself why she was telling her only deep, dark secret to a grubby-minded museum piece she'd known for all of half an hour. Not even Mum knows this stuff.

"One night he went home, packed a suitcase and told his wife he was leaving. As I heard it later, she didn't bat an eyelid, just said if that's what he wanted, fine, but could he collect little Johnny from his tennis lesson first? When he got back with the kid, both sets of parents were there waiting for him. They talked him out of it; I don't think it took them that long. Next day, he stayed at home and his wife came into the office to ask the MD if it was now company policy to hire home-wrecking sluts. His answer was to give me fifteen minutes to clear my desk and vacate the premises. The end."

Grimes went, "Hmmm. And now you've decided you can't be trusted around men?"

Hayhoe couldn't help laughing. "I prefer to think of it as being choosy."

"Well, bear in mind what they say about falling off a horse. You subbed that story with a heavy hand, my dear; one day, when we've got to know one another better, you must tell me the unadulterated version." He heaved himself to his feet. "It's getting a little chilly for these old bones — let's go in."

They went inside. She made him another gin and tonic. He took two greedy mouthfuls, lit a cigarette, leaned back on the sofa, closed his eyes, and spoke fluently and fondly for twenty minutes about his late protégé, Jackson Pike.

She asked, "When did you last speak to him?"

"A month or so ago. He rang up in a foul mood to say he couldn't come over for lunch because they'd had a break-in at the office."

"What was stolen?"

"Next to nothing, which is why I didn't take it too seriously. Jackson was riled because the intruders had fiddled around with the computers; I made a flippant comment on a Luddite theme which, understandably, he didn't find vastly amusing. It wasn't a long conversation."

"So you actually hadn't seen him for a while?"

"No. Jackson had a couple of months in Europe this winter — his first proper holiday for Lord knows how long. The last time I saw him would've been early May, just before he went."

"A guy on the magazine told me he came back from holiday hyped up about something. Would you know what it was?"

"No. The only mention of his trip was to thank me for suggesting a visit to D'Arcy Potterton; he said it was well worthwhile." Grimes' eyes lit up. "Now there's an idea — I'll tell you my Potterton story."

"Is that the writer who died not long ago?"

"By sad coincidence, yes. He wouldn't mean much to your generation, but twenty-five years ago Potterton was the young literary lion. He took himself off to France in a fit of pique, supposedly to live among more civilised folk. I suggested that since Jackson would be in the vicinity, he should drop in on him. I did in seventy-nine and no one had talked to him since. Jackson was lukewarm so I told him about my visit. Now then, let's have dinner and I'll tell you."

Hayhoe protested, in vain. It was all there, ready to go, courtesy of Veronica: just a matter of setting the table, dishing up and pulling the cork out of a bottle of wine — French, he thought, under the circumstances.

They sat at a little table in front of the sliding glass door. Over Veronica's carbonade of beer accompanied by a green salad, Côtes-du-Rhône, and the whisper of high tide thirty metres below, Grimes told his story about the dead writer, D'Arcy Potterton.

"I lived abroad for over thirty years," he began, "all over the place, so I was never much of a one for junkets. Then in seventy-nine, when I was on the brink of retirement, the French tourism people invited me on a gastronomic mini-tour. Well, even the most jaded old hack — which I was — wouldn't knock that back. Someone at the paper suggested tracking Potterton down: it was a few years since he'd brought out that god-awful book portraying us as a nation of fascist yokels and it seemed worth finding out if he still felt that way. I tottered round to his publisher and wheedled Potterton's address and phone number out of him.

"I gave him a ring from Bordeaux. He was wary at first but came around. I think what swayed him was discovering how old I was — people have this extraordinary notion that old age confers benevolence. Anyway, I got the go-ahead and drove down — he lived just outside a village called Levignac, about half an hour from Toulouse. I wasn't expecting the red-carpet treatment so I had lunch on the way and got there mid-afternoon.

"I must say, he'd set himself up rather nicely in a grey stone villa on a hilltop, looking down a little valley with woods on one side and meadows on the other and a stream winding along the valley floor. Behind the house was a large lawn with flowerbeds and lots of fruit trees — mainly cherry, I seem to remember. He even had a couple of fields with a few cattle and some fat geese which the old boy next door looked after for him. It was springtime and we sat out in the garden drinking pastis; I couldn't help thinking that perhaps he'd had the right idea after all.

"He was forty-odd, not a bad-looking fellow; too much hair as they all did in those days. He was perfectly civil, gave me a quick tour, and then, as I say, we sat outside with our pastis and our Gitanes. Now here was the funny thing: as soon as he decently could, he began pumping me for news from home: what was the state of play in politics? What was the gossip in the book world? Then he got on his high horse and raged about Piggy Muldoon, how he was leading the country to rack and ruin and if he got half a chance, he'd stand intellectuals and trade unionists up against the wall. On and on in this vein — he was a tremendous lefty of course — until I got bored and told him he was talking through his hat.

"Things rather petered out after that. He suddenly announced he had work to do and he'd see me to my car. We walked to the front of the house in strained silence just as a little Renault came up the drive. A most attractive woman got out whom Potterton introduced as Madame Dubois, a neighbour, I said hello and goodbye, she gave me a haughty nod and I went on my way rejoicing."

Grimes broke off to make a mini-assault on his meal. Then he pushed his plate aside, refilled his glass, and continued: "I drove away thinking three things: the first was that, despite what he'd said in his book, Potterton hadn't cut his emotional ties with New Zealand; the second was that the people in my daughter's French textbooks were always called Dubois; and, third, it was a bit odd that he'd addressed his neighbour in English.

"By now it was getting on for 6 o'clock; I'd had a couple of pastis on top of several glasses of wine at lunch and wasn't up to driving back to Bordeaux, so I went down to the village and checked into a little inn. I had a nap and got up about ten with a fair appetite. It was a Monday night and le patron was about to close the restaurant, but after some argy-bargy and the inevitable bribe, he agreed to cook something for me. He perked up when I ordered the best bottle on the wine list and invited him to join me and we got talking — by that stage I was starting to get the lingo back. Naturally, he wanted to know what had brought me to Levignac and I told him about Potterton.

"'Ah, l'écrivain,' he exclaimed. 'Il mange ici souvent. Un moment, un moment,' and he scuttled off and rummaged behind the bar. He came back with a Polaroid of a group dining in the restaurant — you know the sort of thing: everyone toasting the camera and grinning like apes. There was friend Potterton and, next to him, the Dubois woman. I pointed to her and said, 'Madame Dubois, n'est-ce pas? J'ai rencontré la madame cet après-midi chez Monsieur Potterton.' You understand?"

"You said you'd met her that afternoon at Potterton's place?"

"Not just a pretty face, eh?" mocked Grimes. "Well, le patron waggled his head most vigorously at this. 'Oh non, monsieur, pas Madame Dubois; c'est Madame Potterton, la femme de monsieur l'écrivain.'

"There'd been no mention of a wife in the files so I asked him if Madame

P. was a local lass. There was much semaphore and expostulation and 'pas du tout monsieur, la madame est Néo-Zélandaise; elle est venue ici avec son mari il y a quatre ans.' So Potterton's wife was a Kiwi and had been there with him all along. By now, the frog was in full flow, jabbering away about what a romantic couple they were, so in love, always holding hands and whispering sweet nothings. I, meanwhile, was wondering why the blazes Potterton had fibbed about it — clearly with her approval."

Grimes glanced at Hayhoe: she was perched on the edge of her chair, eyes wide, nibbling her lower lip. He smiled a private smile.

"I told le patron I'd be off first thing in the morning and fixed up the bill. I got up at five; there wasn't a soul about. On the way out, I slipped into the restaurant and commandeered the Polaroid. When I got back here, I dropped in on the publisher to report how it had gone. I casually produced the Polaroid and pointed to the mystery woman. 'She's rather nice,' I said. 'Do you happen to know who she is?'

"'That's Belinda,' he said, 'D'Arcy's sister. Last I heard she was living in London. I'm glad to see they're getting on so well these days; they used to be very off-hand with one another.'"

Hayhoe stared at Grimes. He leaned back in his chair as if exhausted, but lights danced in his black eyes.

She said slowly, "Spell it out for me, Mr Grimes."

Grimes' loose mouth twisted sardonically: "Well, it would appear that Potterton didn't go into self-imposed exile because his towering genius wasn't sufficiently appreciated or because he feared the fascists would bump him off come the putsch. He cleared off to the other side of the world so he could peg sister Belinda to his heart's content."

11

When the cops at Auckland Central had covered sport, sex and whichever aspect of the job was particularly shitting them off that day, they sometimes got onto the relationship between Detective Inspector Finbar McGrail and Detective Sergeant Tito Ihaka.

They were an odd couple, just about any way you looked at it: McGrail was built like a bullfighter, Ihaka like a bull; McGrail ran marathons, Ihaka had been known to drive to his letterbox; McGrail was pernickety, Ihaka was a slob's slob; McGrail didn't drink, Ihaka could put away a six-pack waiting for a home-delivered pizza; McGrail played chess, Ihaka played poker; McGrail was religious, Ihaka was profane. In a nutshell, McGrail took life very seriously while Ihaka didn't give a rat's arse.

Even so, it hadn't proved all that easy to come up with a nickname which did justice to their double act: "Laurel and Hardy" was too predictable, "Abbott and Costello" didn't stick because hardly anyone knew who the fuck Abbott and Costello were, "Holmes and Watson" was too high-brow, and "The Captain and Tenille" was rejected as too dangerous after Ihaka made a reasonably serious attempt to run over the guy who'd thought of it. In the end, they'd gone for "Jake and the Fat Man", even though the nit-pickers argued that, in the TV show, the Fat Man was the boss.

The big question was: what did they really think of each other? There were guys who "knew for a fact" that, deep down, they hated each other's guts and guys who claimed the opposite. A story did the rounds that McGrail only put up with Ihaka because the Fat Man "had" something on him. Oh yeah? Said the sceptics; what, did he forget to wash his hands after a crap?

Occasionally, there was talk of blow-ups and falling-outs. Like now: those in the know reckoned McGrail had a shitload riding on the APA investigation and was already taking political heat over Ihaka's bolshie attitude towards Wayne Cramp, the SIS man.

Ihaka had heard the rumours so he wasn't too thrilled when, on his way out that night, he poked his head into McGrail's office and found him in conference with Cramp.

McGrail waved him in: "We are discussing this afternoon's events in parliament. Chas Gundry had quite a lot to say about the investigation — much along the lines of Mr Cramp's theory."

Ihaka leaned against the wall. "Gundry, eh?" He looked at Cramp, deadpan. "Great minds think alike."

McGrail took the cue before Cramp could think of a come-back: "That's being too kind to Gundry. I can't imagine him working it out all by himself: I suspect someone's been putting ideas in his head. You wouldn't have a theory on who that might be, Mr Cramp?"

Cramp did his best to look surprised. "It hadn't occurred to me, Inspector." Pause. "Oh, I get it — you think we primed him?"

McGrail smiled thinly. "Well, I must admit, I did wonder. Then I asked myself, why on earth would the SIS think it was a good idea? I suppose a bureaucrat with an agenda might want to get it onto the front page, but for those of us at the sharp end it'll just make an already difficult job even harder."

Cramp, defensively: "Why's that?"

"In Belfast I saw what happens when murder investigations become political footballs." McGrail's voice took on a harder edge. "I can do without rent-a-mob camped outside and civil liberties nuisances bleating every time we interview someone with a brown face. I can certainly do without blowhards in parliament muddying the waters and badgering the minister for information I'd prefer to keep under wraps. If you do come across anyone who might've put ideas in Grundy's head, perhaps you'd be good enough to pass the message on."

McGrail and Cramp locked eyes for a few seconds. The SIS man shrugged nonchalantly and glanced away.

McGrail opened a manila folder. "We've had an update on Pike's autopsy report. In layman's terms, his neck was snapped like kindling. The perpetrator is either very strong or knows some nasty tricks."

"Gang members, maybe?" said Cramp. "Some of them would qualify on both counts and we know the radicals have been recruiting in the gangs."

"Gang guys don't dick around like this," said Ihaka with weary irritation. "This sort of tricky shit isn't their style."

Cramp said: "We obviously move in different circles, Sergeant. I wouldn't have thought there was anything very tricky about shoving people off high buildings or breaking their necks. Anyway, I'm not suggesting this is a gang operation, just that they could be being used as muscle. We're more interested in some of the activists who went to Libya a few years ago, courtesy of Colonel Gaddafi. You're probably not aware of this, but the Libyans have these training camps out in the desert — they're finishing schools for international terrorists."

"I thought those guys went to Libya for some bullshit anti-imperialism conference," said Ihaka.

Cramp smiled, shaking his head as if bemused by Ihaka's naivety. "Sergeant, attending conferences is standard cover for indoctrination and training trips to places like Libya and Cuba, like it used to be for going behind the Iron Curtain. Just for a change, why don't you tell us what you think instead of trying to pick holes in everything I say?"

"I don't have a theory," said Ihaka slowly, "because there's not enough to hang one on. But my gut instinct tells me this isn't a Maori thing."

Cramp laid on the sarcasm: "Oh, so it's your gut telling you, is it? Well, you'll have to make allowances for me: I was trained to use my brain."

"I wouldn't take the sergeant's gut too lightly, if I were you," murmured McGrail. "It's got rather a good track record."

The "Repulse the Republic" meeting began at 8 o'clock sharp that night in the distinctly unimperial surroundings of the Mount Roskill War Memorial Hall in May Road. Chas Gundry MP had an audience of thirty-three, twenty-seven of whom were old enough to vote; they included his bodyguard and a reporter from a Jesus 'n' muzak radio station.

Gundry delivered his usual rant, portraying life in the average republic as a maelstrom of revolving-door governments, corruption, hyper-inflation and uncollected rubbish. He closed with the quip that, under a republic, they'd probably still have a queen as head of state. Not many in the audience got it.

Afterwards, he had a cup of tea and a Girl Guide biscuit and worked the room. He was quickly cornered by four recent arrivals from Britain who whined at him in bewildering accents until his head started to pound. It wasn't until after 9.30 that he managed to lie his way out of the hall. It had been a long, stressful day; now it was time to relax and unwind.

Gundry and his bodyguard ate in an Italian restaurant in Dominion Road. Sergeant Kerry Keene, known as Kay, was a shy, strapping twenty-nine year old who'd been seconded to the VIP Protective Services Unit from the Christchurch police.

As they waited for the bill, Gundry studied Keene carefully: "You married, Kay?"

"No sir."

"Me neither, thank Christ. Tried it once; never again. You got a girlfriend?"

"Yeah." Keene sighed. "Trouble is, she's in Christchurch — I only get to see her once a month."

"Son, in that case, you owe it to yourself to get out and about, have a bit of fun. You'll go blind otherwise."

The policeman's habitual frown deepened. "What've you got in mind, sir?"

"There's this place, sort of members only — you can't get in unless they know you. But once you're in" — Gundry whistled and winked — "it's on for young and old, if you know what I mean."

Keene's eyebrows collided on the bridge of his nose. "Sir, are you talking about a brothel?"

Gundry sat up, scraping his chair loudly. He glanced around the restaurant, then hunched forward, elbows on the table. "Jesus, Kay, keep it down, if you don't mind. And give me some credit: I'm an MP, you're a cop — I'd hardly be suggesting we bowl into the nearest knockshop, would I? This joint's a completely different kettle of fish — it's what you'd call an exclusive private club. The bloke who put me onto it's got a knighthood, that's how classy it is."

"It sounds interesting, Mr Gundry, but I don't think so. My job is to keep an eye on you, not have a good time."

Gundry smirked: "You can forget about keeping an eye on me, pal — I know some blokes don't mind an audience but it puts me right off my stroke."

Keene went slightly pink and looked away.

"You're absolutely sure now? It'd be my shout — well, in a manner of speaking. Shit, every public servant deserves at least one root on the taxpayer."

Keene declined, reflecting that when he'd volunteered for a stint in the VIP Protective Services Unit, he'd expected to be putting his body on the line for a nobler cause than the preservation of Chas Gundry.

They left the restaurant. Gundry drove round the back of Mount Eden Prison, through Newmarket, out towards Parnell. He turned right off St Stephens Avenue into Brighton Road. Halfway down the hill into Hobson Bay, he stopped outside a low-rise apartment block.

"This is it. Last chance, son — you coming in?"

"I'll pass, thanks all the same."

Gundry shrugged. "Suit yourself. Listen, no harm in being discreet: I've got personalised number plates so why don't you park around the corner, in that side street?" He looked at his watch; it was 10.57. "I'll be an hour or so."

At fifteen minutes past midnight, Gundry exited the apartment block. He strolled down Brighton Road and rounded the corner. A dulling but not unpleasant weight of fatigue settled on him: he'd had two large vodka and tonics, a bubble bath, a cursory and unremedial massage, and the most elaborate handjob of his extensive experience.

His Holden Commodore with the number plate PITBUL and the reassuringly solid figure behind the steering wheel was parked twenty-five metres up the street. The MP gave a snappy American-style salute which was acknowledged with a circumspect wave.

Gundry felt an urgent need to urinate. He looked up and down the street: there was no one around and only a couple of chinks of light peeped through drawn curtains. He turned his back to the car and flopped it.

As a teenager, Gundry had been known as Powerhouse because he could piss over the goalposts' crossbar. His favourite trick was to go into the school toilets with a couple of cronies and deposit a golden shower on the unfortunate youth snoozing, dumping or jerking off behind the cubicle door. He could still achieve impressive muzzle velocity, especially with a full bladder. Between his urine drumming on the footpath and his sotto voce rendition of "There is a Rose in Spanish Harlem", he didn't hear the man who crept up behind him and prodded something cold and hard into the nape of his neck.

Not that he knew it was a man until a quiet male voice said, "Finish your piddle, shake your slug three times, put it away, put your hands up and turn around slowly."

When he turned around, he saw that the man was wearing a dark boiler suit and ski mask and the cold, hard thing was a silencer screwed on to a semi-automatic pistol.

The man tapped the silencer against Gundry's front teeth.

"The party's at your place, right, Chas?"

Caught literally and figuratively with his fly open, Gundry was slow to grasp the implications of being in a deserted side-street after midnight with a pistol poked in his face. It was only when a second man in a ski mask and dark boiler suit got out of his Commodore that the full horror of his predicament struck him: he was in deep shit, deep enough to drown in.

The accomplice disappeared into the night. The gunman told Gundry to get in behind the wheel and slid into the back seat.

With as much bravado as he could muster, Gundry demanded: "Who the hell are you?"

"You can call me Betty."

Betty? What the shit? "Are you in the APA?"

"Anything's possible."

"Where's Kay?"

"Would Kay be the minder?"

"Yeah, what . . . ?"

"In that case, he's in the boot."

"Jesus, what did you do to him?"

"Not much. A bodyguard called Kay? Still, who am I to talk?"

Gundry twisted around to ask Betty exactly what he wanted. Before he'd got very far, Betty jabbed him stiffly on the nose with the silencer and snapped: "Shut up and drive. We're going to your place."

"I've had a few drinks," said Gundry shakily. "I'd be over the limit."

"Don't worry your little head about it — if we see a cop, I'll blow you away before he can breathalyse you."

Gundry started the car. He went down Gladstone Road, left into Quay Street, and through downtown, past the wharves. The city had pretty well closed up for the night. He kept fifteen kilometres per hour under the limit until Betty rapped him on the ear with the gun and told him to speed up.

Going along Fanshawe Street towards the harbour bridge, Gundry noticed the van in his rear-view mirror. It followed them over the bridge and along the northern motorway to the Tristram Avenue exit. It was about there it finally dawned on Gundry that he had Betty's off-sider on his tail, not the Seventh Cavalry. From the motorway exit to the turn-off from the Albany Highway into Upper Harbour Drive, they passed two cars: one had no headlights and the other was having trouble straddling the white line.

Eighteen months previously, Gundry had reluctantly come to accept that a headline such as "MP's pit bull gnaws triplets" could do terminal damage to his career. The solution was to decamp from suburban Glenfield and relocate to a brand-new kitset home on a large, fenced-off section in semi-rural Greenhithe. His nearest neighbours were forty metres away in one direction, twice that in the other.

They got there. Betty told him to put the car in the garage. Gundry used the remote control to raise the door and drove in. It was a two-car garage with direct access to the house. As they got out of the car, the van pulled in and parked beside the Commodore.

Betty closed the garage. He walked over to the door into the house and rattled the handle. From inside came a long vibrating rumble, like distant thunder.

"My, he sounds nasty," said Betty. "What's his name?"

Gundry had been counting on an unsuspecting Betty opening the door and getting torpedoed in the groin by a twenty-five-kilogram ball of muscle with a bite like a bear trap, propelled by the mindless fury of a blood-crazed hammerhead. He hung his head, silently cursing himself for ever having bragged to the media about his pit bulls.

"I asked you a question."

"Son of Sam," mumbled Gundry.

"Cute. Al, would you get the minder out of the boot?"

Al hauled out Keene, who was hooded with his hands taped together behind his back.

Betty asked, "How mean is Son of Sam?"

Gundry shrugged.

"Put it this way: does he attack intruders on sight?"

"It depends," lied Gundry. "If he felt threatened, he might."

Betty told Keene: "Whatever you do, Kay, don't threaten the wee fellow."

Gundry babbled: "Jesus wept, what are you going to do?"

"I'm not very good with dogs," said Betty silkily. "Maybe they sense that I'm nervous — that's how it works, isn't it? We'll send Kay in first, to make friends with him."

"Fucking hell, man, you can't do that, not with his hands . . . "

Al shut him up with a backhander across the mouth. As Gundry reeled, Keene pivoted on his left leg and karate-kicked Betty hard in the stomach; he doubled up, making a puking noise. Keene kicked out again, clipping his shoulder. Al picked up Gundry and heaved him at Keene as he launched another kick. They crashed together. Gundry bounced off, scrabbling at the garage door to stay upright; Keene lost his balance and went over. He thrashed blindly on the floor until Al subdued him with a boot to the head.

They dragged Keene to the door. Betty opened it just wide enough for Al to shove the policeman through, then yanked it shut.

There was another throbbing growl which swelled and sharpened into a blood-curdling snarl.

Keene's kung-fu hadn't disturbed Betty's urbane cool: "They don't call them man's best friend for nothing."

Thumps and bumps; Son of Sam's wild snarl rose and fell like the angry whine of a chainsaw. Eventually, it faded to a low hum.

Gundry swayed like a drunk, hands pressed to his face. Betty chided: "Didn't you teach him it's rude to speak with his mouth full?"

Quiet inside. Betty told Gundry. "Okay, your turn."

Gundry was weeping; his voice trembled: "You fucking evil cunt."

Betty protested: "He's not my dog. Now get in there and see if he wants dessert."

Full of dread, Gundry pushed the door open. Son of Sam, his brindle face smeared with blood, quivered a moment, then relaxed. Keene lay awkwardly on his side, his head turned away. The hood was half torn off and blood bubbled from this throat. Ripped flesh gaped behind a shredded trouser leg.

Gundry dropped to his knees. Son of Sam padded forward to lick his master's tear-streaked face. When Al stepped through the door, the dog looked up at him. His lashless, almond eyes were placid and incurious, as if mauling Keene had drained his berserk energy.

Very slowly, Al extended his arm, aiming the stainless-steel Smith & Wesson ten-millimetre semi-automatic which Keene hadn't had time to draw from his shoulder holster when they'd got the jump on him in the Parnell side-street.

Popular usage notwithstanding, people — or, for that matter, dogs — seldom have their heads blown off by a single gunshot. In Son of Sam's case, what was left on his powerful shoulders when the smoke cleared was so inconsequential that only a pedant would have quibbled with the expression.

When Son of Sam's head exploded ten centimetres from his right ear, Gundry uttered a demented screech and rolled into a foetal position, eyes screwed shut and hands clamped over his ears.

He opened his eyes to find Betty kneeling beside him.

"Come on, Mr Queen and Country; time to go to work."

Gundry's mouth moved but no sounds emerged.

"We're going to have a hangi."

Gundry still mouthed silently.

"You know what a hangi is, don't you? I thought you had them all the time."

That got a dazed nod.

"Guess what we're going to cook?"

The MP whimpered.

"You."

12

Leo Strange, the facilitator, was early for his meeting with Brandon Mules. Strange made a habit of being early. It was part and parcel of his policy of doing things at his own pace, which was nice and easy. He'd worked out long ago that, since getting from A to B rarely went exactly according to plan, life was a choice between a stroll and a scuttle, between having to fill in time and having to hurry, between boredom and stress. Being temperamentally suited to hanging around and physically unsuited to hurrying, Strange always allowed more than enough time to get from A to B.

Besides, being early had its rewards. It was amazing the scraps of information you could pick up lurking around a reception area: by cocking an ear to the receptionist's phone conversations perhaps, or by taking your time over signing in and having a quick flick through the visitors book, or by noticing where the couriers were coming from and going to. Spend fifteen or twenty minutes in a company's reception area with your eyes and ears open and you could glean information about its operations that its competitors would pay good money for. And often did.

And when meetings were on neutral ground, the early bird could get a feel for the lie of the land and nab the best position. That might be the spot with the best view of proceedings or the one nearest the exit.

They were just little things but Strange had built a career on little things: pile up enough little things and they made a big thing. A little thing could also give you the edge and in the grey areas where Strange worked, it was all about having the edge.

Thus Strange arrived in the upstairs bar of the Globe at 1.50 p.m. for his 2 o'clock progress review with Mules. He had on a single-breasted navy-blue wool suit with a white shirt and striped club tie and carried the tan leather satchel in his right hand and the oyster-white Burberry draped over his left arm. He bought a Campari and soda and sat with his back to the wall at the far corner table, where he could see everyone in the bar.

When he was satisfied that no one in the bar was sufficiently sober, alert or curious to take any notice of him and Mules, Strange got out his airmail copy of the *Spectator* and began to read. At 2.15, he put down the magazine and checked his watch; looking a little vexed, he got another Campari and soda and went back to his seat and his magazine.

At 2.32, Mules walked into the bar. Ignoring the barman's offer of service, he sauntered over to the corner table and looked down on Strange from his almost two metres with a lazy and not especially respectful grin. Strange glanced up

461

from his magazine just long enough to suggest he got himself a drink, then carried on reading.

Mules pulled out a chair and sat down. "No double Jack today, Leo?"

Strange glanced up again, this time with a brief, patronising half-smile; the intentional rudeness was completely wasted on Mules. After he'd read for another minute or so, Strange put away the magazine and fixed Mules with a cold look: "You're on the payroll now, Mr Mules. I paid you five thousand last week, in case you've forgotten. That enables you to buy your own drinks — and entitles me to punctuality."

Mules responded with a casual toss of the head, dismissing the reprimand like a boxer slipping a punch. "I got held up." After a significant pause, he tagged on, "Sorry," in an ironic tone and with another mocking grin, just in case. Strange thought he really meant it.

Strange frowned. "Well? What progress can you report?"

"Not a fucking sausage," said Mules blithely. "I thought the Trousdale piece was meant to be a full-on nympho? Well, shit, I haven't seen any sign of it — just the bloody opposite, in fact. She's a do-gooder: she takes retards to the park, she does meals on wheels, for fuck's sake. You sure you got this right?"

Strange's well-upholstered poise wobbled: his forehead creased and his normally still grey eyes bulged anxiously: "I'm quite sure; the information came from an impeccable source. You mean she hasn't met up with Early at all?"

Mules snorted: "The little snake hasn't been sighted. I think I'll have one after all."

When Mules came back with a beer, Strange was distractedly plucking his lower lip. "You've got absolutely nothing to show for a week's work then?" he griped.

Mules bristled: "Hang on, mate, don't you go pointing the finger at me. I did what you said, followed the bitch all over town. It's not my fault Early hasn't slapped one up her." He shrugged. "Maybe she's had the painters in."

Strange's mouth twitched with distaste. "So you followed her every day and didn't see a single thing worth mentioning."

Mules gave it some thought. "She went out of town one day — Tuesday it would've been."

"Where to?" asked Strange hopefully.

"Wouldn't know. I stuck with her as far as the end of the motorway. . . . "

"Dammit, man, why didn't you keep after her? That's what you're being paid for. She might've been on her way to meet Early somewhere."

Mules took his time finishing his beer. "You want to know why I didn't stick with her?" He had the cocky air of a man about to turn the tables. "Well, you see, I've got a nine year-old Laser and she's got a hot Merc with a couple of hundred grands' worth of poke — she'd have blown me off as soon as we hit the open road. So what I did was come back and ring Early at his junk barn in

Birkenhead, said I was someone else. When he answered, I hung up. It seemed to me if Early was in Birkenhead and she was south of the Bombay Hills, wherever the fuck she was heading, it wasn't for the end of his wang."

Having put Strange on the back foot, Mules followed up: "You know, I got your outfit's number from directory and gave you a ring. All I got was a recorded message. I must've tried ten times, same thing each time. What's the fucking story, Leo?"

Strange couldn't help blinking with surprise. "I'm semi-retired," he said eventually. "I do project work for a few clients who know how to contact me when the need arises. I didn't think it'd be necessary in this instance; given the complete lack of progress, it was even less necessary than I'd expected."

"Just thought I'd ask." Mules stood up. "See you next week then — same time, same place? Let's hope the root rats pull finger, eh?"

Mules winked at Strange and walked out of the bar. If he'd looked back, he would've seen Strange staring gloomily into his Campari and soda.

Strange was taking stock. He'd underestimated his man: he'd assumed that because Mules was short of money and lazy and lacked character, he'd be more than happy with ten grand. Instead, Mules had gone looking for an angle and had obviously found one.

It could've been worse: if Mules was smarter, he wouldn't have let on.

A little later that Friday afternoon, Clyde Early emerged from his office at the back of the Mr Fixit Hardware store in Birkenhead to tell his secretary Judith that he was off the air until further notice. As if to emphasise his anti-social mood, he shut the door behind him more forcefully than was good for the door or Judith's nerves.

Early sat down at his desk, reached for a pristine A4 lined notepad and one of the high-tech Japanese ballpoints he favoured, and applied his methodical mind to the challenge of avoiding humiliation, divorce and years of child support.

He was past the stage of being angry that his exhilarating sexual adventure with Rusty Trousdale had mutated into a ticking time bomb. He was even past seething with frustration at not being able to do anything about it.

There had to be something he could do, even if it was just kiss his arse goodbye.

Quedley reckoned the blackmailer took the diary because he knew Rusty had been playing around. That made sense, but how did he find out in the first place? Chances are she let it slip — or one of the other boyfriends did. But maybe she and I weren't as clever or as careful as we thought; maybe somewhere along the line we gave the game away.

Early made a list of the people who were present the night they'd met. It was in late April, at a dinner party hosted by a senior executive of a large company which put a lot of sponsorship money into rugby. There were the host and hostess, the Earlys, the Trousdales and the director of the company's advertising agency and his girlfriend.

Maybe one of them caught a vibe and gossiped about it afterwards?

Only if they had the sort of social radar that could pick up a nipple hardening under three layers of clothing across the room. Apart from some cautious eye contact over pre-dinner drinks, he and Rusty had behaved like strangers usually do at dinner parties: they'd politely ignored each other.

Late in the evening, he'd overheard her enthusing about her favourite new coffee place, Café Columbus in High Street, where she often went for a mid-morning latte or post-lunch macchiato. Early began dropping in there regularly. On the seventh day, his ship came in. He was nursing an espresso when she slid into the next high stool murmuring, in a voice which gave him goosebumps, "Who's a clever boy then?"

Early tore the sheet off the notepad and dropped it in his wastepaper basket. They weren't sprung at the dinner party or at Café Columbus, where they'd skirted around what was on their minds until she finished her coffee and said she had to run. She breezed out; he sat there wondering whether to go after her. Then he saw the mobile phone number she'd scribbled on the paper napkin.

After that time in Café Columbus, they didn't meet in bars or cafés or restaurants or anywhere there was a chance of bumping into people who knew them. The assignations took place at Greywater when her husband was overseas and right there, in his office, outside trading hours — on Sundays or at night. When they used his office, they'd rendezvous in the carpark under Aotea Square, drive to Birkenhead in his car, park in the basement and come up the internal stairway.

They always communicated by digital mobile phones so the calls couldn't be answered by others or eavesdropped on an extension. Let it ring four times: if it wasn't answered, flag it away and try again later . . . Early froze as his mind, now in overdrive, seized on a fragment of dim memory: *what about the day I forgot my mobile?*

He jumped up and paced around his desk.

Shit, that's right. It was the Thursday before Queen's Birthday weekend: Trousdale decided to go to Sydney on the spur of the moment and Rusty had to catch me before I left work so I could invent a reason to come back from the lake early.

He sprawled on the sofa and closed his eyes, squeezing his memory. The phone rang: 'It's a Miss Rust from the accountants — she says it's urgent." It took him a few seconds to twig — what the hell's she playing at? Then he heard the delicious, low giggle and didn't care. He said, "Hello," his mouth suddenly dry. She said, "You goose, you left your mobile at home, didn't you? I just tried to ring you on it. God, when I got 'Jane Early speaking,' I just about drove off the road. Listen, Maurice's off to Sydney till Tuesday so the coast's clear at long last if you can swing it . . . "

Early rewound the mental tape. The phone rings, Judith says, "It's a Miss Rust from the accountants . . . " EXCEPT IT'S NOT JUDITH.

He lunged for his diary and pawed through it: she'd written "Judith on holiday!" across the top of the page for Thursday, 1 June. She'd taken some time off and they'd got a temp in.

Sweet bleeding Jesus, it was the temp — the bitch must've listened in.

He grabbed the phone: "Judith, could you dig out the file for the temp who filled in for you over Queen's Birthday?"

When Chas Gundry MP failed to show up at Glenfield College on Friday morning to talk politics with the sixth formers, they heaved a collective sigh of relief and went back to daydreaming about the world without acne. The teacher who'd organised the session was disgusted but not overly surprised: it merely bore out his — and most teachers' — opinion that politicians don't give a toss about education. He didn't bother wasting breath on an indignant phone call to the MP's electorate office.

When Gundry didn't make a midday meeting with a publisher in Takapuna to discuss his idea for a book provisionally titled *The Joy of Pit Bulls*, the senior editor thanked God, which she was later to regret, and went shopping. The firm's publishing committee had given the idea short shrift and she'd been steeling herself for a scene. Dealing with authors every day, she got plenty of exposure to egomaniacs and drama queens but a guy who went gooey-eyed over pit bulls was something else.

When Gundry didn't appear at the North Shore Golf Club for the Glenfield Small Business Association's monthly lunch, the small businesspeople just got drunker than usual, faster than usual. The lunch was Gundry's last engagement for the day: he'd set aside the afternoon for discussing the economic outlook with the GSBA until he fell over or they shut the bar.

About 4 o'clock when the lunchers graduated from throwing cheese to throwing chairs, punches and finally bottles, some of which weren't even empty, the police were called to what was officially classified as an affray.

One of the constables dispatched to the golf club happened to be going out with a teacher at Glenfield College. In the course of their lunchtime phone conversation, she'd mentioned Gundry's no-show.

When the constable reported in, he asked the desk sergeant if it was normal for an MP to just not turn up for engagements which his electorate secretary had confirmed the previous day. The sergeant didn't think so; he looked up Gundry's address and told the constable to swing past and check the place out, seeing he was in the vicinity. The sergeant then called the MP's local office and spoke to his electorate secretary, who was both baffled and concerned by the no-shows.

Shortly before 5.30, the constable reported no one home at Gundry's place; the sergeant told him to hang around. The electorate secretary, a 64-year-old semi-retired bookkeeper, picked up a key to the MP's house from his cleaning lady and drove out there. He unlocked the front door and went inside. The constable, mindful of procedure, waited to be asked in. He didn't have to wait long: the invitation came in the form of a gargling scream which scrambled sparrows from branches and powerlines within a seventy-five-metre radius.

In the entrance hall the constable came across a man who appeared to be dead, a dog which couldn't have been any deader if a tactical nuclear device had gone off in its kennel, and a semi-retired bookkeeper who wasn't going to be the odd one out for much longer judging the way he was clutching his chest and spraying milky-white spittle from bloodless lips.

It was dark when the APA delegation from Auckland Central — Detective Sergeant Tito Ihaka, Detective Constable Johan Van Roon, and the SIS man Wayne Cramp — arrived at Gundry's house. A detective sergeant from Takapuna was standing on the front lawn, smoking grimly.

"What's the go, Pete?" said Ihaka. "I thought murder was against the law this side of the bridge?"

Pete shook his head. "You wouldn't fucking believe it, mate."

"What?"

"We got a dog with its head splattered all over the shop — and a dead cop." Ihaka's eyes darkened and his face set like stone.

"Sergeant Kerry Keene out of Christchurch, according to his ID; seconded to the PSU."

"Gundry's bodyguard."

Pete nodded. "You know the worst part? It looks like the fucking dog did him."

"What about Gundry?"

Pete shook his head. "No sign of him — we haven't done a proper search yet. We found a pistol, though."

"They left a gun?" Ihaka couldn't believe it. "Give us a look."

Pete led them inside. Ihaka took in the scene in one bleak sweep. He nodded to the white-coat crew: "It just gets worse, eh boys?"

Subdued assent.

The pistol was in a tagged plastic bag on the hall table. Ihaka peered at it: "That's a pretty serious unit." He glanced over his shoulder at Cramp who was mesmerised by the carnage. "Hey Wayne, you know what this is?"

Cramp tore his eyes away and came over. He was pale and his fingers shook as he loosened his tie. He looked at the pistol, swallowing hard: "Smith and Wesson ten-millimetre — the FBI use them. Your department brought in a batch last year. I heard they'd been issued — unofficially — to the PSU."

Ihaka said, "Fuck." He walked through the house, ending up in the kitchen at the rear. A constable was stationed at the back door. "You had a look out the back?"

"Just a quick squizz, Sarge."

Ihaka borrowed his torch and went outside. The section sloped away out of the torch's range. Ihaka advanced, swinging the beam of light from side to side. Gundry's back yard was designed for the lawnmower: flowerbeds along both fences and a few well-spaced shrubs.

Ihaka got his first whiff of it as he heard the back door open. He muttered, "Jesus," and quickened his pace. The smell got worse: it was like bad, burnt grease and filled his mouth like a foul aftertaste. He'd smelt it before, at car crashes and house fires: it was the smell of human flesh cooking.

He went on down the slope. The back fence was looming in front of him when the torch beam fell on a low mound of earth. Steam rose from it. He saw a patch of white on the fence and shone the torch: it was an envelope. He was pulling on a plastic glove when Cramp arrived.

"Christ, what's that smell?"

"At a guess, the honourable member."

Cramp goggled.

"See that?" Ihaka aimed the torch beam at the steaming mound of earth. "That's a hangi." He reached out to remove the envelope from the fence. "I think we'll find the APA stuck Gundry in there and cooked the shit out of him. Say what you like about the fuckers, they don't do things the easy way."

13

Around the time that the semi-retired bookkeeper was galvanising sparrows in Greenhithe and about two kilometres due south across Hellyers Creek, Clyde Early was confronting the temporary secretary.

Renée Adlington was a forty-six-year-old divorcee who'd been cute in a pert, snub-nosed way when she was twenty and would resemble a jowly Pekinese by the time she was sixty-five. Right now, she was somewhere in between.

Adlington's main interest in life was her family. Most days, she went to see her eighty-two-year-old widowed mother at the old folks home in Chatswood which backed on to the Kauri Point naval armament depot. Her mother was reasonably compos but a little unsteady on her pins, which necessitated leaving the door open when she went to the toilet in case she fell over and trapped herself. Adlington wasn't sure if it was old age or had gone on for years behind closed doors but, without fail, her mother would fart like a draught horse before, during and after her motions. Listening to the blasts, Adlington would sometimes reflect that, if the armament depot ever did blow up, she probably wouldn't even notice.

Then there was her brother who visited Auckland now and again from his hideaway in the Marlborough Sounds. He was worldly and well informed, so she consulted him on everything from her mortgage arrangements to which wine should accompany the chicken chasseur she planned to serve when she entertained her new man friend.

Finally, there were her daughter and grandson in Cockle Bay, which was on the other side of town and a bugger of a place to get to. She assumed that was why her son-in-law insisted on living there.

When the doorbell of her Birkdale townhouse rang, Adlington wondered if it was the new man friend: he'd been threatening to drop in unannounced since they'd first met, almost a month ago at a mature singles night at Alexandra Park Raceway.

She'd had to be talked into going. Her view was that mature singles nights were just meat markets for people who were old enough to know better; her girlfriend had countered that a healthy diet should include a certain amount of meat. When Adlington thought about it, she found herself wavering. Who said one strike and you're out? Why should men be off the agenda just because she was a grandmother who carried the baggage of a marriage which had curled up and died after nineteen years, having spent half its miserable existence on a life-support machine? She still had her looks — well, some of them, anyway. Her figure wasn't too bad — a bit on the full side maybe but that cut both ways: it wasn't as if Alexandra Park Raceway would be swarming with Brad Pitt lookalikes.

So she'd gone along, vowing to take things very slowly. As it happened, she'd been there all of five minutes when the best-looking man in the room had introduced himself by saying, "Hello darling, I'm Henry. I suppose a knee-trembler would be out of the question?" Completely thrown, she'd blurted that she wasn't that sort of woman. He'd asked the obvious question: what sort of woman was she then? The sort of woman who'd have to get to know a man properly before she'd consider . . . you know. And how long would that take — an hour, a week, a month, a year? A week was rushing things and he didn't seem the type who'd hang around for a year so she'd opted, hesitantly, for a month. Henry had nodded, as if weighing up options, then, announced his verdict: while he wouldn't twiddle his thumbs for ten minutes for most of the old boilers there, he was prepared to do so in her case.

Henry was an experienced seducer of mature single women. Once he'd extracted the information that Adlington had been sexually inactive since the break-up of her marriage, he'd taken to spelling out, face to face and over the phone, what was in store for her when the month was up. These salacious spiels had the desired effects of eroding her inhibitions and, slowly but surely, arousing her anticipation.

"The fact is, when it comes to leg-over, most women need a bit of training," Henry would say. "Frankly, I can have a better time with a filthy video and a jar of coconut oil that the average dame at those singles nights; they haven't got any idea, most of them. You're different: I picked you right from the off as a volcano just waiting to erupt. So we can skip the beginner's stuff. I'm going to throw you in at the deep end, gorgeous — we'll start with analingus."

The word wasn't in Adlington's dictionary but you didn't need to be a professor of linguistics to get the gist. She'd felt queasy for the rest of the evening. By the following morning, though, she was once more tingling with the now familiar sensation of simmering excitement, spiced with a piquant touch of guilt over the sinfulness of it all. The coming week promised to be the longest of her adult life.

But it wasn't Henry at the door, it was Clyde Early. His expression suggested he was itching to do a number of unspeakable things to her but analingus wasn't among them. His hands were thrust deep into the pockets of a shin-length herringbone overcoat and he stared at her with all the benevolence of a vulture watching a lame horse hobbling through Death Valley.

"Mr Early? What brings you here?"

"I want to talk to you," he said ominously.

"It's not really convenient right now — perhaps you could come back some other time?"

"Perhaps I could come back with the police."

She took a short, involuntary step backwards. Early brushed past her and walked into the living room. Adlington rallied and went in hot pursuit: "Who the hell do you think you are, barging into my home like this?"

Early shed his overcoat, which he'd bought in Milan and liked far too much to mothball even though it amounted to sartorial overkill for Auckland's mild, damp winters. "Cut the crap — you know bloody well why I'm here."

She flushed and stalked past him to the telephone on the kitchenette bench. "I will not be spoken to like that in my own home. If you're not out of here in ten seconds, I'm calling the police."

"Are you trying to tell me you don't know why I'm here?"

"I haven't got the faintest idea."

He came closer, his eyes drilling into hers. "When you temped for me before Queen's Birthday, you listened in on one of my phone calls, didn't you?"

Adlington's face went blank, then it went stupid: "I . . . uh, I wouldn't do such a thing."

Early grunted derisively. "Do you know what the penalty for blackmail is, Mrs Adlington?"

"What? What's blackmail got to do with it?"

"The woman who rang me that Thursday, whose call you listened in on, is being blackmailed. I think — no let me rephrase that — I know you're up to your neck in it."

"This is ridiculous. For the last time, I'm asking you to leave . . . "

Early changed tack: "Who'd you tell?"

"What?"

"Who did you tell that we were having an affair?"

Adlington's eyes darted and she gnawed her lower lip.

"You've got the wrong end of the stick, Mr Early," she said without conviction. "I'm sorry about whatever's happened but it's got nothing to do with me."

Early gave a contemptuous shake of the head. He shrugged on his overcoat. "You told somebody and he went and stole the lady's diary. Now he's blackmailing her. Maybe you're part of it, maybe not — I don't give a shit. Tell him to give the diary back and get lost. If it's not back by Monday morning, I'm going to the police."

He threw her a final glare and walked out. Through a crack in the curtains, Adlington watched him get into his car and drive away. Then she crossed the living room, opened the door into the corridor, and called, "You can come out now. He's gone."

She sat in an armchair drumming her fingers impatiently until Leo Strange emerged. He didn't look quite his normal, unflappable self.

In a tone she rarely took with her big brother, she demanded: "Well Leo? I think you owe me an explanation."

When Amanda Hayhoe walked into Vinnie's restaurant in Jervois Road at 8.08 p.m. and was directed to his table, Caspar Quedley was mildly surprised on two counts: he hadn't expected her to be as punctual or as attractive.

He'd missed her at TVNZ that morning and left a message saying he'd call again. The name rang a bell, so Hayhoe looked up his file in the clippings library. The most recent story on him was eighteen months old but she assumed he still looked and behaved like a cad from central casting.

He rang back after lunch wanting a meeting.

"What for?"

"We need to talk. It's a tricky business; better to do it in person than over the phone."

"Oh?" She waited for amplification; none came. "When did you have in mind?"

"Tonight if possible. I'd be more than happy to buy you dinner."

"Tell me, this chat we need to have: would it be professional or personal?"

"The latter. I haven't got a hot scoop for you, if that's what you mean."

"I gave up believing I was irresistible the day I started kindergarten, but just in case this is a roundabout way of asking me out, you should know that I've already had an older man experience. It was underwhelming, to put it politely."

"It happens sometimes: men are like wine — some age better than others. Rest assured, my intentions are beyond reproach. To tell the truth, I'm not too sure I can even put a face to you. I must've seen you on the box but I get all you glam young women mixed up."

"It works like this: the game-show bimbos pout, the weather airheads simper, and us current-affairs bitches do that odd sort of smug frown. It takes lots of practice."

"That's a useful guide. I'd better write it down before I forget."

"Look, I don't mean to be coy but couldn't you give me a tiny clue what this is about?"

"Let's just say it's important — for yourself and others."

Hayhoe stopped fighting: admit it, kid, you're intrigued.

"Okay, I give in — I'll let you buy me dinner. Somewhere decent, I hope?"

"So do I — you choose."

"I like Vinnie's in Herne Bay but we haven't got much show of getting in there . . ."

"I'll see what I can do. If you don't hear back from me, I'll meet you there. Eight o'clock okay?"

It was and she didn't hear back.

Hayhoe scarcely recognised Quedley from his file photo. When she got a closer look, she realised that the big change wasn't so much in what he'd gained — a beard and grey streaks in his hair — as what he'd lost: the livewire glow and that "the joke's on you, sucker" look in his eyes. He looked older, slower, less potent, no longer bulletproof. She wondered if he was wiser.

The restaurant was full. "I'm impressed. How'd you manage it?"

He shrugged diffidently: "I used to be a regular — either that or they felt sorry for me."

A waiter went through the specials. Quedley asked for a jug of water, no lemon, no ice.

"I read up on you." She watched for a reaction. "You were notorious for a while."

His low-voltage smile came and went. "I gave it up."

"Notoriety or public relations?"

"Both."

"So what do you do now?"

"As in a job? Not a thing; I'm unemployed."

Hayhoe had had a couple of drinks after work; she'd come prepared to joust. "Gosh, yet another reason to feel sorry for you."

That seemed to amuse him. "It obviously didn't have that effect on you."

The waiter came for their orders. Quedley still hadn't looked at the menu: he told Hayhoe to go ahead. She ordered salt-roasted chicken, he asked for the fish of the day, whatever it was, grilled and served plain, with a green salad. The waiter looked confused. Quedley handed him the unread menu: "My apologies to the chef."

The waiter offered wine. Quedley referred to Hayhoe, who said she wouldn't mind a glass of chardonnay. He told the waiter to bring her a bottle, a good one.

"Aren't you having anything?"

"I don't think so — I'm out of practice at alcohol, among other things. Besides, I've got to drive to Cambridge tonight."

"What for?"

"I live there."

Hayhoe wondered what the big attraction in Cambridge was but didn't bother asking. Quedley seemed to specialise in cryptic answers.

After the wine had been poured, Quedley said: "I've kept you in suspense long enough: you know Rusty Trousdale?"

Her expression changed several times in as many seconds: "We've met."

"I'm here on her behalf — we go way back. I like Rusty a lot but there's no denying she's been an idiot."

"She can afford to be, can't she?"

"Not this time. To begin at the beginning: she kept a diary in which you rate a mention."

Alarm stirred in Hayhoe's eyes. Her wine glass stopped in mid-voyage and returned to base. "Did she tell you what happened?"

"She told me what happened."

Hayhoe relaxed and refocused on the wine. Quedley lowered his voice: "Amanda, you declined an invitation to have sex with Rusty: that's a rare — possibly unique — distinction. It must've been a blow to her ego because she skated over the fact in the diary."

Hayhoe's eyebrows rose in slow motion and stayed up: "Come again?"

He tugged an ear lobe: "Apparently, the way she described the encounter, anyone else reading it would probably get the wrong idea."

Their meals arrived. As soon as the waiter had departed, she hissed: "You mean she said we had it off?"

"I don't know that she went that far but she certainly didn't spell it out that you turned her down."

"Is she mad or just on drugs? Why the hell did she do that?"

"Beats me. I asked her the same question."

"What did she say?"

"Nothing very enlightening." He refilled her wine glass. "Your chicken's getting cold."

She stared at him for a little longer then began to eat, chewing thoughtfully. He processed his greens without appearing to derive much enjoyment.

"There's more to it, isn't there?" she said. "I mean, you're not buying me dinner just because your old bud implied she got her hand on my woolly."

Quedley struggled to keep a straight face. "Right. I'm buying you dinner because Rusty's got a problem which could become your problem: someone stole the diary and he's using it to blackmail her. You probably wouldn't be stunned to learn that yours isn't the only bedroom scene in which her husband is conspicuous by his absence. The blackmailer wants big bucks — which incidentally she hasn't got, it's all Trousdale's — or else. Or else could mean several things: he might be satisfied with wrecking her marriage; on the other hand, he might get really vindictive and send copies of the naughty bits to every media outlet in the country."

Hayhoe's face fell. She said, "Oh, that's just fucking peachy," loud enough for the people at the next table to hear, and lunged for the wine bottle. "So when can I expect to be outed?"

"She'll stall as long as she can. I'm sure the blackmailer knew what was in the diary before he stole it, which is why I'm going round asking Rusty's playthings whether they told anyone. You're my last call."

She was nonplussed: "I haven't told a soul; I mean, what was there to brag about?"

"I don't know," said Quedley meditatively. "I reckon anyone who gets through a night with Rusty with virtue intact deserves congratulations."

"I presume you didn't manage it?"

"I didn't even get close. Mind you, she was single in those days and I was . . ."

"You were what?"

"Different."

"What's changed?"

"You mean apart from my whole life? Well, for starters, I've been celibate for the best part of two years."

Hayhoe refilled her glass and solemnly raised it. "To the good ship Celibacy and all who sail in her."

"Don't tell me you're celibate."

"That's the way it seems to be panning out."

"That's appalling." He looked as if he meant it. "Why?"

She shrugged: "Whatever's come my way — Rusty, for example — just didn't feel right."

"Maybe you're being a little picky?"

"Isn't that the pot calling the kettle white?"

"It's not the same. In my case, it was part of a" — he stared into space — "retreat from society".

"Permanent?"

"I don't really know. Sometimes I toy with the idea of making a comeback."

"To society or are we still on sex?"

Quedley's eyes lit up. He flashed a lopsided, self-deprecating grin, giving her a burst of the killer charm mentioned in some of the file stories. "I hadn't really thought about sex. First, I'd have to find a woman who didn't feel sorry for me: I'm not proud but I draw the line at sympathy fucks."

Hayhoe giggled. "What are you suggesting — that we join forces to kick the habit?"

Quedley realised that she'd gone from coolly sober to playfully drunk in a single bound, skipping tipsy altogether. "I wouldn't dream of it," he said carefully, "not after what you said about older men."

She inspected him through heavy-lidded, slightly glazed eyes: "You looked a lot younger without the beard."

14

It was still dark when Leo Strange woke up. Rain was falling with the timeless rhythm of a waterfall, as it had been when he'd gone to bed and when he'd woken during the night. For a few minutes, he thought about what he had to do that morning. He wasn't looking forward to it, but he'd studied it from every angle: if there was a better way, he hadn't found it.

He propped himself up, flicked on the bedside light, and checked his watch: 6.09. Only two kinds of people got up at 6.09 on a Saturday morning — those who didn't drink and those who'd got their nuts caught in the wringer. Strange, who'd puked on liquors most people have never heard of, threw back the covers and got out of bed.

He showered, shaved and got dressed in brown brogues, corduroy trousers, a cream lambswool skivvy and a green Harris tweed jacket with leather elbow patches: weekend wear for a man of substance — worthy, solid, respectable. Strange was none of those things but didn't see any point in advertising the fact.

He dawdled over breakfast, having a second cup of tea and a third slice of toast and marmalade. At 7.15 he put the newspaper aside. He rinsed his breakfast dishes and put them in the dishwasher, left a note for his sister, picked up his suitcase, satchel and raincoat, and left the house. He got into the rented Ford Telstar and drove down Birkdale Road towards Birkenhead until he found a phone box.

A minute went by without his call being answered but Strange didn't hang up. He could visualise the scene at the other end of the line: he was connected to a white Bakelite telephone which had done three decades' service in the Paris Office, above the Banque Rothschild on Avenue George V, from which Madame Claude ran her legendary call-girl operation. Now it sat on a Macassar ebony veneer half-moon desk designed by the celebrated French art deco ensemblier Émile-Jacques Ruhlman and which had once belonged to the Maharajah of Indore. The desk was in the study of a magnificent house overlooking the Heretaunga golf course, just outside Wellington. There were no extensions on the number, and house guests, mainly beautiful, transient girls, knew better than to go into the study, let alone answer the white Bakelite telephone.

On the eighty-fifth ring, the white phone was picked up.

"It's Strange."

"What is?" It was a male voice and an unusual one, harsh yet with a breezy undertone. Strange thought it suited the speaker to a T.

He ignored the question. Strange hadn't responded to jokes — good, bad or indifferent — involving his surname since the sixties, when he still thought that if you laughed every time a woman said something she thought was amusing, eventually she'd let you into her pants.

"There's a problem with Operation Early Bird."

"That's one of the things I like about you, Leo. Some people would've said, 'We have a problem.' Not you; you understand that if God had wanted me to have problems, he wouldn't have made me filthy rich. How bad is it? We talking hiccup or fuck-up?"

"There's certainly potential for the latter."

"Should we abort?"

"I think that'd be prudent."

"Well, that's a pity, Leo, a real pity. I thought we were on to something with this one. I could see it having all sorts of applications."

"Yes, I know."

"You got any other bright ideas?"

"I'll give it some thought."

"Okay, I'll leave it with you. I know you don't need reminding, Leo, but seeing you're paying for the call, I'll do it anyway: no mess, no loose ends, nothing that might come back and put me off my game somewhere down the track. Show me a man with a loose end on his mind, Leo, and I'll show you a man who can't putt for shit."

"I'll take care of it," said Strange, because there was no point in saying anything else. They hung up simultaneously.

Strange got back in the hire car. The conversation had gone just as he'd expected, right down to the golf talk. It'd be nice to have nothing more to worry about than playing to your handicap — as opposed to, say, confronting a huge, obnoxious roughneck and forcing him to drop his get-rich-quick scheme.

He heaved a careworn sigh and started the car.

It was coming up to 8 o'clock when Strange parked in a narrow avenue in Kingsland, between the north-western motorway and New North Road. He'd been there before, the same day the whole sorry saga began: the day he found Mules, gave him five grand, and turned him loose on the Trousdale woman.

Mules lived in a granny flat at the rear of a sprawling villa. Strange guessed it was a century old and built of kauri. Intricate fretwork decorated the eaves overhanging the wide verandah but the walls, once white, were a watery grey and the green paint on the tin roof had turned bile-olive and started to peel. The front garden was semi-jungle and trees hunched over the house, branches pressing up to the windows like peeping toms. It looked like the wicked witch's cottage from some dark, cautionary fairy tale.

It was raining again. Strange pulled on his raincoat and reached into the car for his collapsible umbrella. Rummaging in his satchel, he came up with an emergency pack of single malt whisky miniatures. It was a little early in the day for whisky, even for someone as open-minded as Strange, but if this dog's breakfast didn't qualify as an emergency, what the hell would? He selected the Glenlivet and threw it back in two quick hits. He popped the umbrella and crossed the road, feeling the Scotch trickle warmly through him.

He took the path to the rear of the house. The low branches forced him to retract the umbrella just as it began to pelt down. The leather soles of his brogues failed to grip on the slippery concrete and he skidded, flailing his arms like a slapstick comedian.

The door to the flat had a solid-wood border framing latticed panes of frosted glass. The pane nearest the door handle was missing: it had been neatly cut out, leaving a centimetre or so of glass all the way round the lattice. Maybe Mules had been broken into recently — the flat was a burglar's dream, invisible from the street and surrounded by trees.

When his knocking got no response, Strange bent over and peered through the hole: it looked like Mules had had a party.

He was tempted to forget the whole thing. Handling Mules was never going to be easy; if the brute had a mean hangover, it'd be near-impossible and probably hazardous to boot. Strange reminded himself that he was a pro; he had a job to do. There was also the small matter of ensuring he wasn't implicated in blackmail. He knocked again and called through the hole. When that got no reaction, he tried the door. It was unlocked.

Mules' flat had clearly been the venue for some form of group activity, either a party or an all-in brawl. The cushions had been pulled off the two sofas, the coffee table kicked over, and the shelves behind the TV swiped clean, leaving records, CDs, magazines and a few paperbacks strewn over the floor. Strange spotted *The Bridges of Madison County*; it would take more than one book to persuade him that Mules had a soft centre behind the scaly exterior.

More mayhem: the dining table and chairs were overturned; around the corner, in the open kitchen, drawers had been yanked out and emptied onto the floor.

Strange registered the absence of party debris: no empty bottles, no butt-choked ashtrays, no lipstick-rimmed glasses, no cigarette burns, no stains, no miasma of smoke, beer and body odour, no vomit curdling in the pot plants. Maybe Mules was away and there'd been a break-in last night.

Airing cupboard stuff littered the corridor. The bathroom and a closed door, obviously the toilet, were off the corridor to the right; the closed door down the end had to be the bedroom. Strange picked his way through towels and sheets. He knocked: no response. He opened the door.

The bedroom had been done over as well: drawers pulled out, clothes dumped, bedside table overturned, bed stripped, mattress half-pulled off the base.

Strange caught sight of himself in a mirror: with his thinning hair plastered to his scalp, he looked bedraggled and disoriented, like one of those lost souls who tramp the streets gesticulating convulsively and barking to themselves as they wander ever deeper into their interior mazes. He stepped back onto a plastic coat hanger: it splintered with a sharp crack. He yelped, "Fucking fuck."

Shaking hands, fraying nerves.

Let's get out of this dump. Might as well take a leak while I'm at it.

He opened the toilet door. Mules sat on the toilet, head thrown back, arms dangling by his sides, trousers around his ankles. A wooden handle stuck out of his chest and his blue polo shirt was soggy with blood. His face was frozen in a querulous expression, as if he'd died complaining that he couldn't even have a shit without a homicidal maniac barging in on him.

Strange released a long, horrified gurgle. He wrenched the door shut and blundered towards the exit. Then he thought of fingerprints and retraced his steps, wiping door handles. He closed the door to the flat gently and skedaddled to the car as fast as his bulk and the treacherous path would allow. For once, Leo Strange didn't mind hurrying.

He scrabbled in his satchel for a whisky miniature, emptied it in one gulp. He started the car and, forcing himself to keep calm, drove sedately away. He turned right into New North Road and headed south, towards the airport. The lure of his little A-frame house in the Marlborough Sounds had never been stronger.

By the time he was ten kilometres above Tongariro National Park, Strange had worked out his plan. The first priority was to avoid whoever butchered Mules; the second was to stay out of jail. The rest could take care of itself.

When he got to Honeymoon Bay, he was going to lock the door, light a fire and settle down with a bottle of scotch and a Patrick O'Brian book. For about five years.

Amanda Hayhoe didn't sleep well that Friday night either. That was due to too much wine and partly because, like Strange, she'd gone to bed in an unsettled frame of mind.

Around nine, she surfaced from a fitful doze. As recollections of the night before flooded in, her neck flushed crimson. The flush deepened and spread like ink through blotting paper until her face had the velvety, purple-brown tan of a park-bench wino. She groaned and pulled the bedclothes over her head.

It was a few minutes before she was up to assessing the damage.

How awful was it on a scale of one to ten? Item: when Caspar Quedley rang, I implied he was really after my body. Item: I told him I wasn't interested in older men. Item: I had too much to drink and . . . and what? Let's face it, without actually saying so in words of two syllables or less, I invited him to take me home and fuck me till my ears popped.

And that wasn't the worst of it: instead of jumping at this chance, he bolted.

As they came out of the restaurant, he said, "Well, thanks for coming. It was nice meeting you."

Thanks for coming? Nice meeting you? I'm on a date with Forrest Gump.

"Can I drop you somewhere?"

That was more like it. "Well, if you wouldn't mind. I did bring my car but seeing you've plied me with plonk" — flirty look, suggestive smirk — "I'd better leave it here and pick it up tomorrow. I'm only a couple of minutes away."

But when they got to her place, Quedley didn't turn off the motor or even let go of the steering wheel, for that matter. Just a polite smile and: "Maybe we can do this again some time?"

"I take it you don't want to come in for a Milo?"

Another smile, almost pensive this time: "I think I'd better just hit the road."

Seeing you didn't beg, cry or grope him, we'll call it an eight.

Hayhoe got moving: no point sitting around and moping. She scribbled a note to her landlady/flatmate, apologising for losing it when she walked in and the flatmate asked if she'd had a good time. Hayhoe couldn't remember what she'd said but knew it wasn't pretty.

She went into work and pulled D'Arcy Potterton's file from the clippings library. The wire story about his death, dated 18 July, was headed 'NZ writer killed in hunting accident.'

> D'Arcy Potterton, the New Zealand writer who turned his back on his country, was killed in a hunting accident near his home in the village of Levignac, south-west France, on Sunday. He was 57.
>
> Police have released few details but it is understood that Potterton was shot by a hunter while walking in the Forêt de Bouconne, a large forest which is a magnet for the region's many keen hunters. He is thought to have died instantly. The hunter who fired the fatal shot, a local man, has been interviewed by police but is unlikely to be charged.
>
> Potterton left New Zealand vowing never to return after the 1975 'Dancing Cossacks' election which swept the National Party, led by the late Sir Robert Muldoon, back into power. He settled in France and became a full time writer, combining reviews and criticism for various British and American publications with fiction.
>
> His novels and short stories were translated into several languages and earned critical acclaim, particularly in his adopted

homeland. In New Zealand, however, he is probably best remembered for his 1977 collection of essays *She'll be Reich, Mate*, which scathingly criticised the New Zealand way of life and predicted a fascist dictatorship within a decade.

Belinda Potterton, the writer's sister, said her brother would be buried in Levignac as soon as the authorities released his body.

There were follow-up stories with quotes from friends and literary types, including his local publisher, who said Potterton was a "poet and a radical conscience who refused to compromise himself either artistically or politically. New Zealand wasn't ready for D'Arcy Potterton and that was — and is — our loss."

Hayhoe, who'd hit the wall halfway through one of his novels and given the rest of his oeuvre a wide berth, decided she wasn't going to feel unworthy on the say-so of an overwrought publisher.

There was also an excruciatingly precious obituary by Dr Daniel Davenport, associate professor of English at Auckland University: "driven to confront the dark side of human nature . . . callousness of modern society . . . capitalism a juggernaut fuelled by its victims . . . shoulder to shoulder at the barricades . . . driven into exile . . . beloved adopted homeland." Et cetera.

Hayhoe shuddered.

You want an obit? How about this: "D'Arcy Potterton was a writer who got a giant crush on his sister. They went to France and played hide the salami for twenty years. Then a frog hillbilly mistook him for something four-legged and furry and blew him away."

Did she really need this shit?

15

Tito Ihaka's slide show took place in a conference room at Auckland Central early on Saturday afternoon.

His audience consisted of Detective Inspector Finbar McGrail, Detective Constable Johan Van Roon, and the SIS man Wayne Cramp. The gathering was a prelude to a full-scale briefing for the twenty-six-strong Aotearoa People's Army task force, formed following the murder of Chas Gundry MP by live burial in a purpose-built underground oven, a method of assassination largely neglected since the invention of the bow and arrow.

The first slide came up.

"Sergeant Kerry Keene," said Ihaka. "He'd been on Gundry-watch for all of twelve hours. The APA would've picked them up when they left the meeting in Mount Roskill just after nine-thirty. They had a feed in a restaurant in Dominion Road; about eleven, Gundry pitched up at a part-time hooker's apartment in Parnell, big-noting that he was so important he had a personal bodyguard parked outside. They made it easy for the APA: they could take Keene while Gundry was having his knob polished, then just wait for Gundry. Another very slick piece of work — no one around there saw or heard a thing."

Cramp: "What about the hooker — could she've been in on it?"

"Wayne, she's a fucking air hostess."

Slide two: Keene (close-up/deceased).

Ihaka, dispassionately: "Gundry left her just after midnight. They went over to Greenhithe in his Commodore and another vehicle and parked in the lock-up garage. They put a hood on Keene, taped his hands behind his back, and fed him to Gundry's pit bull. It started on his legs, tipped him over, then went for the kill." Ihaka tapped the screen with a pointer. "It got into the jugular, also bit through his Adam's apple and tore up the larynx. Cause of death: air in the jugular."

McGrail: "Sergeant, any leads on the other vehicle?"

"No sightings. We're checking all stolen vehicles that come in. We did a sweep of the main carparks for dumped vehicles first thing this morning: they're being checked now. There were no unidentified prints in the Commodore, by the way."

Slide three: Son of Sam (close up/deceased).

"What was left of the mongrel after they shot it at point-blank range with Keene's gun."

McGrail: "Who looked after it when Gundry was in Wellington?"

"A pet babysitting place in Albany. Gundry would tell them when he was heading back and they'd drop the mutt off so it was there to greet him when he got home."

"They had a key?"

"Yep."

"They checked out?"

"Been in business for thirteen years."

Slide four: Keen's pistol.

"The weapon in question: Smith and Wesson ten-millimetre semi-auto. One shot fired which decorated Gundry's hall with doggy brains. The only prints are Keene's."

Slide five: the hangi.

"Gundry was big on hangis. He had all the gear: stones, sacks, chicken wire and whatnot."

Cramp: "The APA obviously knew that, and about the dog."

"Wouldn't take much," said Ihaka. "Pit bulls and hangis get a mention in bloody near every story ever written about Gundry."

Van Roon: "Hangis take a fair while, don't they, Sarge?"

"Seven or eight hours' preparation, twelve, minimum, for cooking. Say they got going around one or two in the morning, they would've popped Gundry in about eight. As you'll see, he wasn't quite done when we dug him out."

Slide six: Gundry (full-length shot/deceased).

Cramp swore under his breath. Gundry's corpse was slightly charred and grotesquely bloated by massive blisters on the stomach, chest and inside arms and legs.

McGrail, grimmer than usual: "Was he alive when they put him in?"

"Yeah, but probably not conscious — he got a whack on the back of the head."

Slide seven: the APA communiqué.

"And now, a word from our sponsors."

COMMUNIQUÉ NUMBER THREE

DESPITE THE EXAMPLES MADE OF FRECKLETON AND PIKE AND OUR UNEQUIVOCAL WARNINGS, THE POLITICIAN GUNDRY LAUNCHED A BLATANTLY DEMAGOGIC ATTACK ON THE MAORI PEOPLE AND THOSE WHO LEAD ITS STRUGGLE FOR LIBERATION AND SOVEREIGNTY.

WITH THIS ACTION AGAINST A MEMBER OF THE RULING CLIQUE, THE AOTEAROA PEOPLE'S ARMY HAS DEMONSTRATED ITS ABILITY TO STRIKE AT THE VERY CORE OF THE PAKEHA POWER

STRUCTURE. WE HAD NO DIRECT INTEREST IN GUNDRY'S BODYGUARD. HOWEVER, SINCE THE STATE SECURITY APPARATUS IS MERELY THE ARMED PALACE GUARD OF A REACTIONARY REGIME, ITS MEMBERS ARE LEGITIMATE TARGETS.

THE AOTEAROA PEOPLE'S ARMY CALLS ON THE STATE AND ITS SECURITY APPARATUS TO ABANDON ITS OPPRESSIVE TREATMENT OF THOSE ENGAGED IN THE FIGHT FOR JUSTICE. THERE SHOULD NO LONGER BE ANY NEED TO SPELL OUT THE CONSEQUENCES IF THE CALL IS IGNORED.

"It was on Gundry's back fence."

Cramp: "They must've made your surveillance on the TV girl."

Ihaka half-smiled at Cramp's US cop-speak. "Maybe. Maybe they just gave us credit for doing the basics."

"Do we know why they used her in the first place?"

"I suppose they wanted the media to have the communiqués in case we sat on them. As far as we can tell, they picked her at random and she served her purpose. It's a roundabout way of doing it but nothing these guys do is simple; it's all tricky and elaborate, like they're playing a game." He looked at McGrail. "That's it from me."

Ihaka sat down. McGrail told Cramp he had the floor.

Cramp moved to the front of the room. "I don't want to say I told you so, but you'll remember I predicted this." He eyeballed Ihaka: "Everyone's got an opinion but some have more basis than others, eh Sergeant?"

Ihaka yawned.

Cramp pontificated: "I flew to Wellington this morning for a special meeting of the advisory committee of all the security departments. There was unanimous agreement on two points: one, that the country is facing a deadly serious threat to its internal security; two, given that, in addition to the factors I've already raised, Gundry's speech was the trigger for his assassination, given the method of it, and the language in the communiqués, it would be a dereliction of duty on our part not to thoroughly test the proposition that the APA is linked to — if not actually a front for — extreme elements in the Maori nationalist movement. A few moments ago, I heard from Wellington that a cabinet sub-committee chaired by the PM has endorsed that approach." Cramp smiled thinly. "Our political masters want action, gentlemen: right now, there's a bunch of MPs changing their underpants every hour on the hour."

He picked up a marker pen and wrote on the whiteboard, speaking over his shoulder: "I don't have any slides, but there's a few names I'd like to put in front of you. We believe these people are the absolute hard core of Maori radicalism. They're all on record as advocating violence to achieve their ends and, from what our sources tell us, their public comments are tame compared to what they say in private. Our monitoring also indicates a pattern of intensified activity which includes going to great lengths to avoid surveillance."

Cramp finished writing and stepped away from the whiteboard.

There was a knock on the door. A uniformed constable poked his head in: "Excuse me, sir," he said to McGrail, "the commissioner's on the phone for you."

Ihaka scarcely noticed McGrail leave: he was too busy studying Cramp's list. His niece was on it.

No one spoke or moved. Cramp watched Ihaka, who stared at the whiteboard. Van Roon looked from one to the other, feeling something in the air.

Finally, Cramp said: "What's up, Sergeant — I didn't spell one of these wackos' names wrong, did I? Or are you all choked up because your niece made the A team?" He grinned, pleased with his sarcasm. "It wasn't very bright keeping that to yourself, then dumping on me every time I argued the case against them. You've left yourself wide open, my friend."

Ihaka did a slow double-take: "Your friend? You sure know how to hurt a man, Wayne."

Cramp kept his grin going. "Mind you, what else would you expect from Jimmy Ihaka's granddaughter?" He took a sheet of paper from a plastic folder. "Your old man was hard core too, wasn't he? Dedicated communist at the age of eighteen; active in the 1951 waterfront strike: broke with Moscow over the invasion of Hungary; expelled from the Socialist Unity Party but remained a convinced Marxist — quote: 'Communism hasn't failed, the Soviet Union has.' Nineteen sixty-nine, kicked off the Kapuni gas pipeline for general trouble-making; 1970, arrested for assaulting a police officer during anti-Vietnam protests against Vice-President Agnew. And so it goes on."

"Don't tell me you missed the Cuban connection?"

"What Cuban connection?"

"He used to smoke a Cuban cigar every Labour Day — one of those real big mothers, like Fidel Castro."

Cramp's grin was triumphant. "I'm glad to see you've still got a sense of humour — you'll need it. Your name came up at that meeting this morning — as a matter of interest, when did you get offside with the Minister of Police? He's not your biggest fan by the sound of it. Anyway, the heavy hitters aren't impressed by your family tree or your conduct: they think you've got a conflict of interest to go with your attitude problem. You're off the team, Ihaka; I'd say McGrail's getting the message as we speak."

Ihaka got up and headed for the door. "Suits me. I could do with a weekend off."

Cramp fell in behind him. "I know blood's thicker than water, but try to remember you're a policeman: don't contact your niece."

Ihaka stopped dead and turned in a tight circle. They were face to face. "It's not that you should worry about." He said mildly.

"What then?"

"This."

Ihaka shot out his left hand and grabbed Cramp's testicles. Cramp mooed. He started to double up but his face ran into Ihaka's head.

McGrail walked in.

Cramp brayed: "That fucking maniac just headbutted me."

McGrail asked, "Did you, Sergeant?" as if he found the notion a trifle far-fetched.

Ihaka shook his head, more in sorrow than in anger. "He came up behind me, giving me a gobful. I stopped and he just walked into me."

Cramp cupped his genitals and snarled: "What about my balls?"

McGrail swivelled expressionless brown eyes to Van Roon: "What happened, Constable?"

With his blond, almost white, hair, fair skin and deep blue eyes, Van Roon looked every bit as wholesome as the Milky Bar Kid, as Ihaka had dubbed him when he'd arrived at Auckland Central. After six years of appearing in the witness box, he was also adept at information management.

"I didn't really see it, sir — I was taking down the names on the whiteboard. But I've seen the sergeant headbutt a few blokes — in the line of duty, of course — and they came off looking a lot worse than Mr Cramp."

McGrail stroked his narrow nose. "Well, anyway, you're out of each other's hair as of right now: Sergeant . . ."

"I got the message," interrupted Ihaka, "by dildogram. I'm off the case, right?"

McGrail nodded. Ihaka turned to go.

"Hold your horses, Sergeant — that doesn't mean you're on holiday. We've got a knifing murder in Kingsland: you're on it."

"Can I take Van Roon?"

"Under the circumstances, that's probably sensible."

Ihaka winked at Van Roon: "Okay, Snow, let's go beat a confession out of someone. What's the story?"

"The deceased is a white male, thirties, named Brandon Mules . . ."

"The footy player?"

"Do you know him?"

Ihaka shook his head. "I saw him play a few times: he was a bit of a gutless wonder — looked like Tarzan, played like Jane."

Ihaka stood in the toilet doorway contemplating the death of Brandon Mules and wondering if five murders in less than a fortnight was some sort of record.

He glanced over his shoulder at the pathologist: "What do you reckon, Doc? Was he dropping a biggie when he copped it?"

"I haven't had a close look yet; that pleasure is still to come . . ."

Ihaka ho-hoed and sang, "Some guys have all the luck."

". . . but I haven't seen anything to suggest he was killed elsewhere and moved here, if that's what you mean."

"What's the ET?"

The pathologist shrugged: "Twelve hours ago or thereabouts."

Ihaka bent forward to take a closer look at the wooden handle protruding from Mules' chest. "What sort of knife do you reckon that is?"

The fingerprinter, hovering in the corridor, said: "I'd say it's a sharp-pointed stainless-steel cook's knife. Probably his own — there's one missing from the block on the kitchen bench."

Ihaka twisted around: "And who the fuck might you be? The galloping gourmet?"

The fingerprinter smiled wanly. "No; I take cooking classes, though."

Ihaka closed the toilet door and joined them in the corridor. "All right, Antoine, how long's the blade on that thing?"

"Twenty centimetres or so."

"Jesus. Takes a bit of grunt to smack that in up to the hilt, eh Doc?"

The pathologist nodded.

Ihaka and Van Roon went out to the front room. "Okay," said Ihaka, "the killer lifts out a pane and opens the door from the inside. He hears the sound effects of a dump in progress. He gets a knife from the kitchen, kicks open the shithouse door, and nails Mules with one almighty thrust before he can get his arse off the seat. I think it's safe to assume we're not dealing with your average burglar here. Then he tears the place apart. Why'd he do that? He could've taken his time — it wasn't as if he was going to be interrupted. You say there's no one home upstairs?"

Van Roon shook his head. "They're overseas."

Ihaka mused: "This is fucking weird: standard pro B and E access but what sort of burglar pins a gorilla like Mules to the wall then goes through the kitchen drawers and the linen cupboard? Conan the Interior Decorator? What's missing?"

"The VCR by the looks of it, but we don't know what was here. Maybe the word was out he had a stash of something."

"Yeah, could be. Take a couple of boys and do the street. Whoever it was had walked the course, so ask about strange faces, strange cars, anyone poking around recently."

Van Roon set off then turned back. "Sarge, can I ask you a question?"

"Shoot."

"How come you're not pissed off about getting the shove from the APA team?"

Ihaka draped an arm over Van Roon's shoulders and walked him to the door. "Let me ask you something: what do you think of Cramp?"

Van Roon frowned, surprised Ihaka should have to ask. "Well, he's a fuckwit."

"Apart from that," said Ihaka patiently. "Is he any good?"

"Well, he seems to know a lot of stuff, but it's like he's got it all out of a book."

Ihaka clapped him on the back. "Good boy. He's got his anti-terrorist handbook, which would've been written by a twat like him, and he's following it to the letter. If the politicians and the bureaucrats try to run the show from Wellington through Cramp, it'll be the biggest fuck-up of all time."

"Is that why you got me out?"

"That and the fact you'd always be watching your back: he'd be out to get you."

Van Roon shrugged. "He did get off lightly. What about your niece?"

"Jesus, don't worry about her — she'll be as happy as a pig in shit if they pull her in. Those guys want to be taken seriously; they want to be treated like they're a threat to the system. That's the whole point."

When Van Roon left to work the street, Ihaka called over one of the constables who'd found the body.

"We got a tip-off, right? Man or woman?"

"A man, Sergeant."

"What'd he say?"

"Just gave the address and said we should get over here."

"Sift through this crap." Ihaka waved at the mess on the floor. "Pull out letters, bills, names — anything that tells you a bit about Mules or connects him to someone. If you find an address book, you've hit the jackpot."

Ihaka took the bedroom: zilch. He went to see how the constable was getting on: double zilch.

He brainstormed. "You come across his phone books?"

"Over there, Sarge, under those tug maps."

"Go through them page by page: look for names he's marked or underlined."

Twenty minutes later, the constable delivered a tentative report: "I found a few, Sarge, but whether they're any use . . . there's a couple of pizza-delivery places, a dial-a-whore, a hardware shop, and a guy Trousdale in Mission Bay."

16

Leo Strange spent most of Sunday wondering how much strife his sister would be in if Mrs Trousdale didn't get her diary back.

He worked on the basis of "if" not "when" because it wasn't beyond the bounds of possibility that the diary wouldn't be returned: perhaps Brandon Mules' murder had nothing to do with the diary; even if it did, perhaps the killer hadn't found it. In that event, the police would find it, return it, and everyone except Mules would live happily ever after.

It wasn't likely but it was conceivable. Then again, so was peace on earth, a chicken in every pot, and O. J. Simpson becoming president.

A more likely scenario was that the killer had the diary and intended to use it the same way as Mules, in which case there was only one sensible course of action. The reason it took Strange so long to think it through was that, like most devious people, he instinctively distrusted obvious conclusions.

He rang his sister Renée at 7.45 on Monday morning, catching her before she left for a day's temping at the advertising agency in Birkenhead where her duties were answering the phone, making photocopies, sending faxes, and boiling cups of water for the managing director who didn't drink tea or coffee because they gave him erotic dreams about his ex-wife.

Strange got straight to the point: "Just deny everything."

"What do you mean?"

"Ring Early and tell him he's got the wrong end of the stick: say you didn't tell anyone about his affair and had nothing to do with the blackmail."

"Leo, has it slipped your mind that he's threatening to go to the police? It's all very well for you, skulking down there in the Marlborough Sounds, but I'm the one in the hot seat."

"He's bluffing," declared Strange. "If he went to the police, they'd laugh at him — don't forget, he's not the one being blackmailed. The police won't take it seriously unless the woman lays a formal complaint and I bet that's the last thing she wants to do."

"You didn't see Early, Leo. He didn't look to me like he's bluffing."

"Of course he is. Apart from anything else, he hasn't got a shred of proof. Okay, he managed to work out that you listened in on his phone call, but he can't actually prove it and he certainly can't prove that you told the blackmailer. He's bluffing all right, and if he isn't, all the more reason to deny it. Trust me; I've given this a lot of thought."

Adlington doubted she'd ever completely trust her brother again but refrained from saying so. Instead, and not entirely sarcastically, she asked: "I suppose telling the truth would be out of the question?"

Strange detested that sort of talk. He believed that telling the truth was downright unprofessional: there was no percentage in it, no angle, no room for manoeuvre. If you told the truth and it didn't work, what was your fallback? If you lied, on the other hand, you had options: next time round you could embellish the original lie, tell a new one, or mix it up, one part truth to several parts untruth, so the other side had to decide which was which. Pros only told the truth as a last resort and there were a few stops to go before they reached that dismal destination.

"Renée," he said, giving it the quiet emphasis of the last word on the matter, "if you had any idea what the truth was, you wouldn't even think about it."

Adlington rang Clyde Early and followed instructions.

"You're lying," responded Early with daunting certainty. "You're making a bad call, lady," he continued over her spluttered protest. "I offered you a way out but you didn't take it. You won't get another chance."

Early hung up and swung to and fro in his swivel chair. A quick, clean resolution would've been nice but was never likely. Adlington and whoever was the brains behind it weren't going to incriminate themselves by handing over the diary, so the real objective had been to scare them off. Time would tell if he'd succeeded.

He thought about bringing Rusty up to date but decided to leave it for the time being: it wouldn't achieve much beyond raising her hopes and his heart rate.

Amanda Hayhoe wasn't in the best of moods that morning. She'd been sweetness and light for most of the weekend, doing penance for biting her flatmate's head off on Friday night. Now the well was running dry.

Maybe I'm not cut out for TV: the stars don't waste their charm on people; they save it for the camera.

She knew from the cuttings file that D'Arcy Potterton's local publisher was Fraser Merritt at Sceptre Press. She rang him to get Potterton's phone number in France.

"You'll need more than that to get hold of D'Arcy." Merritt's jocularity came as a surprise after the leaden solemnity of his tribute to the late writer.

"Yes, I realise he's no longer taking calls. It's actually his sister I'm after."

"Belinda's back."

"Back where?"

"Back here — in Auckland."

"Really? How can I contact her?"

"Try Fiona Vanarkel's art gallery; she's looking after it while Fiona's in India, finding her inner self — yet again. The bloody thing's as elusive as the Loch Ness monster."

"What's the gallery called?"

"The Gallery."

Whatever it did for the soul, looking at poor people and water buffalo obviously didn't do a whole lot for the imagination.

Hayhoe rang The Gallery and asked the woman with the plummy voice who answered if she could speak to Belinda Potterton.

"You are."

"My name's Amanda Hayhoe. I work for Television New Zealand . . ."

Potterton cut in sharply: "Are you a journalist?"

"Yes, I'm working on a story . . ."

"I'm surprised it took you so long — don't they teach you at journalism school that you can't defame the dead?"

Hayhoe was taken aback: mockery was the last thing she'd expected. "I assure you I'm not gunning for your brother."

"What then?"

"I'm doing a story about Jackson Pike, the magazine editor who was murdered last week. I was interested in what happened when he met your brother."

"As a matter of fact, they got on famously once D'Arcy had recovered from the shock: the man just popped up out of the blue — we hadn't seen hair nor hide of a New Zealand journalist for years. I don't suppose you'd happen to know who put him onto us? I assumed it was Fraser Merritt, D'Arcy's publisher, but he swears it wasn't him."

Hayhoe smiled to herself. "I think it might have been Garth Grimes."

"Who's he?"

"A retired journalist who's either a living legend or a fossil, depending on your point of view. He also dropped in on your brother — in 1979, I think it was."

"Seventy-nine? That's a lifetime ago."

"Yes, and he would've been pretty ancient then."

There was a long pause before Potterton, almost whispering, said, "God, now I remember him — he stole a photograph of us from a restaurant in the village."

Whoops.

"Is he really still alive?"

"Very much so."

"You sound as if you know him?"

"We've met."

Another protracted silence. "Come to the gallery at 5 o'clock tonight. I might have a question or two of my own."

Hayhoe put the phone down and said, "Oh, shit," to her reflection in the kitchen window.

Brandon Mules' next-door neighbour had often seen him in the mud-brown military-style uniform worn by employees of Maximum Security, a security firm with a mixed reputation which operated from a former used-car yard in Great North Road. Early on Monday afternoon, Detective Sergeant Tito Ihaka went there to see Mules' boss, a citizen by the name of Bill Tench.

The first thing Ihaka learned from Tench, who was squat and swarthy and looked like the end product of a cross-breading programme involving several species, none of them Homo sapiens, was that Mules hadn't been well liked by his workmates.

"Why not?"

"You ever meet him?"

"Once — he was dead at the time."

"You probably saw him at his best," said Tench with a lack of sentimentality which Ihaka found refreshing. "The guy was an arsehole."

"Everyone around here's an arsehole, including you. What was so different about Mules?"

Tench put on a wounded tone: "Hey, come on, Sergeant — that's not nice."

Ihaka studied Tench as carefully as a plastic surgeon who'd just heard the magic words "money is no object" and shook his head in silent wonder. "Tench, stop pissing around and tell me something useful."

Tench might have been concentrating, but it was impossible to read anything from his jumble of ill-matched features. "He thought the sun shone out his arse, buggered if I know why, plus he never had a good word to say about anyone. Shit, he was just a nasty piece of work, that's all there is to it."

The second thing Ihaka learned was that Mules had been up to something.

"My oath, he was." Tench wiggled his head like a wind-up toy. "He was bolshie at the best of times but, fuck me, you should have seen the carry-on last week. He kept saying it was just a matter of time till he told me to stick the job up my jacksie."

Ihaka felt it was time for some bluff common sense: "Why didn't you sack the cunt?"

"Beggars can't be choosers, Sergeant. See, Mules might've been a pain in the bum but he was a rare bird in this game, a real big hua who wasn't thick as pigshit. You wouldn't believe some of these drongos. You know they say if you take too many steroids, your tackle shrinks till you end up like a counter-sunk cock? I reckon they have the same effect on the brain."

This little homily drew another bemused look from Ihaka. "Interesting theory, Tench; maybe you should pass it on to the medical association. What about dope? You reckon Mules could've been into it?"

"Sure, why not? He was a lazy bastard; he'd do anything for an easy buck."

The third thing Ihaka learned was that Mules' pay was automatically deposited in an account at the National Bank in Karangahape Road.

He spoke to the branch manager, who told him that the account balance was $2361.28. The manager provided a banker's perspective on Mules' demise, saying it was ironic that just when he'd finally got out of his overdraft, he'd gone and got himself killed. Mules' long-awaited shift into the black had taken place a week earlier when he'd deposited $4500. In cash.

The Gallery was in a mall in the Remuera shopping centre, at the top of Victoria Avenue. At a couple of minutes after 5 o'clock, Amanda Hayhoe stood in the foyer awaiting developments. She was joined by a young man in black who looked her up and down and said, "Yes?" generating as much sibilance as three elocutionists ordering sushi.

Hayhoe told him what she'd come for. He led her through the gallery to an alcove containing two rattan chairs, a low cane and glass table, and Belinda Potterton.

She was about fifty, a faded beauty whose fine bones were diminished by her empty grey eyes and the sardonic set of her wide, thin-lipped mouth. She wore a loose, stylish shadow-check trouser suit with the double-breasted jacket buttoned over a cream silk shirt.

The assistant disappeared. Potterton invited Hayhoe to sit; she lit a cigarette, and blew a stream of smoke at the ceiling.

No beating around the bush: "So tell me, Amanda, when did you last see Grimes?"

"Just last week as a matter of fact."

"And how is he?"

"Well, he's old as Rip van Winkle but he's still got his marbles."

"Did he tell you about his visit?"

Unblinking, lifeless eyes watched her; Hayhoe had to make an effort not to squirm.

"He mentioned it."

"What did he say?"

Hayhoe had known what was coming but it had taken a much more direct route than she'd expected and arrived well ahead of schedule. She opened and closed her mouth, not knowing where to start or how much to say.

Potterton breathed smoke through a cold grin, this time not bothering to avoid Hayhoe's airspace. "I think you'd better tell me everything, don't you?" she said, as if she'd read Hayhoe's mind. "And don't worry about offending me — I'm every bit as tough as I look."

Hayhoe told her Grimes' story.

Potterton listened in silence, although her eyes came to life as the narrative unfolded. When it was finished, she burst into laughter which rang slightly brittle. "That really takes the cake. God, when I think of the lengths we went to . . . and that old snoop sniffed it out in half a day." She leaned back in the chair. "You might as well know that I couldn't give a damn — never did, in fact. It was D'Arcy who lived in dread of being found out. My attitude was that we were two people who loved each other, we were old enough to know what we were doing, and it was no skin off anyone else's nose. I'm having a drink; do you want one?"

Hayhoe said yes. Potterton went into an office opposite the alcove. She returned with a tray containing a bottle of Stolichnaya vodka, a large bottle of tonic, an ice bucket, a lime on a saucer, and a slicing knife.

"Vodka and tonic okay?" Before Hayhoe could answer, she said, "There's some white wine if you want it — people here don't seem to drink anything else. The proles eat chips with everything; the bourgeoisie drink white wine with everything. You go to someone's place and it's white wine before, during and sometimes, God help us, even after dinner. Now I just take my own booze; I feel like a bag lady and the hosts get sniffy, but it's worth it."

Hayhoe said vodka and tonic would be wonderful.

As she made the drinks, Potterton asked: "Did Pike know?"

"I think so. He and Grimes were very close."

She nodded. "He did throw me some odd looks; at the time, I thought he was just another anti-smoking Nazi. So what do you want to know?"

"One of Pike's writers told me that he came back from holiday with a bee in his bonnet but he was so secretive, he wouldn't let on what it was. He did say to Grimes that going to see your brother was well worth it, so I wondered if there was any connection between the two."

"You mean, did D'Arcy put the bee in his bonnet?"

Hayhoe nodded.

Potterton hummed thoughtfully: "He was hardly in the door before D'Arcy started pumping him about what was going on here. One of the differences between us was that I got over being homesick about fifteen years ago, so I pretty much left them to it. I remember them discussing an expat syndrome, which I think was how they got onto the Le Droffs. Does that name mean anything?"

Hayhoe shook her head.

"The Le Droff family owns a lot of land around where we lived. They like to act the landed gentry but I gather they've gone from back street to chateau in a few generations. One of the sons lives here — in Auckland; done very well for himself, apparently. Don't ask me why, but Pike was terribly interested in this fellow, so much so that D'Arcy volunteered to find out a bit more about him. Whether he ever got round to it is another matter, of course; I suspect he felt obliged to make the offer after having grilled the poor sod for most of the afternoon."

17

The next morning, Amanda Hayhoe got Serge Le Droff's file out of the clippings library. There were only a few pasted-up newspaper stories in the manila pouch, which usually meant that the subject's fifteen minutes of fame had led to cell block C or a hole in the ground.

The first and, as it turned out, most substantial item was from April 1987, when he'd started his Eurotours package-holiday venture. Speaking at the launch, Le Droff revealed that he'd been living in New Zealand on and off for several years. "I came here in 1984 purely out of curiosity," the quote ran, "to assess the opportunities created by the opening up of the economy. I found what I consider to be one of the most interesting and rewarding investment environments in the world. As you can see, I believe in putting my money where my mouth is."

Le Droff was described as "an Anglo-French entrepreneur with business interests in Europe and the Middle East". There was a grainy photo of him flourishing the first Eurotours brochure as if it was Jesus Christ's birth certificate. He was mid-thirties with a lean face, dark eyes, curly black hair and an enviable set of teeth. At first, Hayhoe thought there was something vaguely familiar about him but she decided it was just the Latin look; he had the sort of face that has launched a thousand instant coffee commercials.

In early 1989 he scored a mention in an investment magazine's story headed "Riches to Rags: The Big Losers of the Stockmarket Crash".

> It is, of course, much more difficult to get an accurate picture of how the substantial private investors fared but talk around the market suggests that Kiwi-based Frenchman Serge Le Droff took a big hit. The low-profile Le Droff had a reputation as a bold investor partial to entrepreneurial stocks, and market sources believe he was long in some of the crash's major casualties. The encouraging performance of his Eurotours travel business will have provided some consolation.

He also made a few innocuous appearances in *New Nation* magazine's gossip column, *Aucklander's Diary*, where he went from being "saturnine" to "enigmatic" to "debonair". It wasn't clear whether the transition was prompted by biorhythms, hormone treatment or the diarist's thesaurus.

The most recent item was two years old, a snippet in a home and garden magazine about his in-progress conversion of the top floor of a downtown high-rise into a "Manhattan-style" penthouse apartment.

Hayhoe's phone was ringing when she got back to her desk. It was Belinda Potterton doing a passable impersonation of Louis Armstrong.

"You don't sound too good."

"I feel a damn sight worse and it's your fault."

"What did I do?"

"You got me stirred up. I went home and opened my last can of foie gras and a bottle of pink champagne; then I had some Armagnac. When I was nicely sozzled and maudlin, I rang a friend in Levignac. God knows how long I was on the phone — long enough to more or less sober up otherwise I probably wouldn't remember this. I don't know what to make of it — if it wasn't for our conversation last night, I wouldn't have given it a second thought. You know D'Arcy was killed in a hunting accident?"

"Yes."

"Well, the chap who shot him is a farm worker; I'll give you one guess who owns the farm he works on."

Hayhoe had to think about it, but not for very long. "The Le Droffs?"

"Mais oui."

"You're kidding?"

"Some things even I wouldn't kid about."

Detective Sergeant Tito Ihaka stopped in front of the wrought-iron gates of Greywater, the Trousdale residence on the cliff above Mission Bay, and got out of his car. It was 11.51 a.m. on Tuesday, 5 September and, as usual, it was raining. He pressed the intercom button and was squawked at by a foreign-sounding female: "Yes, who is that?"

He told her and had to prove it by holding up his ID for the closed-circuit TV camera. A few seconds later, the gates began to swing open. He drove in.

Greywater was a three-storey, red-brick Georgian mansion with an imposing portico entrance. In the middle of the circular drive was an ornamental pond with a statue of a young woman wearing an off-the-shoulder number and a remarkably serene expression for someone with one brat clamped to her exposed breast and another climbing her right leg.

A grey Bentley was parked out front; a Mercedes convertible and a four-wheel-drive sat in the garage, which still had room for a combine harvester. On the other side of the house, a lush, moss-green lawn, immaculate as newly laid carpet, rolled to the cliff edge.

Ihaka parked behind the Bentley. He walked up the steps to the front door, which was answered by a pretty young Asian in a black maid's uniform. She led him through to a sitting room, saying Mr Trousdale wouldn't be long.

Off the sitting room was a dining room with a massive polished mahogany table laid with silver candlesticks and cutlery and crystal glassware. Ihaka was counting the place settings — there were thirty — when a man came up behind him and said, "I trust this won't take long; I've an appointment in town at twelve-thirty."

The speaker was in early middle age, short and rotund with a fat, wobbly face the colour of grilled salmon. He had very fine, bone-white hair, poached-egg eyes, and a tiny, cartoon-character nose. He wore gold-rimmed spectacles, grey trousers held up with braces, a white shirt with French cuffs and pearl cufflinks, a polka-dot bow tie, and a navy-blue blazer.

Shit the bed — first Tench, now this one. It's the Invasion of the Pod People.

Ihaka said, "Nice place you've got." He hooked a thumb towards the dining room. "Having a few mates around for a barbie, eh?"

"I'm afraid we don't do guided tours," said Trousdale tartly. As is often the case with unsightly individuals whose formative years were spent in boarding schools, his sense of humour hadn't survived the ordeal. "As I say, I'm rather pressed for time so I'd appreciate brevity."

"Time is money, right?" said Ihaka knowingly, one tycoon to another. "The name Brandon Mules mean anything to you?"

Trousdale shook his head decisively. "Never heard of him."

A real head-turner in a figure-hugging dog's-tooth check Chanel suit came in from the entrance hall. She gave Ihaka a nice smile: "I didn't realise we had company."

Trousdale half-turned to her. "Darling, this gentleman's from the police — I'm sorry, I didn't catch your name."

Ihaka sensed rather than saw the woman react. "Ihaka, Detective Sergeant, Auckland Central. Do you know a guy called Brandon Mules?"

She relaxed. "Not me. Do you, Maurice?"

"No, I don't. Who is he anyway?"

"Mules is a dead man. We found him in his flat in Kingsland on Sunday morning with a length of cold steel through the left tit. Your name was underlined in his phone book."

The Trousdales were clearly appalled, either by Mules' fate or his presumption. Her jaw dropped; he exclaimed, "Good God!" getting his hand up just in time to prevent his spectacles sliding off his button nose. "Who on earth was he? I mean to say, what do you know about the man?"

"Mules? Common or garden low-rent white trash. He wasn't a crim — at least, not that we know of. His claim to fame was that he played rugby for Auckland a few times, back in the early eighties."

This time Ihaka knew he hadn't imagined the jolt of comprehension in the woman's eyes. *This is her show, not the blob's.*

Trousdale said, "You access phone records, don't you? You could tell if he'd actually rung here."

"Done it: all that proves is he didn't call here on his phone. He could've used a public phone — or someone else's."

"Well, I certainly haven't spoken to him. Rusty, have you had any strange calls?"

"Not to speak of — I mean, there's always the odd wrong numbers . . ." Rock-steady.

So what? The lies I bet she's told him, she should be good at it.

"I don't think our friend's here to investigate wrong numbers." Trousdale puffed up as if he'd said something stupendously witty. "Look, I really should get going. As you can see, Mr Ihaka, it's a mystery to us why this character marked our name, so I don't think we can be of much assistance."

Ihaka agreed: "Doesn't look like it."

They followed him to the door, coordinating their programmes: she was lunching with Jane in Parnell, then coming back to oversee preparations for his birthday dinner party; he had lunch at the club, followed by a session with the accountants.

Ihaka turned into the first side-street. After the Bentley and the Mercedes had swished past, he drove back up the street and parked outside Greywater. He opened his newspaper, turned on the car radio, and settled down to wait.

Hayhoe was nibbling a filled roll when she got the idea. She was surprised and not altogether pleased to find that she still remembered her ex-lover's direct line. It hadn't changed and neither, it seemed, had he.

"Gary, it's Amanda. Have you got a moment?"

"Amanda?" Surprise gave way to wariness. "Where are you calling from?"

"Relax — I'm in Auckland."

"Oh, right. So how's it going? I've seen you on the box a few times."

She could picture the scene: Gary and Mrs Gary and the kids settling down in front of TV to watch little old her.

"It's going okay but I need a favour."

"I've got to tell you, Amanda, this isn't a good time — it's balls to the wall here. I've got a diary like Bill Clinton's . . ."

"Spare me the corporate slave routine — I've heard it before. You owe me one, Gary; when the shit hit the fan, I left town and went quietly. You never heard a peep out of me and you know damn well I could've kicked up a major fuss if I'd wanted to."

"Maybe," he said flatly. "That was then; you don't have a lot of leverage now."

"Jesus, Gary, don't go all sentimental on me."

"Eh?"

"I was being sarcastic."

She waited him out.

"So what's the favour?"

"You told me once that the bank uses some sort of high-powered corporate information service . . ."

"Did I say that?"

"I remember it distinctly: you said you were clients of this company which specialises in short-notice warts-and-all bios. I think your exact words were, 'They can tell us the last time the guy jerked off.'"

"We're in the information game," he said blandly. "We tap into a range of sources."

"Come on, Gary, can you have someone checked out for me or not?"

"Would it need offshore input?"

"Yep."

"This is a very big ask, Amanda. It means bringing in London or New York and those guys charge like wounded bulls."

"It should leave us about all square then."

"Who?"

"Serge Le Droff."

"The mysterious Monsieur Le Droff?" Gary showed some interest. "What's got you so interested in him?"

"His name cropped up in a story I'm working on — to tell the truth, it's a long shot."

"Amanda, if I do this for you, we're even: you'd be wasting your time with another appeal to my conscience."

"Fair enough."

"What I'm saying is, you only get one wish, so are you absolutely sure you want to use it?"

She said sweetly, "I can't think of anything else you could do for me."

The news broke on the 1 o'clock bulletin. Ihaka was expecting it; he'd had a sneak preview first thing that morning in the form of a frantic call from his sister.

"New Zealand may be on the brink of a race-relations crisis," recited the newsreader in the tragic tones normally reserved for wars, mass murders and beached whales. "That was the widespread reaction to the bombshell announcement that police investigating the Aotearoa People's Army are questioning a number of prominent Maori radicals.

"Following overnight raids on houses in Auckland, South Auckland and Rotorua, seventeen members of Maoridom's radical fringe are being held at Auckland Central police station. Searches of the properties are continuing. The seventeen are being questioned by detectives from the APA task force set up following the murder of MP Chas Gundry and the police bodyguard, and the earlier slayings of radio talkback host Fred Freckleton and magazine editor Jackson Pike.

"Initial responses to the raids from opposition parties, leaders in the Maori community and church and civil liberty groups range from disquiet to outright condemnation. However, the Minster of Police strongly defended the police actions."

They had the Minster on tape: "This is a straightforward police operation with no political implications," he shrilled. "The police are simply following up all lines of enquiry as they are duty-bound to do. I would remind critics that the APA has claimed responsibility for four cold-blooded murders and made intolerable threats against anyone in public life who opposes their aims. I'm confident that ordinary New Zealanders — as opposed to professional agitators and those with a political axe to grind — understand the gravity of the situation and will fully support the police in their efforts to bring the terrorists to justice."

Ihaka said, "Sounds like fun," and flicked off the radio.

Shortly after 2 o'clock, Mrs Trousdale's Mercedes came up the street. He got out of his car and waved at her as she swung into the driveway.

She halted and lowered the car window. "Hello again; did you forget something?"

He leaned against the car, looking down at her. "We need to have a chat."

"What for? I told you I don't know that man . . ."

Ihaka nodded. "Yeah, but that wasn't the cross-your-heart-and-hope-to-die version, was it?" Her face tensed up. "Look, I guess you think you had a good reason for not coming clean but this is a murder investigation — you're legally obliged to spit out whatever you know. So why don't we go in, get Suzy Wong to make us a cup of tea, and talk it over?" He paused. "And what the sugar daddy doesn't know can't hurt him, right?"

She iced him: "That was fucking rude and completely uncalled for."

He nodded, deadpan. "The job makes you cynical — it gets to the stage you can't recognise true love when it's right under your nose."

Reluctant amusement rippled across her face. "How terribly sad for you." She mashed the accelerator and the Mercedes bounded forward. Ihaka muttered, "Thanks for the lift, you tart," and walked up the drive as the rain came down again.

He was in an armchair in the sitting room; she strode in followed by the maid carrying a tray.

He asked: "I don't suppose you could stretch to a sandwich? While you were having lunch with Jane, I was out there listening to my stomach juices foam."

"I can see you've practically wasted away since this morning," she said unsympathetically. "Cecilia, would you mind rustling up a snack for our guest? Something light — a suckling pig, perhaps?"

Cecilia tittered and departed. Mrs Trousdale crossed her legs with a rustle of black silk and gave Ihaka another amused and slightly patronising look. "Well, Sergeant, you wanted to talk: so talk."

Ihaka switched on menace: "You say you don't know Mules and think that's the end of it. Take it from me, sister, it ain't, not by a long stretch. Right now, that line under your name in Mules' phone book is the only lead we've got, so if I have to I'll tear your world apart to find the connection. I've got a feeling old Horace or Maurice or whatever the hell he's called doesn't know what's going on and you want to keep it that way. Well, that's your problem — I don't give a shit."

Her green eyes flashed. "Are you threatening me?"

Cecilia came back with a plate of dainty, cocktail-size sandwiches. He shovelled a handful into his mouth.

The maid left. Ihaka eased off: "I'm not threatening you, Mrs Trousdale; I'm trying to explain that I'll find out, one way or the other. If you help me, then maybe it won't need to go beyond this room. But if I have to do it the hard way" — he shrugged indifferently — "so be it. If it comes to that, just bear in mind that when we start beating the bushes, all sorts of strange things can crawl out."

Ihaka sat perfectly still. He had nothing more to say and nothing showed on his wide brown face. Rusty Trousdale realised that she'd come up against a force which, for all her experience of men, she had no idea how to deal with.

To break eye contact, she reached for a sandwich she didn't want. "All right, there is something going on. But I've got no reason to think it's got anything to do with Mules."

"Yes you do — deep down."

She sighed heavily. "Believe it or not, it's all because Mules was a rugby player."

18

Once Rusty Trousdale's resistance crumbled, she didn't hold back. It was the story of her life.

Assuming Brandon Mules was the blackmailer, then Lusty Rusty's bits on the side also had a motive. Tito Ihaka decided to start with Amanda Hayhoe because that promised to be the most fun. She wasn't at TVNZ so he drove over to Clyde Early's hardware emporium in Birkenhead. Another wasted trip: Early was in Canberra, attending a coaching seminar at the Australian Institute of Sport. That left the frog.

The Eurotours receptionist, a beefy woman with a mouth like a half-healed wound, ran a reptilian eye over his scuffed sneakers, faded jeans and black leather jacket. Despite her natural assets, she was out of her league trading dirty looks with Ihaka. He pulled a scowl which would've killed a cockroach at ten paces and told her who he was and what he wanted.

The combination brought her to heel. She simpered. "Can you tell me why you wish to see Mr Le Droff?"

He squinted at the wall for a few seconds, pretending to think about it: "No."

She snatched the phone to relay the message, then invited him to take a seat.

A minute later, a robust, silver-haired man in a double-breasted suit burst through the door behind the reception desk. He marched up to Ihaka and barked: "Wyatt Bloodsaw at your service; I'm the security bod."

Ihaka scarcely registered that Bloodsaw appeared to be a werewolf — every second person he met these days was some sort of freak. They exchanged a crunching handshake; Ihaka made a mental note to introduce Bloodsaw to Wayne Cramp.

"This way, old chap." Bloodsaw spun on his heel. "By the right."

He stomped over to the door, which he opened with a plastic card. They went up a flight of stairs to another security door; Bloodsaw jabbed in a code and it clicked open. At the end of a dimly lit corridor, double doors opened into a crescent-shaped room. A curved ceiling-to-floor window extended the length of it, providing a panorama of the harbour from the mangroves of Te Atatu around to the silver thread of traffic winding along Tamaki Drive through the eastern bays.

The room, by contrast, was subdued: dark tones, sparse furnishings. There was a bookshelf along the wall and, in the foreground, a matching pair of black leather chesterfields faced each other across a low table. Beyond the chesterfields was a U-shaped work station, set up as two desks with duplicate functions: each had a computer, a stack of trays and a phone.

A man in navy-blue chinos and a pale-yellow sweater sat at the work station. He stared out the window, hands clasped behind his head.

"Detective Sergeant Ihaka, sir," said Bloodsaw. "One of Auckland's finest."

Le Droff gave no indication that he'd heard, even though the announcement had been made at parade-ground volume. He held the pose like an artist's model for half a minute, then slowly swivelled in the chair. He stood up, studying Ihaka impassively. He was wiry, about 180 centimetres, with curly dark hair, olive skin and a blue-black shadow bordering a long-nosed, hatchet face. Ihaka put him in his early forties.

"Good afternoon, Sergeant." The accent was neutral, transatlantic. "Let's sit down."

Ihaka and Bloodsaw sat on one side of the low table, Le Droff on the other. He reclasped his hands behind his head and put his feet up on the table, crossing his ankles.

Ihaka said: "I've been talking to Mrs Trousdale: she sent someone to see you last week."

"He spoke to the colonel." Le Droff tilted his head at Bloodsaw.

"About how she was being blackmailed?"

Le Droff gave a tiny nod. He seemed completely relaxed but his unblinking, light-brown eyes never left Ihaka's face.

"A guy called Brandon Mules was murdered last weekend — you know him?"

Le Droff answered with the barest shake of his head. "I saw something about it in the paper."

"It looks like he was the blackmailer."

"Just deserts, some would say."

"The law doesn't see it that way."

"How do you see it, Sergeant?"

"I'm on duty; I agree with the law."

Le Droff smiled a brief, private smile.

"If Mules was blackmailing Mrs Trousdale, that obviously makes her the prime suspect."

Le Droff raised his eyebrows sceptically. "I seem to remember he was stabbed?"

"With a long-bladed knife; the killer used every inch of it."

"Not a modus operandi one would readily associate with Rusty."

"Oh yeah? So how would she do it?"

Le Droff grinned, showing his perfect white teeth. "She'd kill with kindness."

It was Ihaka's turn to raise his eyebrows. "Well, Mules sure as shit didn't go out with a smile on his face. You had an affair with her . . ."

"I wouldn't call it an affair."

"What would you call it?"

"I call a spade a spade. What we had was a fuck."

Bloodsaw made a noise like a feral pig having an orgasm of a lifetime. The tight, cold smile was back on Le Droff's face.

"A fuck?" said Ihaka. "That's it?"

Le Droff looked at the ceiling. "We met at a party last summer. I suggested she drop in next time she was in town and I'd take her to lunch. A few days later, she did. We came back here after lunch and had sex on a desk in one of the offices downstairs."

"Why?"

Le Droff frowned: "Why what?"

"Why on a desk? Haven't you got a bed?"

"Oh, I see. Well, I was already late for a meeting. It was fast and furious and none the worse for that."

Ihaka's eyes narrowed enviously. "Then what?"

"Then nothing — that's all there was to it, hence my view that it didn't amount to an affair."

"You weren't tempted to go round again — maybe on the photocopier?"

"Oh yes," said Le Droff almost dreamily. "Most definitely."

"Why didn't you?"

Le Droff sighed and rubbed his eyes. "I got the feeling that Rusty was torn: part of her wanted fun and adventure, part of her wanted to leave all that behind and settle down to be a good little wife. Do you smoke, Sergeant?"

"No."

Le Droff took a Marlboro from the packet on the table and lit it with a slim gold lighter.

"I have this problem with cigarettes: I like smoking but I hate being a smoker. I've tried to give up plenty of times and I know how hard it is if you're surrounded by people who smoke. You see what I'm driving at? Besides, I'm not much good at adultery — I can't be bothered with all the intrigue — so I decided the best thing all round was to let it go."

"And she returned the favour by writing it up in her diary? That must've slutted you?"

Le Droff was all worldly nonchalance: "Womanising has its risks — always has and, I dare say, always will. I could do without it but frankly, Sergeant, it's no big deal. I'm not married; I don't have a steady girlfriend; I don't have shareholders to keep happy; I'm not trying to get elected, and my family's twenty thousand kilometres away. I'm in the fortunate position of not having to give a damn what people think of me, so, personally, I really couldn't care if Rusty's diary's serialised in the newspaper."

"Not everyone can afford to take that attitude."

"Obviously not."

"Mrs Trousdale, for instance?"

"Definitely not."

"She's the sort of woman some men would go out on a limb for."

Le Droff looked down, smiling and shaking his head as if he found the notion absurd. "Not this man. Rusty's a big girl; she also happens to be the author of her own misfortune, if you'll pardon the expression."

Ihaka gave no sign that he'd got Le Droff's little joke. "Where were you in the early hours of Sunday morning?"

Le Droff held his gaze. "Tucked up in beddy-byes — where else?"

"By yourself?"

"Yes, by myself. Abstinence obviously isn't as safe as it's cracked up to be: if I'd known I was going to be a suspect, I'd have organised a bedmate. Or two."

"I didn't say you were a suspect."

"I'm relieved to hear it."

"I didn't say you weren't, either."

Le Droff smiled. "On the subject of the diary, I assume you've recovered it?"

"No, we haven't."

Le Droff thought about it. "Then how can you be sure Mules was the blackmailer?"

"We can't. I never said we were."

"Well, okay, but you seem to be working on that assumption. If it turns out it wasn't him, then neither Rusty nor I have a motive."

Ihaka leaned forward, putting his elbows on his knees. "We know Mrs Trousdale was being blackmailed; we know Mules was capable of it; we know he was acting like he'd won Lotto; and there's evidence to indicate he contacted her. I'd say that means one of two things: either Mules was the blackmailer or we've got a motherfucker of a coincidence on our hands."

"Coincidences do occur from time to time."

"Only when it suits us." There was nothing in Ihaka's expression to suggest he was joking.

Ihaka got home just before eleven. He got a couple of beers out of the fridge and went through to the lounge, where he flicked on the TV with the sound down low and flopped onto an armchair.

He'd been at his sister's place. His niece was there, fresh from her brush with the law. She seemed to have enjoyed the experience and was looking forward to doing it again. He had a feeling she wanted to be a political prisoner when she grew up.

The raids had been a fiasco. The house searches turned up a rusty .303, a slug gun, a couple of knives, a Dutch bestiality video, and small quantities of the usual drugs, but not one tiny, tenuous link to the APA. No charges were laid.

The seventeen activists bopped out of Auckland Central into a media love-in, spitting defiance in pre-packaged sound-bites. The government was shitting itself.

Boo-hoo.

Fuck it anyway: he had his own problem — who spiked Mules?

The Trousdales or Amanda Hayhoe? What a line-up — three natural born killers if he'd ever clapped eyes on them. Le Droff? Why would he care? Clyde Early? That felt a bit more like it, especially if he and Mules had bad blood going back. Then there was the mystery man Mules was seen with in the Globe.

The other scenario was thieves fall out: Mules might've had a partner who got greedy, which would explain why they didn't find the diary. One problem: Mules was a loner, everyone said so. Why would he suddenly get a partner if he thought he was going to score big-time? At least there was the tap on the Trousdales' phone now, if someone else had a go . . .

Ihaka felt himself drifting into sleep.

Haul arse, fat boy, before you flake in the chair. You don't want to wake up at four in the morning stiff and cold and feeling like shit.

In fact, it was 3.35 a.m. when Ihaka woke up in the armchair. He was cold and needed to piss and the TV was throwing out a static buzz. Before he could attend to any of those things, there was the small matter of the gun-wielding figure in the dark boiler suit and ski mask looming over him.

Ihaka got halfway out of the chair before the pistol barrel came down across his temple. He grabbed a handful of boiler suit and fell back, pulling his assailant down with him. He glimpsed a second dark figure, then took another metallic crunch on the side of his face. He saw starbursts. He pawed weakly at the guy on top of him who knocked his arms aside and chopped him again with the pistol, driving his head back into the chair. Fingers dug into his left arm and the sleeve was yanked above his elbow. He felt a needle sting in the crook of his arm.

He was in quicksand. He craned his neck to suck in air and clawed at solid ground, trying to hold on. The force dragging him down was relentless and his arms burned unbearably with the strain.

He lost his grip and sank like a stone, all the way to the centre of the earth.

19

It was lunchtime. Amanda Hayhoe was contemplating a quick trip to the cafeteria to top up her cholesterol when she got a call saying there was a package for her in reception. She went down to collect what turned out to be an unmarked, unaddressed white A4 envelope.

"How do you know it's for me?" she asked the receptionist.

"Because the guy said so."

"Did you get his name?"

"Listen, he just shoved it at me, said it was for you and shot through."

"What did he look like?"

The receptionist rolled her eyes: "Get real. We get a zillion people coming in here dropping things off. He was a suit, that's all I can tell you."

Hayhoe went back to her desk. The envelope contained five typed, numbered sheets. There was no letterhead, no covering note, no signature — nothing whatsoever to indicate the source.

She started reading.

> Serge Alain Le Droff was born in Hôtel Dieu Hospital in Toulouse, south-west France, on 11 October 1949, the second child of Jean-Jacques and Penelope Le Droff. His father was a businessman who owned several cafés and bistros catering mainly to blue-collar workers. His mother, whose maiden name was Brackett, was English. His parents had met in 1946, when she accompanied her father, a London wine and spirit merchant, on a buying trip to Gers, the Armagnac-producing region west of Toulouse.
>
> Jean-Jacques Le Droff had been a member of the underground resistance movement during the German occupation. Fiercely patriotic and conservative, he was persuaded to stand for the mayoralty of Toulouse in 1952 but lost heavily to the socialist candidate. Disillusioned, Le Droff moved his family (a daughter, Josette, had been born in 1948, a second son, Dominique, was born in 1954) to the then French colony of Algeria. He settled in Algiers and went into business importing produce from the Gers and Haute-Garonne regions.
>
> In Algiers, Le Droff senior's interest in politics was rekindled. His forceful personality and status as a hero of the resistance

made him a prominent figure among the Algerian French, the Pieds Noirs — 'Black Feet' — as they were known in France. Not surprisingly, he was vehemently opposed to the Algerian independence movement, the Front de Libération Nationale (FLN), which was locked in an increasingly bitter guerilla war with the French security forces.

When Le Droff's political hero General Charles de Gaulle returned to power in 1958 vowing that Algeria would remain French, the Pieds Noirs and the army were euphoric. However, when de Gaulle began negotiations with the FLN, the euphoria was replaced by a profound sense of betrayal.

Le Droff senior publicly supported the 1960 settlers' revolt and the equally abortive 1961 putsch by units of the French army serving in Algeria. While it seems unlikely that he was a member of the Organisation Armée Secrète (OAS), the terrorist group formed following the failed putsch and which made several unsuccessful attempts on de Gaulle's life, it is perhaps significant that the Le Droffs moved to New Caledonia in 1962: Jean-Jacques may have been forced to spend a "cooling off" period there before being allowed to return to metropolitan France. Deals of this kind were struck with particularly intransigent Pieds Noirs; in return, the authorities dropped investigations into their links with OAS. The fact that the Le Droffs moved back to Toulouse in 1966 lends some credence to this theory.

In 1962, at his mother's insistence, Serge was sent to board at Downside in Somerset, England. Even allowing for his bilingual upbringing, he made the transition with remarkable ease. He did well scholastically and excelled in a number of sports, notably cross-country running and fencing.

In 1967, Le Droff enrolled as an economics student at the Sorbonne in Paris. He later claimed not to have taken part in the so-called "Days of Rage", the student riots that convulsed France in May 1968, almost bringing down de Gaulle. While he would have been one of the few students at the Sorbonne not to have participated, that would be consistent with his apparent indifference to politics. In his subsequent career, he has appeared an apolitical pragmatist solely concerned with commercial considerations.

Le Droff left university at the end of 1968 without completing a degree and dropped out of sight for three years. He has occasionally referred to his experiences crewing on charter yachts in the French West Indies, which would account for this gap.

In October 1972, he turned up in the Gulf state of Dubai, part of the United Arab Emirates (UAE), re-establishing contact with junior members of the Dubai royal family whom he'd met at the Sorbonne. He would spend most of the next decade in and around the Gulf, engaged in various trading ventures and middleman activities.

The 1973 Yom Kippur war and the subsequent oil price shock transformed the commercial activity in the Middle East. As vastly increased oil revenues flowed into the region, opportunities opened up for skilful middlemen with connections on both the supply and demand side of transactions. With the Arab states investing heavily in military hardware, Le Droff was once again able to tap personal contacts: in this case, officials in the highly integrated French defence establishment — the military itself and the government-owned armaments manufacturers — who had served with his father in the resistance.

The commissions Le Droff earned from his role in a number of arms deals provided the launch pad for his swift expansion. By the late seventies, he had companies in Dubai, Abu Dhabi and Bahrain engaged in the importation of luxury goods; in addition, he'd continued to earn commissions from acting as middleman or 'spotter' for French companies doing business in the Middle East.

His travels throughout the region included a number of trips to Lebanon, which was embroiled in multilateral civil conflict, and Iraq during its protracted war with Iran. The reasons for these trips are not known.

In October 1980, the classified appendix to a staff study on terrorist activity prepared for the US House of Representatives Committee of the Judiciary was leaked to the publisher of a military/intelligence newsletter. Le Droff's name appeared on a list of known or suspected procurers of sophisticated weaponry for the various groups operating under the umbrella of the Palestine Liberation Organisation (PLO). However, he was not mentioned in the appendix to a full report on the subject which was prepared for the committee several months later and also leaked. A footnote attributed discrepancies to the fact that the earlier study had contained information from a since-discredited source.

The nature of Le Droff's business activities precludes confident estimates of his wealth but there can be little doubt that by 1980 he was a millionaire, probably several times over. He installed his family in a twenty-room chateau near the village of Levignac outside Toulouse and bought several farms in the area. When not on the move around the Middle East, Le Droff himself generally stayed at his home in Cap Ferrat on the Côte d'Azur.

However, the early eighties were not kind to Le Droff. He was involved in several civil-aircraft sales campaigns in Africa and the Middle East, acting on behalf of the European manufacturing consortium, Airbus Industrie. Virtually all these deals went sour when the airline industry slumped in 1982, a slump which coincided with the sharp fall in the price of oil. Most of the customers were the state-owned airlines of nations with oil-based economies and they reacted to these twin blows by reducing, indefinitely postponing or cancelling their orders.

Le Droff is believed to have invested heavily in these deals in the form of bribes paid to airline executives, government officials and members of the ruling group or family, in the expectation of earning substantial commissions when the sales were finalised. Even those sales which did eventuate were effectively oil for aircraft barter transactions, meaning Le Droff was forced to take his commissions in kind, i.e. oil, which he then had to sell at a loss on the spot market. He was also rumoured to have invested in Middle Eastern arms dealer Adnan Kashoggi's catastrophic Sudan venture.

With the Middle East no longer such a profitable environment, Le Droff looked for fresh fields. Having scaled down his holding in the Gulf, he visited Latin America in 1983 and Australia and New Zealand in 1984. Impressed by what he saw as the potential for growth in the New Zealand financial sector as a result of the deregulatory policies embraced by the Labour government, Le Droff moved to Auckland in mid-1984. He rented a house in Kohimarama and acquired a shelf company, Craxus Holdings Ltd, which he renamed Brackett Investments Ltd. He took office space in Air New Zealand House in Queen Elizabeth II Square and began trading shares.

When the market boomed in 1985/86, Le Droff's focus shifted from blue chips to high-yield entrepreneurial stocks, a switch that left him heavily exposed when the market crashed in October 1987. Although no hard information is available, market watchers believe the losses wiped out a good percentage of his gains of the previous three years. He is believed to have resumed share-trading within the last two years, although on a lesser scale.

In April 1987, Le Droff launched Eurotours, a wholesale travel company specialising in middle and upmarket package holidays to lesser-known regions of France and Italy. The Eurotours product was seen as offering quality and value for money and was well received. As a result, the company was able to weather the post-1987 recession and capitalise on the surge of offshore travel when the economy eventually picked up and the New Zealand dollar strengthened.

Once again, however, events conspired against him: Eurotours was caught in the consumer backlash against all things French triggered by the resumption of nuclear testing at Mururoa Atoll and is understood to be trading on sharply reduced volumes.

Le Droff is seeking to diversify. He has approached the New Zealand aviation authorities with a proposal for a charter airline operation linking New Zealand (and possibly Australia) with Europe. He is believed to have agreed terms with Airbus Industrie's used-aircraft division for the lease of up to three A310 wide-body jets and secured in principle approval from the French authorities, as well as stopover/pick-up rights in Singapore. The New Zealand authorities are favourably disposed towards the proposal but the Minister has put further consideration on hold until the furore over French nuclear testing has abated.

In 1986, Le Droff obtained the right to permanent residence in New Zealand. In 1993, he bought the top floor of the First Pacific Bank building in Quay Street and converted it into a penthouse apartment. The property is mortgaged to the Banque Nationale de Paris for NZ$2.5 million. He also leases the ground and nineteenth floors for Eurotours' sales and corporate offices respectively. His various other commercial operations are also located on the nineteenth floor.

For a wealthy man, Le Droff has very little in the way of an entourage. His personal staff consists of a cook/valet, a Corsican named Pascal, and Colonel Wyatt Bloodsaw, who could best be described as his right-hand man. Le Droff met Bloodsaw, formerly of the British Army's Thirteenth Parachute Regiment, in Sharjah in 1982. Bloodsaw was an old Middle East hand, having served in Oman and Qatar while on attachment to the SAS. He left the army in 1979 to take up a position as a military advisor and trainer in UAE. In 1982, Bloodsaw joined Le Droff's organisation as an executive assistant with responsibility for security. He appears to be Le Droff's closest associate.

Little is known about Le Droff's personal life. He is private to the point of being reclusive but is said to be relaxed and adept when he does socialise. Those who have had business dealings with him describe him as an accomplished performer in meetings and negotiations. His social contact is largely confined to a small group of acquaintances in the financial community that date from his early share trading days.

He has never married but the inevitable rumours of homosexuality appear to be baseless. Indeed, he earned a reputation as something of a ladies' man among the expatriate community in UAE and is known to have had a number of short-lived relationships with Auckland women.

He owns a house on the eastern side of Waiheke Island in the Hauraki Gulf where he spends most weekends, and a 12-metre yacht, *Lady Penelope*, which is moored at Westhaven Marina. He has always been fitness-conscious and reportedly remains in good physical condition. He visits his parents at least once a year and also makes regular trips to Tahiti and New Caledonia, where his family retains ties.

Hayhoe finished the report and announced, "The plot thickens," in a dramatic voice.

She saw the producer coming her way, looking even more harassed than usual. When he reached her desk, he put his hands on his hips and said ominously: "If I was in your shoes, I'd unthicken it. Double quick."

"Why, what's up?"

"I've just heard that news is preparing a one-hour special on the APA to go to air next Monday — fronted by Ainsley Tarr."

"Eeek."

"Exactly. If our story isn't a quantum leap forward from whatever they come up with, two careers will crash and burn. My kids are relying on you, Amanda."

Massive bladder pressure finally woke Tito Ihaka. The dense, throbbing pain in his head reminded him that he was in the shit.

He was fully clothed, lying on a thin rubber mat with a blanket over him. When he rolled onto his back, he felt a tug on his left wrist and left ankle. He threw off the blanket: his wrist and ankle were handcuffed to what proved to be a leg-press weight-training machine. He tried to shift it but only succeeded in confirming the obvious — it was too heavy — and making his head pound like a fishing-trip hangover.

He sat up and looked around. He was in a windowless room, a basement maybe, about six metres square with whitewashed plaster walls and an old carpet. The leg press and another weight machine, a bench press, were against the wall facing the door. On his right was a wine rack which must have held 100 bottles; on his left, an old chest of drawers, a few cartons and a stack of magazines. The room was chilly and dimly lit by a single-bulb light.

He looked at his watch: 2.43 p.m. on the sixth. He'd only missed two meals.

Well, maybe not. On the floor beside him were two plastic buckets, a bottle of mineral water, a roll of toilet paper, a packet of aspirins, and some sandwiches in Gladwrap.

Well, fuck me, I've been kidnapped by the Salvation Army.

He got a bucket, manoeuvred himself into a semi-kneeling position, and had the longest daytime piss of the twentieth century. It was the biggest thrill he'd had for a while.

He checked the damage: the left side of his face was swollen and he had three lumpy welts between hairline and cheekbone. The skin was broken and there was dried blood on his fingers when he took his hand away. He popped a couple of aspirins, washing them down with water.

He hollered a few times but nobody came and it just made the thumping in his head worse. He decided to have lunch. There was a choice of cheese or ham; he went for ham.

The first swallow came back up a lot faster than it had gone down. It triggered a power-spew, accompanied by epileptic shudders and sound effects which would've made a torturer gag.

Ihaka lay propped up on his elbows waiting for the nausea to recede and surveying the mess. He knew he'd had a lot to eat at his sister's place the night before, but he was surprised and mildly embarrassed to see just how much.

A little later, he sat up and reached for the rest of the sandwich with a trembling hand.

20

Detective Constable Johan Van Roon thought nothing of it when Tito Ihaka didn't turn up at work on Wednesday morning.

There was any number of possible explanations. Ihaka was unconventional: he didn't always go to bed at night and get up in the morning and brush his teeth after meals like most people.

But when Ihaka failed to show for the 2 o'clock Mules investigation briefing, a faint alarm bell rang. You could accuse him of a lot of things — and he'd give you one of his 'up yours' grins and admit to most of them — but at the end of the day he was a pro: he fronted up. Ihaka didn't miss murder briefings come hell, high water or the sort of hangover that drove lesser men to their first AA meeting.

There was no answer at Ihaka's house and his mobile was switched off. Van Roon checked with the switchboard: he hadn't reported in but, as the operator pointed out, "So what's new?" He had a look on Ihaka's desk, which was as neat as could be because Van Roon himself had spent an hour the previous day creating order out of chaos, as he did every few weeks; the fact that it was still in that state meant Ihaka hadn't been near it since. Van Roon didn't go through the drawers: he was concerned but not that concerned.

Van Roon went back to his desk and tried to do some work. What am I worrying about? Any minute now, he'll barge in and abuse me for not reminding him about the meeting.

Ihaka would've been out in the badlands, sidling up to back doors for whispered conversations or putting the squeeze on some loser in the back bar of a dead-beat pub. He'd look round with that sour expression, as if he'd just walked into someone's fart fog, and say something charming like, "Hi there, homos: am I too late for the circle jerk?"

But no matter how hard Van Roon tried to put it to rest, it just kept nagging away at him. Finally, for his own peace of mind, he decided to take a quick run out to Ihaka's place.

Ihaka's car was in the drive but the curtains were drawn. That was odd: if he was home, he would've opened the curtains; if he wasn't, why was his car there? The front door was unlocked: he never bothered to lock it when he was there but usually remembered when he went out.

The house was clean and tidy. A few months earlier, Ihaka had got sick of living in his own private Black Hole of Calcutta; he'd decided to get a cleaning lady in once a week. A couple took one look at the place and declined the gig; the third one agreed to take it on at time and a half and on the condition that he started showing a little house pride.

Van Roon called out but didn't even get an echo. He checked the house room by room and looked in the car and around the back yard: Ihaka definitely wasn't in residence. He went back inside to use the phone and saw the envelope slipped under the receiver. It was unsealed; he flipped it open with a ballpoint pen and slid out the note.

The news could have been worse, but only just.

> THE POLICE HARASSMENT OF 17 MAORI PATRIOTS WAS AN OUTRAGEOUS PROVOCATION AND CLEAR PROOF THAT THE STATE IS NOW ON A WAR FOOTING VIS-A-VIS RADICAL ELEMENTS. THE AOTEAROA PEOPLE'S ARMY HEREWITH VOWS TO STAND SHOULDER TO SHOULDER WITH THOSE THREATENED BY THE POLICE STATE'S ONSLAUGHT AND TO RESIST IT WITH ALL THE MEANS AT OUR DISPOSAL.
>
> THE POLICE STATE SHOULD UNDERSTAND THAT RETALIATION FOR ANY FUTURE ACTIONS OF THIS KIND WILL BE SWIFT AND DECISIVE. TO DEMONSTRATE THIS, THE APA HAS SEIZED THE POLICEMAN, IHAKA. HE IS A TRAITOR TO HIS PEOPLE AND WILL BE TREATED ACCORDINGLY, SHOULD THERE BE ANY REPEAT OF THE INDISCRIMINATE, RACIST AND FASCIST POLICE ACTION AGAINST THOSE IN THE VANGUARD OF MAORIDOM'S STRUGGLE FOR LIBERATION AND SOVEREIGNTY.
>
> IT IS NOT TOO LATE FOR THE STATE TO ABANDON ITS TOTALITARIAN COURSE. IF THE AUTHORITIES ARE PREPARED TO APOLOGISE FOR THEIR ACTION AND GIVE AN UNDERTAKING THAT IT WILL NOT BE REPEATED, IHAKA WILL BE RELEASED UNHARMED. IF, HOWEVER, THEY ARE INTENT ON VIOLENT CONFRONTATION, HE WILL MERELY BE THE FIRST OF MANY CASUALTIES.

Van Roon, who'd had a religious upbringing and didn't take the name of the Lord or any of his immediate family in vain, said, "Holy Mother of God."

At 5.39 that evening, the SIS man Wayne Cramp paused outside Detective Inspector Finbar McGrail's office. He loosened his fat Windsor knot and breathed hard through his nose, then knocked and entered.

McGrail was ready to call it a day: he had his jacket on and, as he did every evening before leaving the office, he'd cleared his desk except for a copy of the APA's fourth communiqué.

As Cramp lowered himself into a chair, McGrail tapped the communiqué with his index finger. "Well, Mr Cramp, it seems our little exercise on Monday night achieved something after all. I think you'd concede it's not quite the outcome you predicted."

Cramp loosened his tie some more and cleared his throat. "If you remember, inspector, I did predict they'd strike at police officers. I think it shows we're on the right track."

McGrail studied Cramp as if he had a mildly interesting deformity. "Oh really? And how did you arrive at that sanguine conclusion?"

Cramp, with a hint of bluster: "Well, why else would they've grabbed Ihaka? Okay, we mightn't have hit the target on Monday night but this tells us we got too close for comfort. It's obvious from the communiqué what they're up to — they're trying to make us back off."

"I see." McGrail nodded slowly. "Can I take it, then, that your department's advice to the Minster will be carry on regardless?"

Cramp thrust his chin out: "Absolutely. In fact, we'll advocate turning up the heat."

"Well, if nothing else, that should eliminate the slightest chance Sergeant Ihaka has of remaining in one piece."

"Look, inspector, I'm gutted about Ihaka, but you know as well as I do he's a goner. We can't cave into these bastards: there's no way in the wide world the government can let a gang of criminal subversives dictate terms to them. The APA know that too; that stuff about letting him go is just posturing."

McGrail nodded dolefully.

Sensing he was winning the argument, Cramp pushed on: "With all due respect, we'd be kidding ourselves to think otherwise. They wouldn't dare turn him loose now: the guy's an experienced officer — he'd know far too much about them. I'm sorry to say this, I really am, but my guess is he's already dead."

McGrail sighed. "Thank you, Mr Cramp. I think I'll go home now."

The conversation had confirmed what McGrail already suspected: the government had already written Ihaka off. Only his friends could help him now. The question was, would they?

McGrail didn't go home. He drove out to Sandringham, to Ihaka's place, where he wandered around trying to keep out of the way of the lab boys who were going through it with a fine-tooth comb. When he'd found what he was looking for, he drove back towards the city, crossing Newton Gully and Great North Road, and went into Grey Lynn the back way, up the hill.

He parked outside a restored villa in a short street off Richmond Road, went up the steps to the verandah, and knocked on the door: no one was home. He got back in his car and called his wife to say he'd be late. Then he sat and waited, still and contemplative as a mystic.

It was almost eight before his patience was rewarded. A Peugeot 305 zipped past, its showroom sheen reflecting the street lights. It halted in front of the garage; the man McGrail was waiting for got out, opened the garage door and drove in.

McGrail stayed put. The man locked the garage. Without looking left or right, he walked towards the steps up to his front door. Instead of going up the steps, he circled around the rear of McGrail's car on cat's feet and wrenched open the driver's door.

McGrail looked at him, a glimmer of amusement in his bleak brown eyes: "I'm pleased to see you're still on the ball."

Duane Ricketts smiled quizzically. "Detective Inspector McGrail, as I live and breathe. What are you doing, lurking around outside my humble abode?"

"It's a long story. If you could spare me half an hour . . ."

"Why not? I can go to the opera any old night."

They went inside. Ricketts offered McGrail a drink; he said a cup of tea would be nice. Ricketts put the kettle on and got himself a beer. He sat down opposite McGrail and made a perfunctory "cheers" gesture with the bottle.

"It must be a year," said McGrail. "You look healthier."

The last time they'd met, Ricketts wasn't long out of a Bangkok jail. He'd been on the scrawny side and sunken, wary eyes and hollow cheeks had accentuated his sharp, slightly foxy features. Now he'd bulked up to lean and had an expensive haircut to go with the smart suit and boldly patterned silk tie. Add the new house and the new car and Duane Ricketts seemed to be doing quite nicely, thank you.

The packaging was different, flasher, but McGrail was sure the product hadn't changed: the mind behind the knowing grey eyes would be just as quick and calculating. Not for the first time, McGrail reflected that Ricketts would have made a very good policeman if he hadn't been expelled from the force all those years ago. It was before McGrail's time and he'd never really got to the bottom of it: a newspaper was slipped a police photograph from an unsavoury sex case and somebody — presumably not the horse — kicked up a fuss . . .

"Yeah, well, staying out of jail helps."

"Work's going well by the look of things?"

Ricketts nodded. "I'm getting heaps of work from Trubshaw Trimble and a couple of other law firms. Your recommendation certainly didn't hurt."

"It might've got you in the door, that's all."

Ricketts went to make the tea. McGrail called through the kitchen: "Have you been following the exploits of our home-grown terrorists?"

"Pretty hard not to." He came out with a tray. "They don't muck around, do they? You on to them yet?"

"We're still chasing shadows, I'm afraid." McGrail sipped his tea. "They struck again last night."

Ricketts decided he was about to find out why McGrail had come a-calling. He put down his beer and paid attention.

"They've got Sergeant Ihaka."

Ricketts stiffened. He opened and closed his mouth, as if McGrail wasn't a suitable audience for the comment he had in mind. "You mean they're holding him prisoner?"

"Yes."

"What are his chances?"

"Poor to non-existent." McGrail could've been predicting the weather. "He may be dead already. His release is conditional on government compliance with demands which can't or won't be complied with. Unless they're completely crackers or completely naive — and I don't believe they're either — they know that perfectly well, so the offer isn't worth the paper it's written on."

Ricketts shook his head. "So what are you doing, ripping the town apart?"

"We're doing the usual things with an unusual degree of urgency. There's a complication: the APA says it's retaliation for the other night's blitz on Maori activists and he's for the chop if it happens again."

"Why would you do it again? It was a big fat zero, wasn't it?"

"That hasn't deterred our anti-terrorism experts . . ."

"Who're they?"

"Some gentlemen from the SIS: they're convinced that the APA are Maori extremists and that view seems to hold sway in Wellington. They see what's happening to Ihaka as a vindication — it shows we're getting warm."

"What do you think, Inspector?"

"Initially, I was inclined to go along with it, if only for a lack of alternatives: who else out there displays the obsessive rage that drives people to political violence? I know from my Belfast days that, over time, terrorist organisations attract romantics and psychopaths and bandits, but they're founded on single-minded fanaticism which derives from a burning anger over some real or perceived historic injustice. Who else in the community does that apply to? Sergeant Ihaka was sceptical from the outset but, as you know, he tends to operate on gut instinct, which the bureaucratic mind-set doesn't value. As you probably also know, he believes a fool should be allowed to suffer the consequences of his foolishness, so he didn't pursue the argument with any great degree of persuasiveness. In fact, it reached the point that his attitude got him dropped from the investigation. Now the APA wouldn't have known that, but if they are some sort of Maori extremist faction, you'd think they'd know about his niece."

"What about her?"

"She was one of the strident seventeen hauled in for questioning. Don't you think that abducting her uncle is an odd form of retaliation? The niece certainly does: I spoke to her mother late this afternoon — the girl's beside herself."

"Maybe the APA didn't know . . ."

"Maybe — she does have a different surname. I'd be surprised, though — when all's said and done, they're a pretty select group and I would've thought word would get around."

Ricketts poured McGrail another cup of tea and got himself a second beer and a packet of potato chips. McGrail apologised for keeping him from his dinner; Ricketts told him not to worry about it, he wasn't looking forward to it that much anyway.

"Something else bothers me about the Maori radicals theory," said the policeman. "The APA has carried out four operations without leaving a trace. No one's seen anything, no one's heard anything — we haven't got a single, solitary lead, not even a sketchy vehicle description. That's the hallmark of experienced professionals, not a bunch of beginners."

"So why the hell grab Ihaka?"

"That's the sixty-four thousand dollar question, Mr Ricketts, and I don't have the answer. Perhaps the sergeant stumbled across something on one of his solo forays."

Ricketts stared thoughtfully at McGrail: "Okay, Inspector, what's on your mind?"

McGrail stared back: "When I was churning over this earlier, it occurred to me that you're probably the best people-finder in the business. If anyone can find him, you can."

Ricketts started feeding chips into his mouth, nodding as he crunched through them. "Sure, I'll have a go. I owe the fat bastard: if it wasn't for him, I wouldn't be in this place . . ."

McGrail coughed: "Yes, I'm not sure I really want to hear about that."

Ricketts grinned. "What have you got?"

McGrail flipped open his briefcase and brought out a plastic folder. "That's everything worthwhile on the APA, which doesn't amount to much. I even included Ihaka's case notes . . ."

"Jesus, since when did he make notes?"

"In the loosest sense of the word — they're more a collection of rather disturbing doodles. There's also some background on the case he was transferred to . . ."

"You're sticking your neck out, aren't you?"

McGrail frowned. "I suppose so. Not as much as you are, though: you do realise that, whoever these people are, they're completely ruthless?"

"It's a fine fucking time to bring that up, now that you've talked me into it."

"The art of salesmanship, Mr Ricketts." If he hadn't known better, Ricketts would've said McGrail's expression verged on affectionate. "Don't draw their attention to the fine print until they've signed on the dotted line."

21

It was well past Finbar McGrail's bedtime.

He liked to be at his desk by 7.45 a.m. having jogged, made his toilet with an attention to detail which suggested a degree of vanity, had a tasteless but reliably laxative breakfast, and chaired the family discussion on the day ahead. This routine meant getting up at 5.30. Seeing he wasn't one for burning the candle at both ends, his head normally hit the pillow at half past ten.

That Wednesday night was an exception. If his arithmetic was correct, there was a seventeen-hour time difference between New Zealand and the state of Georgia on America's east coast, so midnight in Auckland was 7 o'clock in the morning there. Seven in the a.m. was as early as most people cared to get their phone calls.

McGrail dialled a number from the address book he'd taken from Tito Ihaka's house earlier that night. After half-a-dozen rings, a man answered in a down-home drawl: "I'm listening."

"Good morning, I'm trying to get hold of C. C. Hellicar."

"You've got the next best thing, bubba. This here's C. C.'s daddy."

"Mr Hellicar, I'm Detective Inspector Finbar McGrail of the Auckland police — that's Auckland, New Zealand. I'm sorry to be ringing so early . . ."

"Hell, that's okay, the whiskey ain't biting too hard this morning. And call me Willard. What time you got where you're at?"

"It's shortly after midnight."

"Midnight, huh? Would that be midnight last night or midnight tonight?"

"Tonight — we're seventeen hours ahead of you."

"Is that right? Well, if you're seventeen hours ahead, you must be a long ways away; and if you're a long ways away, you'll be wanting to get down to the nitty-gritty. C. C. ain't here; matter of fact, this ain't been C. C.'s home for nigh on ten years."

"I wonder, could you tell me where I can get hold of her? As you know, she came down here last year . . ."

"Hold your fire, Finbar — did I get that right?"

"Yes."

"That's a New Zealand name?"

"No, Irish. I'm from Northern Ireland originally."

"I could tell you had an accent of course but, hell, anyone from outside of Walton County sounds a little strange to me. What I was fixing to say, Finbar, was it's news to me my little gal's been down to your part of the world. See, the thing is, C. C. wasn't inclined to tell me a damn thing about her job. I remember one time not long after she'd gone to work for that outfit in Arizona, she came visiting and happened to leave her passport lying around. When I picked it up, it just kind of fell open, you know the way they do, and I couldn't help but notice she had a stamp for Mozambique. I said, 'C. C., what in the hell you been doing in Mozambique?' Well, sir, she just looked at me with those pretty blue eyes and said, 'Daddy, I can't tell you on account of it's a matter of national security.' So ever since then, we've had ourselves an arrangement: I don't ask and she'd don't give me the high hat." His voice dropped. "Not that I didn't have a good goddamn idea what she was doing: I mean, the government didn't send her to Fort Bragg to learn touch typing, right?"

While C. C. Hellicar was undeniably attractive, McGrail felt that only a fond father would refer to her pretty blue eyes, since they were the coldest, palest shade of blue imaginable, like frozen meths. But that wasn't the comment which really made McGrail prick up his ears: "Willard, you said 'what she was doing'..."

"Check." His voice got flat. "C. C. quit — she don't do that stuff no more. It's a sad story: about midway through last year she started stepping out with a fellow in Phoenix, professor at the college there. I'll tell you, Finbar, you wouldn't have looked at C. C. and this boy and said straight off they were made for each other. I'd always figured that any man she got serious about would have to be like her and then some, you know what I mean? This Oliver, he was a gentle guy, real earnest — shit, he was a professor, what can I say? But he sure was sweet on her and I guess that counts for a lot. Anyway, to get right along, something bad happened when they were on vacation in England last fall — the professor bought the farm. C. C. don't talk about it; all she said was her past caught up with her. She quit and went off to Hawaii. She's working in a fitness club there run by an old friend of hers. The point is, Finbar — and I apologise for taking the long way round — if you had in mind for C. C. to do a job for you, the plain fact is, she's retired."

"I see." McGrail didn't try to hide his disappointment.

"Why don't you give that company she worked for a call? They must have other folks who do whatever the hell it was exactly C. C. did."

"The problem with that, Willard, is this isn't an official call. It's a personal matter: someone C. C. got to know when she was here is in a terrible bind."

"Well shit, why didn't you say so? The way she is these days, there's no telling which way she'll jump, but C. C.'s always been one to side with her friends. You hang there two shakes and I'll find her number for you."

C. C. — for Candice Clara — Hellicar dozed in the single bed in her poky mid-town Honolulu apartment. The apartment bore a passing resemblance to a cell in one of the looser nunneries; like a lot of things, it had seemed like a good idea at the time.

As she often did in the dreamy haze of her slow awakenings, Hellicar was retracing the sequence of events that had brought her to Hawaii. She'd decided some time ago that the connecting thread, if there was one, was sex.

It began in late fall 1993. She was working for a security company based in Scottsdale, Arizona, which provided advice, training and protection to a range of international clients. The company was a CIA front — 'a proprietary' in agency terminology — and Hellicar was a CIA agent. A very special type of agent: she belonged to a unit so shadowy that its very existence was a matter of conjecture within the US security and intelligence apparatus. The unit's members were known as the "cleaners"; they were the US government's instruments of last resort for ridding itself of rogue agents who, in intelligence jargon, had "gone bamboo" — become the menace they had been charged to combat.

Drew Hobbs was one such rogue. He was tall and blond with an appealing 'aw shucks' country-boy manner and good enough at the game to have gone a long way. Instead, he'd gone seriously off the rails, teaming up with Cuban intelligence to run dope into Florida. The Cubans had been doing it ever since the revolution. It was just about the perfect anti-Yanqui operation: they piped poison in and sucked greenbacks out. Hobbs didn't see himself as a criminal, let alone a traitor. The way he looked at it, any fool could see that Cuba posed as much of a threat to the US as the Canary Islands. He was just meeting a demand and getting rich in the process and wasn't that the American way?

When Hobbs' superiors at CIA headquarters in Langley, Virginia, finally caught on, they took a diametrically opposed view. They assigned Hellicar the task of conveying their extreme disapproval in any way she saw fit, providing it (a) caused Hobbs' death; (b) couldn't be traced back to the agency; and (c) didn't exceed budgetary guidelines.

The set-up was a variation on the honey-trap. Hobbs was in Miami, staying at the Bellevue Hotel on South Beach. He was a compulsive skirt-chaser, so around 10 o'clock he'd hit the Bellevue's cocktail bar, one of the hot spots along the beach, where a twenty-one-year-old Cuban-American calling herself Carmelita would be sitting alone at the bar.

It was a sure thing that Hobbs would zero in on Carmelita, whom Hellicar had recruited from one of the ferociously anti-Castro Cuban exile groups in Miami, because she made every other babe in the bar look like Courtney Love on a bad smack day. She had a mane of glossy black hair, a heart-shaped face, hot eyes and a soft-lipped, crimson pout. She wore spray-on leather pants and a skimpy white singlet which barely contained bulging, centrefold breasts and exposed a swathe of flat, satiny midriff. When Hobbs got a load of Carmelita, he'd be putty.

She'd let him come on to her. When he suggested adjourning to his room for some meaningful interaction, she'd reply that they knew her in the bar and she didn't want a reputation as an easy lay. Why didn't he go on up to the room and set out a few lines of coke? She'd go powder her nose and be up in a few minutes.

Hobbs would drift off; Carmelita would give Hellicar the nod on her way to the ladies' room. When she knocked, Hobbs would open the door with a flourish to find a silenced Heckler & Koch VP 70 nine-millimetre semi-automatic pointed at the small gap between his front teeth.

Except it wasn't Hobbs who opened the door of room 1053. It was a brunette wearing a see-through black peignoir and an expression of glazed expectancy. Hellicar knew her from a photo in Hobbs' file: she was his wife, Diann. What wasn't in the file was the information that Diann didn't mind her husband playing around as long as she could join in. She'd flown into Miami late that afternoon for some three-way action.

Diann screamed a warning and tried to slam the door, but Hellicar punched the pistol butt into the side of her jaw and squeezed into the room. Naked except for his stainless-steel Rolex Oyster Sea-Dweller, Hobbs was squirming across the king-sized bed trying to get to the gun in the bedside table drawer. Maybe his erection got snagged in the bedclothes, because he'd only just got the drawer open when Hellicar's first round hit him below the left armpit.

Hellicar tore up the sheet to tie and gag the new widow. She hung a 'Do not disturb' sign on the doorknob, took a cab to the airport, and caught the midnight flight to New Orleans.

Diann Hobbs might have been a tad kinky but she wasn't stupid; in fact, the joint venture with the Cubans had been her idea. So when the Miami police department started dragging its feet, despite having a fairly accurate description of the shooter, she assumed they'd filed Drew's killing under Spook Shit. The question was: whose spooks?

The Cubans got word to her that it wasn't them. Three weeks after Drew's termination, an elegant middle-aged woman followed Diann into the restroom at a Georgetown café and told her it had been a CIA hit. Their sources inside the anti-Fidel movement said the hitwoman had a southern accent and used the name Clara Monroe.

Diann thought it over. "If I find out who she is, will you waste the bitch?"

The middle-aged woman looked offended. "You mean me personally?"

Diann rolled her eyes. "Your people. Cuba."

"I doubt it," said the woman, "but you can always ask."

Diann Hobbs knew that several of Drew's colleagues had a permanent hard-on for her. She casually asked the best-looking of them to see what he could find out about a statuesque operative with eerily pale blue eyes and a southern accent who used the field name Clara Monroe. He was happy to oblige.

He reported back a couple of weeks later that the description appeared to fit a Candice Clara "C. C." Hellicar, current status and whereabouts unknown. Trawling through the computer, he'd come across a bio listing which described her as an electronics specialist and mentioned the fact that she'd attended high school in Monroe, Georgia.

That was good enough for Diann. She flew down to Mexico City and went to the Cuban embassy, where she asked to see an intelligence officer. They said, "Come back tomorrow." The next day she asked the fat man in the safari suit who'd flown in from Havana if his government would avenge Drew's murder. The fat man smiled politely and craned his neck to get a better look at her bare, brown thighs.

When the fat man realised that she was serious, he said his government was very sorry about the death of her husband, who was an enlightened man and a valued ally, but was unable to help her. She asked why not. He explained that Cuba was seeking to improve its relations with the United States, so inserting an assassination squad, even in such a worthy cause, would be viewed as counter-productive. He stood up, took a lingering, regretful look at her legs, and said that if she could alert them in advance, with detailed information, when Hellicar ventured beyond US borders, then . . . he shrugged expressively . . . perhaps the matter could be reassessed.

Diann re-enlisted her late husband's colleague, urging him to find out everything he could about Hellicar. That amounted to next to nothing: Hellicar obviously worked in a highly sensitive area, probably covert operations, because accessing her full file needed a whole lot more security clearance than he had. Diann threw him a motivational fuck and asked him to try again. He didn't get any further and warned her that if he kept trying, someone would notice him poking his nose where he wasn't authorised to poke it.

She took him to bed again and went through the manual. Afterwards, she gave him a tear-jerking and largely fictitious account of her husband's death. It went in one ear and out the other: he didn't give a foaming fuck who'd aced Drew or why. The important thing was that Diann was alive and kicking — and scratching and biting for that matter. He was prepared to play along with whatever dumb-ass scheme she had going if it meant some more of that wild sack-time. He had a buddy in the office of personnel in the Support Directorate; maybe he could find out something.

By early summer, Diann was running out of patience with her lover's inability to deliver the goods in either sense when his buddy came through with Hellicar's itinerary for the overseas holiday she had planned for the fall. It was routine procedure for agency staff going on vacation to submit an itinerary and contact details to the office of personnel so they could be reached in an emergency. Covert ops were an exception, as they were to most things, but the Plans (Clandestine Services) Directorate had sent Hellicar's programme through anyway. There was no particular reason for it: it was just another of the countless bureaucratic screw-ups that occur in Washington DC — and every other government town — on a daily basis.

Diann returned to Mexico City for another audience with the fat man in the safari suit. He studied Hellicar's itinerary and remarked that Britain was hardly the ideal country in which to mount such an operation, but he'd see what could be done. In the meantime, perhaps she might like to give some thought to what she could do in return for Cuba's assistance. Diann shrugged and said she picked up lots of stuff from her CIA friends and their wives which she was happy to pass on; apart from that, she'd consider any reasonable proposition.

The fat man smiled until his faced creased like a baby's. He pushed his chair back so he could see her legs under the table. She'd worn an even shorter dress this time.

Hellicar and her beau, Oliver Kirsopp, flew to London in the first week of October. For Kirsopp, a professor of English literature at Arizona State University, the trip was both a romantic interlude and a pilgrimage. His Mecca was the Welsh seaside town of Laugharne where his hero, the poet Dylan Thomas, had lived and, having cemented his reputation by drinking himself to death at the tender age of thirty-nine, been buried.

They spent a few days sightseeing in London, then drove down the M4 and across the Severn bridge into Wales. They'd rented a cottage near Worm's Head on the Gower Peninsula and, after the visit to Dylan's grave and the boathouse where he'd worked, they explored the soft green countryside. They drove down impossibly narrow lanes, tramped across fields, picnicked on the banks of the Towy, wandered in dark woods, and climbed Sir John's Hill in the mild twilight. Kirsopp knew much of Thomas' work off by heart: in each location, he'd recite an appropriate poem, imitating the dead poet's celebrated bardic chant. His light Louisiana tenor was a far cry from Thomas' rich baritone but Hellicar didn't care: she could've listened to him all day long.

On their way home, they'd stop for a drink in rural pubs where they were mostly welcomed as guests, occasionally shunned as tourists and Yanks to boot. Back at the cottage on the cliff, they'd have dinner, drink wine, make love and fall into deep, country sleep.

Kirsopp had no idea what Hellicar really did: she'd told him that she designed and supervised the installation of state-of-the-art electronic security systems. So when a noise woke them at 3.13 one morning, he insisted that she stayed put while he went to investigate. Against her better judgement but feeling that it was a little late to admit to knowing more ways of killing a man with her bare hands than Ezra Pound had mental breakdowns, she acquiesced. He got up, pulled on his black kimono with the dragon rampant on the back and stepped out into the corridor.

About half a minute later, there was a noise like a suppressed sneeze followed immediately by a fabled grunt, another suppressed sneeze and a series of thuds. The average person might have assumed that Oliver was having a sneezing fit, had tripped in the dark and fallen over; Hellicar knew the sound of a lover being shot dead with a silenced pistol when she heard it. She sprang out of bed, hoisted the window, and dived through it. She did a forward roll as she hit the ground, bounced to her feet, and sprinted into the night. Behind her, doors slammed, footsteps pounded and voices were raised in a gabbled exchange.

It wasn't freezing but it was too cold to be playing hide and seek in nothing but a pair of Calvin Klein underpants. She was wearing underpants because she had herpes and because Oliver slept naked and was inclined to get amorous in his sleep. With exquisite timing, the herpes had made one of its infrequent appearances the previous day, ringing the usual bells: the joke — "What's the difference between love and herpes? Herpes is forever"; the scumsucking ex-boyfriend; and the vow to track the scumsucker down and tattoo the joke on his dick with a jackhammer. Not that there was room.

The rented cottage was a good killing ground: the nearest house was a kilometre away and the cliff twenty metres from the back door cut off escape. It was dark, though — low cloud blocked out the night sky — and there was cover from the overgrown garden dotted with clumps of trees and a low stone boundary wall.

Pin-drop quiet. Don't run; hide, wait. Let them come. You'll hear them; they'll have to see you.

Hellicar crouched in a stand of trees by the wall, about forty metres from the house. Someone was coming. She dropped onto her stomach and inched backwards into the knee-high undergrowth that grew along the wall. Thorns raked her bare back.

A squat figure shuffled up to the trees, right arm extended, swinging to and fro like a windscreen wiper. He edged through the trees and bellied up to the wall. She could smell cigarette smoke on his clothes.

He was almost on top of her when she erupted from the undergrowth, like a missile from an underground silo. She caught his right wrist, wrenching it down, and pulped his nose with the heel of her other hand. His head whiplashed. She slipped a leg behind him and flipped him. His skull pinged off the wall as he went over. She ripped the pistol from him, jammed the silencer into his ear and pulled the trigger.

The gun was a Colt Woodsman .22. Hellicar tossed the silencer: they were into stealth; she was more concerned with accuracy. She tore at the buttons of the dead man's jacket until a gravelly crunch told her the other gunman had crossed the drive. She forgot the jacket: exposure was the least of her worries.

The dead man lay half in, half out of the undergrowth. As she lifted his feet into the long grass, his trouser leg rode up his calf. He had an ankle holster with a Harrington & Richardson Young America .22 calibre revolver; seven more rounds. She stuck it in the waistband of her underpants, at the small of her back.

Hellicar crawled on her belly through the undergrowth to the line of trees and shrubs along the cliff edge. The Atlantic Ocean boiled over rocks fifty metres below. She knelt behind a tree, in the firing position, straining her ears and eyes for a rustle or flicker of movement.

Then the tree trunk exploded, blasting wood fragments into her face. She lurched backwards, losing her footing and the Colt. The ground dropped away and she slid on her stomach. She wrapped her right arm around the base of a sturdy bush growing out from the lip of the cliff. Her feet swung into space and she pawed frantically for a toehold on the cliff face.

She had both arms around the base of the bush hauling herself up when the second gunman appeared above her. He wore a dark tracksuit with a woollen cap pulled down to his eyebrows and dangled a pistol in his right hand. He lowered himself onto his haunches, elbows on thighs, wrist uncocked, the fat tube of the silencer pointed downwards.

He said, "Well now, darling," in a broad Irish accent, "and how long would you be thinking you can hang on there?"

"Not for long."

"You look a bit cold." A low chuckle: "Your nips are standing to attention like grenadier guards."

"Who are you?"

"Ah, now that would be telling."

"Why did you do this?"

He showed off a toothy grin. "Let's just say we're doing some friends a favour . . ." He broke off, noticing the Colt: "That's Davy's — I don't much like the look of that. What have you done with him?"

"He's over there."

The Irishman looked over his shoulder. "Where now?"

Hellicar dropped her left arm and plucked the revolver from the waistband of her underpants. When he looked back at her, she shot him twice through the left eye. The Harrington & Richardson must have pulled right because she'd aimed at the bridge of his nose.

The dead gunmen turned out to be members of a deactivated IRA hit squad. The IRA had taken on the job at the request of the Libyans who, after all, hadn't asked for much in return for the moral and material support they'd provided over the years. The Libyans, for their part, were doing a favour for the Cubans. Hands across the water.

Hellicar's rehashes always led to the conclusion that Oliver was dead because of her. Sometimes, she wondered whether she'd feel any worse if she'd been in love with Oliver, as opposed to very, very fond of him. Occasionally, she'd reflect that if it hadn't been for the herpes attack, she'd probably be dead too.

She never dwelt on that notion for long: the ironies were too bitter.

Hellicar looked at the bedside clock. Five after eight: she'd be late for work — again.

In Auckland, about 8000 kilometres to the south-west and across the international date line, it was 6.05 the following morning. Finbar McGrail had treated himself to a half-hour sleep-in after his late night.

The phone rang. Hellicar's past was reaching out for her again.

22

As a rule, Rusty Trousdale didn't bother keeping up with the dreary parade of trivia, humbug, acts of God, and man's inhumanity to man that we call "the news".

Massacres in the Kwa-Zulu, tidal waves in the Bay of Bengal, bone-pits in the Balkans, baby-faced crack whores on the south side, family fatals on the motorway — shit happens, as they say, always has done, always will. Rusty wished it otherwise but as the old prune who'd taught her French at boarding school used to say: "You can wish till you're blue in the face, ma petite; that won't make it so."

This morning was different. Today's top billing victim-wise was someone she knew: Detective Sergeant Ihaka. A couple of days earlier, he'd sat in the next room wolfing sandwiches and bullying her ragged; now there he was on the front page. The photo, a blow-up from a news shot taken at a crime scene, captured Ihaka in all his sensitive new-age glory. It cried out for a cartoon balloon — something like, "Get the fuck out of my face."

The accompanying story reported that Ihaka had been abducted by these terrorists whom Maurice and everyone else she came across insisted were wild-eyed Maoris. While Rusty didn't actually know any Maoris personally and didn't pretend to understand what made them tick, she found it hard to fathom why a bunch of angry, disaffected Maoris would take it out on one of their own. Surely there were plenty of Pakeha policemen to choose from?

She was reading the Police Minister's statement and thinking that the stuff about not making deals with terrorists didn't sound too promising for Ihaka when her mobile phone rang. It was Clyde Early, in a better mood than last time they'd spoken.

"I got your message. Sorry I didn't get back to you sooner — I've been in Australia."

"That's okay. The reason I called is there's been a development."

"I've got some news too." He sounded positively cheerful.

"Good news?"

"I'd say so."

"Well?" she coaxed. "Don't keep me in suspense."

"Have you heard from the blackmailer this week?"

She hesitated. "No, why?"

"I reckon I've scared him off." He told her how Renée Adlington, the temporary secretary, had found out about their affair by listening in on the phone call, how he'd figured it out and put the wind up her.

"So she's in it with the creep who rang me?"

"Yeah, obviously. I don't know who he is but . . ."

"Did she confess all?"

"Course not. She lied through her teeth, just as you'd expect her to. You should have seen her, though — she was packing shit."

Rusty went, "Hmmm."

"What's the matter? You don't sound all that pleased."

"Well, it's just that . . . you know that ex-rugby player who was murdered?"

"Mules? I'll say. I sacked him once, in Italy. I could've told you he'd come to a sticky end. What about him?"

"Remember I said it sounded like the blackmailer knew you?"

"Yeah."

"The police think Mules was the blackmailer." She told him about Ihaka's visit and the underlining in Mules' phone book.

There was a long silence as Early digested this information. He asked slowly, "Does that mean the cops know about us?"

"Afraid so."

"But they didn't find the diary at Mules' place?"

"This cop . . ."

"Detective Sergeant Ihaka."

"Right — he thinks whoever murdered Mules has got the diary."

"I suppose that's a reasonable assumption."

"Shit." Early was struck by another unpleasant thought: "Jesus, what about Maurice? Does he know?"

"No. Ihaka's more subtle than one would think."

"Well, thank Christ for that."

"Getting back to your temp for a moment: Ihaka made Mules out to be a nasty piece of work, which is certainly how the blackmailer came across. It's not that I don't think you've been very clever, because I do, but is that how you see Renée Whatsername?"

"Probably not, but then I didn't see her as the sort who'd listen in on phone calls. You know, we should tell Ihaka about her: she might know something about the murder."

"As a matter of interest, Clyde, have you read today's paper?"

"Just the sports section. Why?"

"Have a look at the front page. You'll see that Ihaka's got rather a lot on his plate just now."

In fact, Tito Ihaka hadn't had as much as a crumb on his plate for eighteen hours.

Gnawing hunger was just the start of it: he still had a booming headache, still felt queasy after-effects of whatever they'd injected him with; he was also cold and his body ached from enforced discomfort.

Then there was the smell. During the night, room service had emptied the buckets and left him a sponge and an old towel to mop up what had missed and what had splattered, but he couldn't clean up what he couldn't reach. He'd woken up that morning with an urge to surge and ended up sludging on an industrial scale. Now that was mingling with the residual puke and really starting to hum.

Then there was the boredom. He was running out of things to think about, ways to pass the time.

Analysing his plight hadn't taken long. The APA had got him. They'd known where to find him because he was in the phone book, bravado he now regretted. Why him? He'd been named in a couple of early APA newspaper stories and they weren't to know he'd been arseholed from the task force. The fact that he was still alive might mean they planned to use him as some sort of a bargaining chip. Then again, it might mean they were dreaming up a really warped way of sticking it to him.

Stewing on it wasn't going to help, so he'd turned to other subjects. He'd chosen the best and worst All Black teams of the past twenty-five years. He'd picked his top ten films, top ten albums, top ten Bruce Springsteen songs, ten biggest fuckheads on TV, ten sleaziest people in town, ten sportsmen who could be closet homos and the ten people he'd most like to beat within an inch of their lives — give or take an inch. Interestingly, that list had almost as many cops as criminals. He'd gone for Steve McQueen in *Bullitt* as his favourite movie cop, ahead of Gene Hackman in *The French Connection*. Ellen Barkin in *Sea of Love* bolted home in the cop's squeeze category.

From there it was a natural progression to the ten women of his acquaintance he'd most like to fuck. Over half of them, including Rusty Trousdale, who made a strong late run coming in at six with a bullet, were married or de factos. Not a very healthy state of affairs but that was the way the cookie crumbled. He tried the ten women he'd most like to fuck again but that proved overly ambitious; even five was tough going. His ten most fuckable movie actresses reflected the enduring influence of his uncle's *Playboy* magazines with which he'd whiled away many a happy hour in his youth. Claudia Cardinale just pipped Brigitte Bardot for top spot.

Now what? Ten policewomen you'd like to fuck? Settle down. Try "wouldn't knock back on a wet Sunday afternoon" and you could probably scrape up a few. How about ten known or suspected dykes you'd like to . . . No, I don't think so. Okay: ten women you know, or have reason to suspect, don't wear undies? Well, for a start there's . . .

A key rattled in the lock. The man who stood in the doorway was in his mid-fifties, tall and wiry with receding grey-black hair, olive skin and deep-set, unblinking black eyes in a thin, lined face.

Psycho.

Ihaka said, "What's for lunch?"

The man ignored him. He sniffed, wrinkling his nose in disgust, and produced a wide-bladed commando knife from behind his back. After he'd given Ihaka a good look at the knife, he put it away and removed the crap-bucket. He came back with a bucket of water, sluiced away what was left of the vomit, and threw the empty bucket at Ihaka.

"Who are you?"

The tall man's forehead furrowed as if he'd been asked the square root of 187 trillion. Then he casually kicked Ihaka in the stomach and walked out. He returned a few minutes later with a bottle of water and some food: a few slices of salami, a lump of cheddar cheese, buttered bread and an apple.

Ihaka said, "Pig's bum."

The tall man grinned unpleasantly, revealing uneven yellow teeth. He kicked Ihaka again — in the ribs this time and quite a lot harder — and exited, locking the door.

Ihaka looked at the food: all of a sudden, he wasn't that hungry. The fact that the mute with the cut-throat eyes had showed his face meant that they were going to kill him. It was just a matter of time.

The words every journalist dreads hearing are: 'There's someone out here who wants to talk to you.'

Members of the public who hawk their wares around newsrooms generally fall into one of two categories: those who've been gang-banged by little green men from the planet Zorb and those who think their petty obsessions — the wrangle with the gas company over the sum of $28.76, for instance — are of cosmic significance.

For female journalists, particularly those who appear on TV or have picture by-lines, there's the third category: the admirer.

The admirer is almost never a well-adjusted hunk with a fascinating past and more frequent flyer points than the Duchess of York. He's more likely to live with his mother and wear woolly orange socks with leather sandals; or to belong to a cult which worships the midget from *Fantasy Island*; or to smell like a badger and break out in medieval skin disorders at full moon; or to have the world's largest private collection of ladies' bicycle seats.

Most of them will get a hearing, though, on the same basis that people buy lottery tickets: sooner or later someone will walk in off the street with an earth-shattering story. Maybe this one is the one; maybe this guy isn't a loony; maybe he really did see Lord Lucan roller-skating along King Edward Parade.

Thus Amanda Hayhoe was wary when she got the call to say there was a man in reception waiting to see her. His name meant nothing so she asked the receptionist to find out what it was about. Answer: Detective Sergeant Ihaka.

"What about him?"

Another hiatus. The receptionist came back on the line: "He said, 'What sort of question is that? I thought she was a journalist.'"

Hayhoe said, "I'll come down."

At first sight, Duane Ricketts seemed normal. They sat on a settee in the reception area.

"Okay," she said briskly, "what about Ihaka?"

"I'm trying to find him; I was hoping you could help me."

"Don't you think you should leave that to the police?"

"There's nothing I'd like more."

"So what's stopping you?"

Ricketts didn't answer straight away. "Ihaka's a mate of mine. More to the point, a senior cop came round to my place last night to ask me to have a crack at finding him. That's what I do for a living, by the way — I find people. He thinks the task force is barking up the wrong tree. He gave me some background on the APA, which is how I got on to you."

Hayhoe couldn't believe her ears. "Are you telling me that a senior police officer thinks the task force doesn't know what it's doing?"

"Put it this way: they're working on the assumption that the APA are a bunch of radical Maoris; he doesn't share that view."

"Jesus, this is all pretty . . . irregular, isn't it?"

"You can say that again. His arse is hanging out, big time. Keep that in mind."

"What's that supposed to mean?"

"It means that if word gets out, he'll be in deep shit."

"Well, excuse me," snapped Hayhoe. "I don't remember asking you to come in here and tell me about it. And in case you've forgotten, I do happen to be a journalist."

"I haven't forgotten," said Ricketts mildly. "I haven't forgotten Ihaka either."

They locked eyes for a few seconds.

Ricketts said, "I told you about it because I'm asking you for help and I figured you were entitled to know the background. But if I'd thought it was going to cost the guy his job, I wouldn't have told you, would I?"

Hayhoe was sure she'd find a flaw in his logic when she got round to putting her mind to it. "Well, I'm not making any promises. Anyway, what makes you think I can help?"

"I had to start somewhere. And I was intrigued that you bobbed up in both of Ihaka's recent cases."

"What do you mean, both? What's the other one?"

"A guy called Mules was murdered last weekend. Ihaka reckoned he was black-mailing a Mrs Trousdale over her sex life — which apparently you featured in."

The ghost of a smile that flitted across Ricketts' face only added to Hayhoe's fury: "Where the fucking hell did you get that from?"

"I told you, the cop filled me in on what Ihaka was working on. Relax — I can keep a secret. I'm sure you can too."

Hayhoe's eyes flashed dangerously. "You're pushing your luck, buster."

Ricketts smiled.

It was a nice enough smile, as smiles went, but Hayhoe was in no mood to be charmed. "Look, I'm flat stick right now, doing a story on the APA as it happens, so could you get on with it? Whatever it is."

The smile vanished. "Why do you think the APA left those communiqués on your car?"

She shrugged impatiently. "Ihaka asked me that. I didn't have a clue then, still don't."

"How long have you been chasing the APA story?"

She frowned: "Since Freckleton. Why?"

"What've you come up with?"

"How do you mean?"

"Ihaka seemed to think you were pretty smart. I just thought that if you'd been on it since the start, you might have some bright ideas."

That doesn't sound like Ihaka. "When did he say that?"

"In his notes. He did add 'for a TV reporter' but hey, a compliment's a compliment — especially from him."

Hayhoe started to say something, then stopped. "The cop who came to see you — he doesn't think they'll find Ihaka?"

Ricketts shook his head slowly. "The way he sees it, I've got forty-eight to seventy-two hours. After that, he's history."

Hayhoe didn't want to seem callous, but she had her own problems: she was under big pressure to come up with something new, break a major story, scoop all-comers. She had her hunch but standing it up wasn't going to be easy . . .

Brainwave: why not do a deal with Ricketts? Use him — wind him up and let him go, see what happens. You've got nothing to lose. Ihaka's got even less.

She said, "This has got to be a two-way street: I get something in return."

"What?"

"Everything you pick up, you pass on to me, right? And I mean everything, whether it's from following my lead or not."

"So you can put it on TV?"

"If it's any good, you bet. It won't go to air until the weekend after this at the earliest. If your cop friend's right, by then it won't matter either way."

Ricketts nodded. "True."

"So, do we have a deal?"

"We do." He put out his right hand. Hayhoe thought a handshake was overdoing things but she went along with it.

"Okay," she said. "Can you find out if the cops found any floppy discs at Jackson Pike's place and, if so, what was on them?"

"Yep."

"What about what was on his home computer's hard drive?"

"Yep." After a pause: "Did you say something about a two-way street?"

Hayhoe finally smiled. "Have you heard of a guy called Serge Le Droff?"

23

Duane Ricketts: closing in on forty, unattached, looking like staying that way.

It wasn't that he was under-powered in the sex drive department or quirky — at least, not according to late twentieth-century sexual etiquette. But he was choosy. Contrary to the usual trend and, perhaps, common sense, the older he got, the choosier he became. These days, he just never seemed to meet suitable women.

Instead he met: wives who gave him the eye while hubby wrote the cheque; solo mothers floundering in cask wine and self-pity, looking for a saviour or someone to take down with them; lady lawyers whose wish lists didn't stretch to a man with a past but without a degree, a man who only knew three types of pasta and fell asleep during *The Piano*; law firm secretarial chicks.

Holy shit.

Last summer, he'd gone to the mat with a twenty-two-year-old secretary at Trubshaw Trimble. She made his mouth water, she wore a fake diamond in her belly button, she thought he was cool. So far, so good. And she kept it real basic. So what do you want to do, Nicole? Nicole shrugged: "Grab some Thai, check out the Empire, then go back to your place and pump it, baby — what else?" Well, if you insist. Ricketts gave it his best shot; then he gave it what he had left. Then he rolled over and went to sleep, thank you and goodnight. Nicole smoked a joint, sank a can of Beam 'n' Coke, then shook him awake: "Hey man, don't flake on me, I'm just getting warmed up." Honey, have you got a licence for that thing?

So Ricketts was sleeping solo when the bedside phone went ape at 6.57 on Friday morning. He groaned, raised his head to look at the alarm clock, which was set to go off at 7.30, groaned again, and flopped his face on the pillow, mumbling filth. A few rings later, he lunged for the receiver.

Whine: "I don't remember asking for a wake-up call."

"Have I read you wrong, Mr Ricketts?" enquired Detective Inspector Finbar McGrail. "I picked you for an early riser."

"I thought I was."

"I wanted to be sure of getting hold of you," said McGrail, as if that settled the matter. "Any progress?"

"Maybe." Ricketts sat up and shook himself awake. "I need a favour — could you run a check on one Serge Le Droff, a frog businessman resident in our fair city?" He spelt out the name and gave McGrail a taste of him.

"You think he's got something to do with it?" McGrail's politeness couldn't muffle his scepticism.

"It's clutching at straws time, right? Think of Le Droff as a straw."

"Point taken. Now then, have you got much on this morning?"

"This and that," said Ricketts unhelpfully.

"Could you pick someone up from the airport?"

"Hang on, inspector. I signed on to find Ihaka, not run a fucking limo service . . ."

McGrail cut him off but without heat: "Don't be daft, man — it's someone to watch your back."

"Oh." Ricketts knew he should have known better. "Who?"

"C. C. Hellicar."

"Jesus."

"She's on the Air New Zealand flight from Honolulu, arriving at ten past ten."

"So for once in his life Ihaka wasn't bullshitting."

"Come again?"

"He always said they started a fire."

McGrail's description was typically terse: late twenties, pale-blue eyes, short dark-blonde hair, serious accent.

Hellicar would meet her pick-up at the Air New Zealand ticket desk. Ricketts worked on half an hour to disembark, retrieve luggage and queue for immigration, but didn't allow for a closed lane on the motorway and a two-kilometre crawl. It was after eleven when he got there. A woman with a straight back and a gymnast's bum had her elbows on the counter, reading a paperback. The hair was shoulder-length, though, and more blond than dark.

The guy manning the ticket desk was standard-issue airline camp: blow-dried hair, signet ring, manicure, fluttering hands. Ricketts asked him if he'd sighted a Ms Hellicar, just in from Honolulu. The blond looked up: "I'm C. C. Hellicar." Butter-wouldn't-melt drawl.

Check those eyes.

Hellicar was tall, maybe 170 centimetres, long-legged, square-shouldered. She had great cheekbones and wore black jeans, a denim shirt over a white T-shirt, and canvas sneakers.

"McGrail said you had short hair."

"It grew." Not rude, just jet-lagged into indifference.

He offered his right hand: "Duane Ricketts."

She goggled: "The dope fiend?"

Now that's rude.

Ricketts froze for a couple of seconds, then let his hand drop. "Nice to meet you too." He picked up her large metal suitcase, felt his testicles retract, and looked around for a trolley.

"Leave it," she said. "I can carry it."

He put it down. "That makes one of us."

They exited the terminal. He asked: "What was that in aid of?"

"Dope fiend? That's a direct quote from Tito," she replied coolly. "You ought to know I seriously disapprove of that shit."

Ricketts stopped dead and gave her what was intended to be a cold stare. The one she sent back was the real McCoy. He did an eyes front and kept walking. When they reached his car, he flipped open the boot and stood aside as she heaved the suitcase in.

He eyed her across the roof as he unlocked the car: "Seeing we're going to be working together, can I make a suggestion? If you find yourself disapproving of me, try minding your own business. It works for most people."

She drilled him with another ice-coated laser beam: "Well, excuse me all to hell. You want to screw around with hard drugs, don't expect folks to pat you on the back."

They got into the car.

He said, "Once upon a time" — laying it on — "I smoked half a heroin cigarette. It ended up costing me fifteen grand and three weeks in a Bangkok piss-tank. Isn't that enough for you?"

"I don't enter into it. The point is, it obviously wasn't enough to put you off."

"What are you talking about?"

She sniffed contemptuously. "You know goddamn well — that big mess of coke you and the rest of that trash were panting after."

Ricketts frowned. "Didn't Ihaka tell you what happened?"

"I haven't been in contact with Tito since the day I flew out of here."

"Not even a postcard?"

"You do the job, you move on." She looked straight ahead. "Besides, he didn't strike me as one of nature's pen pals."

"Now you're back — so what's changed?"

"A shitload." Read: mind your own business. "Did my ears deceive me back there or did you mention us working together?" The honeyed accent somehow added sting to the implication that the prospect made her skin crawl.

McGrail had obviously told her the bare minimum, which didn't include a character reference.

"Guess whose back you get to watch?"

She raised her eyebrows: "You're the one's going to find him?"

"I'm going to try."

Neither spoke till they hit Mangere Bridge. "I've got to tell you" — shaking her head — "this is a real kicker."

Ricketts said nothing, kept his eyes on the road.

"I have this very clear recollection: we're driving back from Tito's beach house and he's cussing you out . . . goddamn, I ain't heard nothing like it, ever. Where it all led to was, once you were behind bars, he was going to induce the biggest, ugliest, meanest dudes in the joint to . . . well, I guess you can figure it out."

Playing dumb: "No, what?"

"You know . . ."

He shook his head.

Hellicar gave him a look, not sure if he was for real. "Hose you," she said eventually. "Often."

"Oh, I get it: the old prison diet — pork every day and twice on Sundays. And you approved of that?"

"It seemed reasonable at the time." She giggled like a schoolgirl. "But seeing as how you and McGrail are holding hands these days, I've got to assume you walked? Picked your moment and cut a deal, huh?"

"Something like that."

"That figures. I have to admit, in between the many less flattering comments, Tito did concede you were smart."

Ricketts remembered the lie he'd told Amanda Hayhoe. "Let's hope he's right."

Coming down Manukau Road, he asked her where she was staying. McGrail had booked her into the Centra.

"Who's picking up the tab, if it's not a rude question?"

"Me so far," she said, "but the inspector said he'd fix it."

"Is that right?" By reputation, McGrail was as tight as a bull's arse in fly season.

"Why, would that be a problem for him?"

"He's got a young family; I doubt he's rolling in dough."

She shrugged. "It's no big thing."

"Why waste money — yours or his — on a hotel? I've got a spare room. I've got a spare bathroom, come to that."

She thought about it. "Makes sense, I guess, seeing as the reason I'm here is to wet nurse you. And if it turns out you ain't a gentleman — well, I can't get too shook up over a guy who can hardly budge my suitcase."

By the time they got to Rickett's place, Hellicar was fading fast. First, though, she wanted to hear what they were up against. He told her about the Aotearoa People's Army and McGrail's doubts about the investigation.

She said: "Let's say he's right and this-all ain't about the natives getting restless: what percentage of the population does that eliminate?"

"Talking about the real hot-heads? Depends on who you believe."

"Just roughly."

"Less than one per cent."

Hellicar went, "Uh huh. Well, it's a start."

"This guy interests me." He showed her the material on Serge Le Droff, the spoils of his horse-trading with Amanda Hayhoe.

She skim-read it. "Well, there's no denying he's interesting — unusual even — but it sure doesn't read like the profile of a left-wing terrorist."

"There's more." He covered the Mules case and the Jackson Pike–D'Arcy Potterton connection.

Hellicar rubbed red-rimmed eyes. "So not long after they got together, the writer gets whacked in a hunting accident — by someone who just happens to work on this boy's farm — and the editor has his neck broke by the APA. That the way it was?"

"Yep."

"Shit, I can't make head nor tail of that."

"Let's call it a coincidence. Here's another: on Tuesday afternoon, Ihaka goes to see Le Droff about Mules and the blackmail; that night, the APA grabs him."

Hellicar nodded thoughtfully. "That's a little better."

She went to get a sweatshirt. "You wouldn't have a gun by any chance?" she called out, "because I don't."

"No. What did you do last time?"

"Last time, I was on assignment — from DC with love; my piece came in the diplomatic bag."

"I'll mention it to Uncle Finbar."

She came back into the living room yawning like a big dog.

Ricketts stood up. "Why don't you get some sleep?"

"I could use some — we flew out of Honolulu at 1 o'clock in the morning and I don't sleep on planes the way I used to. What about you?"

"I've got some things to do, but I should be safe enough in the Land Titles Office."

As he was showing her around, he asked how she'd managed to make it at such short notice.

"There was nothing much to stop me."

"How come?"

She got sombre. "I was in your shoes, I wouldn't want to know."

It was shaping up to be one of Amanda Hayhoe's better days.

In the morning, she persuaded Belinda Potterton to talk on camera about her brother and Jackson Pike. Then she took a camera crew over to Takapuna to film Garth Grimes' eulogy to the late editor. She also extracted an unadulterated version of why he'd put Pike onto D'Arcy Potterton in the first place. As she'd expected, the old perv proved to be great talent.

In the afternoon, she and the crew went to the *New Nation* office for some footage and a few 'the Jackson Pike I remember' sound bites. Afterwards, she had a coffee with Justin Hinshelwood, the staff writer.

Hinshelwood bolted his and ordered another. He was acting like a man with something he wanted to get off his chest. When he'd made a start on the second cup, he got to it: "You know something? I feel like shit every time I hear his name."

"Pike's?"

He nodded. "I didn't tell you this, but Pike and I had a huge falling out. In fact, we weren't on speaking terms when he was murdered."

"What happened?"

Hinshelwood squinted anxiously: "This is between you and me, right? I mean, you're not going to use it?"

Hayhoe sighed and gave a smile which was both reassuring and gently reproachful. She said nothing.

"A few months ago, he got me to do a story on the tenth anniversary of the *Rainbow Warrior*. I threw a tantrumette — I mean, when it reaches the stage of *Rainbow Warrior, The Musical*, it's a pretty good sign there's not much flesh left on the carcass, wouldn't you agree? It didn't get me anywhere. So I rocked up to the *Sunday Star* — we've got access to their clippings library — pulled out the files, and did what I thought was a reasonably comprehensive overview. A cut and paste job, in other words. Well, Pike spiked it — with extreme prejudice." Hinshelwood put on a grating voice; Hayhoe assumed he was mimicking the dead editor: "'No self-respecting cadet reporter on the suburban free-sheet would submit this sort of crap; I should've known that if I want something done properly, I have to do it myself.' Et cetera, ad nauseam. Not long after that, he swanned off to Europe for a couple of months. While he was away, I did a piece on Ron Rangi . . ."

"Who?"

"An All Black in the sixties — a rough-round-the-edges Maori boy. He blotted his copybook: it was real so-what stuff, you know, routine rugby boofhead carry-on, but they sent him to Coventry on a slow train. He hit the skids, died a semi-derelict at the ripe old age of forty-seven. It was a bloody good read if I say so myself — pissed all over the usual sports profile hero-gram. When Pike got back, he pulled it on the grounds of who gives a fuck? It was obviously meant to teach me a lesson: this is what happens when you take short cuts on my story ideas. I thought it was vindictive, not to mention unprofessional. It was our last conversation, if you could call it that. The very last thing I ever said to him was, 'You wouldn't know a decent story if it shat on your lap.'"

Back at TVNZ, Hayhoe got a call from Ricketts. He was keeping his end of the bargain, letting her know that the cops hadn't found any floppy discs at Pike's place. He'd seen a police summary of what was on the home computer's hard drive: it was innocuous stuff, mostly admin — budgets, staff files, planning for upcoming issues. Nothing to die for.

She tried the *Sunday Star* clippings library but they'd knocked off for the day.

Ricketts got home just after six. Hellicar, in bicycle pants and a *Pulp Fiction* T-shirt, was exercising on the living room floor. The T-shirt featured Samuel L. Jackson doing his bad motherfucker thing, about to blast someone into baby food. The caption read, "And you will know my name is the Lord when I lay my vengeance upon you."

He asked how she was feeling: a little fuzzy. She followed him into the kitchen, wanting to hear his news.

Ricketts leaned against the bench and popped a beer. "You know that stuff on Le Droff mentioned he had a yacht moored at Westhaven Marina? I got his mooring from the boating register and went and had a look at it. I got chatting to this old guy mucking around on the boat on the next mooring; turned out he's retired and goes down there most afternoons. I asked him how much use *Lady Penelope* got. He said about every second weekend but funny you should ask: just this week, he'd gone down first thing one morning and it wasn't there. When he went back after lunch, it was."

He paused to sip his beer.

She said: "You're going to tell me that when you jogged that old boy's memory, it transpired that it was Wednesday morning? Am I right?"

Rickets grinned. "I didn't have to jog his memory. He plays in a golf four at Devonport every Wednesday and sometimes drops in at the marina on his way over. It's the only time he's ever there in the morning."

"You're thinking maybe they put Tito on the yacht and took him over to that island?"

He got a map of the Hauraki Gulf from his work-room and spread it out on the bench. "I did a search at the Land Titles Office." He put his finger on a small bay on the eastern side of Waiheke. "Le Droff's place is here, Sutcliffes Bay — he owns the whole bay. This is the unfashionable end of the island: it's pretty rugged, access by water or four-wheel-drive. This time of year, there'd be hardly anyone around anyway. It's a big, old house, built in 1905, so there'd be a few nooks and crannies to stash someone away — even a lard like Ihaka."

"You've been a busy boy."

"One other thing . . ."

"You do keep saying that."

"A friend of mine lives over there. This afternoon, he took his Pajero down that end of the island and got up on top of a hill with a pair of binoculars. He didn't see anyone but there was smoke coming from the chimney."

"You talked to McGrail about this guy?"

Ricketts nodded. "As far as the cops are concerned, he's a model citizen."

"What does he think?"

"Same as you: Le Droff's interesting but there's nothing to justify kicking down his door. He's also rich, which tends to make cops tread extra-carefully."

"He's getting more interesting all the time. It might be worth a call to the States."

Ricketts pointed to the phone. "Help yourself."

He had a shower and was watching the news when she came through from the kitchen.

"That was my old boss in Phoenix. He's going to call round a few of his buddies inside the company, see if any of them have heard of Le Droff."

"The company?"

"The C . . . I . . . A."

"Oh, that company."

"No harm in trying. This boy's been around — hustling God knows what in the Middle East, getting himself named in that report. He'll get back to me in the morning. So what now?"

"Well, thought we could go out, have dinner somewhere . . .?"

Hellicar planted her hands on her hips. "I meant, what now in the race against time to save our friend Tito's ass?"

"I don't know about you but I plan to have a nice dinner and get a good night's sleep because tomorrow we have to go exploring."

"I don't want to harp on it but, as of right now, we ain't equipped for a showdown."

"We will be by lunchtime tomorrow — Uncle Finbar's on the case."

24

Saturday came in on a warm wind, like a change of season.

Duane Ricketts and C. C. Hellicar were having breakfast on the rear deck when the phone rang. Ricketts answered and got a sagebrush twang: "How's it hanging, amigo? You got a house-guest by the name of C. C. Hellicar?"

"Hang on, I'll get her."

"Tell her Bobby G. in Phoenix has got some news for her."

Ricketts put her on, then strolled down the path to inspect his vegetable garden: it was out of control, a mission for Agent Orange.

Hellicar joined him. She zoomed in on the horticultural freak show through her Ray-bans: "Jesus, Duane, Johnny Greenfingers you ain't."

Ricketts grunted. "What'd Bobby G. have to say?"

"Just that Le Droff used to be a spook."

"A what?"

"A French intelligence agent. That middleman stuff — pushing hardware to the rag-heads — was a cover: he was really working for DGSE. It explains why his name disappeared from the congressional report: Langley would've slipped word to the committee that old Serge was fighting the good fight for Christianity and cheap oil."

"What did he actually do?"

She shrugged. "The usual. The French are forever playing spook games in the sub-Sahara, places like Chad and Guinea. I never met anyone could explain exactly what the point of it all was, aside from the fact it pissed Gaddafi off, which made it just dandy as far as Uncle Sam was concerned."

"How'd he rate?"

"Not bad," she nodded. "Smart, capable, played hardball when he had to."

"Now he's retired — you're two of a kind."

"Ain't we just?" said Hellicar sardonically. "A couple of ex-spooks living the good life in well-earned retirement. It kind of makes sense him coming all the way down here, though: you don't put in ten years' field-work in camel country without getting on a few hit-lists."

"Why would a retired French . . ."

"Intelligence agent be tied up with a way-out terrorist outfit? You got me. It's hard enough to figure a big-shot businessman moonlighting as a left-wing terrorist without adding the fact he used to be a spy. The French secret service culture is hard-line right-wing — okay, tell me one that ain't — but, boy, they are out there. On top of that, his family background's ultra-conservative."

"Sounds to me like you think we're sniffing the wrong lamppost?"

"Shit, who knows? I sure hope you've got a Plan B, though."

At 10 o'clock that morning, Amanda Hayhoe rang the *Sunday Star-Times'* head librarian to ask if Jackson Pike had used the library in the few months prior to his death.

"Yes, I think he came in not so very long ago, the poor man." The head librarian sounded middle-aged and gentle.

"Do you remember what he was researching?"

"I wouldn't have the foggiest, dear, but Amy might. She was a friend of his, she always looked after him when he dropped in."

Amy came on the line, saying she was more of a friend of Pike's ex-wife, the first one that was. Not that she had anything against the guy but then she'd never been married to him. Hayhoe asked which files he had used.

"All the old *Rainbow Warrior* stuff."

"Anything in particular?"

"It was to do with the tenth anniversary. I remember him saying he might end up with egg on his face because he'd bawled out one of his writers . . ."

"Justin Hinshelwood?"

"That's right. Justin had been in a couple of weeks earlier: spitting tacks he was too — he didn't want a bar of it."

"So Pike went through the files. Then what?"

"Then he went away happy."

"Why?"

"Oh, he'd found an angle. That was Jackson: if there was something there, he'd find it."

"Did he say what it was?"

"No offence, but that's a pretty silly question."

"I work for TV, remember? They're always telling us: don't be afraid to ask the dumb questions."

Amy laughed. "A few of your colleagues deserve VCs. No, all he said was something like, if you dig deep enough, you'll always find a nugget."

Hayhoe asked if she could come over and dig through the *Rainbow Warrior* files. Amy couldn't see why not — no one else was likely to want them.

The man who ignored the doorbell to pound on Ricketts' front door was tall, thin, mid-thirties. He had blond hair, greasy and pony-tailed, a wedge of white fluff hanging off his lower lip and tattooed forearms. He wore ear-studs, wrap-around sunglasses, cowboy boots, black gloves, too-tight jeans, and a white T-shirt which read, "Nuke the Whales". He had a big gym bag, the sort pro tennis players use, slung over his shoulder.

Rickett's take: low-life slime.

He said, "You Ricketts?"

"Yeah."

"I got something for you."

"Who are you?"

"Blair."

"Is that your first name or your second name?"

"What the fucking difference does it make?"

Ricketts shrugged. "I might want to send you a Christmas card."

He led Blair through to the rear deck, where Hellicar sat in the sun, looking good in white shorts, white polo shirt and Waikiki tan.

Ricketts told her: "This is Blair. I think he's going to solve our equipment problem."

Blair panned from Hellicar to Ricketts: "I have come to the right place? I mean, you two look like tennis-club geeks."

Hellicar hummed softly. Ricketts said, "And you look like you fuck dead cats, so what? What've you got?"

Blair showed pointy teeth. He dumped the gym bag on the jarrah table and unzipped it. "We have: one Remington semi-auto twelve-gauge shotgun, two boxes of cartridges, one Browning semi-auto handgun, and two mags — nine mil parabellum load."

Ricketts asked Hellicar, "You want to have a look?"

She checked and loaded the guns with casual assurance. "They'll do."

Blair stared at her; she smiled lazily, unreadable behind the dark glasses. He shook his head. "Weird fucking set-up, man."

He put the guns and ammunition back in the bag and zipped it up. "All yours, Ringo. I don't know what you've got in mind and I don't want to know. But should the unfortunate occur and you wind up down at Pig Central having to explain some major fucking carnage, you got this gear from a short, dark, Italian-looking dude you met in a K Road skin joint. Let's call him . . . Frank. Okay?"

Ricketts wasn't sure if he was serious. "Frank, eh?"

Blair scanned the back yard. "You know, mate, you could really do something with this place: start by ripping out the crap you got in those flowerbeds, make a nice little rose garden . . ."

Hellicar drawled, "There's a real impressive vegetable patch down yonder, beyond that tree."

"I'm a flower man myself: any retard can grow veges."

"You want to bet?"

"Well, I'll leave you kids to it," said Blair affably. "Remember: eat what you kill and vice versa."

Ricketts walked him out. Blair stopped in the doorway and turned around. "I've tagged you now — you're the guy who stitched up Bryce Spurdle."

Ricketts nodded, thinking, undercover cop.

"That was slick work. I guess you and Emmy Lou know what you're doing after all."

Hayhoe drove over to Eden Terrace. The *Sunday Star-Times* building was a three-storey box in New North Road, on the city side of the Dominion Road flyover. Amy collected her from reception and took her down to the library, which was tucked away at the back of the building, off the carpark — out of sight and out of mind, like an idiot step-child's bedroom.

The files were in ceiling-to-floor walk-in movable cabinets. Amy pulled a stack of thick manila envelopes and told Hayhoe, have fun. She found a desk in the corner and got started.

Marsden Wharf, Auckland Harbour, 10 July 1985: just before midnight, two explosions blow the arse out of Greenpeace vessel *Rainbow Warrior*, about to lead a flotilla to French Polynesia to protest nuclear testing at Mururoa Atoll. Collateral damage: one dead Portuguese photographer.

Boat-owners spending the night on their boats in Hobson Bay to deter thieves see a man pull an inflatable rubber dinghy ashore and run to a Toyota Hiace camper-van in Tamaki Drive. The dinghy gets left behind.

Suspicion falls on the crew of a New Caledonian charter yacht, the twin-masted ketch *Ouvea*, which left Auckland for Norfolk Island after the bombing. Police fly up there to interview them. The Australian attorney-general's department gives them 24 hours to issue extradition warrants, not enough time to get the results of forensic tests of suspected — later confirmed — traces of explosive in the bilges. The *Ouvea* is allowed to leave Norfolk and promptly disappears, believed scuttled.

16 July: Police detain Alain and Sophie Turenge when they drop off the Hiace at Auckland airport. They're Swiss; she's a professor, he's a manager. Well, that's their story.

The passports are false; Sophie turns out to be Captain Dominique Prieur, attached to the French Ministry of Defence, Alain is Major Alain Mafart, an officer at a training centre for DGSE frogmen. DGSE equals Directorat Général de la Sécurité Extérieure equals French intelligence.

In Paris, President Mitterrand tells his prime minister to conduct a rigorous inquiry, internationally recognised bureaucratese for: whitewash this shit out of my hair.

In Auckland, the evidence points to an elaborate operation by the French intelligence services. The abandoned dinghy was bought in North London by one of the *Ouvea* crew, three of whom turn out to be NCOs from the DGSE underwater combat school on Corsica. By now, they're supposedly lying low in the former French colony of Guinea.

A map found on the *Ouvea* was drawn by Frédérique Bonlieu, a dykey mademoiselle who'd shown up at Greenpeace headquarters in Auckland a few months previously with a letter of introduction from a French anti-nuclear activist. She turns out to be Christine Cabon, a French army lieutenant attached to DGSE. She sends Greenpeace a postcard from Israel.

The theory is that Prieur and Mafart collected the limpet mines off a French container ship, *Hélène Delmas*, and passed them to the *Ouvea* crew: the bombers got away clean while the support team sits in Mount Eden prison sweating on a murder/arson/conspiracy rap.

22 November: Mafart and Prieur plead guilty to manslaughter and wilful damage and are sentenced to ten years' hard time.

Conspiracy theories are dime-a-dozen.

That the British knew about it, let it happen, then tipped off New Zealand to get even with the frogs for selling Exocet missiles to Argentina during the Falklands war.

That the CIA and ASIO, Australia's spy outfit, knew in advance but didn't tell because New Zealand was out of the ANZUS information loop over its no nuke policy.

That the French did it because Greenpeace was infiltrated by the KGB, who had spies and surveillance equipment on the *Warrior*.

That the French did it because they feared the protest flotilla would trigger insurrection in French Polynesia.

That Prieur and Mafart and the *Ouvea* crews were decoys to distract attention from the real strike team.

That the French had sent a hit-team to silence Prieur and Mafart.

That it was all a plot to compromise France's intelligence apparatus, a plot to drive France out of the South Pacific, a plot to stop Gérard Depardieu from winning an Oscar.

Hayhoe rolled on.

The French defence minister resigns; the French prime minister resigns; France heavies New Zealand over butter access to Europe; the New Zealand government says no deal on Mafart and Prieur come hell or high water. The deal goes down — Mafart and Prieur are transferred to a Pacific atoll for three years; the frogs welsh — Mafart and Prieur are sprung from Club Med after less than eighteenth months.

Fuck the deal, fuck New Zealand, vive la France.

Whatever Pike found, she'd missed it. She started again.

She'd been skimming clippings for five hours and her brain was cutting in and out like a bad satellite feed when she found it. It was buried in the second to last paragraph of a Reuters story out of Paris, dated 8 February 1986.

This week's issue of *Paris Match* reported that an unidentified businessman living in New Zealand had collected the mines from the container ship *Hélène Delmas* and passed them to the sabotage team, a role previously thought to have been taken by Prieur and Mafart.

Now what?

A monster story was lurking out there but could she corner it and get it to air? Did she have enough time? Pike/APA — the unanswered questions: who broke into the *New Nation* office and went through the computers? What were they looking for? Why didn't the police find floppy discs at Pike's place? Bring in the bee in Pike's bonnet; bring in Potterton and Le Droff — if the lawyers would let her. Would Le Droff do an interview? Unlikely, given his publicity phobia. So what would she do for pictures? Christ, she didn't even have a proper still of him, just a two-column pic from an eight-year-old newspaper clipping.

The papers ran a lot more business news than TV did: maybe the *Sunday Star-Times* had a pic. She asked Amy, who checked the picture library: negative. Amy said the business section had its own picture library upstairs, mainly mugshots sent in by PRs.

They went up to the newsroom. Deadline fever: frazzled people in fast-forward; sub-editors raging at computer screens; reporters hunkered down behind grey partition screens, beating their keyboards like bongo drums.

The business section was deserted — they had an early deadline. Amy showed her the gun-metal filing cabinet and left her to it.

Hayhoe looked under names beginning with L and drew a blank. She tried D; strike two. The filing system was haphazard: sometimes by the person's name, sometimes by their company's. She tried E. Bingo: a paperback-size black and white print of Serge Le Droff, chairman and chief executive of Eurotours Ltd.

The photo was of a similar vintage to the one in the newspaper clipping but much better quality. Once again, Hayhoe had the nagging feeling that she'd seen the face before. She willed herself to make the connection but it was like Rubik's cube: the fragments of memory wouldn't click into place.

She wrote, 'For pic of Serge Le Droff of Eurotours, see Amy in library' on a piece of pad paper and left it in the E folder. She took the photo downstairs and asked Amy to keep it in a safe place until she'd got permission to use it.

Hayhoe drove home. Going down Ponsonby Road, she passed a liquor store advertising a French champagne special: 'Prices slashed on top brands — Veuve, Moët, Bolly'.

The memory flash hit like an electric shock.

A Saturday night in late February; a friend from her investment banking days called to invite her to a birthday party. She dragged her heels — she didn't know the people. He said they wouldn't mind: Amanda was on TV — that made her somebody. She'd never get a better chance to see how the other half lived — these people were loaded. He talked her into it.

Remuera Road: the rustle of wind in tall trees, the rustle of old money. In through big gates, down a winding drive to 700 squares of red brick and gables. Round the back, a huge patio with a harbour view and steps down to a pool, a hundred people swilling Bollinger. The host was a stockbroker whose wife and daughter shared a birthday. That explained why the guests came in two packages: young and pretty, middle-aged and well preserved.

Hayhoe spotted a couple who didn't fit in either — they were worldlier than the young crowd, sexier than the old.

The woman had striking chestnut hair; what was revealed by the plunging neckline of her caramel-coloured Donna Karan dress wasn't ho-hum either. When the woman noticed Hayhoe watching them, she smiled enigmatically and locked eyes until Amanda looked away. When she glanced back half a minute later, they were watching her. The woman still had the enigmatic smile but her green eyes glittered. The man looked amused.

Before the night was out, Hayhoe would discover that the woman's name was Rusty Trousdale and she was every bit as worldly as she looked.

The man, she now realised, was Serge Le Droff.

25

He was so clean-cut and earnest, he had to be a missionary — direct to your doorstep, all the way from Salt Lake City. Renée Adlington wasn't buying but she couldn't help feeling sorry for him: what a way to spend your Saturday afternoons.

The young man with the peaches and cream complexion and neat blond hair said, "Mrs Adlington? I'm Detective Constable Van Roon."

Adlington hadn't come that close to wetting herself in twenty-five years. Then: an unbearably hot January night in the Bay of Islands; toss the blanket, toss the sheet, strip off the shorty nightie, peel off the knickers — finally cooled down enough to sleep. She'd woken up goosebumped at first light to find a giant weta nesting in her bush.

Van Roon asked if he could come in. Adlington nodded, catching flies.

Inside, a florid heart-throb going to seed had his feet up watching TV. He saw Adlington's spooked expression and said, "Trouble at the mill?" in a Monty Python voice. Van Roon would've bet on him having a repertoire of them.

He was Henry Pye, Renée's admirer from the mature singles night. The clock had ticked down on their month-long moratorium the day before, not a moment too soon for Adlington. Pye had her pawing the carpet by portraying himself as a sex wizard who worked women over in ways Masters and Johnson hadn't documented.

As so often happens, the bigger the build-up, the bigger the let-down.

Henry had come over for an intimate dinner. He'd "had a few" at the pub with the people from work; after the lion's share of two bottles of chardonnay and a barrage of Tia Marias, his nose had more of a glow than the candles.

They'd adjourned to the bedroom. He'd promised to blast her into orbit but she never even got off the launching pad. To top it off, he had the hide to suggest that a spot of 'throat' would be just the ticket. She'd feigned ignorance and grimly fumbled between his legs: getting him to half-mast almost gave her tennis elbow.

But to hear him tell it this morning, he'd been a pork-pumping ball of fire; he'd left her chewed, screwed and unglued. She retreated to the kitchen in a daze, trying to decide if he'd had a booze black-out or was simply a shameless bullshit artist.

Van Roon introduced himself. Pye's eyebrows formed question marks. He zeroed in on Renée, mock-teasing: "What have you been up to, sauce-pot?"

She blushed beetroot. Van Roon picked up the vibes: "Would you be Mr Adlington?"

Pye leered: "No, we're just good friends, as they say."

"Well, Mrs Adlington and I have a few things to discuss if you wouldn't mind leaving us to it for an hour or so."

"I won't get in your way . . ."

Adlington said, "Henry, please." Van Roon unbuttoned his sports jacket and put his hands on his hips.

"All right, I get the message." Pye snatched his car keys and headed for the door. "You'll see me when you see me."

Van Roon asked, "May I?" before sitting down. He produced a pocket notepad and ballpoint.

"Is this something to do with Clyde Early?" she asked nervously.

"He's been in touch with us."

She blurted: "Honestly, that man — he barged in here accusing me of listening to his phone calls. I sent him away with a flea in his ear."

"Yes, he said he'd talked to you. Mrs Adlington, do you know a man called Brandon Mules?"

She screwed up her face to show she was doing her best.

"The ex-rugby player who was murdered last weekend," prompted Van Roon. "You might've seen something about it?"

"Oh, yes, I thought I'd heard the name — I saw something about it on the news."

"We think Mules was blackmailing Mr Early's friend." He paused to see if she'd caught on, but nothing moved on her face. "Obviously, him getting murdered makes it a whole new ballgame."

Bull's-eye: Adlington went toilet-bowl white. She could hear Leo lecturing her in his big-brother-knows-best voice: 'Renée, if you had any idea what the truth was . . .'

"Let's start from scratch, Mrs Adlington: did you overhear Mr Early talking to his girlfriend?"

She lowered her eyes. "I didn't mean to. I wasn't sure if he'd picked up the phone . . ."

"That's not important. What's important is whether you told anyone about it?"

"I swear I didn't tell a soul."

Van Roon no longer bore such a resemblance to the mummy's-boy hot gospellor from Squaresville, USA. He drummed his ballpoint impatiently on the notepad: "Mrs Adlington, I wonder if you realise how serious this is. It's gone way beyond your dispute with Mr Early: you're in the middle of a full-scale murder investigation. Now, if you can't convince me you've told the whole story, I'm going to have to ask you to come in to Central and go through it by the book."

"I am telling the whole story," she pleaded. "I had nothing to do with the blackmail and I'd never heard of Mules until he was on the news."

"You'd never met him, never spoken to him?"

She waggled her head. "On the Bible."

Van Roon flipped through his notepad: "What about this bloke? He'd be in his fifties, well dressed — suit, tie, cufflinks — pink complexion, a bit overweight, going bald. He goes round with a brown-leather satchel and a white raincoat — oh yeah, and he drinks top-shelf scotch. Any of that ring a bell?"

Adlington gulped air. Van Roon saw her hands shake. "No, I don't know anyone like that."

"He was seen with Mules a week ago yesterday; Mules was murdered that night. Think hard: are you absolutely sure you've got no idea who he might be?"

She clamped her hands between her legs. "Positive."

Van Roon stood up and went to the sideboard, where a set of framed colour photographs of Renée Adlington's nearest and dearest were displayed. One of them featured an owlish, middle-aged man with round, pink cheeks and thinning hair.

He took the photograph back to where Adlington sat squirming and thrust it under her nose: "So who's this joker?"

Amanda Hayhoe was hyped.

She buzzed on the story, on the implications of Rusty Trousdale's party huddle with Serge Le Droff, on the ambiguous feelings stirred by memories of the girls' night fizzle. She tore home, found the number, and made the call. Rusty answered.

"It's Amanda Hayhoe here."

Crackling silence ended by a brittle titter: "Oh dear, how embarrassing. What can I say, Amanda, except that I'm abjectly sorry? I know I should've made contact myself but to be perfectly honest, I wasn't up to it. Caspar said you took it very well."

Quedley, shit. She'd almost managed to wipe that epic fiasco from her consciousness. "Did he now? What else did he say?"

"Only that you were kind enough not to tell the world about me." She sounded on the level. Maybe Quedley had taken pity on her; maybe he really was a changed man.

"I wanted to ask you something. That guy you were with at the party was Serge Le Droff, right?"

"Well, I wasn't with him as such: I didn't arrive with him and, as you know, I didn't leave with him. But yes, that was Serge. Why?"

"Does he know who I am?"

"I beg your pardon?"

"Yes or no, Rusty." The words came out clipped. "Does Le Droff know me?"

Another silence. "Why do you ask?"

Hayhoe snapped. "Why can't I get a straight fucking answer? Is that too much to ask?"

Rusty said, "Don't get mad at me, Amanda." She made it sound like tears were just another snarl away.

Hayhoe soothed, marvelling: what a scene-player.

"This is what happened." The tremor had gone from Rusty's voice; now you hear it, now you don't. "That night at the party, I mentioned to Serge — apropos of what I'm not quite sure, general boudoir goss I suppose — that I'm partial to the occasional roll in the hay with someone of the female persuasion. Part of life's rich tapestry and all that. He was fascinated: for some reason, girl-on-girl stuff gets most men fizzing. He wanted to know if there were any women there who got me hot and bothered. That's when I saw you."

"And?"

"And I said, 'Yes, Mandy Pandy over there,' I knew you from TV, remember? I told him who you were."

"Have you talked about me with him since then?"

"God, I don't know. I couldn't swear not but I can't remember it. At the risk of getting told off again, can I ask what this is in aid of?"

Hayhoe ignored her. "Did he know you were going to . . . make a move?"

"Did he ever — he practically suggested it."

"Then surely he wanted to know what happened?"

"That's the point: he wanted a full account — anti-climaxes all round."

Hayhoe hardly heard her. She was being jolted by another memory flash: RUSTY DROPPED ME HOME THE NEXT MORNING.

"Rusty, this is important: did you tell Le Droff where I live?"

"Gosh, maybe. I mean, I might've. Come to think of it, I probably did. I drove you back to your place in the morning, didn't I, so I expect that's how I finished my report. Don't say he's been hassling you?"

"No, it's not that."

"Thank God for that. Mind you, it would be a feather in your cap: normally, Serge is the one ducking for cover. I hope I haven't put my foot in it — you haven't fallen for him, have you?"

Hayhoe couldn't help smiling: talk about a one-track mind. "No, it's not that either."

"Don't do it, darling. He's charming when he puts his mind to it but he doesn't feel a thing."

Duane Ricketts and C. C. Hellicar got the 3 o'clock ferry to Waiheke Island. Ricketts' friend "Bum" Yandall met them at the Matiatia Bay wharf. Bum had an unusual shape and a salesman's body language.

They climbed into his Pajero. Hellicar said, "It's probably one of those questions a body shouldn't ask, but how'd you get stuck with a name like Bum?"

"I'm not stuck with it." Yandall admired himself in lurid sports sunglasses in the rear-vision mirror. "Ricketts is. You can call me Derek like everyone else."

He drove through Oneroa, which swarmed with weekending yuppies and day trippers making the most of the balmy weather. They swung inland. Tarseal gave way to gravel; hillside paddocks gave way to jungly native bush.

Ricketts' mobile phone rang.

Amanda Hayhoe said, "You did give me the number."

"I'm not complaining."

"You sound like you're en route to Pluto in a concrete mixer."

"Not quite: I'm on Waiheke."

"Waiheke? Are you going to Le Droff's place?"

"Yeah. Thought I'd have a sniff around."

"This should interest you then: I've just found out that Le Droff knows who I am and where I live, and has done so for months."

Ricketts focused, made the jump: "Which could explain why you got the communiqués."

"Couldn't it just? Want to hear my latest theory? It's a real . . ."

They crested a ridge and dropped down into a hollow. Hayhoe went off air. She came back on, along with a blizzard of static, as they climbed out the other side. Ricketts said he'd call her back later.

He looked over his shoulder at Hellicar: "Le Droff just firmed in the betting."

Tito Ihaka's guts churned when he heard the key in the lock. It was too soon for room service: the psycho had only just slung him a sandwich and emptied the bucket.

The psycho stood silhouetted in the doorway. He flicked on the light and stepped deferentially aside. Serge Le Droff sauntered in, hands in pockets, a cigarette slanting from the corner of his mouth.

Ihaka gasped; he goggled; he — reflex action — scratched his balls.

Le Droff enjoyed the reaction. "Cat got your tongue, Sergeant? A simple hello would be nice."

Ihaka propped himself up on his elbows. "Where the fuck am I?"

"Let's just say you're my guest."

"Well, thanks for nothing: the service is ratshit and every time I open my mouth, Herman Munster there puts the boot in."

Le Droff blew smoke. "I gather you've made life unpleasant for him. As for conversation, you're not missing much. Pascal speaks very little English — for that matter, he's not exactly a chatterbox in French."

"Where'd you find him — the serial killers' hall of fame?"

Le Droff dropped the butt and stood on it. "You're being disrespectful to a brave man. Pascal served with distinction in the French Foreign Legion for almost three decades. He has a wide range of expertise including, as you may soon discover, interrogation."

Ihaka's colon writhed like an eel but he managed to keep his voice steady: "You mean he's a sadist?"

Pascal's ears were burning. He peered at Le Droff: "Quoi? Qu'est-ce qu'il a dit, le flic?"

Le Droff glanced at him. "Il pense que vous êtes sadique."

Pascal shrugged indifferently: "Et alors?"

Le Droff liked it: "Roughly translated, that means, you better believe it."

Ihaka lay back and stared at the ceiling. "So what's going on?"

"If I told you that, I'd have to kill you." Le Droff was laugh-a-minute.

Ihaka turned his head and beamed poison: "You're going to kill me anyway, cock-breath."

Le Droff threw his head back and hooted. "Well, now that you mention it . . ."

They were on a hilltop, 200 metres above the road. Beyond the road, the hill slid steeply down into Sutcliffes Bay, where *Lady Penelope* bobbed at anchor. A barbed-wire fence ran alongside the road and a cast-iron cattle-stop gate barred entrance to a drive which spiralled through tall pines down to the waterfront house and a few out-buildings.

Ricketts lowered the binoculars. "So there're at least two of them, assuming whoever lit the fire yesterday's still around."

"There'd be more than two, wouldn't there?" said Hellicar. "You couldn't sail that thing solo."

"Why not? People sail around the world single-handed. The old guy at the marina said *Lady Penelope* was state-of-the-art, auto-everything."

Yandall piped up: "I could find out for you."

Hellicar and Ricketts exchanged raised eyebrows. He said, "And how do you propose to do that, Bum?"

"I'm a real-estate agent, remember? I know people who'd kill for a place like that: an old four- or five-bedroom kauri house in a private bay, off the beaten track. I've got one guy who's ready to kick loose up to two-and-a-half mill for the right place."

"Get to the point, Bum."

"The point is, I can go down there, knock on the guy's door, hand over my card, and tell him if he's ever thinking about selling to give me a yell because I've got a serious buyer lined up. Shit, I do it all the time: He might say piss off, in which case we're no worse; or, when I spill the magic words 'two point five million,' he might cream his jeans. The second rule of real estate, Duane: everyone's a seller at the right price."

"What's the first?"

"Position, position, position."

"I still don't see what . . ."

"Where's the downside?" Yandall was already into his sales pitch. "He'll either shut the door in my face or he won't. If he doesn't, I'll ask for a quick look inside so I can give the client a feel for the place. Then I can have a bit of a ferret and see how the land lies."

"Can you get in that gate?" asked Hellicar.

"It's not padlocked — I checked yesterday."

Ricketts asked her what she thought.

"What I think is, a little recon wouldn't go amiss. The case against this guy still isn't exactly iron-clad — I wouldn't want to go in blazing and find him serving milk and cookies to the local orphans."

"The local orphans eat grass and shit standing up."

"You know what I mean. For all we know, he could have friends over for the weekend or there might be a posse in there. We could ride with Bum — I mean Derek: put the seat down and stretch out. If he parked between those buildings out back, they wouldn't see us coming. The alternative is, we wait till it gets dark and go in blind. Darkness works both ways: it gives us cover but they know the terrain."

Ricketts was edgy but it made sense.

"Okay, Bum, we'll do it your way. Just remember what this is all about: if you fuck up down there, you could be waving goodbye to a lot more than a commission."

"Duane, look, just relax, would you? Christ, I've been a real-estate agent for almost twenty years — I can talk my way out of anything."

Ricketts punched numbers on his mobile phone. Hellicar said, "Who is it this time?"

"Uncle Finbar."

She nodded. "Just remember to switch the goddamn thing off when you're done."

26

Serge Le Droff got down to business.

Pascal fetched a director's chair and plonked it down in the middle of the room. Le Droff sat, legs crossed. Pascal leaned against the wall, giving Tito Ihaka the evil eye.

Le Droff said, "Let's begin with an assessment of the APA investigation."

"Suck shit."

"A word of advice: don't play the hero." Le Droff's tone was almost avuncular. "If you invite Pascal to do his worst, he'll be happy to oblige. You look tough enough and that go-to-hell manner may be the real thing. On the other hand, the ones who wear their toughness on their sleeves often break like little girls. Why make it hard on yourself?"

"Why don't you make it easy?"

"How?"

"Uncuff me — I've been lying here like this for four days."

Le Droff shook his head.

"Well, what about taking one of them off? At least let me sit up."

Le Droff thought about it, shrugged, rat-tat-tatted French at Pascal. He handed over a set of keys, then held his knife under Ihaka's chin while Le Droff unlocked the ankle-cuff.

Ihaka hoisted himself into a sitting position and flexed his legs. "Shit, that's better. Tell you what, I could go a drink."

Le Droff rolled his eyes. "I should've just left it to Pascal. What do you want?"

"You got any bourbon?"

"Don't drink the stuff. There's some good cognac."

"That'll do."

Pascal was dispatched.

Ihaka asked, "Are we in Auckland?"

"You're answering the questions, Sergeant."

"How the fuck would I know what's happening? I got the shove from the task force a week ago and I've been here, chained up like a rabid dog, since Wednesday."

"What was the state of play then?"

"It was going nowhere fast — you'd know that better than anyone."

"Why was that?"

Pascal returned with a tray: Hennessey XO cognac, Pernod, a small ice

556

bucket, a jug of water, and three glasses. He mixed Pernod, ice and water in tall glasses for Le Droff and himself and poured a dollop of cognac into a brandy balloon. Ihaka gulped and felt the spirit roar through his bloodstream.

"We had no leads and no witnesses, plus we were chasing our tails because the anti-terrorism experts in the SIS had sold the government on the APA being a front for Maori extremists."

"What did the police think of that?"

Ihaka shrugged: "Some thought it made sense; others didn't like being told how to do their job by armchair experts. That shit comes and goes — you go along with it until it runs out of juice."

Le Droff sipped. "Explain."

"Until whoever's driving it loses interest or gets cold feet."

"When will that happen?"

"Yesterday. Maybe the day before."

"Why?"

"Because we would've turned over every Maori tub-thumper in the country and had fuck-all to show for it."

Le Droff smiled. "You haven't factored in the latest communiqué."

"What was that about?"

"You, of course." His superiority complex was showing.

"I can see you're dying to tell me about it."

"The communiqué announced that your abduction was retaliation for the harassment of the seventeen Maori patriots and that you'd be released if and when the government apologised and promised not to do it again." The smile became a grin; Le Droff was having fun. "I'm afraid we called you a traitor to your people — a little poetic licence."

Ihaka aped the grin: "I don't know why you're looking so pleased with yourself, Napoleon: no one's going to believe that."

"And why not?"

"One of those seventeen Maori patriots was my niece."

Le Droff's face rearranged itself. "Merde." After a few seconds, he said, "That might need some finessing. What about the Mules business?"

"What about it?"

"Just curious — I'm a bit player in the drama, after all."

"I'd say Mules had a partner and they fell out. The partner zapped him and grabbed the diary. He'll wait for the heat to die down, then put the bite on Lady Hotpants again."

"Any leads?"

"We've got a description of a guy Mules met — and had a row with — on the day of the murder." Ihaka finished his drink. "I wouldn't mind a few answers myself."

Le Droff studied him: "You want a reason, right?"

Ihaka stared back: "It'd help."

Le Droff nodded. "The condemned man's last wish — to comprehend his fate." He lit a cigarette. "First of all, I'm an officer in the Directorat Général de la Sécurité Extérieure, the French intelligence service; secondly, there's no such thing as the Aotearoa People's Army. Once you know that, it all falls into place."

Le Droff told his story as if they both had all the time in the world. Ihaka didn't complain.

France, May 1968 — revolution in the air. Students riot, workers strike, the government teeters on the brink. Knowing his family background, the DGSE approaches and recruits Le Droff.

Marseille/Corsica/French Guiana, 1969–1972 — training. He learns that the enemies of France are everywhere; he learns to be a chameleon, he learns to sense weakness, to corrupt, to seduce, to terrorise, to destroy.

He learns that the end justifies the means.

The Middle East, 1972–1983 — agent in the field. His cover: trader/middleman, seeded with DGSE money. He exhibits networking skills and entrepreneurial flair; his superiors encourage his money-making. They let him keep twenty per cent, he skims another ten; the rest goes into a slush-fund for off-the-books operations — emergencies, last-minute scrambles, the desperate, dirty jobs that no one wants to sign off on.

The seventies are good years but the eighties start badly — a few business ventures turn to shit.

Lebanon, 1983 — a dirty job: spring a hostage before his captors — the Popular Front for the Liberation of Palestine, extremist PLO splinter group — discover he's a French agent and blow France's intelligence network in the region. Le Droff's team snatches a PFLP big-wig and tortures the hostage's whereabouts out of him. The big-wig cracks just in time; he dies a few minutes later.

The end justifies the means.

Do the usual — blame it on Mossad. One slight hitch; the dead Palestinian was a Mossad mole who'd worked his way through the ranks to sit at PFLP head honcho Dr George Habash's right hand — a priceless intelligence asset. The Israelis howl for blood.

Two members of Le Droff's crew, Maronite Christians, are car-bombed into small pink pieces in Beirut. A DGSE agent is garrotted with piano wire in Nicosia. Time to get the fuck out of Dodge.

He tells his bosses he wants to quit, disappear, get rich. They offer a deal: go south but stay inside — there's work to be done down there. The money you make from here on is all yours.

Auckland, 1985 — Greenpeace prepares to lead a flotilla to French Polynesia to protest the nuclear testing at Mururoa Atoll. Paris is Paranoia City. DGSE head Admiral Pierre Lacoste revives a 1978 plan to rat-funk Greenpeace by sinking its flagship, *Rainbow Warrior*. Defence Minister Charles Hernu says GO.

Inside Service Action, DGSE's dirty tricks brigade, the plan gets a few refinements.

President Mitterrand brought communist filth into his government; President Mitterrand dumped public shit on the DGSE for poor intelligence — on the Falklands war, on the USSR, on the 1984 Libyan invasion of Chad. The refined plan: sink the *Warrior* but blow the operation — humiliate Mitterrand, force him to defend the DGSE against international criticism, maybe even bring down the government.

Three teams are assembled: the patsies, the decoys, the hit team. Target zone operation coordinator: Major Serge Le Droff.

The plan works: the *Warrior* is sunk, the police home in on the decoy team on board the *Ouvea*, the patsies get caught, the conspiracy is revealed. The louder New Zealand protests, the more intransigent France becomes. Mitterrand throws Hernu and Prime Minister Laurent Fabius to the wolves and is forced to bring right-wingers into the government. Gaullist Jacques Chirac, his arch-rival, becomes prime minister. Major Le Droff goes back to making money, in between keeping an eye on pro-independence trouble-makers in France's South Pacific colonies.

Ihaka said, "So the two we caught . . ."

"Prieur and Mafart."

". . . had nothing to do with it?"

"They were the onshore support decoy team. They never knew they were set up to be the fall guys."

"Weren't you worried they'd finger you?"

"A, they wouldn't talk; B, they didn't know I was involved — that was my precondition. They reported direct to Paris — remember they actually rang a Ministry of Defence number from their hotel?" He shook his head. "Unbelievable."

"Did you rat them?"

"I made an anonymous phone call to pass on the number of their camper-van but I think half of Auckland beat me to it. Whoever selected that pair of imbeciles did a good job."

"Did it feel good when they got put away?"

Le Droff shrugged dismissively: "Intelligence agents, even incompetents like them, understand the principle of expendability."

Cut to: *New Nation* editor Jackson Pike researching a *Rainbow Warrior* tenth anniversary story finds a reference from *Paris Match* to a New Zealand-based businessman allegedly involved in the bombing. (The leak came from inside the national gendarmerie's Sixth Section anti-subversion unit, which was monumentally hosed off with the DGSE for turning Paris into the mercenary recruitment capital of the world.)

Pike works a contact in the immigration department, gets details of French-passport-holding businessmen resident in New Zealand in 1985. He concentrates on Auckland-based ones, eliminates those not in New Zealand when the bombing took place, those who'd been in New Zealand for more than ten years, those over sixty. That leaves three names. He asks around; bad vibes spread rapidement through Auckland's tiny French community.

Le Droff alerts Paris: new president and hard-core big bang man Jacques Chirac is about to press the button at Mururoa — seriously bad timing for a new *Rainbow Warrior* scandal. Any time is a bad time for a DGSE scandal. Monitor and report.

Pike goes to France. The process of elimination has made him hot for Le Droff. He hangs out with D'Arcy Potterton, expat Kiwi writer living near Toulouse, soaks up scuttlebutt on local boy made good, Serge Le Droff. Potterton hears that Serge's borderline ga-ga old man Jean-Jacques has been known to boast about "my son the master-spy".

Humungous bingo.

Back in Auckland, Pike requests an interview with Le Droff, get's stone-walled by his security man, Colonel Wyatt Bloodsaw. Pike tells Bloodsaw, "I'm going to nail your boss."

Consult Paris: does this pest know anything about Service Action's domestic political agenda in 1985? Any airing of that could seriously compromise the DGSE.

Le Droff breaks into *New Nation*, searches Pike's office, scrolls through his computer files. No joy.

The family takes out Potterton — Pike still doesn't get the message.

Consult Paris: this is unthinkable; the story must not appear.

Think: two birds with one stone — stop Pike, deflect public/politicians' attention from Mururoa tests. Think: classic black propaganda — commit atrocities and frame the enemy. Think: the Aotearoa People's Army.

The end justifies the means.

Launch the Freckle from a high place; snap Pike's spine and burn his floppy discs; back Gundry. Put out communiqués full of red freedom-fighter mumbo-jumbo. Sit back and enjoy the fun: watch them blame the Maoris, watch Pike get lost in the confusion.

"So, pinning it on Maori radicals was the idea all along?"

"I know how the counter-intelligence mind works, Sergeant. When the

Cold War ended, your counter-intelligence people would've focused on the Maori nationalist/separatist fringe as potential subversives. I mean, let's face it, how else were they going to justify their existence? The tendency to take the perceived threat's chest-beating at face value is the counter-terrorist's occupational hazard. Eventually, your people would've convinced themselves it was only a matter of time. I simply pandered to that mind-set."

Ihaka rubbed his face. "You mean that's all it ever was — a way to stop Pike exposing you in his magazine?"

Le Droff sighed. "Haven't you understood a word I've said? This has got nothing to do with me, personally; it's about defending the integrity of the most vital elements in France's security and defence structure."

"You're fucked in the head, pal."

"How very profound. Contemplate this, Mr Small-Town Policeman: within a decade, a fascist madman will come to power in Russia; Islamic militants will complete their takeover of the Arab world and launch an undeclared war on the west; we shall enter the age of atomic and biological terrorism. America's response will be isolationism; seal the borders and retreat behind the missile shield. Without the world's policemen to maintain a semblance of order, international affairs will become chronically unstable. There will be wars involving nuclear weapons on the Eurasian land-mass, in North Asia, and on the Indian sub-continent, causing unimaginable refugee crises. The world is sliding into chaos — it may even reach this beautiful backwater. Only nations with the will and the means to defend themselves will escape it."

"So you've read Nostradamus," said Ihaka with maximum rudeness. "Big fucking deal."

Le Droff got up. "It's all very well for you," he said, quite unruffled. "You don't have to worry about the future."

"You still haven't explained why you picked on me."

"Ah, well, that's another story — you can thank Rusty Trousdale for that."

Le Droff had lied about his relationship with Rusty — there was more to it than one desk-top wham bam, although that pretty well set the tone. He would've passed a carnal-knowledge test with flying colours but there were lots of other things he didn't know about her — like the fact that she could read French.

About once a fortnight, usually after lunch, she'd show up at his office/penthouse expecting him to drop everything, including his trousers. One afternoon, before they'd had a chance to lock on, he got called down to the nineteenth floor. She was flicking through the magazines on his desk looking for something to read when she noticed a fax in the top tray. It was in French, from his brother in Levignac, reporting that D'Arcy Potterton was sniffing around asking questions, obviously on behalf of Jackson Pike. Le Droff had scrawled a reply on it and faxed it back: "On m'a dit que l'écrivain fait souvent une promenade à la Fôret de Bouconne — c'est dangereux pendant la saison de la chasse, n'est-ce pas?" I hear the writer often goes for walks in the forest — that's dangerous in hunting season, isn't it?

A week later, Potterton was shot dead while walking in the forest: a hunting accident. Rusty wrote about it in her diary.

> Freaky or what? At Serge's the other day, I saw a fax saying that D'Arcy Potterton, the writer, is stirring up trouble in France — something to do with Jackson Pike, presumably the same one who runs the mag. Confused? Moi aussi. S. wrote on the fax — a propos beats me – that DAP's hobby of going walkies in the forest is a trifle high-risk during hunting season. Hey presto, Potterton gets potted. A case of many a true word spoken in jest? I don't suppose DAP saw the funny side of it.

The affair cooled. A month later, Rusty was in her Merc with the radio on. The news was full of Pike's murder. At a slow set of traffic lights, she scribbled a diary entry.

> First Potterton, now Pike — creepy coincidence, non? Alternatively, Serge is up to something sinister. Not sour grapes, but I almost think he's capable of it — that cold, detached side to him. Maybe I'm better off out of it. I'll miss him a tad, though — on a different level than the rest. Not to mention très GIB!

The lights went green; Rusty shoved the diary in her handbag and drove to her next meals on wheels drop. She hardly glanced in her rear-vision mirror, didn't notice the blue Laser that had dogged her since she'd left home that morning.

Brandon Mules was intrigued by the diary references to Potterton and Pike. Once he'd read up on their violent deaths in the public-library reading room, he had no doubt that Le Droff was up to something sinister. He saw neon dollar signs ten metres high.

Mules rang Le Droff: "I've got the slut's diary; there's stuff in it that could cause you a fuckload of grief."

"What do you want?"

"A million dollars."

Le Droff asked for proof. They rendezvoused in Twin Oak Drive in Cornwall Park; Mules handed over photocopies. It was Friday afternoon: Le Droff said he couldn't get the money till after the weekend. Mules said, Monday — same time, same place.

Mules waited till Le Droff had gone before he walked to his car parked by the tea-rooms. He drove west out of the park, into Royal Oak, through

Onehunga and Te Papapa, then left into Great South Road, looping back around Cornwall Park. Bloodsaw and Pascal tailed him in separate cars linked by mobile phones, swapping positions every couple of minutes. Mules led them right to his lair.

They broke in that night. Pascal skewered Mules; they found the diary and trashed the place. No more Mules, no more blackmail.

Then Ihaka turned up. Le Droff was impressed at how quickly he'd got Rusty to own up to the blackmail, worried that if he kept at her, she'd start squawking Pike/Potterton.

Think: two birds with one stone. Think: stop Ihaka, tweak the APA/Maori connection by linking it to the police raids. Think: fake hostage snatch.

The end justifies the means.

Ihaka asked, "Why didn't you just whack her and be done with it?"

Le Droff dead-panned: "Exactly the question I'd expect someone in your position to ask. Whatever Rusty's vague suspicions, I very much doubt that she'd dwell on them long enough to draw any conclusions. And even if she did, I doubt she'd act on them. It may yet come to that but I'd much prefer it didn't: I have a weakness for beautiful women who don't give a damn."

Ihaka clicked his tongue. "You know your problem? You're just too soft for your own good."

Le Droff laughed: "You're quite right. I'd prefer to spare you too, Sergeant, sentimental fool that I am. Sadly, it's just not within the realms of practicality."

"Shit, don't worry about me — I can keep a secret."

Colonel Wyatt Bloodsaw, wearing dark-green corduroy trousers and a cream Pringle golf sweater, walked in.

He said to Ihaka: "Hello, old son. How's the noggin?" He noticed the cognac: "I say, jolly old XO — don't mind if I do." To Le Droff: "There's a real-estate johnny at the door; says he's got a punter ready to fork over a king's ransom for a place like this."

27

Real-estate salesman's jabber.

"As I was telling the other gentleman, I know a few people — one bloke in particular — with very deep pockets in the market for a property like this. What they're after — well, you know the story: they'd rather have their own little shelly beach down the quiet end than share half a mile of sand with the rest of the island, not to mention the ferry-fodder."

Rave on: privacy, space, houses like this, kauri timber, they did things properly in those days, cowboy builders, architects with ponytails . . . Christ, didn't the man ever stop to draw breath?

Bum Yandall was on a roll but Serge Le Droff had stopped listening. He was thinking about the ticklish state of his finances: Eurotours was cash-flow negative; the charter-airline venture was stalled; the mortgage on the penthouse was burning money like an heiress's coke habit . . . if this clown really could wheel in a serious, top-dollar buyer, it'd take the pressure off.

Le Droff said, "I'm sorry, I didn't catch your name."

"Derek Yandall, Island Realty." He dealt Le Droff a business card.

"Well, Mr Yandall, the short answer is yes, I would entertain a serious offer in that price range."

Yandall rubbed his hands together. "That's what we like to hear."

"When would your client want to inspect?"

"Just on that subject, I was wondering if it'd be convenient for me to have a quick walk-through now? Knowing this client, he'll bombard me with questions and the more I can tell him, the more fired-up he'll be."

"Go ahead. Take your time."

Le Droff had no particular reason to distrust Yandall but he was suspicious at the best of times and this was one of them. He went out onto the verandah to summon Wyatt Bloodsaw, who was practising chip shots on the lawn. After he'd instructed Bloodsaw to stick close to Yandall, he sent Pascal to scout around the back; while Pascal was at it, he could check Yandall's car for flyers, open house signs — anything to show he was who he said he was.

There was a double garage behind the house. Visitors usually parked on the turning area in front of it: not this one. Pascal set off down the shingle drive towards the guesthouse.

The drive ran between the guesthouse and a garden shed before beginning its climb up to the road. Yandall had parked there so the raiding party couldn't be seen from the house. C. C. Hellicar had circled around the shed, skirted the large vegetable garden, and come down the side of the garage; now she was in position on the far side of the house, behind a pair of immense oleanders. Duane Ricketts was behind the shed, waiting for Yandall.

The day had dwindled to a crisp, still twilight. Rickets heard someone coming and gripped the Remington tighter. The car door opened. Bum was back, in one piece. Ricketts hurried around the corner of the shed.

Jesus fuck.

Pascal was in the Pajero, going through the glove box. He saw a flicker of movement out of the corner of his eye and looked up. Ricketts froze; he held the shotgun across his body, radiating uncertainty.

He doesn't know what to do next, thought Pascal. Get on top of him before he snaps out of it.

He got out of the Pajero, waving, and walked round it. He didn't hurry, just kept coming.

Ricketts put the shotgun to his shoulder, legs braced: "Stop there."

Pascal stopped — the gap was seven metres. Ricketts told him to lie on the ground, face down.

Pascal heaved an exaggerated shrug — no speaka da lingo. He said, "Comprends pas," and took another step. Six metres.

Ricketts waggled the shotgun. "Fucking . . . get . . . down."

Pascal moved again. Five metres.

His right hand was out of sight, behind his back. A voice in Ricketts' head screamed, IF HE BLINKS, SHOOT HIM.

Pascal bared his teeth; yellow fire raged behind his deep-set black eyes. *Wild man.* SHOOT HIM NOW.

Steel glinted by Pascal's right thigh. He charged.

Ricketts squeezed and Pascal was airborne. He hung in mid-air for an instant, coming apart, like a bug exploding on a windscreen.

Ricketts pumped the shotgun and ran for cover.

Le Droff heard the shotgun blast from his study. He took a Glock 17 semi-automatic pistol from the desk drawer and went into the corridor.

Bloodsaw came out of the dining room dragging a hollering Yandall by the hair. He swung him over to Le Droff and got out of the way; the colonel didn't want exit wound splatter on his Pringle sweatshirt.

Le Droff jammed his Glock under Yandall's chin. "How many are there?"

Yandall trembled and stammered; he looked far too frightened to lie: "One."

"Who?"

"A mate of the cop's."

"Is he a cop?"

"No."

"Do the police know he's here?"

Bad shakes. "No."

Le Droff's eyes slid to Bloodsaw. "Pascal didn't have a gun."

"Rather unsporting."

Le Droff stepped back and put the Glock in Yandall's face, holding up his left hand to block head-shot blowback.

Yandall's eyes were screwed shut. He chanted, "Oh God, please God, please God."

Le Droff hesitated.

Yandall moaned, "Please don't kill me . . ."

Le Droff pistol-whipped him unconscious.

Bloodsaw raised his extraordinary eyebrows: "I'd call that hedging your bets — has it come to that?"

"Maybe. Someone certainly knows far too much about us."

"You'd better make tracks. I'll cover you and clean up here."

Le Droff rummaged in his pockets for Pascal's keys. "I'll dump Ihaka."

Drumbeat footsteps on the stairs; the cellar door wrenched open; Le Droff, galvanised, pointing a pistol and throwing Ihaka keys.

"Uncuff yourself, snap the cuff on the other wrist, throw the keys back."

Ihaka, gagged, made big eyes.

"Do it or you're dead."

Ihaka did it.

"Move."

Ihaka stood up. His legs were jelly: he took a couple of steps, lurching like an amputee.

"Up the stairs," barked Le Droff. "Move it."

Ihaka staggered up the stairs. Bloodsaw, cradling a compact black sub-machine gun, called down to him: "Get those knees moving, old son — chop, chop."

Ihaka came up through a trapdoor into the hallway. Bloodsaw grabbed him by the shoulder, spun him and sent him stumbling towards the front door.

Le Droff caught up with him. "We go down to the beach and get in the dinghy; you row us out to the yacht. Do anything I haven't told you to, I'll kill you on the spot. Go."

He pushed Ihaka out into the wide verandah and followed him down the steps to the lawn. They were halfway across the lawn when Ricketts, on his belly in the line of trees which curved from the guesthouse down to the beach, yelled: "Drop the gun." He was about twenty metres away, aiming the shotgun.

Fuck me sideways, thought Ihaka; that's Ricketts.

Le Droff pressed up close, holding the Glock to Ihaka's temple. "I don't rate the sergeant's chances in a fire-fight," he yelled back. "If I don't get him, you will." He hissed at Ihaka: "Keep moving."

Ricketts, stymied, lowered the shotgun and watched them go.

The aluminium dinghy was a couple of metres above high-water mark. Le Droff told Ihaka: "Get in the water: I get in, you get in, you row."

Ricketts was watching the beach; he didn't see Bloodsaw in the shadows of the unlit verandah.

Hellicar had slipped in the back door. She moved down the corridor as carefully as a tight-rope walker, two-handed grip on the Browning. She stepped around Yandall: he had dents in his face but his jugular pulsed.

Hellicar heard the verandah creek. She eased through the last doorway off the corridor into a sitting room with a view of the bay through french doors. A big, silver-haired man stood on the verandah, his back to the windows. He turned side-on and she saw he had a Heckler & Koch MP5 with a back-up mag scotch-taped upside down to the magazine: 80 nine-millimetre rounds, rapid-fire. Heavy duty.

Ihaka got out of the tide into the dinghy; Ricketts got to his feet and stepped out of the trees; Bloodsaw brought up the MP5.

Hellicar put four rounds through the window. The impact slammed Bloodsaw through the railing, out onto the lawn. There were three red holes in his cream sweater, a fist-sized crater behind his left ear.

Le Droff was in the bow, watching the shore. Ihaka saw him recoil at the gunshots, saw his face twitch and jump. He glanced over his shoulder; Le Droff chopped his knee with the pistol, told him: "Row, shithead."

Ihaka was in the stern: he had to row in reverse, push instead of pull, but it was only forty metres to the yacht. He brought the dinghy up alongside. Le Droff made the transfer in one smooth, gymnastic motion; Ihaka didn't.

Le Droff made Ihaka handcuff himself to the yacht's railing. Ihaka looked back: in the gloom, he could make out two figurers on the lawn. One was Ricketts.

There, in front of the house: someone down. It had to be Bloodsaw — the other guy must've popped him.

The other guy took off his black baseball cap and shook loose shoulder-length blond hair.

Shit, that's a woman. It couldn't be her, surely to Christ . . .

Le Droff auto-raised the anchor and started the engine. *Lady Penelope* chugged out of Sutcliffes Bay.

It was blowing a nor-wester, about 15 knots. Once they'd cleared the bay, Le Droff press-buttoned up the mainsail, cut the engine, and pointed *Lady Penelope* north, out into the gulf.

He removed the gag. Ihaka said, "We going fishing?"

Le Droff sat across the cockpit from him, one hand on the tiller. "Think of it as a cruise." He was his old, coolly ironic self again.

"Where to?"

"New Caledonia's nice this time of year."

"You're dreaming, pal. You won't get as far as Kawau."

Le Droff started to say something confident, then thought of Yandall: that dogshit real-estate agent probably lied about the police too.

They crossed Man o' War Bay. Night fell, so did the temperature. Le Droff went below and came back up wearing a three-quarter length oil-skin. He tossed one to Ihaka, who pulled it over his shoulders as best he could.

Off Kauri Point, Ihaka sat up straight, cocking his head.

From behind the dark hills away to their left came a faint thump-thump-thump of rotor blades. The sound got steadily louder until blinking lights appeared over the Waiheke skyline. A searchlight blazed; the helicopter went into a left-hand swoop and came pounding over the water, straight at them. Then it was overhead and blinding light strafed the yacht. A loud-hailer boomed: "*Lady Penelope*, this is the police. Turn around and return to Sutcliffes Bay, otherwise you will be intercepted and boarded. I repeat, this is the police: alter course to return to Sutcliffes Bay. Signal your compliance immediately."

Le Droff stood up, waving. The searchlight dimmed and the helicopter backed up. He tacked and the yacht swung through 180 degrees.

Ihaka taunted him: "You're not giving up that easily, are you? Why don't you swim for it? You could hide out on Ponui and fuck donkeys."

Le Droff shook his head. "As appealing as that sounds, it's simply not practical — I sail a lot better than I swim."

He ejected the Glock's magazine and flipped it overboard. He wiped off the gun and tossed it to Ihaka, followed by the keys to the handcuffs. "I surrender into your custody, Sergeant. For your information, the pistol's never been fired in anger."

Ihaka uncuffed himself: he was going to live after all. Just when he'd convinced himself that being dead wasn't as bad as it was made out to be.

He pulled on the oil-skin, eyeing Le Droff suspiciously: he was a fucking sight too relaxed for a man staring down the barrel of humiliation, disgrace, and twenty-five years' wear and tear on the chocolate speedway.

"You don't seem too worried."

"Why should I be? My conscience is clear; I've got nothing to answer for."

Ihaka did a silent-movie double-take: "Well, there're a few what we law-enforcement types call technicalities — to wit: five murders and an abduction."

The superior-being expression was back on Le Droff's face. "Not my doing."

"That's not quite what you just told me."

"You're imagining things, Sergeant. If not, produce my signed confession."

Ihaka's eyes slitted: "You're fucked. There's no way you're going to weasel out of this."

"I can see I'll have to be more careful what I say to you — you're obviously prone to getting the wrong end of the stick."

"No jury will believe I made it up — all that stuff about the *Rainbow Warrior* and your spy games in the Middle East."

"The Middle East was long ago and far away. As for the *Rainbow Warrior*, it sounds to me as if my employees told you some tall stories while I was in town working my derrière off. Should I say, my late employees — I don't think Pascal will be telling any more tales either."

"Oh, I get the idea — blame the dead."

Le Droff chuckled. "Succinctly put."

"Prieur and Mafart all over again, eh? Did the loyal dogsbodies know they were being set up?"

"That scarcely matters now, does it?"

"You had a fall-back rigged up all along, right?"

Le Droff oozed smugness: "One thing about intelligence work, it teaches you to plan for contingencies."

Ihaka stood up, stretching and flexing. "I've got to hand it to you — you're a smooth operator."

Le Droff's grin gleamed. "You don't know the half of it."

The chopper had dropped further back; its dimmed searchlight illuminated the white bubble in the yacht's wake.

Le Droff stared into the night, whistling softly. Ihaka shrugged off his oil-skin and swung. Le Droff glanced up, turning his face into the punch. It hit like a wrecking ball: the shock ran up Ihaka's arm to jangle nerves deep in the socket. Le Droff slumped, his head flopping. Ihaka hauled him upright and shook him to and fro, as if they were wrestling. The searchlight was cranked up to high beam again; when it flooded over them, Ihaka sucked air and rolled overboard with Le Droff hugged to his chest.

The sea was breathtakingly cold but that was okay: he was built for it.

He was going to be down there a while but that was okay too: he'd been diving for crays and shellfish without a tank since he was a kid. What's more, he'd never smoked, not even a puff on one of his old man's Cuban cigars.

Ihaka had a very efficient set of lungs.

Epilogue

On Sunday morning, Detective Constable Johan Van Roon flew to Nelson. A local cop picked him up from the airport and drove him out to Honeymoon Bay to see Leo Strange.

Strange had his story worked out: his sister, Renée, had told him about the Clyde Early/Mrs Trousdale affair. He was in the information business: knowledge was power and power was money. Put together adultery, the Trousdale fortune and Early's high profile, and it spelt opportunity. He'd hired Brandon Mules to get proof. When he realised that Mules had his own, shady agenda, he'd baled out. Next thing he knew, Mules was dead.

As far as Strange was concerned, it was just a speculative venture which hadn't paid off: you win some; you lose some.

Van Roon asked, "How much did you pay Mules?"

"Five thousand."

The policeman whistled. "Where did the money come from?"

"Out of my own pocket or, to be precise, out of a safety-deposit box at an offshore bank — my special projects fund." Strange smiled ingratiatingly. "I assume you have a reciprocal arrangement with Inland Revenue — they tell you nothing and vice versa?"

Van Roon ignored the feeler. "Mr Strange, can you explain to me exactly how you expected to make a profit on that five grand without breaking the law?"

Strange got pinker. "I don't pretend to be a saint, Detective Constable, but I can assure you I am not a criminal. The scenario I had in mind was this: I believe the Trousdale marriage was ill-advised and I don't expect it to last. Given what's at stake, I'd expect the break-up and settlement to be contentious, to put it mildly. Had things gone to plan, I would've been in the position to provide Mr Trousdale with information which might've given him some, shall we say, leverage in the negotiations."

Van Roon saw no reason to go on being polite to Strange: "Some people would call you a parasite."

Strange could handle that: "I've been called worse."

With both the blackmailer and the blackmailer's killers dead, there was no interest in prolonging the investigation by pursuing Strange on comparatively minor and probably unprovable charges.

Case closed.

On Monday morning, the police team searching Serge Le Droff's Waiheke Island home found an envelope Sellotaped to the back of a drawer in the bedroom used by Pascal. It contained Pascal's account, typed in slang-ridden, un-grammatical Corsican-French, of how he and Wyatt Bloodsaw had planned and carried out four murders and an abduction in the guise of the Aotearoa People's Army. According to the document, Pascal belonged to a French neo-fascist secret society, Les Fils de Charlemagne. The Sons of Charlemagne's sacred mission was to "cleanse" France of foreigners, whom Pascal lumped together with the roughly translated heading "sand niggers". They were also big on the need to preserve France's empire, as they characterised the motley handful of overseas territories. The Sons were convinced that New Zealand was hell-bent on driving France out of the South Pacific; the long-running anti-nuclear-testing campaign was just part of that master plan.

The APA was intended as a pay-back and a warning that two could play the destabilisation game. The Sons of Charlemagne's leadership in France had devised the strategy; the tactics and implementation had been left to Pascal. He'd enlisted his fellow employee, Bloodsaw, as advisor, back-up and wordsmith.

It transpired that after each APA operation, US$10,000 had been deposited by electronic transfer into Bloodsaw's account at the National Westminster Bank in the Haymarket, London. The money trail was traced back to the Union Bank of Switzerland in Zurich and thence to a nominee company in Vanuatu. The nominee company's directors, two partners in a local law firm, declined to reveal whose nominees they were.

That afternoon, Tito Ihaka and Duane Ricketts recorded an exclusive interview with Amanda Hayhoe. Ihaka and C. C. Hellicar then headed north, to his family's beach house at Tauranga Bay, on the south head of Whangaroa Harbour.

They had supper on the deck. Afterwards, Hellicar put on a Lloyd Cole tape and shimmied over to Ihaka. She draped her arms around his neck and got in close.

"Okay, big boy, where were we before we were so rudely interrupted?"

Ihaka got instant, jumbo tumescence.

She looked up at him, wide-eyed: "Goddamn, you really are pleased to see me."

After being heavily promoted all week, Amanda Hayhoe's story went to air on Sunday night. It created a predictable sensation.

The next day, the French Embassy in Wellington issued a press release.

> The Government of France wishes to make the following points
> in response to last night's *60 Minutes* programme concerning the
> so-called Aotearoa People's Army:

1. Serge Le Droff resigned from the Directorat Générale de la Sécurité Extérieure (DGSE) in 1983.

2. In December 1984, M. Le Droff was asked to cooperate with an internal investigation into possible misuse of DGSE funds entrusted to agents stationed abroad during the 1970s. He refused. The investigation subsequently uncovered evidence which suggested that M. Le Droff had diverted DGSE funds into his private business ventures. In May 1985, M. Le Droff was advised of the investigation's provisional conclusions and invited to respond. He declined to do so. There has been no contact between M. Le Droff and any agency of the French Government since that time.

3. The dispute between France and New Zealand arising from the sinking of the Greenpeace vessel *Rainbow Warrior* was resolved by arbitration in 1986. Under the terms of the settlement, France paid New Zealand substantial compensation. It is the French Government's view that dubious rehashes of that regrettable incident do not serve any useful purpose nor are they conducive to friendly and productive relations between the two countries.

4. The French Minister of the Interior has asked the New Zealand Minister of Police to pass on any information obtained by the New Zealand authorities relating to an organisation called Les Fils de Charlemagne. While the organisation is not known to France's law-enforcement agencies, the French Government undertakes to fully investigate any firm evidence linking Les Fils de Charlemagne to the Aotearoa People's Army.

5. The French embassy has asked the relevant New Zealand authorities for a full account of the circumstances surrounding the recent deaths of French citizens Serge Le Droff and Pascal Borgo.

Naturally, the Government of France deplores the criminal acts committed in the name of the Aotearoa People's Army and extends its sympathy to the victims' families.

Late on the morning of the first Monday in December, Caspar Quedley was sitting at the dining-room table in his Cambridge cottage working on a business plan for the new public-relations consultancy he aimed to set up in the new year.

Quedley had regained weight and cut back his facial hair to a neatly trimmed moustache and Van Dyk beard. He felt that the moustache/beard set, together with his roughened-up good looks and longish, grey-flecked hair, gave him the air of a well-bred if somewhat jaded pervert in an arty continental film. It was an image to which he'd long aspired.

There was a knock at the door. His visitor was a plump, owlish, middle-aged man wearing a navy-blue linen suit and a white panama hat. He removed the hat and said, "Good morning, Mr Quedley."

Quedley said hello.

The visitor put out his right hand. "This is a real pleasure. If I may so, sir, you're a legend in our profession. My name's Leo Strange."

They shook hands. Quedley said, "I thought you'd retired."

Strange seemed to find that amusing. "You never really retire from this game, do you? Take yourself — I hear on the grapevine that you're poised for a comeback."

"Word gets around."

"Indeed it does. Can I have a moment of your time to talk business?"

Quedley said, sure. They went in and sat facing each other across the dining-room table.

Strange said, "I also heard that Maurice Trousdale's wife enlisted your help during her little blackmail imbroglio."

"I stood in for her at a couple of meetings — it didn't amount to much."

Strange cleared his throat: "I have to admit to being partly responsible." He told how he'd set Mules on to her.

"Why?"

"My interest was in Clyde Early, not her. One of my clients wanted dirt on him."

Quedley frowned slightly and leaned back in his chair. "Why are you telling me this?"

"Because it relates to the proposition I'd like to put to you."

"I'm all ears."

"A year or so ago, I was reading about yet another British politician coming to grief in a sex scandal. It struck me that I knew some pretty fruity stuff about a number of our leading executives. It further struck me that, from time to time, there are situations in the normal course of commercial activity — hostile takeover, say, or boardroom power struggles — in which that sort of information, judiciously used, could influence, if not determine, the outcome. I discussed it with a long-standing client of mine who gets involved in a fair amount of corporate argy-bargy — between you and me, it was Benny Strick . . ."

"The boy wonder?"

Strange nodded. "He's hardly a boy anymore but the tag seems to've stuck. Anyway, Strick was interested. As is his wont, he requested a free sample: he set me the challenge of derailing Early's coaching career."

"Why the hell would he do that?"

"Various reasons. Apparently, when he really was a boy, Early spurned his request for an autograph. Young Mr Strick is not the forgiving kind."

"I take it you're joking?"

"Well, that was a minor factor. Strick's a fanatical rugby fan with a deep — one might say mysterious — emotional attachment to his home town of Wellington. More to the point, perhaps, he also has a considerable financial stake in our capital city. I'm not a rugby man myself, so excuse me if this is a bit hazy, but Strick was — still is, I presume — convinced that Wellington would benefit significantly if a Wellingtonian became the All Blacks coach.

"He assured me there's ample precedent for it: the centre that supplies the coach tends to get more players in the All Blacks and is the venue for more big matches; the big matches bring the spectators from out of town who spend lots of money; promising players from round the country gravitate to the centre thinking they'll have a better chance of making the big-time; that boosts the local team, whose success in turn has various commercial spin-offs. I'm sure you get the idea. Strick's premise is that it would do wonders for Wellington rugby and give the place a shot in the arm morale- and business-wise.

"He's got a candidate lined up — bear in mind, he's looking a couple of years down the track. He's also identified and assessed potential rivals and considers Early the biggest threat."

Quedley shook his head. "Now I've heard everything."

"Unfortunately, using Mules was an error of judgement on my part and the trial run was a flop. I'm convinced, though, that the principle is sound."

"So what's the proposition?"

"A joint-venture niche-market corporate information service: you and me, Mr Quedley, joining forces to supply red-hot, absolutely reliable scuttlebutt to big corporate players engaged in no-holds-barred fights. Twice the contracts, twice the dirt. What do you think?"

"Well, it's certainly an intriguing concept."

"I thought you'd like it — and the beauty of it is, if we keep our arrangement secret, we could supply both sides. I can see it being a most rewarding little sideline for us." He slid a card across the table. "Think about it and give me a call. While you're at it, why not bend your mind to the question of how we might capitalise on Mrs Trousdale's penchant for adultery? I haven't given up hope of recouping that investment."

"I'll give it some thought."

Quedley saw Strange out then went through to the kitchen, where Rusty Trousdale was standing over the stove stirring a casserole. She wore cut-off jeans, battered sneakers, one of Quedley's old shirts, and a new apron.

They clinched like honeymooners.

Quedley bent over the pot. "That smells fantastic. What is it?"

"Risotto alla Sbiraglia — chicken risotto to you."

He pulled her to him again. "Still no second thoughts?"

Rusty glowed: "Does it look like it?"

He sat down at the kitchen table. "Did you catch much of that?"

"Enough. Does he look as sleazy as he sounds?"

"Not really. That's probably how he gets away with it."

"What are you going to do?"

"Well, first of all I'll ring Early and warn him he's going to have a fight on his hands."

"Then?"

"Then I'll ring Benny Strick to let him know Leo's been telling tales out of school."

Rusty knew her man: "And then?"

Quedley got a dreamy look in his eyes. "Then we'll weigh up their offers."

About the Author

PAUL THOMAS is the author of six novels and a short story collection. *Inside Dope*, the second book in *The Ihaka Trilogy*, won the Crime Writers' Association of Australia's inaugural Ned Kelly Award for crime novel of the year. His fiction has been widely published internationally, and translated into several languages. He has also written a number of books on sport.